PENGUIN BOOKS

The Simple Rules of Love

The Simple Rules of Love

AMANDA BROOKFIELD

PENGUIN BOOKS

PENGUIN BOOKS

Published by the Penguin Group
Penguin Books Ltd, 80 Strand, London WC2R ORL, England
Penguin Group (USA) Inc., 375 Hudson Street, New York, New York 10014, USA
Penguin Group (Canada), 90 Eglinton Avenue East, Suite 700, Toronto, Ontario, Canada M4P 2Y3
(a division of Pearson Penguin Canada Inc.)
Penguin Ireland, 25 St Stephen's Green, Dublin 2, Ireland
(a division of Penguin Books Ltd)
Penguin Group (Australia), 250 Camberwell Road,
Camberwell, Victoria 3124, Australia (a division of Pearson Australia Group Pty Ltd)
Penguin Books India Pvt Ltd, 11 Community Centre,
Panchsheel Park, New Delhi – 110 017, India
Penguin Group (NZ), cnr Airborne and Rosedale Roads, Albany,
Auckland 1310, New Zealand (a division of Pearson New Zealand Ltd)
Penguin Books (South Africa) (Pty) Ltd, 24 Sturdee Avenue,
Rosebank, Johannesburg 2196, South Africa

Penguin Books Ltd, Registered Offices: 80 Strand, London WC2R ORL, England

www.penguin.com

First published 2006
1

Mrs Dalloway by Virginia Woolf, 1925. Reproduced by permission of The Society
of Authors as the Literary Representative of the Estate of Virginia Woolf.

The moral right of the author has been asserted

Set in 11.35/13.5pt Monotype Garamond
by Palimpsest Book Production Limited, Polmont, Stirlingshire
Printed in England by Clays Ltd, St Ives plc

ISBN-13: 978-0-141-02182-9
ISBN-10: 0-141-02182-9

For my godchildren, Gabriel, Kiki, Hebe and Maddy

'Moving, mysterious, of infinite richness, this life'
Virginia Woolf

Acknowledgements

Help came from many directions during the writing of *The Simple Rules of Love*. Sara Westcott and the neonatal staff at Queen Charlotte's Hospital, Dickie Scarratt, Henry Sutton and Angela Brookfield all assisted me with invaluable research. For support of a vital but more invisible kind, I must thank Clare Ledingham and Stephanie Cabot, whose faith held firm when mine wavered. Lastly, but so importantly, my warmest appreciation goes to Barbara Ryan, whose artful physiotherapy eliminated pain as a reason not to sit at my desk.

February

By the time the mourners followed the coffin out of St Margaret's arched Norman doorway, the sun had burned the leaden screen of cloud to harmless grey tufts, which floated over the distant ridge of the South Downs like puffs of smoke. It had been a wet winter and the grass of the churchyard, pitted here and there with clusters of daffodils, was long and lush, asserting more than words ever could that, though bodies might rot beneath it, life, on the surface at least, went on.

The surviving members of the Harrison family, the edges of their dark clothes flapping in the brisk breeze, made their way slowly down the path and into the graveyard, moving with the seamless ease of a flock of gliding birds. They came to a stop in a sheltered corner by a hedge of ripening privet where a deep, rectangular hole had been dug next to the other, variously weathered family graves.

'Ashes to ashes, dust to dust . . .' The priest issued his valedictions in a tone of almost bored familiarity, casting a handful of earth, which caught on a gust of wind and blew back against his gown.

As the coffin was lowered into the hole, Pamela Harrison, at seventy-nine now the oldest living member of the family, found her attention drifting from the demise of her sister-in-law, Alicia, to the grassy mound that covered her husband's remains. After two years the plot still looked new and plump, as if John had changed his mind and was trying to punch his way through the rows of winter pansies she had planted on top, wanting a final gasp of air, or maybe the chance – so regularly sought in his life – to have the last word. With his ailing eighty-three-year-old heart, death had been expected but, for Pamela at least, none the less shocking. Six decades of marriage had bound them together as firmly as the twisted roots of the old oak that guarded the entrance to the drive of Ashley House, their beloved family home on the other side of the village. Passing the tree as they set out for the church that morning, Pamela had caught herself staring through the dots of her veil at its sprawling canopy of boughs, remembering how John had loved to sit beneath it, one hand cradling his pipe, the other absently stroking the silky ears of Poppy, their beloved springer spaniel. She had gripped her little black handbag as she studied the tree's heaving base of tangled roots, wondering at the surgical possibilities of removing just one, and how so old and convoluted a structure would respond to such an assault.

For her own part Pamela had concentrated on the dignified but wearisome business of *continuing*, discovering in the process the comfort of pursuing all the myriad daily routines that, at various times in her life, she had despised for their sameness. As she twisted her thinning white hair into its customary bun, walked Poppy up the lane, browsed through the paper in the drawing room, with the lavender visible through the windows and the inviting green mouth of the pergola beyond, she was aware that it was precisely the familiarity of these actions and their landscapes that held her together: they required no thought, thereby offering at least a semblance of the business of living.

It was performing tasks beyond this routine that Pamela found hard. Like choosing a hat for the funeral – a hat for John's rickety-hipped sister Alicia, who had clung to life with all the irascibility and obstinacy that had made her impossible to regard as a friend. Pamela had fretted for hours at her dressing-table, hat-boxes strewn across the counterpane of the bed, as paralysed with indecision as one of her fashion-conscious twin granddaughters. She liked hats and had several elegant black ones in various styles. With lace or without? Wide brim or narrow? Cocked to one side or straight? She had still been deliberating when Charlie, her second son, had shouted up the stairs that it was time to go. There was an edge of impatience in his voice, so reminiscent of John that, for a few seconds, Pamela had imagined that her husband might be waiting for her in the hall, his face creased with frustration, his elbow ready to loop through hers for the walk to the car. She had seized the nearest hat and reached for the enamelled box that contained her hatpins. John would never wait for her again, she reminded herself. Charlie and Serena lived with her now, and Ed, their seventeen-year-old, who made the walls of Ashley House vibrate with his music, who used the old oak tree to shield the smoke of his illicit cigarettes, and who claimed so vociferously not to miss Maisie and Clem, his twenty-year-old sisters, that it was obvious he longed for them all the time.

Even now the hat Pamela had chosen didn't feel right. There was a growing sore spot where one of her treasured mother-of-pearl hatpins was pushing through her bun into her scalp. And she had pitched it so far forward that the brim now obscured the view of the sky and rolling hills, precluding what would have provided a welcome visual escape from the sombre expressions of those around her. She made do instead with looking at the ground. Next to John's grave an empty patch of grass was reserved for her. Pamela squinted at it through the fine gauze of her veil, trying to imagine the cold comfort of death, but thinking instead, with sudden yearning, of a nice cup of tea.

'All right?' Peter, her elder son, patted her hand where it gripped his arm. He and his wife Helen had driven down from London that morning, electing not to bring their four- and thirteen-year-old girls, Genevieve and Chloë, and apologizing for the absence of Theo, their eldest, who was in the thick of his second term at Oxford.

Pamela nodded, pressing her fingers into the soft cashmere of Peter's overcoat. With his wide, balding grey head and determined eyes, he was so like John at a similar age that every time she saw him, these days, she wanted to weep at the complicated poignancy of life's relentless echoes, so comforting yet so disquieting.

Her other three children, ranged among the small crowd on the opposite side of the grave, were less obvious physical replicas of their parents' union, though people often remarked that Cassie, still striking at forty-two, with her petite frame and long curly blonde hair, looked as she had in her prime. The middle two, Charlie and Elizabeth, with their much heavier features, dark hair and wider girth were like peas from an altogether different pod – apart from their eyes, which were blue and deep-set like her own. And Elizabeth had her father's chin, reflected Pamela, feeling a little spurt of fond compassion, as she always did, for her somewhat clumsily assembled second child. In her long black coat she was as close to smart as Pamela could remember. Only the thick-soled boots protruding from below the coat hem bore testimony to the faintly anarchic style she had adopted in recent years, a style that involved not only heavy-soled footwear but layers of shapeless clothes and, on particularly misguided occasions, two thick, squaw-like plaits. It was no way for any woman to dress, in Pamela's view, least of all a fifty-three-year-old secondary-school maths teacher with an impressionable teenage son to consider.

Dear Roland. Pamela sighed as her glance shifted to the fifteen-year-old, whose six-foot frame towered above his mother and whose cheekbones jutted out under his huge, long-lashed brown eyes with a man-boy innocence she would have done anything to preserve. To be so handsome was almost unnatural, and would lead to trouble, she was sure. As she watched,

Elizabeth slipped an arm round Roland's waist and leant into him, resting the side of her face against his upper arm. *Depending* on him, as usual, Pamela noted with despair, marvelling as always at Roland's still unspoilt good nature and that Elizabeth's split from Colin five years before seemed – contrary to all traditional wisdom – to have proved far less traumatic for the boy than for his mother. Elizabeth had rebounded, with predictably disastrous results, into the arms of her first husband, Lucien Cartwright, and then there had been a series of other unlikely characters, each promising much but delivering little. Pamela had seen it all coming, just as she could see that Elizabeth leant too heavily on her only son in consequence. She saw such things but no longer tried to speak of them. Voicing opinions, no matter how accurate, changed nothing, she had discovered, especially if one was old, lacking in confidence and struggling, publicly now, with the disconcerting embarrassment of a failing memory.

The funeral cars were waiting for them in the lane, their shining black bulk taking up almost the entire space between the church wall and the hedge on the other side. At the sight of them Ed's spirits lifted. He nudged Roland, the only one of the cousins to have been subjected to the ordeal of their great-aunt's send-off, and made a face. 'We could do a royal wave through the streets of Barham. The lords of the manor, returning to their country seat.' He slung out an arm to demonstrate, accidentally catching his aunt Helen's ribcage with his elbow. 'Whoops. Sorry.'

'You two will probably go with Sid in the Volvo,' said Helen, sharply, absorbed not by any real irritation at her nephew so much as a strong desire to get back to Barnes, where the demands of her two young daughters awaited her, with a brief-case of work on a difficult deal for her law firm's latest, most prestigious corporate client. Fitting in Aunt Alicia's funeral had blown the week off-course, just as she had known it would. Angling with Peter to be let off the hook – the demise of a prickly family ancient hardly constituted a tragedy – had got her nowhere. Peter, as was his wont on any matter relating to his family, had been intractable. A good turnout was essential, he said, to support his mother, not to mention Charlie and Serena, on whom would fall the burden of orchestrating the event. So here they were, and with the wake still to get through, God help her. It would be seven o'clock at least before they got home.

'Isn't Sid a bit on the doddery side for driving, these days?' asked Ed, sliding his fingers through the quiff he had sculpted with some care that morning, using gel and a few blasts of Serena's hair-dryer. 'From what I've seen he can hardly manage a lawn-mower.' He cast a mischievous glance at Roland, hoping for a glimmer of approbation in his younger cousin's pale, grave face. As far as his own hardening adolescent heart was concerned, the best thing about Ashley House's old gardener – Sid was so long-serving that he was almost an honorary member of the family – was his granddaughter, Jessica, who lived in Wandsworth with her mother but was always popping down to Barham on one pretext or another. As children they had all found Jessica a pain. She would appear at Ashley House when she was least wanted, whining to join in their games and running to Sid with tales of their unkindness if they didn't let her. Lately, however, this same plump, whingeing creature had re-emerged as a curvaceous sixteen-year-old, with a come-on smile and a taste for tight clothes. Ed had almost lost his footing on the stairs that morning, glimpsing her tottering along the hallway with a tray of glasses in a mini-dress that paraded both her size-able chest and the outline of her knickers. 'What do you reckon, Roland?' Ed pressed, cheered at the prospect of Jessica playing waitress at the wake. 'Should we trust creaky old Sid with our lives?'

6

Roland's hands were in his pockets and he was kicking a stone with the tip of his shoe. 'Sid's okay,' he murmured, shrugging his broad shoulders. He could feel the tension crackling between the adults and didn't want to make it worse. Nor did he care much which vehicle transported them back across the village. He would have been happy to walk. After the heavy smell of lilies in the church – the oppressive atmosphere of sorrow – it was a huge relief to be outside. Personally he thought it daft that anyone should mourn the loss of a grumpy eighty-year-old who, to his recollection, had always displayed a clear preference for television and Turkish Delight over the company of her family. She'd had a nasty habit, too, of using her walking-sticks to get attention, banging them on the floor or jabbing their rubber ends into her great-nephews' and -nieces' shins and ribs, so hard sometimes that Roland, as a small boy, had often swallowed tears.

Church, in Roland's opinion, was a lot of mumbo-jumbo. He far preferred the sound of religions where families partied at gravesides, quaffing wine and telling funny stories. He hadn't felt sad until they'd assembled at the graveside when he had thought of his grandfather, whom he still missed, and his little cousin Tina, whom he didn't – you couldn't pine for a toddler – but whose death six years before was still a vivid memory and, in his view, a much more obvious cause for mourning. He was sure that his aunt Serena, nose in a soggy tissue for most of the service, was thinking far more of her dead daughter than of the witchy occupant of the coffin parked in front of the altar. And he suspected that his mother's tears had much more to do with being on her own and the fracas with Richard, her latest ex-boyfriend, rather than sadness about her aunt. He was on the verge of telling Ed he'd prefer to walk when Sid appeared round the side of the church, looking even more craggy-faced and rheumy-eyed than usual, jangling the keys to the Volvo.

'I think you two are with me,' he growled, so firmly that both boys barely exchanged a look as they followed him to the line of smaller cars parked further down the road.

At the sight of Ashley House, crouched, with its mossy walls and crowning glory of polished slates, waiting to greet them like a huge, shy friend, Peter felt a familiar wrench of affection. His decision, five years before, to hand over to his younger brother Charlie the right to inherit it wasn't one he regretted. For one thing, Peter didn't believe in regret. Life was about paths chosen. It was pointless to look back and play 'what if' based on nothing but imponderables and hypotheses. For another, all the reasons behind the decision – neither he nor Helen wanting to commute, loving London and their spacious Barnes home, avoiding upheaval for Chloë, their thirteen-year-old, recognizing that Charlie and Serena, with their country ways, were far more the *natural* inheritors of this family jewel – still stood. Yet it was hard sometimes because he loved the place so. Built by his great-great-grandfather and lived in by Harrisons for two hundred years, Ashley House was an integral part of his childhood landscape, something he could not have surrendered even if he had tried. Since moving in, Charlie and Serena had kept the open-house policy upon which they had all agreed – he, Cassie and Elizabeth had their own bedrooms and visited often – but it wasn't the same, Peter reflected, as he helped his mother out of the car and scowled at the precarious angle of the cockerel weathervane, the three loose slates on the garage roof. Had he been in charge, his perfectionism would have had him on to anything like that in a flash. Leading the way through the gate and down the steps to the front door he couldn't help noticing other things too – the squeak of the gate hinge, a section of loose grouting in the garden wall, the unsightly eruption of three molehills on the front lawn – and wondered whether Charlie's idle streak or shortage of funds lay behind it. A talk was called for, Peter decided, easing off his mother's coat and handing it to Jessica, who was hovering nearby, clearly briefed to deal with such matters but too shy to say so. A brotherly chat, nothing too heavy-handed, ideally – if he could engineer it – over a pint at the Rising Sun that evening.

'Let's not stay *too* long, darling,' pleaded Helen, once Jessica, staggering a little under the coats, had turned for the stairs.

Peter shot a glance of disappointment at his wife and noted that she looked tired. The shadows under her still striking brown eyes were as dark as fingerprints and her usually kempt hair had been blown haywire by the wind that had gusted across the churchyard, tugging at their clothes like an attention-seeking child. Although she visited the hairdresser regularly the grey showed through quickly, these days. Thanks to the assault of the February breeze it was clearly visible now, crusty patches of white along her hairline and parting, as if dabbed there by an inexpert painter. She looked old, Peter realized, recalling the wholly uncharacteristic fervour with which she had appeared to pray in church, fingers locked, eyes cast down, lids trembling, as if she was seeking something. Usually she stared straight ahead, as he had, in a pose of respectful but defiant agnosticism. 'But we haven't been here since Christmas,' he said at length, his expression softening. 'In fact, I was thinking of staying the night. It would do us both good, don't you think, a night out of town?'

'Staying the night?' echoed Helen, shrilly.

Jessica, half-way up the stairs, paused to peep through the carved oak spindles of the banisters.

'Of course you can stay,' Serena assured them smoothly, catching a thread of the conversation as she emerged from the kitchen into the hall. 'You know you're *always* welcome,' she added, while her mind leapt, with rather less enthusiasm, to the dusty, unready state of Peter and Helen's room. And she would have to change her scribbled order to the milkman too, from three pints to four – or maybe five, if Roland and Elizabeth ended up staying too, which was likely, given the gusto with which her elder sister-in-law appeared to be tucking into the wine.

'No, thank you, Serena. It was just a lovely but perfectly ridiculous idea of Peter's . . .'

'Ridiculous?' Peter snorted with irritation, all tenderness forgotten, his blue eyes blazing in a way that regularly made juries sit to attention, no matter how hopeless the position he was defending.

Even Jessica, who was used to being in the thick of uglier confrontations, took a step back on the landing, using her bundle of coats to shield all but her green eyes and high forehead, ivory-white against her freshly dyed black hair. There was an undeniable thrill in watching people you didn't like fighting with each other, especially when they were unaware of it and you didn't give a toss about the outcome.

Serena, who did care about the outcome, decided it would be best effected by her absence. 'Just let me know what you decide,' she murmured, hurrying through to the drawing room, grateful that she had fallen in love with the infinitely less fierce second son, Charlie, and thinking how baffling the behaviour of other couples could be, even those one had known and loved for two decades.

'I just meant,' persisted Helen, too used to her husband's quick temper to be cowed by it, 'that we ought to get back for the girls.'

'It's Friday and we have a nanny, don't we?'

'A nanny who has the evening off to go the cinema.'

'Who *always* has the evening off when we need her.' Peter tugged at his starched cuffs, one eye on the doorway into the drawing room where everyone else had already gathered. He could hear the spit and crackle of the freshly lit fire, laid by Sid, no doubt, that morning, and Charlie's booming laugh from the far end of the room. 'Well, perhaps *I* could stay, then – catch the train up tomorrow. Would that be all right?' There was an edge of sarcasm in his voice.

'Of course! And don't be such a crosspatch,' Helen scolded, sealing her peace-offering by brushing a fleck of dust off his suit, then adjusting his tie.

Peter grunted to acknowledge the truce, feeling, with his chin lifted and his wife's deft fingers at his collar, both cornered and mollified.

'I would stay if I could,' Helen added, stepping back to admire her handiwork, too relieved at the resolution of the dispute to question whether this was true. It was certain, though, that without Peter her evening would be infinitely more productive: she could snack instead of preparing a proper meal, then sit up in bed with her papers for as long as she liked, glass of wine in hand, with the prospect of sleep uninterrupted by thunderous snores.

With the chairs and side-tables pushed against the walls, the drawing room offered almost too large a space for the thirty or so assembled guests to lose themselves comfortably. A smaller room would have pressed them all together, forcing jollity and cohesion. As it was, they stood in small, awkward groups – islands amid the sea of blue Axminster – making small-talk and picking food off passing trays like timid strangers. In the broad stone jaws of the hearth, with its handsome, fluted black-marble surround, Sid's expertly laid fire lashed and burned vigorously, looking spectacular but belting out so much heat that Serena, with a surreptitious glance at her mother-in-law, who liked greenhouse temperatures all year, hurried from radiator to radiator, turning them down. Even so, the line of windows overlooking the veranda, known to the family as the cloisters, and garden, each like a miniature stage, with its frame of heavy blue velvet curtain, was soon misted. Almost, mused Serena, pausing to rub a porthole in one with a tissue, as if the spring mist, now seeping towards the house from the South Downs, had found cracks in the walls and crept inside. The thought made her shiver, in spite of the heat. She was getting a headache, she realized, pressing the wet tissue to the bridge of her nose, which still felt blocked from crying. The tears had started with the opening hymn – 'Abide With Me' – then continued to pour out of her throughout the service. Like a sluice gate opening, letting all the old sadnesses flood out – missing John, Charlie's lovely dad, and her own mother, felled by cancer years before. And Tina, of course. Always Tina, loved and lost, but not lost because nothing so truly loved could ever disappear. In the church she had found Charlie's hand and squeezed it, aware that he knew how she felt, reminding herself that he would help her bear it.

Now she felt better, in spite of the headache. Crying always helped. Purging or *something*. Serena smiled to herself and then at Charlie, who was springing round guests with a bottle, his unruly hair even wilder than usual and his funeral tie slung over one shoulder. Every so often he reached with his free hand for an absent tug at his waistband, clearly forgetting that he was in a new fat phase so his trousers had no alternative but to slip down to his hips, defeated by the substantial bulge of his belly. After Tina he had taken up running and got rather slim. Serena had been equivocal about it, even at the time, feeling dimly that a part of him was literally running away from her – from their grief. When the weight had begun to creep on again she had relished reacquainting herself with his teddy-bear bulk, the lovely sensation of being small in his arms. Aware that a few people were staring at her, alone by the window, Serena crossed the room to see to things in the kitchen, tossing her wet tissue into the fire as she passed.

Roland, seeing it land, went to watch the tissue burn, a livid yellow bundle, before it subsided among the blackened logs and coal. Ed joined him, lobbing in paper napkins until their uncle

Peter tersely suggested they find less childish and more useful occupations than setting the chimney on fire.

As Charlie worked hard to link the still stranded groups with cheery remarks and offers to top up glasses, he could feel perspiration spreading across his forehead and back. He glanced at the gilt-framed portrait of his father, which hung above the fireplace, dominating the room, and couldn't help thinking that the old man would have managed the occasion better: seeing to every detail with his usual, often irksome, fastidiousness, asserting himself, exuding the quiet, infectious confidence of the truly self-assured. Maybe he himself was an impostor, Charlie reflected, with uncharacteristic bleakness, as he paused, bottle in hand, to meet John Harrison's penetrating gaze. He felt for a moment as if they were locked in one of those blinking games he had once played with his siblings, staring each other out till their lids ached and their eyes streamed.

'All right, old thing?'

Charlie blinked, and turned to see that his elder brother's broad, earnest face was softened with affectionate concern.

'You were lost there for a minute.'

'I was.' Charlie grinned. 'Do you think the old man's watching over us all, thinking we're making a botch of things?'

'Of course not . . . Here, let me take charge of this.' Peter seized the wine bottle. 'Go and find yourself a glass. I was thinking of staying the night, by the way, if that's okay – thought we might treat ourselves to a pint in the village later.'

'Fine. Did you, er, mention it to Serena for catering purposes and so on?'

'I did indeed,' replied Peter, with a formal click of his heels as he set off to distribute the wine. Charlie remained where he was, torn between gratitude at his elder brother's unfailing pragmatism, his ability to take command, and a dim sense of having been outmanoeuvred. He watched Peter launch into the role of genial host with which he himself had been struggling, breaking into a little throng of Alicia's bridge-playing friends, then approaching their sister, Elizabeth, who was standing alone by the table of family photographs, staring at them, as if they were a gallery of strangers. Peter said something to her and Elizabeth's face lit up. Observing the exchange, Charlie's spirits lifted. *He* might have his wobbly patches, but Peter would hold it all together. He always did, Charlie reflected, recalling the inspirational dry-eyed determination with which his elder brother had helped to shoulder Alicia's coffin that afternoon, just as he had helped to bear the body of their father two years before. He had stood tall and stoical while the rest of them bowed their heads and dabbed at their faces with handkerchiefs. And giving him Ashley House – Christ! Charlie experienced a fresh, dizzying rush of gratitude at the extraordinary magnitude of the gift. Announced a couple of years before the death of their father, while he and Serena were in the thick of grief after losing Tina, the family home had dropped into their laps like a lifeline, a way forward without which they might have drowned.

Pamela stood for as long as she could, listening but not hearing as Alicia's son Paul told her about life in Canberra. She nodded, as if his words meant something, but inside she fought vainly to merge the tanned, paunchy-faced man in front of her with the pale, shy twenty-five-year-old who had left England forty years before, breaking his mother's heart. Alicia had never said as much, of course – one didn't talk about such things, in those days – but that was when the acerbity had started, the closing of the door on friendship. She had been jealous, probably, Pamela mused now, losing her one child while Pamela and John had four to fill their hearts and their beautiful home with clatter and energy.

'I think I'll sit down,' she said, even though Paul was in mid-sentence. 'I have a bad back,' she explained, looking for the sofa, which had been moved from its usual place in front of the fire to a stretch of wall between a Georgian bookcase and a cabinet of ornaments. 'Never used to. John was the one – terrible time with his back for years, not that he liked to admit it . . . Ever since he's been gone, virtually from the day he died in fact, I get this pain, almost as if –' She broke off, aware that Paul's round face was sinking in bafflement. 'I'll just take myself off for a sit-down, then,' she murmured, moving towards the sofa. And it *was* baffling, she mused, sinking back against the cushions with a sigh of relief – utterly insane – to imagine that a pain could be passed on, bequeathed like a piece of jewellery or a house, when it was just the crumbling of her ancient spine. Seeing Jessica approach with a tray of asparagus rolls, Pamela waved her away and closed her eyes. The funeral had drained her. She might not miss Alicia *per se* but with her gone she felt fragile and exposed, like a last flower standing up to a gale.

Annoyed, feeling like a troublesome insect, Jessica took her offerings to Cassie and her fiancé, Stephen Smith, instead. The pair had positioned themselves by the largest of the windows overlooking the arched stone veranda fronting the garden and were using the windowsill to sort through a stack of white envelopes.

'Oh, Jessica, thank you.' Cassie took a roll, waited for Stephen to take one too then started to eat. Jessica was about to move on when Cassie seized her arm and announced to Stephen, through her mouthful, 'Darling, you remember Jessica, don't you? Sid's granddaughter – she used to play with my nephews and nieces.'

'Of course. Nice to see you again. Good of you to help out.'

'Yeah . . . right.' Jessica blushed, unsure how to respond given that she was being paid for her services rather than performing them as an act of charity.

'We're getting married,' gushed Cassie next. 'Did you know?'

'Yeah, Mrs Harrison told me . . . That's great. Are them the invites?'

'These?' Cassie glanced at the envelopes. 'Oh, no, they're for our engagement party. The wedding isn't going to be until next year. January, we've decided, as the deadline for Stephen's new book is Christmas and we think a winter wedding, if done properly, could be lovely, don't we, darling? The thing is,' she continued, before Stephen had had a chance to reply, 'what with the funeral and so on, we were wondering whether it really was the moment to give out these invitations – whether it might look a bit *unfeeling*. What do you think?'

Jessica gripped her tray, alarmed at having her opinion sought. 'I think people always want a party, don't they? A reason to let their hair down, have some fun . . .' The pair nodded happily and exchanged a look that made Jessica feel it was more than time to move on. She scanned the room and, with only one asparagus roll left on the tray, her eyes alighted on Ed. He was crouched in a corner rifling through a stack of CDs in front of the mahogany unit that housed his parents' music centre.

He stood up as she approached, grinning and shaking his head at the tray. 'Not for me, thanks, I'm stuffed.' He slapped his hand to his stomach, drawing attention to his untucked shirt and revealing a couple of inches of white skin. 'What are Mum and Dad paying you, if you don't mind me asking?'

'I bloody do mind – it's none of your bloody business.'

'Use language like that and they might not pay you at all.'

'Bollocks.' Jessica took a bite of the last remaining canapé and dropped it back on to the tray with a grimace. 'Gross.'

Ed laughed. 'Asparagus – I hate it too. It makes your pee smell, did you know that?'

Jessica giggled. 'No way.'

'Hey, you couldn't get us another glass of wine, could you?'

'I might,' she replied archly, not enjoying the reminder that she was at everyone's beck and call. She snatched Ed's empty glass and took the nearest route back to the kitchen, through the adjoining door to the music room, with its soft green carpet and black monster of a piano, and out again into the bit of hall that ran past the downstairs cloakroom. The house, as she had tried occasionally to tell some of her Wandsworth schoolmates, was as giant and grand as a museum, but also sort of homely, with furniture that was posh but somehow *used*-looking and comfy, like the deep armchairs in the TV room and the big yellow sofa in the kitchen, which was easily as big as her mum's bed. She couldn't look at it without wanting to kick off her shoes and wallow around in its huge, faded cushions.

Entering the kitchen now Jessica gave an involuntary sigh of pleasure. As a small girl she had spent many happy hours in here, sitting on her grandfather's lap usually, nibbling biscuits while he swigged his mid-morning mug of tea and chewed at the end of an unlit roll-up. She remembered hiding once under the big oak table, peeping out from between the chair legs, pretending she couldn't hear him calling, pretending the table was her own grand house, not wanting ever to be found. Even now, with the grown-up perspective that made everything seem smaller, she noted that the table remained big enough to provide a roof for several people. The rest of the place – the huge quarried floor tiles, the gleaming blue Aga in the old fireplace, the two stainless-steel sinks, the oak cabinets and the marbled surfaces connecting it all together – was like something out of one of those glossy magazines at the hairdresser's, with pictures of houses and swimming-pools that made you wish you could dive into them and leave all the crap behind.

Completing the picture of perfection, Samson, the elderly ginger tom, was curled up on the back of the sofa in a pool of sunshine, his head on his paws, tail tucked round him like a draught-excluder. Jessica, who didn't much like cats, kept a wary eye on him as she poured wine into Ed's glass and took a good

17

long swig. Dogs were better, she thought, remembering the lovely chocolate Labrador called Little Boots who had been run over a few years before and feeling a stab of pity for Poppy, whom she could hear yelping in indignation at her enforced confinement in one of the garden sheds.

'You're a lucky puss,' she muttered darkly, taking another gulp of wine, tempted suddenly to throw a cloth or cork at the cat to disturb things a little, make them more *real*.

'Ah, there you are,' exclaimed Serena, sternly enough to indicate that she had seen the hasty lowering of the wine glass. Allowances had to be made, she told herself, tugging the oven gloves off the Aga rail and bending down to check the trays of sausage rolls and vol-au-vents she had put in to heat earlier. They were employing Jessica as a goodwill gesture to Sid, she reminded herself, and because they had heard enough over the years to recognize that it was something of a miracle the child was still in one piece, let alone capable of waitressing for the afternoon. 'Could you take some of these into the drawing room?' she asked sweetly. 'And thank you so much, you're doing *such* a good job.'

Jessica watched, chewing her lower lip and feeling awkward, as Serena tipped the pastries on to a large serving plate decorated with blue and gold flowers. 'Pretty, isn't it?' her employer murmured, pausing to stroke the edge of the plate. 'Hand-painted. An ancient wedding present from some distant relative to my husband's grandparents.'

Jessica smiled politely, though inwardly she felt cross about the glare she had received for swigging the wine. One drink was hardly a big deal. In the same instant she recalled how bloody amazing she had once thought all the Harrisons were, with their big house and polite talk. It wasn't until she hit her teens that she realized the only difference between her and them was money and all the good fortune it brought with it. She didn't think any of them were amazing now, except perhaps

Ed, whom she'd always liked best, ever since he had devoted an entire July afternoon to teaching her how to do kick-ups with a football. She was sure he'd have forgotten it now and, in a way, she hoped he had because she had been so useless – anything to do with sport, and bits of her body tried to go in different directions. That day Ed had persisted for hours in spite of these handicaps, being funny and patient and kind, and telling Roland and Chloë to piss off when he spotted them spying and giggling behind a bush. Even now, five years on, the memory of that hot afternoon, the pleasure and pride of being defended by Ed, with his skinny legs and Arsenal shirt, made Jessica feel funny inside.

The change in him since those days was remarkable. The skinny legs had thickened and lengthened so that now he was several inches taller than his dad. The football strip had been replaced either with the smart suit trousers he was wearing that day or baggy designer jeans, slung so low on his hips that he looked like he had no bum at all, and exposing a good four inches of his underpants. He had one of the latest phones too, one that could go on the Net and take pictures, and a mini iPod with neat little white head-phones that would cost Jessica half a year's worth of Saturday wages, if she could be bothered to save for that long. All of which made the old feelings of liking him more complicated: part of her wanted to tell him to go to hell while another part didn't because he was right to think he was cool. In spite of his designer clothes and expensive gadgets he was never remotely stuck-up like his cousin Theo could be, or his twin sisters, for that matter – she remembered them going round the place holding hands, sniggering behind their long hair like members of a secret club.

'Wow,' remarked Ed, when she returned with his drink. 'My lucky day, is it?'

'Might be.' Jessica grinned, enjoying the way he was looking at her.

'I was thinking of slipping off to the pub later. Do you want to come?'

'Dunno.' She frowned, looking suddenly anxious and much closer to six than sixteen. 'Granddad's cooking tea and then I've got to get the train back to Wandsworth. I work Saturdays, in a hairdresser's.'

'Do you? Mine will need a cut soon – would you be up to that?' Ed ran his fingers through the vertical wall of his fringe, keeping an eye on her expression. The ratio of girls to boys at the Chichester sixth-form college where he had persuaded his parents to let him do his A levels had proved disappointingly uneven. The decent ones had boyfriends already. The rest were ugly, or stuffy, or tediously conscientious, particularly now with their exams just a few months away. Jessica with her lippy comebacks and Saturday job was a breath of fresh air.

'Cut that lot?' Jessica giggled, playing for time, reluctant to tell him that all she ever did was run the broom over the lino and wash the thinning scalps of the purple-rinse brigade. She was still deciding how to answer when Charlie, concerned for the canapés, tapped her shoulder and suggested she circulate a little more widely. 'And you should be helping look after our guests,' he scolded Ed, giving his son a fond rap on the head, 'instead of flirting with the waitress. Have a word with your uncle Peter, while you're about it. He's kindly offered to look into a work placement for you in the holidays. I know law might not be your thing but it would look good on your CV and might help you make up your mind about university courses.'

'Great,' said Ed, doing his best to look earnest but wanting only to avoid a parental diatribe on his lack of plans for the next four years. He couldn't think beyond his A levels, which loomed in view like a range of mountains, blocking out anything on the other side, good or bad. A recent careers talk on the armed forces had stirred dim thoughts of joining the Royal

Marines, or even the SAS, but not convincingly enough for him to share them with anyone else.

'Ed?' His father was still standing, arms akimbo, like some sort of bodyguard, waiting for him to move.

'I'm *going*, okay? Unless you want me to leave these like *this*?' Ed gestured at the fallen pile of CDs, as if their state of disarray was a matter of profound concern, when all he really felt like doing was giving them a good hard kick: a gesture of his annoyance at being treated like a five-year-old.

Pamela, still on the sofa, was experiencing the horrible blankness that came over her when she was tired. A stream of kindly people had taken it in turn to talk to her: first Cassie's nice young man, Stephen Smith, who she knew wrote crime novels, though she couldn't remember any of the titles; then Cassie, radiant as a bride-to-be should be, brimming with impossibly detailed questions about her and Stephen's wedding plans. Should the marquee be attached to the cloisters or stand free on the main lawn? Would the banns have to be read at St Margaret's as well as at her and Stephen's local church in Camden? How many heaters would they need to shield two hundred people from the inclemency of January? Was velvet appropriate for bridesmaids' dresses? Pamela had done her best, regretting that she was too weary to manage the proper mother–daughter repartee owed to such a momentous subject. She regretted, too, that her youngest had taken so long to decide on her Mr Right that John would not walk her down the aisle.

'Mum? Did you hear what I said?'

'Oh, Cassie, darling . . . yes . . . yes, of course. I was just thinking about all those clever detective stories Stephen writes and how that would have thrilled your father. He loved a good book.'

'Yes, he did.' Cassie had sighed both at the memory of her father and the waywardness of her mother's thoughts, which drifted hopelessly, given half a chance. 'Here, I've got something for you,' she continued, pressing a starched white envelope into Pamela's hand. 'We debated long and hard as to whether to hand them out today, then thought it would give everyone something to look forward to. It's a housewarming, too, though we haven't put that on the invitation.'

Pamela, unsheathing the gold-embossed card announcing the engagement party, had struggled to look pleased. 'How lovely,' she had murmured, kissing Cassie's cheek, but not managing to think beyond the two long car journeys that a party in London would entail, how her spine and bladder would ache, and all so that she could endure the strain of feeling left out or in the way.

Two of Alicia's bridge companions had approached to offer thank-yous and goodbyes. Mabel and Iris. Or had it been Mavis and Irma? Pamela closed her eyes, experiencing a sharp stab of fear at the way the edges of her life were losing their certainty. Contrary to all the platitudes about time and healing, life without John seemed, if anything, to get harder as the weeks and months ticked by. She longed more and more for the world they had shared for six decades, a world of distinct shapes and sequences, in which she had felt both commanding and at ease. Charlie and Serena were kind but it wasn't the same. Nothing was the same.

Her forgetfulness didn't help, of course, descending always when she was tired and could most have done without it. At such times the simplest words or thoughts could sit, tantalizingly unreachable, in some dark corner of her brain, remembered but not remembered, like a confused dream.

When Pamela opened her eyes Roland was sitting next to her.

'Hi, Gran.'

'Roland, darling, you sweet soul.' Pamela grasped his hand and squeezed it, fighting the urge to cry at the sight of him, so grown-up and beautiful. 'I miss you, darling,' she said tremulously. 'I loved it when you and Mummy lived at Ashley House.'

Roland smiled patiently. This was a familiar theme. The period to which his grandmother referred had been when he was ten and hadn't lasted long. And they had not lived in Ashley House but had lodged in the barn conversion until the settlement of his parents' divorce, when he and Elizabeth had moved to a cottage near Midhurst where he now went to school. 'We liked it too, Gran, but we're not far away, are we?'

'No, and you visit us whenever you can, I know.' Pamela let go of his hand and stared at the sea of faces in the room, all of them looking suddenly disconnected and unfamiliar. 'Are they all here?'

'All who, Gran?'

'The other children . . . the . . . your . . . cousins.' Having struggled to find the word, Pamela released it with a little gasp. She kept her gaze pinned on Roland's kind brown eyes, aware that she was having one of her bad patches and willing him to help her out of it.

'Ed's here,' said Roland, gently. 'He's over there, talking to Uncle Peter.' He pointed across the room.

'Ah, yes, of course.' Pamela hesitated, listing Charlie and Serena's four children in her mind. But no longer four, she reminded herself, because darling baby Tina had been killed by that hateful motorbike. Which left the twins, Maisie and Clem, nineteen now, or twenty? 'And Maisie and Clem, are they here?'

Sometimes the fact that his grandmother was losing her marbles made Roland feel too sad to try to talk to her. At others it simply tried his patience. But since Ed was being anti-social and the grown-ups boring, he did his best, telling Pamela things she knew already, content to be talking to someone instead of staring into space with his orange juice. 'Maisie's gone to Mexico to teach English, but she's coming back in the autumn to go to university. Clem is . . .' Roland tailed off. Clem, as he had discovered from several overheard snippets of conversation between the adults, was a cause for concern. Unlike her twin sister – and in spite of equally excellent A-level grades – Clem had shunned the notion of further education and traded the comforts of Ashley House for a poky flat in Camberwell where she divided her time between working in a wine bar and singing in her boyfriend's band. Which sounded fine to Roland. Hopeless at exams himself, he had already set his heart on heading to London and art college. When the dullness of country life got him down he sometimes fantasized about what making such a move would entail – sharing digs with Clem, perhaps, or wearing outrageous clothes and shaving interesting lines into his hair. He was fond of all his cousins. To him, as an only child, they were almost like siblings. He had spent many happy hours sharing rooms and bath-water with them all during family sojourns at Ashley House when his grandparents, instead of his aunt and uncle, had been in charge. Clem, in spite of her moods, had always been a favourite. She didn't talk much but she didn't make demands either – not like Maisie, with her know-it-all defiance, or Theo, with his seriousness and scary brain-power, more like a middle-aged man than a nineteen-year-old.

'Clem couldn't make it,' he said eventually, 'and Theo's in Oxford.' Seeing bewilderment cloud Pamela's face, he rounded off this summary with the observation that Theo's two little sisters, Chloë and Genevieve, were probably at home in Barnes with Rita, their nanny.

'But you're here,' said Pamela, clinging with some desperation to this simple fact, fearful of the darkness awaiting her on the other side.

'I'm here,' echoed Roland. He let his eyes drift from the imposing portrait of his grandfather to a much smaller still-life on the wall behind the sofa. A vase of pink roses, two oranges and a pear. The colours were electric but the objects looked as if they were floating in mid-air, revolving round each other like planets in search of a moon. A bad picture, Roland had always thought, relishing each time the certainty of his opinion. Many things in life left him giddy with doubt – subjunctive verbs, his mother's mood-swings, the recent alien feel of his childhood friend Polly's tongue in his mouth – but when it came to art the ground felt solid. With art he just *knew* things, like where to move his pencil or brush on the paper, which colour to mix with which, where and how firmly to press his thumb into a lump of clay to tease out the life crouching within . . .

His grandmother had fallen asleep. Her chin lolled on to her chest and loose wisps of thin white hair from her bun were falling over her face. Roland reached out a hand to nudge her awake, then withdrew it. She looked a little silly, but also rather peaceful, he decided. He slipped a small cushion behind her head.

By the time Helen set off for London it was already quite dark. Peter, waving in his shirt, shivered with cold. He watched until the rear lights of the car disappeared round the bend in the lane, then stood in the drive for a little longer, his jaw and fists clenched against the icy February night, while his heart swelled with the curious blend of pleasure and dissatisfaction that seemed to characterize so much of the business of being a father to young children. Each morning, escaping the mêlée of breakfast and school run, he sat in the leather seat of his BMW, tuned into John Humphrys and felt a similar confusion – at once regretful that he wasn't *indispensable* and grateful that, with the formidable organizational skills of Helen and Rita, he didn't have to be.

Now, turning back to the house, Peter found himself fondly picturing the scene as it would unfold in their handsome Barnes home that evening – Genevieve catapulting her tea across the table and Chloë flouncing, as only Chloë could flounce, about television or sweets or how late she could stay up – bewildered by how he could long for something yet at the same time grateful to be absent from it.

The steps down to the front door were slippery with evening frost. Peter felt his way gingerly, holding on to the slim tree trunk Sid had erected as a handrail and pondering what wonderful, incomprehensible things families were, millstones one minute and life-saving anchors the next. He would call Helen later, he decided, apologize again for being short-tempered. He would try to explain how wanting a night away didn't mean he wouldn't miss them, how nothing, not even Ashley House, was quite the same without them at his side.

Peter grinned when Cassie emerged from the drawing room with her arm looped through Stephen's. He'd always had a soft spot for his little sister, the baby of the family, no matter how their respective ages advanced. The relief and pleasure that at last she should have found the man with whom she wanted to share her life was beyond words. When she had asked him, that afternoon, pulling at his sleeve and whispering shyly, if he would walk her up the aisle, he'd been almost too choked to speak.

'Off so soon?' he exclaimed, in dismay, noting that they were already in their coats.

'Afraid so. Lots to do and all that.' Cassie released Stephen's arm and gave her brother a hug, having to reach up because even though she was in her high-heeled suede boots he was so much taller. 'But you're coming to our party, aren't you, you and Helen?'

'Of course,' Peter assured them warmly, shaking Stephen's hand. 'Wouldn't miss it for the world.'

'It's not just to celebrate *us* and our new house,' explained Cassie, happily, 'Stephen's just signed a new contract for *three* more books.'

'Cassie, really!'

'Have you? That's fantastic. Congratulations.' Peter turned to

26

his soon-to-be brother-in-law with genuine admiration, liking the man all the more for having made no mention of it during their various exchanges that afternoon. Coping with the Harrisons *en masse* couldn't be easy for anyone, he reflected, let alone a quiet sort like Stephen who, from what Cassie had told them, had nothing comparably rowdy or solid in his own background. 'More detectives?'

'Still the same one, I'm afraid. Good old Jack Connolly.' Stephen made a face. 'Nothing to threaten the Booker shortlist. Pays the bills, though,' he added, offering the sort of man-to-man look that he knew would be appreciated, while anxiety about his capacity to steer his character through yet more implausible adventures churned in his mind.

'Okay, who's ready for a pint?' called Charlie, striding along the hall to join them, battling with the inside-out arms of a tatty brown anorak. 'Lizzy and Roland have already scuttled back to Midhurst, Ed's cycled off to a friend's house and Serena says she's too whacked to go anywhere.'

'We're away too, I'm afraid,' said Cassie, blowing him a kiss as Stephen steered her out of the front door.

'So that leaves you and me.' Charlie beamed at his brother. 'I thought we'd walk, unless . . .' he glanced at Peter's smart leather shoes '. . . you'd prefer to drive. Trouble is, I reckon I'm already over the limit. Christ, funerals give me a thirst – black hats, doom, gloom, ghastly things.'

'I'll drive,' said Peter at once. 'It's freezing out there and I've only had one drink.'

Crossing the landing to fetch his coat, Peter noticed that the door to his mother's bedroom was open and the light on. She was lying on her back, fast asleep, a cup of untouched murky tea on the table next to her. Peter studied her for a few minutes, tenderness flooding his heart. As he was reaching to turn off the light her eyes fluttered open. 'John?'

'No, Mum. It's Peter.'

'Oh, darling, of course . . . Just for a moment, I thought . . . So silly.' She closed her eyes again, so quickly and heavily that Peter, switching out the light and closing the door quietly behind him, wasn't sure she had been awake.

Ed, cigarette in one hand and pint in the other, had a fraction of a second in which to register the appearance of his father and uncle before he ducked into the corridor by the phone-box and lavatories. Jessica, similarly equipped, but with a Bacardi and Coke instead of beer, didn't react so quickly. She looked at Ed's disappearing back and then at the bar, uncertain what to do. Catching Peter's eye, she waved, and Charlie waved back. 'All right over there?'

'Fine thank you, Mr Harrison.'

'On your own?'

'I was meeting this friend, only he didn't turn up.' Lying, Jessica had discovered, was easy, if done with enough conviction. 'Spending my waitress wages,' she added, patting her denim backpack and producing her toothpaste smile, designed to stop all living creatures in their tracks, especially men.

'Ah, yes, well done. Serena and all of us were most grateful. And to your grandfather, too, of course, for all his sterling work with the car-parking and so on. Is he here?'

Jessica shook her head, her glossy black ponytail swinging. 'He's having an early night. Gets a bit tired these days, does Granddad.'

'Of course he does. Well, thanks again. We'll be over there if you need us,' Charlie added gallantly, indicating an empty table.

'Thank you, Mr Harrison and Mr Harrison.' Jessica grinned with studied innocence, offering them another little wave.

'There's something about that girl . . .' murmured Peter, once they were seated out of earshot with their pints.

'You mean she's bloody cheeky?'

'Yes. And something else . . . I don't know . . .' Peter frowned. 'She's so young, but something about her seems very *old*.'

'Really? Can't say I'd noticed. Ed's keen on her – but, then, he's at the age where he'd be keen on a chair if it was decked in a short enough skirt. Remember those days? Christ . . .' Charlie threw back his head and laughed. 'Testosterone raging . . . Oh dear, I wouldn't go back to all that for anything, would you?'

'Certainly not.' Peter smiled, feeling a little superior but trying not to show it. Until Serena, his brother's love-life had been messy and exuberant. He, in contrast, had had only one long relationship before Helen, whom he had recognized at once as someone attractive and intelligent enough to be his ideal partner for the long haul. From the first he had been proud of how independent and career-oriented she was – quite the opposite of Serena, who'd made it no secret that her ambitions did not stretch beyond motherhood. Helen was hard-working too, which Peter liked, and had a passion that matched his for the detail and idiosyncrasies of English law.

'Talking of which, how's Theo getting on?' Charlie chuckled. 'Finding time to enjoy himself, I hope?'

Peter, swelling visibly with fatherly pride, was about to deliver an account of the sporting and academic prowess of his eldest when they both noticed Jessica sauntering over to their table, swinging her denim bag. 'Excuse me, sorry to be a bother and all that, but . . . I mean, like, you said if I needed anything?'

'We did,' Charlie assured her, avoiding the stern look in Peter's eye.

'It's just that I've got to catch the train back to London and I've just phoned and the last one leaves in fifteen minutes and I won't get there if I walk, and I've really got to catch it as I have this job in a hairdresser's at the Arndale on a Saturday.'

'Do you indeed? Right. In that case –'

'Would you like us to call you a taxi?' suggested Peter,

reluctant to abandon his pint and the conversation, which hadn't even begun to steer in any of the directions he had planned.

'I've tried that.' Jessica fiddled with the thick sleek hair, momentarily uncertain. 'But there's only two that work in Barham and they're both booked up.'

'I see.' Charlie glanced at his empty glass, then at Peter's, which was still half full. 'I say, Peter, perhaps . . .'

'Of course.' Peter stood up. 'I'll run you over there.'

'Thank you so much, Mr Harrison.'

'No problem.'

'And I'll keep your beer warm,' Charlie promised, as the pair left the pub.

Outside Ed, hovering behind a large wooden tub of tight-budded rhododendrons, leapt back as his uncle, the cause of his wait in the cold car park, strode out through the door. He heard enough of the conversation to gather that Jessica had wangled a lift to the station, and pressed himself against the stone wall, murmuring curses. He had been well in there. *Well* in. Peering through the foliage and glimpsing Jessica's pale bare legs, splendid beneath the frayed hem of her mini-skirt as she clambered into the car, he groaned.

Ed smoked a cigarette as consolation, dropped the stub into the flower tub, then popped a stick of gum into his mouth and retrieved his bicycle from under the hedge where he had hidden it half an hour before. He pedalled slowly down the lane towards Ashley House, distracted by keen disappointment and a dim disquiet that on a day when he should have been con-templating the demise of his great-aunt he had allowed himself to be so preoccupied by less edifying matters. He always wanted sex, of course – what seventeen-year-old virgin male didn't? – but today it had been particularly bad. All through the service, the hymns, the prayers for the departed, he had been able to think of little else – which made him feel sort of guilty but also annoyed. It wasn't like he was religious or anything and watching someone being buried was bound to make one think of a pleasant alternative. Wasn't it?

Ed was half-way down the lane now, far from the lights of the pub but not yet within sight of home. On the outward journey he hadn't noticed how dark it was, or how cold. He had been too excited, his groin aching at the recollection of Jessica's tongue in his ear and her promises during their few snatched moments among the coats upstairs. Now, however, with the trees crowding overhead, blocking out the meagre light coming from the fingernail of moon, the darkness seemed as thick as treacle. A creature scuttling in the undergrowth to his left made him start.

Thinking that only an idiot would be scared of a familiar country lane, and of how the man from the Royal Marines would laugh, Ed began none the less to pedal faster, no longer bothering to steer round the numerous pot-holes and puddles pitting the way. Soon he was blinking sweat from his eyes, trying to fix his gaze on the spot where he imagined the bend in the lane to be, fearing that when he reached it he would find not the illuminated squares of Ashley House's numerous latticed windows but yet more darkness.

'Did you have a nice time?' called Serena, when she heard the front door.

'Yep.' Ed, the panic still upon him, hovered in the doorway of the television room where his mother was lying on the sofa with one eye on a book and the other on the screen. She had her new glasses on, half-moon ones that made her look like an old lady, but not old because her hair was still silky soft and mostly brown, and her skin like smooth soap.

'Give us a hug, then,' she said, patting the sofa.

Ed hung on by the door, the fear gone now and the desire for sex too – with Jessica or anybody else. He longed to nestle up to his mother, but hesitated, aware of the unused Durex in

31

his back pocket. 'Just going to the loo,' he called, racing up the stairs two at a time and sprinting along the top landing to his bedroom, which was nicely away from everyone at the far end of the corridor, with its own bathroom alongside. It took a few seconds to clamber on to a chair and return the Durex to the secret bag he kept on the dusty top of his wardrobe. Then he smeared toothpaste round his teeth, washed his hands and raced back to the television room. 'What are you watching?' he asked, a little breathless as he flopped on to the sofa.

'It's something telling us what to do in a terrorist crisis – buy tins of baked beans, hide in a cellar if you've got one, that sort of thing.'

'Oh.' Ed scratched his head. 'Well, we've got a cellar anyway.'

Serena laughed. 'Yes, that's smelly and damp and so full of your uncle's wine that we could hardly fit ourselves down there, let alone food supplies and blankets.'

'There's that new reality show on the other side,' ventured Ed. 'Can we watch that instead?'

Serena yawned. 'I suppose so . . . I'm too tired to care. Ugh – imagine cameras watching *us* all the time,' she added cheerfully, once Ed had switched channels and that season's contestants appeared, slouching on bean-bags and drinking beer. 'Imagine everybody knowing what you were up to twenty-four hours a day, all the little things you keep hidden . . . Would you like that?'

Ed paused, console in hand, alerted by something in her voice, a certain *knowingness* that made his stomach twist. Was it possible that she knew all about the pub and not working and Jessica and the dusty box on top of the wardrobe and the locked suitcase of magazines? On screen, one of the contestants had pulled out a dildo and was dipping it into her mug of beer. 'Actually,' he muttered, 'that terrorist thing did look quite interesting.' He switched channels again and dropped his head on to her shoulder.

'That's better.' Serena tucked an arm round him and kissed the crown of his head, smelling smoke but not saying anything because, these days, such moments of maternal physical closeness were rare and she missed them.

Side by side on their own much smaller sofa some ten miles away, Roland and Elizabeth watched the same programme, the remains of their supper on plates at their feet. Through the gap in the curtains, which had been designed for their old sitting room in Guildford and didn't close properly, a stream of car headlights flashed past, as regular almost as the ticking of the second hand on the clock above the fireplace.

'All right, sweetheart?'

'Mm.'

'I always think the only good thing about a funeral is the hymns.'

Roland nodded. She was trying to be jolly, he knew, talking for the sake of it so he wouldn't guess how miserable she was. After the funeral she had gone straight upstairs to the phone in her bedroom and closed the door. There had been quiet talking, then a bit of louder stuff and some crying. Roland, making a pot of tea, had tried not to listen, but it was hard with the bedroom being right above the kitchen and the walls of the cottage so thin. A little later she had come downstairs with a red nose and puffy eyes, full of questions about what homework he had for the weekend and whether he thought it too early for her to start preparing supper.

Roland had played along for a bit, then said, 'Was that Richard?' Whereupon his mother had burst into tears and hugged him hard and said yes, but it didn't matter because he had been a shit and she was well rid of him, and what she needed was a strong drink. When Roland said he'd made tea, she patted the pot and squatted down to pull out a bottle from the wine rack set between the two cupboards underneath. Eight slots for eight bottles, filled and emptied each week with exactly the regularity as the slots for the eggs in the fridge door and the jars of pasta ranged above them. Roland had handed her the corkscrew, then carefully stirred two heaped sugars into his mug and retreated into the sitting room.

He wouldn't miss Richard, he decided, casting a look at his mother, who had kicked off her heavy shoes and was resting her stockinged feet on the chair next to the sofa. There was a small ladder in one, showing the yellow ridges of her big toe nail. Richard, in his view, had been noisy and unreadable from the start, the sort of man who repeated jokes and still expected you to laugh, ignoring Roland one minute, then asking him impossible questions the next. He had an ex-wife whom he called 'the old cow' and an open-topped sports car that was always breaking down. His job was something boring to do with the Arts Council, though he talked about it as if he was running the country. His breath smelt too, sometimes so badly that Roland had wondered how his mother could bear to be anywhere near him, let alone press her lips to the scratchy thicket of his beard.

'What about a biscuit or two? There are some of those nice chocolate ones, I think. Would you like one?'

'Not really, but I'll get them if you want.'

'I shouldn't.' She patted the swell of her stomach dolefully. 'I'm far too fat already.'

'No, you're not,' Roland replied, partly out of duty but mostly because he never thought of his mother as fat or thin. She just *was* and he couldn't imagine her otherwise. He fetched the biscuits and she ate two, very quickly.

'Did you see this?' she said, when she had finished, waving Cassie and Stephen's invitation. 'As it's a Saturday I thought we could make a day of it – go to an exhibition or something beforehand.'

Roland was loath, after the tedium of the afternoon, to

commit himself to another adult party, but did not want to ruin all the effort she was making to be cheerful.

'She is your godmother . . .'

'Yeah . . . I know.'

They were silent for a few minutes until Elizabeth, still studying the invitation, let out a long sigh. 'Funerals and weddings . . . Sometimes I wonder why we bother.'

'Look, I'll come to Aunt Cassie's party, okay?' said Roland, fiercely, detecting the glum turn the conversation was taking and wanting to put a stop to it.

'Oh, thank you, darling.' Elizabeth's expression had switched in an instant from slack despondency to watery-eyed joy. 'Do you realize it will be you lot next, my darling – Maisie, Clem, Theo, you, the next generation – getting married, starting families. Oh, my goodness, I shall enjoy that – becoming a grandmother. Oh, my goodness.' Elizabeth laughed, a rich, natural laugh, full of amazement at the pleasure this image afforded, like a little window on to a better world.

Roland stood up, in a hurry suddenly to be alone in his room with the cotton-wool solace of some music and one of his art books. It happened like that sometimes – like suddenly he couldn't bear to be near her a moment longer, not because he didn't love her but because he understood her so well that the pressure was simply too much. 'Going upstairs . . .' He stuffed his hands into his jeans pockets and sauntered out of the room, forcing himself not to break into a run when he reached the steep little stairs connecting the ground floor to the two bedrooms and bathroom above. There was an attic too, a lovely huge space, which he peered at longingly sometimes from the top of the pull-out ladder that led up to it. One day it would be his, his mother had promised, when she had enough money for a conversion. Which, with his dad in America and not sending cheques any more, would probably be never, Roland reflected, casting a wistful glance up at the trap-door in the ceiling before he slipped into his bedroom.

Downstairs Elizabeth tipped the last inch of wine into her glass and reached for the biscuit packet. She ate several more in quick succession, doing her best to concentrate on their sugary sweetness instead of on the sourness of her own self-loathing.

By the time Charlie and Peter got back from the Rising Sun, Serena and Ed had retired upstairs to bed. The two brothers were greeted in Ashley House's wide oak-panelled hall by Poppy, who leapt gleefully from her bed in the kitchen at the sound of the car and trotted along the passage, dragging her blanket with her by way of welcome. She bleated with particular pleasure at the sight of Charlie, burrowing her nose and blanket into the back of his knees for attention.

'Shush, you daft dog,' he scolded, tugging her silky ears. 'You'll wake the household.'

'That's what Dad always called Boots – and Little Boots, come to that. Do you remember?'

'What?'

'Daft. You daft animal, he'd say.'

'Did he?' Charlie frowned. 'I don't remember. I remember many things, but not that.' He cast a look at Peter as they eased off their coats. The pub had been good, but not quite right, somehow. Picking up his beer after dropping Jessica at the station, his brother had launched into an unwelcome and unexpected diatribe on the upkeep of Ashley House, as if he had been secretly scrutinizing the place with a magnifying-glass. Charlie did his best not to take offence but had been offended none the less. It had taken all his natural affability to ride the discussion without losing his temper. It had been a far cry from the easy exchange of news and views he had hoped for and he was determined now to set things right. 'A nightcap?'

'Excellent. A malt, please . . . and a few left-overs if there are any – those pub sandwiches were disgusting.'

'Coming right up.' Charlie headed for the kitchen, closely followed by the dog. When he went into the television room a few minutes later with a tray of drinks and food, he found Peter sitting squarely in the large leather armchair, so often frequented by their father that the smell of his pipe was still faintly detectable in its beaten leather folds.

'Aah . . . good man,' growled Peter, 'that's *exactly* what I need.'

'Cheers.' Charlie stretched out on the sofa, balancing his own drink and a heaped plate of left-over canapés on his stomach. It was weird, he mused, seeing his brother in the old man's chair, looking so like him yet not because Peter was so much leaner, his nose was longer and instead of John's big-lobed ears, his were markedly small and delicate. Weird but nice, Charlie decided, raising his glass, feeling pleasantly – mildly – drunk. 'To Aunt Alicia, and all who sailed in her . . . to Cassandra and Stephen . . . to the Future . . . Talking of which, Serena and I were thinking of changing the layout of this room a bit – knocking down that wall there, left of the door, easing access to the kitchen, useful for TV dinners and so on . . . and upstairs, we thought we might convert the green dressing room into an *en suite* one day, take the pressure off the top-floor bathroom so that when Elizabeth's staying she can relieve herself without having to stomp down the hall and wake up the rest of the house in the process. And then there's the old toolshed, which I'd love to turn into a proper studio for Serena . . .' Charlie faltered, discouraged by the expression on Peter's face. 'Improvements, as you were suggesting in the pub . . .'

'What I was suggesting in the pub . . .' Peter felt for the signet ring on the little finger of his left hand and twisted it so that the face was next to his knuckle. 'What I was suggesting,' he pressed on, soothed as always by this small correction to the ring, which had belonged to his father and was seal-engraved with the family crest, 'was merely the replacing of a few missing roof tiles, regrouting the front wall, getting those weeds out before they crack the patio to smithereens and maybe setting that weathervane on an even keel before it topples off in the next high wind and kills somebody.'

'Oh.'

'Not – as I said earlier – that I want to interfere or criticize.'

'No.' Charlie eased himself to a more upright position and stared hard at the patterns criss-crossing the sides of his crystal whisky tumbler. 'But that's what you're doing, isn't it?' His usually jovial face was slack with dismay.

'No, it isn't,' insisted Peter, quietly. 'I love this place – I can't help wanting it to be looked after.'

'And so it is . . . and always shall be.' Charlie drained his glass. 'Okay?'

'Okay.' Peter swirled the remaining swig of his whisky, telling himself not to be surprised at Charlie's resistance, but feeling suddenly as if they were perched on a tightrope, unbalancing each other in their efforts not to fall off. 'And as for the other . . . er . . . more extensive alterations you mentioned, go easy, won't you? Too much change might upset Mum.'

'Upset Mum or upset you?'

'Don't be ridiculous. Each custodian of this house has made his mark. I fully support your right to do as you wish . . . within reason.' Peter looked up to meet the gaze of his brother's blue eyes, which seemed both bold and terrified. 'It's your house now. And I'm delighted it is. I gave it freely and stand by that gift.'

Slowly Charlie let out his breath. 'Good . . . that's good to hear. The plans are still just vague ideas,' he added carefully, 'and would probably cost far too much to carry out anyway. I'm a civil servant, remember.' He pulled a comic face, wanting to puncture the bubble of tension that was now in danger of ruining the evening. 'A civil servant who – very happily, I might add – settled for bricks and mortar instead of cash. When Mum goes, whatever remains in the bank will be for you three – you, Lizzy and Cassie – and I'm happy about that too. Peter? Don't go all stony-faced on me. I'll deal with all the things you mentioned, I promise. You were right to point them out. The truth is, Sid doesn't keep on top of repairs any more and Serena and I are already thinking about a replacement. Now, let's drink some more Scotch and stop behaving like grumpy old men.'

Peter grunted agreement and reached for the whisky. He filled Charlie's glass before his own, tipping the bottle slowly and carefully, then adding water from the jug Charlie had brought from the kitchen. 'I'm the grumpy old man,' he muttered, placing one hand briefly on his younger brother's shoulder. 'Ask Helen. I'm always biting her head off. Don't know how she puts up with it.'

'Nor do I,' joked Charlie. The hand on his shoulder had meant everything. Peter was good like that – a dragon at one minute, then so conciliatory and understanding that you had to forgive him.

'By the way,' said Peter, after a few moments of a now thoroughly companionable silence, 'how does Umbria in August sound?'

'Umbria in August?' Charlie echoed, laughing.

'It was Helen's idea. She's found this spectacular farmhouse-villa in the hills outside Todi –'

'Where's that?'

'Near Orvieto – well, not far. Anyway it's got seven bedrooms, a massive swimming-pool, hot and cold running maids, that sort of thing. We thought it might be fun to get the whole family out there – move Ashley House to Italy, so to speak. In fact, we've already shelled out a deposit. Places like that, you have to move quickly.'

'Who's moving Ashley House?' said Serena, appearing in the

doorway in a pair of Charlie's pyjamas, hair tousled, face pale with sleepiness.

Charlie swivelled into a sitting position and reached out a hand to draw her to the sofa. 'Sweetheart, did we wake you?'

'No,' Serena assured him, yawning as she clambered on to the sofa and tucked her legs under her chin. 'It was your mother – I heard her walking round her room, then a sort of bump, and I was just about to go in when it all went quiet again. Then I heard an owl hooting, and Poppy barked. *Then* I heard you.' She yawned again.

'Poor baby,' Charlie whispered, reaching out and stroking her hair. Serena smiled and closed her eyes, tipping her head towards his hand.

Watching them, Peter felt a shiver of something between admiration and envy, not of Serena, whose beauty, while obvious, had never stirred anything but the purest appreciation, but for the way they *were* together: the effortless intimacy of their partnership. In many ways they were an old-fashioned couple, Charlie earning the money, calling the shots, but it worked – by God, it worked. Helen's hair, thicker and shorter – more *bristly* – than Serena's, didn't lend itself to stroking, but even if it had flowed like silk to her waistline, Peter would never have touched it in that way, in all the twenty-five-odd years he had known her, at such a moment, with such protective tenderness. He and Helen were tender when they made love, of course, more so if anything as the years trickled by, but outside the bedroom they had always been businesslike, running their hectic lives like a well-oiled machine.

'Peter and Helen have booked an Italian villa for us all to go to in the summer,' Charlie explained.

'Have they? What heaven.'

'Umbria . . . Big enough for the whole family.'

'Including your mother?'

'Certainly,' replied Peter, firmly. 'I know she's not keen on flying but it would do her so much good, don't you think? Her first proper break without Dad – I'll tie her to the plane if necessary.'

'Now, that I would like to see,' said Charlie, as he heaved himself off the sofa, pulling Serena gently with him. 'Come on, my petal, it's way past our bedtime.'

'I'll follow shortly,' Peter told them, pointing at his glass, in which half an inch of whisky remained, but really just wanting to stay a little longer in the deep armchair with the quiet tick of the old house around him and the wind rattling the windows like an excluded guest.

It was almost eleven o'clock by the time Jessica tottered along the platform towards the exit at Wandsworth station, high heels clacking on the concrete. She had fallen asleep on the train and woken just before her stop to find a bloke with bushy hair staring at her with the look men had when they were interested. She'd given him her best fuck-off stare and crossed her legs so that he couldn't ogle up her skirt. He'd got off in front of her and was striding up the platform now, the only other person in sight, shoulders hunched under a dirty green anorak. Jessica slowed a little so there was no chance of catching up and checked her phone for messages. Ed would have turned his off by now, she knew, but she punched in 'c u soon J', then tried her mum and got no answer.

At the flats the lifts weren't working, though few people were dumb enough to risk them at night anyway, what with all the nutters who used them to piss in or trade gear. Jessica took off her shoes to climb the stairs, partly so that none of the estate's retards could hear her coming and partly because her toes, squashed into the tight pointy plastic all day, were killing her. At the door of the flat she rummaged in her bag for her keys, keeping a wary eye on the dank hallway that stretched on either side. From inside she could hear the sound of the television and guessed her mum would be asleep on the settee in front of it, her ciggies and an empty can on the floor next to her.

'Where've you been, then?' said Maureen, the moment the door opened, not asleep but leaning against the kitchen door, like she'd spent all night waiting up.

'Nice to see you too.' Jessica tossed her shoes and bag on to the floor and pushed past her into the kitchen. 'Anything to eat?'

'Haven't you had any dinner?'

'I wouldn't want anything to eat if I had, would I?'

'Where've you been, then, love?' asked Maureen, in a softer voice, putting a fresh cigarette into her mouth and watching as her daughter moved round their coop of a kitchen, fixing herself a sandwich.

'I stayed on a bit with Granddad.'

'Oh, yes, and how was he?' inquired Maureen, green eyes narrowing with suspicion.

'We had a cup of tea. He's fine. Then I went to the Rising Sun and had a couple of drinks.'

'*Very* nice. And that Harrison boy was there, I expect, was he?'

'Might have been.'

'You're wasting your time, girl. Having a grandfather who's their gardener and playing waitress at their fancy funerals doesn't get you into their world, you know. He's pissing around with you, that's all.'

'Like you would know, wouldn't you?'

'I know a bloody sight more than you, young lady,' snapped Maureen, tapping ash into a saucer.

'Fat lot of good it's done you.' Jessica pressed the two halves of her sandwich together and bit into it, keeping her eyes, which were as green as Maureen's but brighter and more hostile, fixed on her mother. Such skirmishes were part of their daily routine, how they talked to each other. Once, they had upset her, but now, at sixteen, with the end of her schooldays and a bit of independence in sight, Jessica had got better at not caring. Her mum's life, by her own, moaning admission, had been a mess: men who'd run off, including Jessica's father, jobs in pubs and cleaning people's houses, offloading Jessica to long-suffering neighbours or, when she really couldn't cope, at Granddad's in Barham – it had always been a case of holding things together, making do, railing at disappointment. Jessica had seen enough of it, felt too much part of it, to want anything like that for herself. 'I would have stayed over – Granddad said I could – but I've got to be at the hairdresser's by nine thirty.'

'Oh, yeah, this job of yours . . .' Maureen inhaled deeply on her cigarette and folded her arms. 'How much did you say you're getting?'

'I didn't.' Jessica took a bite of sandwich, letting half of it splurge out on purpose so that she looked gross. 'None of your bleeding business.'

'Come on, Jess, don't be like that.' Maureen dropped her cigarette into the saucer and advanced upon her daughter with open arms. 'Be nice to your old mum, darling, I do love you, you know.'

'Yeah, whatever.' Holding her sandwich out of the way, Jessica allowed herself to be embraced. She even let herself relax a little, taking in the familiar smoky scent and thinking that a hug was nice, even if it was the whiff of extra cash that had prompted it. 'Thirty quid plus tips, Jerry said.'

'Jerry. You want to watch him an' all.'

'I can look after myself,' replied her daughter, archly, pushing Maureen away and going into their little lounge to finish her sandwich in front of the television. She ate slowly, leaving the crusts, which were brittle, on the arm of her chair, positioning them in a little line across all the ring-stains left by years and years of too full, too hot mugs of Cup-a-soup, coffee and tea. Her mum telling her to watch out for Jerry was a laugh. How did she think she'd got the fucking job in the first place? Saturday jobs were hard to find, especially with girls like Shona and Aileen trawling the same possibilities, with their pushy mums to back them up. Jessica had used her own wiles, not letting him go all the way, but undoing his jeans and giving him what he wanted with her hand – it never took long with men like him, full of flirt but worried all the time that someone might come in or the wife might get on the phone.

'You can work here for as long as you want, darling,' he had grunted afterwards, when she was wiping her hands. 'So long as we can have a cuddle now and then.' He'd kissed her and patted her arse, then strolled back into the salon. And when Jessica had bumped into Shona and Aileen in the precinct later that day she'd held her head high and asked how was *their* job-hunting going?

March

Stephen hovered in the doorway, avoiding eye-contact with his guests as he scanned the packed sitting room for Cassie. It was a few moments before he spotted her, in the corner by the bookcase, deep in conversation with Charlie, always the most convivial of her three siblings. She was laughing at something, throwing back her cloud of blonde hair and opening her mouth wide, every sinew of her face and body alert with pleasure and interest. At forty-two she was still beautiful, alive with energy, so open and giving, so impossible not to love. Watching her, Stephen experienced a fierce urge to elbow his way through the throng and lay claim to her, to kiss her laughing mouth, taste the joy of whatever she was sharing with her brother. He stared hard, willing her to turn her head, fighting a momentary un-edifying prickle of envy. Sibling, friend or stranger, the world engaged her so. She was lost in conversation with Charlie, just as she lost herself in anything she did – advising clients on colour schemes for their homes, reading a book, watching telly. She managed to fall asleep the instant she put her mind to it. In contrast, Stephen had spent many of his thirty-seven years struggling with the sense that he was standing, arms akimbo, watching an irreversible video of his life. Even at his desk, on the rare occasions that his fingers flew over the keys, steering his Irish detective through another intricate case of murder and skeletons-in-cupboards, half his mind remained not just obstin-ately unabsorbed, but separate and critical of his endeavours.

The weeks since Cassie's aunt's funeral had been dominated by preparations for the party. Rushing to finish the decorating, haggling with the local deli over revised estimates for the food and drink, Stephen had wondered many times whether it would prove worth the effort. Only Cassie's infectious enthusiasm had kept him going. 'We've so much to celebrate,' she had reminded him, just the night before, as they lay side by side on the sitting-room floor, nursing headaches from the petrol smell of fresh gloss and surrounded by yards of the sticky masking tape that had protected their new bottle-green carpet from stray paint dribbles on the skirting-boards. 'Let's see now . . .' She held up her fingers and began, literally, to count their blessings. 'Your contract, owning this *beautiful* house and . . . I'm sure there was *something* else.'

Stephen rolled across the carpet and pulled her into his arms, so eagerly that a nest of tape caught in her hair.

'Ow – bugger!'

'Hang on – stop pulling, you're making it worse. Don't move.' He sat up and held her head still to inspect the damage, trying to appear serious but thinking how dear she looked with the tape in her hair and such a furious expression. 'Now, don't move.' He went to fetch some scissors and then set about teasing free each strand, doing his best not to hurt her. He worked slowly, sucking his lower lip in concentration, aware of her mounting irritation and that he enjoyed having her at his mercy. 'There, all done.'

Cassie rubbed her scalp. 'Are you sure there isn't a bald patch?'

'Well . . . only a small one.'

'Where?' she squealed, then caught sight of his face. 'Oh, Stephen! How mean! It's too late for teasing – I'm tired.' She lunged for a newspaper and flung it at him, catching his shoulder. He threw it back far more vigorously, scattering pages, which flew briefly – like drunken birds – before subsiding across the furniture. Then, because she was starting to smile, he threw a sofa cushion as well, one of the old ones, which landed square on her chest, releasing a cloudburst of feathers. Moments later they were wrestling, then tugging frantically at the zips and buttons of each other's clothes. They toppled into the biggest armchair where they made ungainly love, as feverishly enthusiastic as they had been the first time, three years before, when the passion Stephen had nursed for so long had been rewarded by an explosion of reciprocity.

Now Stephen glanced at that armchair and saw that Cassie's square-jawed barrister of an elder brother, Peter, occupied it, looking grave and a little too self-important. Stephen couldn't help laughing. They had left a wet patch, he remembered gleefully, right in the middle of the cushion. Cassie had scrubbed at it with Fairy Liquid and a J-cloth while he finished peeling the masking tape off the carpet.

'What's the joke, then?'

Stephen spun round, caught off-guard by the familiar voice of his old friend, Keith Holmes, whom he hadn't seen arrive. 'I . . . There's no joke, no, at least not one I'm prepared to share.' He blushed, feeling as wrong-footed as he had when Keith had erupted with delighted expletives out of a small book-signing queue a couple of months before. 'Glad you could make it, mate,' he added, so awkwardly that a trace of something like pain flashed across Keith's rugged face; a beaten-up face, these days, Stephen thought, as if the man had spent two decades in a boxing-ring or fronting a rugby scrum.

'Still can't believe it, eh? After all these years.'

'No, I guess not.' Stephen blew out his cheeks, shaking his head. 'Our days at Kelsey Grammar seem a long way away.'

'Thank God. What a dive that was.' Keith grinned, producing a more familiar version of his features – the lips a little lop-sided, the dark eyes flashing with charm. 'Stephen Smith a thriller writer – I tell you, I'm still pinching myself.' Keith chuckled and reached for his cigarettes, only to recall that he was in a no-smoking zone. He ran the palm of his hand across the top of his head instead, reassured, for no reason he could have defined, by the feel of the short, thick bristles of his crew-cut. Looking round at the elegant furnishings and polite wine-sipping guests, he let out a low whistle. 'You've done all right, Steve, I'll say that for you. Talk about landing on your feet.'

'Well, Cassie is an interior designer . . .' Stephen faltered, aware that he was sounding pompous and remembering, with sudden distressing vividness, the ugly, cramped box-rooms and the scrubby back gardens in which he and Keith had played out their mutually unsatisfactory childhoods in the suburbs of Hull. Seeing him in the Camden bookshop, he had felt a confused surge of pleasure and anxiety. They had been good friends – the best – but had lost touch when Stephen had done a TEFL course and gone to South America, returning twelve years later to forge a new life in London. Keith, from what Stephen had gathered during the course of their drink after the signing, had stayed in Hull, married a local girl and followed his father into the building trade. He hadn't made the move to London until his early thirties, and within a year of doing so was eking out a living on building sites. His wife had headed back north with their two sons.

'Cassie's great,' Keith remarked, nodding appreciatively as he recalled her firm handshake at the door. On learning who he was, she had promptly kissed him on both cheeks, doing the any-friend-of-Stephen's-is-a-friend-of-mine routine, which was corny but bloody nice all the same. 'Classy,' he added, casting a sidelong look at Stephen, reappraising the leather-tasselled loafers, the crisp blue chinos and white linen shirt, the mani-cured nails and floppy Hugh Grant haircut. The Stephen he remembered was a sallow-faced seventeen-year-old, with dark, angry eyes and a gallery of bruises round his torso and thighs, varying in colour according to their age and the degree of severity with which his old man had chosen to swing the belt. His hair had been long and greasy then, often held back in a ponytail or shoved up under a cap, particularly when they were skiving off school at the bus station or in shopping malls, trying not to look like truants. Spotting Stephen's picture in the bookshop window, the groomed appearance, the enigmatic smile, had been like having two realities running side by side. Then, when they got talking afterwards, the two pictures had merged and Keith had felt this shout of joy inside – not just for Stephen but for himself – like the revival of hope. 'How did you two get together, then, you and such a classy bird?'

Stephen hesitated, wanting to do justice to the extraordinary business of meeting Cassie Harrison and the certain knowledge that such a task would be impossible. Explaining love at first sight was a tough call at the best of times, let alone to someone with whom he felt so out of touch, who was clearly down on his luck and who, Stephen thought, should have stayed in the box of the past to which he had hitherto confined him. Though he was on Christmas-card terms with his parents, these days, cutting loose from the first eighteen years of his life had been as fundamental and deliberate as a snake shedding a dead skin. 'I was doing some research on Cassie's uncle for a book – my first – about unrecognized heroes of the Second World War. I went to interview Cassie's parents about him at their place in Sussex.' Stephen paused, as an image of Ashley House shimmered in his mind, with its frothing ivied walls, and chimney-stacks rising like periscopes out of the angled sea of its grey slate roof. 'And, well, Cassie was there too. I ended up staying for supper. We played Scrabble and . . .'

'Scrabble?'

Stephen looked away quickly, cursing himself for even beginning to attempt to lead his friend on to such hallowed ground. How could Keith or anyone else understand what had happened to him that day? A bachelor and a cynic, he had fallen in love so instantly and deeply that even now, six years on, he trembled to remember it. A long period of mad pursuit had followed, while Cassie had remained indifferent, going through her own private tortures over a married man who had promised to leave his wife but never quite managed it.

'Scrabble?' Keith repeated with an irreverent guffaw, thinking for no good reason of Stephen's sister, Claire, whom he had screwed once, really quickly, standing up in the little alleyway that ran alongside their house, leaning against the cold wall for support. She'd never given him a second glance after that, though personally Keith would have been happy to keep the thing going. She was in Canada now, Stephen had said, with teenaged kids and a husband who spoke French.

Stephen was searching for a way to change the subject when Elizabeth, frumpy in spite of a glittering black dress and crimson lipstick, bounced up to him. 'The house is lovely, Stephen, just lovely. I've been having a snoop upstairs, I hope you don't mind.'

'Not at all. This is Keith Holmes, a very old friend from my dim and distant youth. Keith, this is Elizabeth, Cassie's elder sister. She lives in Sussex too, very near Cassie's mother. And now, if you'll excuse me . . .' Stephen edged away. Cassie chose that moment to catch his eye. She smiled and the rest of the room melted away. Stephen mouthed, 'I love you,' and held up ten fingers, silently pronouncing the words 'Ten months to go.' He had to do it twice before she laughed in happy recognition, mouthing 'I love you too,' as she manoeuvred her way to Pamela, who was sitting alone on a high-backed chair, staring about her with the air of a bemused child.

'Your mother doesn't seem too good,' whispered Helen, perching on the arm of Peter's chair. She touched his shoulder briefly, wondering whether to inquire after the back muscles he had strained exercising the day before. Since his aunt's funeral – maybe even *because* of it, Helen mused – he seemed to have cranked up his fitness regime to a new level. If he didn't get to the gym from chambers he had taken to punishing himself for an hour in the evening, alternating between the bike and the rowing machine now installed in the games room of their new extension. 'Definitely worse than at the funeral.'

'Do you think so? I think she looks rather well.' Peter glanced across the room, relieved to see that Charlie was taking his turn at Pamela's side. 'In fact, she's done bloody well to come. Managing these things without Dad must still be hard for her.' He ran his hand across his forehead, briefly fingering his eyebrows – so bushy, these days – and the contrastingly smooth small circle of his bald patch. As one got older, hair grew in all the least desired places, he was discovering, while simultaneously absenting itself from where it was most needed. 'Would you go ga-ga if I died?' he asked after a pause, making a ghoulish face.

Helen chuckled. 'I hope not. What a horrible thought. And, anyway, I didn't mean to suggest for a moment that your mother is remotely ga-ga.' She hesitated, twisting her rope of pearls round her index finger as she pondered her mother-in-law, whom she had always found tricky – one of those quiet but immensely strong characters, who dominated a room, or an atmosphere, by saying nothing at all. 'She just sort of *floats* sometimes and . . . well, she is repeating herself more, isn't she? She must have asked after Genevieve at least three times tonight.'

Peter flexed his shoulders, grimacing at the knots of resistance that had taken root inside. 'At seventy-nine a little absent-mindedness should be perfectly allowable,' he growled, feeling as if he was defending something beyond the mental agility of his mother. 'For years your dear parents couldn't find a butter-dish without each other's help. And of course she's going to ask a lot about Genevieve because she adores Genevieve and having lost one little granddaughter she probably wishes she saw more of this one.'

'Talking of which . . .' Helen tapped a fingernail on the face of her wristwatch. She was in no mood to have her spirits dampened by references to the tragedy of their niece; neither did she want Peter to tell her, for the umpteenth time, that they didn't spend enough weekends with his family in the country. Ashley House was lovely, of course – rather like a grand hotel – but Genevieve was just as happy playing with her little friends in their own substantial house and garden in Barnes, while Chloë had netball matches, parties and increasing piles of homework to get through. More crucially, Peter often returned from the place in a fractious mood. After his funeral stop-over he had been positively stormy – from a hangover, he claimed, but Helen suspected that something more was going on, some fracas with Charlie, who was a dear but could also be maddeningly bumbling and indecisive. Probing had got her nowhere. The only good result of the visit, as far as she could see, was that her idea about the Italian villa had apparently received rapturous approval. She had confirmed the booking just that morning, emailing credit-card details and contact phone numbers, then gone to another website to reserve five very reasonably priced return tickets to Rome. Afterwards Helen had felt elated. They had spent far too many precious summer breaks making do with patchy sunshine and Ashley House's sludgy lake, reserving escapes to warmer climes for snatched weeks in the autumn. Working for years against Peter's obstinacy, Helen had been nothing short of ecstatic at his acceptance of her new plan. The rest of the Harrison clan accompanying them, while not ideal, was an easy price to pay. She was fond of her husband's family, and would feel even fonder, she was sure, under blue Umbrian skies, surrounded by olive groves, with a swimming-pool, not to mention a maid, who would shop for essentials, provide fresh towels and wipe their wet footprints from the villa's spectacular marble floors. 'I told Rita we'd be back by eleven,' she said now, her mind leaping from track to track as it always did – as it had to – to stay on top of things. 'It wouldn't be fair on either of them if Genny wakes for any reason – you know what she's like.'

'Indeed I do, and it's not yet ten,' Peter replied, wearily noting his wife's capacity to worry about arrangements to leave a place just minutes after she had crossed its threshold. He was weary, too, of the pain firing like electric shocks across his upper back, making hard work of what should have been an enjoyable occasion. But they had done the long trek from Barnes to Camden and he was determined not to let the demands of their delightful but exhausting four-year-old interrupt it prematurely.

Helen got off the arm of the chair and impatiently smoothed out the lap of her blue silk dress, which showed off her skinny figure but creased at the slightest ruffling. 'And there's Chloë too. We've got to collect her from her sleepover at eight tomorrow morning, so a late night wouldn't be a good idea.'

'Really, Helen, stop *fussing*.'

'Sorry,' she muttered, in such an uncharacteristic and sudden change of tack that he glanced at her in surprise. Helen looked away quickly, fiddling with the clasp on her evening bag, wishing they were leaving for Umbria the next day instead of in five months' time. Peter was right, she *was* always fussing. It was like a reflex she couldn't control. She hadn't always been like that. When she was pregnant with Genevieve a wonderful tranquillity had descended from nowhere, making her feel unworried, powerful and at peace. Filling her, unbidden, like some holy grace, it had ebbed away again, leaving her as she was now – as she had been when Theo and Chloë were small – whirling like a dervish between appointments and commitments, dragging anxiety and maternal guilt behind her like a ball and chain.

'Hello, you two. Are you all right over here? Peter, someone said you'd hurt your neck.'

'It was my shoulder, but it's fine, Cassie, thank you.' Peter heaved himself out of his chair with as much agility as he could muster and kissed his sister on both cheeks. 'Congratulations again. We're so happy for the pair of you, aren't we, Helen?'

'Delighted,' said Helen, smoothly. 'Though I gather we've all got to wait until January for the happy day.'

'It's not ideal, is it?' gushed Cassie, too happy with the evening and life in general to mind the dryness of her sister-in-law's tone. 'But there's so much to factor in, what with our work commitments and so on. What it does mean is that we have heaps of time to organize the thing properly. Charlie and Serena are being fantastic, saying Ashley House will be at our disposal. We're looking at marquees already; it turns out you can get special ones for the winter and in all sorts of exotic shapes too – Stephen's current favourite is like a cross between Tower Bridge and the Taj Mahal.' Cassie paused for breath, aware amid her exuberance of a faint temptation to disclose the possibility of another momentous event on the horizon, an event connected to the fact that as of that morning her period was officially three days overdue. Three whole days! It had been one day late before – two once, but never three. Stephen, still wary of the whole concept of parenthood, insisted it was far too early to make plans, but Cassie couldn't help thinking that if she was pregnant they might have to rush the wedding and maybe focus a big Ashley House gathering on a christening instead. 'So, all in all it'll be a bit like your fiftieth, Peter,' she continued gaily, 'a big tent on the lawn, slap-up food, and probably a jazz band because Stephen's mad about jazz.'

'How super,' murmured Helen, unmoved by her sister-in-law's girlish enthusiasm. To her a big white wedding seemed faintly ridiculous for a woman of almost forty-three, even if it was the first time down the aisle for both parties. There was something theatrical about Peter's younger sister that never failed to annoy her, as if she lived for display rather than substance, perhaps from having spent too many years focusing on wallpapers and carpet swatches, Helen decided, casting a beady look at Cassie but saying sweetly, 'How lovely for your mother to have another family wedding to look forward to, and at St Margaret's, too, where she and John married all those years ago.'

'Oh, yes, Mum *is* pleased.' Cassie cast an affectionate glance at the upright figure perched alone now on a high-backed chair. 'I'm so glad she came tonight – I'm so glad all of you came – it means the world to me, and to Stephen, not having a family of his own to speak of . . . at least, not like ours. His sister lives in Canada and he's on such poor terms with his parents that he says he doesn't want me to meet them before the wedding. He isn't even sure he's going to invite them, which is *so* sad, don't you think? Mum does seem frail, though, doesn't she?' she added, gazing wistfully at Pamela. 'All I can say is, thank God she's got darling Charlie and Serena to look after her. It takes the worry from all of us.'

'Thank God indeed,' murmured Helen. Without Peter's extraordinarily bold decision to pass the inheritance of the family home to his younger brother, such a fate might have been hers. She wasn't good with frailty. Even when the children were ill she felt a sort of deep impatience with it all – the sticky plastic spoons, the waiting, the endless *uncontrollability* of their recovery, perky one minute and floppy the next, just when you'd got your hopes up. Attempting to look after Pamela would have driven her mad. All her set ways and naps and cups of tea, and with no end in sight other than increasing fragility and *death*. It made her shudder just to think of it. At least with a child's soaring temperature or one of Peter's awful fluey colds, when she often wanted to shake the self-pity out of him as much as the illness, one could hold on to the cheering thought that it was *finite*. Remembering his strained shoulder suddenly, fearing it might be the start of some lingering malaise, she reached up and rubbed her palm tenderly across his upper back. 'And as for you, a visit to the physio might be in order.'

Peter flinched. 'Maybe.'

'I know a brilliant one,' put in Cassie, brightly. 'She's not far from you either, in Richmond. She works from home – it's a beautiful house, right on the river. I tell you, decorating the place was pure heaven. Her husband's a corporate lawyer or something – *loads* of money. She sorted out my clicky ankle, and Stephen's been to her a couple of times for his neck, which seizes up from sitting at his computer all day. I'll give you her number, Peter – don't let me forget, will you? Now I'd better circulate. Catch you later.'

'Sometimes I think I preferred your sister when she was single and subdued,' muttered Helen, darkly.

'Now, now,' scolded Peter, but with a twinkle in his eye because he knew exactly what she meant. 'Come on, we'll *circulate* too – for twenty more minutes before we get out of here.' He began to move, then grimaced, gripping his sore shoulder.

'I'll get that number off Cassie,' said Helen, alarmed at the pain on her husband's face. He was fifty-five, after all, she reminded herself, just three years older than her. People might well boast that fifty was the new forty, but it was meaningless if one didn't hang on to one's health.

Sitting on her chair with her handbag on her lap, Pamela kept her eyes down. Everybody, she felt, was watching her. She was watching herself. It was hateful. It made her feel *unsafe*, on constant red alert for a slip of memory, tongue or digestive system. Everything was worse if you worried about it, she knew, but it was impossible *not* to worry, especially being away from Ashley House in a place where nothing was familiar. Just the thrum of the London traffic that evening, the sirens, the car radios, the rumble of buses, had made her draw away from the window, reluctant even to peer out at such an imposing, alien world. And then, arriving at the party, she had been bursting for the loo, as she had known she would be, even though she had restricted herself to one cup of tea all afternoon. It was ridiculous to need the loo after so little, and all down to worry, of course – much more to do with her head than her waterworks – but what good was it to know that when the worry wouldn't stop and the ache in her bladder was as keen as a twisting knife? 'Cassie, dear, I need to go,' she had whispered, as soon as they were in the hall and being offered drinks.

'But you must use our *en suite*,' her daughter had insisted kindly, delivering hasty instructions about going up the stairs and turning right and left and second and third doors, then leaping away to let in more guests. Arriving on the landing, panting from the long flight of stairs, Pamela stared about her blankly. She tried various doors, tentatively at first and then with real urgency as the ache in her stomach grew unspeakable and a dreadful sensation of clammy wetness seeped into her pants. Stumbling at last on the main bedroom and its handsome *en suite*, she closed the door only to find there was no lock. Precious seconds were wasted while Pamela absorbed this unsettling fact, pitting her mounting desperation against visions of her soon-to-be son-in-law barging in to find her straddled on the loo, wad of paper in hand, every remaining shred lost of her already crumbling dignity. Desperation had won in the end, though the vision of Stephen opening the door remained throughout, rushing her unpleasantly as she relieved and cleaned herself as best she could. Afterwards, looking at her reflection in their mirrored wall above the basin, Pamela had held up her hands and watched them tremble. 'Hopeless old woman,' she had scolded herself, digging courage from her anger and squeezing her hands into fists. 'Stop being such a fool.' She had felt better after that, even humming a little as she powdered the shine from her forehead and filled the thinning line of her mouth with lipstick.

Walking back through the bedroom, she was able to take more notice of her surroundings – the forget-me-not blue curtains, the pretty trellises of flowers on the wallpaper, the long soft pile of the new cream carpet, the creaseless white duvet and pillows as plump as ripe fruit. Like the proverbial clean sheet, Pamela had thought wistfully, pressing a dimple into the duvet with one fingertip and remembering all the wonder of new love and the rich, complicated map of marriage that followed.

Going out on to the landing she almost bumped into Roland. 'Hello, darling, are you looking for the loo?'

'No, Gran,' mumbled her grandson, blushing. 'Stephen said if I was bored I could come up to his study and play on his computer. He's got loads of games apparently – says he prefers them to writing his books.' Roland glanced over the banisters, aware that if his mother saw him he'd be hauled downstairs again.

'Is Ed here too?' Pamela peered over his shoulder as if expecting his cousin to pop out of nowhere.

'Er . . . I think he stayed at Ashley House, didn't he? To do some revision for his A levels.'

'Of *course* he did. Silly Granny. I say, darling, would you mind giving me a little hand down the stairs? I'm feeling just the slightest bit dizzy and would so hate to fall and cause a fuss.'

Roland had led her to the high-backed chair and then gone back upstairs. She had stayed where she was, doing her best to seem happy and self-contained when she didn't feel either. 'Were they good games, dear?' she murmured, having glanced up and seen her grandson once more hovering nearby.

'Great,' Roland assured her, although his grandmother wouldn't have thought too highly of Lara Croft's plunging cleavage and the improbable arsenal of weaponry that had enabled her to save the world. He was still pondering the matter when Pamela gripped his wrist. 'What's that noise, dear? Do you hear it?'

'Uh – it's my phone, Gran. Excuse me a minute, I've got a

text.' Roland pulled his mobile out of his pocket and studied the screen. '*In pub. Pls warn when M & D on way home. Cheers, Ed.*'

'Someone nice?' inquired Pamela, whose own mobile had yet to be removed from the box in which Peter and Helen had presented it to her two Christmases before. 'Really,' she added, on a lovely burst of confidence, 'so many phones these days – I don't know what you all find to talk about.' At which point Serena, poised and elegant in a grey chiffon dress that made the few threads of silver in her chestnut hair shine like silk, tapped her mother-in-law's shoulder and said it was time they went home.

'*On way now,*' typed Roland, keeping the screen tipped away from his aunt, only to find his mother accosting him from the other side.

'Roland, really! Put that thing away.'

'Are we going too?' he asked hopefully, slipping the mobile into his pocket.

'Not quite.' Elizabeth smiled in a way that meant she had drunk enough to start enjoying herself.

'We could drop Roland back if he's had enough,' offered Serena, unable to resist patting her nephew's glossy dark hair, and feeling a swoop of motherly concern at the thought of her darling Ed poring over his history files at the kitchen table. 'I don't know why we didn't all come in one car – silly, really.'

'No, thanks. I'll stay with Mum,' replied Roland, grandly, putting an arm round Elizabeth's shoulders. 'Honestly, I'd like to stay . . . to, er, talk to Aunt Cass a bit. She *is* my godmother, after all.' He shifted from one foot to the other, torn between meeting his mother's gaze of gratitude and the darker expression on the face of his aunt.

'Do you think she enjoyed it?' Serena whispered, glancing over her shoulder at Pamela, who had fallen asleep, the tartan car blanket tucked under her chin. In the dim light the old dear's face, dusted still with a few traces of makeup – pink lipstick, a kiss of lilac eye-shadow – looked as delicate and pale as that of a china doll.

'Hard to tell, but I think so.' Charlie yawned widely and opened the window. The night air, icy even for March, hit his face like a cold shower.

'God, that's freezing! Do you have to?'

'Sorry, darling, I'm bushed.' Charlie began to wind it up but Serena reached across to stop him.

'Leave it open. I'll just turn the heating up a little.'

Charlie left the window open a crack and slowed his speed, in spite of the inviting black ribbon of the A3 under the beam of the headlights. Alone, he would have driven fast in spite of his fatigue but Serena, he knew, was now alert to the possibility of him falling asleep at the wheel. He could feel the fear pulsing out of her, drawing him in. It was six years since Tina had been run over. They had coped – moved on – but it had changed them, introduced moments, like this, when anxiety at the prospect of misfortune bulged out of all proportion and shadows of pain flitted between them.

'Good party, eh?' he said. 'I must say, Stephen grows on me. I wasn't sure, at first, about him and Cassie – different backgrounds and so on – but they really seem good together, don't you think? And he's done bloody well with those books of his.'

Serena, relaxing as he had intended, kicked off her shoes and flexed her toes in the warm blasts of heat circulating round their feet. 'I've always liked Stephen . . . and he's devoted to Cassie, which, at the end of the day, is all that matters, isn't it? They've settled on a date by the way – the fourteenth of January – which I said was fine.'

'They're mad. Whoever heard of a January wedding? What's wrong with the summer?'

'Apparently Stephen has a book deadline and Cassie says it will give them enough time to prepare. You know your little sister, she'll want synchronized colour schemes, hand-made dresses and food too beautiful to eat. She's praying for snow too, she said.'

'Snow?'

'You've got to admit it would look nice – St Margaret's steeple and all the gravestones crusted in white, holly berries and snow drifts –'

'Black ice and breakdown vehicles.'

Serena giggled. 'Spoilsport. Anyway, the rest of the year's going to be busy enough, what with Italy and Ed's eighteenth.'

Charlie groaned. 'Oh, God, I'd forgotten that ordeal. Can't we persuade him to have a twenty-first – put it off for three years?'

'The girls had an eighteenth.'

Charlie sighed and wound up the window. 'At least it's after his exams. Once they're out of the way we might all feel like a party.'

'He's working hard.'

'Is he now?' Charlie eyed his wife doubtfully, envying her faith in their easy-going seventeen-year-old. Returning his attention to the road, he found himself wishing, for by no means the first time during the last six years, that they had gone on to have another child. He had wanted to, very badly, but Serena had declared that Tina couldn't be 'replaced', that it would be wrong even to try. And now she was forty-nine, like him, which was definitely on the ancient side to become parents again, although, as he liked to remind her, Helen had been forty-eight when Genevieve was born, with nothing but joy all round.

Aside from whatever emotional gap a new baby might have filled, Charlie worried about the simple fact that, with the girls no longer at home and Ed almost through school, his wife did not have enough to do. The move to Ashley House had been a useful diversion and, during their first year, she had channelled her considerable artistic talents into a wheel and kiln she had set up in one of the outhouses. She would start her own cottage industry, she had said. But for months now all her little pots and vases had been gathering dust on shelves that were home to spiders, beetles and fieldmice, seeking warm bolt-holes during the winter. 'Had quite a chat with that friend of Stephen's,' he ventured now, as an idea took shape that he realized might solve several niggling problems simultaneously. 'Keith Holmes – nice bloke, rough round the edges, but a good heart. A builder apparently, said he was between jobs.'

'Oh, yes?'

'I just thought a man like that might be just the sort of Sid substitute we've been looking for. There would be loads he could do, including fixing up that draughty box you call a studio – put in some heating, make it really comfy. We could give him that as a first project, try him out.'

'Maybe.' They were off the motorway now, in the thicker darkness of the countryside. Specks of rain were flecking the window, running races with each other as they slid down the glass. Her husband still worried about her, Serena knew. And that was good, she told herself. 'Speak to him, if you like,' she murmured, 'though I'm never firing Sid – even if he turns up in a wheelchair, the darling. Such a part of the landscape. Pamela adores him, and he can still manage the lawn-mower and the shears.'

'Of course we won't fire Sid. As you say, he's part of the landscape . . . Hey, what's up?'

'Nothing.'

'Yes, there is.'

Serena let out a heavy sigh. 'I was just thinking of Roland, how protective he is of Elizabeth. It's not right. He asked me tonight if I had any ideas as to what he could do for her birthday, which is weeks and weeks away. Could you imagine Ed asking that? Or one of the girls, for that matter?'

Charlie chuckled. 'I could, actually. Anyway, did you have any ideas?'

'I told him we'd sort something out – a surprise get-together of the family. Was that okay?'

'Of course.'

'It falls on the first Saturday in May, which should be easy. I've already told Cassie and Peter. They've promised to keep it free – make a weekend of it.'

'Clever girl.'

'If only things had worked out between Elizabeth and Lucien. I was so sure they would.'

'If only a lot of things, eh?' said Charlie, softly, swinging the car into the lane leading to Ashley House, where the trees arched like the vaulted ceiling of a dark cathedral and the pot-holes were so deep and broad he had to slow to a crawl to negotiate them.

As the car swayed Pamela woke. She had been dreaming of God and of John, a tangled dream of torn loyalties. Not knowing for a moment where she was, she patted with small frantic movements at the space around her, feeling the cold door on one side, the empty space on the other, the roughness of the blanket over her and the wetness on her chin where she had dribbled in her sleep. 'I've been asleep,' she called, her voice high with alarm.

'It's okay, Mum, we're home now,' came a voice she knew was Charlie's, dear Charlie. And there, indeed, was home, her beloved Ashley House, a huge, comforting bulk in the darkness, its downstairs lights blazing and the spectral army of silver birches whispering to their left as the car rolled the last few yards up the drive.

Lying in bed that night, Cassie stroked her palms across her tummy. Closing her eyes, she pressed gently with her finger tips, trying to feel beyond the warmth of her skin to her sense of something else inside. Another life. A pencil-dot quivering in her womb. Serena had told her once that she had known with all her children the instant they had been conceived. Her body had felt different, she said, softer, more tender, ripe. Cassie spread her fingers wider and pressed a little harder. She did feel different – excited but also serene. And her breasts were tingling – that, too, was a sure sign. 'All good things come to those who wait,' she quoted in her mind. It had been a once annoying adage of her recently deceased aunt. And she had waited, for years not wanting children particularly, and then, with Dan, longing for them until his wife, Sally, had become ill and the possibility of him abandoning his marriage had shrunk like a tired dream. With Stephen she had waited again – although she had been almost forty when they had finally started going out together – partly because she had wanted to be sure of her feelings for him and partly because of his own troubled reluctance. With parents like his, she would have been reluctant too.

Turning her head but keeping her hands on her belly, she studied Stephen's profile in the dark, thinking how good things in life might come with waiting but how they could also be unexpected too, like her feelings for Stephen transmuting slowly, steadily into love. Dan had let her down but Stephen had proved constant, adoring her resistant, broken heart until it melted and adored him back. He worried, he said, that parenthood might change them, that it would force him to share her with someone else when he didn't want to share her with anything or anyone *ever*. Recalling the sentiment, moved afresh by its sweetness, Cassie reached out and stroked the sandpapery roughness of her fiancé's cheek. She had talked him round, of course, as she had always known she would, explaining the yearning, the hunger, gnawing inside and citing her lovely bunch of nephews and nieces as examples of how great children could be. Her secret favourite was Roland, perhaps because he was her godson, but Stephen had developed a soft spot for Helen and Peter's little Genevieve, with her auburn curls and freckles, spoilt rotten but endearing all the same. It was after a stay at Ashley House the previous year, when this particular niece had spent many of her waking hours clambering on and off Stephen's lap, that he had pronounced himself ready to try for a family, regardless of which month they settled on for their wedding.

Since then there had been no stopping them. They made love almost every day, whenever the mood took them, between unpacked boxes, among paint pots and once, somewhat uncomfortably, on the kitchen table, which had left Cassie's lower spine bruised and aching for days. After two decades of assiduous precautions *not* to get pregnant it was nothing short of liberation to focus on the act of conception as her primary aim. It added a new dimension to the pleasure, Cassie had discovered, that felt at once erotic and curiously virtuous. Pulling Stephen into her in recent weeks, she felt as if no penetration could be too deep or too furious, that every electrically charged fusion of their sweat and flesh – focused as it now was on the momentous miracle of conception – was somehow blessed.

Turning again to study Stephen's face, Cassie experienced a surge of motherly protection. He didn't always drift off easily. Even now, she could see his eyes rolling under the soft milky-white eyelids, as if he were seeking a way out of the dark, or watching the unknowable slideshow of his dreams. His broad mouth with its beautiful Cupid's bow and curling corners – a mouth born to smile, she had always thought, even before she fell in love with him – trembled with each breath. In the half-dark, with his wavy hair splayed against the pillow, showing none of the grey smudges creeping into the sideboards, he looked younger than thirty-seven. 'I'll be a menopausal crone just as you hit your stride in your early forties,' she had joked recently, 'and then you'll start fancying the socks off nubile creatures with no smile-lines and firmer breasts.' Instead of laughing as she had intended, he had exploded with hurt that she could suggest such a thing, and protested his love with a vehemence that had made Cassie, with her knowledge of having loved before, almost afraid.

She was concentrating again on her belly, certain now that it felt strangely tight, when she heard the squeak of the front gate followed by the crunch of footsteps on the little path that led up to the front door. She eased herself out of bed, then peered through the window, half wrapping herself in the curtains for warmth.

Stephen sat up and rubbed his eyes. 'Hey, babe, what are you doing?'

'I heard something,' she whispered. 'Someone outside.' As she spoke the doorbell rang.

'Bloody hell! Who is it? Can you see?'

Hugging herself and dancing with cold, Cassie shook her head. 'It's raining and dark.'

'I'll go. You stay here.'

'No, I'm coming too. If you're going to be shot we might as well go down together.'

'Mad woman,' he whispered, pulling on his dressing-gown and throwing hers across the bed. 'Come on, then. It's probably kids playing a prank. Keith and I used to do it all the time.'

Which was why Cassie laughed when Stephen – with her peeping over his shoulder – opened the door to reveal Keith, hair standing up in wet spikes and rainwater dripping off his coat.

'Sorry, mate. Cassie, hi, sorry about this.' He shot several glances over his shoulder, clearly contemplating the possibility of retreat.

'Come in,' said Cassie at once, pulling her dressing-gown more tightly across her chest. 'You're soaked.'

'The thing is . . .' Keith stepped into the hall, shaking himself like a wet dog '. . . I've run into a bit of a hitch on the accommodation front. I'm sorry, Steve, I didn't know where else to turn.'

'You want to stay?'

'Just for the night,' said Keith. 'On the sofa. Won't be any trouble, I promise.'

'Poor you. Has something terrible happened?' said Cassie, feeling the need to make up for the undisguised flatness of Stephen's response. She stepped forward to help their visitor with his sodden coat, then carried it at arm's length to one of the spare hooks under the stairs.

Keith grinned sheepishly. 'Nah, not really. Just lost my keys, and this friend I'm living with has gone away for the weekend.'

'One night will be fine,' said Stephen, sounding a little more amenable. 'No need for the sofa, though. You can have the spare room.'

'Poor old Keith,' murmured Cassie, once they were back in bed, 'losing his keys like that.'

Stephen snorted. 'Keys, my arse. He's been kicked out by some woman, I expect.'

'I thought he had a wife.'

'He did, but it fell apart a few years ago. I get the impression his whole life is a bit of a mess, but he doesn't want to talk about it.'

'Typical man,' Cassie murmured, snuggling closer and rubbing her frozen toes up and down Stephen's warm calves.

'I don't mind helping him, but we're not running a charity, okay?'

'Okay. He's your friend, darling – whatever you say.' She pressed her nose, which was also cold, into the crook of his neck.

'Hey, you're an ice-box.'

'Mm. Warm me up, then,' she whispered, shifting herself on top of him. 'But gently, gently . . .' She leant forwards and

67

planted kisses on his ears, letting her hair trail across his face. 'We don't want to disturb whatever might already be inside.'

Or Keith, thought Stephen, but not saying so because it was hardly a romantic or helpful notion, given the circumstances. He nuzzled her hair instead, wishing he could erase the small, persistent squeak of their bed and the unsettling image of his friend lying in the next room listening to it.

Scrolling through emails the next morning, perched at the little roll-top desk she had been allowed to bring with her to London, Clem wondered if she should have made the effort to go to her aunt's party after all. Her mother, usually reluctant to make electronic contact, had written to her twice about it.

> Ed, poor love, is snowed under with revision, but Elizabeth says Roland's going. It would be nice just to see you, darling. With Maisie in Mexico, Dad and I are feeling quite bereft! Call us soon, won't you? Sometimes it feels as if you're as far away as your sister! All love, Mum

And then again, two days later:

> About Cassie and Stephen's party, couldn't you take one night off from your job at that wine bar? Lots of love, as always, darling. Look after yourself, won't you?
> Mum

Aware that time was ticking towards her lunch shift, Clem made two decisive swipes at the delete button and switched off her laptop. It was annoying to be fussed over, especially in the clumsily disguised way her mother did it, with all her exclamation marks and quips about looking after herself, which really meant 'Don't forget to eat' – because for a time in her teens she had got so thin that they'd whisked her off to a specialist and had watched her like hawks ever since. Getting away from all that vigilance had been part of the appeal of moving to London where she could skip meals or binge at leisure, secure in the knowledge that however she chose to burn the calories afterwards – by frenetic exercise or, if she was in one of her desperate moods, sleeping with the windows open and the covers off – there was no chance of anyone remarking on it. Her two flatmates, a pair of music students called Flora and Daisy, were openly envious of her slim figure. Always on diets themselves, in furious competition usually, it never occurred to them that Clem was locked into an intricate battle of her own, with checks and balances at every turn.

In contrast, Clem had found herself watching the friendship between her two companions closely. Oscillating on an almost daily basis between suffocating intimacy and icy hostility, it reminded her in many ways of the complicated business of having a twin sister. It made her feel left out sometimes, yet glad not to be in the thick of things getting hurt. With their plump figures, blonde hair and blue eyes, the pair could easily have passed for twins, unlike her and Maisie, who were about as different as it was possible to be: Maisie had Serena's shining chestnut mane and honey skin, while Clem was pale and dark-haired like their father, with angular features and eyes that seemed too big for her face.

Closing her laptop, Clem reached for the modest pile of recent letters she kept in the central compartment of the desk. Before she read any she pressed them to her nose, smelling the familiar scent of wood and polish and something floral – lavender, maybe – that made her think of her grandmother and Ashley House. The desk had belonged to her great-grandmother, Nancy Harrison, and had lived for as long as Clem could remember in the top-floor bedroom, which had been Aunt Cassie's before it became hers. It was made of walnut, a soft toffee colour, pitted with defunct woodworm holes and polished scratches, so deep they looked like veins. Its legs were coiled and spindly, with little brass wheels at the bottom, causing it to wobble badly at times because each had worn differently over the years.

Clem knew that the desk didn't look right in her poky room. Squashed between the bed and the window, with the lino tiles curling round its pretty feet and the ugly backdrop of anaglypta, it reminded her a bit of a delicate wild animal – a gazelle or a fawn – trapped in a cage. Clem felt sort of guilty to be responsible for its entrapment, but glad to have it there. She sat at it at least once a day, even if all she did was stare at the bobbles in the wallpaper or study the sky, sailing past the window next to her in seascapes of blue, white and grey.

Among the letters there was a postcard from Maisie. 'Having fantastic time! My Spanish developing worrying Mexican drawl! Teaching a bit of a drag, but going on scuba-diving course this weekend. Trust you're having a wild time in London . . . !'

Clem stared at it glumly, despising the false cheery tone. Given how badly they had parted she would have preferred the honesty of silence. On the card there was a picture of two smiling, coffee-skinned girls in bright striped ponchos with bowler hats on their heads and babies strapped to their backs. Two sisters, maybe, mused Clem, liking the image in spite of everything. Two sisters . . . or maybe just young mums taking time out between herding goats and fetching water, or whatever the hell young mums did in rural Mexico. She gave the card a last long look before dropping it into the wastepaper-basket and turning her attention to the rest of the pile.

Two bank statements and a phone bill later, she came across what she was looking for – an invitation from her cousin Theo to accompany him to his college ball in May. 'If you're free?! Thought it might be fun!'

Clem gritted her teeth, wishing suddenly that exclamation marks could be banned, or at the very least their users heavily fined. In spite of the exuberant punctuation, she remained in no doubt that her shy, stiff-faced cousin had no one to take to his party and had turned to her as a face-saving last resort. The wastepaper-basket yawned invitingly, but Clem resisted it. She liked Theo. He was clever and kind. When they were children he had always taken her side, even – on the rare occasions that they fell out – against Maisie, who was an intimidating and fearless adversary, felling all comers with her sharp tongue and fiery glare. Picturing his boffin solitariness, his pale, pimply face and earnest brown eyes, imagining the courage – the pride-swallowing – it must have taken to invite her, Clem reached for her pen and a pad: 'Most honoured – will reorganize work shifts accordingly. Hope I don't have to wear LONG!!!'

And where was her own courage? Clem asked herself, sealing the envelope and experiencing a fresh stab of regret at not having gone to her aunt's party. Much as her parents irritated her, she felt now a swoop of longing for their familiar faces – her mother's solemn blue eyes, the low rumble of her father's voice – for the easy, comforting business of being a child and feeling cared for, even if she resisted that caring. She thought of Roland too, with whom she'd always got on well, and then of Stephen, her soon-to-be uncle. It would have been the perfect opportunity to take him to one side and confess that she, too, hoped to be a novelist one day, that after eight years of religious diary-keeping she was planning to embark on something more creative and potentially commercial.

Irritated now rather than sad, Clem rammed the letters back into their cubby-hole and slammed the lid, hating the desk suddenly for being beautiful and reminding her of things from which she was working hard to break free. A ringing emptiness followed. Clem listened to it for a few seconds, then pushed her way out of her bedroom, managing in the process to knock over a music-stand that lived behind the sitting-room door. It toppled, then daintily righted itself, like a skeletal ballerina regaining her balance. Clem kicked it, and watched with some satisfaction as it clattered to the floor, landing neatly between Flora's cello and the battered black leather box that contained Daisy's flute. Their endless practising got on her nerves. In fact, anything to do with music got on her nerves. It reminded her too much of the band – of Jonny, whom she hadn't seen since January. 'You're overreacting,' he had said, racing after her when she stormed out of his flat. 'A bit of snogging behind the science block – ancient history. It meant nothing.' All of which was so close – so uncannily close – to what Maisie had said that Clem's misery had flared to new heights, fuelled by the ugly suspicion that with their secret out, blown by the casual remark of an old schoolfriend, the pair had got together for a private consultation, agreeing statements like guilty accomplices. Ancient history or not, and Clem still wasn't sure, she felt strongly that it was her history too, and she had had every right to know about it.

Singing, Clem had since discovered, was connected to joy. Once, she had longed for the times when Daisy and Flora were away so that she could belt out her favourite numbers without fear of a critical audience. Occasionally Jonny, skipping a lecture, would be there too, in an armchair, his long legs folded under him, humming and strumming encouraging accompaniments on his guitar. Probing for a tune now, however, as she moved round the flat, determined to raise her mood before she left for work, Clem felt her throat muscles close in protest. Even taking up a determined stance in front of the bathroom mirror didn't help. 'Baby, feel my heart, as a part of you . . .' All great soul singers were heartbroken in one way or another, Clem told herself, trying harder to relax, to ease out the notes, but managing only a thin, edgy sound, as if some tone-deaf stranger had hijacked her voice-box.

Giving up, she closed her mouth, then reached for a hair-brush and her makeup bag. A few minutes later, with the support of a little mascara, her gaze had resumed its habitual striking blue glare, and her lips, rubbed with pink, looked more sure of themselves. This is coping, she told herself fiercely, scraping her thick mop of dark hair into a taut ponytail and pulling on her usual work outfit of black trousers and a white shirt. This is being grown-up. It was why she had come to London, why she didn't need anyone, why she was going to be okay.

By the time the heavy front door of the flat closed behind her, Clem felt ready for anything, even the grizzled American with the thick grey hair who took his usual table by the window and made two coffees last for two hours, watching her as always from behind a haze of cigarette smoke, his eyes like shadows under the arch of his heavy brows.

Sitting with *The Times* folded open next to his lunchtime plate of bacon, eggs, sausage and baked beans, Theo read as ravenously as he ate. After an early morning excursion on the river and three hours finishing an essay entitled 'Jurisprudence – science or philosophy?', his appetite for relaxation and food was keen. He had an hour before his tutorial with Dr Beresford, a beak-nosed Keble don, who wore livid bow-ties and munched sweets as he taught, sometimes hurling one into his students' laps, whether for reward or his own amusement Theo remained uncertain. After the general dullness of the sixth form at his Surrey boarding-school, he enjoyed such eccentricities as much as he relished fixing his bicycle clips to the bottom of his trousers and pedalling round Oxford's cobbled centre with the proverbial dreaming spires towering around him and his gown flapping behind him like a sail. Many of his peers claimed less contentment with their surroundings; some who hadn't boarded missed home, others worried about intellectual inadequacy or adopted irritating socialist postures of rebellion, too eager, in Theo's opinion, to criticize the institution from which they were benefiting.

'You'll have a heart-attack if you eat that lot.'

Recognizing the voice of Charlotte Brown, an earnest theology student from Jesus with whom he had managed an undignified, alcohol-inspired fumble at a beer-cellar party a couple of weeks before, Theo took several seconds to respond. Even a less awkward encounter would have been unwelcome. He had been enjoying both the anonymity of the café and an article on terrorist infiltration of London's Islamic community. Having recently started to use some of his precious spare time to work on a film script with a terrorist theme, he had been on the point of making a few notes. 'Charlotte, how are you?' He moved his laptop off the spare chair and folded his newspaper. Charlotte dropped her bag to the ground and herself into the chair with a weighty sigh. Clearly she had a cold, Theo observed gloomily, hearing the wheeze in her breath and noting a flaky rawness round her nostrils. He recalled in the same instant, with some astonishment, the fervour with which he had pressed his mouth to hers in the steamy heat of the party. Her lips, he couldn't help thinking, were decidedly unkissable now, dry, and parted slightly to aid in the business of breathing. 'Would you like a coffee?'

Charlotte produced a bottle of water from her bag and shook her head glumly. 'I'm doing a detox thing, trying to drink two litres of water a day. It's bloody hard.' She began picking at the label on the bottle. 'I know I look a sight.'

'Don't be silly.' Theo moved his last piece of bacon round his plate, cutting a neat swathe through the remaining egg yolk. It had been a good egg, spilling a lake of orange the moment he'd touched it with the point of his knife.

'I just . . .' She sniffed, then burrowed again in her bag, this time for tissues. 'You said you'd call and you haven't. I just need to know where I stand, Theo. Is that so much to ask?' She blew her nose.

'Not at all.' Theo wiped the back of his hand across his mouth, aware that a prickle of embarrassment illuminated his cheeks. Clem was wrong in assuming he received no attention from girls: he knew he wasn't good-looking in any conventional sense – his hair was too thick and wiry, his eyes too small, his nose too long – but since arriving at university he had had more encounters than he could have dared hope for. It was the follow-up that Theo wasn't so good at: the discovery that he was *fussy* – though many might have considered him in no position to entertain it. Charlotte Brown, like a couple of her predecessors, with whom he had been more sexually adventurous, did not strike him as meriting the effort of further exploration. Even Isabel Markham, with whose aid he had disburdened himself of his virginity a few months before, had inspired little zest in him for the more pedestrian business of developing a relationship. They had given it a go for a while, with Isabel reading Spanish poetry to him by candlelight and Theo spending more than he could afford on taking her out to pubs and restaurants, but when she had transferred her attentions to a member of a more prestigious rowing squad, Theo had listened to her tearful apologies with something like guilty relief. He liked sex well enough – it had proved empowering for his self-esteem and his body – yet he had discovered that, for the time being at least, he could manage perfectly well without it too.

'Theo? I'm asking where I stand.' Charlotte drank deeply from her bottle of water, studying him with pleading eyes.

Theo cleared his throat. 'I like you a lot, obviously, but . . .'

'Is there someone else? Is that it?'

'Well . . .'

'That's a bloody shame, Theo, is all I can say, because I thought we really, like, hit it off – all that talking we did about what we like and so on. We had so much, Theo, so *much* . . .' She reached again for her Kleenex, though whether the need was generated by her cold or heartbreak, Theo found it hard to be sure. '*And* you said I could be in that film you were going to make. The lead role, you said.'

'Did I?' Theo had no recollection of any such invitation and could not conceal his dismay. If his film project ever got off the ground he would want someone willowy and striking for the main part. To have considered Charlotte, with her wide, flat face and cushiony body, meant he must have been very drunk indeed.

Perhaps detecting some of these uncharitable thoughts in his expression, Charlotte rammed her bottle back into her bag and stood up, so abruptly that her chair tipped over, knocking into a neighbouring table and causing a ripple of chaos in their cramped section of the café. 'I take it you don't recall inviting me to the Keble ball either?' she said, once apologies had been issued and her chair righted.

Theo's dismay deepened. 'I couldn't have . . . I've already –'

'So there *is* someone else. Fine.' Charlotte tugged fiercely at the zip of her anorak, sealing herself up to her chin. The anorak was padded and silver-coloured, bearing a close resemblance, Theo couldn't help thinking, to body armour. 'Who is she? Might I at least be allowed to know that?'

'Look, there isn't anybody –' Theo seized on the notion that the existence, no matter how fantastical, of an alternative girl-friend would provide the cleanest, shortest exit from the conversation and any possibility of further entanglement. 'She's called Clem and she lives in London.'

'As in *Clementine*?' Charlotte laughed nastily, rolling her eyes. 'My *darling* Clementine, eh? Well, good luck to the pair of you.'

Women were a bloody pain, Theo reflected, pedalling past the Parks a few minutes later, hunched over his handlebars so that the top of his head bore the brunt of the icy wind as it cut partings into his hair. And that included Clem, he decided, blocking out any guilty qualms for having used his cousin as a smokescreen. Inviting *her* to the ball was something he remembered only too well, since it had been done under protest, after pressure from his mother. The poor thing needed to be *taken out of herself*, Helen had insisted, using the steely tones that served her well with recalcitrant clients. Charlie and Serena, she claimed, clearly relishing the chance to pass on news from the thick of the family grapevine, were beside themselves with concern. Charlie had secretly told Peter all about it. Clem was barely keeping in touch, refusing offers of help on all fronts. Perhaps because she doesn't need any, Theo had suggested, only to be curtly informed that instead of snide remarks the family should make an effort to rally round.

Taken out of herself, indeed, mused Theo, pausing at the entrance to the Parks to scan the nearest pitch, where a women's lacrosse match was in full swing. It struck him as an absurd phrase to use, given that being 'out of herself' was precisely what Clem – albeit in a rather unimaginative way – was clearly trying to achieve.

An attempt to put this view to his father during the Michaelmas vac, however, had proved as fruitless as trying to argue with his mother. To get grades like hers, then use them for nothing more than waiting at tables was a bloody crime, Peter had thundered, banging the table with outrage on his brother and sister-in-law's behalf. Watching the crockery shake, Theo had wondered what his parents would have said if he had confessed to some of the more rebellious impulses crouched in his own heart: like the simmering resentment he felt at the way his father had handed over Ashley House to his uncle – handed over his birthright, without consultation or apology, as if it might have no more significance to Theo than a packet of sweets. Or the urge, vividly experienced for a time, to tear up his UCAS form and apply for a place at the London Film School. The crockery would have rattled then, he was sure, even though his parents had encouraged his passion for film, giving him a video camera at thirteen and applauding all the clumsy creative efforts that had followed.

The allure of Oxford, however, had proved overpowering.

Alighting from the bus in the middle of the high street on the day of his interviews, Theo had stared about him in awe, not just at the obvious glories of the colleges, their towers and walls a glossy gold that day in the autumn sunshine, but at the town-and-gown bustle of city life in which he had wanted, instantly, to play a part.

Disappointed by the lacrosse players who – apart from a little blonde thing, who never looked his way – were mostly hefty creatures with blotchy thighs, Theo pushed off from the gates and cycled on towards Keble. He parked his bike among a bunch of others along the front wall and went into the porter's lodge to check his pigeon-hole, then hurried across the main quad towards Dr Beresford's staircase. As he walked the wind dropped and the sun slid into view between two clouds, illuminating the quad with the effect of a picture light on a painting. Theo slowed his pace and looked about him with a fresh, joyful sense of belonging. The red-stoned Victorian Gothic grandeur of the place had been a shock at first, so much more imposing than the other more ancient colleges, but now Theo couldn't imagine being – or wanting to be – anywhere else. The sheer scale of Keble's architecture was stimulating: each time he glanced up at its towering dark-red walls he could almost feel the eyes of the college's venerable founders and members watching for how he, this tiny integral link in the chain of history, would make his mark. As a couple of second-year students strolled past, chatting intently, Theo called out a greeting to them, seeking expression for the new exuberance bubbling inside him. The pair, a girl and a boy, smiled acknowledgement, faintly surprised. Theo hurried on, not caring what they thought, not caring what anyone thought, lost, for those moments at least, in an almost visionary contentment with his place in the world. Charlotte Brown, however messily, had been despatched. His essay was good. His body tingled pleasantly from training. He was fit, alert, young, and with more hopes and plans than he could number.

At the bottom of the stairs he checked his watch, took a deep breath and set off at a gallop. Dr Beresford's study was on the top floor, with views over the Parks. If he took the steps two at a time he'd be there on the dot of three. And it was good training, Theo mused, breathing hard as he raced upwards, hoping that his tutor would be in the mood to share whatever confectionary he had selected to get him through the afternoon.

Sitting astride the bike parked in the corner of the games room, Peter worked the pedals gingerly, trying to ignore the ever-present tightness in his upper back. A week had passed since Cassie's party, most of which he had spent in court, fighting on behalf of a GP: the man had failed to diagnose meningitis in a thirteen-year-old girl, who had died. A hopeless case, as Helen had pointed out many times, even though the GP was good and kind, and the family, in the years before their loss, had invaded his surgery on so many spurious pretexts that it was little wonder he had sent the girl home with a prescription for paracetamol.

Sometimes there *was* no right and wrong, Peter reflected bleakly, glancing at his blurred reflection in the windowpane next to the bike, then looking quickly away, as a distressing sense of futility threatened to take hold. In the gym he used near chambers, surrounded by others working as keenly on similar pieces of equipment, it was far easier to maintain concentration. There was an atmosphere of camaraderie and competition, the vague sense that one was on show and therefore required to put on a decent performance. There were mirrors too, in which the sight of his straining face was pleasantly offset by the glimpse of pumping muscles, instead of this grey half-image in the glass next to him, shimmering like a troubled ghost.

Having set himself an arduous course of three long hills, Peter was soon sweating hard. He kept his eyes on the little cinema of information flashing between the handlebars – remaining kilometres, calorie count, gradient – trying to keep his thoughts focused on these immediate, achievable targets rather than his sore shoulder and the niggling sense of failure that had trailed him out of the courtroom like a bad smell.

'You are *wet*,' shrieked Genevieve, pedalling in through the doorway on her scarlet tricycle. She pointed at his sweat-sodden T-shirt and shorts. 'And *your* bike doesn't move like mine. Look.' She hunched over her handlebars and set off across the room, working her stout little legs furiously.

Peter wiped the sweat from his eyes and laughed. 'Jolly good . . . but shouldn't you be in bed?' He threw a hopeful glance in the direction of the palatial new utility room into which Helen had disappeared, clutching a pile of laundry, ten minutes earlier.

'Not – tired!' shrieked his youngest, her voice ringing with a newly discovered, worryingly Chloë-like defiance, as she steered the tricycle between two bean-bags and turned sharply past the french windows backing on to the garden. 'Look, Daddy, look.'

Peter looked, only to see the tricycle tip slowly on to two of its three chubby wheels – causing its rider to squeal with glee – then on to the floor, which prompted a squeal of a more strident, less positive kind. At which point Helen charged into the room, her arms still full of crumpled clothes.

'She's fine,' Peter called, shouting over Genevieve's impressive orchestra of sobbing. 'Bit of a tumble,' he added, more defensively, as Helen, with a sharp look, dumped the washing on a bean-bag and scooped her daughter on to her hip.

'There now, sweetheart,' she whispered, stroking Genevieve's gingery curls until the sobbing had shrunk to hiccuping sighs. 'There now, tired girl . . . Theo just called,' she added, addressing Peter over her daughter's head in an altogether different voice. 'He asked Clem to go to that ball and apparently she's agreed.'

'Well done, Theo,' Peter murmured, trying to focus on the last hill in his programme but for some reason finding it hard to do so with Helen watching, all tender and fierce at the same time.

'He'll be home in a couple of weeks for the spring vac. He said to warn you his squash has improved beyond measure. He sounded really well.'

'Good.'

'Sorry about your case.'

Straining now against the resisting pedals, a hair's breadth away from giving up, Peter managed a half-shrug. 'It was just as you said it would be. A lost cause. The jury were never going to budge.'

Helen turned for the door and paused, hitching Genevieve's solid little body higher on to her hip. 'And that shoulder of yours?' Her tone had hardened again. 'Have you called Cassie's physio yet?'

'No, I –'

'Call the physio,' she snapped. 'It's bound to flare up again, the amount you're exercising, these days.'

Peter laboured on up the last hill, in thrall to gloom again. Helen was right, of course. She was good at being right – an endearing but maddening quality. He pondered, for a moment, the sheer density of married life, the good and the bad so entwined that it was impossible to see them separately. Remembering the news about Theo, a fresh surge of adrenaline obligingly flooded his tired legs. His son beat him at squash, eh? He'd see about that. Gripping the handlebars, forgetting the lost case, his wife's bossiness – even his aching shoulder – Peter managed a bursting sprint to the end of his programme.

As he got off the bike he slapped the saddle in satisfaction. Physical exercise always made him feel better. He slung a small towel round his neck, headed into the main house and skipped upstairs, suddenly looking forward to seeing his youngest daughter's freckled nose peeking over the edge of her duvet and a gentler conversation with his wife. It was Friday night, after all. Two silvery trout lay in a dish next to the oven, with a handful of new potatoes and two wine glasses ready for the bottle of St Véran chilling in the fridge. They would drink and eat with their customary pleasure and then, maybe, retire upstairs for an early night and a little loving in the dark.

On the stairs he met Chloë coming down. She had changed out of her grey school uniform into a T-shirt that stopped at her navel and jeans that trailed several inches over the soles of her shoes.

'And why are you looking cross, little one?' Peter ruffled her dark curls, ignoring her efforts to duck out of reach.

'Mum made me turn my CD off because Gen's going to sleep, and even though I'm starving she says I can only eat cereal or *fruit*.'

'Probably best to do as your mother says,' replied Peter, cheerily. 'A lot safer for both of us, eh?' He winked, then went on up the stairs, thinking that happy families was all about playing the game, and that if he pulled himself together instead of moping he was more than up to the job.

Cassie was lying on the sitting-room floor, sketching dress designs on a large white pad, when the dull cramps in her abdomen sharpened in a way that was only too familiar. Waking that morning to a headache and a limp feeling in her face and hair, she had resisted both painkillers and the notion that such symptoms might have anything to do with her menstrual cycle. Now, however, there was no denying the signs.

She stopped drawing, put down her pencil and rested her head on her arms. There was no hurry. There never was at the beginning of her period. She lay quite still, staring at the flecked green fibres of the carpet, breathing slowly and deeply, wanting somehow to mark the moment – this dreadful moment – when all her hopes were crushed again.

Stephen had gone on one of his early-evening walks, which he did sometimes if he'd had a bad day at his desk. There had been several such days that week – because of Keith, he said. It was almost a week since the party and his old friend was still with them. It was impossible to concentrate, Stephen claimed, with Keith lumbering around, turning the telly on and off, making endless cups of tea, calling up the stairs to ask if there was anything he could do. Each night, in the sanctity of their bedroom, they would agree that enough was enough and he had to leave, yet each morning they had shrunk from the task, mown down by Keith's cheery face, the news of imminent job and accommodation possibilities. The latest was an office redevelopment site in Pinner – months of work, he had assured them over breakfast the day before, biting into a doorstep slice of toast and slurping his tea. The money would be good enough to 'see him right' for the rest of the year. He had licked his fingers and looked so pleased that Cassie hadn't known whether to feel exasperated or admiring.

She could hear him now, moving around the kitchen, trying to make up for the inconvenience of his presence with the preparation of yet another meal. Lamb chops, this time, with mashed potato, carrots and peas. He had shown off the chops proudly on his return from the butcher; thick and bleeding with edgings of white fat as stout as fingers. Cassie, thinking of the ordeal of eating them, with her tummy sore, her heart broken and no chance of a moment to herself with Stephen, began, very quietly, to cry.

Keith padded in from the kitchen in his socks to ask how she felt about grilled tomatoes and paused, imagining, with some reverence, that he was witnessing a moment of intense artistic concentration. 'Did you have any plans for these?' he ventured at length, tossing two tomatoes into the air. 'Not everyone's cup of tea, grilled tomatoes, I know . . .' He faltered, losing confidence. 'Hey, are you all right down there?'

'Fine.' Cassie reached for her pencil and, beginning to go over lines she'd already sketched, pressed the lead so hard it cut the page.

'You don't look fine.' Keith peered at her. 'You're upset.'

'I am a bit. It's nothing, really.' She managed a sort of laugh and wiped her hand across her nose.

'Nobody cries for nothing,' replied Keith, solemnly, kneeling on the floor next to her. 'It's me, isn't it? I'm in the way, aren't I? Getting on your tits – I mean, shit . . . Sorry, that sounded bad.'

Cassie couldn't help smiling. 'No, it's not you, Keith, although . . . I think if you *could* find somewhere else soon, that might be best.' She swivelled to a sitting position, sniffing freely now and feeling a little better. 'If this thing in Pinner comes through, I mean. It's just with both Stephen and me working at home the place does feel a little . . . crowded.'

'Say no more.' Keith held up his hand. 'I'll find somewhere else right away. You've been great, both of you, really great. Something will come up, it always does in the end.' He sighed so wistfully that Cassie felt tempted to retract her ultimatum. 'Are you worried about your wedding dress?' he ventured, using the uncertain tone of one making a valiant effort to understand the incomprehensible and pointing at the page of what looked to him like magnificent drawings. 'Is that it?'

Cassie laughed and then, finding she was almost crying again, stopped abruptly. 'No . . . nothing like that. It's . . . Well, the truth is, I thought I was pregnant and it turns out I'm not.'

'Oh dear.' Keith stared at the tomatoes, wondering what on earth to say. 'That – that is a shame. Mind you,' he stammered, 'kids are more trouble than they're worth a lot of the time, the little blighters. Sometimes I think me and June might have got on a bit better without them – not that I don't love my boys, give anything to see more of them, but, of course, *wanting* kids,' he added, 'that's how women are, isn't it?'

'Well, I never used to want them,' confessed Cassie, 'and then, a few years ago, my little niece died and it changed the way I looked at things. I was in a hopeless relationship then – no prospects of making babies, though I fooled myself there was for a while.' She picked at the pile of the carpet, lost in the recollection of her rollercoaster year with Daniel Lambert, all that belief and energy coming to nothing.

'What did she die of then, your niece . . . if you don't mind me asking?'

'She was hit by a motorbike in Oxford Street. The bastard drove off. Just one of those dreadful things that happen to people who don't deserve them. Serena, Charlie – the whole family – we were all distraught, but life moves on, doesn't it? I think they're all right now, with Ashley House to look after, not to mention my mum.' Cassie made a face and got to her feet. 'Certainly puts my little loss into perspective, doesn't it? Keith?' Instead of coming back with the quip she had expected, he had rammed a cigarette into his mouth and was fumbling for his lighter. 'Not in here, please,' she reminded him.

'What?'

'The cigarette?'

'Oh, bloody hell. Sorry. Of course. I'll just pop out the back, then,' he muttered, looking peculiar and awkward, and hurrying out of the room.

Cassie ran after him. 'I say . . . can I join you? Have a fag, I mean. I shouldn't, really – I'm supposed to have given up – but I could just do with one.'

Ten minutes later Stephen returned from his walk to find his fiancée and his friend huddled in coats on the small patio, shrouded in smoke and the steam of their warm breath against the cold night air. 'Darling . . .' Cassie dropped her cigarette and ran to hug him, wanting to communicate some of her own distress and to erase the dismay on his face. 'I'm not pregnant after all,' she whispered. 'I felt so sad.'

'Poor baby,' Stephen murmured, hugging her back but keeping a dark look fixed on Keith, busily smoking his own cigarette down to the filter.

'I've had an idea,' announced Keith, when they were all back inside, seated a little stiffly in front of mountainous plates of chops and mash, the meat charred from overcooking and the potato clogged with lumps. 'At your party that brother of yours, Cassie, Charlie, he said he might need some work doing down at his place in Sussex. I should have heard about the Pinner job by now, to be honest, so I'm thinking why not give him a ring, see if he's still interested? Cassie said you two want me gone . . .'

'Did she?' exclaimed Stephen, looking at her with barely concealed admiration. 'Well, I . . . We're glad to help out obviously but, yes, that sounds like a good plan . . . a very good plan. I seem to recall someone mentioning the old house was in need of attention – but it was Peter, not Charlie. Mind you, the place is a couple of hundred years old at least, so it's hardly surprising . . .' Stephen, aware that this rambling response was charged only by ignoble relief at the prospect of waving goodbye to his friend, gave up and put a forkful of food into his mouth.

Cassie nodded. 'I, too, think that sounds like a great idea. I don't know about general repairs. All Charlie said to me was that he wants to turn the old toolshed into a proper studio for Serena, who's always been quite arty but never done anything about it. There are all these outhouses and barns and things, Keith. My father converted one into a cottage, but the rest just sit there . . . empty.' Cassie dropped her eyes to her plate, acutely aware suddenly of her own aching emptiness, crouched inside her, so in need of private, intimate consolation that it was all she could do not to run from the table.

As it was, consolation, like all things intimate that week, had to wait until after the washing-up and the ten o'clock news and Keith asking for Charlie's number. It felt like hours before she and Stephen were upstairs in the soothing privacy of their own bedroom.

'My period came,' she explained bleakly, pulling her nightie over her head and climbing into bed.

Stephen rolled over and hugged her. 'Poor baby.'

Which was what he had said before. Cassie did her best to be satisfied but felt, somewhere deep inside, that she needed something more, some inkling of comparable distress on his part. 'I feel so sad,' she whispered, pressing her mouth to his chest, breathing the faint saltiness of his skin.

'Well, smoking's hardly going to help, is it?'

Lying with one cheek pressed against his chest, Cassie went very still. She could feel the quiet pulse of his heart against her head. 'What did you say?'

'All I meant was . . .'

She was fighting her way out of his arms now, feeling like a diver thrashing upwards for air. 'One measly cigarette is hardly going to make any difference, is it?' She was almost shouting. 'It's not as if there's a foetus to damage, is there?'

'Hang on, Cass, I know you're disappointed –'

'Do you?' She grabbed a pillow and hugged it to her chest.

'What is this?' he asked, his voice light, incredulous. He tried to prise one of her hands off the pillow, but she resisted.

'I don't think you do know. You've spent all week worrying about Keith being here and how your work's going. The truth is, you don't care as much as me about having a child and never will.'

'That's not true. Of course I care as much, of course I do.' Stephen made another, more successful lunge for her hands and pressed them to his lips. 'There's nothing wrong with loving you more than the idea of a baby, is there?' he urged softly. 'I love you so much,' he continued, encouraged by the way her fingers were softening against his lips, 'that coming in tonight, seeing you with Keith on the patio, I wanted to punch his face.'

'Really?' Cassie exclaimed, genuinely amazed. 'Whatever for?'

'For standing close to you . . . close enough to smell your lemony hair and see the dark flecks in your wondrous blue eyes.'

'Oh, *please*.' She let out a short laugh, diverted from her unhappiness but also faintly alarmed. 'Well, Keith is one thing we *won't* have to worry about any more, judging by how well the conversation went with Charlie. He's up to the job, isn't he? It would be too awful to offload him on to Ashley House if he wasn't.'

'Oh, he'll be good,' Stephen assured her, turning off the bed-side light and pulling her back into his arms. 'His dad was a joiner – Keith packed in school to be an apprentice to him. I'm sure he'll be fine.'

'Good.' Cassie wriggled into a comfortable position, closed her eyes, then opened them again. 'Stephen?'

'Hm?'

'I was thinking . . . if this goes on, the not getting pregnant, I'd like to see a doctor . . . maybe even look into the possibility of IVF.'

He was silent for so long that Cassie thought he might have fallen asleep. 'Okay, baby, okay,' he murmured at last, reaching up and stroking the wisps of hair off her face. 'Anything for you. Anything.'

Anything for *us*, she thought, but did not say because it was a momentous thing to have asked and he had acquiesced so easily.

Roland altered the position of his Anglepoise lamp so that it was shining more directly on to the canvas and took a step backwards to study his picture. He had painted the background the day before – a thick black at the bottom graduating to midnight blue at the top. Now he was working colours on to it, yellows mainly, and some red, all so heavily applied that the paint sat in coils and ripples, as densely textured as wet sand. He had pulled back the curtains at the window next to the easel, even though it was well past midnight and the ivory crescent moon had no power to illuminate anything but the dusty streaks of cloud crossing its face.

He was painting because he couldn't sleep, which in itself wasn't unusual. Roland often found that crawling into bed and turning the light out had a stimulating rather than relaxing effect on his mind, as if it had been waiting for just such a time to address the issues swimming round his subconscious. Normally he just lay there and let it pass or, if that didn't work, flicked on his table-lamp and read until his eyes closed of their own accord. Tonight, however, every time he shut his eyes, colours had crowded in, jostling for space like pieces of a jigsaw demanding assembly.

Yawning hard, Roland had pulled on tracksuit bottoms and a jumper, rubbed the chill from his hands, then started to squeeze coils of paint on to one of the wooden boards propped next to the end of his bed. With the house so quiet – the gurgle of the central heating had long since subsided – and the darkness outside, he had at first felt almost too self-conscious to work. It was as if he was watching himself perform some cheap charade of inspiration, the sleepless artist, working into the small hours, alone in his garret, when in fact he was a recently turned sixteen-year-old schoolboy who was seeing colours probably because they were marginally less confusing than some of the more literal images pressing for his attention. Images like maths coursework – how many equations were there for fitting squares into rectangles and triangles into pyramids? – and the freezing tedium of rugby, running only to keep warm, hoping the ball would never come his way, and Carl Summers, the first-fifteen captain, with his big, square body and staring eyes: he couldn't pass Roland without a look, a tease and a nudge, but it was all gently done, so gently that Roland had wondered – hoped – that underneath the banter and joshing there lurked . . . what? Genuine interest? Mutual understanding? The very thought made Roland blush. As well as heading the rugby team Carl was head boy – sporty, clever, popular and as burly as a thirty-year-old. Girls from year nine upwards sighed when he passed them in the corridor. It was absurd to entertain hopes of friendship with such a creature – absurd, yet so appealing that Roland couldn't stop thinking about it.

He picked up a fresh brush and began to stab dashes of brown and orange among the yellow. The picture was of his mother, he decided, all her colour and gloom, the shining bits and the messy edges – all those disparate parts that, he was beginning to realize, constituted the business of being human. Certainly he was a mass of good and bad – lousy at maths but good at drawing, loving his mother but recoiling from her too, getting goosebumps talking to Carl, yet feeling sick with terror at what that might mean. No one was entirely *knowable* even to themselves, Roland decided, putting down his brushes at last and stretching out the stiffness in his arms. It was all a fucking mystery.

Before climbing into bed he had another look out of the window. The moon had disappeared, leaving the darkness complete. Yet not complete: pressing his nose to the pane Roland could make out the shadowy lines of the treetops at the end of the garden and the shape of next door's chicken coop. Nothing was black and white, if you looked closely enough. He rubbed away the steam of his breath from the glass and narrowed his eyes, wondering suddenly if he could really see the trees and the coop or whether he was imagining them because he knew they were there.

Turning out the light a couple of minutes later, his elbow caught the edge of a card that had arrived from Cassie that morning. Would he consider being an usher at her wedding? An *usher*! The idea of him doing something so stuffy and pompous had made both him and Elizabeth laugh. 'And come and see me in the Easter holidays,' the note continued. 'We could go to a film and maybe buy something for your birthday – a new phone or some clothes. I hardly know what you teenagers are into!'

Which was very nice of her, Roland decided, closing his eyes with a happy sigh, relieved to discover that all the blobs of colour had been replaced by the cheery face of his godmother waving her cheque book. At which point his dad tried to enter the dream too, stepping off an aeroplane with that look of earnest expectation he wore, holding out his arms for a hand-shake, one of the American sort, in which, he had learnt, you seized the forearm for a double squeeze. Roland took control at once, shooing him back up the steps and making the plane fly away, till it was no more than a dot in the sky. By which time Cassie had flown away too and there was only the bliss of nothing for company.

April

'So you want the shelves there – on the right of the door – and the worktop over here, next to the window?'

'Yes . . . At least, I think so.' Serena squinted at the bare brick wall, trying to imagine a worktop sprouting out of it and herself seated at it, moulding one of her clay vases or, better still, reframing the numerous collages of family photos, which, currently situated on various corkboards round the kitchen, were yellowing and losing their moorings. 'What do you think?' She studied Keith from under her long sandy eyelashes. It was only three days since his arrival and she was still trying to make him out. He had the faintly lugubrious, lived-in face of one who had known suffering, yet there was an energy to him – in his voice, his quick hand movements and crooked, ready smile – that suggested something far brighter and determinedly positive. He had an ex-wife and two children in Hull, she knew: after agreeing terms of work with Charlie he had promptly disappeared for three weeks to visit them. Serena wondered what had driven Keith and his wife apart, and thought how desperate anyone must be to move voluntarily away from their children. With her own three so grown-up, she felt more keenly every day that she wouldn't have missed a second of mothering, not one tottering step or tantrum. She wouldn't have missed a precious second of Tina either, not even if an angel had swooped down to warn her of what lay in store, fast-forwarding her to the roadside where she had cupped her daughter's crushed skull in her palms.

In the three days since Keith's arrival she and Charlie were already wondering how on earth they had managed without him. As well as being an excellent handyman he was good with Sid, offering the old man cigarettes during their tea-breaks and seeking his opinion on everything, from nail sizes to what the weather would be doing. Nor did he seem to mind Sid's grudging responses, the old man's resentment as visible as the now righted cockerel on the garage roof.

Charlie was especially delighted with their new employee because she would get her studio, he said, although Serena suspected it had just as much to do with proving to his meddling brother that they were on top of things. She could picture the scene when Peter came down for Elizabeth's surprise dinner the following weekend: how her husband, so keen to please, so incapable of rancour, would tug him round the place, pointing out what had been done, as eager for approbation as he had been when they were little boys and Peter had chosen all the games. Charlie was, and would always be, the younger brother, she reflected, looking past Keith through the open door to the garden, bursting on all sides with a spring growth that she felt little inclination to tame. He was vulnerable to Peter's dominance just as Ed could still be crushed by the will of his elder sisters, and Chloë, for all her naughtiness, would do anything to earn a smile from Theo. Such sibling patterns were forged in the cradle and you had as much hope of changing them as of kneading granite.

'It's your decision,' prompted Keith, eyeing his new employer with equally guarded curiosity, aware that her attention wasn't fixed on the issue in hand but not minding much. He still couldn't believe the turn his life had taken – bumping into Stephen, then stumbling on employment with the Harrisons and accommodation thrown in. Opening his eyes each morning to the barn's timber and stone walls, with its handy little kitchen and living room, the simple comfort of its furnishings, views of trees and fields on all sides, Keith felt at times as if he had fallen into a parallel universe. Don't blow it, he told himself now, trying to gauge Serena's mood, whether she would welcome an opinion or find it irritating. 'Personally, I'd want to work by the natural light from the window and that wall there would be best for the shelves as it's so large . . .'

'Great.' Serena pressed her hands together. 'Let's do that, then. And the floor – I want pine boards, like the ones in the barn. Are you okay in there, by the way, got everything you want? The fridge doesn't close sometimes. You need to give it a shove.'

'The fridge is fine. Everything's fine.'

'I guess we'll need a proper estimate,' Serena added, pausing at the door, feeling faintly fraudulent because she wasn't good with things like estimates. The way he was looking at her made her wonder suddenly if he thought she was just some bored rich housewife who would never use a studio for anything more than dreaming in and showing off to friends. And maybe he would be right. Maybe she was just going through the motions, these days, filling life instead of living it. Seeing Helen at the party in London, hearing her stories about Chloë and Genevieve, the trials and tribulations of juggling work and home, Serena had been aware of a sensation akin to envy. It had intensified when Cassie – in hushed promise-not-to-tell whispers – had broken the happy news that she and Stephen were already trying for a baby, that they had decided the race against the biological clock was too tight for them to care about upsetting Pamela or anyone else by not doing things in the conventional order.

Pondering it all now, it seemed to Serena that her own maternal duties had shrunk to a sort of deluxe housekeeping service – the regular preparation of large meals (Ed's appetite was boundless) interlaced with laundry duties. Neither Pamela nor Charlie was anything like as demanding, and they were grateful, too, with a form of caring politeness that seemed to be as alien to teenagers as a foreign language. With Ed, these days, it was bear-hugs or silence. In fact, Serena mused wryly, if there was any equivalent of a small child in her life now it was Ashley House. With its creaking three storeys, seven bedrooms and five bathrooms, all serviced by temperamental heating and water systems, it generated as much need for attention and organization as any petulant young charge. Just that morning she had been diverted from changing the sheets by the sight of a bulging patch of green behind Charlie's and her bed; on closer inspection she had discovered several more, less verdant outcrops, confirming that the entire wall was succumbing, chicken-pox style, to some dreadful case of spreading mildew.

Standing precariously on the edge of the bed to check the severity of the problem, Serena had been diverted yet again by hundreds of tiny red spiders partying along the dado rail. Remembering them now, and the blotched wall, she said, 'I might need you to look at a patch of damp in our bedroom at some stage and also . . . little red spiders. Do you know anything about them?'

'Spider mice?'

'Is that what they're called? I keep finding them in the house.'

'Check the pot plants, they'll be nesting in those – silvery webs coating all the leaves. You have to get really close to see them but they'll be there, all right.'

'Will they? Thanks.'

'Some sort of bug-killer will sort it out – an aerosol. Do you want me to . . . ?'

'No, it's all right, I'll get some. Spider mice . . . thanks.'

'As for the damp, I'll have a look this afternoon, if you like.'

'Oh, *would* you? Thanks so much.' Serena beamed at him, thinking again how lovely it was to have someone other than the doddery Sid to turn to, someone so relatively young and willing.

Making her way back up to the house a few minutes later, she noticed Pamela, in a too-big mackintosh of John's, wellingtons and a headscarf, heading towards the vegetable garden. She was walking purposefully, carrying an empty basket and a pair of secateurs.

'Pamela?'

Her mother-in-law stopped and looked about her, then shook her head and continued with the same purposeful strides.

Serena sighed and continued up the narrow stone path that led round the side of the house towards the kitchen door. Pamela wouldn't find much to put in her basket. Thanks to Sid's decline, the vegetable garden had produced paltry pickings all year. She had done a trawl herself the day before, finding nothing but a few withered carrots and a couple of Brussels sprouts stalks, both badly mutilated by some of the munching assailants that Pamela had once energetically helped Sid keep at bay. Delving into Pamela's library of gardening books to get to grips with such matters was high on Serena's never-ending list of Things to Do. In the meantime she had scattered an entire canister of slug pellets between the rows, then toured the perimeter fence, cutting her fingers in her efforts to tug rusting chicken wire over the holes.

Maybe Keith knew about vegetables as well as floor tiles and red spiders, she mused, hurrying on at the sound of an approaching car, consoling herself with the thought that searching for non-existent vegetables was a better pastime than writing Christmas-card lists, which was how Pamela appeared to have spent most of the morning. Christmas in April . . . Taking a cup of tea into the study, where Pamela was perched like a dainty queen in John's winged Jacobean desk chair, Serena had had to bite her cheeks to stop herself smiling. How quaint, she had thought. How quaint and sweet. Peering over her mother-in-law's shoulder at the names she had been sufficiently enchanted to remark on the number with black lines through them, joking at how many friends had obviously fallen out of favour.

'They're the ones who have died, dear,' Pamela had replied, so mildly, so matter-of-factly that Serena was half-way to the door before the awfulness of what she had said hit home.

'Oh, Pamela, I'm so *sorry*.'

'It's quite all right. I didn't like many of them very much. There are only a few people one really likes in the end.'

Recalling the conversation as she arrived at the back gate, Serena felt again the awfulness of the moment and thought how typical it was of Pamela to have taken it so well – to be so *stoical*. Her mother-in-law was one of a dying breed, she reflected fondly, a generation that had known world wars, rationing, strict upbringings, for-better-or-worse marriages and, as a result, were so much better at *accepting* things instead of complaining and lunging after happiness as if it were some God-given right. Sometimes she felt positively flimsy in comparison.

But perhaps not as flimsy as her sister-in-law, she reflected, peering over the gate and seeing that the car she had heard coming up the lane belonged to Elizabeth. Dear Elizabeth, with her wide, sad eyes and dreadful statement-making clothes. At fifty-three she was so obviously still in search of herself that it pained Serena sometimes to bear witness to it. She was always having 'fresh starts' – most recently landing the maths job at Midhurst Grammar and meeting the odious Richard – only to discover, as any of them could have told her, that the job was far more stressful than teaching primary children and Richard was interested in no one but himself. No wonder she'd started drinking too much. Serena still shuddered at the recollection of the dinner she had organized in an attempt to welcome this new beau into the family circle. Between revealing the table manners of an oaf, he had spent the evening lecturing them on the terrorist threat to the Western world and how Charlie should single-handedly reform the civil service.

At least that horror had gone away, Serena reminded herself, resting her elbows on the back gate and watching in some amusement as Elizabeth made a to-do of parking the car, reversing, turning and going forwards again, as if she was negotiating a busy street rather than Ashley House's spacious rectangular drive.

Elizabeth took several deep breaths before she turned off the engine. She could see Serena fiddling with something by the back gate but wasn't yet ready to greet her. Feeling desolate was one thing; letting other people – even her sweet-natured sister-in-law – know the extent of it was quite another. Friday was her day off and she usually spent it full of preparations and optimism for the weekend. But this weekend was the start of the Easter holidays and Roland had gone to London to see Cassie so there was no one to prepare anything for except herself. Waving her son off on the station platform that morning, she had been enveloped with such a strangling sense of emptiness that only raw determination had kept her smile in place until the train was out of sight.

It was insane, of course. The poor child was only going away for two days to his godmother, dear Cassie, her own little sister, who would meet him at Victoria, spoil him rotten, then post him back on Sunday, his stomach bulging with junk food and his rucksack full of frivolous expensive gifts. There had been similar excursions in the past, but Elizabeth had always gone too. Not to be included on this occasion – because, as Cassie rightly pointed out, Roland was old enough to manage the journey on his own – had contributed to her irrational flood of abandonment. Deep down she wondered if Cassie didn't want to see her, whether, in her new feverish happiness as prospective bride, she wanted to keep some distance between herself and the sibling who had managed to cock up not once but *twice* on the marriage front. As if Elizabeth was bad luck or simply too jaded with her own disappointments to be truly happy on Cassie's behalf. All of which was rubbish. No one in the world deserved happiness more than her little sister, bravely ploughing her own furrow for years and years when she was so pretty and capable. Seeing her and Stephen together at the party, all that touching and eye-contact, so clearly in love, had made Elizabeth nothing short of joyful on their behalf. Only the tiniest bit of her had felt sad, and that wasn't out of jealousy so much as recognition that marriage closed certain doors, that having sworn loyalty to her husband some of her and Cassie's patchy sibling intimacy would be lost for good.

That morning, however, it was the greater, more subtly looming milestone of losing her son that Elizabeth had found so oppressive. Standing on the platform, watching the train lumber away, she had had a sudden sharp presentiment of the pain she would feel when Roland flew the nest. All rational consolations – the futility of feeling miserable in anticipation of a prospect, Roland having almost three years of school still to go – failed to have any effect. She was losing him already. She could *feel* it – in his new silences, his closed bedroom door and the thump of his music pulsing through the floorboards. Her sweet son, her lifeline, her darling, was pulling away, as he had every right to, as she had known he would. What she had not known was the extent of the isolation she would suffer. The foretaste of it that morning had induced a deep, physical fear the like of which Elizabeth had never before experienced – a million times worse than discovering Colin had been screwing around, or the hollowness in the pit of her stomach when Lucien had picked up his car keys and said hanging on to memories was better than sticking around to destroy them.

After she'd got back to the cottage she'd staggered upstairs to Roland's empty bedroom and hugged his pillow, feeling quite mad but not caring because there was no one to see, and hugging the pillow was better than hugging nothing. Among the laundry smell of fresh linen she could detect traces of his recently acquired aftershave and beneath that, if she inhaled deeply enough, the little-boy scent of his skin. She had pressed the pillow to her face, drinking every last drop, until the linen was wet and there was nothing to smell but the musty dampness caused by her tears.

Then she had moved about the room, picking things up and putting them down again, fondly noting the teenage mess of his belongings and pondering the curious fact of loving something annoying. He hated her coming into his room – hated her tidying. In spite of this she could not resist scooping up his abandoned pyjamas, still faintly warm, and laying them neatly on the end of the bed.

Crossing to the window, she had tried to shake a little sense into herself by staring out at the sharp, clear-skied brilliance of the day. The sun was shining, summer was coming, her sister was getting married and her son had gone away for two days. It was laughable to feel so sad. Laughable and pathetic. Elizabeth had turned, resolution burgeoning, to leave the room, only to be stopped in her tracks by the picture propped on the easel, an explosion of colours, messy, but somehow not messy, just . . . beautiful. Elizabeth sighed, incomprehensibly moved not just by the picture but by the brushes and paint tubes laid out so neatly on the table next to it, an oasis of extraordinary order, as clean and precise as operating instruments. She had run her fingers over each one, then run from the room, all the love and fear spilling inside like a pain.

Downstairs in the kitchen, she had made herself some coffee and topped it up with a generous shot of brandy. After she had drunk it she felt both a little better and a little worse. The alcohol soothed her, as she had known it would, but to require soothing so early in the day made her ashamed. Fearful that she might be tempted to repeat the exercise, she had set out to visit Ashley House, chewing gum all the way to neutralize her breath.

'It's only me,' she trilled, feeling soothed in an entirely different way by the sight of Serena, still leaning on the gate, her long chestnut hair loose and blowing across her cheeks, her pretty face kind and concerned. 'My day off – thought I'd drop in, see how Mum is, how you are. I hope I haven't picked a bad moment.'

'Of course not.' Serena opened the gate and beckoned her through. 'Your mum's on one of her little walks round the garden, Ed's pedalled off to the library and I've been pretending to our new handyman that I know what I'm talking about.'

'Oh, yes, that friend of Stephen's . . . We were introduced at the party and I couldn't think of a word to say. Is he any good?'

'He appears to be excellent,' Serena replied, fighting annoyance at the way Elizabeth had pushed open the kitchen door and flung herself with easy familiarity on to the big yellow sofa. 'Coffee?' She ran the tap a little more violently than necessary, wondering whether her and Charlie's open-house-to-family policy was sustainable. Their gratitude to Peter for giving them Ashley House was huge, of course, beyond articulation, but with Elizabeth sprawling on the sofa and Peter's latest interference fresh in her mind, Serena found herself thinking how awful it would be for her and Charlie to have to spend the rest of their lives demonstrating their gratitude, as burdened and beholden as freed slaves. She'd married Charlie, after all, not his trio of siblings.

'How do you do it?' wailed Elizabeth, sweeping her unruly thatch of greying hair off her face and letting it fall back again. 'How do you look so *fabulous*?'

'Do I?' Serena laughed, thinking that, for all her faults, how guileless her sister-in-law was compared to most women, how impossible *not* to like. 'I can't say I feel it.' She glanced doubtfully at her off-white T-shirt and long denim skirt, so old it was fraying along the hem, and the black plastic flip-flops she had slipped on because she couldn't find any clean socks.

'Soon I'll be fifty-four,' continued Elizabeth, morosely, 'but today I feel more like a *hundred* and four. My hair – Christ! It's like an old brush.'

'Don't be silly,' said Serena, observing that Elizabeth was indeed rather more dishevelled than usual, like a badly wrapped parcel. 'Here you are – milk, one sugar.' She made a cluck of concern as she handed over the mug, calmed as always by the easy business of being nice to someone and thinking that the now imminent surprise party was exactly what her sister-in-law needed to bolster her spirits.

'And you've been through so much,' gushed Elizabeth, thoroughly into her stride now, thanks to the brandy and no breakfast. 'I mean, all I've had to contend with is two failed marriages while you . . .' She blew on her coffee. 'Do you still miss her . . . Tina?'

'Of course.' Serena eyed her sister-in-law steadily over her mug. She was well past the stage of experiencing any obligation to explain her feelings to anyone. The loss of her child was simply part of her, walled inside, as integral to each breath as her pumping heart. 'Do you still miss Lucien? Or Colin?' she countered deftly.

Elizabeth groaned. 'Well, it's hardly the same . . . but Colin, no, I'm still too angry. If it wasn't for Roland I wouldn't care if I never heard from him again. As for Lucien . . . that's harder. To have tried a second time and failed . . .' She sighed, remembering again how she had watched him drive away, taking with him, she sometimes felt, every ounce of her fragile self-belief. 'We should never have got back together. Never. It's always a mistake to go back, don't you think?'

'Probably,' replied Serena, thinking suddenly that maybe the entire Harrison family spent too much energy trying to go back to things, to cling to some idyllic past, instead of adapting to the realities of change. Sometimes she even thought she and Charlie might have got over losing Tina more quickly if they had resisted Peter's offer and moved somewhere else. Their youngest had spent so many happy hours of her short life at Ashley House that at first it had been almost as hard as being in their old house in Wimbledon, with memories waiting round corners like thugs with cudgels. But, then, memories were a comfort too, she reflected, her thoughts switching to the lifebelt of the past that clearly sustained her mother-in-law, all the little rituals and recollections that propelled her through each day. 'Pamela's well,' she said brightly, the tail end of the thought slipping out of her.

'Oh, good . . . I ought to go and see her, I suppose.' Elizabeth glanced at the kitchen window, as if expecting Pamela to appear on the other side of it. In truth she didn't really feel like skipping out into the garden, playing the role of attentive daughter. She was still too preoccupied with her own woes, too unsteady. Besides, she and her mother had never enjoyed the most relaxed of relationships: clashing temperaments and personalities, middle-child syndrome – variously confronted over the years, these demons had taught them tacitly to accept that each was a lot easier to love at a distance. 'Just finish my coffee . . .'

Serena, her own mug empty, glanced in some despair at the kitchen clock.

Elizabeth, mired in her own closed world, asked after her nephew.

'Oh, Ed's fine.'

'Roland is too, I think, except . . . he spends a lot of time in his room, painting and listening to music. Sometimes I think he's a bit too solitary – he doesn't even see that friend of his, Polly, much any more. I think they've had some sort of falling out . . .'

'We have to let our children *be*,' interjected Serena, with some frustration, both at Elizabeth's dogged occupation of her kitchen and the difficulty of putting such wisdom into practice herself. Roland might be more publicly stifled by his mother but in some ways she and Charlie were just as bad. Every text, every email from their twin daughters was read and reread, treasured and worried over, just as they worried ceaselessly over Ed – his often lacklustre approach to work, his recent, astonishing announcement that he had consulted the school careers teacher about going into the army. The army! Serena's mouth had dried with terror as her mind flooded with images of mutilated limbs, body-bags and tours of duty in barbaric far-flung places. Charlie, on the other hand, had been delighted. It was the first sign of initiative on any front, he said, and they should welcome it. 'Our children are gifts and owe us nothing,' she declared firmly, speaking as much to herself as to Elizabeth and beginning, pointedly, to rinse out the coffee pot.

Ed had been hoping to make a discreet entry into the house via the back door, but saw his mother and aunt in the kitchen and hurriedly ducked under the window. If they spotted him they would ask awkward questions, like how was his A-level revision going and why had he made a trip to the library with a rucksack containing nothing but his phone and a bottle of water.

Head down, he trotted round the side of the house and walked along the cloisters, trying first the door to the music room and then the one into the drawing room. He rattled the handles impatiently, inwardly bewailing that, in recent weeks, his home life had degenerated into a non-stop game of cat-and-mouse with his parents. He didn't like it and wasn't sure how it had happened, except that suddenly all the things he felt most like doing – going to the pub, having a smoke, hanging out with Jessica – were things of which he knew they'd disapprove. His twin sisters were partly to blame, of course, for taking off at the same time, casting him in the unforeseeably horrible role of Only Child. With no one else to quiz, chivvy or encourage, the full beam of parental attention had swung his way just when he could most have done without it. It made him wonder how Roland had borne it all those years, and with Aunt Elizabeth too, whose intense concern and clinginess made his own mother seem positively neglectful.

Ed took off his rucksack and slumped down on to the cloister bench to consider his options. His legs were trembling slightly, from the vigour with which he had worked his bike pedals and the rather more enjoyable form of physical exercise that had preceded the journey home. He closed his eyes for a moment, reliving the sex, smelling it, tasting it, hearing Jessica's short breaths in his ear, urging him on, saying things that had helped excitement overcome his terror. Once, a few years before, a particularly bold biology teacher had informed his class of sniggering thirteen-year-olds that sex was enjoyable, that the Lord had made it so to ensure the survival of the human race. Though admiring of the teacher's courage, Ed had sniggered along with the rest, not then having the wherewithal to imagine enjoyment beyond an ice-cream or the delicious, explosive drive of sexual desire. Now he knew. Boy! He knew, all right. Ed clapped his hand to his mouth and laughed, elated again at having disburdened himself of his virginity, not clumsily either but – though he said it himself – pretty well. Jessica had seemed pleased enough, clinging to him afterwards, her body sticky with sweat, whispering that she'd never been so happy in all her sixteen years on the planet. Ed had returned the compliment, but when she'd hinted at heavier feelings he hadn't responded so easily. The encounter, though satisfying, had had nothing to do with anything deep on his side. Jessica was a laugh, someone to cut his teeth on, way off any hazy notions he might have of the Real Thing.

Ed wondered if he should simply stroll in through the front door. He felt exhausted suddenly – too tired, too contented to move. Since their thwarted clumsy assignment in the pub after his great-aunt's funeral, the prospect of a second, better chance with Jessica had built inside him like a gathering storm. Wherever he had been – trying to sleep, trying to work, listening to the careers teacher's nasal drone on the challenge of getting into Sandhurst or the Royal Marines – he had thought of little else. It had been like trying to live two lives – the normal, boring, necessary one and the other shimmering, imagined one, kept alive by the beep of his phone and Jessica's stream of texts, suggesting possibilities that kept falling through. She seemed to understand that what they were doing had to be kept secret. Her mum didn't even know she was on the pill, she had confessed that morning with a giggle, pressing herself against him as they lay hip to hip on Sid's narrow box of a spare bed, sharing a cigarette. 'And my mum and dad want me to concentrate on my exams,' Ed had replied, looking from Jessica's flushed face to the crumpled sheets, then laughing so hard he had choked till his eyes streamed.

'Hi, there.'

'Oh . . . hi, Keith.' Ed struggled to his feet, almost choking now at the sudden appearance of his parents' new employee, who was standing by the rosebushes that skirted the lawn.

'Enjoying the holidays?'

'Yup.' Ed picked up his rucksack as casually as he could. 'Got to work, though, which is a pain.' He sauntered on to the lawn and kicked idly at a molehill, wishing Keith would go away instead of staring at him like he knew everything. 'See you, then,' he muttered, strolling towards the front of the house.

Keith watched the boy till he had disappeared, thinking he looked up to no good, then chuckling because most seventeen-year-olds *were* up to no good – it went with the territory. He pulled his notepad out of his back pocket and checked the list he had made of materials for the studio job, wondering whether to set off to the shops Charlie had recommended or wait until after lunch. A nice crusty loaf and a packet of ham were waiting for him back at the barn, and his tummy was rumbling.

The shopping could wait, he decided, and turned to admire the view beyond the garden, where the South Downs guarded the horizon like a fairytale border to another land. A moment later he had set off briskly past the rosy cage of the pergola towards the gate at the bottom of the garden. Beyond it there were a couple of fields and then a small wood – the copse, they called it – which sat like a plump green mushroom in the distance, as soft as the cushions of moss sprouting along the garden walls. There was a lake right in the middle, Charlie had told him, pointing out various landmarks on the day of his arrival, a wayward thing that ebbed and flowed to its own rhythms, bog one minute, deep enough to swim in the next.

Keith had never lived in the country and felt a distinct surge of pleasure as he clicked the garden gate shut behind him and strode across the field. Worth missing his sandwich for a walk like this, he told himself, imagining the lake and thinking how great it would be if he could make the job stretch to the summer and maybe have a picnic or two sprawled next to it.

He began to whistle, thinking how right it felt that he had come to work for the Harrisons, how maybe life had a way of shaping itself even when you thought you weren't in control. He wondered, too, what it felt like to be in possession of so much land you couldn't even see all of it without taking a walk, and whether such luxury precluded the possibilities – so wretchedly familiar to him – of feeling hopeless and unhappy. The Harrisons certainly didn't look hopeless or unhappy but, then, if life had taught him anything it was that you could never be sure what anyone was feeling about anything. Charlie seemed the jolly kind, bouncing off in his Volvo to catch the train every morning, not getting back till seven or eight, always with a cheerful word on his lips, while Serena . . . Keith took in a deep breath and let it out again. What did she really feel about life? She smiled a lot, but in a dreamy, fragile way, as if she was a chisel-tap away from collapse. Like something that had been mended. Perhaps because of her little girl . . . Keith tried to stop his musings there, loath to erase the sparkle from the day with difficult thoughts. His own two kids hadn't died, but sometimes he thought they might as well have, with their mum poisoning their minds against him and their lives so full he hardly got a look-in. Even when he had parked himself in Hull for three full weeks the previous month – staying on his sister Irene's couch, borrowing money off her for treats – it had been like getting blood out of a stone, with his wife June on his case all the time and the boys lippy and cold, ruder to him than they'd have dreamt of being to anyone else's dad.

There was a path in the trees, hard to follow in places because of the bracken and brambles sprouting on all sides. Keith picked up a broken branch and used it to beat back the worst of the green tentacles, more for the pleasure of wielding a stick than because he needed to. The lake appeared as he rounded a bend, glistening under the open sky like some huge looking-glass. It was such a lovely sight that it took Keith a few seconds to register that he was not the only one enjoying it. The old bird, Mrs Harrison, was there too, standing in her wellies on the edge with her back to him, both arms looped through what looked to be a heavy basket, her silk headscarf fluttering in the breeze.

Keith was debating whether to retreat or call a greeting when, stiff-necked, her gaze fixed on the far bank, she began to wade into the water. He watched in astonishment, waiting for her to stop, wondering dimly if he was witnessing some weird rural ritual that was normal to grand families with grand houses. But she kept walking until her mac was floating round her hips and the weight of whatever was in the basket tipped her forwards, like a feeble boat losing its balance. Keith dropped his stick and leapt clumsily through the tangle of long grass, bracken and nettles that still separated him from the water's edge.

'Hey! Mrs Harrison! Hang on! What are you doing?'

She stopped, half turned her head, then sank lower still, with a soundless grace, as if she were merely bending her knees rather than out of her depth. By the time Keith had wrenched off his fleece and trainers the water had lapped over the trailing tip of her headscarf so that it pointed like a dark arrow down between her shoulder-blades.

'Mrs Har— Christ!' The water was achingly cold. Keith pushed at it with his knees, gasping as it splashed up his stomach and chest. Only when his feet sank into the thick muddy bottom, which squelched between his toes, sucking him down, did he remember that he could not swim. The word 'impossible' slid into his brain. He turned back for the bank. There would be a long stick, surely, a coil of rope – something. But as he turned the old lady – or, at least, the last visible bit of her – sank below the surface of the water. The lake closed over her in an instant, like the magical healing of a wound. 'Mrs Harrison!' Keith croaked, weeping now. He took another big stride, at which point the sludgy ground sucking at his toes, keeping his own head above water, disappeared. It was like stepping off an invisible cliff, with no time to brace himself, no instant in which to gulp some preparatory air before the water swallowed him. For a few long moments Keith flailed wildly, forgetting the old woman, forgetting everything but his bursting lungs. I'm going to die and it's right, he thought. But then, out of nowhere, came the recollection of what Serena and Charlie had lost already and he fought the water more steadily, groping downwards to where he imagined Pamela might be. A moment later his fingers made contact with something soft, a straggle of weeds, then something much harder – the fucking basket! It weighed a ton and the old biddy was still clinging to the handle – clinging as if her life rather than her death depended on it.

Had his kicking legs not found a foothold at that point, a miraculous solid something on which to perch among the reeds, Keith might have had to return all his efforts to saving himself. But he was able to stand – to take a breath – and then, because he was strong, to duck down and pull the basket, which was full of stones, from her grasp. After that it was easier. He plunged again finding first a fistful of sodden cardigan, then an arm and finally her waist. A couple of minutes later he was hauling Pamela on to the bank, a wet, spluttering bundle now, all the silent stiffness gone. But when she looked at him, through bloodshot eyes, it was with an expression so much more akin to horror than gratitude that Keith wondered, even in the extraordinary trauma of the moment, how monstrous it was that some treasured lives were fought for and lost, while others were so wilfully thrown away.

'Could you take two deep breaths for me, please? That's it. In and out. Slowly. And again. That's it. Back pain – all pain – is a funny thing, you see. It starts with an injury, sometimes something very small, then increases as the muscles tighten to protect it. Then, because everything is out of kilter, the rest of the body moves differently to accommodate it, which can start a chain of other problems. Before you know it you've damaged something else. I've seen it time and time again, a sore ankle or hip, say, which stems from an unsolved problem in the back for which the sufferer has subconsciously been compensating. Looking at your stance now . . .' Peter heard the physiotherapist take a step backwards '. . . your entire body is leaning slightly to the left. Did you know that?'

'Nope.' Peter felt meek and foolish standing there in just his trousers, being studied like a beast in a zoo. On arriving at Delia Goddard's Richmond house – far more splendid than he had pictured in spite of Cassie's exuberant description – he had been half hoping to be sent packing with a couple of stretching exercises and a prescription for some decent painkillers. Whatever was going on between his shoulders certainly hadn't got any worse. In recent days he'd only noticed it if he turned sharply without thinking or sat for too long in one position.

'You're compensating for the pain.'

'Am I? Right.' Peter began to fold his arms, then hastily let them drop to his sides as she had instructed. He stared out of the window, trying to lower his right shoulder. Two fat pigeons were on the lawn, one pecking at the ground as the other strutted round in circles, puffing out its chest and ruffling its feathers.

'So, there was no specific moment when you felt the injury occur?'

'No . . . That is . . .' Peter tried to remember the evening session in the gym before Cassie and Stephen's party. 'I did my usual – the bike, the rowing machine, a few weights – and it just sort of stiffened up afterwards. It's nothing like as bad as it was – though I had a tough game of squash the other week, against my nineteen-year-old son, which probably didn't help.'

'Who won?' she inquired, with a chuckle, straightening the paper sheet covering the consulting bed and indicating that he should lie on it face down.

'Me,' Peter shot back, absurdly glad that the question had been asked.

She washed her hands at a basin in the corner of the room, then returned to the bed. 'Tell me when you feel pain. It's hard, I know, but if you could relax . . .' She pressed her fingers down either side of his spine, starting at the base of his neck, then working outwards across his shoulders. 'I think it's here, isn't it?' She pressed a little harder at a spot just below his left shoulder-blade and Peter, struggling to relax, flinched involuntarily as an agonizing spasm pierced his upper back. 'Sorry. Yes, I thought so. Very tender, isn't it? But easily fixable, with a little ultrasound, a little common sense . . .'

'Common sense?' Peter grunted, his mouth full of the papery sheet.

'The correct exercises, a little rest, some anti-inflammatories, no more squash matches against teenagers.' Her hands continued to work, painfully, but also soothingly. 'Now this will be a little cold,' she warned, a few minutes later, spreading gel across the afflicted area and pressing some buttons on her ultrasound machine. 'You should feel a little prickling – nothing too bad.' She rolled an implement over the gel. 'So, you're Cassie's brother,' she remarked, after a couple of moments, her tone light and conversational now.

'That's right. She recommended you.'

Delia laughed. 'Well, that's good because I've recommended *her* to several people – such a good eye . . . It's one thing knowing how you want a place to look and quite another having the innate wherewithal to achieve it. A real talent.'

'She's getting married,' Peter said, relaxing as he got used to the pinpricks rolling across his back. 'To a chap who writes detective stories.'

'Is she? That's nice. And do you have just the one child?'

'No, we've got three. A recently turned five-year-old, a thirteen-year-old and the squash player. What about you?'

'Married, one child, currently on his gap year. Once upon a time I was in marketing but took time out after maternity leave, then retrained as a physiotherapist when Julian started school. I never did understand women who can make a career of motherhood. I'd have gone mad if I hadn't found something else to do – baking cakes, coffee mornings, not my thing at all.'

Peter chuckled. 'My wife's exactly the same, although . . .'

'Yes?'

'Well . . . she works hard and there's our little one, Genevieve . . . It sometimes feels like we never get a moment to ourselves.'

'And then, if you're not careful, you get a moment to yourselves and don't know what to do with it.'

Peter was still wondering how to respond to this when the machine beeped and she began, with swift, firm strokes, to wipe the gel off his back with a tissue. 'There. Now I'm going to stretch you a bit – nothing too drastic, I promise. If you could begin by putting this arm up here . . . like that . . . and the other down here . . .'

These manoeuvres were interrupted by the jaunty ring-tone – chosen for him, with some insistence, by Chloë – of Peter's mobile.

'Sorry.' Peter tried to sit up. 'I thought I'd turned the damn thing off.'

'No worries. Take the call, if you want. I'll get it for you. Is it in here?' She trotted to the chair over which he had draped his clothes and fished round in his jacket pockets. 'Believe me, I'm used to it. My husband only turns his off when he goes to sleep. But that's corporate lawyers for you.' She hurried back to the bed and handed him the phone.

Peter turned on his side to take the call, frowning as he recognized the Ashley House number and wondering what on earth Serena could want from him on a Friday afternoon.

'Bit of a drama here,' said Charlie, who had jumped on a train to Sussex the moment he'd received the news about Pamela. 'Sorry, Peter, tried the office first, expect you're busy, but it's Mum.'

'What's happened?' Peter heaved himself up on to one elbow.

Charlie, his usually jovial voice flat and grey, pressed on: 'She appears . . . Christ, Peter . . . the fact is she *appears* to have tried to take her life.'

'She *what*?' Forgetting Delia, who had made a tactical withdrawal to her desk, and his back, Peter sat up, swung his legs over the side of the bed and pressed the phone to his ear. Charlie proceeded to deliver an account of the morning's events, pieced together from Serena, Keith and Ed, all of whom were now clustered in the kitchen keeping an eye open for Dr

Lazard's black Vauxhall. Pamela had been given brandy and put to bed where, amid mumbling apologies, she had lapsed into fitful sleep.

'Christ! The *lake*? *Stones*? What the hell . . . ? Thank God she's all right . . . and thank God for Keith. Jesus, this is *unreal*! Look, I'll come down at once, okay? I'll sort things out this end – talk to Helen and so on. I was taking the afternoon off anyway. I'll be there as soon as I can.'

'Oh dear,' said Delia, quietly, raising her face from her papers and watching as Peter lowered the phone.

Peter looked at her, trying to focus. The columns of flowers on the walls of the consulting room were spiralling madly in and out of his line of vision. He had to go, obviously, put his clothes on, excuse himself, but somehow he couldn't move. He opened his mouth with the intention of explaining this – apologizing for it – and found himself saying instead, 'My mother has tried to kill – to drown herself. We've got this lake, you see – or, rather, we have this big family house where my brother lives, with our mother. Our father died a couple of years ago, and I suppose she . . . *Christ!*' Peter looked at his watch, then at the phone. 'I ought to go. I *must* go.'

'No.' She had materialized at his side and placed a steadying hand on his arm. 'At least, of course you must go, but not before you've had something – a cup of tea, a whisky. We've time left, and I haven't got another patient till four. Call your wife. I'll put the kettle on.'

A few minutes later she returned with a mug of tea and a small glass of whisky, by which time Peter had left a message for Helen, who was in a meeting, and put on his shirt and shoes. He had tried to put on his tie but had been prevented from completing the task by a curious trembling that began at his elbows and travelled down to his fingertips. He stuffed the tie into his pocket and examined his hands in some amazement, as unnerved by this evidence of shock as the appalling news that had prompted it. Normally he was up to any crisis – knew just what to do and say, whom to call. It was why he was so effective in the courtroom, why, when there was any family drama, his siblings turned to him for advice, relying on him to lead the march, show them all the way through. 'That's very kind,' he murmured, taking the drinks from Delia and swigging the whisky first, swallowing a good half in one gulp.

'Come to the sitting room,' she suggested gently. 'It's much more comfy.' She led the way along the hall and into a chic conservatory-style room with leather furniture, a marble floor scattered with rugs and a glass wall that overlooked a platform of handsome decking, covered with terracotta pots of trim bay trees and rosebushes.

'I really should be going,' muttered Peter, sitting down and sipping his drinks.

'You stay right where you are until you're ready.' Delia crossed the room and stood looking out at the garden, arms folded. 'My brother killed himself,' she said, after a few moments. 'Out of the blue. Secret money worries, which turned out to be nothing when we looked into them. Stupid bastard. It still makes me cross.'

'Cross?' Peter glanced up in surprise. He felt upset, guilty even, but anger hadn't yet occurred to him.

Delia turned to him, the colour rising in her cheeks. 'It is the most selfish of acts. He left a wife, two children and a family all banging themselves over the head, wondering what they could have done to prevent it. Whatever we go through in our lives – however unhappy we are – we have a duty of care to those around us . . . There are ways of finding fulfilment without damaging those closest to us. Don't you think?' She was staring fixedly – passionately – at him, her eyes shining.

Preoccupied as he was, Peter sensed at once that this display of feeling, while emanating perhaps from the recollection of losing her brother, was connected to other, more immediate, more personal things. Confused, he dropped his gaze to his shoelaces. 'Your own brother . . . How awful. I'm so –'

'It was a long time ago,' she murmured, unfolding her arms. 'I only told you because I thought it might help.' She left the window and came to sit next to him. 'Your mother's okay, then?' Her crossed legs, he noticed, were a couple of inches from his knees. Shapely legs, he couldn't help observing, hitherto concealed by the panels of a plain black skirt. Peter looked away. It felt criminal to make such an observation at such a time and in such circumstances, yet . . . something about her manner, the way she was presenting herself – opening herself – seemed to invite it.

'Apparently she's, er, she's in bed resting, my brother said . . . not offered any explanations as yet . . . in shock, of course.' I, too, am in shock, Peter reminded himself, wanting to account for his renewed stammering, when in fact the whisky had settled his nerves. His hands, resting on his thighs, felt normal now – more than up to the trickiest of ties. His heart, on the other hand, appeared to have embarked on a private gallop towards an invisible finish line. Because of what? A set of decent legs? Surely not. Like any man he had an eye for a good female body: Samantha Harding, one of their junior barristers, had a stunning figure – he had joked with Helen several times about how it helped to disarm judges and get juries on her side. No, something else was going on, something intense and intangible, almost as if an invisible veil of intimacy had floated down from nowhere and was ensnaring him in its folds.

The timing of Charlie's phone call was in part to blame, Peter decided, hunting frantically for explanations. It had introduced a personal note into what should have been a thoroughly impersonal encounter; and then, of course, he had dealt with it badly – talking when he should simply have taken his leave, then accepting the invitation to move from the clinical safety of the consulting room to the contrasting sensuality of the wide brown leather sofa. Sitting at Delia Goddard's desk half an hour before, answering questions, he had noticed only a woman in her late forties, with a sensible coiffure of dyed blonde hair and a figure that was neither remarkably thin nor fat. Now, however, he could see that the physiotherapist's hair was prettily coloured with streaks of ash and honey – several strands had fallen into her eyes, which she made no attempt to brush away – and her eyes, without the enhancement of makeup, were a soft, sultry green and ever so slightly slanted. Like a cat's, he thought, slamming his palms decisively against his thighs – slamming away the thought – as he stood up.

'I've taken up more than enough of your time.' He gripped his empty glass and half-drunk tea. 'My family need me,' he added grandly, looking over her shoulder out of the window, ransacking the patio for some solution to his discomfort. 'We're a close family, very close indeed.'

'How lovely,' Delia replied, so normally, so enthusiastically, that for a few glorious moments Peter wondered if all the weirdness had been conjured by his own wild imaginings. He was in quite a state, after all. His dear mother, a paragon of contented endurance, an exemplary light in all their lives, had tried to commit suicide. The shock of such news might warrant all sorts of forgivable insanity.

'How old is she?'

'Seventy-eight – no, nine . . . Almost eighty.' Peter studied the remains of his tea, which was strong and very tasty. Earl Grey, maybe, or some related blend. A single tealeaf floated on the surface, bobbing against the rim.

'Are you sure you don't want to finish it?' All the strangeness was there again, not imagined at all. She was standing so near to him that Peter felt the need to rock back slightly on to his heels.

'I . . . The tea? Oh, no, quite sure . . .' He thrust mug and glass into her hands and strode towards a door, which turned out to be a cupboard of crockery and crystal. He closed it, muttering apologies, his face burning.

'I'll show you out,' she said, leading the way through another door into the hall. 'Poor you and your family. I do hope everything sorts itself out.'

'Oh, it will, it will.' He was jolly now, light-headed with desperation to be gone. 'Thank you again, very much. You've been most kind.'

It was a relief to be outside. He looked up at the sky, which had crowded since his arrival with menacing dark clouds, and breathed deeply, feeling suddenly as if he hadn't breathed for hours, as if he'd forgotten the simple necessity of it, for life, for lucidity. He shook Delia's outstretched hand – firmly, cursorily – then strode towards his car, which he had parked on the curve of the little crescent-shaped drive, facing towards the street. With each step his head cleared a little more. The rest of the day was unfurling in his mind like an open road: he would get back to Barnes before the start of the rush-hour, call Helen again, pack an overnight bag and his briefcase, head down to Sussex, get what sense he could out of his mother, help Charlie and Serena decide where on earth they went from here.

Delia stayed on the doorstep, rubbing her arms as if she was cold and looking – Peter decided with some relish – rather lost. As he was about to get into the car she called, 'I do hope everything works out. And I need to see that shoulder again, okay?'

He waved in response, a single dismissive sweep, then slammed the door and edged out into the road. He might well have another appointment, but not with Delia Goddard, he thought savagely. Never with Delia Goddard. Already what had happened – what hadn't happened – seemed risible, preposterous and shameful, given the drama with his mother. 'Sad old bag,' he said out loud, glimpsing Delia again in his rearview mirror, still on her doorstep, tiny against the backdrop of her large, handsome house. He accelerated away noisily, noting that his shoulder felt tender but a little looser, as if some invisible knots had been untied. It made no difference, he told himself. No matter how good a physiotherapist she was, or how much of the afternoon's extraordinary disquiet had been fabricated by his own imagination, some dim animal sense remained, humming at the back of his mind, telling him that there had been a scent of danger in the house and he would return to it at his peril.

When it started to rain Clem almost turned back. She didn't want to arrive damp and bedraggled, with her hair, specially washed that morning, all frizzy. Though the American had said it didn't matter what she wore, that he liked his subjects to look *natural* – entirely themselves – she had deliberated for hours in front of her meagre rail of clothes, struggling with the notion that she didn't know what 'being herself' meant. It felt increasingly, these days, as if she had many different selves, depending on her mood and the company she was in – meek and mousy for her flatmates, raunchy and wild with a microphone, brisk and neutral as a waitress, self-contained and distant with her family . . . Which, if any of these, to choose when posing for an artist was almost impossible to decide.

In the end, feeling fake in anything pertaining to glamour, aware that she had a bus ride to get through, with the possibility of gawping strangers, Clem had settled on a long grey skirt and black T-shirt, making up for this conservatism with a more than usually lavish application of makeup. Staring at her reflection afterwards – the glowing cheeks, highlighted eyes and crimson lips – she had smiled shyly, both at the notion that she was confronting a new and interesting person for the first time and because it felt comforting to have assembled some sort of armour against the now frighteningly imminent ordeal of being scrutinized.

Flora, languishing in an armchair with a heavy cold, had squealed with delight as she emerged from her bedroom. 'Gorgeous!' she shrieked, her voice thick with catarrh. 'I hope he's worth it.'

'We'll see,' Clem had murmured, unearthing her handbag from under a cushion and heading for the door. She hadn't told Flora or Daisy or anyone about Nathan Chalmer. Just as she hadn't yet told anyone about the thin, but growing manuscript in the bottom drawer of her desk. Aside from fearing the possible ridicule that such confessions might invite, the private smirking (who does she think she is, writing a *novel*? That scarecrow, a *model*?), there was something about the secrecy of these new ventures that Clem couldn't help relishing. Perhaps, she mused, slamming the flat door behind her, because with Maisie breathing down her neck for twenty years she had never felt private enough. Looking back, she wondered how she had put up with being a twin for so long – shared bedrooms, shared teachers, shared birthday parties. Any normal sibling would have protested violently at such enforced overlaps. It had made them close, of course, unbelievably so for a time – with a secret language and an almost telepathic empathy – but, as Clem had discovered, being close to someone was as burdensome as it was nice. It opened one up to pain, made one vulnerable. Far better – far simpler – to be self-contained and on top of things, to forge one's own separate path, as she was now doing, blissfully far from the possibility of comparison and competition.

As she turned into the narrow street just short of London Bridge station – sketched for her by Nathan on the back of a paper napkin – Clem's phone beeped. Recognizing the number and in no mood for her mother, she let it ring. A couple of minutes later a text arrived. 'Darling, could you call home? Love Mum.' Feeling vaguely harassed, as if her parents had somehow found out about her escapade and wanted to put a stop to it, Clem dropped the phone back into her bag. It beeped again a moment later, this time with a message from Roland, saying he was staying with Cassie and Stephen and could she meet them for lunch on Sunday? Families clung so, Clem reflected crossly, remembering with a swoop of dread the impending ball with Theo, and a still unanswered missive her aunt had sent her, full of sketches of bridesmaid dresses: leg-o'-mutton sleeves, frilly necklines, giant Easter-egg ribbon sashes. Clem had riffled through the pages in horror, wishing, for a few unguarded moments, that Maisie could have been there to help her see the funny side.

Nathan Chalmer lived on the top floor of what looked from the outside like an old Victorian factory. It had tall, imposing red-brick walls, lined with rows of small arched windows, the larger ones fronted by bulging wrought-iron balconies. Like miniature prison cells, Clem couldn't help thinking, digging deep inside herself for the final burst of courage necessary to push the button next to his name. A few moments later there was an audible click, releasing the lock on the heavy black front door. She pushed it open cautiously, blinking as her eyes adjusted to the darkness of the hall. Inside, a stone staircase curled round a black iron Tardis of a lift. Its concertinaed metal doors seemed to fight her attempts to open them, then slid shut easily behind her with a clang. A moment later, there was a whoosh of compressed air and the lift rose, so swiftly that the pit of Clem's stomach dived towards her knees.

Nathan Chalmer was waiting for her at the top, arms folded, with an air of studied patience. Like a craggy, ancient-faced statue, Clem decided, wondering how old he was. He dressed like a teenager – baggy combats, a white T-shirt – but his face was like crumpled leather. He had to be sixty at least. Her uncle Peter was fifty-five and didn't look anything like as old. And whereas her uncle had pale-skinned hands with neatly filed nails, Nathan's were huge and hairy with bulging violet veins.

'Welcome,' he said, smiling more grooves into his face, and

staring his steely, grey-eyed stare from under the shelf of his eyebrows. 'It was good of you to come. I thought you might change your mind.'

'Why?'

'Fear, maybe?' He cocked his head at her, looking amused, as he turned to lead the way into his flat, which wasn't really a flat at all but one huge room partitioned into various functions only by the arrangement of its furniture – a single divan bed, a cluster of armchairs, a semi-circular bar of a kitchen and, taking up most of the space, a forest of tables and easels covered with sketches. 'An old guy watches you for a few weeks, then asks if he can draw you. It would be enough to make anyone afraid.'

'I'm not afraid,' retorted Clem, taking off her coat, then hugging it hard. 'I just fancied some extra cash.' She glanced about her, taking in the high ceilings – twice as high as anything at Ashley House – and the wall of windows overlooking a muddled landscape of rooftops, chimneys and railway track. She stepped over to the nearest and peered out. In the same instant a train appeared, like a toy in a model railway but making such a clatter that she could feel the faint vibration of the floorboards beneath her feet.

'I like trains. Do you like trains?' He had come to stand next to her, so close she could see a thicket of white hairs curling over the neckline of his T-shirt.

'Not particularly.'

'Tracks and carriages, all that coming and going, people on different routes in their lives . . . starting points and destinations . . . making choices about where to begin, where to end . . . Life is all about such choices, don't you think?'

Clem shrugged, lacing her fingers together more tightly under the protective shield of her coat. Everything felt unreal, as if she had drifted on to a stage without a script. 'I guess so . . . I mean, I chose to come here, didn't I?'

'You did.' He took a sideways step and began, brazenly, to study her, half closing his eyes and rubbing his fingers back and forth across his chin.

Clem stared back, determined not to be cowed. 'Look . . . what exactly is the deal here? What do you want me to do exactly?'

'Take that lot off for a start.'

Her worst fears realized, Clem blushed violently and glanced round for the door.

'No, not your clothes – unless you would like to. I can assure you it would be a delight and a privilege to draw your naked body . . .' His fingers had moved to his mouth, smothering a smile. 'Maybe when we know each other a little better, eh? No, I was referring to your makeup. I don't like face paint on my models.' With his American accent he rolled each syllable as he spoke, as if tasting it before releasing it from his mouth. 'Would you mind washing it off before we start? There's a bathroom over there, the blue door beyond the sofa. Don't get me wrong, you look great, but it's the *underneath* I'm interested in, those Slavic cheekbones, that quite extraordinary hunger you have about you.'

Clem blushed again, this time with indignation. 'Slavic? Well, I can assure you –'

'It was the first thing I noticed – doing that job of yours, serving all that food and looking starved, like your entire being was focused on self-deprivation.' As he spoke he sauntered towards the semi-circle of kitchen units, floating like an island in the middle of the room, and began pulling things out of cupboards and drawers.

'That's dumb.' Clem laughed uncertainly.

He returned from his foraging with two heaped plates of food – one a precarious mountain of plums, fat purple grapes, strawberries, apricots, the other a more solid stack of biscuits, each one a different shape and flavour. 'So you like eating, do you?'

'Of course I like eating. I eat what I want,' Clem retorted, taking a plum and then a biscuit and biting into each, trying not to frown as the flavours and textures collided in her mouth.

'That's good.' Nathan took a biscuit for himself and disposed of it in two wolfish bites. 'And now that warpaint of yours . . . if you don't mind?'

Clem scurried towards the blue door, licking her fingers and despairing at the oddness of it all. When she returned, feeling scrubbed and vulnerable, a few minutes later, he was sitting on a stool next to the most central window, his head bent over a large pad of paper.

'Would you stand there for me?' He pointed without looking up at a space on the floor – a nowhere-space, as it appeared to Clem, with yards of nothing on either side. 'No, there.' He left his stool and placed one hand on each of her shoulders to propel her to the exact spot. 'I want you to look towards the window. I want you to think of the trains and who you are and where you're going. I want you, above all, to relax – to breathe and move as you have to, to fill, to *own* this space. I want you to be Clementine Harrison, to let all that you are fill your heart and your face . . .' He circled her as he talked, at one point brushing a single hair off her forehead and tugging at a crease in her skirt. 'That's it . . . Now, *unfreeze* yourself, unclamp your jaw. Let your fingers float . . . There, that's better. Now we're getting somewhere.' He left her for a few minutes, returning with a small table on which he placed the biscuits and fruit, and a glass of freshly squeezed orange juice, complete with bits of pith and pips. 'Drink when you're thirsty, eat when you're hungry,' he commanded, settling himself on his stool and picking up his pencil.

Clem stood for a few moments, trying vaguely to comply with this list of instructions, but managing only to feel silly. Her cheeks and lips tingled unpleasantly from the vigorous scrubbing in the bathroom. Her arms felt heavy and ridiculous, whatever position she chose for them, while her feet looked odd and awkward, as if they had been grafted to her ankles. What did he mean *own* this space? It was ridiculous. Ridiculous and impossible, she decided crossly, glancing at Nathan's inscrutable, downturned face, the quick, sharp movements of his pencil – convinced that he was just a mad old man enacting some sick fantasy. Once this thought took hold she couldn't get rid of it. Soon, in the quiet turmoil of her mind, it seemed hilarious. Within a few minutes giggles were rippling through her, as unquenchable as the urge to cough or sneeze. Like a schoolgirl, a pathetic schoolgirl, Clem berated herself, biting her cheeks, swallowing, digging her nails into her palms, while the laughter continued to spiral out of her, until she was doubled up and slapping her knees. 'Oh, God . . . sorry . . . sorry, it's just . . . I feel . . . God, if my sister – my family – could see me . . . they'd . . . she'd have a fit . . .'

'Tell me about your family,' said Nathan, quietly, ignoring her shameful childish convulsions so completely that for a few moments Clem found herself laughing even harder. Through streaming eyes she watched Nathan's pencil continue to move feverishly, his leonine face set in concentration.

And then, quite suddenly, the laughter subsided, draining out of her as quickly as it had arrived. Clem took a deep breath and wiped the back of her hand across her nose, which was running. She felt shaky but also more relaxed. She let her gaze drift out of the window. The rain was falling steadily now, lending a grainy texture to the grey skies and sprawling rooftops. Framed by the windows, the scene looked like a sepia snap-shot of concrete and iron, sprouting a patchy forest of chimneys and TV aerials. Here and there Clem could make out the odd abandoned belonging – a battered trainer, a deflated ball – lying like clues to the unsolved mystery of the lives whence they came. It was like seeing a new layer of the world, a populated space between the ground and the sky.

'I've got a brother called Ed,' she said at length, screwing up her eyes to follow the progress of an aeroplane as it tracked across the grey backdrop of cloud. 'He's okay most of the time but also a bit of a twit. He looks like my dad, who has a boring job in the civil service but isn't boring at all. My mum doesn't really do anything, except cook and clean and look after my gran. I've also got a twin sister called Maisie, who's on her gap year in Mexico. We're not at all alike but used to be really close. Then I found out she'd been seeing my boyfriend, which made me glad she was going away. I had another sister, too, but she died when she was a baby. Two years ago we moved to live in this huge house in the country that's been in the family for centuries. My uncle was supposed to inherit it but he told my dad he could have it instead. It's really beautiful but also kind of dull as it's in this tiny village called Barham, which has nothing but a pub and a church . . .'

An hour later he was pressing a twenty-pound note into her hand and seeing her to the door. 'Good start. Same time next week sound okay?'

'I . . .'

'It's a date, then,' he growled, kissing the top of her head and sending her on her way with a pat on the backside. Which was a bloody cheek, Clem decided, performing a little skip as she stepped back out into the street. Trotting towards the bus stop, she found herself carefully placing her steps between all the pavement lines, just as she used to do with Maisie sometimes, walking home from school. *Tread on a square marry a bear, tread on a line marry a swine.* Dodgy alternatives, Clem had thought, even as a little girl. Though a bear was better, of course, frightening but splendid somehow. Both she and Maisie had aimed for the bear.

On the bus she parked herself at the front of the upper deck, put her feet on the window-ledge and got out her phone. 'Yes,' she texted to Roland, 'am free Sun lnch. Wen n where?' After a deep breath she phoned home.

'Ed? Hi, it's me. Mum asked me to call.'

'Right . . . er, hang on.'

'Ed? What's up?'

'Nothing. Why?'

'Dunno . . . You sound odd.'

'I'll get Mum.'

'Is something the matter with Ed?' Clem asked, once Serena was on the line.

'No, not that I know of.'

'Right . . . good. Well, you asked me to call.'

'I did. How *are* you, darling?'

'Fine, Mum, I'm *fine*.' Clem looked out of the window in front of her feet. She loved being so high up, with the bustle of the city scrolling by like a video on a wide screen. I occupy this space, she thought. I am between the ground and the sky.

'Well, I wanted to know that, of course, but also to ask if you could join us all for your aunt Elizabeth's birthday dinner next month. I thought if I asked you well in advance . . . It's going to be a surprise. She's been a bit low recently . . .'

'Mum, I'm supposed to *work* on a Saturday night.'

'Surely you could take a day off or swap your shift or something? Clem, we haven't seen you since Christmas and it would mean *so* much to your aunt.'

'Yeah, right . . .' Clem hunched against the window, not looking out of it now, not feeling she had any space at all. 'I'll see what I can do, okay? I'll let you know in a couple of days . . . There's a girl called Sarah who might swap with me.'

'That's wonderful, darling, thank you. And how have you been?'

'Like I said . . . fine.' Clem fought annoyance with her mother and herself, for not being more communicative, more *glad*. 'And you lot, Dad, Gran . . . everybody there . . . are you all okay?'

'We . . . we . . . That is to say, yes, we are all fine too.'

' 'Bye, then.'

''Bye, darling. Hope to see you soon. Just let us know.'

A moment later Clem's phone beeped with a fresh text message: 'Gran tried to DROWN herself in the lake. She's ok. Thght u shd no. Pls cum soon. Luv Ed.'

Since when, Cassie asked herself, had the world become so populated with pushchairs and pregnant women? When she had been walking to the tube station with Roland that morning, the streets had been full of young parents, jogging behind buggies, and expectant mothers in low-slung trousers and short T-shirts, showing off their taut white bulges to the April sun; showing off to *her*, Cassie had felt, as if the entire female world was bent upon some conspiracy to make her feel empty and unbabied.

Then, for most of the stops to Oxford Street, they had sat opposite a glum-faced dark-skinned girl so hugely with child that Cassie had wondered quite seriously how she had managed to wedge herself into the seat. A buggy parked by her feet had contained a squirming, unhappy toddler, with watery eyes and a gooey nose, who had whimpered and received nothing but withering looks for its pains. Studying the pair, Cassie had felt a mounting anger at the mother's insouciance – to be in possession of such treasures and look bored with them seemed almost criminal. Catching the toddler's eye, she tried out a smile, thinking that no one in such dire need of a handkerchief could be expected to take pleasure in anything. The child squirmed harder under her scrutiny, inducing in Cassie a fierce, absurd sense of failure. Perhaps she would be a bad mother anyway. Perhaps she wasn't designed for it. Perhaps loving Stephen should be enough. Since Keith's departure he had been attentive, caring, consoling. At times she felt almost unreasonable for wanting anything more.

As they pulled out of Baker Street the toddler had chuckled. Cassie glanced to her right, and noted with delight that her godson was pulling monstrous faces – crossing his eyes and sticking out his tongue. When the mother looked at him Roland exacted a smile from her too, a huge, glittering crescent grin that transformed her instantly from a picture of sullen exhaustion into a velvet-skinned beauty. Still smiling, she patted her toddler's curly head, then sat back and tucked both arms protectively round her balloon-belly.

'So . . . jeans, we decided?'

'Uh . . . I don't really need any.'

'But you would like some?'

'I would . . . at least . . . I mean, they don't have to be expensive ones.'

Cassie laughed and looped her arm through Roland's. 'You aren't a typical teenager, do you know that?'

Roland shrugged. He felt uncertain walking down Oxford Street with his aunt hanging on to his arm. It felt weird having a grown-up so much shorter than him when he could recall, as if it were yesterday, being no higher than her waist. She was trying to treat him as an equal, he could tell, which was sort of flattering but also difficult because it didn't feel natural. Sitting in the coffee shop after the tube ride, she had pulled out a pack of cigarettes and even offered him one, which he turned down, saying she wouldn't tell on him if he didn't on her. While she smoked, she had asked him all sorts of intense questions about school and who his favourite artist was, and when he said Edward Hopper, she made him describe in real detail why that was and tell her all about his favourite picture with the couple and the dog looking in different directions outside the white clapboard house. He was still talking when she had leant across the ashtray, stroked his cheek and said her sister was lucky beyond words to have such a boy and that she wouldn't have missed being his godmother for the world. To which Roland couldn't think how to respond other than to say that he wouldn't have had another godmother in the world either, which sounded too corny and unbelievable so he hadn't said anything until, forced by her silence and worryingly weepy-looking eyes, he had blurted, dishonestly, that he was looking forward to being her usher.

'Oh, I've been thinking about that too,' Cassie had exclaimed, stubbing out her cigarette with a flourish and batting at her eyes as if the smoke had made them water. 'We'll hire you a morning suit for the day, of course, but what about *shoes*? Could I buy you some smart black ones? Could you bear it? Would you mind? If we do the jeans first and then have lunch, McDonald's, if you like – *do* you still like McDonald's?'

'Yeah . . . whatever. Great,' Roland replied, though he didn't particularly.

'And the Tate – you never got there with Elizabeth when you came up for the party, did you? I thought we could do that tomorrow – with Stephen, too, I hope.'

It was at this point that Roland, daunted by the prospect of such unadulterated intensity for the entire weekend, had fumbled for his phone and shyly introduced the idea of meeting up with his cousin.

'Clever you – of course! Ask her now. We'll have brunch somewhere – there's this lovely place near the Barbican that does full English, or eggs Benedict or Spanish omelette . . . *heaps* of things. Stephen and I have been there several times and poor Clem won't want to come all the way to Camden, so it would be perfect.'

In the jeans shop she went round all the rails pulling off different styles, not looking at the price tags as his mother would have done and not minding when he pointed at a pair that was ripped at the knees and full of darned holes.

'Oh, yes,' she said, 'I like those – I *really* like those.' And they had been the ones he had chosen eventually, after much bashful to-ing and fro-ing from behind the change curtain, with Cassie standing outside, nodding or shaking her head, like she was his best friend with absolutely nothing better to do than spend an afternoon watching him parade around in different outfits.

The shoes took even longer. There was only one place to go, Cassie insisted, hailing a cab and bundling him inside. It turned out to be in Bond Street, more like a sitting room than a shop, full of leather sofas and men in pinstripe suits flapping tape measures and shoehorns. Torn between pleasing himself (tricky, since he disliked all of the styles on offer) and a sense of obligation to his aunt, who seemed to be enjoying the agony of indecision, Roland began to feel that his life might end in that shop.

'Those – definitely those,' said Cassie at last, slapping her knees. 'That is, if they're as comfy as those other ones.'

'They are . . . very comfy, but . . . the thing is . . . my feet might grow,' Roland stammered. His mother never bought shoes until the last minute before they were required, and often made him opt for a pair that was half a size too big so they would last longer.

'Might they?' For a moment Cassie looked at him as if he had confessed to something indecent. 'Haven't they finished?' She stared at his feet as if expecting his toes to sprout out of the shoes at that very minute.

'He's a tall chap,' said a smooth voice behind her. They turned to see a man with tanned skin, in a grey charcoal suit, standing behind the sofa. A perfect white triangle of a handkerchief protruded from the breast pocket, highlighting the whiteness of his shirt and the crisp trim of his cuffs.

'Frank!' exclaimed Cassie, leaping up and kissing him on both cheeks.

'Cassie, how are you?'

'I'm in heaven. This is my godson Roland. We're buying him smart shoes because he's going to be an usher at my wedding – aren't you, darling?'

Roland nodded. The man was staring at him in a way he

didn't like, an appraising, sizing-up kind of way, as if he was a cow at an agricultural show.

'How's the house? No peeling wallpaper, I hope? No regrets about the pink bathroom?'

'None whatsoever.'

Frank tipped back his head and laughed loudly, revealing huge white teeth pitted with several gold fillings.

'A regular client,' confided Cassie, once they were safely outside, the shoes bought. 'A sweetie – lives with that actor who's just done *Lear* at the National, though never seems to do anything himself. Spends money like water. He'll be phoning in a few months saying he wants the whole place done again. Gay, of course, but I expect you could tell that, couldn't you?'

'No,' muttered Roland. 'At least, I didn't think about it.'

'Not that that bothers me in the slightest. In fact, I love gay men – in many ways they're so much easier to talk to, so much more in touch with their *feminine* side . . .' Cassie chattered on, charmed by her godson's embarrassment, thinking it would go away if she talked for long enough. She thought, too, of how openly she would discuss such things with her own children, so they'd never suffer the embarrassment of ignorance or be afraid to turn to her for help, or want the ground to swallow them whole, as Roland clearly did, given the concentration with which he was staring out of the taxi window.

'I still think we should have told everybody straight away. It doesn't seem right somehow, not telling. It feels like *pretending*.'

'We could put an advert in *The Times*, I suppose, announce it to the whole world . . .'

'Charlie!' Serena cast a despairing look at him. They were standing in the garden, huddled at the mouth of the pergola and talking in whispers like conspirators, even though the only creature within earshot was Poppy, busily ripping bark off a stick with her teeth. 'A few more minutes and Elizabeth would have been here when it happened. Don't you think she, at least, has a *right* to know?'

'And my mother has a right to some privacy, some respect.'

Instinctively they cast a furtive glance at the house, at the little lamp shining on the windowsill in Pamela's bedroom. Although the garden was still bathed in late-afternoon sunshine, its power to penetrate the house – for that day at least – had died. 'Of course she does. But telling people – telling the family – doesn't diminish that does it? Ed knows, for goodness' sake.'

'Yes, and he knows not to tell anyone too. Our son may not be the most reliable creature, but in this I trust him absolutely.'

'And then there's Keith, of course.'

'I trust him too,' said Charlie stoutly. 'A good man . . . a very good man. We should give him something, don't you think? A bottle of champagne, whisky . . . *something*.'

'Absolutely,' Serena murmured, seeing again Keith's arrival in the kitchen, soaked and wretched, Pamela a seeming corpse in his arms, her hair plastered like netting across her face. And Ed in the doorway behind, gawping and incredulous, until Serena started barking instructions about running a bath, calling the doctor, finding the brandy. Ed had skidded off down the hall in his socks, knocking against furniture, then raced back and asked which of all these things he should do first. 'And Peter . . .'

'Of course we had to tell Peter. He's so good with Mum. He'll know just what to do, how to play it.' Charlie glanced in some desperation at his watch. Peter was on a train from London, a delayed train, as it had turned out, thanks to a faulty signal outside Gatwick. 'Look, I'm not saying we shouldn't tell the rest of the family, I just want a chance to talk to my brother about it first. I should be going – twenty minutes late, he said, didn't he?'

'Thirty. There's still plenty of time.'

'What was she playing at? What, in God's name, was she

thinking?' Charlie slapped his hand against the frame of the pergola so hard that several rose petals burst out of the foliage and floated to their feet. 'I thought she was okay. You did too, didn't you?'

Serena nodded, suddenly too close to tears to speak. The guilt, which had been hovering at the edges of her consciousness all day, pressed in on her. In the rush of crisis management there had been no need – no opportunity – to acknowledge it. Now she remembered her mother-in-law's silence at breakfast, the sad Christmas-card list of dead friends, the scurrying with the empty basket. 'She wasn't herself, but . . . but I didn't see it. I didn't *see* it.'

'Don't start,' Charlie growled, checking his watch yet again and pulling out his car keys. 'None of us saw it. Not even her, by all accounts,' he added, in a reference to Pamela's faltering attempts at explanation, the heartrending, childlike apologies before she had fallen asleep. 'We'd better go in. You look cold.'

'Not really.' Serena sniffed. 'Just my feet.' She glanced down at her flip-flops, recalling, like some ancient image of a past life, her conversation with Elizabeth that morning. In retrospect it felt somehow treacherous that they should have been enjoying such a cosy mundane exchange while Pamela, not many yards away, had been spiralling towards calamity. She knew Charlie was right – that for any of them to feel guilty was both groundless and unhelpful – but the response was there none the less, uncurling inside, like a dark flower, taking her back to the other, deeper guilt, which she'd thought she had erased for good. She had been with Elizabeth that day too. Lunch in Oxford Street. Tina toddling between tables. A busy restaurant. The hubbub of cutlery, crockery, conversation. The opening door, the brush of cold air on the back of her neck, the screech of rubber on Tarmac, the roar of the motorbike as it sped away.

'Darling? You're crying.'

'I know. Sorry. I can't help it . . . A part of me does feel *responsible* . . . just like I did when . . . when . . .' Serena didn't need to complete the sentence.

'Stop this, do you hear me? This is *utterly* different.' There was fear as well as reprimand in Charlie's voice, and the hand that stroked her bowed head was more firm than tender. 'You weren't to blame then and you're not to blame now. In addition to which my mother, in case you had forgotten, is lying safely in her bed, sipping soup and reading a magazine. Her guardian angel has had a busy day but, thanks to Keith, she's *okay*. You heard her, she's sorry, she doesn't know what came over her, she's not going to try anything like it again. Now, give me a hug and tell me you're not going to torture yourself. If you're responsible, so am I, so are all of us. What we *are* responsible for however,' he continued, sounding suddenly like Peter, 'is helping her through it.'

Serena shuffled into her husband's arms, cursing herself for having added a new layer of concern to an already difficult day. 'I guess I'm a bit shocked, that's all. Now, you go and get your brother and I'd better see to supper. I was thinking of inviting Keith – do you think that's a good idea?'

'Excellent. It's the very least we can do.'

Pamela lay perfectly still, listening to the sounds of the house: the faint gurgle of the radiator next to her bed, the thump of Ed's CD-player, footsteps along the hall and back again. The smell of supper was in the air too – onions, meat – a stew of some kind: something with wine, beef or maybe *coq au vin*. Serena was a good cook. Pamela could imagine her moving round the kitchen, chopping, stirring, lifting lids, humming to herself, enjoying the solace she herself had once known so well. Feeding, *providing* for the family. She didn't understand women who failed to enjoy domesticity. Women like Helen, with their microwaves and home-helps, happier with a brief-case than a wooden spoon. It was one of the reasons she had readily agreed to the plan of Serena and Charlie taking over Ashley House, recognizing in her daughter-in-law the potential of a true inheritor to the way of life that she had so cherished. What she hadn't anticipated was the trauma of abdication; becoming a spectator rather than an orchestrator; grateful, of course, but sidelined, like a retired animal put out to grass.

Pamela made herself dwell on this feeling now, wondering how much it had contributed to the course she had taken that day. An astonishing course, as it already appeared. Her apologies to Serena and Charlie – to the poor man who had fished her out – had been heartfelt. As she rose out of the water there had been a moment of pure anger, followed – as the cold air tore back into her lungs – by the purest unutterable shame. What had led her to that moment? Pamela wondered now, trembling in spite of the warm soup and the hot-water bottle at her back under the duvet. Feeling sidelined was just a tiny part of it. No. Something else had happened that morning, something connected to the empty ticking of the old carriage clock in John's study as she had pored over their shrinking list of friends. And then, later, in the garden . . . Pamela drew in her breath, recalling the bare stumps in the vegetable patch, her sad, empty basket. There is nothing here, she had thought, nothing anywhere. She had picked a stone out of a mound of earth, then another and another, scrabbling for them as if they were buried potatoes. I am dying anyway, she had thought, striding across the field towards the copse, her arms aching from the weight of the basket. We are all dying. Why wait, when the waiting is so hard, so empty?

Downstairs the front door slammed. Footsteps on the stairs were followed by a tentative knock on her door and the appearance of Peter at her bedside.

'Mum?' He was still in his overcoat, his newspaper in one hand, briefcase in the other. 'You've given us all quite a scare.'

'Darling . . . I'm so sorry . . . So silly . . . to cause such a fuss.'

'But you're all right now,' he announced firmly, pulling up a chair and easing himself out of his coat. 'That's all that matters. Are Dr Lazard's pills helping? Charlie said he'd given you some.'

'Yes . . . at least . . . Yes, I do feel a little better.' Pamela tried to sit up but Peter pressed his hand to her shoulder.

'Rest now. Lots of rest, eh?'

Pamela let her head sink back into her pillows. 'So kind . . . Everybody has been so kind.'

Peter leant forward, resting his arms on his knees and clasping his hands. 'We're all here to look after you. We all want the best for you . . . If . . . if ever you feel low you must *tell* us, Mum, okay? Tell us and then we can help.'

'Yes, of course . . . I don't know what happened. I feel so bad . . . for Serena and Charlie . . . Tell them, darling, how sorry I am . . . Tell them I won't . . . that it won't happen again.'

Peter picked up one of her hands and pressed it between his palms. He felt solid on the chair, his feet planted firmly on the floor, but weak inside. He wished he had something to offer her other than platitudes. Some form of concrete comfort. 'We miss Dad too,' he ventured quietly, 'but he would want us to carry on . . . to be happy . . .' He lost heart at the sight of her face, which was trembling visibly.

'Oh, yes, John would be cross,' she murmured, her trembling mouth settling suddenly, miraculously, into a smile. 'Very cross,' she added, closing her eyes and chuckling softly.

'He certainly would.' Peter pressed her hand to his lips, delighted at this evidence of a corner turned, musing that no problem was insoluble if one dared to face up to it boldly enough. He laid her hand gently on the bed, as if it were a delicate creature in its own right. Her fingers, swollen-knuckled, these days, with rheumatism, stroked the duvet a few times, as if checking their bearings, then relaxed. Peter watched, chest tightening at the recollection of how the same fingers had once deftly flown over piano keys, worked knitting and threaded silk into miniature needles. *We have a duty of care.* The sentence slipped into his consciousness so easily that it took Peter several moments to recall that the physiotherapist had planted it there. A good one, he mused, in spite of its dubious source. He rolled his shoulders, enjoying the new muscular freedom between them, and the wonderful distance he now felt between the present moment and the shock of Charlie's phone call. 'We want to look after you, Mum,' he said. 'We *want* to, okay?' he repeated, his voice ringing with fresh self-belief and a vivid, lucid sense of his and his siblings' place in the world – in the family – poised between generations, caring for the elderly who had produced them and the youngsters they themselves had spawned.

Ed popped his head round his grandmother's bedroom door a few minutes later, and drew back in surprise at the sight of his uncle sitting at the bedside with his eyes closed, smiling benignly, like a Buddha. His grandmother was smiling too and squeezing his hand in a way that wasn't entirely normal, but the atmosphere in the room was far from the funeral kind, for which Ed had braced himself.

'Er . . .'

'Ah, hello, Ed.'

'Hi . . . Just to say . . . ten minutes till supper, Mum says.'

'Splendid. And what is for supper?'

'Er . . . not sure.'

The two adults exchanged a look as Ed, feeling the vibration of his phone in his pocket, bolted from the room and up to the second floor. 'Hi, Jess, how are you?'

'All right, I guess. How are you?'

'Fine, thanks,' Ed retorted, compelled by something irritating in her tone – something sarky and flippant – to add, 'apart from the fact that my gran tried to kill herself this morning.' Even as the words left his mouth Ed felt a tingle of shame. Not just because he had already defied his father's plea for discretion by telling Clem but also because he knew that so easy a disclosure of such a dreadful piece of news was wrong. Texting Clem had been justified. She was his sister, after all, one of the few people who might understand the bizarre, harrowing spectacle of their grandmother being carted into the kitchen, dripping and limp, pondweed trailing from her clothes. Their *grandmother*, with her Mrs Pepperpot bun, tapestry kits and cups of tea, trying to *commit suicide*. If it wasn't so horrible it might have been funny. Clem would understand that, too, just as she would the awfulness of their mother's ashen face as Serena had rushed across the landing with blankets and towels, while downstairs Keith, the saviour of the hour, had sat at the kitchen table nursing the brandy bottle, pressing his teeth against the rim of his glass to stop them chattering.

Calm had been restored with the visit of the doctor, Keith striding back to his bolt-hole in the barn, and the arrival of their father, full of refreshing normality and reassurance. Feeling forgotten during the numerous hushed consultations that had followed, Ed had retreated to the TV room with a plate of buttered toast. He had eaten ravenously, watching a Spanish football match on Sky, fighting the mounting sensation that a curtain had been lifted on a world he neither understood nor wished to understand. Communicating with Clem had felt like he was making contact with something real, bringing it all down to earth. He had felt a surge of longing for Maisie, too, who was so good at not being afraid, but reasoned that it wouldn't be fair to muck up her trip with bad news.

'Bloody hell,' said Jessica, which, while exactly the response Ed had hoped for, made him no happier. 'How?'

'Tried to drown herself in the lake in the copse – walked into it carrying all these stones, like Virginia bloody Woolf.'

'Virginia who?'

'Woolf. You know – the writer. I'm doing one of her books.'

'What's it called?'

'Jess, really.'

The book you're doing, what's it called?'

Ed sighed, wishing more than ever that he'd kept his mouth shut. *Mrs Dalloway.*'

'Right.' Jessica, who was lying on the sofa in her flat, scribbled the name on a cigarette packet, not daring to ask for the spelling. 'Look, I'm sorry, Ed, for your gran and stuff. My mum tried to top herself once – took a load of pills – but she was just pissed and feeling sorry for herself as usual. Granddad took her to the hospital and she had her stomach pumped. Put her off ever trying anything like that again, she said.'

'Right . . . Er, Jess, they're calling me for dinner – I've got to go.'

'Hang on, Ed – when can I see you again? You said you might come up to London.'

'Yeah . . . but it's hard – I've got a load of work and –'

'What about next weekend, then? I could get away early after school on Friday.'

Ed hesitated, aware suddenly that talking to Jessica was a lot more complicated than touching her, a bit like being on board a moving vehicle with no controls. 'Maybe. I'll call you, okay?'

'Promise me, Ed Harrison.'

'For Christ's sake! I promise, okay?'

'Don't you want to see me, then? Don't you want to do what we did again?'

'Of course,' he whispered, glancing at his bedroom door. 'Of course I do.'

Jessica let out a whoop of glee, so piercing that Ed held the phone away from his ear. 'Look, Jess, my mother's calling – I've got to go.'

'All right. Love ya,' she sang, then clicked off the phone.

For a few moments Ed remained motionless, relishing the silence of his bedroom. His mother hadn't called him down to dinner. Why had he lied? He crossed to the window and rested his forehead on the pane. And why, when he knew full well that Jessica wasn't the One, had he agreed to see her again? Ed straightened and traced a line through the smear his forehead had left on the glass. Outside, he could see the treetops at the bottom of the garden swaying in the wind, silhouetted against the inky black sky like flailing arms. It felt shitty to have lied, even about something so small. He didn't want Jessica, he wanted sex, Ed reflected, miserably, and it wouldn't do, it just wouldn't. He rubbed angrily at the window with the sleeve of his jumper. He would see her at the weekend, he decided, but only to tell her it was over. Whatever 'it' had been.

Downstairs he heard his mother banging the little gong in the hall, which was what she did when she didn't want to holler up three flights of stairs.

'Coming,' he yelled, taking the stairs three at a time, then vaulting over the banisters on the first landing and continuing in the same fashion down the second flight. He arrived, breathless and tousled, in the kitchen a few minutes later to find his parents, his uncle and Keith already seated in front of steaming plates and full wine glasses.

'All right, darling?' asked Serena, with concern, her face all hot and pink from cooking.

'Yes . . . I am, in fact,' declared Ed, his heart swelling with gladness at the prospect of eating and at the sight of all the grown-ups ranged round the table, so ordered and on top of things. 'I'm so glad Gran's okay,' he burst out, feeling he might cry from the relief of being young and alive. As he loaded his fork with food, he thought again about Jessica. The drama with his grandmother had shifted something, he realized, made him see stuff differently, made it clear that there was only one *decent* option open to him. It had made him – possibly – more grown-up, he mused, approaching the notion warily, uncertain as to whether it was something for which he was truly ready to strive. Did decent mean boring, he wondered, piercing a few extra peas on the end of his fork? Did it mean snoring in front of the news like his father or swirling wine noisily round his mouth like his uncle? Preoccupied both with these thoughts and his now mountainous forkful of food, it took Ed a few moments to register that the adults were staring at him, waiting with their glasses raised.

'To you, Keith,' said Peter, gravely, once Ed had reluctantly lowered his fork and picked up his glass. 'From the bottom of our hearts, thank you. Life is full of turning points and today you made sure that a potentially disastrous one went the right way.'

May

Stephen pressed *word count*, then leant back in his chair, hands laced behind his head, and stared out of the window. It was a relief not to look at the screen, not to see the sorry reminder of how far behind he was with his weekly target. His readers, his editor had assured him at their last meeting, wanted more of the same: more Jack Connolly, with his troubled private life and weakness for malt whisky; more pretty widows with trembling emotions, more murders, abused children and grisly post-mortems. Cassie, reading his mood as they lay in bed with cups of tea that morning, knowing it had been a barren week, had been full of gentle encouragement. There was no need to rip himself apart over each story, she had said. He should stay detached, see it as a *craft* at which he excelled, assemble it with the clinical approach of a mathematician – clues, dilemmas, resolution. While welcoming her comfort, Stephen had tried to explain that it wasn't like that, that, if anything, he felt *too* detached. Sitting at his desk now, he felt even more strongly that he didn't care enough about Jack Connolly. The man was paper-thin, a walking cliché, a mish-mash of convenient re-actions, each one linked clumsily to the necessities of an equally clumsy plot. The detective had been beaten up as a child, which made him a lousy adult. So what? So bloody what? If Stephen didn't care, why the fuck should his readers?

Cassie had gone now. He had seen her off at the door, wiping a smear of butter off her cheek, wishing her luck, managing not to say that he didn't want her to go. Managing not to quiz her on *where* exactly she was going to be for every minute of the long day that stretched ahead. She had shown him her work diary earlier in the week, murmuring in amazed despair at how busy she was, saying it was no wonder her body was stalling over making a baby. Stephen, keen to keep the option of consulting a doctor at bay, had held her hand and said there was plenty of time and not to worry and maybe she should consider turning down projects instead of accepting them. At which point a man called Frank had telephoned to request a William Morris makeover for his dining room. Double-quick, double-money, Cassie had exclaimed, flushed with sheepish pleasure as she came off the phone. Good old Frank, and all because she had bumped into him while she was shopping with Roland. Just like her bad ankle had led to all that work in Richmond. Wasn't life funny?

No, Stephen mused now, life wasn't very funny. Even with love, even with money, he still felt *unsafe*. If he failed as a writer the money would dry up. If he failed Cassie, love would dry up too. In the euphoria of getting engaged it had never occurred to him to entertain such doubts. Life, it felt then, had reached a point of such completeness that he could never doubt anything again. And yet here he was, just a few months on, nursing irrational terrors and jealousies of just about everything. Even having Roland to stay the previous weekend had been a struggle for him. Well-mannered and easy-going as Cassie's godson was, Stephen had, at some seedy, dim level, resented the boy's presence in the house, just as he had resented Keith's a few weeks before. It didn't help that Cassie had fluttered round him like a bee at an open flower, attentive and adoring, pandering to his every need, even when it was perfectly clear the lad would have preferred to be left alone.

By Sunday morning Stephen had been counting the hours until Roland's train. Feeling guilty that he was capable of such mean-spiritedness, he had tried to make up for it by dropping them at the door of the brunch place in the Barbican so that only he had to endure the inconvenience of finding somewhere to park. When he got to the table, Cassie's niece, Clem, had been there too, reed-thin in a pair of high-heeled boots and a long black dress, her kohl-rimmed eyes like holes in her face. She had eaten one toasted muffin, picking bits off with her fingers while the rest of them feasted on eggs and bacon, hash browns and sausages. They talked of art mostly, Cassie leading the way, teasing opinions out of the young with a patience that Stephen had found both admirable and alienating. This is how it will be, he had thought suddenly. With a child, this is how it will be. I will lose her. Then she had touched his arm, asked if he was okay, and his heart had ached with shame. Of course she wanted a child, of course *he* wanted a child, a fusion of their love. How could he not? As they were saying their farewells Clem had reached into her satchel of a handbag and pulled out a battered yellow folder. The start of a manuscript, she had said shyly, thrusting it at him. If he had time, could he possibly . . . she knew he was busy . . . Charmed, delighted, feeling integral to the family gathering at last, Stephen had assured her that it would be no bother at all.

Staring at the yellow folder now, however, Stephen felt rather less avuncular. He had perused its thirty or so dog-eared pages on Monday morning, slurping his first coffee of the day, glad to have what felt like a legitimate diversion from his own creative efforts, expecting only to be faintly entertained. His twenty-year-old soon-to-be niece writing a novel – it was, as Cassie had said, rather sweet. For it hadn't crossed her mind either that it would be good: that, while Clem fell occasionally into the obvious traps of youthful, autobiographical indulgence, her writing would contain a raw power, for which Stephen dimly remembered striving when he had been younger and less afraid.

Stephen plucked at the rubber band holding the folder together. It had split open down one side allowing part of a page to protrude. *I wake to the sound of my own breathing. I listen in the dark, hearing the silence outside my body, so thick it has the quality of sound. I am alive but alone, in limbo, between earth and sky, a lost child, a would-be woman . . .*

He wanted badly to look at it again – he had promised a critical appraisal, after all – yet he feared the effect of it. All those heated young thoughts. He was surprised the thing hadn't burned a hole in his desk. As if afraid it might do just that, he picked it up, slipped it into the bottom desk drawer and kicked it shut.

His foot on the drawer handle, he tipped back his chair and peered out of the window down into the garden: a patio, a patch of grass bordered by two flowerbeds and a pretty, trailing tree whose name they didn't know. It was a modest but heartening sight, especially since the tree's lacy green skirt had thickened that week into a layered tutu of yellow and emerald, dotted with buds of crimson pink. Maybe Jack Connolly could possess such a tree, Stephen decided wildly, maybe it would illuminate his detective's stunted, gritty, urban life. Maybe . . .

'Stephen, darling, sorry to disturb you . . . and it's a terrible line too. How's it going? Is the muse with you?'

'Absent without leave, as usual.'

'Poor you . . . Look, I haven't got long, I just rang to ask if you could possibly get something for Elizabeth's birthday?'

'What sort of something?'

'Oh, God, I don't know – I never know what to get her. Do you have any ideas?'

'She's your sister.'

'Don't say it like that. I *meant* to get something yesterday but ran out of time. It would be too awful to turn up empty-handed tonight.'

'But the big dinner isn't until tomorrow. We could go shopping together in the morning – in Chichester or somewhere.'

Cassie groaned. 'Spend our precious Saturday sitting in bank-holiday weekend traffic for three hours? No, thank you. Oh, darling, anything will do – you could go to that gift shop in the high street, get her a scarf or some really expensive body lotion or a picture frame or –'

'Okay, I'll see what I can find,' Stephen promised, sounding defeated but actually pleased to have been reminded of the approaching weekend in the country. Visiting Ashley House was always pleasurable, particularly since Charlie and Serena had allocated them the roomy first-floor bedroom with its four-poster bed and views towards the downs. On this occasion there was the grand birthday dinner to look forward to, in the splendid mahogany-panelled dining room, with its jewelled candelabra casting intricate shadows across the ceiling, and Cassie's ancestors ranged round the walls, smiling like benign spectators. A veteran now of such Harrison gatherings, Stephen knew that they induced in him a joyous sense of belonging, of *safety*. At such times he felt as if he had fallen in love with Cassie's family as much as with Cassie herself; not so much for their wealth as for their cohesion, the way they all still wanted to criss-cross their lives, to build and strengthen the web that bound them together. His family was a trailing thread in comparison, disparate and pointless, too infused with ugly memories and resentments for it ever to be anything else. Peter and Helen, with their high-flying legal careers and huge salaries, could be pompous at times, but he was fond of Charlie and Serena, Elizabeth too. As something of the unacknowledged black sheep of the Harrison brood, Elizabeth's life always helped to quash any lingering doubts about his own credentials. And he could see Keith, Stephen realized, with a start, testing the prospect with some caution and finding that not having seen his old friend for two months, this, too, held considerable appeal.

'You're an angel.'

'Hm . . . I might need to remind you of that one day. Where are you anyway?'

'Fulham – but I've *got* to go. I was due at Frank's ten minutes ago.'

'Frank's . . . I see. When will you be back tonight?'

'Stephen, *please* . . . I don't know – not too late obviously. I'll call when I'm on my way.'

Stephen returned his attention to his computer where the three-dimensional electric green cube he had chosen as a screensaver was performing somersaults. He stabbed at the return key and started to write, not caring that it was Clem's manuscript that remained in the forefront of his mind.

Jack ducked under the orange ticker tape and walked round the side of the house to the garden. He stood for a few moments feeling the silence thicken, aware only of the sound of his own breathing. In the corner of the garden a small tree sported a ballgown of lemony green dotted with pink flowers . . .

Dear Mum and Dad,
   Been meaning to email you for a while, just to say that I really enjoyed the vac

Theo scowled at his laptop, wondering how much padding to put in before he broached the question of money. His parents weren't stupid. No matter how many pleasantries he stuck in first, the request for an injection of cash would stand out with all the subtlety of a scarecrow in a field.

   particularly our game of squash, Dad. Don't worry I'll get you next time!

Theo stopped again, rubbing his fingers along his jawbone where, thanks to his new abstinence from the razor, the bristles were thickest. He had tried to start the process in the holidays but had given up after a few days, defeated by the itching and the relentless remarks of his family. His little sister Chloë had taken particular pleasure in commenting disparagingly on the beard's progress, calling it gross and ugly and dumb, and saying he looked exactly like her physics teacher. Nor was the squash game a particularly happy memory.

'You need your head looking at,' Helen had scolded, returning from shopping with the girls to find her husband and son in shorts and trainers in the hall.

'No, his *back*,' Chloë had quipped. 'It's your back that needs looking at, isn't it, Daddy?'

And although his father had laughed it off in the car, saying he was going to see a physio just in case and that the pair of them were surrounded by fussing women, Theo had walked on to the squash court with a heavy heart. When he saw how hard his father tried for every single shot, careering between the walls, drenched in sweat, grimacing against pain and fatigue alike (it was impossible to tell which), Theo's heart grew even heavier. I could beat him, he had thought. He is getting old and I could beat him.

He lost both games, triggering a riot of back-slapping and affectionate taunts from his father, which he had weathered with difficulty, nursing not hurt feelings, as Peter had supposed, but the new knowledge of his own physical superiority and the complicated cowardice of not having dared to act upon it.

Sorry to say, I am also writing to confess to a certain cash-flow problem

Pausing to look round the clutter of his room for inspiration, Theo's eyes alighted on the gold embossed invitation to the Keble ball.

largely caused by having to shell out £160 for the Keble ball, to which, as you know, I am – under orders! – taking Clem. To be quite honest I would probably have given it a miss otherwise – there's such a demand I could easily sell it back, but obviously I wouldn't want to let Clem down at this late stage. All of which is to say, could you possibly give me an advance on next month's allowance? Am planning to stay up here and work in college for a couple of weeks at the start of the summer vac – playing scout and waiter for conference delegates – so should have no trouble making the money up in the long term.

Hope all well otherwise. Sorry to have to pass on Aunt Elizabeth's birthday dinner – there's just too much going on here to get away.
Love, Theo

Peter glanced up from his papers and peered at the digital clock he kept on his desk, inwardly cursing the slowness with which the dial came into focus. He could almost feel his eye muscles labouring – long vision, short vision. Nothing came without a struggle these days. It was four o'clock already. In a couple more hours he'd have to leave to catch the train for his sister's birthday surprise in Sussex. A quiet Friday afternoon was a luxury and he had somehow let most of it slip through his fingers. His in-tray was a pagoda of papers, the brief before him – a complicated case involving the death of a student on a school sailing trip – barely touched. Usually he relished the challenge of a new case – that clean-slate feeling, with everything to play for, all the subtleties of the arguments to be teased out, like buried fragments of something whole. Yet that afternoon the stamina, the patience, whatever it was, simply hadn't been there. Instead he felt both sleepy and restless, utterly without the wherewithal to prevent his mind wandering down pointless little cul-de-sacs and back again. Almost, he reflected, taking off his glasses and cleaning them on his handkerchief, as if his brain was searching for something, flexing its muscles – much as his eyes did – in a bid to bring a hitherto blurred but important fact into focus.

He was worried about his mother, of course, Peter reminded himself. What she had done, or attempted to do, was not easily forgotten. He had heard the shock lingering in Charlie and Serena's telephone reports all week. She was doing well, they assured him, arranging flowers, walking Poppy, even testing Ed on some French vocab – correcting her grandson's accent like a fierce schoolmistress. Apparently she was also thoroughly entering into the spirit of the approaching secret dinner party, advising Roland over the phone on how to cajole Elizabeth out of the house, saying that no female victim of a surprise party would ever want to be caught without makeup or clean hair.

Peter couldn't wait to get to Ashley House to see evidence of such improvements for himself. He was keen, too, to see the fruits of the indispensable Keith's labours, which Charlie had described at length. Helen, on the other hand, had phoned that afternoon sounding martyred and fraught. Genevieve was running a temperature, she said, and with Chloë's netball practice to fit in, they wouldn't be able to set off until six at the earliest. She was exhausted already and the traffic would be dreadful and . . . Peter had gone into a mild daze as she talked, interjecting reassurances, resisting the urge to surrender his own, infinitely less stressful plan of catching a train by offering to help out. Helen never wanted to spend time with his family, these days. Although she had been supportive about the recent trauma with his mother, he had detected an underlying impatience too. If Pamela was seriously depressed – if Charlie and Serena couldn't cope with her – she should be put into a home, she had said, apologizing for her brutality. Her own mother was happily ensconced in an old people's residence in Portsmouth, she had reminded him, playing canasta and bingo, free of domestic and emotional stress, surrounded by on-tap care. It was best for everyone.

Remembering the conversation, Peter sighed. Helen's parents were as pragmatic as their daughter. They had been on the waiting list for the Portsmouth home for years and moved there together when their health began to fail. It had good views, a duckpond and comfortable furniture. They had slipped into it as easily as they had transferred themselves to the practical geography of an ugly bungalow ten years before. They had never been ones for attaching themselves to their surroundings in anything but the most clinical terms. They had been attached to each other, all right, in the crotchety way that many old couples managed, sparring over ancient domestic rituals – hot toast or cold, soft eggs or hard, windows open or closed – but when her husband died Helen's mother seemed to have left them behind happily enough too. She had a new friend now called Mr Boulder, who wore bow-ties and sucked his false teeth when he was dealing cards. Peter shuddered to think of Pamela in such surroundings. She was too sensitive, too integral to her family and her home. Moving her to any sort of institution would be like uprooting a flower and expecting it to thrive in the North Pole.

Peter was interrupted from these reveries by the muffled trill of his mobile phone. He patted his pockets, then realized it was buried in his briefcase. Scrabbling underneath his umbrella and a brochure detailing the splendours of their Umbrian villa, which he had packed to show the family, he experienced a faint, familiar twinge between his shoulder-blades. By the time he got to the phone it had stopped ringing. Angry with himself, life, the fresh twist of pain in his upper back, he swore loudly as he punched in the buttons to return the call.

'Hello?'

'Peter?'

'Who is this?'

There was a laugh. 'You called me.'

'Yes, but only because you . . .' Peter dried up. It had taken him just a couple of seconds to place the rather low female voice, the soft consonants, but now the image of the physiotherapist was in focus, as sharp as a knife. 'How did you get my number?'

Delia laughed again, more freely. 'You filled in a form, remember?'

'So I did.'

'How's the shoulder?'

'Funnily enough, it's taken a turn for the worse in the last couple of minutes.'

'Really?' She sounded amused.

'My phone was buried in my briefcase. I had to twist under my desk to get it.'

'I see. Perhaps you should make another appointment.'

'Oh, there's no need for that – no need at all. I'm doing the exercises on that sheet you gave me and, overall, it's *much* better – great, in fact.' Peter cleared his throat, then swapped the phone from his right to his left hand.

'And your mother, how is she?'

'She's good too. Thank you for asking . . . most kind.'

'And you? How are you?'

'Me?' Peter changed hands again, glad that she could not see the heat in his face, feel the ridiculous clamminess in his palms. 'I'm fine, obviously.'

'I don't think it's obvious,' she replied quietly. 'It must have been a momentous shock for you all, being such a close family, especially as, from what I gathered, the suicide attempt came quite out of the blue.'

'Yes, it . . .' Peter faltered, quailing at her choice of words. *Suicide attempt.* None of them was calling it that. 'Out of the blue . . . indeed. Now she seems better but . . .'

'You must all feel on edge about it, scared she'll try again.'

'Exactly.' End the call, Peter told himself, end it now. 'Do you show such concern for all your patients?'

'No.'

'Ah.'

'I was wondering if you'd like to have lunch.'

'Absolutely not. Thank you for asking, but it's out of the question.'

'Why?'

A long silence followed while Peter battled with what to say, what not to say. He cleared his throat again. 'Because, Delia, it would, I fear, be . . . inappropriate.'

She made a small noise, something between a laugh and an intake of breath. 'What are you afraid of?'

'Afraid? I'm not *afraid* of anything.'

She paused again. 'How fortunate . . . not to be afraid of anything. I envy you.'

'Well, there we are.' Peter felt exuberant. He had outwitted her. He had seen her off. Kicked her into touch. He would tell Helen, make her laugh at the woman's audacity. Being propositioned, at his age, by a lonely physiotherapist . . . It was nothing short of hilarious.

'I felt we connected,' said Delia, not sounding kicked into touch at all. 'I would like to get to know you better. Besides, the business with your mother, it may help you to talk to someone who has been through something similar, someone outside your family. I could be that someone. I could be your friend. Where's the harm in that?' She proceeded to tell him the number of her mobile phone, speaking slowly and clearly, as if dictating a letter.

'I won't call,' he said, when she had finished. 'And don't call me . . . please,' he added, wishing instantly that he hadn't because his voice had shrunk to a pleading whisper, reverberating with all the terror he had sought to deny.

After the call Peter sat very still, his elbows on his pile of papers, hands clasped as if in prayer. That's that, he told himself. He breathed deeply. In and out. That was it, that was better. Forget the whole thing . . . Forget the telephone number certainly. He closed his eyes in an attempt to perform this small feat, but his mind, having found its focus at last, refused to let go: the numbers filed into his memory, as determined as marching soldiers.

It was mid-afternoon by the time Ed set off for his rendezvous with Jessica. He had spent the morning working in his room, head and heart ablaze with a sense of self-virtue and a desire not to engage with the rest of the household. Ever since the drama with his grandmother, there had been an atmosphere of impenetrable, determined cheerfulness, which he found hard to stomach. His mother in particular was so full of caring and smiles that Ed wondered if her face might crack from the strain of it. It reminded him of how she had been during the months after his sister had died – pretending so hard to be normal that there wasn't a trace of normality in her. To make matters worse, Clem had phoned while he was packing his books to warn him that she wouldn't be coming for the weekend after all. She couldn't face it, she said. Ed had found himself shouting at her, saying he couldn't face it either but he had to, and how would she feel being the only one stuck at home in such circumstances? He had even tried the black-mail route, saying how much their grandmother was looking forward to seeing her when, as far as he knew, Pamela had said nothing of the kind.

All of which lent a certain fierceness to the manner in which Ed swung his leg over his bike saddle and set off down the lane. Sid was going to an agricultural show, Jessica had explained gleefully, so they would have the place to themselves. He had tried to respond with enthusiasm, rationalizing that there was no point in alerting her to his recent decision until the moment of its delivery. Sailing past the hedges through the village, birds tweeting overhead and the wind in his face, Ed had half wondered whether he might change his mind. Was sexual gratification such a crime, after all, if carried out between consenting couples? Then he remembered how the phone call – every phone call now – had ended with a breathy 'I love you, Ed Harrison' and his resolve hardened. Much better to get out now before things got any more complicated. Anyway, he had received an interesting text that week from a girl called Melanie, whom he'd always fancied from afar. 'Having party do you want to cum?' Of course he bloody well did – preferably without feeling that he had to explain himself to Jessica Blake. Given the choice, he'd go for Melanie, with her long, fair-skinned limbs and pierced belly-button, any day. Jessica's puppy curves and black ponytail were nothing in comparison – *nothing*.

'Hey, Ed.' She was waiting for him at the gate outside the cottage, her hair loose for once, with a line of mousy brown along the parting where the dye was growing out.

'Hey.' She tried to kiss him, surprised and hurt when he pulled back after only a couple of seconds.

'Let's go in, shall we?' he muttered, looking anxiously over his shoulder, as if his reticence stemmed purely from fear of observation. Be a grown-up, he told himself, when they were inside. Be a fucking grown-up. 'Jessica, there's something . . .'

But she had sprung on ahead, down the little hallway and into Sid's box of a sitting room, with its brown sofa and electric heater wedged into what had once been a fireplace. 'Look, Ed, I've been reading it.' She was holding out a book, her face pink with pride and uncertainty. 'I'm not sure I get it – I mean, it's all about a party, isn't it? That Mrs Dalloway buying flowers and stuff – which is weird, not like a story at all – but I sort of like it . . .'

'Jessica . . .'

'I thought maybe you could, like, explain it to me a bit – tell me all the clever stuff you learn at that posh school of yours.'

'Jessica . . . I . . . don't think we should see each other any more.'

She laughed. 'You what?'

'It's just . . .'

'Has this got something to do with your nan trying to top herself?'

'No, of course not,' snapped Ed, fury flaring both at the suggestion and the icy casualness of her tone. 'It's just . . . going out with you – it's not working. At least, not for me. I'm sorry, I . . .'

'Sorry, are you? Well, that's fucking nice, that is.' She flung the Virginia Woolf book on to the sofa and folded her arms, looking not so much heartbroken as belligerent. 'Well, let me tell you, Ed Harrison, I don't get fucking treated like this. I just don't, okay?'

'Look, I know you're upset —'

She stepped towards him and poked a finger into his chest. 'You know fuck-all.'

Ed took a step backwards, looking over his shoulder for the door. He'd made a botch of it, he knew, but at least it was done. It would be funny, in retrospect, he reassured himself, and suddenly remembered a story his father had told him about a rejected girlfriend who had camped outside his door for four entire days, howling whenever she got a glimpse of him at a window. He was *allowed* to break up with this girl, Ed reminded himself. He was only seventeen, after all, allowed to make and break as many relationships as he wanted. 'It's not like we're *married*,' he said, alarmed at the expression on her face, thinking it might be best for both of them if he made a run for it.

'Have sex with her and drop her, is that it?'

'No . . . I never meant . . .' He turned for the door but she had somehow got there first and was leaning against it, arms folded again, so ugly and robust he wondered how he had ever found her attractive.

'Well, that's a shame,' she snarled, 'seeing as how I'm expecting your kid.'

Ed tried to smile, to sneer in the way that she was, but his mouth wouldn't move. 'You can't be. We only . . .'

'Did it once? Is that it? Well, it only takes one go, mate, in case you didn't know.'

'But . . .' Ed felt as if his lips had solidified. 'But the pill — you said —'

'Did I now?' She held out her hand and studied her fingernails.

'You lied,' whispered Ed, feeling as if the walls of the poky room were closing in on him.

'Yeah . . . and before you ask, no, I don't want to get rid of it. So you just go home and have a think about that, eh? It's not like your lot couldn't afford to provide, with that fucking great house of yours. And I'd marry you an' all,' she added slyly, peering at him from under her hair. 'Jessica *Harrison* . . . Yeah, I wouldn't say no. And it's not like I don't love you . . .'

Ed lunged past her, groping for the door handle, heavy-limbed, as if he was moving in slow motion. Jessica stepped aside to let him pass.

'Look, think about it, okay?' she called after him. Her voice had changed again. It was sweet and breezy now, as if she was asking him to consider nothing more compelling than which bus to catch or whether to have a second pint. 'Call me, yeah? I'm not going anywhere.'

Ed blundered down the path towards his bicycle. He couldn't look back – at her, at Sid's loathsome little cottage. His life had ended – a life, he saw now, with terrible clarity, that he hadn't appreciated. The tedium of revision, the lack of a girlfriend, the shifting moods of his parents seemed like Paradise now. A lost Paradise. He thought, too, of his grandmother, no longer childishly baffled by her despair but *understanding* it. No way out, that was how she had felt, and that was how Ed felt now, pedalling like a madman under the inky blue sky, along the hedgerows, past the faded pub sign of the Rising Sun, seeing none of it, hating all of it for remaining so unchanged, so oblivious to his misfortune.

It was hot in the kitchen. Serena, standing elbow deep at the sink, felt the dampness of her forehead as she wiped a stray hair from her eyes with the back of her hand. Next to her the steam from several pans was spiralling upwards and outwards, curling like mist round the strings of garlic and dried flowers that dangled from the beams. The aromas travelled with it: simmering apple for a crumble, minted boiling potatoes for mash, sizzling liver and bacon for that night's casserole. Ed would complain, of course – animal guts, he called it – but it was a particular favourite of Pamela's. Peter's too, Charlie had assured her, slipping his arms round her waist and planting a kiss on her neck when he got in from work. Helen and the children were running late, he told her, stuck in traffic on the A3. Peter was arriving by train at eight. Cassie and Stephen might be later still, coming from north London. He had rubbed his palms together gleefully, saying how much he was looking forward to the weekend, how supper smelt great, how he was going to rush upstairs to shower and change.

A moment later Pamela had appeared, already changed for the evening, her face freshly powdered and her hair pinned tightly off her face. 'What can I do, dear?' she had asked, smoothing her skirt, lacing and unlacing her fingers, patting her hair. 'Although you don't look as if you need me at all.'

'Of course I need you,' Serena had replied briskly, handing her mother-in-law an apron and a bag of broad beans. 'If you could pod those, then get Ed to help you with the table. Where is Ed? Have you seen him?'

'He went off on his bike.'

'Did he now? And how long ago was that?'

Pamela frowned, tensing at her daughter-in-law's tone, wanting to get it right, to be helpful. She had felt all week like a child who had done wrong – dreadful wrong. To break the rules like that – admit to despair when only a few years before she had counselled Charlie and Serena about the importance of carrying on, being brave, accommodating bereavement – felt tantamount to betrayal. In the immediate aftermath, she had made several faltering attempts to explain the weight that had crushed her into behaving so unforgivably. Yet each time, seeing the concern in their faces, sensing that their own still wounded hearts had no desire to be dragged through more emotional turmoil than was necessary, she had switched to the easier route of apologies and assurances that it wouldn't happen again.

Inwardly Pamela remained less certain. If such desolation could descend once, seemingly from nowhere, like a red mist, what was to stop it returning? It was this fear that had made her swallow Dr Lazard's tablets, like an obedient child, even though the calm they induced felt almost second-hand, like a feeling passed on rather than one that sprang from inside. Without it she was sure she might have been able to recollect now exactly when she had seen Ed disappearing down the lane, sitting up on his bike seat, whistling some incomprehensible tune, steering – terrifyingly – with one hand, the other wielding his mobile phone. 'We could call him,' she suggested brightly, 'on his telephone.'

'Good idea.' Serena tugged off her rubber gloves and offered her mother-in-law an encouraging smile. 'But I'll give him a bit longer. Chasing teenagers, I find, makes them slow down. Could you keep an eye on the potatoes? I'm going to get some air . . . Won't be long.' She stepped outside into the lemony evening sunshine, closing the back door carefully behind her before she set off down the garden path. She hummed as she walked, the tension floating out of her at the sight of the burgeoning green of the garden, poised for summer like one huge, exotic, budding flower. The lawns, cut by Keith that afternoon, shimmered under the long rays of the sun, like Hoovered carpets. Along the wall of the vegetable garden the honeysuckle was already running riot, playing host to lazy bees and a couple of butterflies, their wings a flash of velvet orange against the creamy yellow flowers.

'Lovely, isn't it?'

Serena turned to see Keith in paint-spattered jeans and T-shirt, emerging from the direction of the toolshed where he had been labouring on her behalf all week. 'Yes, it is. Thanks for mowing the lawns.' She inhaled deeply. 'God, don't you just love the smell of freshly cut grass?' She smiled at him, noting the myriad flecks of paint across his forearms, face and hair – even his eyelashes – as if he had been dunked in icing sugar.

'Got all the family coming for the weekend, then? That's nice.'

'Yes,' Serena murmured, 'very nice. Though not quite all. One of our daughters is abroad and the other, her twin . . .' She hesitated, biting her lip. Clem wasn't coming. She had sent an email that morning. An email, not even a phone call. 'Sorry but just impossible to get away . . . have a great time.' Serena had had the strongest sense of the family fragmenting, flying away from each other like shards of smashed glass. Unsettled, she had phoned Charlie, only to receive a scolding for getting things out of perspective again, all delivered in the new don't-you-dare-crack-up-on-me tone he had been using since the crisis with his mother; a tone with which Serena had some sympathy. She didn't want to crack up again either, though from what she could recall of the blur that had become her life after Tina's death, it wasn't a state of mind over which one exerted any control. Pamela's attempt to drown herself had unlocked something, certainly, but so had Aunt Alicia's funeral and her father-in-law's death two years before. All grief was connected, Serena mused now, like a fault line running through each life, lying dormant at one minute then surging with energy when one was least prepared for it.

Serena blinked at Keith, aware, in a moment of almost visionary lucidity, that there was a big picture, and that the paint-spattered man in front of her, who had ridden into their lives from nowhere, restoring order – saving a *life* – was part of it.

'Daughters, eh?' Keith was saying. 'I can imagine they *are* a worry. Now, boys, they're a much simpler breed.'

'You might be right there,' Serena murmured. 'Though Ed's thinking of going into the army – now *that* worries me, I can tell you.'

'Good career, though. Solid. And he's strong, too, isn't he? I should think it'll suit him very well.'

Serena sighed, letting her gaze drift to the view beyond the garden, where the fields were a bulging counterpane of yellows and browns and greens. 'I just want all my children to be . . . safe.'

'Of course you do, what with . . . of course you do. Same for me,' Keith added, wanting to erase the sadness from her face. 'June's got this new man now and I just hope he's treating my two right.'

'What you did,' interjected Serena, 'it meant so much to all . . .'

'You've said your thank-yous,' Keith assured her quickly. 'I did what anyone would have done. How is Mrs Harrison, anyway? I saw her picking roses this afternoon – that's got to be a good sign.'

'Oh, yes, a very good sign. She's doing fine, I think. Talking of which, I'd better get back – I've left her in charge of supper. Enjoy your weekend, won't you?' She turned away, but stopped, moved by the expression of gentleness on Keith's dusty face. 'I'm sorry if this embarrasses you, Keith, but what I was trying to say just then was that your coming here feels like – like a gift.' With that she skipped back on to the path and hurried towards the house.

Watching her, Keith let out a groan. Arriving at Ashley House, he had wanted to make them all pleased, *indebted*, even. Yet now, having been given the most extraordinary opportunity to earn such gratitude, he felt utterly weighed down by it. Unworthy. He would finish the studio conversion, see to the damp in the bedroom, then leave. He was getting too sucked in, beginning to care too much – about the old lady, about Charlie and Serena, even about the wastrel of a son who was forever lurking behind bushes with his phone and his fags, looking lost in a way that reminded Keith, in spite of all the obvious differences, of his own troubled teens. That man-child stage, he remembered it only too well. It seemed incredible that he had once idly pondered the possibility of dragging out the work through the summer. There was a lifetime's work here, if he wanted it. And he didn't, Keith realized miserably. All that dependence, all that needy gratitude, he couldn't handle it.

Rounding the last bend in the lane, Ed glanced over his shoulder in time to see a black BMW edging towards him, his aunt Helen sitting erect and tense behind the wheel, her driving glasses perched on the tip of her nose. Not wanting them to catch him up, not wanting, in fact, ever to have to talk to anyone again, Ed stood up on the pedals and pumped his tired legs in a last frenzied dash for the garage. A few moments later he leant his bike against the wall behind Keith's motorbike and crouched in the chilly dark, like a thief, holding his breath, until the sound of the car arriving, doors slamming and voices had died away.

With trembling fingers Ed lit a cigarette, only to find that he was too choked to smoke it. He dropped it on to the concrete floor of the garage and swiped at his tears, digging his knuckles into his eyes until his head was popping with pain and his vision was a blur of fuzzy orange and yellow. Never in all his seventeen years had he felt so wretched. Nothing, not even his sister dying, came close. Appalled by the thought and his predicament, Ed wept harder. His only hope, he knew, was to get Jessica to agree to an abortion. He had thought of nothing else all the way home. And yet it seemed a desperate, futile hope, given what she had said about money – about *marriage*. He would rather *die* than marry Jessica Blake. It was unthinkable. Monstrous. Almost as monstrous as the thought of spending the rest of his life paying for a baby, a child – *his* child – like some loser in a tabloid or a crap soap opera on television. It wasn't possible. There had to be another way.

There just had to be. Ed hoicked up his T-shirt and dropped his face into it, aware through his tears of the smell of laundry, the smell of *home*, of a life now lost for good. If it was money she wanted, he would have – somehow – to give it to her. For an abortion, if nothing else. He blew his nose on his T-shirt, remembering, with a small gust of hope, that he was only a couple of months off his eighteenth. He had been promised driving lessons and . . . Ed swallowed, trying to keep his focus. Driving lessons and access to the five-thousand-pound trust fund left to him by his grandfather. So far Clem had refused to touch hers, but Maisie had used some of hers to pay for her travels. He had been planning to buy a car with his. But now . . . Ed sniffed deeply, feeling fractionally more composed at the materialization of this feeble glimmer of salvation. Hung in the balance against his happiness – against the entire stability of his life – a car seemed piffling and stupid. Five thousand pounds. He'd use the fucking lot, if necessary, to buy her an abortion followed by a one-way ticket to Timbuktu. In the meantime he had somehow to get through the rest of the day, the weekend, his life . . .

Ed dropped his forehead on to his knees, seriously contemplating, for the first time, telling his parents. He tried to imagine himself explaining what had happened, but all he could see was his own burning shame and their stricken faces. He couldn't do it, he simply couldn't. They were annoying – they nagged and worried – but they had been through a lot too. For a time after the death of his sister they'd got on so badly he had even thought they might break up. Now they were beside themselves with anxiety about his grandmother. How could he add to such woes? It was unthinkable. They were concerned enough as it was about his poxy A levels, Ed reminded himself, with a bitter half-sob of a laugh, and whether he'd get into Sandhurst. How they would react to the news that he had fathered a child with Jessica Blake did not bear thinking about. He thought instead, with huge and vivid longing, of his sisters: Maisie, he was sure, would be cool and practical, but Maisie wasn't due back for months, and Clem, he reminded himself fiercely, was looking out for no one but herself. Which meant he was alone, Ed reflected bleakly, as alone as it was possible to be.

'You all right there?'

'Oh, Keith . . . hi . . . yes, fine, thanks.' Ed pretended to study something on his bike wheel before standing up. He tried out a smile, glad of the garage's dim lighting.

'Found someone here looking for you,' Keith continued, eyeing Ed intently and beckoning Chloë, who was hovering by the bumper of Serena's Mondeo. 'Here he is, love, turned up like the proverbial bad penny.'

'Hi, Chloë.' Ed tugged at his jeans and scuffed his still smouldering cigarette out of view.

'Hi, Ed.' Chloë grinned, noting that her cousin looked even bigger and more grown-up than she remembered from Christmas and wondering if he would ignore her to the extent that her brother had during his Easter holidays. She took a step closer to peer at him, squinting in the half-dark to make out whether he, too, was growing a beard. 'Everybody was wondering where you were so I said I'd have a look and Keith said he'd help.'

'Well, I'm here,' snapped Ed, leading the way out of the garage, trying to look purposeful but feeling as if his legs might buckle under him. If seeing Jessica had felt like a double life, he reflected, then trying to keep the lid on this new secret calamity would be like straddling the Grand Canyon.

Chloë trotted after him, with Keith following more slowly behind, then ran ahead to swing on the front gate in the way her parents always warned would damage the hinge.

'I'll be getting back, then,' said Keith, and added, when Ed didn't reply, 'If ever you want a break from your nearest and dearest, you come and find me, okay? We could have a beer, if you like, and . . .' he lowered his voice '. . . a smoke maybe?' He winked, trying to engage Ed's still averted gaze, feeling, in spite of his earlier resolutions, an irresistible desire to find out what had driven the boy to weep like a toddler in the garage.

'And me,' called Chloë indignantly, peering upside-down through the slats in the gate, her face puce. 'Can I find you too?'

'Sure, pet, any time.'

Once Keith had gone, she hurdled off the gate and caught hold of Ed's arm as he tried to escape down the steps. 'Do you get hay-fever too?' she asked, staring with unabashed curiosity at his puffy face.

'Yeah . . . a bit.' Ed shook her off.

'Horrid, isn't it? I have to take pills every day in the summer for mine. Do you take pills for yours?'

'Nope.' Ed yanked open the front door and made a run for the staircase. He had got to the bathroom on the top landing and was splashing cold water on to his face when Charlie found him.

'Are you hot or something?'

'Yup – bike ride. Bloody hot.'

'I see – and by the way, no swearing in front of your little cousins, okay? We may have brought you up a lout but I know my brother still entertains loftier hopes for his brood. Now, look . . .' Charlie glanced down the corridor to check there was no possibility of being overheard '. . . just wanted to remind you, not a word about what happened with Granny, okay? Peter and Helen have agreed that it's best for all, that it will help *her* get over it. So, with your aunts this weekend, and Stephen, mum's the word. Got it?'

'Got it,' Ed echoed, reaching for a towel. He dabbed vigorously at his face, fighting a renewed urge not only to weep but to throw himself against the rotund bulk of his father and spill the whole sordid story. But Charlie was already looking at his watch and turning away. Peter was waiting for him downstairs, he said. He was going to show his brother all the sterling work that Keith had been doing around the house and grounds. 'Help your mother lay the table, won't you?' he commanded, bounding off down the corridor, the change rattling in his pockets as he swung himself round the banister post on to the stairs.

'We're thinking of offering him a job for life,' said Charlie, as Peter ducked his tall frame under the doorway of the half-completed studio.

'I can see why. Quite the jack-of-all-trades, isn't he?' Peter pulled the door shut behind him, and dusted a patch of white powder off his suit jacket. 'It all looks great – much more ship-shape. Well done, old chap.'

'I haven't *done* anything,' replied Charlie, mildly irritated by the note of condescension in Peter's tone. He reached round his brother and locked the shed door. 'Keith landed in our laps when we needed him.'

'He certainly did,' murmured Peter, falling into step beside Charlie to continue their tour of the garden. 'Where is the man anyway?' He squinted in the direction of the barn, whose gingery-tiled rooftop was just visible through the trees behind the toolshed. 'I'd like to thank him again.'

Charlie chuckled. 'Serena says he's getting fed up of people thanking him. She's also starting to say,' he added, with a snort, 'that Keith was somehow *meant* to come here, that fixing the place up, saving Mum, is all part of some grand design.' He shook his head, glad for once to be able to laugh at his wife's volatile state of mind instead of worry about it.

'Is she now?' Peter turned towards the garden, putting his hand to his brow to shield his eyes from the still powerful red disc of the sun perched on the skyline of trees behind the copse. Coming to the country, re-engaging with his family, seeing his mother so well had soothed him, as he had known it would. The phone conversation with Delia Goddard felt wonderfully distant in consequence, a pinprick of an incident, beyond anxiety or relevance. 'A grand design, eh? I'm not sure I find that very comforting,' he murmured, planting himself on the old wooden bench that overlooked the largest of the lawns, offering views across the fields towards the village. 'I mean, if there was such a thing, the choices we make wouldn't matter, would they? It would all be meaningless. And,' he continued fervently, as the pinprick began to swell to a less manageable size, 'choices *do* matter – they always matter.'

Charlie eased his much wider frame into the remaining space on the bench and eyed his brother uncertainly. 'Are you trying to tell me something?'

Peter laughed. 'No, not at all. Ah, there's Ed. How is he? Has he got any further with his gap-year plans?'

They watched as Ed, oblivious to an audience, ran on to the lawn kicking a half-deflated football. He ran fast, keeping the ball at his toes, dodging imaginary opponents, then fired a shot at the fence. It bounced off the top bar and back towards his chest from where he somehow manoeuvred it on to his knee, then to his foot and back to his knee.

'I thought we told you – he's thinking of applying to Sandhurst. Serena's horrified, but it might be just the thing.'

'Yes, it might . . . so I'll forget the work-experience thing, shall I?'

'Oh, Peter, sorry, I'd forgotten about that – yes, for the time being, anyway.' Charlie touched his brother's arm to reinforce the apology, then got to his feet. 'Hey, Ed, kick it over here, won't you?'

Looking across the garden in surprise, Ed hesitated, then let the ball drop to the ground. He swung his foot at it with such force and accuracy that it landed squarely against his father's ample stomach. Charlie gasped, laughed at his own incompetence and recovered himself sufficiently to manage three kick-ups, then steered the ball back to his son, the keys and change in his pockets jangling like a mini orchestra. 'Aha . . . reinforcements,' he shouted happily, as Chloë and Genevieve came into view, interested but shy.

Helen appeared next, her frown lifting at the sight of the game, and her husband, relaxing on the bench, surveying it. She waved and Peter waved back, motioning to her to join them. As she sat down he picked up her hand and kissed it. 'Glad we're here?'

'Of course,' Helen murmured, staring in some surprise at the spot where his lips had touched her skin. 'Except that Genevieve slept for the entire journey so we haven't a hope of getting her to bed.'

'Never mind. She can curl up in the TV room with a DVD while we eat. That'll get her sleepy again.'

'I wouldn't bank on it,' muttered Helen, darkly, turning to study their youngest, who had seized the football in both hands and was marching back to the house like a hunter with a trophy. Chloë was shouting after her, throwing up her arms in despair. The situation was saved by Charlie, who ran after his youngest niece, scooped her into his arms and tickled her until she released the ball. Then, seeing Ed sidling towards the house, he hurled it into his path and nodded fiercely in the direction of Chloë, who was fiddling with a strand of her hair trying not to look disappointed.

'I surrender,' Charlie gasped, tipping his niece gently on to Peter's lap. 'I'm past it – way too old, way out of practice. In fact,' he straightened slowly, prodding at his lower back with his fingertips, 'I might have done myself a serious injury picking you up, young lady.' He growled and pretended to swipe at Genevieve's freckled button nose. 'Damn! Missed! Here it comes again . . . the *nose-eater*! Aaargh!' His niece squealed in delight, trying to burrow deeper into Peter's chest.

'Seriously, have you hurt yourself, Charlie?' asked Helen, detecting real pain beneath this display of avuncular bravado.

'A touch. Nothing bad, I'm sure. Old man's pains, as Ed would call it. Come on now,' he clapped his hands together, 'we'd better get back inside – Serena will be wondering where we've all got to.'

'Because,' persisted Helen, 'Peter has seen this amazing physio whom Cassie recommended. I know it might seem a long way to go but –'

'She wasn't that amazing.'

'But you said –'

'She was okay, but nothing special. Actually, she . . .' Peter lifted his daughter off his lap, put her down and began to walk backwards towards the house. Tell her, he told himself, tell all of them about the phone call. Legitimize it. Make the choice, the right choice.

'Actually she what?' inquired Helen, but only half attending, since Genevieve had settled to a game of grass-plucking, yanking fistfuls out by the roots and piling them up into a small messy mountain between her legs. She glanced anxiously at Charlie, fearing for the lawn, and almost forgot she'd asked the question.

'She just wasn't that good,' repeated Peter, still walking backwards, feeling as if each word of the sentence was glued to its predecessor.

'I tell you, I don't need a physio,' protested Charlie, doing a little skip to prove the point as he drew level with Peter. 'Hey, that sounds like a car arriving. Cassie and Stephen must be here. Excellent. Just like old times, eh?' he exclaimed, punching his brother fondly in the arm. 'I can't wait to see Lizzy's face tomorrow night – all of us here for her in her hour of need.'

'Hour of need?' echoed Peter, puzzled. 'I thought it was her birthday.'

'Yes, of course, but Serena, who's usually right about these things, says she's down in the dumps about that horrible man Richard. Another birthday, another broken heart . . . dear old

Lizzy. Some things never change, do they?' he added merrily, hurrying on ahead, wanting to be the one to greet his little sister and her fiancé at the gate.

The following evening, once his mother was safely submerged in a deep bath, with thick swirls of the aromatic foam he had given her as an interim present, Roland tiptoed into his bedroom and pulled out his recently completed painting from behind the chair where he had hidden it. Unable to find a sheet of wrapping-paper big enough, he made do with old newspaper, folding and Sellotaping most of its pages into an unruly parcel, which he then carried out to the car, and stowed carefully in the boot under an old picnic blanket. He knew it wouldn't exactly be a surprise – she must have seen it on the easel during its early stages – but she would still be pleased, he was sure, to have it presented to her, particularly when he explained that, in its unobvious way, it was a portrait. Another aspect of the gift that made it special, for Roland at least, was that he knew it was far and away the best thing he had ever done. More exciting still was that when he had tentatively confided as much to Clem during their brief meeting in London his cousin had made the astonishing promise that she would show it to someone in the art world. She was developing certain connections, she said, smiling mysteriously, and would be happy to help in any way she could. An introduction to the right person at the right time . . . she would see what she could do. Fleeting and rushed though this promise had been, offered whisperingly out of earshot of the adults, it had sat in Roland's heart like a jewel ever since, something he took out, looked at, treasured and put away again. He had started several new projects since, all in the same new bold style, uncertain where it might lead but wanting to be ready when the moment – whatever form it took – arrived.

Keeping half an eye on the steamy lit window of the

bathroom, Roland leant against the car and phoned Ashley House on his mobile, explaining to his grandmother, who took the call, that they were running a little late.

'I'll tell Serena,' Pamela promised, before inquiring – to Roland's despair – if Elizabeth was making herself look nice.

'Yes – at least, I think so. She's having a bath.'

'Oh, good,' Pamela murmured, then went on to recount, yet again, the story of when his grandfather had arranged a surprise party for her, for which she had been so underdressed and badly coiffured that she had found it hard to enjoy herself.

Hearing the click of the garden gate as he put away his phone, Roland looked up to see Jessica Blake standing on the pavement watching him.

'Hi, there.'

'Jessica . . . hi.' He approached the gate, smiling a little nervously, wondering how long she had been standing there. 'What are you doing here?'

'It's a free country, isn't it?' She was wearing a denim miniskirt, high heels and a plunging white T-shirt that showed off the deep cleft between her breasts.

'Yes . . . I . . . We're just going out,' Roland stammered, alarmed at the notion that she might expect him to invite her in. In spite of the number of hours they had spent playing alongside each other as children, Roland had never felt at ease with the Ashley House gardener's granddaughter. Even as a ten-year-old there had been a sort of fearlessness – an unpredictability – about Jessica that had frightened him.

'Still doing your drawings, then?'

'Er . . .' Roland glanced at the car, wondering if she was making conversation or whether she had seen his makeshift parcel and known what it contained. 'I guess so.'

'You drew me once. Do you remember? When we were kids.' She laughed, tossing her hair off her face and tightening her hold on the strap of her handbag. 'Wanna draw me now?' She turned to show off her profile and sucked in her cheeks. 'I got Granddad to drop me off – he's gone to meet some mates at a pub down the road so I've got plenty of time.' She puckered her lips.

'No . . . I . . . Like I said, we're going out.'

'Yeah, yeah, I know. You're all off to the big house, aren't you? Your mum's *surprise* birthday party.'

'How . . . ?'

'Ed told me. Ed tells me a lot of stuff,' she added slyly, dropping her head and looking up at him through the curtain of her thick black hair. 'I want you to tell him to call me, okay? When you see him tonight. Just say, Jess says to call her. You'll do that, won't you?'

Roland hesitated, his mind working furiously. He had seen his cousin flirt with Jessica at the funeral and thought it stupid. Yet if Ed now didn't want to speak to Jessica that was his business and he saw no reason to get involved.

'What's your fucking problem?'

'Nothing.' Roland blushed, hating her fat pasty legs and pouting lips, thinking he wouldn't draw her if she paid him.

'Look, just tell him that, okay?'

She was pleading suddenly – close to tears, Roland realized, in some amazement.

'I know you don't think much of me, but Ed does – at least he did – and then we had this sort of . . . row, and now he's turned his phone off and I don't know what to do and they all like you and listen to you so I just thought . . . I tell you what, just forget it, okay? Fucking forget it. You can all go to your fancy fucking party, see if I care. You lot, you bloody Harrisons. My mum was right. You can all fuck off.'

'I'll tell him,' said Roland, moved, in spite of himself, by her obvious distress. 'No need to get upset. I'll tell him, all right?'

She sniffed noisily. 'Right. Thanks. 'Bye, then.'

'Who was that?'

Roland turned to see Elizabeth standing in her dressing-gown at the front door, her hair dripping round her shoulders, her face mottled from the heat of the bath.

'No one.'

'I see.' Elizabeth folded her arms. 'A female no one, by any chance?' She raised one eyebrow and grinned knowingly. 'It's all right, darling, I wasn't born yesterday, there's no need to keep secrets from me. Besides, as I've tried to tell you, with your looks, and Polly out of the frame, girls will be round you like bees at a honey-pot. Now then,' she continued cheerfully, 'what should I wear for wherever we're going? Trousers or something smarter?'

'Smart, I should think,' Roland muttered, kicking at a little twig that was lying on the path, all his pride and excitement at the prospect of the evening quite gone. The encounter with Jessica, he could cope with. What he couldn't stomach was his mother's persistent jaunty posturing on the subject of the opposite sex, all her supposed *knowingness*, when she knew nothing. How could she possibly know anything when he was in a state of such confusion himself? She clearly loved the idea of him having a girlfriend, so much so that it was impossible to tell her that the only thing he missed about Polly was their friendship, that he would have given anything to go back to the times when all they did was listen to music and help each other with their homework. In the meantime the sight of Carl, even at a distance – across the playground or the playing-fields – sent bolts of electricity into his stomach and down his legs. Passing him at closer quarters, Roland found himself literally freezing with pleasure, unable to speak or move. Was this hero-worship? The other boy was like a god after all, bursting with all the brawn and social confidence that Roland knew he would never have. Or was it love? If it was, did that mean he was gay? The very thought made Roland dizzy with terror, both on his own account – could one really be gay and *happy*? – and because of his family: his mother, his strait-laced uncles and aunts, his *cousins* . . . Christ, Roland could hear them laughing now, so vividly that he suddenly envied the silliness between Ed and Jessica, strutting round each other like peacocks, so sure of themselves, being daft in the way grown-ups liked to complain about but seemed to expect. He could never be like that, Roland reflected sadly, stamping on the twig and snapping it in two. Gay or not, he didn't have the confidence. And he didn't want to be like that anyway. He was different – more solitary – like Clem, he decided, deriving consolation from the thought. She was on her own now, she had told him, and had every intention of staying that way.

Elizabeth, to the satisfaction of her assembled family, shed tears of pleasure at the sight of all their eager, smiling faces in the hall, clutching gifts and calling birthday greetings. She hugged and kissed each of them, smearing lipstick across their cheeks and proclaiming many times that she could have sworn Roland was taking her to the cinema. They moved into the drawing room, where Charlie and Serena had put out full flutes of champagne with bowls of crisps and peanuts. Peter, exclaiming at the beauty of the evening, opened the doors on to the cloisters while Serena hurried upstairs to fetch Pamela a shawl.

Elizabeth parked herself on one of the cloister benches and tore at the wrapping-paper on her presents like an excited child, exclaiming that everything was lovely even before she had opened it. 'For Italy,' said Peter, when she got to Helen's inspirational choice of a pair of designer sunglasses.

'I can't wait,' exclaimed Elizabeth, putting on the sunglasses, and slinging the silk scarf Charlie and Serena had given her round her neck. 'How do I look?'

'Like a film star?' ventured Roland, guessing it was the sort of answer she wanted, then wishing he hadn't because she got up and hugged him in front of everybody.

'And I shall smell lovely with those soaps you gave me, Mum,' gushed Elizabeth, returning to her seat, 'and the picture frame is beautiful, Cassie and Stephen. Thank you so much. And what can this be I wonder?' she murmured, beaming at Roland, as she reached for his bulky newspaper parcel. 'A jigsaw, maybe?'

Blushing and suddenly terrified, Roland took a step backwards. Peering over his aunts' and uncles' shoulders and glimpsing his mother's hands peeling off the layers of newspaper, he felt as if some private inner part of him was being exposed for scrutiny. 'Oh, darling, how . . . It's beautiful.' The rest of the family gathered round the picture, cooing in appreciation.

'It's you,' said Roland, blowing out his cheeks with relief once the moment of revelation was over.

'Oh.'

Ed began to laugh but stopped quickly.

'At least, it's meant to be. All the . . .' Roland dried up, rendered inarticulate by self-consciousness. Yet he felt proud too, proud and pleased. The picture looked great – *bloody* great, in fact.

'I love it,' said Elizabeth, stroking the frame. 'You clever darling, I love it. Such colours . . . I'm so glad it's me.'

As the grown-ups led the way into the dining room, Roland hung back to deliver Jessica's message to Ed, who was solemnly working his way through the abandoned contents of the champagne glasses.

'She came to see *you*?'

'Obviously,' muttered Roland, not liking the expression on his cousin's face, fearing he had prompted some sort of ridiculous jealousy. He wondered in the same instant if Ed could possibly be jealous about the picture too, given how the adults had praised it. 'Like I said, she just wants you to call her,' he explained, wanting desperately to get things straight.

'Did she say anything else?'

'No, I don't think so. Look, are you two . . . ?'

'No, we are not. Okay? We are *not* and never fucking will be.'

Roland watched him stride off into the house with a heavy heart, thinking that being liked by adults definitely had its drawbacks and that he would choose the allegiance of Ed over that any day. Then he saw his picture leaning up against the cloister bench and thought that Ed and the rest of the world could go to hell. He would paint and live alone, he decided, carefully picking up the picture and carrying it through to the drawing room. He didn't need anything but that. Clem was going to help him make a name for himself. Why should he care about anyone's future but his own?

They ate chilled asparagus soup followed by rolled sirloin of beef, cooked to such a delicate pink that Chloë turned up her nose at the blood and was told off by Peter for lack of manners. She hadn't liked the soup either, she muttered, first to Ed, who ignored her, and then to Roland who responded, more encouragingly, with the news that pudding was to involve a chocolate birthday cake as well as meringues and whipped cream. Feeling Poppy brush against her knees, she slipped the bloodiest piece of meat off her plate and under the table, assuming a pose of studied innocence as the dog licked her fingers.

'Is that dog in here?' barked Peter. 'Chloë, is she?'

'I'm not sure, Dad.' She ducked her head under the tablecloth, glad of the chance to conceal her expression, which she knew, from considerable experimentation during the course of thirteen years, would betray guilt, no matter how hard she persevered to prevent it.

Serena came to her niece's defence. 'Peter, it's okay. We let Poppy come in here. She's usually very good, isn't she, darling?'

She looked hard at Charlie, wanting him to help her make some sort of stand. Since Peter's arrival he had shown off all Keith's handiwork like an anxious pupil, just as she had predicted. Worse still, he had let Peter take over the carving of the beef, laughing with his bottomless good-humour when his elder brother pointed out the messy progress of his own endeavours. 'Like a traffic accident,' Peter had said, pointing with the knife. 'A mess on the road.' Everyone had laughed, except Serena, who had experienced a breathless moment of something like pure hatred. She counted to ten while the moment passed, like a fever. She was on edge and it had been a difficult week, she reminded herself, wondering in the same instant, when – if ever – such remarks would lose their power to wound. It was six years after all; well over a thousand days. No wonder the possibility of causing offence hadn't crossed Peter's mind. 'Poppy, darling,' she called, a little hoarsely, then turned to her mother-in-law when the summons had no effect. 'You call her, Pamela, she always comes to you.'

Looking pleased, Pamela clicked her fingers and the dog trotted out from under the table, tail wagging hopefully. 'Here, darling.' Poppy cast a last wistful look at Chloë, then flopped down behind Pamela's chair, dropping her head on to her outstretched paws with a loud sigh.

The incident left a small ripple of tension, which Cassie elected to smooth away by turning to her mother and remarking that she had been rather quiet and was she feeling all right.

'Much better now, thank you, dear,' murmured Pamela.

'Better? Why? Have you been ill?'

'No . . . that is . . .' Pamela looked helplessly at Serena, then Charlie, lost in confusion as to who among the assembled throng knew what.

'Mum has agreed to come to Umbria with us all in August, haven't you?' pitched in Charlie, gallantly. 'For the whole month.'

'Really? That's great.' Cassie glanced from her mother to her brother, wondering if she had precipitated a moment of awkwardness or merely imagined it. In truth, she was having trouble losing herself in the weekend's celebrations. Normally she and

Stephen found Ashley House the easiest place in the world to relax, but on this occasion they seemed to have packed their worries with their toothbrushes. She had returned from Frank's the previous evening to find Stephen in a state of frenzied impatience. While she packed he had paced the hall like a caged beast. Who was Frank anyway? he had demanded, once they had joined the rush-hour traffic heading south. Why did he matter so much that she not been able to turn the job down? Frank was a good customer and gay, she had retorted, too outraged at the absurdity of this childish display of jealousy to deliver the reassurance nicely. Stephen had tried then, clumsily, to back down, rambling on about not wanting her to overdo things, about the importance of her being relaxed if she was to conceive a child, but in so convoluted a fashion that Cassie had remained deeply, bitterly, unconvinced. A silence had descended, so dense and smothering that Cassie, staring fixedly out of the windscreen, had wondered that something essentially so empty could have such force. She had wondered too, for the first time, about the ferocity of the emotions of the man she was about to marry. His love for her had been like an obsession, bewitching in its intensity. His sheer refusal to take no for an answer was what had eventually won her round, made her believe – as Stephen had from the first – that the paths of their lives were destined to cross intimately and for ever. It had never occurred to Cassie that such obsession had its darker side; that loving her so much meant he would fear losing her with equal passion.

'Please, don't start getting jealous, Stephen, will you?' she had whispered at last, all her thoughts converging into this one vital plea as they swept past the sign for Barham.

'Jealous?' he had scoffed, smacking the steering-wheel. Of my work, she had said, of people like Frank . . . Keith. He had rounded on her then, bumping the car into the grass verge in his distraction. Jealous of Keith? What bollocks was this? On the patio that time, she had reminded him, trying to be gentle, the two of them smoking together, standing close. He had said – he had said – Stephen had pulled over on to the verge, deliberately this time, and yanked on the handbrake. What he had said, he corrected her, was that smoking endangered the likelihood and process of getting pregnant. The comment about Keith had been a joke; she was cruel and wrong to consider it otherwise. He had dropped his head on to the steering-wheel. All he wanted was for them to love each other. Nothing else mattered. Nothing at all. And if she didn't agree she'd better tell him now.

Of course she agreed. Of course. Cassie had reached across and run her fingers up the nape of his neck. She was sorry. She was tired. He was tired. They had pulled into the Ashley House drive a few minutes later, misty-eyed and holding hands. After supper they had gone upstairs early and made love. 'We're going to make a fucking baby,' he had whispered, the four-poster creaking gentle reluctance as he moved on top of her. 'You – and – me – now.' Cassie had locked her legs across his back, pressing her teeth into his shoulder, thinking that if will-power helped conception, they would surely succeed. The row had seemed like a good thing: it had brought them closer, sharpened their desire, their focus. In the morning, however, after their visit to Keith in the barn, its shadow had crept back over them, as smothering as the silence in the car.

Around the table they were still talking about Italy. Peter had produced a brochure and was passing it round. Cassie patted Stephen's leg under the tablecloth. 'We don't have to go to Umbria,' she whispered, wondering still at the origin and persistence of the shadow, wanting more than ever to get rid of it. 'Two weeks of my family . . .' She made a face.

'But I love your family,' Stephen insisted, seeming puzzled rather than reassured. 'The villa looks fantastic. We'll have a great time. Are you looking forward to it, Ed?' He leant across her to address her nephew, who had slouched with disappointing teenage surliness throughout the meal.

Ed blinked hard in an attempt to bring Stephen's face into focus. He had drunk a lot of champagne and he didn't know how many glasses of wine. During the flurry of pudding being served and Pamela announcing her decision to go to bed he had even tipped some of Cassie's into his glass, draining it in one swig. Every conversation of the evening could have been in a foreign language, for all he cared. He couldn't imagine Italy, or August, or finishing his exams. He couldn't think how he was going to get through the next day, let alone the next week. 'Dunno . . . haven't really thought about it.'

Stephen returned his attention to Cassie, slipping his hand over the one she had placed on his leg. Things still weren't right between them, he knew. In spite of the argument in the car ending well – the love-making that had followed – he still felt bruised. He had lain awake for most of the night, trying to make sense of it, mulling over all the things that were worrying him – the stuttering progress of Jack Connolly's latest case, Cassie's obstinate absorption in her work, the pressure of the decision that they should have a child and behind it all the creeping, destructive sensation that, while the woman sitting next to him might have agreed to marry him, he still didn't really *have* her, not in the way he needed.

By the time the steely dawn light crept through the cracks in the curtains Stephen had found himself confronting the new, even bigger fear that maybe all this signified some fundamental shift in his fortunes, the inevitable downturn after the climax. He had had a good run, after all, meeting the love of his life and launching a successful career as a writer. Had he really been naïve enough to imagine it would continue, that the unhappy ugliness of the first eighteen years of his life wouldn't re-emerge in some form, belittling his efforts to be strong and happy? Having looked forward to seeing Keith, and finding him later that morning, with his feet up on the barn's cosy oatmeal sofa, full of chat about his work at Ashley House and what Serena thought about this and Charlie thought about that, had only magnified these fears. Heading back to the main house with Cassie afterwards, Stephen had been beset by the insidious, unsettling notion that just as his life had hit a difficult patch Keith's had turned a corner, as if they were on some sort of invisible see-saw with the Harrisons planted in the middle. Up on one side, down on the other.

Absurd, Stephen told himself now, squeezing Cassie's hand still harder as he surveyed the splendour of the dining room, magnificently arrayed with antique glass, crockery and gleaming silver. This was his new family, his new life, he reminded himself; precisely the place where, not long ago, he had dreamed of being. How silly to be there and not enjoy it! How ridiculous. He had all that a man could want and more – more, certainly, than Keith would ever have. 'I've been a pig,' he whispered. 'Forgive me?'

'Of course,' she murmured, kissing his cheek. It wasn't as fervent a kiss as he would have liked, but it made him feel a lot better – a lot safer.

Serena was on the point of asking Charlie to see to coffee when Peter stood up and tapped his wine glass with a knife. She sat back in her chair exhaling slowly.

'I would just like to say,' Peter began, 'how excellent it is to have so many of the family gathered together and to wish you, Lizzy, the happiest of birthdays and to –'

'Could I say something?'

'Cassie?' In spite of an attempt at a generous smile, Peter was put out. He had intended, as had been his father's wont, to grace the evening with a few well-chosen words, to give them what appeared to be a much-needed sense of occasion; to remind them of how unified and strong they were; to remind himself of what, at all costs, needed protecting.

'I'd just like to say . . .' Cassie searched for Stephen's hand under the tablecloth. She hadn't been listening to Peter or to anything very much except the racing of her own thoughts. A way of putting a seal on the new uneasy peace between her and her fiancé had come to her at last: a mad way, perhaps, but for those instants too heartfelt to resist. 'The fact is . . . Stephen and I . . . that is, we are . . . trying for a baby. I had told Serena but I wanted to tell all of you so that . . .' Cassie faltered, panicking for a moment at the expressions on all their faces and the clamminess of Stephen's palm. 'I know it's a very *personal* thing to say,' she pressed on, propelled by the conviction that her declaration was tantamount to a public profession of their love, their mutual commitment – just the sort of reassurance Stephen needed. She felt, too, as she spoke, as if the utterance of her hopes made them all the more real, more *possible,* 'but it means so much to me – to us – that I wanted you all to know.'

There were collective murmurs, first of surprise and then encouragement. Stephen stared at his dessert plate, focusing on the melting blobs of cream, willing himself to be pleased instead of panic-stricken.

In the hubbub of the moment no one heard Ed's quiet groan of despair triggered by the word 'baby'.

Keith, peering in at one of the windows, seeing the burnished mahogany table and the family ranged round it, their faces lit by the shadowy light of the chandelier, sighed at the perfection of the scene, glad to see his old schoolfriend enthroned at the heart of it. He was glad, too, that maybe he had contributed to the happiness of this family gathering with the rescue of the old lady. I have done what I can, he reminded himself, ducking out of sight.

Chloë, a little tense still at her aunt's announcement, her imagination unpleasantly fired with images of grown-ups having sex, pointed at the window and shrieked, 'I saw a face! Mummy,

Daddy, I saw a face – a face looking at us. A ghost! Do you think it was a ghost?'

'Don't be silly, Chloë,' Peter barked, still hopeful of resuming his speech, feeling rather like the captain trying to regain control of his listing ship.

'It was probably Keith,' murmured Serena, who had stood up and put her arms round Cassie and Stephen, sensing from their shell-shocked faces that what had been said had been unplanned and arisen from some sort of desperation. 'It's great,' she whispered, squeezing their shoulders. 'If it's meant to be, it will be.'

'If it was Keith, we should probably invite him in,' said Charlie, crossing to the window and squinting out into the darkness.

'Why?' asked Elizabeth, who had been struggling throughout the meal with the sensation that while the evening was ostensibly in her honour, it had had little to do with her presence. Unveiling Roland's extraordinary, wonderful portrait had definitely been the highlight. Ever since then she had been struck by how preoccupied everyone seemed. Helen had said barely a word, Peter, while trying to hide it, was obviously in a bad mood, and Serena had fired so many beady looks at Charlie that she wondered her brother's face wasn't peppered with holes. It had made her long for all the family gatherings they had enjoyed under the aegis of her dear father, when everything had felt so effortlessly ordered and her own future had seemed an open road rather than a dead end. When Roland had asked if he could slip off to the television room she had been almost tempted to join him. And then, when Peter had seemed about to impose exactly the sort of order she craved, tapping his glass to make his little speech – to remind them of why they were all there – Cassie had snatched the limelight by blurting out her quest to have a child. Which was moving and wonderful, of course, but also, Elizabeth couldn't help thinking, a little selfish. Cassie, as usual, thought the world revolved round her, when in fact, Elizabeth mused a little sadly, they were all at the centre of their own worlds, spinning like planets, held together only by the gravitational force of the family. 'Why on earth should we invite Keith in?' she repeated, noting, with some puzzlement, a series of hasty exchanged glances between Charlie, Serena, Helen and Peter.

'Just because . . . the man's a star. He's done so much. We don't know where we'd be without him,' Charlie faltered. 'Thank you, Stephen, for introducing him into our lives.'

Stephen managed a nod, while inside the maelstrom of all his new doubts assailed him with fresh force. He felt as if he had entered some diabolical maze in which every route he tried failed to produce a way out. Without a baby, Cassie would be unhappy. With a baby, he would not only lose her but, worse still, disappoint her with his own, inevitable ineptitude as a parent. With only his own vile upbringing to go on, how could he not? Cassie knew some of it, of course – the regular beatings, the way his mother had put her hand to her eyes as his father swung the belt. What she didn't – couldn't – know was the snivelling self-doubt, the self-loathing, the certainty of failure and disappointment that those beatings had induced. Only Keith knew that – Keith, who had parachuted back into his life from nowhere, trailing, as it now seemed, all the sourness of their past in his wake. Like a bad smell, Stephen decided, wishing he had turned his back on him in the bookshop instead of inviting the man into his home – into his life – letting him taint it all with his crooked smile and meddling efforts to turn the tide of his own bad luck. 'Keith is a good man,' he began, forcing the words out, only to find himself interrupted by a loud, irreverent cackle from Ed.

'Bed for you, mate,' growled Charlie, realizing, with guilty consternation, that his son was extremely drunk.

'Bed for *you*, Chloë,' muttered Helen, and steered her daughter – still murmuring about ghosts – from the room.

'Come on now, Ed . . .'

Ed surveyed them all through half-closed eyes. 'The point is . . .' He twirled his empty wine glass, fed up suddenly with the throbbing in his head and all the pussyfooting around – all the exhausting aching business of secrecy. 'The point is, Granny tried to drown herself and Keith rescued her. In the lake in the copse. But, ssh . . .' He raised an unsteady finger to his lips. 'Mum's the word.' He lunged for his aunt's full wine glass and fell off his chair.

Keith was leaning on the fence watching the red glow of his cigarette in the dark when he heard footsteps coming towards him through the pergola. He braced himself, wondering who it was and what to say, ashamed suddenly of how he had spied on them through the dining-room window. The footsteps stopped, though the entrance to the pergola remained gaping and dark. It was probably the boy, Keith decided, turning as quietly as he could and resting his elbows on the fence. He waited, not wanting to scare him, expecting at any minute to see a small cloud of smoke drifting through the roses to join the wisp of grey spiralling from his own cigarette. A gust of wind caught the trees to his right, sending a flurry of blossom into the air. Keith watched as the petals fell like huge snowflakes on to the lawn, thinking with longing of his own sons and vowing to get back up north as soon as he could, no matter how menial the work he had to accept to stay there. He might have helped the Harrisons, but they had helped him too, more than they would ever know.

Something moved at last. Whoever it was had sat down, he realized. He tossed his cigarette over the fence and stepped closer to peer through the tangle of branches. He was on the point of tiptoeing away when he heard the unmistakable hiccup of tears. Female tears, he knew at once. Not Ed, then, but one of the women. Keith stepped sideways, trying to get a better view, only to find himself treading on a small branch, loosed from the trees by the wind. It broke with a loud snap.

A moment later Elizabeth hurried out of the pergola, her face tear-streaked and pale with fright. 'Christ, you gave me a jump.' She was breathing hard, both hands pressed to her chest.

'I'm sorry I . . . I was taking a bit of air. I didn't mean to scare you. Sorry,' he repeated, 'I was on my way back anyway.' He turned to go.

'No . . . I . . . I . . . It's my birthday,' she blurted, starting to cry again.

Keith swore under his breath, trying to equate the cosy scene through the window with such a startling demonstration of unhappiness. 'Should I . . . Would you like me to fetch someone?'

'No,' Elizabeth wailed, hugging herself and shaking her head from side to side. 'Just . . . could you . . . would you give me . . .' She dropped her arms and looked at him through the straggle of her hair. 'Actually, I could do with . . . a *hug*,' she sobbed, taking a step towards him, then jumping backwards, waving both arms over her head as if to fend off an attack. 'I'm sorry, ignore me, I'm out of my mind. I've drunk too much, I'm a disgrace – forgive me.' She lurched back towards the pergola.

By the time Keith caught up with her she was half-way down the tunnel, taking big strides and still sobbing furiously. 'Steady on.' He put a hand on her shoulder, tentative because he felt awkward and also because, sealed as they were from the moonlight by thickets of laburnum and roses, it was very dark. 'A hug, is it? Well, that's not so difficult.' He put his left hand on her other shoulder, then almost lost his balance as she fell against his chest. He patted her back, much as he had sometimes attempted to console his sons – when they allowed it – and murmured a few inanities about cheering up and life not being so bad.

'I just feel so . . .' Elizabeth hiccuped and swallowed, trying to compose herself. 'I'm fifty-four, so of course it doesn't matter. I mean, birthdays aren't supposed to matter when you get older, are they? I knew all along Roland wasn't taking me to the cinema, that we were coming here, and I was so glad . . . I didn't mind pretending to be surprised. I mean, my family is all I've got, really, and then it went so *wrong* somehow – like we were here as we used to be but *not* here because, of course, the children are going their separate ways and my brothers and sister are so tied up in their own lives. It's like we can't function as a family any more – at least, not like we used to – and then, as if that wasn't bad enough, it turns out you stopped my mother *killing* herself.' She lifted her face and hit his chest with the palm of her hand. 'I mean, Christ, what the fuck is going on? I've never exactly got on with my mother, but she's always been this sort of *rock* so if she goes and does that, there's no hope for any of us.'

'Of course there is,' muttered Keith, uncertainly, glancing towards the house, wondering what on earth he would say if one of the others came looking for her. 'Your mum just . . . I guess she just . . . had a bad day.'

'A bad day . . . yes . . .' Moved by this ridiculous, kind, gentle understatement, Elizabeth found herself laughing. 'A bad day . . . she certainly did. Oh dear . . . now I can't stop . . . I . . .' She looked up at Keith, eyes streaming, nose and lips wet, aware suddenly both of her own dishevelment and the closeness of his face. He smelt of tobacco and an aftershave she didn't recognize. In the dim light the whites of his eyes were very white and the pupils as black as coal. 'I am so *very* sorry . . .' she began, then found, to her amazement, that his lips were pressing against hers. Soft, kind lips. She had to breathe, with difficulty, through her nose. Could one suffocate from kissing? she wondered, but she was finding air somehow because the rest of her body had liquefied with pleasure, so much so that without his arms round her she might have sunk to the ground.

'Sorry,' she gasped, staggering a little as they pulled apart at last. 'I don't know how – You don't want to come anywhere near me, I assure you. I'm a mess. I've got two ex-husbands to prove it. I drink too much. I'm old.'

'Don't tell me what I want,' Keith growled, stroking her cheek, wanting to remind himself of its softness. 'I've got an ex-wife of my own, thank you, and feel most of the time like I'm about a hundred and five.'

'I didn't come out here looking for you, you know . . . I never thought . . .'

'Of course you bloody didn't. I wasn't looking for you, come to that. But that's how it is sometimes, isn't it? You find something when you're not looking.'

'Oh, God, what are we going to do?' Elizabeth whispered, wringing her hands, suppressing an urge to giggle at quite how packed with surprises her 'surprise' birthday had turned out to be.

'We could do what we just did again?' ventured Keith, enjoying the extraordinary turn the evening had taken far too much to care about consequences. For those moments the entire family could have danced into the pergola and he wouldn't have minded. It was a long time since he'd kissed anyone, let alone felt such instant, mutual attraction. It was chemistry, like an engine firing, rare and inexplicable. Her age didn't bother him in the slightest. He liked her full figure. And she had a strong, interesting face and the hopeful deep blue eyes of a girl. He took her in his arms again, nuzzling her neck with his nose, wondering why he hadn't taken more notice of her at the party all those weeks ago, wondering too how skin could smell so edible.

'This is mad,' protested Elizabeth, weakly. 'We don't even know each other.'

'Well, let's find out,' Keith murmured, slipping his hands into her coat in search of the zip on her dress.

'No . . . Keith . . . I . . .'

He stopped at once, dropping his hands to her waist.

'I'm just too . . . I'm not sure I'm ready . . . or that we should . . .' Elizabeth faltered, her heart quailing at the thought of what everyone would say, all the surreptitious rolling of eyes – Elizabeth launching herself into a doomed relationship, again, with the *handyman* of all people. 'I can't help thinking that if you really knew me – knew all about me – you'd run a mile.'

Keith rested his chin on the top of her head. 'Well, that makes two of us.' She snuggled against him and he sighed. Outside the pergola the wind was picking up, hissing through the twists of leaves and flowers, teasing at their hair and clothes as if to remind them of the real world.

It was impossible, of course, Keith reminded himself, chemistry or no chemistry. He was leaving. He had to, for reasons he hoped never to have to explain to anyone. 'Yeah, well, I'm leaving here soon, anyway,' he confessed, 'I'm going back to Hull . . . try to see something of my boys.'

'Really?' Elizabeth pulled away, astonished and dismayed. 'Do Charlie and Serena know?'

'Not yet. I haven't told anyone . . . except you.' He nibbled the tip of her nose. 'I will tell them soon, though. I must.'

'I see. There we are, then.'

'There we are,' he echoed, tightening his embrace and starting to kiss her again.

'I was thinking of going to church tomorrow,' said Helen. She was standing at their bedroom window, rubbing cream into her hands.

Propped up in bed with a book, Peter peered at her over the frames of his spectacles. 'Really? Whatever for?'

Helen made a face. 'Don't worry, I'm not expecting you to come. Though I'll take Genevieve and Chloë, if I can persuade her.' She tugged at the window latch, her hands slipping on the metal. 'A bit of quiet time in St Margaret's, praying for other people and so on, will do them good.'

'Hmm . . . very virtuous.'

'Don't be scornful.' Helen hit the window frame, releasing it at last. 'With all that's happened we could all do with a little praying.' She breathed deeply, inhaling the dense, complicated scent of the night air.

'I'm not being scornful. I've simply never believed in God – as you well know – and don't intend to start now.' Peter glanced, with some longing, at his book. It had been a long evening, a long day. He was in no mood either for God or for any notion that might encourage feelings of divergence from his wife.

'I'm not sure I believe either. I just want to . . . I don't know . . . give Him the benefit of the doubt for a while. See where it leads. Do you have a problem with that?'

'Of course not. Look, are you coming to bed or what?' He patted her pillow impatiently.

'In a minute.' Helen pushed her head further out of the window, thinking that the air could smell as nice as it liked but it would always be a relief to go back to London, away from all the noise and neediness of her husband's family. It had been quite a night, what with Cassie's emotional announcement and Ed's shameful drunken outburst. Although, as she and Peter had since agreed, it was far better that everyone should know what had happened. Knowing things, after all, meant one could deal with them.

'Darling, do come to bed,' Peter pleaded.

'I'm coming . . . I thought I heard voices.' Helen strained her eyes in the darkness, making out nothing but the silhouette of tall trees skirting the fields and the lacy tunnel of the pergola snaking between the lawns like a giant caterpillar.

'Ghosts?' Peter snapped his book shut, maddened at her inability to sense that all he wanted was the reassurance of a comfortable silence and her warm, familiar body next to his.

'Maybe ghosts are just things and people that haunt us.'

'You don't say.'

Helen left the window open and pulled the curtains shut. 'No, I mean like memories rather than spirits . . . images of things you miss or hate or . . . Are you listening?'

'Of course,' Peter muttered, turning on to his side. 'Memories like ghosts, spirits of the past. Things you hate or want –' He broke off as an image of Delia Goddard blazed into his mind. A moment later it was gone, like a light switching off.

Helen approached the bed and stood looking down at him. 'You've been in a weird mood recently.' She folded her arms and frowned. 'A bad one, in fact.'

'Nonsense. There's been a lot going on, that's all.'

'Yes, there certainly has,' she conceded, with a sigh, dropping her arms and pulling back the duvet. 'You'd tell me if there was anything else, wouldn't you?'

'Anything else? What's that supposed to mean?'

'I'm not sure.' She rolled on to her back and pulled the duvet up to her chin. A few moments later she was breathing heavily, and every so often an arm or a leg twitched as she reached or ran for things in her dreams.

In contrast Peter remained wide awake. Serena's chocolate cake still sat heavily in his stomach, while his mouth and teeth felt dry from too much wine. *Anything else.* The words sent little electric shocks up and down his spine. There wasn't *anything else*, he reminded himself fiercely. There never would be. In the meantime, the evening's dramas had instructed him more than words ever could that the family needed his full focus more than ever. Ed had been banished to his room while the rest of them retired to the drawing room for a much-needed briefing about Pamela and all that had happened. Cassie and Stephen had sat hip to hip on the sofa through it all, looking so united in the face of adversity that Peter wished they'd get the wedding over with instead of keeping everybody waiting until

January, when Cassie – if their hopes were fulfilled – would be in no shape for a wedding gown anyway. Elizabeth had taken it pretty well too, albeit with the aid of a large brandy and a napkin on which to wipe her nose. Roland had stood behind her, as impressively silent and composed as a man twice his age.

And now they could put the whole wretched business behind them, Peter mused, trying to ease some of the duvet from under Helen's arm. His nephew's lamentable behaviour had, in this solitary respect, been a good thing. As a family they could now pull together, as they always did in times of crisis, steer the ship back into calmer waters . . . except Peter could feel something blocking his mind, snagging the mental tranquillity necessary to sleep. His mother? No, that wasn't it. She was frail still, but definitely better, and now that everyone knew, that was better too. What was it, then? Why did he feel so peculiarly alert, so afraid?

He knew why, of course. He just didn't want – even in the privacy of his own brain – to articulate the reason. *You have done nothing wrong*, crooned his conscience, *nothing at all*. With which solace Peter slept at last, pressed up against his wife in a bid to claim his share of the bedding.

Ed slept deeply for several hours, then woke to be violently sick. Staggering back into his bedroom, he dug his phone out of his jeans pocket and turned it on. There were seven messages from Jessica. 'Plse call . . . love you . . . plse plse call . . . plse Ed . . . I need you.'

Ed knelt beside his bed, clutching his aching head while he tried to think what to say in return. 'Will call 2morrow,' he typed at last, his fingers feeling like jelly. 'Needed time 2 think. Have good plan. Plse tell NO ONE.'

Then, still clutching his phone he pressed his face into his palms and prayed. *Dear God, if you're there get me out of this, please. Get me out of this and I'll believe in you until the day I die.*

June

Peering out of the kitchen window at the leaden skies, Serena was tempted to hang the photo collages back on the walls and find something more useful than picture-framing to fill her Friday afternoon. Apart from anything else, the grimy grey squares left by their absence looked dreadful. Like walled-up windows, Pamela had remarked, swiping at them with a cloth so that the smears of dirt looked even worse. 'Maybe Keith could redecorate in here before he goes,' she had added, moving to the sink and making a big to-do of rinsing and squeezing out the cloth, holding it up to the window to check for remaining specks of dirt in a way that made her daughter-in-law want to wrest it from her hands and hurl it out of the window into the flowerbed. 'It's a shame the man is leaving,' she remarked, not sounding as if she minded at all.

'He wants to spend more time with his family – well, his sons, anyway,' said Serena, trying to sound accepting rather than resentful. She was still baffled at Keith's recent announcement that he would be leaving Ashley House at the end of the month. Baffled and hurt. She and Charlie had tried everything to dissuade him – more money, fewer hours, long weekends so he could get up north. She had even suggested he should bring his boys to Ashley House for the summer, her heart surging at the prospect of having two little ones running round the garden with sticks and nonsense games, being wild and innocent in the way that only children could be, in the way that her own prickly semi-adult brood would never be again.

'Time with his family . . . Ah, well, that's as it should be,' clucked Pamela, draping the cloth over the Aga rail to dry and then, spotting a teaspoon, returning to the sink to give that a thorough wash as well.

'I'm going to my studio to put these into proper frames. Is that okay?'

'Of course, dear.'

'I'm not sure how long I'll last. It's been such ages I'll probably be all fingers and thumbs.'

'No, you won't.' Pamela turned, drying the teaspoon now, breathing on it and polishing it as if it were some treasured piece of silver instead of one of the old stainless-steel ones that Charlie and Serena had bought from an Argos catalogue when they shared their first flat. 'You're very creative. You always have been.'

Serena nodded her appreciation at the compliment, glad of this evidence that her mother-in-law was in a positive frame of mind. 'Thank you,' she said, trying not to track the progress of the spoon as it was placed in the cutlery drawer, then removed again for a final rub-down. 'And I haven't forgotten your hair appointment this afternoon. Five o'clock, wasn't it? We'll leave at quarter to . . . or four thirty,' she corrected herself, as a flicker of alarm crossed Pamela's face. She'd be parked in the hall by four o'clock anyway, Serena reflected gloomily, headscarf on and handbag packed, checking her watch every few seconds. She pondered with equal gloom that, while her mother-in-law's recovery appeared to have been unimpeded since the disintegration of the family birthday dinner, her own state of disequilibrium had returned with a vengeance.

As Serena opened the back door it started to rain. Swearing under her breath, she put the clipboards of photos under her arm and made a run for it, dodging puddles and dripping branches. Just that morning the radio forecasters had prophesied the wettest summer for years, linking it to holes in the ozone layer and melting ice floes, the changing rhythms of the world. As she looked round the breakfast table at Ed, hiding behind a pile of revision notes, at Charlie, snatching bites of toast between finding his mackintosh and his mobile, at Pamela, her bun loose and lopsided, the powder too thick on her nose, Serena had been unable to resist the thought that changing rhythms were indeed afoot and not confined to the global stage.

Once inside her studio she set down the photograph boards and admired again the cosy arrangement of shelves, worktops and freshly painted walls. Running water, heating, electricity – in doing up the place Keith had thought of everything. He had even dusted off a little blue velvet armchair from the attic and set it in a corner next to the sink, the kettle and her small collection of art books. Surveying it all, recalling how keen she had been to believe that their new employee's presence was part of some grand design – a gift – a new integral cog to the intricate faltering mechanism of the family, Serena felt close to tears.

She had composed herself sufficiently to remove the photos from their clipboards and start sifting through them when there was a knock at the door and Ed appeared, his hair plastered to his forehead, his school blazer dark with rain. 'Sorry to interrupt.'

Serena's spirits lifted at the sight of her son. 'Darling, you're not. Come inside quickly, you're drenched. How was the exam?' She tried to pull off his blazer but he shook off her hands, keeping her at arm's length, as he had since his drunken outburst at Elizabeth's dinner. Trust mattered, Charlie had roared, bursting into Ed's bedroom the following morning, slamming the door with such violence that Serena, standing at the airing-cupboard on the landing below, felt a tremor ripple along the walls and beneath her feet. Creeping upstairs, she had hovered outside the top bathroom to hear the rest of it, torn between motherly compassion for her blundering son and wifely loyalty for Charlie, who never shouted and who would, she knew, emerge trembling and downcast once it was all over. When Ed had shouted back that life was crap and he didn't care, Charlie had responded with a thundering declaration that his son could consider himself gated until the end of his exams. Ed had been sullen and silent ever since, even when his penitent and equally long-faced father had commuted the sentence by several weeks.

'The exam was fine,' Ed grunted now, slumping into the chair and sniffing in a manner that, had their moods been lighter, might have prompted Serena to remind him of the invention of the handkerchief.

'Was it? That's fantastic,' she gushed instead, tempted to say how pleased she was to have been sought out, even if it was to be sniffed at and given sulky inadequate answers to her questions. 'Only a few more to go . . . and the gating ends today,' she reminded him brightly, glancing with some longing at the photograph uppermost in her pile, which showed Ed in his too-big prep-school tracksuit, holding up a trophy for the camera. His face had been freckled in those days, open and grinning, showing off the chipped front tooth, which they had since had capped at huge expense by a dentist in Chichester. 'Look at you,' she murmured fondly, 'mud and a ball and you were happy.'

Ed gave the picture a cursory glance, then turned to scowl out of the window at the rain, still teeming down in fat grey rods outside.

'I know it's been tough lately,' Serena ventured gently, 'but Dad and I are both *so* proud of the way you've buckled down to work . . . I mean, from that point of view Dad's punishment probably even helped, didn't it? You've always been a bit of a last-minute merchant, just like him.'

'I'm not like Dad,' Ed said fiercely, getting to his feet and ramming his hands into his pockets. 'I'm not like anyone, okay?'

'Okay,' Serena echoed, at a loss as to how to elicit even a glimpse of the freckled cheerfulness staring up at her from the photograph. It occurred to her in the same instant that maybe Ed's open, easy-going nature really was lost for good, mislaid somewhere in the vile dark tunnel of adolescence and academic pressure. Then I will have lost all my children, she thought. The studio heaved, a raft pitching on a storm. Tina, Maisie, Clem, Ed . . . Serena gripped the worktop for support as all the anxiety she was fighting so hard to contain pounded through her veins. Silly, silly, silly. She could hear Charlie saying it now, dismissing each of her worries the minute she expressed them – his mother was fine, there were other handymen in the world, a little discipline would do their son no harm at all – while behind each breezy reassurance clanged the warning: *Don't you dare fall apart on me, not again.*

'And I've decided I don't want an eighteenth,' Ed declared stoutly, keeping his back to her, loath to see the expression on her face, all the kindness, all the wanting to understand. Being gated *had* helped, but only because it had provided a legitimate pretext for not facing Jessica. But now she was waiting for him at the bottom of the lane, looking bigger already, she had said, managing as she delivered this sickening piece of information to sound both coy and *proud*. Getting off the bus after the phone call, Ed had lurched down a footpath away from the road to throw up, only to find that there was nothing to eject but spittle and spasms of air, like he was puking his own panic.

'No eighteenth?' Serena exclaimed, sufficiently astonished at the announcement for her own terrors to slide away.

Ed cleared his throat and braced himself. He had a plan, he reminded himself, a way out, if he played his cards right. 'Maybe get the cousins round or something but I don't want a big party. I'd like the money instead, if that's okay,' he said, making a conscious effort not to speak in a rush, not to sound nervous. 'And I've decided I don't want to go into the army either – at least, not for the time being.'

'Well, I'm sure . . .' Serena faltered, glad of any opportunity to wave goodbye to images of body-bags, but suspicious of her son's jerky voice and averted gaze. 'Do you know what you want to do instead?'

'Travel . . . I want to travel for at least a year, like Maisie.'

'Right, I see.'

'And I would like to use Granddad's trust money, if that's okay. You and Dad have always said it's for us to use as we choose. Well, I'd like to spend mine on travel. In fact, I'm going to need some pretty soon. I've been looking at these gap-year websites and lots of them want deposits. There's this placement in Sri Lanka that looks good – a turtle sanctuary . . .' Ed clenched his lighter inside his trouser pocket, needing to hold on to something so he wouldn't lose courage. He did indeed want to travel – far away and for ever, like his great-uncle Eric – but how much money he would have left for such a purpose was a different matter. Jessica was half playing along with his plans and half resisting, one minute agreeing to a termination, the next changing her mind. There were pills, she said, that would do the job more gently, but the weeks were ticking by and she had refused so far to do anything about getting some. She seemed to like him trying to cajole her, as if she thought it was all a big game. If he lost his temper, as he had phoning her on the bus that day, her viciousness knew no bounds. 'Your mum of all people wouldn't want a baby terminated, would she?' she had hissed. 'Maybe I'll go and tell her and see where we get to.' The nausea had started then, unlocking memories of his mother's zombie-like unhappiness after the death of his little sister and, worse still, the muffled arguing behind closed doors. People thought grief drew families together. Ed felt like he was the only person in the world who knew that it tore them apart. He couldn't stir all that up again, he just couldn't. And with sufficient funds he wouldn't have to, he reminded himself fiercely. Money, as his uncle Peter was fond of saying when he'd had a glass or two, was power. Beneath Jessica's brassiness

Ed guessed that she was as terrified as he was – as eager for a way out. Money could provide that. 'Then I thought I might go to South Africa or Kenya or somewhere,' he continued, in such an enthusiastic tone that he even felt half convinced, 'to work in one of the game parks, but I need money to book it up now so – so would you ask Dad?' He shot his mother a pleading look, then dropped his eyes and scraped at some invisible mark on Keith's newly laid honey-coloured floorboards with the scuffed toe of his shoe.

'Turtles?' Serena laughed, with happy incredulity. 'Since when have you been interested in animals, Edward Harrison?'

'But will you ask Dad,' Ed persisted, 'about the party money and the trust? Pave the way sort of thing?'

'I suppose I might,' she replied carefully, 'if you promise to stop sulking.'

'Sure. Thanks, Mum! Awesome!' Ed managed a lopsided grin.

'Anything to help endangered species.' She smiled back, then started to arrange the photographs on large white pieces of cardboard, feeling that the perfect order in which to frame them was there, if only she could find it.

In the hairdresser's Pamela found herself sitting next to Marjorie Cavendish, which was nice but also a little embarrassing as they hadn't seen each other since the Cavendishes' fortieth-wedding-anniversary party many years before. It had been a good party, Pamela remembered now, held in the garden on a balmy evening with twinkling lights spangling the trees and a string quartet playing waltzes. She and John had drunk too much champagne and danced like young lovers, ignoring both the lateness of the hour and their aching knees.

'I heard about John,' said Marjorie at once, 'I'm so sorry. Geoffrey passed away last year. A heart-attack on the golf course. Just like that.' She clicked her fingers.

'Oh dear, how terrible for you,' Pamela murmured, shy both

of her own recent crisis of misery, and the hairdresser teasing her thin silver strands on to rollers, showing the pink patches of her scalp. Marjorie's head of much shorter, thicker hair was far further along in the process, already pruned and permed to a resilient and elegant helmet of ivory waves. 'I have my second son and his family living with me now,' Pamela explained, 'keeping an eye on me.' She rolled her eyes as if the idea amused her rather than making her stomach heave with shame.

'How *lovely*,' replied Marjorie, slipping two pound coins to the girl sweeping the floor and carefully easing herself out of the chair. 'I've had to sell up. The tax man.' She made a face. 'I was going to buy a bungalow but my son found out about this place called Crayshott Manor, a retirement home for people like you and me, my dear. Except that it's not like a *home* because it's grand and beautiful and the food's top-class and you get a little suite of rooms so you can have all your most precious things around you. Costs an arm and a leg, of course, like a five-star hotel, but I thought, Why scrimp for the last few years to leave something behind, when neither of my two needs money and the wretched chancellor will snatch most of it anyway? I've met some of the other residents and they seem so nice, *just* the sort of people one would want to spend time with. The grounds are splendid – the place belonged to some lord or other once upon a time – with a lake and a croquet lawn, and they're always organising little parties and concerts and . . . But listen to me, rabbiting on, when I've got both my sons coming for the weekend to help me go through the attic. There's not much in the end that one *does* want, don't you find? So much *clutter* – it will be a joy to be rid of it.'

'A joy indeed.' Pamela glanced at her reflection. The curlers were all in place now, pulling uncomfortably in places, making her look like a shrivelled hedgehog. I was once beautiful, she thought. I turned heads and broke hearts. Now there is only clutter and death. She could think such things now without being overwhelmed by them. The pills were splendid in that regard – like little cotton-wool plugs against reality – letting her keep dreadful things at a distance so they didn't seem dreadful at all. And her memory was better, too, not letting her down nearly so often. Yet she didn't want to take pills all her life: it seemed cowardly, somehow, as if she wasn't really coping. Pamela shifted her gaze to Marjorie, now tying a plastic scarf round her sculpted white head and talking loudly to the receptionist about dates and next appointments. Pamela stared till her eyes clouded, envying the woman's energy, her obvious sense of a future.

'You must come and see me before I leave,' insisted Marjorie, returning to Pamela's side, 'or when I've settled into Crayshott. We're allowed to do as we please – like boarding-school but without the rules.' She chuckled. 'I loved boarding-school.'

'I might but I – I've not been well,' Pamela murmured, moved to the confession by the pressure of her companion's cheerfulness and her inability to compete with it.

Marjorie's dimpled face sagged with concern. 'You poor dear. What sort of not well?'

'Oh, nothing serious. I just . . . I suppose I miss John,' admitted Pamela, once the hairdresser had moved out of earshot.

Marjorie sighed, so deflated now that Pamela felt almost guilty. 'Yes, I know, believe me, my dear, I know. Being left behind is always the hardest thing. I got a taste of it when the boys went off to university and Geoffrey was so busy I hardly saw him – I was bereft for months, a mother, a wife, with no one to look after, much as I am now.' She hesitated, closing her eyes, as if summoning some deep reserve of hidden strength. 'But Geoffrey hated me moping then and it would make him positively *furious* if I did it now. And, besides, missing someone means you loved them, doesn't it? And, really, I wouldn't have had it any other way. All the broken marriages, these days, we were so lucky, you and I, finding the right men, staying together all those years. One couldn't really ask for more, could one?' She looked at her watch, all businesslike and cheerful once again. 'I must dash. I'm on a meter – a pound a minute now, isn't it? Call me, Pamela, please? We could *do* lunch, as they say,' she added gaily, tightening her plastic headscarf and scurrying out of the salon.

Serena was in the greenhouse at the bottom of the garden, picking through broken flowerpots and crispy brown skeletons of dead plants when she looked up to see Charlie pressing his nose flat against one of the misty panes, grinning and making ghoulish faces. 'For you,' he said, trotting round to the entrance and producing from behind his back a large, somewhat battered bunch of red roses. 'For my wife, my angel, who puts up with ungrateful children, difficult grannies and resigning handymen, who has had a hard time and deserves a treat from her loving, hopeless husband.'

'Oh, Charlie . . .'

'I'm taking you away, sweeping you off your feet.' He put his arms round her and began to dance her round the greenhouse, bumping into the flowerpots and bin-liners of rubbish.

'Away? Where?'

'To a luxury hotel, luxury food, luxury beauty treatments, where they'll massage your feet and your face but only when I've had a go first.' He pulled her head into his neck and kissed her hair. 'I've a good mind to take you now, ravish you in the glasshouse, with the rain pounding around us. We did that once, do you remember, in this very place, just before we told my parents we were getting married? We destroyed several trays of Sid's seedlings.'

'Of course I remember.' Serena laughed softly, pressing her face into the familiar rough warmth of his skin, loving the way he knew her, the way he was trying to cheer her up. 'But we can't possibly go away –'

'Oh, yes, we can, no buts allowed.' He pressed his finger to her lips. 'It's all arranged. I've spoken to Keith, and Lizzy's coming over to help hold the fort. I've persuaded Peter and Helen to join us at the hotel – use that overpaid nanny of theirs for once. We need ties for dinner and swimsuits for the pool. Dinner is booked for eight so we should start packing.'

'But I've got to pick your mother up from the hairdresser,' protested Serena, her voice ringing with dismay, not because of Pamela so much as the news that they would be sharing their treat weekend with Peter and Helen.

'No, you haven't.' Charlie looked down at her, enjoying this final moment of triumph. 'She phoned just now, moments after I walked into the house. She's getting a taxi home, she said, the lovely Paulo is arranging it for her. So you see,' he continued, hugging her again, as if he might press all his hope and good humour into her, 'there's no escape. My mother has decided she can look after herself and I've got you cornered, with every intention of reminding you why you married me.'

Theo arrived at the station with so much time before Clem's train was due that he sat down on a bench and pulled his laptop out of his rucksack. The rain, which had been falling steadily all morning, had finally retreated, allowing the clouds to part like curtains and reveal a livid sun. The bench was still wet but Theo was soon too absorbed to notice. He dipped into some lecture notes and that week's essay, making amendments here and there, then scrolled to his now almost complete film script. Disaffected student recruited by terrorists. A female Serbian, orphaned by the Bosnian war, a nihilist in search of her own end, who agrees to plant a bomb, only to fall in love twelve hours before she's due to detonate it. He was still working on the ending. A Hollywood feel-good or a dark, life-affirming tragedy? That was the question. Did his heroine get to be with her lover or blow herself up?

Theo rubbed the now substantial field of bristles covering his upper lip and chin as he pondered, enjoying the quandary and the diversion from the prospect of having to take his cousin to the Keble ball. A sore reminder of why he had been persuaded to initiate the invitation had accompanied the welcome injection of cash from his parents.

Clem not keeping in touch is in our view very poor behaviour. What with your grandmother's recent trauma and Ed being difficult, Charlie and Serena have quite enough on their plates without worrying about her as well. So, darling, we are all relying on you to report honestly on what you find. Our biggest fear, of course, is that Clem is losing weight again and sinking back into the clutches of that dreadful disease. I know we can rely on you, Theo, to tell us if you think that's the case. The four of us are taking a much-needed break at a country hotel this weekend, so if you need us try our mobiles. Fondest love, Mum. PS Don't spend the enclosed all at once!

Reading it had made Theo feel like a spy. It had also made him worried about what he would be meeting off the train. He remembered only too well how his once dumpy cousin had shrunk into a bony, hollow-eyed stranger, who hid behind books and attempted to disguise her scarecrow thinness in baggy tracksuits. If she was going that way again, the weekend would be an ordeal beyond his worst fears.

It was with genuine delight therefore that Theo glanced up from his laptop to see a tall, striking young woman emerge from the main entrance to the station and look about her with somewhat imperious and indifferent curiosity. Her hair had grown considerably since the previous summer and hung in sleek, dark waves round her shoulders. She looked slim but attractively so, displaying her figure in boot-cut hipster jeans, and a T-shirt that stopped half-way down her rib-cage, revealing the pearly white slope of her stomach and a small gold ring in her belly-button.

'Clemmy,' he called, waving.

'I thought you'd forgotten,' she shouted, grinning and waving back as she tottered down the steps towards the bench, dragging a large suitcase.

'How could I? Highlight of my term.' Theo sprang to his feet, stuffing his laptop into his rucksack. 'Sorry, I meant to meet you off the train . . . Forgot the time . . . Was doing a bit of work on a script.'

'A film script? I thought you'd given all that up. My God, do you remember when you asked me to be your producer and we made that dreadful film about the family? We managed to get everyone to contribute except Sid, who agreed but then got stage-fright and ran away.' Clem dropped her bulging case, laughing, partly out of pleasure at the memory but also from relief. She, too, had been dreading the ball, regarding its approach on her calendar like an unavoidable missile. It was nothing short of astonishing to find herself pleased to be there. Pleased to see Theo, she realized, with his funny stubble of a beard and wide, interesting face, boffin-like still, but exuding a new easy-going confidence, as if he had grown into his big, square features at last.

'The film wasn't dreadful.' Theo frowned, then laughed. 'Well, maybe just a tad. Everyone's got to start somewhere.'

'Yeah, they have,' agreed Clem, popping a stick of bubble-gum into her mouth and thinking of Stephen's continuing silence with regard to her own tentative efforts. It had to be bad obviously, or he would have been in touch. Though Nathan, bolstering her as he always seemed to, had said that this wasn't necessarily the case and the opinion of one person meant nothing anyway. Art was subjective, he had said. As long as it came from the heart, that was all that mattered.

'You've got a beard,' she remarked, nudging Theo when they were wedged into seats on the bus with their bags.

'And you've had your stomach pierced,' quipped Theo, inwardly despairing at how every member of his family seemed determined to make a big deal of his decision not to shave. Friends at college had barely remarked on it.

'It looks okay . . . No, really, it does . . . quite cool, in fact. You've got enough hair, that's the main thing –'

'Right, thanks,' Theo cut in, wanting to stop any further analysis of his face. 'And when did you decide to mutilate your stomach?'

'A few weeks ago,' Clem murmured, chewing her gum and looking out of the window, because the piercing had been Nathan's idea and she couldn't think how to broach such a fact with her cousin. *I like an older man. A much older man. He draws me and tells me I'm beautiful. He feeds me exotic foods and calls me his muse. He has asked me to take my clothes off and I think I'm going to. I want to, because he looks at me as no one else ever has: as if I am good and pure and worthy of reverence. I tremble under his scrutiny but I love it too. The hours I have spent sitting for him are the best I have known. I live for them. When he comes into the wine bar the plates and glasses shake in my hands.*

'They're all worried about you,' Theo blurted, needing to get at least some of his sense of duplicity off his chest.

Clem rolled her eyes and blew a dainty pink bubble with her gum. He didn't have to say who *they* were. She knew only too well. 'Like they haven't got enough other things to worry about right now,' she said, once the bubble had made a satisfactory pop and she had scraped all the last little bits off her lips with her teeth. 'I presume you heard about Granny?'

Theo sighed. 'Yeah. Unbelievable.'

'Totally. I mean, what's that all about? *Granny* . . .' Clem's eyes filled with tears as she tried for the umpteenth time to equate the desperation of suicide with the cosy image of her grandmother in one of her soft wool twin-sets, pearls round her neck and in her earlobes, a knitting pattern on her lap, her veiny stockinged feet resting on the footstool in front of the fire. Telling Nathan about it, she had cried like a baby. He had stroked her back, then given her a white silk handkerchief and a glass of wine. While she sipped it he explained that the drama of living never ended, that age meant nothing when it came to pain or loss or love. He had uttered the last word very softly, so softly that Clem had experienced a frisson of something else within the consolation, something that had burned like a flame inside her ever since.

'They weren't even going to *tell* me about it, did you know that?' she continued now. 'It was good old Ed who did that –' She broke off, recalling with some discomfort her brother's now impregnable sulkiness – he was punishing her, she knew, for resisting his plea to attend their aunt's birthday party. He hadn't said as much – he didn't have to – but when she phoned now he was too busy to talk and if she sent a text he never answered, not even if she wrote 'TMB' at the bottom. 'When Mum finally deigned to fill me in I had to pretend I was hearing it for the first time, as poor Ed, from what I could gather, was in enough trouble.' Clem let out an affectionate groan, then plucked out her gum. 'The family . . .' she sighed, moulding it into a tiny perfect ball between her thumb and index finger '. . . It's like they want us to be involved but on *their* terms, don't you agree?'

'Sort of,' said Theo, watching with faint disgust as the gum-ball was pressed flat and popped back into her mouth. He decided in the same instant that he had never encountered anyone less in need of looking after. His cousin was more confident than he'd ever seen her, and more beautiful, with a new womanly elegance to offset her huge blue eyes and sharp cheekbones. In fact – Theo's eyes widened, as an idea, glaring, simple and fantastic, exploded in his mind. Clem looked like his Serbian heroine. She *was* his Serbian heroine. How had he not seen it before? How could he ever have considered the snivelling, chubby-cheeked Charlotte Brown for the role when he had known his perfect leading lady all along? He would make the film. He bloody well would. He would use the trust fund left by their grandfather. Five thousand pounds wasn't exactly a Hollywood budget but it would be enough if he was clever and careful and saved from his job in the summer. Theo was so excited he wondered that Clem didn't turn from the window and remark on it. He would ask her later, he decided, sitting on his hands, then releasing them to hug his bag, needing to make some outward gesture of the energy – the inspiration – surging inside. He would wait till the moment was right – after a few glasses at the ball, perhaps. He had planned to set much of the action in London anyway. Clem's flat might work for some of the interiors. It would be perfect.

The bus was now locked in Saturday traffic, edging its way along the high wall guarding Worcester College from the road. Two dishevelled drunks were reeling along the pavement, drinking from cans and waving the stubs of their cigarettes at each other as they talked. 'Don't you envy people like that some-times?' murmured Clem, pressing the tip of her nose against the window.

Theo peered across her and snorted happily, his mind still on his film. 'Not at all. Whatever for?'

'No ties . . . no one to disappoint . . . no expectations . . . I mean, Mum and Dad pretend they want to see me all the time, but really, deep down, they're worried and disappointed because I'm not doing what they'd hoped I would. They'll be all over me with innocent questions and references to Maisie – and *you*, no doubt,' she poked Theo in the ribs, 'the star of the family with your big Oxford brains. My dear parents can't accept that I'm twenty years old with my own life to lead. I'm doing okay. I earn good money. I'm *happy*. And I eat,' she added slyly, 'more and more, these days, as it happens.' Seeing the look on Theo's face she burst out laughing. 'I know how they think, you see.' She wagged a finger. 'Which is why, just right now, I don't particularly want to see them.'

'I see,' murmured Theo, disarmed and impressed in equal measure, thinking in some wonderment of his mother's letter and how Clem couldn't have presented a better account of herself had she read it. 'But you'll have to go home at some stage, won't you?' he ventured, gallantly taking charge of her bag as they scrambled off the bus and headed towards Keble Road.

'Oh, sure. Ed's eighteenth is coming up for a start. If he has a party I'll definitely go, especially with Maisie away. And you'd come, of course, and Chloë, I suppose' – she made a face – 'and Roland, who's turning into such a sweet dark horse, all introverted and artistic. God, do you remember what a wimp he used to be, always crying and wetting his bed and taking medicines? Now he's so into his painting, and handsome enough to model for *Vogue*, if he wanted to.'

'Is he?' murmured Theo, not really listening because they had arrived at the top of his staircase and he was too primed with hope that she would remark on the beauty of his rooms to think about anything else. 'I share with a chap called Ian, but he's away this weekend so you can have his bed. His room is through that door and mine's here and we share this sitting room in the middle, with our desks there and there – well, you can see that – and the sofa and the fireplace, which is gas but still looks quite good and . . .' Theo rushed round picking up stray items of clothing and books as he talked. 'The windowseat is rather fine too.'

But Clem had already dropped her bags and flung out her arms. 'It's *fantastic*, Theo, like something out of bloody *Brideshead*.'

'Except I'm not remotely like Sebastian Flyte,' put in Theo, laughing, 'and from what I can recall of the book Keble barely gets a mention.'

'I want to go punting. Can we do that?' Clem exclaimed, sprawling on the windowseat and stretching her arms. 'And eat strawberries and cream and visit all the famous colleges, and Christchurch Meadows and Magdalen Bridge.'

Theo shook his head in happy despair. 'We've got twenty-four hours and it's starting to rain again.'

'I don't care. Nathan said I would love it and he was right.'

'Nathan?'

'A friend,' stammered Clem, leaping off the windowseat and unzipping her bag.

'An instead-of-Jonny sort of friend?'

Clem, kneeling on the floor now with her back to him, shrugged. 'Suppose, sort of.' She flung back the lid of her suitcase and slapped her hands on her thighs. 'Now then, to more important matters. I didn't know what to wear so I brought quite a few options. Tell me which you think.' And with that she began pulling dresses out of her suitcase and spreading them out on the floor.

Theo sank back on the windowseat to watch, any lingering curiosity about the new boyfriend giving way to dismay. He wasn't good on dresses or colours or saying the right thing in such situations. Clem might have been his cousin, his old play-mate, but she was also a *girl,* he reflected gloomily, studying the mounting pile of outfits and thinking they'd be lucky to get to the ball in time, let alone the boathouses for a quick punt beforehand.

'You've lost weight,' remarked the designer, managing to sound accusing in spite of the pins wedged between her lips. 'We'll need to take it in here – and here.' She tugged at the white silk, extracting the pins one by one to mark out a fresh seam. 'It's weddings that do it – I was the thinnest I've ever been for mine, been downhill ever since, especially since *that* one arrived.' She nodded at the Moses basket parked behind the mirror, between a mannequin and a tea-chest. 'Breastfeeding makes you starving, which doesn't help – I'm currently on about six meals a day, and that's not counting night time snacks.'

While the designer, Sylvie, talked, Cassie's gaze drifted from her own reflection in the mirror to the Moses basket. The baby, she had been told, was five months old and called Noah. He was lying on his back, naked except for a nappy and a square of muslin, which he clutched in one tight fist while he slept. His skin was a soft olive brown, from his father, Sylvie said, who had an Italian mother. His arms and legs were plump with little dimples in his knees and wrists. He had slept for the entire consultation, moving his head from side to side occasionally and making little smacking sounds with his lips. Cassie didn't know when she had last seen anything so beautiful. Every time she looked at him she felt an ache deep in the pit of her belly, right in the middle of the new flatness that had prompted Sylvie to tighten the seams.

Since Elizabeth's dinner such feelings had sharpened, almost as if blurting out her hopes to her family had given free rein to the true vehemence bottled inside. The ensuing shocking revelation about her mother's plunge into despair had, if anything, honed this desire still further. Happiness was so precarious. One had to lunge for it with both hands, hold fast no matter how it slithered between one's palms. Reaching for Stephen in the safe cage of the four-poster afterwards, icy cold and shaking with shock, she had murmured such thoughts into the warm bulk of his chest, enjoying the comfort and closeness, the tickle of his wiry chest hair against her lips. 'To think she was so unhappy and we never knew . . . to think she misses Dad that much . . .'

Stephen had stroked her head, from time to time pressing his lips against her hair. Then, when she was finished and almost asleep, he had said, 'I hope you would love me that much.'

Remembering the moment now as she stared at the fairy-tale image of herself in the mirror, her blonde wavy hair and creamy skin rising out of the frothing silk, with Sylvie on her knees working at the hem, Cassie felt her breath quicken. 'Love you enough to kill myself?' She had tried to keep the gasp from her voice, to sound merely inquiring.

'I'd do it if I lost you,' Stephen had said simply. 'Without you I wouldn't want to live. But I don't think you feel like that. I think you want a baby more than you want me. You didn't used to, but you do now.' He had sounded both matter-of-fact and accusatory. 'The way you felt able to tell everyone our private business tonight made me realize that, and I find it hard, Cassie, really hard.'

Cassie had murmured to him not to be silly, astounded by this new revelation of the feverish workings of her fiancé's mind, so different from hers, like another world. 'You're right, I should have consulted you before I said anything, but it doesn't mean I don't love you. And although I wouldn't wade into the lake if I lost you it doesn't mean that my love isn't fantastic and strong. Please, Stephen, trust me,' she had begged, remembering again the ridiculous argument in the car and feeling suddenly as if they had taken a wrong turning on the journey down and had yet to find their way back to the right road.

Since then Stephen's attentiveness had reached new heights: chocolates on her pillow, love-notes in her handbag, and small gifts – a book of poetry, a pair of earrings, a phial of perfume – had materialized within the folds of her underwear, like lucky charms. The accusatory note in his voice had gone but they would not, he had insisted several times, be consulting a medical expert. He had decided, he said, to let nature take its course. When Cassie, swallowing her disappointment, had mentioned a device she'd seen in the chemist's that took a woman's temperature to indicate her precise level of fertility he had argued against that too. It would be like bringing maths into the bedroom, he claimed, remove all spontaneity, reduce sex to an obligation instead of a pleasure. Cassie had bought the device anyway and hidden it at the back of the bathroom cupboard behind the spare toilet rolls. She had taken to going up to bed before him to use it, locking the bathroom door slowly and silently, like a thief, feeling devious but justified. Her future husband needed careful handling, she had realized, now more than ever. Telling her family about their quest for a baby had clearly been a serious miscalculation and she had to make up for it.

'You're swaying,' scolded Sylvie, sitting back on her haunches and adjusting the train so that it fell into an elegant pool behind Cassie's feet. 'Look, have I shown you this?' She reached into the tea-chest and pulled out a fat roll of chiffon. 'I thought we could put a little strip of it round the neckline and at the cuffs.' She began to unravel the material, feeding it lovingly through her fingers and draping it round the dress. Like a web, Cassie thought, watching in the mirror, resisting the urge to shake off the gossamer strips dangling from her neck and arms.

'Are you all right? You're a little pale.'

'I . . . A sit-down, I think . . . I feel . . . My legs are aching a bit.'

'Sure, I'll make some tea. Look, his lordship's waking anyway. He'll want a feed.'

The baby had opened his eyes and was screwing up his face, making little punching movements with his fists.

'Pick him up, if you like, while I put the kettle on. Here, you'll need this.' She pulled a white cloth off the back of a chair and threw it at Cassie. 'So he can't do any damage. Hey, you, nothing but trouble,' she scolded, bending down and giving a gentle poke to the tight little swell of the baby's belly, then disappeared into the kitchen.

Noah whimpered, then fell silent. Cassie stepped towards

the basket. 'Hey, little one, you be good now. Mummy's only gone to the kitchen.' At the sight of her face – the wrong face – Noah, with no notion of virtue beyond his own wants, clutched frantically at the air with his fists and then began to cry, firing each sob from the back of his throat with terrifying machine-gun ferocity. 'Oh dear, oh dear . . . Come on now, stop this.' Cassie dangled the cloth over the basket, trying in vain to distract him. She had held all her nephews and nieces as babies but had never been very good at it. Even with little Tina she'd kept such attentions to a minimum, in spite of Serena being the sort of mother who plonked her little ones into the arms of anyone who happened to be passing. She had had even less practice with her youngest niece, Genevieve, not seeing her eldest brother's family quite so much and with Helen being the antithesis of Serena, displaying the sort of devoted, control-ling approach that precluded intervention, even from Peter a lot of the time.

'Oh, blimey, all right, here goes.' Cassie arranged the cloth carefully across her shoulder and bent down to pick up the baby. He stopped crying at once and stared at her with big blue-black eyes. Holding him at arm's length, like a dangerous parcel, she stepped between the piles of material and pin boxes to the sofa. He seemed to like dangling and kicked happily with his chunky bare legs, curling and uncurling his toes; but the moment she sat down he was squirming and whimpering again, turning his face to her chest, opening and closing his mouth against the folds of the cloth like a fish.

Sylvie, returning with the tea, laughed. 'Come on, Noah, no milk there, darling.' She flopped down next to Cassie, hitched up her shirt and reached for the baby in one easy movement. 'There you go, my poppet . . .' She glanced dreamily at Cassie as Noah's mouth slid round her nipple. 'Latches on like a vice, as usual.' Cassie sipped her tea trying not to watch as the baby guzzled, cradling the curve of his mother's breast with almost adult earnestness in his little palms. The tea was too hot but Cassie drank it quickly, relishing the comfort of its warmth in her empty belly.

After his feed Noah refused to settle and Sylvie, with many apologies, brought the session to a close, promising to find a child-minder for the next one and saying how much she was looking forward to getting started on the designs for the brides-maids. Mother and son stood on the doorstep to wave her off but it was raining heavily and Cassie urged them to go back inside. As the door closed she embarked on a battle with her umbrella, which had a habit of sticking, particularly when she was in a hurry and needed it most. Usually persistence and determination met with reward, but that afternoon, grappling among the folds of nylon with the jammed catch, while the rain streamed down her neck and flung itself against the bare backs of her legs, Cassie felt as if she was in combat with some monstrous demon. I need help, she thought suddenly, looking about her. Nothing is working out and I need help. Giving up on the umbrella, she reached for her mobile, blinking the rain from her eyes as she stared at its little panel of numbers. She should be happy, she reminded herself. In six months she was getting married; she was on the cusp of a new beginning, a new life with a man who would die for her. Yet all she could think of was the clutch of Noah's little hands, the warmth of his small, writhing body and Sylvie's laughing words: *no milk there*. Maybe there never would be. Maybe she was barren, an old crone in spite of her still-youthful looks; a sham of a woman, a kernel, hollow inside . . . Cassie continued to stare at the phone, tears now mingling with the rain on her cheeks. She should call Stephen, of course, tell him how she felt, how she needed his support more than ever. But, these days, she feared the effect such a confession might have. *Careful handling*, she reminded herself, thinking unhappily of her lover's bottomless demands for reassurance, his new predilection for interpreting her needs as a threat to their happiness.

Who to call, then? She didn't have many friends. She had always been a man's woman, not the sort to pour out her woes to female confidantes over glasses of wine. Before Stephen there had been Daniel, and before him a string of steady, respectably long relationships, each one providing all the emotional solace her undemanding nature had required.

Cassie began to walk, holding the phone in front of her like a torch in the dark. Other daughters might talk to their mothers in such circumstances, but then other people's mothers hadn't . . . She didn't want to think about that. There was Elizabeth, of course, a good sister in many ways, but so messed up in others – not an obvious candidate for the counsel Cassie craved. Her brothers were out of the question too: she could imagine the bafflement in their voices, all that manly incomprehension at such feminine despair, and from her too – Cassie – the one who wound life round her little finger and did as she pleased. Which left . . . Serena, of course. Why hadn't she thought of it before? Her dear, perceptive, gentle sister-in-law, who had been through so much, who alone of all people had seemed to comprehend the magnitude of her quest to become a mother. Cassie, fighting tears, was so pleased to have identified a source of help that she hardly minded when her call to Serena's mobile was put through to voicemail. 'Serena, it's Cassie. Could I talk to you . . . urgently? Could you call? I need your . . . I need to meet, just to talk through a couple of things . . . Would you mind? Thanks so much.'

Cassie dropped her phone into her pocket and had another go at the umbrella, which opened smoothly and sweetly into a sleek black flower, as if all it had been waiting for was the injection of a little self-belief into the effort.

Seeing Cassie emerge from Sylvie's house, Stephen stepped back behind the protective shelter of the bus stop. He had chosen

217

his lookout carefully, near enough to watch the door but not in the path of her route back to the car. The street had been easy to find once he'd double-checked the postcode in Cassie's address book with the various options presented by the *A–Z*. On the way to the tube station he had stopped off to post Clem her manuscript, with a dog-eared copy of the *Writers' and Artists' Yearbook* and a note that had taken most of the morning to compose.

> A very brave start to a story. Well done you! But I'm afraid it's not really my sort of thing . . . far better to send it to an editor or agent – the enclosed book might help. It's a few years out of date but lists all the main ones. Sorry not to be more helpful. Keep it up!

Handing the parcel across the post-office counter, Stephen had felt as if he was unburdening himself of something far weightier than the modest brown package suggested. He couldn't believe he had allowed the manuscript to sit in his bottom drawer for so long, undermining – jinxing – his own creative efforts with the quiet invisible force of its presence, just as Keith worming his way into Ashley House had undermined him, upsetting his sense of balance within his future wife's family. But now the manuscript was off his hands and Keith was leaving Charlie and Serena, heading back north where he belonged. Hearing the news via Cassie that week, Stephen had felt a lump of joy clog his throat. Everything was going to get better, he could *feel* it. All that remained was to get things back on an even keel with Cassie, pull her back into the circle of his love, where things like her work and having babies were secondary preoccupations instead of obsessions.

It was all a question of perspective, Stephen mused, fighting the temptation to rush to Cassie's aid as she fought with her umbrella. She was so vulnerable, so in need of his protection.

If only she could recognize that instead of retreating into herself all the time, putting the wrong interpretation on things. Like the business with her mother, which had been dreadful but Stephen had felt he understood at once. Poor Pamela, bereft without her soulmate, living like a guest in her own home. No wonder she had wanted to end it all. It was terrible, but glorious too, as terrible things often were. But Cassie couldn't see it that way and trying to persuade her otherwise had proved so detrimental that Stephen had given up.

He was *wooing* her instead now, Stephen reminded himself happily, peering round the side panel of the bus stop and experiencing a fresh wrench of pity at the sight of his beloved's bedraggled hair and rain-soaked jacket. All he wanted was to rush down the pavement and grab her, lick the rain off her cheeks and tell her he loved her. Yet it was exciting too, he had to admit, watching but not touching, safely screened inside the bus stop. In many ways it reminded him of the days when she hadn't yet reciprocated his feelings, when he had prowled outside her flat like a stray in search of a home, leaving flowers on her doorstep and scratching messages into the icy windscreen of her car. Halcyon days, Stephen reflected wistfully, though he hadn't known it at the time. He dropped his gaze to his damp shoes, pondering how simple early love was, how pure, how driven by the energy of its own conviction. Where had that simplicity gone? How had he become a man watching his lover from a bus shelter on a dank June afternoon? A man with cold toes and an aching heart. Jack Connolly might behave in such a way, but not him, surely?

And yet he was doing no harm, Stephen reasoned fiercely, fighting the wistfulness now, digging deep inside himself for reassurance. It wasn't like he had *planned* to come. It had been a whim, blown into being by the oddness of Cassie's manner the previous evening, the reserve with which she had yielded her itinerary for the day. There had been a certain *stealth* (there was no other word for it) about the way she had slipped upstairs afterwards – while he was still finishing his wine from dinner – and bolted the bathroom door. *Bolted* it. After letting him in she had jumped back into the bath like a shy schoolgirl burying herself under the bubbles and smiling awkwardly – weirdly – almost as if she didn't want him to see her nakedness. Any normal lover would have thought it odd, let alone one who'd already had doubts about a chap called Frank and who feared deep down, within the rubble of his terrified heart, that she might find someone else to make a baby with, someone keener and more sure of themselves, someone who'd had a decent dad of their own and didn't live with the terror that everyone he cared about would either hurt him or disappear.

Cassie was hurrying down the path now and out into the street. Her hair was so wet it hung in black rats' tails round her face. She stepped carefully in her high heels, avoiding the worst of the puddles. The rain had eased slightly. High in the sky a minute patch of blue had appeared like a teasing hope. Noting its presence and experiencing a sickeningly lucid glimpse of the absurdity, the sheer seediness of what he was doing, Stephen stepped out of the bus shelter to declare his presence. As he did so Cassie lifted her face sufficiently for him to observe, with some shock, that she was crying. He noticed, too, that she was holding her mobile phone and on the point of dialling a number. *His* number, Stephen realized, his chest tightening with panicky excitement as he hastily stepped out of view. Who else would she call if she was sad? Who else but the love of her life, her future husband, who would die rather than live without her? He pulled his own phone out of his pocket and waited, so sure it would ring that when Cassie began to talk he tapped its little screen, dimly wondering if there was a faulty connection. But then, suddenly, she was walking away, clearly talking but out of earshot, wiping the tears off her face, then laughing – he was sure he'd heard a laugh. Stephen stared after her through the Perspex wall of the bus shelter in disbelief. Why had a dress-fitting for their wedding made her sad? Why had she phoned someone else for consolation? Why was his world crumbling, no matter how hard he tried to prop it up?

When a bus pulled up several minutes later he was still standing there, all the doubts he had sought to allay ganging up against him, mocking him like the bullies at school who had poked his bruises and told him he was a loser, until Keith elbowed them away. Until the next time. There had always been a next time. There always would be, Stephen mused bitterly. No matter how far he tried to remove himself, pain would always be waiting round the corner, ready to get him in the end.

The doors of the bus slid open with a hiss and an old lady got off, clinging to the handrail as she lowered herself gingerly to the pavement.

'You getting in or what, mate?' shouted the driver.

'Yes . . . no.'

'Make up your mind.'

'No . . . thanks, that is . . . I'm not sure where I'm going.'

'Who does, mate?' laughed the driver, returning his attention to the road as the doors closed.

Peter swilled the wine round his mouth, swallowed, scowled, then peered over his spectacles for a second look at the bottle being held out for him by the sommelier. Next to him Helen chewed a piece of bread and checked her phone for messages. Serena tried to catch Charlie's eye, but he was too absorbed in his brother's antics to notice. Absorbed and admiring, mused Serena, despairingly. She caught the sommelier's eye and beamed at him, wanting to make up for all the silliness. The wine was priced at thirty-five pounds and had a beautiful label and a lovely long French name. Of course it was all right. Peter was just being Peter, showing off as usual.

'Is Monsieur not happy with the wine?'

'I'm not sure . . . Charlie, see what you think?'

'Could I see what *I* think?'

'Of course, Serena. Be my guest.' Peter offered his sister-in-law an indulgent smile and pushed the glass across the tablecloth.

She sipped. 'It's heavenly,' she declared, patting her lips with her napkin.

'Good,' murmured Peter, unperturbed. 'Helen, darling? Do you want a taste?'

Helen, replying to a text from Chloë who had asked if her Saturday-night curfew could be extended from ten thirty to eleven o'clock, shook her head absently.

'Your turn then, Charlie.'

Charlie looked anxiously from his brother to his wife, aware, as he swallowed the remaining mouthful of wine, of a tension that he didn't want to explore. Serena was looking cheerful, that was the main thing – the purpose of the exercise in fact. 'Doesn't seem too bad . . . but I'm no expert,' he said.

'Well, I don't think it's at its best,' declared Peter, returning his attention to the sommelier.

'I will fetch Monsieur another bottle,' said the waiter at once, his face a mask as he bowed and left the table.

'Good. Well, that's sorted that, then. No point in settling for second best.' Peter rubbed his hands. He was enjoying himself enormously, far more than he had dared hope. Far more than he deserved, probably, he reflected, turning to catch something Helen was saying and detecting – from his cheek or collar, perhaps – the faintest but most deliciously distinct trace of Delia; not so much a perfume as an animal scent, a combination of skin and soap so alluring that he had wanted to lunge across the checked tablecloth of the bistro in which they had lunched that day and bury his face in her neck. He hadn't, of course. They had enjoyed a civilized meal instead. Steak and

222

frites and a green salad, washed down with mineral water and a glass each of merlot. They had talked about the wet summer, their children, their jobs and, eventually, Pamela, who had provided the justification for the meeting in the first place. *I know some of what you're going through . . . the shock . . . I could be a friend, someone to talk to about it all.* The memory of those words, the simple offer of comfort – not to mention the indelible imprint of her phone number across his brain – had proved too vivid for Peter to resist. Helen, with increasing regularity, was seeking comfort in church, so why shouldn't he do the same in a new, unexpected friendship? And Delia had proved a friend indeed, sharing details of the events surrounding her brother's suicide, offering all sorts of gentle wisdom in the process. The scent of her was from a parting kiss: her lips on his cheek; a momentary burning. And here he was a few hours later, treating his wife to a well-earned break, strengthening brotherly bonds, accommodating the now ever-present tetchiness of his once easy-going sister-in-law. So, no harm done. In fact, if anything, Peter mused, he felt warmer towards his family than he would have done if he *hadn't* met Delia for lunch. It had boosted him, as all good friendship should, he assured himself, experiencing, as the trace of scent vanished, an absurd momentary urge to sniff his shirt collar like a dog. 'Darling, you're as bad as Chloë with that phone.'

'No, I'm not,' murmured Helen, pressing the *discreet* option and setting it down next to her side plate.

'Our dear daughter is plugged into machines of one kind or another *all* day,' Peter continued, turning to Charlie and Serena. 'She even dries her hair, preening herself like a film star. Teenagers, eh! Who would have them? Talking of which, how's Ed getting on?'

'Ed's fine,' said Serena, a little sharply. 'His exams have gone really well. He's got one left on Monday, then his eighteenth to look forward to – though he's decided against a big party.'

'His latest plan, apparently,' put in Charlie, glancing at his wife, 'is to use both his trust fund and the money we would have spent on a party to go travelling.'

'Is it now?' Peter folded his arms and leant back in his chair. 'Forgive me for being old-fashioned, but I thought gap years were supposed to be about earning one's own way. Give them too much and they'll start blowing it on drink and drugs. Theo's planning to hang on to his trust fund until he needs a mortgage.'

Serena's mouth was full of wine from a second, approved, bottle. She almost spat it across the tablecloth. 'A *mortgage* – at his age?'

'Oh, you know Theo,' said Helen, smoothly, doing her best to sound proud rather than smug. 'He likes to think ahead.' She smiled at her sister-in-law, enjoying, as always, her sheer straightforwardness but thinking with something like pity that offspring were invariably the product of their parents and upbringing. Ed, for the most understandable reasons, had been spoilt. He had his father's easy charm and a mollycoddling mother – a lethal combination, she and Peter had agreed many times. She had been in no mood for a weekend away with the pair of them, no matter how luxurious the setting, but Peter had talked her round. Charlie and Serena were still reeling from the trauma of his mother's recent breakdown, he reminded her, they needed cheering up, and he and Helen might have a good time in the process. All of which had made Helen grateful that Peter, in contrast, seemed to have recovered his own high spirits. Lately his mood had been verging on ebullient – because his shoulder was better, he said, and because his case was going well, and because he could still beat his son at squash. He had been singing so loudly in the shower all week that Chloë, who had just turned fourteen and was more self-obsessed than ever, had been moved to remark on it herself, delivering such a hilarious rendition of his operatic wailings between mouthfuls of cornflakes that all of them – including Genevieve, banging her spoon against the table in encouraging and uncomprehending glee – had laughed till their sides ached.

'Oh, look,' said Helen, picking up her phone as it hummed for attention. 'A message from Theo . . . about to go to that ball of his with Clem. She's fine, he says, better than he's ever seen her.'

'And why wouldn't Clem be fine?' inquired Serena, stiffly, looking from her husband to Peter, then to Helen.

'No reason. We knew she hadn't been in touch much lately and –'

'What else have you told them?' Serena interjected, glaring at Charlie. 'Have you said you're worried about me too? That that's why we are all here – to *cheer me up*?'

'Darling, really –'

'I'm perfectly cheery, thank you.' She lanced one of the little scallops she had chosen as a starter, wondering when her husband had started looking to his brother for support rather than to her, or whether he had always been that way and she had been too dense to notice. She popped the coral into her mouth and chewed slowly, aware that as the architect of the now ringing silence round the table it was her responsibility to dispel it. The scallop was sweet and buttery, melting between her teeth. 'Sorry.' She rolled her eyes and made a face. 'It's been a tough couple of months, what with . . .' she breathed deeply '. . . all that's happened. And, yes, Peter, you're right, teenagers are a *nightmare.*' She chattered on about Ed's exams, Keith leaving and Pamela improving, until the gusts of relief from Charlie were almost palpable.

'Well done,' he said, once they were safely back upstairs in their sumptuous bedroom, which had been tidied in their absence – towels folded, curtains drawn and the sheets turned down, as white and smooth as envelope flaps. 'I should have brought you here alone, shouldn't I, my petal?' He took her hands in his and kissed each palm. 'I just felt the need to include Peter and Helen . . . I mean, they're cut up too, about Mum and so on.'

'I know.' Serena cupped his face in her hands. 'Because you're kind and loyal and I love you for that. I also know that you've been worried about me and bringing us here was a lovely idea – I'm truly grateful – but we don't *owe* them anything, darling.' She moved her fingers over his face, feeling the strong ridges of his cheekbones. 'Sometimes I wonder whether you're trying in some way to make up for the fact that Peter gave us the house but – hush, let me finish – we didn't ask him to, remember? He insisted, just as your uncle Eric insisted your father should have it. John and Pamela didn't spend the rest of their lives trying to make up to him and neither should we.'

'I'm just trying to keep him . . . involved,' muttered Charlie, sheepishly, inwardly marvelling at his wife's capacity – no matter what else was going on inside her head – to see to the heart of things. 'And I'm sorry for telling them we were concerned about Clem. I meant it for the best.'

'I know, and I'm glad Theo says she's fine. That was good to hear. The family tom-toms signalling across the country. It's good that we all watch out for each other.' She had moved into the circle of his arms now and was pressing her body against his, offering signals of a rather more immediate nature. 'There are chocolates on our pillows, look,' she murmured, peering over his shoulder. 'Shall we unwrap them and have a choco-latey kiss?' She ran her tongue round his ear-lobe, enjoying his breath against her neck and the knowledge that twenty-five years of marriage had not dimmed her ability to stir her husband's passions. 'A sticky wet kiss, my bear . . .'

When the phone rang a few minutes later Charlie, negotiating the stubborn zip on his wife's dress, growled at her to ignore it. 'It will be the daffy one at Reception, asking which paper we want. I don't care what they give us, the *Sun*, *Gardeners' Weekly*,

Worm Lover's Gazette . . .' The dress parted as he spoke, revealing the soft, inviting expanse of Serena's back, the skin on either side of her spine like two smooth pages of an open book.

'Sweetheart . . . we should . . .' Serena wriggled near enough to the bedside table and picked up the receiver. 'Pamela . . . hello . . .' She made a face at Charlie, who groaned and rolled over to the other side of the bed, clutching his head in mock-despair. 'Is everything all right?' She tried not to look at Charlie, contorting his face and slicing his finger across his throat. 'No, of course, not a bad time at all . . .' She manoeuvred herself into a sitting position, while her husband began, with exaggerated, noisy attention, to lick her toes. 'Ed? What about Ed? Is he there? Could I . . .' She was prevented from finishing the sentence by Charlie who, alerted to the possibility of crisis by her sudden change of tone, lunged across the bed and snatched the phone. 'Mum . . . oh, Ed, it's you. What's going on? Are you all right? He's drunk,' he hissed to Serena, who had wriggled on to her knees beside him and was wringing her hands. 'There are other things in life than alcohol, you know, Edward,' he barked into the phone. 'Behaving like this again the moment our backs are turned, when you're supposed to be looking after your grandmother, is just not on, do you hear me? Just not *on.*' Serena was tugging at his arm, mouthing at him to be kind, but Charlie, with his romantic evening shot to pieces and his son slurring at him about, of all things, needing *money*, felt little inclination to be gentle. 'I know you want to get your hands on your trust fund – your mother has told me about it. But I can tell you now you won't get a penny of anything, my boy, until you can learn to hold your drink or, better still, not drink at all. Do you understand? Now, apologize to your grandmother and get yourself to bed. You're a disgrace, Edward, do you hear me? A bloody disgrace.'

'I think we should go home,' moaned Serena, after Charlie had slammed down the phone.

'Now? It's ten o'clock at night. Don't be ridiculous.'

'I just feel . . . I . . .' Serena, still kneeling on the bed, her dress dangling round her waist, dropped her face into her hands. The panic was welling inside her again, feeding off this new drama as it seemed to feed off everything. 'I *want* to go home . . . Everything feels *wrong* . . . I . . . Ed needs us.'

'Ed needs a good hiding, that's what Ed needs. Exams or no exams, his behaviour recently has been unacceptable. You can't cling to him, you know,' he snapped. 'You've got to let him *go*.'

Serena could not have felt the force of the remark more if he had slapped her across the cheek. 'Like I let Tina go?' she whispered. 'And your mother? Like I let her wander off to pick vegetables that didn't exist?'

'Sweetheart, don't –'

'Don't *sweetheart* me.' She got out of bed and pulled off her dress, leaving it in a heap on the floor. 'Somewhere, somehow, you've stopped trusting me, Charlie.'

'Of course I trust you. What is this?'

'My feelings.' She slapped her bare chest. 'You don't trust my feelings. You're afraid of them. You don't want to *deal* with them. For months now, ever since your aunt's funeral, you've been treating me like an invalid, like – like your bloody mother, tiptoeing around everything for fear of stirring it up. Well, I am *stirred up*. I don't know why and it may not be pleasant, but I am. And since you refuse to let us go home I'm going to send our – my – son a text, telling him I love him because in the end that is *all* that matters and if he's getting drunk he needs reassurance not a bollocking.' She dug her phone out of her handbag as she talked, listening absently to the brief message from Cassie before she punched in a few words to her son: 'It will be all right. We love you. Let's have a proper talk tomorrow.'

After that they lay side by side in the dark, as cold and rigid in their respective misery as stone figures on a tomb. Around

228

them the shadowy shapes of the room's opulent furnishings stirred in a breeze from an open window, each rustle like a whispered accusation of failure.

'Come closer. There, that's better. Are you comfy?'

'Oh, yes, very . . . You have the most perfect body, has anyone ever told you so?'

Keith chuckled. 'Not for a while . . . a long while. Hey, have you seen the moon? It looks fake it's so perfect.'

Elizabeth raised herself on one elbow to gaze across Keith's bare chest through the open window next to the bed. A glistening yellow full moon shone in the middle of it, a burning hole in the black sky. 'People go mad at full moon, don't they? Werewolves and so on?'

'Oh, yes.' Keith pulled her back on to the bed and rolled on top of her. 'Haven't you seen my teeth, lady?'

Elizabeth giggled. 'I have . . . nice and sharp and . . . Oh, Keith, don't leave this place, please don't. I can't remember when I was last so happy. Why leave when we've only just found each other?'

Keith rolled off her with a sigh and reached for his cigarettes. 'Your mother saw us tonight, you know. I'm sure she did.'

'I don't care. I gave up worrying what my mother thought about me years ago.' Elizabeth laughed softly. 'I'm fifty-four, for God's sake. So she saw us kissing in the drive. So what? If anything, she should be pleased for me.' She stroked his chest, watching the smoke curl out from between his lips and float towards the window. 'I'm pleased for me,' she whispered, her voice breathy with a neediness she feared but was past disguising.

Keith feared it too. Feared it and relished it. The way she had fallen into his arms on the night of her birthday, a bundle of yearning, still felt extraordinary. Chemistry apart, it was a long time since he had felt the intoxicating empowerment of being wanted. Ever since that first encounter he had felt as if someone had pumped extra air into his trainers, like he was floating instead of working. The dullest, hardest jobs – rehinging the barn door, lacing fresh barbed wire round the vegetable garden – had felt sweet and effortless, as if something had re-energized his joints as well as his heart. 'I can't stay here, Lizzy. I only meant to help out for a bit. I've got my boys to think of.'

'Let's play a game,' said Elizabeth. She didn't want to think about his boys. She had seen pictures of them, front teeth missing, hair sticking up from broad, innocent foreheads, eyes full of mischief. They were two years apart, he had told her, but could have been twins, with their tufty blond hair and snub noses. She couldn't deny him his boys, couldn't begin to compete with them. If they were the reason he was going, it was fair enough. She would have crossed continents to bring up Roland, walked on water, through fire – anything. Wanting to share in his sons' upbringing only confirmed what she knew already: that her new lover was a good man.

'What game, babe?' Keith stubbed out his cigarette, carefully blowing the last of his smoke away from her towards the open window.

'A truth game.'

'I don't like the sound of that.' He pulled her more tightly into the crook of his arm. 'Do I have to play?'

'Yes, you do. It's what young lovers do . . .'

'Young lovers, that's a laugh.'

Elizabeth giggled, happily aware of her straggling grey hair and unfashionable curves. Keith, she had discovered, liked the light on to make love. He also liked to talk as he touched her, asking her if she was enjoying what he was doing, telling her how good she felt and tasted. There was nowhere to hide – no room for shyness – and it was fantastic. It made her wonder how she had put up with Colin, who only reached for her if he was in a good mood, or Lucien, who liked to be drunk, or Richard, who kept his eyes closed and ground his teeth as he came, then gave reprimanding pats to the swell of her stomach afterwards, as if he liked her in spite of the way she was rather than because of it. 'You ask each other questions and have to tell the absolute truth when you answer. I'll go first. What's your favourite colour?'

Keith chuckled. 'Begin easy, eh? Blue . . . blue, like your eyes.' He pushed the hair off her face and planted a kiss on each eyelid.

'That's cheating – and distracting. One answer only. Your turn.'

'Hmm . . . what's your favourite food?'

'Toad-in-the-hole with peas and mash and baked beans.'

Keith roared with laughter. 'That's great. I like that. Better still, I can *cook* it.'

'What are you most afraid of?' said Elizabeth next, very quickly, while he was still laughing.

'Ah, in for the kill now, are we?' He sucked in his cheeks and blew out his breath, which smelt sweet from the orange juice he had been drinking. 'That's a tough one. I'm not sure.'

'I'm going to have to hurry you,' she teased, taking a sip of the white wine he had poured on her arrival, noting happily that it was warm from neglect and thinking that falling in love was a bit like getting drunk: euphoria, dizziness, laughing at tiny things . . . but without the price of a headache. No wonder people said it made the world go round. Keith had surprised her by opting for orange juice. He hadn't had a drink for years, he had admitted, giving her a look that had made her curious to know more, to peel off his layers, unwrap him like a parcel, get to the core of him. 'Come on,' she urged now, getting impatient. 'I know what scares me.'

'What?'

'Being alone.' Elizabeth breathed deeply, feeling less afraid already as she released the confession. Keith might go north to be near his children, but he wasn't leaving the planet. They would work something out.

'Mine is . . . being found out.'

'Found out?' Elizabeth laughed, happy and incredulous. 'In what way?'

'As a bad person . . . someone who never did the right thing.'

Elizabeth let out a dismissive whoop. 'That's mad given that doing the right thing is clearly your forte –'

'It's not, Lizzy, it's not,' he interrupted, his voice low and urgent.

Elizabeth felt his arm stiffen under her head. 'Keith, what is it?' She sat up, wanting to look at him, wanting to read his expression and fathom the urgency, but he had swung away from her, planting his feet on the floor and facing the window so that all she could see was his bare back. There was a scar, she noticed, a faded silvery snake curling in from the tuck of his waist and down to the cleft of his bottom. She reached to touch it, delighting in yet another discovery, but he flinched. 'Keith, what is it?' she said again.

He got off the bed, slipped a towel round his waist and went to the window.

'Look it's just a silly game, I'm sorry I started it . . . The last thing I wanted was to upset you. I just wanted us to get to know each other better.'

He glanced at her over his shoulder, with an expression so forlorn, so haggard, that Elizabeth let out a cry of dismay both in compassion and at her own foolishness. She didn't yet know him, nor could hope to do so by firing a few questions at him. Knowing someone took months – years – of sharing and effort. 'Keith, I've been an idiot. Forgive me.'

'No, you haven't. You Harrisons think the best of people. Why do you do that?' He pressed both hands against the wall and dropped his head between his arms. 'I'm going to tell you why I have to leave this place, Lizzy.' His voice was muffled, directed at the floor. 'It's a . . .' he made a growling sound '. . . a hard thing to do because I like you lot, and when I tell you, you won't like me. But at least you'll understand why I have to leave. At least things will be . . . clear between us.' He sighed, shaking his head and raising his gaze to the moon, which glowed still, like a perfect pearl on a dark cushion. 'We . . . I should never have let things get this far . . . I never meant to . . . I just liked you and . . .'

'And I like you,' Elizabeth wailed. 'Oh, please, don't tell me anything you don't want to, Keith. I never meant to pry or make you so unhappy. Please, let's enjoy –'

'I ran over a child. Coming home from the pub, soon after June and I moved to London. I ran over a child and I didn't stop. She appeared from nowhere, between two parked cars. Dark hair, dark clothes, I never saw her. There was just this noise, a weird soft noise – nothing, really – and then she was in the air. I saw her land, her head at a bad angle – I knew it was a bad angle – and I drove away. I drove home and June made me a cup of tea and asked how the pub had been, and I said I hadn't liked it much and wouldn't go there again.'

'No, Keith, no . . .'

'The police found me anyway because I'd shot a red light and they caught it on film. A witness said it wasn't my fault, that the girl had run out into the road, which was true but, still, I could – I should – have avoided her. I should, above all, have *stopped*.' He turned to face her, leaning his head against the wall and crossing his arms. 'I got two years. June made a few visits, then left. I didn't – I don't – blame her. I'd have killed one of my own sons rather than that little girl. She was ten years old, her parents were Pakistani . . . an only child apparently. I tried to see them after I got out but they had left the country. I stayed in London, got odd jobs, tried to keep my head together . . . even had counselling for a while – six sessions, courtesy

233

of the NHS. Are you getting all this, Lizzy? Are you seeing where it's going?' he snarled, reaching for another cigarette and watching her intently as he lit it and inhaled. All he could see of Elizabeth now were her eyes, wide and horrified. She had drawn the bedclothes round her, as if trying to protect herself from his words . . . protect herself from him, of course, as he had known she would. Even without the niece – that dreadful, extraordinary parallel revealed to him unwittingly by Cassie four months before – her reaction would have been the same. He had killed a child and run away. No matter that it had ruined his life – that the crime had indeed proved to be the punishment – he had still done it, branding himself untouchable in the process.

'The funny thing was,' he continued, feeling almost relaxed now, but manically so, as in his sessions with the counsellor when it all poured out like the vomit it truly was, 'bumping into Steve after all those years felt like a turning-point. He'd had a crap deal as a kid and there he was, polished and success-ful, different clothes, different accent, a different man. And I thought, I can be different too, turn myself round. I felt *inspired*.' He laughed, the sound thick with self-recrimination and smoke. 'When I first heard about Tina – from Cassie – I felt even better. I thought, Here's a chance to do some good, to help put things right. That's why I took this job – that, and being sort of *curious*, I suppose, wanting to see the other side . . . I mean, how the fuck do people get over losing a kid, Lizzy? How? And then I get here and it's unreal – saving the old bird, the kindness, the gratitude, it made – it makes – me want to throw up, because I don't deserve it, because I'm a fraud and –'

'Serena and Charlie must never know,' said Elizabeth, sitting up and drawing her knees into her chest. 'As for me, it changes nothing.'

'What?'

234

'It changes nothing,' she repeated, dropping the side of her head on to her knees and staring at him. 'I can see now why you want to leave, but even if you do, my feelings . . . they . . .' she wrapped her arms round her shins '. . . they remain the same.'

'Bloody hell,' Keith murmured, picking up his packet of cigarettes and putting them down again, not knowing what to say, what to do, where to look, even. 'You can't mean that,' he gasped at last, 'you can't be sure . . .'

'I've never been more sure of anything in my life,' said Elizabeth, simply. 'How you deal with that is up to you.'

Ed saw the light on in the barn as he crossed the drive. He paused, toying vaguely with the notion of taking Keith up on his offer of a beer and during the course of it telling him everything. The man was all right, he knew that now, not just because he'd risked his neck in the lake when it turned out he couldn't even swim but because he'd seen Ed late, drinking or smoking, countless times and Ed had known he wouldn't say a thing. He watched, sometimes in an almost spooky way, but he was always kind and solid, like it would never cross his mind to *judge* what he saw, unlike all the other adults Ed knew, who spent their lives passing judgement about things being good or bad or disappointing, like they had some secret agenda for how every kid ought to be to pass muster as a human being.

Above the roof of the barn, the moon shone like a golden eye; a spying eye, Ed decided, shivering a little as he turned his back on the house and set off down the lane. He was still a little drunk. Three beers with Jessica and a load of vodka after getting home, it was little wonder. He had been lying on the floor by the drinks cabinet in the dining room when his grandmother had stumbled on him, bottle in hand and cabinet door open in the hope that he might be able to conceal the evidence of his wantonness should the need arise. Except that when his grandmother's thin, stockinged calves had come into view, moving slowly, cautiously between the table and chair legs, Ed had been too slow and drunk to do anything much except sit up, groan and then laugh at his own ineptitude. Without the laughter he suspected his grandmother might have let him off but, as it was, she bristled and tutted, then turned on her heel for the telephone. Ed remained slumped on the dining-room carpet, trying to consider his options, but managing only to see all the images he had hoped the vodka would hide: Jessica showing off the new barrel of her belly, the popping buttons of her skirt, wheedling for affection one minute and hurling abuse the next, threatening to tell her mum – his mum – and then sobbing that she wouldn't do anything he didn't want, that she loved him to death and was his to command. Except for having an abortion . . . There would be no commanding there. It was their baby, she said, and she wanted it. A schoolfriend had had a kid, she said, and it was really cute and nice. *Cute* and *nice*? Ed had found himself stumped and powerless at the sheer inanity – the absolute understatement – of the words. A baby would make her happy, she claimed, even if he kept away and only sent money and never loved her. Come what may, she was going through with it.

So, when Pamela had returned with the phone, holding it out to him like a baton, all Ed could think to tell his father was that he needed money, if not for Jessica then for himself, so that he could get away. And when his father yelled and scolded, saying he would receive nothing, Ed had settled upon the idea of leaving anyway. Broke or not – he had forty-four pounds and thirty-two pence in his bank account – his imagination had stalled at the point where he could think of no other course to take. It would solve nothing, of course. He was leaving a time-bomb ticking, but at least he wouldn't be around when it exploded.

Ed walked quickly down the lane, grateful that in the moon-light he could avoid the sludgiest puddles. He tried not to think of how eerie the trees were, or where he was going or what might happen. Instead he remembered a time when he had run away as a little boy. A time before Tina, when his sisters must have been about ten and they were spending the summer holidays – as they always did in those days – at Ashley House with their grandparents and cousins. He couldn't remember the cause of his complaint, only his burning outrage. He had taken a KitKat and a carton of juice and run down the lane, flying and furious, only to take fright at the main road and run all the way back to hide in one of the barns. He had hidden and waited . . . waited with mounting hope that he would be found, while outrage gave way to hunger. Eventually, after what had felt like hours, he had crept back to the house, only to find that no one had registered his absence. A different outrage had descended then, which prompted him to seek out his mother. 'I ran away,' he sobbed, 'and you didn't notice.' She had hugged him hard and said she was on the point of noticing and would have found him, no matter what.

Something hooted to Ed's left and he started to run, his bulging rucksack thudding against his back. He didn't like to think of his mother, or her text, or the brief two words he had scribbled on a piece of paper next to his bed. *Don't worry.* Of course they would worry, but he didn't want them to find him, not this time.

July

On the way to the park Keith stopped at the newsagent's to buy cigarettes and a paper for himself and a couple of bottles of Coca-Cola for the boys. They insisted on having crisps too, even though June had said no snacks in case they ruined their appetites for lunch.

'Okay, but not a word to your mother,' he warned, dangling the packets out of reach till they had agreed, relishing the simple pleasure of buying them something they wanted even if it led to trouble. They skipped along at his heels munching happily, then raced ahead when the playground came into view, shouting taunts at each other as they dodged buggies and toddlers and old ladies enjoying the sunshine.

Keith parked himself on a nearby bench and flicked through the paper to the jobs page, as he had every morning of the week since his return to Hull. His sister had promised to ask around on his behalf, but it would be tough, he knew. Building and decorating always went dead in the summer. People were already in the thick of having work done or too busy saving for their holidays to want to start. He studied each advert intently, hopes high, telling himself to keep an open mind, that any form of paid employment would be better than benefits and the lumpy discomfort of Irene's sofa. Soon, however, he was skimming the small print, puffing disconsolately at a cigarette. Computer skills was all people wanted, these days. He could hardly work his sister's DVD-player, let alone a computer. His mobile was so old the boys had complained that he should get a new one with a flip-up screen, loads of games and a camera. One like Barry's, they said. Keith had replied that he liked the one he had and, anyway, his fingers were too big to work the buttons on a smaller pad – anything to avoid conceding inferiority to Barry who was June's new property-developer boyfriend; he had thick hairy wrists, a Rolex and a smile that felt like a punch in the nose.

'Hey, are those two yours?'

Keith lowered his newspaper, glancing from the woman who had spoken to his sons. They were attempting to climb the wrong way up the slide, tugging at each other's T-shirts in a bid to be the first to the top. Peering down from the platform above them, more angry than afraid, was a doll-like creature with blonde ringlets and small gold loops in her ears. 'Craig, Neil, stop that! Can't you see there's a little girl trying to get down?' When they ignored him Keith stood up and slapped his newspaper against his thigh, so hard he felt the sting through his jeans. 'I said, get off,' he yelled, trembling with anger, because he had no computer skills, he missed Elizabeth, and his sons, despite his love for them, seemed so obstinately disconnected from him that he thought sometimes they might as well have done a runner – like Ed Harrison, whose selfish bolt had cast such a dreadful shadow over Keith's last days at Ashley House. Serena had carried her son's note with her everywhere, keeping it up her sleeve, pulling it out to show to members of the family, and to the young policeman who had called to ask questions, unfurling it each time like an ancient treasure that might crumble upon exposure to the world.

Engaged in the mental preparation of leaving the Harrisons, Keith had felt the pull of her unhappiness with an intensity that bordered on resentment. He had his own troubles – he didn't need theirs. Yet when Serena had asked him to use what remaining time he had to help in the search he had thrown himself into the task, trawling country lanes and nearby towns at a snail's speed, peering over hedgerows and into the hooded faces of loitering youngsters, certain that it was futile, yet unable to resist trying. When Roland, quiet but as desperate as the rest, had said he suspected something had been going on between Ed and Jessica Blake, Keith had rushed to visit Sid, persuaded the old man to phone his daughter in London, then spoken to Maureen himself, only to be told curtly that Ed Harrison had never shown his face at their flat and neither did she expect him to. When he asked for Jessica, Maureen had said wasn't her word good enough, and put the phone down.

'I've lost them all,' murmured Serena, when he returned empty-handed. 'All my children . . . all gone.' Charlie had taken the week off work to deal with the crisis and put his arm round her. Catching Keith's eye, he had reminded her gently that their son was nearly eighteen and long overdue for rebellion. When Serena shook off the arm he had shot Keith a pleading look. 'Isn't that right, Keith? Teenage rebellion takes many forms, doesn't it?'

Keith had agreed heartily, then fled to the barn to pack, cursing under his breath, as he flung clothes out of drawers, at the hopelessness of the situation and his inescapable urge to help.

Later that evening Elizabeth had found him sitting on his bed staring at the photo of his boys, a tell-tale heap of cigarette butts in the ashtray. Since the night of his confession he had done his best to avoid her, hiding behind a flurry of finishing-off jobs and the drama of Ed's disappearance. 'The other night,' she said now, 'what you told me about the little Pakistani girl . . . Like I said, it doesn't change anything.'

Keith had looked at her sadly, knowing from the defeat in her voice that she had come to realize that, noble as such sentiments sounded, words were powerless; that what he had told her had, indeed, changed everything. There was no hope for their relationship with such an ignoble secret at its heart, not with a family as close as hers. Even without the new trauma of Ed, which had so clearly – so painfully – cast Serena back into her earlier, more terrible bereavement, it would have been unthinkable. That Elizabeth believed her feelings strong enough to override the situation – to forgive him – was irrelevant. The truth was that Keith still hadn't – and probably never could – forgiven himself. Seeking atonement in volunteering his limited skills to the Harrisons seemed in retrospect so laughably naïve that he blushed to think of it. Getting close to such a family had only made him more painfully aware of the damage he had inflicted on himself and the Pakistani couple, who had sat so silently in court, heads bent, hands clasped like the one remaining link in a broken chain. He could never make up for what he had done, Keith knew that now. All he could do was live with it and try, for ever after, to do the right thing, beginning with being around for his boys, creating something from the rubble of his own family. It would be like building a wall, one brick, then another. Every task, every journey, no matter how huge, began with a single step.

'I'm sorry if I've made you sad,' he said at length. 'I never meant to. But you're stronger than you think. And that lot,' he jerked his thumb in the direction of the main house, 'they need you more than I do. Roland needs you. So let's end as we began – with a hug – and be done with it. I'm leaving early tomorrow . . . I won't see you.'

'Oh, Keith . . .'

'Don't speak.' He had held her tightly, wishing he could squeeze the choke out of her voice. 'I'm going and that's the end of it. It's for the best.'

'Nice to have a bit of sun, isn't it?'

Lost in thought, Keith started. His cigarette had burnt down to the cork and put itself out without him noticing. The woman, clearly having forgiven him for his haphazard parenting, had sat down on the bench. 'All that bleeding rain . . . They say there's more on the way too, that we should make the most of this.' She snorted. 'English bloody summers, don't you love them?'

Keith was in no mood for conversation, but he smiled and nodded, then glanced at his watch. The woman gave him a puzzled look and got out her mobile phone, at which point Keith's own phone rang inside his pocket. Thinking – because she had been in his mind – that it might be Elizabeth, breaking the silence on which he himself had insisted, Keith sprang up from the bench to take the call. But it wasn't Elizabeth, it was Stephen.

'Is there news?' asked Keith at once, disappointment subsiding with the instant hope that his friend might have something positive to report on the Ed front. Popping into Camden *en route* up north, he had made Stephen promise to inform him of any developments, knowing that otherwise he would only succumb to temptation and call Ashley House or Elizabeth himself.

'Nah. Bloody kid. They're all sick with worry. Selfish brat. I know what I'd do if I came across him.'

'And have you seen the family at all? Do you know how they are?'

'No, we've been too busy – that is, Cassie's been too busy, working weekends, out and about all the time, and if she's in she's buried in paperwork or guest lists or dress designs for bridesmaids. I – we're sort of hanging on for the big holiday, to be honest.'

'Big holiday?'

'Umbria next month. Peter and Helen have booked a seven-bedroomed villa for the entire family.' Stephen, who was sitting in a deckchair in the garden, reading through a section of his manuscript, checked himself. Umbria, he realized suddenly, was a far cry from Hull. How ridiculous he had been to tie himself in knots about Keith and the Harrisons when there were so many more important things to worry about. 'So, anyway,' he continued quickly, 'what with all that's happened, Charlie and Serena are threatening to pull out, which would be mad, especially as Elizabeth has offered to stay behind . . .'

'Has she? That's nice of her . . . bloody nice . . . and she's okay is she – Elizabeth?'

'I think so,' said Stephen, sounding sufficiently puzzled for Keith to rush on with inquiries as to the health of every other member of the family. He was even more glad in retrospect that knowledge of their brief liaison hadn't become public. Elizabeth might not care what her family thought, but he certainly did. Given the off-stage shambles of his life, the Harrisons' belief in him – their sadness at his decision to leave – meant a lot, an awful lot. 'Blimey,' remarked Stephen, in a voice that was not altogether pleasant, 'and there was me thinking you'd have had enough of the Harrisons to last a lifetime. At least, that's what you said when you came by last week.'

'Did I?' murmured Keith, wondering suddenly, and with great sadness, where the easy companionship of their childhood had gone. Six months had passed since their 'rediscovery' of each other in the bookshop and still they were no better than strangers. He felt he'd tried hard enough but Stephen, he saw, had not let down the barriers. Keith found it hard to imagine why this should be. As children they had looked out for each other, pricking fingers to share their blood, uniting against boredom and bullies alike. A new wardrobe, a new haircut, a healthy bank balance shouldn't affect that sort of bond, surely?

'Actually, it was because of that that I rang . . . at least partly . . . You see . . .' Stephen cleared his throat. He had spent more time planning the phone conversation than working on his notes yet, poised now at the purpose of his call, his courage was failing. 'The thing is, I have a dilemma and I could do with your help.'

'Really?' Keith exclaimed, unable to keep the pleasure from his voice. Maybe there was something of the old closeness, after all. Maybe he should tell him about Elizabeth, get some of the ache off his chest. 'Fire away, anything for an old pal.'

'What I have to say is in total confidence, you understand.'

'Of course,' agreed Keith, eagerly, moving so that he could keep an eye on the boys, who had traded the thrills of the playground for a wrestling match on a square of grass next to the playground.

Stephen tucked the phone tightly to his ear and lowered his voice. 'It's Cassie . . . she . . . I think she might be seeing someone else.'

'Are you sure?' Keith laughed, incredulous.

'No. That's the trouble, I'm not sure. But I need to *be* sure and I wondered if you knew anyone who could – it's just that otherwise I'm left with the *Yellow Pages* and any dope can put an ad in there.'

'Hang on a minute.' Keith laughed again, but with less delight. 'Let me get this right. You want to *spy* on your fiancée and you're asking me to recommend a man for the job?'

'Or a woman.' Stephen was too relieved to have got out his request to pay much attention to the edge in Keith's voice.

'For Christ's sake, why don't you just ask her?'

It was Stephen's turn to laugh. 'Because she'd deny it, wouldn't she? I mean, I already have – sort of – and she's said no.'

'Maybe she's telling the truth.'

'*Maybe* being the operative word. Look, all I'm saying is give it some thought.'

'No, I won't. It's sick. If you don't trust her you shouldn't be marrying her.'

'Blimey! Well, thank *you* for your support. And there was me thinking we were old mates . . .'

'Yeah, I thought so too for a while, but you've been weird from the start, behaving a lot of the time like I was *intruding* on your patch. It took me a while to see it because I'm a daft bastard. And I was down on my luck and you looked like you'd found everything a guy could hope for and I guess that stopped me seeing clearly. Well, I'm seeing clearly now, all right, so, as your *mate*, I'll tell you that you're a lucky bastard and that if you're having doubts about marrying Cassie Harrison you should be talking to her about them not me.' He disconnected the call.

Craig had started crying. Neil was hovering next to him sheepishly. They were both spattered with mud from the grass, which had looked verdant but was so sodden that Keith, hurrying over to them, felt it squelch under his trainers. 'Hey, you two.' He crouched down and pulled them close.

'He *hurt* my arm,' sobbed Craig, scowling at his elder brother. 'I *hate* him.'

'No, you don't. Here, let's have a look . . . Hmm, do you think it could still carry an ice-cream or is it too hurt for that?'

'Yeah . . . it could . . . I think.'

'Okay, well, the deal is you have to say sorry, Neil, and then you both have to be friends, because brothers should always be friends. We'll go to the ice-cream van, then we're going to play footie with that ball over there, which someone has conveniently left for us, and then you'll go back to your mum's for lunch.'

When June opened the door an hour later, all three hung their heads, chocolate smears round their mouths and mud clods on their clothes and shoes, like guilty accomplices. Keith looked up first, his expression defiant. 'We found a football and had a great time.'

'So I see.' She folded her arms. 'You'll have to take those off for a start,' she pointed at the boys' footwear, 'and go straight up for a bath.'

'Thanks,' muttered Keith, kissing the tops of his sons' heads as they were ushered inside.

'Barry doesn't play football,' she said, offering him a half-smile before she closed the door.

Jessica was lying in the bath when she heard the door slam. She lay very still, listening to the sound of her mother's heels clack along the lino, praying she had only popped in to pick something up. It was Friday morning, her day for cleaning at Mrs Dawson's in Pelham Road, usually a five-hour stint, although she brought the ironing back sometimes if she was running late. The footsteps sounded purposeful. Jessica sank deeper into the water, her hopes rising. She'd run a hot bath, the hottest she could bear. Her feet were already blotchy and pink, and there was a clear line at the top of her arms – like a sunburn mark – indicating where the water reached. She'd read a magazine article once about a woman who'd got rid of her baby by drinking a pint of gin and jumping into a boiling hot bath. There had been some business about a knitting needle too, which Jessica didn't want to think about. Just the idea of the gin made her feel queasy, but there wasn't any in the flat, just a solitary can of Boddington's, which she hadn't been able to bring herself to drink, not at eleven in the morning when she was feeling dodgy anyway. Getting the bath so hot had been an experiment more than anything, like challenging Fate to say, 'Okay, here's a helping hand if you need it.' Yet thinking through the consequences made Jessica feel even sicker. She'd heard about miscarriages often enough, but never before imagined what they looked like, how one got rid of whatever came out, how much of it there would be. She wasn't good with blood. A nosebleed almost made her faint.

The footsteps came out of the kitchen, receded towards the front door, then grew louder – and much brisker too, as brisk as Jessica's beating heart. A moment later the door handle was twisting this way and that, like it had a life of its own.

'Are you in there?'

Jessica put the flannel over her mouth and sucked out the water through her teeth.

'I know you're in there, so there's no point in pretending. I've had that head of yours on the phone – again. Why aren't you at school? Jess . . . you are in there, aren't you?' She sounded less shrill suddenly, much more uncertain. 'Come on, love, talk to your mum.'

'I didn't feel well,' Jessica snapped. 'And school's a waste of time cos I've messed up all the exams anyway and I'm leaving the stinking place for ever in two weeks.'

'Are you going to open this door, or what?'

'No, I'm not. Piss off.'

'Well, that's nice, isn't it, with me trying to find out if you're okay? You can piss off too, for all I care, the way you've been acting lately.' There was a final vigorous rattle of the door handle followed by steps clomping back down the hall and the angry thwack of the front door.

Jessica shouted, 'Fuck you,' after it, then closed her eyes only to find tears streaming out of them, mingling with the perspiration on her cheeks. The bath was hot – too hot, she realized, sobbing quietly as she heaved herself out and reached for the grey towel, which was still damp from her mother having used it that morning. She pressed her face into it, breathing in the damp mildewy smell in a bid to banish both the tears and the dizziness, which she knew soon – any minute – would convert itself into the need to throw up. The only thing that stopped the puking was food, but there was only a couple of yoghurts and a lump of rock-hard cheese in the fridge and she'd eaten so much lately to suppress the sickness that she feared all the thickening round her belly was nothing to do with a baby, just flab.

She unlocked and opened the door to let in some air, then sat down on the loo, pulling the towel round her like a cape and using a corner to wipe her nose. She wasn't normally one for crying. She despised girls who turned on the waterworks all the time to get what they wanted. But since getting pregnant she'd found she wanted to bawl her eyes out most days, especially when she was alone and not having to pretend that everything was okay and normal, nothing to worry about but finding a decent job on no qualifications, and how to stop Jerry pawing her every time she had to go to the store room. 'You started it, you little tart,' he had hissed the last time, his breath all fishy and vile, making her feel so bad that she'd let him have a grope, saying eventually that she had to go back into the salon. He was right, she had started it, back in the days – centuries ago – when she had thought sex was a laugh, a bit of fun, a way of getting what you wanted, getting noticed – like landing the job in the salon, or wearing a short skirt to waitress at the old aunt's funeral and letting the hem ride up to her knicker-line when Ed's uncle Peter drove her to the station. She had seen the old man looking, felt the heat of his interest, a sucker for a bit of flesh, like all blokes. She'd even considered taking it further, offering more, just to see where it would lead, show the old geezer that he wasn't so different as he imagined. It was the thought of Ed that had stopped her, poor Ed, freezing his bollocks off in the car park. And she had been so glad of that later, when the pair of them got together properly at last and the sex hadn't seemed like a laugh but something deep and fantastic, and as romantic as anything she'd ever seen in a film. Who could blame her for not wanting to ruin it by asking if he had a condom? They were ugly, stupid things. When the biology teacher had put one on a banana Jessica and her mate Sue had almost wet themselves laughing. Letting Ed think she was on the pill had been so much easier and hadn't felt risky: getting pregnant after one screw – what were the chances of that? She'd got away with it before, after all.

Jessica lifted the lid of the toilet and got her head within reach of the bowl just in time. She'd had a cup of tea earlier so at least it was more than retching, though she couldn't stop crying while she was doing it and ended up with the taste of sick up her nose. After she'd finished she rinsed her mouth and padded into her bedroom to lie down. She checked her phone, which she had left charging, hoping as always that there was something from Ed. When there wasn't she read his last message several times, though she knew it by heart already. 'I've left home to think things through. Don't worry, I will take care of everything, whatever you decide. Please say nothing to anyone until you have heard from me. Ed xx' She liked the way he'd written it in full words like a letter, and how he'd signed it too, with two kisses, like he really cared, after all.

Jessica kissed the smeary little screen and turned on to her side clutching it to her chest. She could feel the sleepiness descending like a hammer-blow, as it always did now, like she was drugged. She wanted badly to give in to it. Being asleep was the only time she felt okay, or rather, felt nothing, which amounted to the same thing. Yet this time the worry wouldn't let her go. All her life she had worked at not caring about things, not letting the crap get to her. But now the not caring was like this paper-thin outside of her, while underneath she felt like she was hurting all over. She didn't *know* anything any more – what she cared about, what she really wanted, what to do. She had never meant to sling out the news to Ed about her being pregnant as she had, firing it like a missile. She had envisaged something much softer and better, *sharing* it gently, and then Ed being loving and concerned, and the two of them talking it through like a proper couple. It was him trying to end things that had done it, casting her off like she was a piece of rubbish, like he could just stuff her into the bin when he'd had enough. She had wanted to shock him, hurt him but, above all, to keep him.

Of course it would be sensible to get an abortion. Three months was the deadline everybody talked about for that, and she was only just into the fourth, so she still could presumably. It would make Ed happy, but she'd lose him just the same. On top of that, Jessica honestly wasn't sure how she felt about abortion. Blood and doctors and pain, all to get rid of a little life? It didn't seem right. Sometimes, blocking out the crap, she could picture herself with a pushchair and a baby with tufty hair in cute outfits and her being a great mum and Ed coming round and the pair of them making something of it together, something patchy maybe, but good. With him being a Harrison there would be money, so it wouldn't be like when she was little, her mum raising her on benefits in a string of mouldy flats shared with whatever bit of scum happened to be passing, all of it tacky and difficult, full of shouting, and her, Jessica, in the middle, feeling always like the *reason* for all the problems. No, it wouldn't be like that at all, not with Ed. And what else had she to look forward to anyway, except some lousy job and hoping to find someone else as rich and handsome and funny? Fat chance. Better to dig in with what she had, see it through, wherever it took her.

Aware of something stirring in her stomach, Jessica pulled back the towel and stared at the moist pink bulge of her belly. It was too early, surely, for the baby to move. She tensed, wide awake suddenly. If it was moving then it really was too late. You couldn't kill something so alive – you just couldn't. In a panic now, Jessica gripped her phone and wrote a message to Ed. 'I need u 2 call. Can't keep this secret 4ever.' As she typed the last word, an acrid bubble of air belched out of her and the tension in her belly eased. Indigestion. But she sent the message anyway. Ed couldn't hide for ever. Neither, in spite of her past threats, did she want to spill the beans about their situation without him at her side. He was all she had. However her future turned out, he would be a part of it.

Driving past the churchyard as she left the village, Serena glanced over the wall at the familiar zigzagging lines of headstones pitched at different angles in the sloping grass, their patches of lichen gleaming in the midday sun like swatches of green velvet. Charlie, back at work, had made a big to-do of the blue sky that morning, clapping his hands as he drew back the curtains, as if the respite to the damp summer offered hope for them too. Serena had pulled the duvet up to her eyes, unmoved either by the weather or her husband's efforts to be cheerful. He would cut the grass over the weekend, he declared, maybe even make a start that evening as it was Friday, get a grip on things. What were her plans? Uncertain even of her grip on the duvet, Serena had murmured that she had none, beyond an invitation to lunch from Elizabeth, which she was thinking of cancelling, and a trawl round the supermarket for food.

'Lunch with Lizzy? That's nice. Send her my love.' He had swung his tie round his neck, then asked for help with a cufflink, holding out his arm like a challenge for her to move, show some sign of normal marital affection. Serena had responded without eye-contact, struggling with the stiffness of the cuff, which Pamela, who got to the ironing pile before her, these days, had over-starched.

'Do you think he will ever come back?' she whispered, letting his arm drop so abruptly that a glimmer of hurt flashed across Charlie's face.

He tweaked the cufflink. 'Of *course* he'll come back. You heard the police – they've seen this sort of thing a thousand times. Money, food, home comforts – he'll be back.'

'But why did he leave?'

Charlie turned away to tug open the curtains and hook the tie-backs round to keep them in position. Bathed in morning sunshine, the South Downs looked blue and huge, as if a bank of water was rolling across the fields, preparing to swallow them whole. 'As to why he left, there's no point in going through all that again.'

Serena sat up, latching with some gratitude on to the anger that had risen like bile in the back of her throat. It was never far away now, especially where her husband was concerned. It was a new, disturbing state of being, but something to hold on to. 'Well, I want to go through it again. Why did he leave? What did we do wrong? Other than not return when he needed us.'

'Oh, here we go! I might have known! You don't want to discuss Ed at all. You want to beat me about the head *again* for daring to tell him not to behave like a drunken imbecile. For daring to behave like any decent father.' Charlie snatched his suit jacket off the bedroom chair and made for the door. 'Even if we *had* come straight back from the hotel he would have been long gone . . . at least that's what my mother reckons, isn't it? And anyway,' he continued, regrouping quickly, 'if my telling-off triggered Ed's departure then he's got even more to learn than I thought. I'd do the same thing again, I tell you, the bloody *same*.'

'How can you say that? How *can* you?'

Charlie, half out of the door, glanced longingly at the spindles of the banisters marking the start of the stairs at the end of the landing. A few strides and he would be safely out of the front door, cushioning himself from this hateful reality with a CD in the car, the paper on the train, meetings and phone calls and all the other blissfully impersonal, absorbing demands of the office. Just as he had when Tina died. What they were going through now was so resonant of those days it was impossible to ignore. Yet it was worse too, as anything bad a second time round was worse and because Serena hadn't been hostile then: she had closed down like an animal in hibernation, doing only what had been necessary to survive, adapting to the grief as if it were a new element in which she had to learn to live. It had been hard on him – on all of them – but this . . . This was in another league, like fighting on a cliff-edge, sick with the knowledge that they were adversaries when they should have been allies. She had been fragile all year, Charlie knew, but hadn't he done his best? Just as he had with Ed. He felt wretched about his son's absence, more wretched than he could express to

Serena or anyone else. It riled him beyond words that she seemed unprepared to acknowledge this, that she was instead busy taking this crisis – as she took every crisis, he reflected bleakly – and trying to make it hers. But Ed *had* needed that talking-to, no matter how his mother tried now to twist things, he bloody had. And even when he turned up, as Charlie was sure he would, nothing – no amount of joy and relief – would make him stand down from believing that.

'The truth is,' continued Serena, her voice tremulous now, the tears not far away, 'we have failed as a family.'

Charlie groaned, dropping his head against the door.

'We have, Charlie. We have. First Tina . . . that was bad enough – *my* failure, if you like – but then taking up the reins of Ashley House, trying for the fresh start, trying to keep everyone together, we've failed at that too. I mean, what with your mother . . .' Serena swallowed, though her mouth was dry. 'And then there's Helen, she hates coming here, while Peter behaves as if he owns the place, as if he is so *superior* to you . . . and you just *let* him. Nobody knows who's in charge any more or where they're going. Elizabeth's a disaster, her birthday was a disaster. Maisie's gone, Clem's gone, Ed's gone. We couldn't even persuade a handyman to stay with us. At this rate we might as well give the house back to Peter because there'll be no one left in our family to run the place. It's all a *mess*, a fucking mess, and it's our fault,' she wailed, burying her face in her hands.

Charlie went to sit on the bed with a heavy sigh and handed her his handkerchief. 'Maisie will be back in September. Clem is only in London. The various travails of the rest of the family are not our fault.' He patted her head, but without conviction. There was too much distance between them for him to believe any longer in his capacity to offer comfort. He was too much a part of what she was railing against, too much the enemy. 'As for handing this place back to my brother, believe me, the thought has crossed my mind more than once. Peter is not only considerably wealthier and wiser, but in possession of a son who shows some kind of willingness to behave like a responsible adult . . . Look, I've got to go or I'll miss my train.' He felt exhausted suddenly, all the fight gone out of him. 'See Elizabeth, it will do you good. Ed will come back. He's asserting himself, being a teenager, blind as they all bloody well are to anybody's feelings but their own.'

Trembling at the recollection of the argument, Serena pulled up on to the grass verge that ran along the church wall and got out of the car. The same sun is shining on Ed, she thought, squinting at the sky and trying to imagine where her son might be, what secret venom had turned him against them. Charlie was wrong – they had failed. Misery had made her overstate things, but the kernel of truth was there. No secure, well-loved child ran away, no matter how selfish. And the family had been falling apart all year, scrabbling for a foothold, a direction – she had been aware of it for months, in spite of Charlie's efforts to reassure her. The only truly decent, joyful thing to happen in ages had been Cassie's engagement. Serena moved closer to the wall, resting her forearms on the warm stone and seeking solace in the prospect of the wedding: pin-stripes and top hats, a crisp frosty morning, Ed adorably handsome in a hired morning suit, Clem and Maisie reluctant but radiant brides-maids, Cassie at the centre of it all, buzzing around in a cloud of white lace like a queen bee at a flower. Maybe they would all feel some sort of proper cohesion then; maybe it was just what they needed.

The images shimmered inside Serena's head, refusing to form clearly, as if they were too fictional to materialize, even in the wide universe of her mind. At the same time a dim bell rang deeper inside her consciousness – a bell relating to Cassie. Her phone message, of course, on that terrible Saturday night in the hotel. *Could I talk to you . . . urgently? . . . I need to meet, just to talk* . . . Serena slapped the wall, irritated and even a little afraid that she should have forgotten such a thing. In the aftermath of Ed's disappearance Charlie had called round to alert the family. She hadn't spoken to anyone but Pamela, Elizabeth, Charlie, and hapless, gormless boy-policemen for days. Serena pulled out her phone, then put it away again. She was already late for Elizabeth, and she didn't want to use her mobile in case Ed chose that moment to get in touch. Cassie's call had no doubt been about something trivial, she decided, turning back to the car, something about arrangements for the wedding – where to pitch the marquee, whether to have salmon or beef, which field to use for parking. Whatever it was could wait.

Elizabeth had gone to a lot of trouble with the lunch, laying her small kitchen table with mats, wine glasses and linen napkins. She greeted Serena on the doorstep, keeping her arm round her as she stepped inside, as if she was too unstable to cross the threshold alone.

'No news, then?'

Serena shook her head, aware suddenly of how their roles had changed and not liking it much. To have Elizabeth all purposeful and taking care of her felt both peculiar and *wrong*.

'Roland has been calling everyone he can think of to ask if they've heard or seen anything. He says he'll ask around at the station too – he's off up to Clem's on Sunday to show her a couple of his paintings. And Clem's calling everyone she can think of as well – at least, that was what Charlie said.'

'Did he?' murmured Serena bleakly, feeling almost as cut off from the rest of her family as she was from her missing son.

'Anyway, what about his bank account? Can't they trace withdrawals or something?'

'Tried that. He took all his money out on the first day – Chichester apparently.'

'He's working something out,' said Elizabeth, firmly, once

they were sitting at the table in front of steaming plates of lasagne, which had seemed like a good idea when she prepared it that morning but looked now too huge and glutinous for a hot day. 'Something in his head . . . He's just working it through. Or maybe he's mucked up his exams and can't face it,' she added, desperate to trigger some flicker of hope in her sister-in-law's grim expression and thinking, for by no means the first time, how unfair it was that one so kind, so well-intentioned, should be made to suffer so. It had certainly put her own troubles into perspective. Roland was growing up, growing away from her, but at least he was *there*. He would never leave in such a manner, she was certain, and she loved him all the more for that. Since his cousin's disappearance he had been particularly sweet, making an effort to tell her where he was going, what he was thinking, responding as he so often did to needs of which most children would have remained oblivious. And as for Keith . . . Elizabeth gripped her knife and fork, tensing as always as the longing swelled inside. Curiously, the Ed business had helped there too. Not just by offering a distraction but because Keith had been right to point out that her family needed her. She called round at Ashley House most days now, not saying much, but knowing she was helping by being there, doing the odd bit of washing-up and deflecting Pamela, who so far seemed oddly disengaged from the drama, almost as if she didn't want to admit it was going on.

Elizabeth glanced again at Serena's pallid face, recognizing how impossible it would have been to tell her about the little Pakistani girl. Keith had been right there too. It was too pertinent, too dreadful, especially now with her sister-in-law so haunted again, drowning in this new, equally dreadful bereavement.

Elizabeth eased her grip on her cutlery and began to eat steadily, taking dainty sips of her wine as she tried to do these days, so that sometimes the cork went back into the bottle instead of being lobbed straight into the bin. She liked it that Keith had been right. She liked loving someone who was right. 'I thought we could go for a drive after this,' she suggested cheerfully, 'to Chichester – maybe stop at a few hostels and ask some questions. I've got a picture all ready to show them. Look.' She reached behind her for a brown envelope and pulled out a photograph of Ed sitting on the bench in the cloisters at Ashley House, looking towards the camera as if he hoped it might take him more seriously than the rest of the world. 'It's the one Theo took last year when he was doing stills of all the family. Do you remember? Trying out one of his endless lenses . . . Oh dear, oh, Serena, don't cry, please don't cry.' Elizabeth hurried round the table to comfort her. As she did so Roland, still half asleep and dressed only in his boxers, appeared in the doorway. At a nod from his mother, he grabbed the box of tissues that lived by the toaster and put them on the table next to his aunt's plate of untouched food.

'A girl at my school ran away this term,' he ventured, after Serena had blown her nose. 'Turned out she was camping in a shed at the bottom of the garden. She was scared of her A levels, apparently. They've said she doesn't have to do them. She's going to train to be a nanny instead. You only need a few GCSEs for that.'

'There, you see?' exclaimed Elizabeth, smoothing a strand of hair off Serena's forehead. 'Exam pressure, the poor loves, that's all it is.'

'I should get my GCSE results just before Italy,' added Roland, momentarily diverted from the effort of consolation.

'We might not be going to Italy,' countered Elizabeth, quickly. 'If Ed isn't back, we're holidaying at Ashley House instead, remember?'

'If Ed isn't back,' said Serena, quietly, plucking shreds off her tissue as if they were petals on a flower, 'I'm not going

257

anywhere either. I would rather die than go to Umbria still not knowing if he's safe.'

After Serena had left for her lunch with Elizabeth, Pamela put on her wellingtons and took Poppy down the lane. The dog trotted at her heels for a few yards, then darted off in pursuit of a squirrel, emerging from the undergrowth a few minutes later with a fat muddy stick between her teeth.

'I'm not throwing that for you,' said Pamela, crossly, stepping over the stick when the dog, with irrepressible optimism, dropped it at her feet. 'You'll have to find one a lot smaller – and *cleaner*, come to that, silly girl.' Undeterred, Poppy retrieved the stick and bounded on ahead, tail high. Pamela slowed her pace, her feet uncomfortably hot in the wellingtons she had worn because of the still muddy state of the lane, thinking how wonderfully simple pets were, how beyond upsetting or taking offence, how loyal. How unlike human beings, she mused wistfully, as her thoughts turned to her grandson and she began to scour the hedgerows and thickets of brambles, as if Ed might pop out, like a conjuror's rabbit from a hat. In running away, loyalty had been the last thing on the child's mind. Nor would he have paused to contemplate the catastrophic effect on his family of his behaviour. He couldn't have: one glimpse into the parlous state of affairs he had evoked at Ashley House would surely have persuaded him to return. Being privy to the agonies that Serena and Charlie were going through – the endless laments and tail-chasing conversations, the ugly recriminations – was so painful that Pamela had withdrawn to the fringes of the life they shared, busying herself with domestic matters, the ones she could manage, like ironing, polishing the banisters and cleaning the silver. The girl Serena used was nothing like as good as her own dear Betty had been, and always crying off for some reason. There were a million things to do, Pamela had discovered, once one started looking.

She had taken to reserving her own very real anxiety about her missing grandson for Marjorie, whom she had met for lunch a couple of times since their encounter at the hairdresser's and with whom she now conversed regularly on the telephone, usually from within the sealed sanctuary of the study. There was a pragmatism about her friend, which Pamela greatly admired and which, she could see now, she had disregarded during the days when their acquaintance had been enmeshed in their marriages. Sharing fears about Ed's whereabouts with such a sympathetic outsider had the immediate effect of defusing the worst. Ed was almost certainly all right, they had agreed, merely testing boundaries and steeling himself to turn up soon enough like a bad penny. Pamela had found herself admitting how much this particular grandson reminded her of Eric, John's elder brother, who had been a lovable rogue and lived life dangerously, appearing on doorsteps with gifts and smiles just when everyone had given up on him. She had even told Marjorie about the affair she had had with Eric early in her marriage, how passionate they had felt but how right it had been to give each other up. Marjorie had said Geoffrey had fallen for someone else too and how forgiving him had been the hardest – and best – thing she had ever done. It was new to Pamela to engage in such confidences. A long, strong, self-sufficient marriage, such as hers and John's, had, she saw now, largely precluded the possibility of such friendships. It made her understand how lonely widowhood had made her, how desperately in need she had been of like-minded company. It made her begin, too, to comprehend the madness that had reached its crescendo five months before and – a little bit anyway – to forgive it.

'We're going back now,' she called to the dog, when they were still only half-way down the lane. 'I've got things to do. Come on.' Ignoring Poppy's imploring look, Pamela turned on her heel and began to pick her way back, avoiding the worst of the mud in spite of her footwear. Brisk walking was good for her back she had discovered, but it was too hot to enjoy it. And at her age, she was discovering, one could start in small ways to do as one wanted, without the nagging fear of letting people – or animals – down. Poppy would love her, no matter what, just as Serena and Charlie would love Ed, in whatever state he returned to them, she reflected. Maybe animals and humans weren't so different after all, at least not the ones who loved each other. Love was all that mattered in the end, she mused, pausing to stroke the gnarled ridges of the old oak that arched across the entrance to the drive, its branches reaching over and round her like welcoming arms.

Two days later, just when everyone had got used to its presence, begun even to take it for granted, the sun withdrew behind a wall of thunderous cloud and the rain resumed its domination of the summer. On TV weather presenters' satellite maps, the entire British Isles appeared as a swirling smudge of black and grey.

In Hull that Sunday Keith went to Toys 'Я' Us and spent money he could not spare on a Subbuteo game, so that he and his sons could enjoy the delights of football sprawled on his sister's living-room floor. Parked stony-faced in the sidelines on an armchair, wearing a thick jumper she had hoped not to see again until October, Irene announced that when she returned from a now imminent two-week holiday in Skiathos she would like to have her place to herself again. Perhaps Keith would bear that in mind, not that she wanted to be unfriendly.

Arriving in Camberwell, Theo told Clem it was too wet to film outside and too dark to do interiors, so why didn't they hope the skies would clear and go to the pub instead? His mother, on the other side of London, hearing the rain on the new extension roof and wondering about the safety and whereabouts of her nephew, decided it would be a good morning to attend church and try out the power of prayer. On hearing her plan, Peter turned his head gratefully into the pillows to think about the physiotherapist, whose naked body he had imagined so many times now he felt he knew it better than his own.

In Camden Stephen left Cassie sleeping and went downstairs to prepare a breakfast tray of freshly squeezed grapefruit juice, camomile tea, wholemeal toast with honey and, by way of a finishing touch, a single rose, plucked from a bunch he had given her the day before.

'Surprise,' he exclaimed, balancing the tray on the end of the bed and crossing the room to open the curtains. Outside the drizzle was flecking the view of sky and terraced houses in a way that made it resemble a grainy old photograph. 'I want to spoil you, make you glad you met me.'

'Of course I'm glad I met you,' replied Cassie, keeping a wary eye on the tray as she eased herself upright, aware through the blear of sleep that such responses to him had become automatic. She wondered if it mattered. It would have been more honest to say that she was mostly glad she had met him, but sometimes, increasingly, she wasn't so sure. However, that, Cassie knew, would lead to trouble and she'd had a hard week, what with work being manic and worrying about dear Ed, not to mention the period that had started and not ended, which the doctor had said could be down to stress or, worse still, the earliest signs of the menopause. Cassie had found herself blurting out a tearful confession about her desperation to become a mother, about Stephen not wanting to go for tests, about the little machine that told her when she was fertile but so far with no result. The doctor had given her a plastic cup of water and sat back in his chair while she talked, his face such a mask of patience and understanding that, for a while, Cassie had forgotten about the crowded waiting room outside.

Afterwards, although the doctor had said nothing except to come back if her next period was the same and that stress was bad for conception, Cassie had felt a lot better – a lot more *philosophical*. Her predicament was simple enough: She (mostly) loved a difficult man who did not share her need to have a child; it was hardly a life-threatening equation – certainly nothing like as bad as having a child and losing it as poor Charlie and Serena had done, first with Tina and now – albeit in a milder way – with the wretched Ed. God alone knew what the boy was up to. And no wonder that in attempting to deal with the situation Serena hadn't got round to replying to her plea for help. Cassie felt bad for having left the message in the first place, imposing such a demand when her sister-in-law had so much else to worry about.

The tray wobbled and Stephen picked it up. He waited for Cassie to lever herself upright so that he could place it on her lap. 'Damn, I forgot the napkin – do you want one?'

'No, this is great. Thank you, darling, so much.' Cassie kissed his cheek, trying not to mind how he was hovering, hungry for approval. 'Are you not having anything?'

'Just tea. I left that downstairs too, stupid bastard that I am.' Stephen hurried off, aware as he did so that his words had been too harsh, too revelatory of his real state of mind; aware, too, that 'bastard' was the word Keith had used when he had thrown Stephen's plea for help back in his face. *Lucky bastard.* Stunned by the response, Stephen had sat in the garden for a long time afterwards, heedless of the sun curling the edges of his notes and burning his nose and cheeks. *You are on your own*, he had told himself. *You always were, you always will be. Every man for himself. That's how it is.* He had decided in the same instant that he would trust no one's vigilance but his own, that in spite of the detrimental effect on progress with his manuscript, he would continue to keep track of Cassie. Keith was wrong to call it spying. He simply needed to be sure of her, to feel safe, to erase all shadows of doubt before they got married. Any normal man would feel the same – would want to know whether his lover truly loved him, whether there was someone else, whether having a baby was all she really cared about.

On returning with his mug of tea to find that Cassie had abandoned the tray with the toast only half eaten and tunnelled back under the covers, Stephen felt a small, familiar sting of rejection. He took off his dressing-gown and got in beside her. 'Hey, babe . . .' He stroked her hair, her neck, the smooth mounds of her shoulders, then the top of her chest, at which point Cassie changed her position, rolling over, bunching up her knees and tucking her arms together. Like a little fortress. A fortress against him. 'Cass . . .' He started to touch her with more determination, running his fingers up the back of her thigh and along the soft cleft in her bottom.

'Hmm . . . sleepy.'

'That's nice, being sleepy . . . Let me wake you up . . .' He began to kiss the downy nape of her neck, licking gently in the way that she had once, many months before, described as inducing a state of ecstasy. *Ecstasy.* That was what he wanted, for his woman to feel *ecstatic* about him. Nothing else, nothing less, would do.

'Stephen, please.' Cassie slithered further away, and tugged her nightdress down round her hips. 'Been a long week . . . need sleep . . . maybe later.'

Not ecstatic, then, not even close. 'I want to make you happy.'

'You do,' Cassie muttered, wading now, with monumental effort, through all the thoughts that had been preoccupying her – her still tender belly, her missing nephew, the long list of things waiting for her on the pad in the kitchen. 'You *do* make me happy,' she repeated, unfolding her limbs and turning towards him with a sigh, wondering, as she began to return his attentions, kissing the peeling tip of his sunburnt nose, whether it was her failing or his that his relentless, innumerable displays of kindness should feel so controlling, so like demands for his happiness rather than hers.

'Ohmygod, *Roland*,' exclaimed Clem, rushing up to Theo just as he had fought his way through the crush at the bar. 'I can't believe I forgot. He's arriving today . . . *now*,' she wailed, looking at her watch. 'He's coming by train, bringing his paintings. I said I'd show them to – I'm sorry, Theo, but we've *got* to go.'

'Flopsy and Mopsy can let him in, can't they?' replied Theo, mildly, referring to Clem's flatmates, whom they had left curled up on the sofa in their dressing-gowns nursing bowls of cereal. 'Half an hour won't make any difference,' he added, suppressing a surge of impatience at the way the day was turning out – not a single shot of anything and Clem too distracted even to have a proper look at the script.

'It *will*. Sorry, Theo, it'll make a lot of difference. Poor Roland, it'll look dreadful if I'm not there, like I don't care. And what with Ed . . . Imagine if Flora and Daisy have gone out and Roland arrives, wanders off and gets lost.'

'Okay, okay.' Theo sighed heavily and put away the ten-pound note he had been waving at the barman. They'd already done the Ed conundrum to death, Theo managing during the course of their discussions to be bland and supportive rather than expressing his parents' – and his own – fears about hard drugs. In all the years he had known Ed, Theo had never witnessed his younger cousin do anything but puff – rather inexpertly – at a joint, but Ed had exactly the sort of reckless, reactionary spirit that he had seen drive other less close acquaintances to the treadmill of addiction. 'Showing Roland's paintings to someone, eh? That's nice of you. Who exactly are you going to *show* them to? It wouldn't be this Nathan person, would it?' he pressed slyly, opening his umbrella for her to share once they were out in the street.

'It might be,' muttered Clem, walking so quickly that Theo had to reach out to keep the umbrella over her head.

'Does that mean we all get to meet him?'

'No, it doesn't.'

'Is he a great painter or something?'

'He's . . . I don't know about great but he's an artist, yes. He's been drawing me, as a matter of fact.'

'*Drawing* you? Blimey, why didn't you say so before?' exclaimed Theo, delighted to have stumbled on this small verification of his cousin's dramatic talents. She was posing for an artist and he had asked her to star in his film: it all linked up, made sense.

'He's finished the drawing stage and moved on to paints now, but it's no big deal,' added Clem, cursing herself for having said too much, wondering what her cousin – or any of her family – would have said if he had seen her lying on Nathan's sofa the previous afternoon, naked apart from the blue satin throw he had arranged under and around her, its folds high-lighting the whiteness of her skin. 'Show me yourself,' he had said, moving an arm to expose more of her chest. 'You trust me now. Show me that trust.' He had tweaked the satin so that it covered one foot and pressed her knee to straighten it, removing Clem's last small hope of masking the neat dark tri-angle between her legs. Clem had burned and breathed, wondering that he did not remark on the heat of her skin, won-dering too what she would do when he began – as he surely would – to touch her differently. The expectation was blissful; so blissful that she had felt a momentary shame to experience such exaltation with all the hell that had broken loose in the now peripheral world of her home-life: Ed on a park bench, for all they knew; her mother, by all accounts, in pieces; her father sounding so angry and unhappy on the phone, telling her on no account to bother Maisie with messages about what had happened, that he was sure her brother would resurface when he was good and ready. Without Nathan immediately to hand, she had found herself stumbling from that first revelation of the news into the arms of Daisy and Flora, telling them not just about Ed but about the death of her little sister and being anorexic and falling out with Maisie over Jonny Cottrall. The pair had responded generously and sweetly, with soft bosomy embraces, Pringles and so much wine that Clem had only just managed to refrain from blurting out everything about her feelings for Nathan too. She was glad she hadn't, especially when Nathan not only hadn't touched her but had turned his back while she got dressed, firing kind inquiries about Ed while he cleaned his brushes, as if nothing had happened except that . . . well, except that he had *painted* her. Clem was still puzzling over it, wondering how he could hold himself back, whether the next session – the last, he said – was what he was waiting for.

'I thought *something* was going on,' exclaimed Theo, happily, as they reached the front door of the flat, 'when you mentioned him at the ball. I could just tell it was something special. Hey, look, it's about to stop raining. I might leave you to Roland for a bit and check out a couple of locations – I need to find a park for that scene where you've got the bomb but are having second thoughts.'

'Great. Whatever,' murmured Clem, anxious now to see whether Roland had arrived and not sharing her cousin's optimism about the weather. Not yet sharing his faith in her acting abilities either, she was also quite glad to have a good reason to defer putting them to the test. 'See you in a bit.' She took the stairs two at a time, preparing apologies for Roland in her head – preparing, too, to explain that she would show the paintings to Nathan later in the week, that her spare time that day had to be shared with Theo.

'We let them in,' said Flora and Daisy in unison, as she opened the door. Dressed now and with handbags over their shoulders, they hurried out, casting looks of sympathy over their shoulders.

'Drunk,' mouthed Daisy, before they disappeared round the bend in the stairwell.

Clem thought she must have misheard the word, since she had rarely seen Roland take a sip of anything alcoholic, not even when they were all experimenting behind the backs of their parents and grandparents as youngsters. She returned her attention to the room.

'Hi,' said Roland, emerging from the flat's little kitchen, clutching a pot of coffee and a mug. 'I thought I'd better try to sober him up. It's Ed,' he added, somewhat unnecessarily, pointing to the armchair at which Clem was already staring in slack-jawed astonishment. 'I found him on the doorstep.'

'Oh, Ed! Ed, you pillock.' She ran to her brother, tripping over his outstretched legs in her eagerness to embrace him. Ed blinked at her with bloodshot eyes, managing a sort of shrug within the circle of her arms. 'You fucking eejit! If you knew – bloody hell!' cried Clem, punching him and hugging him at the same time. 'What the *fuck* have you been playing at? I'm going to call Mum – have you called Mum, Roland?'

Roland was pouring coffee and stopped mid-flow, spilling a few drops on to the carpet. 'Oops, sorry.'

Clem got to her feet and snatched the half-filled mug from him. 'Roland, for Christ's sake, have you called Mum and Dad?'

'No . . . It's a bit . . . I would have, but . . .' Roland noted that the coffee spill, between two faded brown flowers, might have been part of the carpet's design.

Ed chose this moment to come to life in the chair. 'No one,' he growled, craning his neck to get them both in his line of vision, 'is to call anyone.'

'Don't be ridiculous, Ed,' wailed Clem, kneeling beside him, close to tears. 'If you knew how worried they – we – have been – Christ, where did you go anyway?' she asked, with fresh

267

incredulity, noting his lank hair and the crumpled state of his clothes. He smelt a bit too, a mulchy smell of unwashed body and junk food.

'Brighton,' grunted Ed. 'I've been in Brighton . . . I . . . Oh, what the fuck does it matter? Go on, Roland, tell her the rest. I really can't be arsed.'

'Have you become an alcoholic, Ed?' asked Clem, aware that the question sounded prim and silly, but not knowing how else to tackle it. 'Because if you have, there are . . .'

Ed began to laugh, tweaking at the greasy strands of his hair, which, deprived of his styling gel and Serena's hairdryer, had spent two weeks dangling irritatingly in his eyes. 'Sadly not. Didn't have the money. I'm pissed because I found a half-bottle of Scotch at the bus station – amazing what you find if you look . . . *Amazing.*' He drew breath in wonderment at the recollection of this serendipitous start to his morning, how it had eased the desperate decision to give up the increasingly hopeless task of trying to survive on a couple of pounds a day and seek the help of his sister. 'Money is what I need and then I can return to the family fold . . . the prodigal . . .' he struggled with the syllables and giggled '. . . son returns.'

'Money? What for?'

'I could lend you money,' ventured Roland, shyly, setting the coffee-pot on a pile of magazines and perching on the end of the sofa. 'I've got three hundred pounds in my savings account.'

'That's very decent, mate, thanks.'

'What do you need money for?' persisted Clem, shrill with exasperation.

'Roland, I asked you to tell her, didn't I?' Ed pressed the tips of his fingers to his forehead and closed his eyes.

'Tell me what?' wailed Clem. 'What's he done? What's happened?'

Theo, who had found the door ajar, froze in the hallway.

Roland took a deep breath. 'Ed . . . and Jessica – Jessica

Blake – had this . . . *thing* for a bit and, well, apparently she's pregnant. Ed needs the money to . . . er . . . sort it out. He asked your parents for his trust money but they said no and that's why he ran away. He got a job selling deckchairs but the rain meant he didn't earn very much so he couldn't pay the rent on his bedsit.'

Roland, having delivered the most lucid version of the disjointed summary Ed had given on stumbling into the flat half an hour before, folded his arms and looked from cousin to cousin. This was a crisis, he knew; he was glad to be the youngest present and therefore not required to do anything but repeat facts and do his best to remain composed. For his own part, he felt too detached from the concept of Jessica Blake having a baby or Ed being its father to react to any of it. He even felt a little twinge of compassion for his canvases, which he had rolled and tied with such excitement, but which were now leaning unattended and forgotten behind the door. The only thing of which he remained convinced was the cruelty of prolonging the agony of uncertainty at Ashley House – but he had already tried to explain that to Ed and got nowhere.

'Pregnant?' The word came out of Clem's mouth as a small shriek. 'You *can't* have, Ed . . . *Jessica?*'

'Oh, yes, he can have,' said Theo, darkly, striding into the room in a way that made all three of them, even Ed, feel a little reassured. 'Edward, it's a relief, of course, to see that you are well.'

Ed groaned, burying his face in his hands. 'I need your help, guys,' he moaned, 'I asked for my trust money but Mum and Dad said no . . . I need money . . . lots of it.'

'For an abortion, presumably,' said Theo, taking the mug of coffee from Clem and thrusting it into Ed's hand.

'Yes, or maybe to . . . You see, the worst of it is she sometimes says she *wants* the baby.'

'Dear God,' Theo murmured, looking, though none of them

269

grasped it, exactly as his father did when he was absorbing difficult evidence that threatened to blow an argument off course. 'That does make things awkward.'

Clem was still gawping incredulously at Ed, but let out a gasp of a laugh at this understatement. Yet she was glad Theo was there. He was famously sensible, so much more likely than any of them to know what to do.

'I'm going to persuade her,' said Ed, struggling into a more upright position and taking his first proper swig of the coffee. 'If we set it all up, find a place for her to go, I'm sure I still can.'

'Who knows about this?' demanded Theo.

'No one,' growled Ed. He was feeling a little better, not just sober but hopeful too. Talking about it, after so long, after so much soul-searching, was such a relief. He looked at his sister and cousins, basking in the sense of their allegiance. 'And no one must know either.'

Theo was leaning against the wall next to the fireplace, arms crossed. He cocked his head at his cousin. 'That will be hard . . . impossible, even.'

'No, it won't,' cut in Ed, fiercely. 'She gets rid of the baby, she gets a load of cash – that's all that needs to happen. Deep down she's as terrified of everyone finding out as I am. She hasn't even told her mum and I don't think she will, not if I handle it right. No one must know – do you hear me?' He looked desperately at all three of them. 'Swear you won't tell . . . *swear* it. If Mum and Dad find out I think I might . . . *die*.' He burst into tears, his head dropping into his hands, his shoulders heaving.

'Of course we won't tell,' murmured Clem, hugging his legs and laying her head on his knees. 'Dear Ed, don't worry, we'll sort this out together – won't we?' She looked pleadingly at Theo and then Roland, who was chewing his lip anxiously at the recollection of his mother and his aunt returning from their trawl round Chichester on Friday afternoon, pale and crestfallen. 'They must be told you're all right, though,' he ventured, after a pause. 'I mean, you should see how it's been – how they've been, especially your mum, not knowing where you are . . .' He faltered, defeated by an inability to explain the level of desperation he had witnessed and to think more deeply into how the situation might be resolved.

'Roland is quite right,' said Theo. 'We'll tell them you're okay, that you're staying with Clem for a bit and take it from there. Clem?' He was already pulling out his mobile phone. 'Can he stay here?'

'I guess so – I'm sure Flora and Daisy wouldn't mind it for a bit, though he'd have to sleep on the sofa, of course . . . but Mum and Dad will want to *talk* to you, Ed, to know what's been going on.'

'Yes, they will,' agreed Theo, starting to punch numbers on his phone.

At which point Ed heaved himself out of his seat and made a lunge for his cousin, knocking the mobile out of his hand. 'Sorry,' he moaned, scrabbling under a chair on his hands and knees to retrieve it, then checking fearfully to see if the call had gone through. 'I know they need to know, but – but not just yet, okay? I'm pissed, for Christ's sake. I have to think what I'm going to say. Please, Theo . . .' His cousin was staring down at him, steely-faced. 'When I'm ready, okay? When we've talked all the other stuff through . . . I need you to lend me the money,' he continued, starting to sob again, 'and to promise to keep quiet about – about Jessica. Will you do that? Will you promise, all of you?' Clem murmured that she would while Roland nodded solemnly. Ed, still cradling the phone, looked up beseechingly at his eldest cousin. 'Theo?'

'Of course, mate.'

'Thanks,' whispered Ed, handing back the phone and wiping his nose noisily on the back of his sleeve as he clambered to his feet.

'Would you like a bath?' ventured Clem.

Ed nodded, smiling for the first time. 'I bloody would.'

Clem stood up, glad to have something concrete to do. 'I'll run it. Roland, perhaps you could make some more coffee? And we could have some toast, too, and jam – Granny's homemade. I brought jars of it from home when I moved in here.'

Ed emerged, scrubbed and shiny-cheeked, from the bathroom ten minutes later, then ate ravenously and with mounting happiness as Theo put forward a plan to do with lending his own trust fund to his cousin and agreeing to help talk sense into Jessica. He had been on the point of asking for the money anyway, Theo explained, deliberately avoiding mention of the film project for fear of complicating matters.

'You're fantastic – all of you,' Ed muttered. 'I feel it's like us against the rest of the world, us against the adults sort of thing.'

'We are adults,' said Theo, gravely. 'That's why this has happened.'

'Yes, of course, but you know what I mean,' insisted Ed, undeterred. He tipped his head back with a sigh and had fallen fast asleep a minute later, his mouth open, emitting the snores of an old man.

Theo studied him for a few moments, then reached, with some weariness, for his mobile. 'We *are* adults – some of us, that is.' He smiled quickly at Roland. 'But this is too big. We can't handle it alone.'

'Theo, what are you doing?' whispered Clem, fiercely, glancing at Ed and putting her hand to her heart. 'Theo, you promised him . . .'

'Yes, I know I did, and don't think this isn't hard. But sometimes the hard things are the *right* things. Ed needs help, but we're not the ones best placed to deliver it. He can't see that, but we can and I, for one, am prepared to act on that knowledge.'

'I'm going to write to Maisie,' said Clem hoarsely. 'She has a right to know too.'

Roland, not wanting to hear the conversation, retreated to the kitchen and began to wash up. He worked slowly and methodically, scrubbing at the brown stains in the mugs, and thinking how full of surprises life was, how awful sometimes but how interesting, how a million paintings couldn't begin to do justice to it.

Shortly after twelve thirty Peter went into the kitchen and peered, with some concern, at the sizzling state of the rolled sirloin Helen had instructed him to put into the oven. He was anxious about the roast potatoes too, which appeared to be browning haphazardly and with far less efficiency on the shelf above. Helen had told him when to put them in, giving him the exact times for turning and basting so that all that would be required of her on her return from church was to boil the vegetables and whisk up the gravy. But, thanks to a long phone conversation with Delia, Peter had put the potatoes in late, then got into a muddle about how far up to turn the temperature dial and when to do the basting. Helen understood the oven much as one knew and accommodated the idiosyncrasies of an old friend. One glance at the overcooked meat and the under-cooked potatoes and Peter was sure she would know that he had failed to do as she asked. He trembled to think of it, imagining in his feverish state that such knowledge was a hair's breadth from his wife discovering everything else too – his outrageous fantasizing after she had left for church, the phone call he had made in his dressing-gown, needing to hear Delia's voice, to introduce a toehold of reality into his overheated brain. Instead he had babbled about wanting her, how it was driving him mad. She had laughed softly and said it was driving her mad too, and when could they meet, she wasn't talking about lunch. At this crossroads, Peter had said not that he was too busy or too married or too full of conscience but that, with Umbria only a couple of weeks away, he had been winding down his workload, instructing clerks to keep major assignments until the autumn and that he was hers to command. What day would suit her best?

Thinking back on the conversation, as he stared hopelessly through the clouds of acrid steam issuing from the meat tin, Peter was incredulous at how easy it had been. The line, so firm, so indelible, so huge, so resisted, had been crossed at last and with such a little step too – with a mere skip, a leap of the heart. Not that long ago, hearing or reading about people whose marriages had buckled under adultery and who had used phrases like 'it just happened', and 'we couldn't help ourselves', had made Peter snort with impatience. Such action didn't happen *to* people. They were responsible for it. Yet, examining his state of mind now, Peter genuinely felt as if he had been swept along by powers – needs – beyond his control. He could imagine nothing less than his own death keeping him from the tryst he and Delia had agreed for Wednesday. His desire was simply too strong – like nothing he had ever before experienced, not even during the early days with Helen and certainly not with the meagre conquests that had preceded her.

It was *wrong*, of course. Peter knew that with a clarity that felt at once awesome and irrelevant. It was wrong, but he would go anyway. He had stopped resisting. He was in a new territory – a new world – as alluring as it was terrifying. Never had he wanted another human being in the way that he wanted Delia. How could he not explore such feelings? How could he creep deeper into humdrum middle-age, closer towards increasing decrepitude and death without having explored them? Just the thought of her made him feel more alive than he had for years: the grass was greener, the sky less grey, the smiles of his daughters more vibrant. She *illuminated* him.

Lost in such thoughts, Peter did not hear the key in the front door. So that when Helen strode into the kitchen, dumping her handbag on the table and reaching for the oven gloves in one swift movement, he started guiltily. 'Have you checked the meat? It smells overcooked.' She sniffed suspiciously while he stepped out of the way, part of him still fearful that his wife's formidable perspicacity might detect matters of greater import than the blackening meat and the too-white potatoes. 'It's done to death,' she cried, tugging out the tin. 'No wonder you're looking sheepish. Pass that plate, could you, so we can keep it warm in the top oven? That's it. God, and the potatoes have hardly begun . . . What have you been up to?' She laughed and ruffled his hair.

'I . . . I . . .'

'It's okay, darling, I didn't marry you for your culinary skills. Church was good, by the way. Even Chloë listened to the sermon. He's one of those lovely priests who manage to make religion sound *normal*.' She moved busily round the kitchen as she talked, draining off fat from the meat, reaching for a spoon, putting on the kettle for water, calling with mounting impatience for Chloë to lay the table, weaving round Peter as if he was one of the kitchen fittings.

'I'll bet she's plugged into her iPod.'

'Probably. You okay?'

'Fine.'

'Good.' Helen smiled, holding out a wooden spoon for him to taste the gravy.

They were still waiting for the potatoes when the phone rang. Peter answered it, mouthing, 'Theo,' at Helen, when he heard his son's voice. A moment later his expression had darkened so visibly that Helen was dancing round him in concern. 'Dear God,' he murmured, when Theo had finished reporting on the events of the morning, concluding with the view that his father should be the one to break the good – and bad – news to his uncle and aunt. 'Absolutely . . . of course . . . and well done, Theo, you've done the right thing – absolutely the right thing. Ed himself, I'm sure, will see that in time. Christ, what a mess. Don't tell Ed you've told us yet, in case the wretched boy takes himself off again . . . What a business! It beggars belief.'

'What?' cried Helen, when he had finished. As Peter relayed Theo's news she sank into a chair and groaned, clapping a hand to her mouth as Chloë charged into the kitchen waving a Barbie doll out of reach of her little sister.

'What's happened?' said Chloë, absently handing the doll to Genevieve as she glanced from the stricken expression on her mother's face to her father, who was still clutching the telephone.

'It's good news,' said Helen brightly, firmly, reaching out to smooth the curly auburn mop of her youngest's hair, which sprang back the moment she withdrew her hand. 'Your naughty, unbelievably selfish cousin has returned at last.'

'Ed? He's home?'

'Well, he's at Clem's flat, but no doubt will be going home any minute, yes.'

'Well, that's good, isn't it?' pressed Chloë, who was old and intelligent enough to wonder that such longed-for information had not elicited a more jubilant response.

'It's fantastic,' said Peter, smiling at her. 'We're so relieved.'

'Ed – is – home – Ed – is – home,' chanted Genevieve, making her doll dance to the rhythm of the words along the edge of the kitchen table.

'He's safe and well, and that's all that matters,' said Helen, smoothly, 'and it's all thanks to your clever, clever brother that we know about it.'

'Theo? What did he do?' asked Chloë, scornfully, picking out a carrot as her mother tipped them into a serving dish.

'He *told* us, that's what he did, even though Ed didn't want him to,' explained Helen, starting to put the food on to the table, then lifting Genevieve on to a chair. 'He knew what was the *right* thing to do and he did it . . . and Ed is *safe*,' she exclaimed happily, struck, in the midst of all the shock about the other dire aspects of her nephew's situation, by the excellence of the news. Not dead in a ditch, or dealing in drugs, but fast asleep on his sister's sofa. 'Isn't that *wonderful*, girls? And do you know what is just as wonderful? I prayed for it this morning. I prayed for it and it happened.'

'I'll go to my study to call Charlie and Serena,' said Peter quickly, riled by his wife's increasing readiness to put a religious spin on everything. If a deity was responsible for such chaos then it certainly wasn't one with whom he wished to become acquainted.

'Why can't you use that phone?' asked Chloë, pointing across the kitchen.

'Because I don't need Barbie's squeals and your chomping in the background, young lady. Now, eat up. I won't be long.'

Shutting the door of his study behind him, Peter leant against it and closed his eyes. The news was still sinking in. Ed, his nephew, screwing Sid's tart of a granddaughter and getting her pregnant. It was unbelievable. Appalling. Breathtaking. He felt, in the same instant, huge compassion for his brother and sister-in-law and gratitude that he was on the fringes of the calamity, rather than at its core. A termination would have to be arranged, of course, maybe counselling for the girl. Such a slut too, Peter reflected, recalling the ride he had given her to the station on the evening of Alicia's funeral, how she had simpered and squirmed in the passenger seat, crossing and uncrossing her legs, making no effort to conceal her chunky thighs or the jagged holes in her tights. How terrible that Ed had succumbed to such dubious, cheap attractions. How fortunate and fantastic that Theo was built of the sort of mettle that meant he never would. How . . . Peter opened his eyes, wanting to stop his thoughts there, before they hit the wall of his own rather less virtuous predicament. Delia . . . He tried out an image of her in his mind, half hoping that something would have shifted. Was he up to cancelling their meeting after all? Was he up to doing the so glaringly obvious right thing, to behaving, in short, in precisely the way he found so commendable in his son? Maybe, he reflected wildly, there was a deity, after all, one who had organized the whole thing to shame him out of his intentions.

'Peter?' Helen caught him in the back as she opened the door. 'I wondered how it was going —' She broke off, clearly surprised to find him nowhere near the phone.

'Just . . . collecting my thoughts,' he stammered, hurrying to his desk, rubbing his back where the door handle had jabbed into him. 'Not that easy.'

'No,' she agreed, and added, a little harshly, 'Best to get on with it – not fair to keep Charlie and Serena waiting.'

'Of course.'

'Your lunch is in the oven.'

'Thanks.' Peter waited until she had closed the door, then picked up the telephone. Even then he hesitated, preoccupied, to his dismay, by the thought that if he did keep his rendezvous on Wednesday he'd better make damn sure he had a condom.

Three days later a wood-pigeon chose to lament the dawn of another grey sky from the vantage-point of Ed's bedroom window. Surfacing slowly, reluctantly, to consciousness, Ed thought for a moment that he was still in Brighton where each long day had started with the gulls wheeling round the roof of the hostel, screeching for breakfast. Not ready to deal with his despair, he turned his face into his pillow, thinking how soft it was, how perfectly wonderful. Then the cooing stopped and a different, much more whiny, persistent sound took its place. Opening his eyes, Ed saw Samson at the window, miaowing furiously and scratching at the frame. 'Bugger off,' he growled, not angry with the cat so much as the avalanche of unpalatable thoughts concomitant upon the fact that he was in his own bed, with his sordid secret public knowledge and nothing to look forward to but the unspeakably diabolical prospect of a meeting in London that afternoon with Jessica and her mother. And it was his birthday. This thought depressed Ed almost more than all the others. He was eighteen, to which he had once looked forward with such longing, imagining it as the gateway to freedom, to power, the beginning of the bit of his life that really mattered. But it was none of those things. He had never felt less free or less power-ful. His mother's suggestion that he could still have a party had made him laugh violently. There was nothing to celebrate, nor ever would be again.

Samson, seeing the lump under the bedclothes move, redoubled his efforts to be noticed, pressing his whiskered face against the windowpane and scratching so aggressively that Ed could hear the shredding of wood and paint. Swearing under his breath, he got out of bed and undid the latch. The cat leapt past him on to the bed where it purred happily, arching its back to be stroked. Ed ignored it and burrowed back under the covers, losing himself to contemplation of his horrible day and the fact that every time he thought things couldn't get any worse they did. The way Theo had betrayed him – gone behind his back to his father after all his plans and promises – still made him feel physically sick. The first he had known about it was the ring of Clem's bell and the sight of his parents staggering through the door, his mother reeling towards him as if she was falling, as if the only thing to prevent her losing her balance was him.

'It's okay, darling,' she had said, over and over again, 'every-thing's going to be okay.' He had let her cling to him, aware of his father hovering in the background, wide-eyed and stupid, like he didn't know what to do with his arms, legs or face. Ed had started to weep, partly at the peculiar painful pleasure of seeing them and partly because all his meagre hopes – of resolving the whole miserable business discreetly, of retaining a shred of dignity – were lost for good. Ever since the shame had been crushing, like a steel clamp round his lungs and heart, as bad when they berated him as when they tried to cover up their disappointment with kindness and futile promises about everything being okay.

Hearing a timid knock on the door, Ed closed his eyes and turned towards the window. Pamela, who had heard the cat and often spent the early-morning hours awake with the radio for company, opened the door and peered in. Samson rolled on to his back and purred loudly in the hope, at last, of receiving some attention. Pamela tiptoed to the bed and ran her fingers along the cat's soft gingery tummy, noting as she did so that her grandson's eyes were far too tightly shut to denote genuine sleep.

'I thought you'd be awake,' she said softly. 'I wanted to say happy birthday.'

Ed kept his eyes closed. He couldn't deal with his grandmother. He couldn't deal with anything. If it were at all possible – if they weren't all watching him like hawks – he would have run away again.

'Difficult times,' she murmured next, 'but they will pass, they always do, just like the good ones. Nothing stays the same. All things pass in time. I'm making hot chocolate by the way, and some of my eggy-bread – lots of sugar. Come downstairs if you want some.'

Ed kept his eyes shut, ears ringing, heart thumping. He was aware of his grandmother's stillness, of her watching him. Then he felt her scoop the cat off the bed. 'Naughty puss,' she crooned, 'bothering Ed when he's in no mood for you. You come with me. You've had a rabbit, haven't you? That's why you're not hungry . . . Horrid cat, I can't think why I bother with you . . .' Ed heard the rustle of her moving across the room and then a gentle click as she closed his bedroom door.

Serena drove carefully, tussling with the urge to try to penetrate the silence of the hunched figure next to her and the wiser instinct to leave him alone. The day was moist and muggy, the sky like a dark, swelling sponge. Her dread at the prospect of seeing the Blakes was, she was certain, equal to her son's. Yet her heart, ever since Sunday, had been bulging with joy. To have Ed back, to have him safe, made everything else bearable. Shock, outrage, anger – all the things that made Charlie still choke and stutter through every effort to discuss the situation – were to her a sideshow. Plainly, Ed had been stupid, not just in getting Jessica pregnant but in imagining he could solve anything by running away. How she *felt* about their son, though, was unchanged. If anything, she loved him *more* for getting into such a mess, for so obviously needing their help and being unable to ask for it. She had wanted, every minute of every hour since stumbling into Clem's flat, to try to make him understand that – to explain that nothing he had done, or could do, would ever endanger the huge solidity of her love for him. After the trauma of his disappearance and the mounting sense of foreboding that had preceded it, the certainty of this feeling was, to Serena, like floating in a warm sea, like stepping into sunshine, like seeing beyond all the anxieties of living to a universal truth.

'If you want to talk, darling . . .'

Ed squirmed, huddling deeper into his seat.

'Such a shame that it had to happen – this meeting, I mean, today of all days, but it was simply the only time everybody could manage. We'll have to celebrate your birthday properly another day. I've phoned the driving school already, by the way, booked a couple of lessons before we go to Italy . . .'

Ed wound down the window and stared at the fields and

houses streaking past the car until the colours blurred and he couldn't tell trees from grass or sky. Of course he didn't want to talk. There was nothing to say. It didn't matter that it was his birthday, or that he had been given driving lessons, or that they were all going to Italy. Nothing mattered. He could think only of the ordeal ahead, being paraded like a guilty criminal in front of Mrs Blake and Jessica, the horrible, shameful secret laid bare to be picked over by his parents and his uncle . . . Dear God, his uncle.

'Why does Uncle Peter have to be there too?' he burst out.

'Dad thought it was a good idea, to cover the legal side of things.'

'The *legal* side? What does that mean?'

Serena sighed, her thoughts on the matter as hazy as Ed's. She wasn't sure she wanted Peter there either. Yet her redoubtable brother-in-law had been involved from the start, not just because Theo had referred to him first but because he had turned up at Clem's flat too, ostensibly to drive Theo back to Oxford but exuding such irresistible energy and confidence that even she had been grateful for it. It had reminded her that in crises the Harrisons rallied round, that was how they were, why they survived so well. While Charlie made the initial, intensely difficult call to Mrs Blake, Peter had stood by his side, nodding sombre-faced encouragement and shooting looks of sympathetic consternation at her and Ed, who remained curled in the corner of the sofa throughout, clutching himself as if he had been shot.

Maureen Blake, both on this first occasion and throughout their subsequent conversations, had been as shocked and anxious to clear up the whole sorry business as they were. A termination, she agreed, was the only way to proceed. It was Peter who had pointed out that, relieved as they all were to hear this, compensation might be required and he would be happy to attend the meeting to help handle it. In the intervening two days he had also taken it upon himself to compile a shortlist of reputable clinics where the procedure could be carried out, with possible dates and prices.

'Have you spoken to Jessica again?' ventured Serena, gently. They were just two muddled teenagers, after all, she reminded herself, caught up in that early tangle of sexual feelings and emotions. She thought, too, of the happy fact that it had been this, rather than any failure on her or Charlie's part, that had compelled her son to run away.

Ed shook his head miserably. He hadn't spoken to Jessica since Sunday night when she had screeched at him about breaking his word, about how she had hung on for him and he had let her down, about how her mum had called her a worthless whore. He had shouted back that if she had agreed to get rid of the thing in the first place it would all have been easier, how it was her fault that everything had got so out of control.

'The poor girl. This is so hard for both of you.'

'She's not *poor*,' Ed snorted, 'she tricked me into it. She *said* she was on the pill, that I didn't need to use a –' He snapped his mouth shut, unable to say the word, hating in that moment the fact that his parents knew he had had sex almost as much as the sad truth that he had done so without taking the necessary precautions.

'Did you – do you have feelings for her?'

Ed snorted again. He had feelings, all right, but none that he dared express. 'I screwed up, okay? There's nothing more to say. I know you and Dad are trying to help with this *meeting . . .*'

'It's not easy, darling, for any of us,' murmured Serena, changing down a gear as they hit the speed restrictions on the final approach to London, 'but please try to see that it's not the end of the world either, that there are worse things that could have happened –'

'Oh, yeah, like what?'

'Like . . .' Serena hesitated, thinking inevitably of Tina – her

283

reference point for any calamity. That unspeakable loss, she saw now, had weakened her in some ways but strengthened her in others. The demise of near relatives, her mother-in-law's breakdown, herself being at loggerheads with her husband, her son getting a sixteen-year-old girl pregnant – none of it came close to touching the nerve of grief awakened by the death of her child six years before. Yet the troubles of the year had shown, too, that she was still raw about the tragedy, that the nerve was still so easily stirred. 'Like you deciding never to come home to face the music,' she continued firmly, 'folding deckchairs all your life, leaving us all beside ourselves with worry.'

'I'm sorry,' said Ed, bitterly. 'I told you not to worry.'

'That's okay, sweetheart.' Serena patted his leg. 'I understand.'

Ed resumed staring at the countryside, puzzling at how her kindness could be just as hard to take as his father's unguarded glances of disappointment. Reacting to either of them, he often felt like a boxer punching at air, a boxer who would have preferred the reassuring collision – the pain – of a fist against a target.

Even without such dire circumstances, a gathering of the Blakes and the Harrisons would never have prompted an easy cohesion. Maureen knew them all by sight, just as they knew her, from the times in the past when she had collected or dropped Jessica to play under the eye of her grandfather at Ashley House. She came home early that afternoon to prepare for them, giving the flat more of a spring-clean than it had had in years, darting to and from the concrete balcony that overlooked the street in the hope of some warning before the doorbell rang. Her daughter, meanwhile, kept to her room, as she had since their shouting match on Sunday, emerging only to forage for food among their meagre stocks and to turn away her head if her mother so much as looked at her.

In spite of her attempts at vigilance, the knock on the door took Maureen by surprise, as did the unreal sight of Serena and the three tall Harrison men filing into her narrow hall. The boy *was* a man, Maureen thought, unable to resist gawping at Ed, whom she had last seen as a skinny fifteen-year-old with clusters of spots round his nose. Loath though she was to admit it in the circumstances, she could see now why Jessica had got so keen on the lad; had she herself been twenty years younger, she wouldn't have said no either. She even felt a momentary pang of something like sympathy for her daughter. After all, she hadn't been much older when she'd had Jessica, and that hadn't been planned either.

After an unspeakably awkward series of handshakes, Serena took the lead on efforts to break the ice, saying Sid sent his best regards and offering to help make tea. Elbow to elbow with Maureen in the tiny kitchen, she lamented the unfortunate circumstances of the meeting, emphasizing their concern for Jessica and how they all just wanted to help the children put it behind them. Maureen, busy with tea-bags and mugs, agreed heartily, at the same time privately doubling the figure she and her mate Dot had agreed she should ask for.

Sitting knee to knee with Charlie and Peter in the sitting room next door, Jessica and Ed eyed each other like wary animals, both too overwhelmed, too entrapped in their separate wretchedness, to speak. The two brothers did their best, taking it in turns to ask Jessica if she was well and telling her not to worry, that between them they would sort everything out. After a long, awkward silence Charlie, catching sight of a dog-eared copy of *To the Lighthouse*, picked it up and said it was one of his favourites and who was the reader.

'That would be Jess,' replied Maureen, appearing in the doorway with a mug in each hand. 'She's good at books and that, aren't you, love?'

Jessica scowled, her gaze fixed on the floor.

'Well . . .' Charlie took a sip of his tea and cleared his throat. 'Now that we're all assembled, I would like to begin by saying that I – that all of us – only wish you two had come to us at once instead of . . . However . . .' he tried the tea again, which numbed his lips because it was so hot '. . . be that as it may . . .'

'The main thing is that you're all right,' cut in Serena, a little desperately, wishing she could steer Jessica's gaze to something other than the carpet. The girl was so forlorn that her heart ached with pity. Even allowing for the early stages of pregnancy, her figure had swelled unattractively since the funeral. Her hair, with its curious line of black where the dye continued to grow out, was dry and neglected, while her pasty face was pitted with small angry patches of livid pink, which she kept picking at with her fingernails. 'Jessica? Are you okay?'

'Yeah, fucking brilliant,' she hissed, her eyes sliding briefly towards Serena and back to the floor.

'You watch your tongue, girl,' snapped Maureen, rising out of her chair towards her daughter, then reaching for her cigarettes instead.

'We are all agreed, I think,' said Peter, speaking quietly and gravely, 'on the appropriate course of action.'

Maureen tapped a sprinkle of ash into a saucer and exhaled a plume of smoke towards the ceiling, which was a faint brown from a steady stream of similar assaults over the years. 'Oh, yes, she's seen sense on that, all right, haven't you, Jess?'

'I have here a couple of suggestions for places that would carry out the procedure privately,' Peter continued, getting out his list and putting on his glasses. 'All that remains is to find a time that would suit you, Jessica – and, of course, you, Maureen, as I'm sure you would want your mother by your side.'

Jessica laughed. 'Oh, sure, yeah, by my *side*.'

'Or maybe a close friend,' put in Serena, gently, 'someone who –'

'Ed was my *close friend*, weren't you, Ed?' Jessica peered at him from under her hair, her face such a mixture of resentment and pleading that, for a moment, none of them, least of all Ed, knew how to respond.

Ed shook his head slowly. 'Jess, this is crap, I know, and I'm truly sorry.'

'And then,' continued Peter, firmly, 'there is the question of what we can do to make up for this most upsetting state of affairs – that is, to compensate Jessica for the distraction she must have suffered, not to mention the distress . . . Charlie, perhaps you . . .' He gave his brother, who was looking dazed, a sharp nod of encouragement. In spite of his confidence in his own abilities to develop this sensitive aspect of the subject, even Peter could see it was one that Charlie, as father of the unfortunate Ed, should manage himself. The pair of them had, after considerable discussion, agreed on the figure of two thousand pounds, erring on the side of generosity as an expression of regret, and recognition of the part Ed's lack of responsibility had played in the whole sorry business.

'The point is,' stammered Charlie, giving up on his tea and gripping the mantelpiece, 'we want you to be all right after the operation, Jessica, so anything you need – anything at all – we would like to make sure that you get it, and to that end we thought we would give you some money so that –'

'How much?' asked Maureen, dropping her cigarette into the dregs of her tea, where it fizzled briefly like a damp firework.

'We thought, maybe, two thousand pounds would cover anything that –'

Maureen was trying not to look too pleased. Her doubled figure had been eight hundred. Her dad had said Jessica had got what she asked for and the Harrisons owed them nothing, but what did an old gardener know? 'That's generous, Jess, isn't it? Very generous.' She folded her arms, nodding happily. 'Anyone for another cuppa?'

Everyone said, no, thank you. 'Perhaps I should leave this with you,' said Peter, relief evident in his voice as he handed Maureen the list of clinics. 'Just let us know –'

'What about me? Shouldn't you be showing me your *private* clinics?' snarled Jessica, getting up from her chair and snatching the piece of paper.

'Of course. I'm so sorry,' said Peter, masking his shock at the speed with which the girl had moved, the viciousness in her tone.

'I tell you what, though,' continued Jessica, her eyes darting from the paper to those watching her, 'Ed's right. This is crap. All of it, a pile of crap. You see, I'm not having an *operation*. It's my bleeding baby and I don't want to *kill* it. So you can all fuck off, especially you, *Maureen*, doing anything for a bit of cash as usual.' As she spoke Jessica started to tear the page in two, holding it out so that there was no danger of any of them missing the spectacle.

'You stupid bitch,' said Maureen, her voice throaty with smoke and anger. 'What do you think you're doing?'

'I'm *having* it,' screamed Jessica, ripping the paper again, then screwing it into a ball. 'Just cos you wish you'd got rid of *me* – it would have made your life simpler, wouldn't it? Nothing but trouble, that's what you always say. Well, guess what? You're right, I am *trouble* and you'll just have to put up with it. But I tell you what, it's *my* baby and I'm fucking well going to have it with or without their stinking money.'

'I knew she'd ruin everything,' gasped Maureen, lighting another cigarette, her eyes filling with tears. 'Stupid cow, she always does.'

'Now, now . . .' Peter stretched out his arms and flapped his hands in the manner of a grand speaker trying to calm a noisy crowd. 'You're upset, Jessica, that's understandable. It's not an easy decision and I apologize profusely if any of us have given the impression that we thought otherwise.'

'It's just that it's the *best* thing for you,' pitched in Charlie, desperately. 'Both you and Ed are far too young to have children – you're still children yourselves.'

'Oh, yeah?' she sneered. 'Then how come men want to have sex with me? Not just Ed, but men like *him*.' She pointed her finger at Peter, who, while trembling inside, stared back at her with strong, stony eyes.

'As I said, child, you're upset. You don't know what you're saying. I think we should leave you now to think through everything. I'm sure you'll see sense in due course.'

They all stood up, except Serena, who had listened to the exchanges with mounting sorrow.

'Darling?' Charlie touched her arm. 'We should go.'

'We should listen to Jessica – to how she feels . . . It's such a big thing, after all.'

'Of course,' Charlie murmured, pulling rather less gently at her sleeve. 'She needs time to think.'

'I don't,' said Jessica, leaping from her chair and running to her bedroom. 'I *have* thought and you can all fuck off.'

'I wonder how it's going,' murmured Cassie, reaching across Stephen for the wine bottle and topping up her glass. They were sitting side by side on the sofa, wrapped in after-dinner tranquillity. Her fiancé, she could tell, was in a good mood – from a successful day on his book, she presumed, although he hadn't said as much, merely greeted her with a fond kiss and talk of the veal he had bought for supper and left marinating in lemon juice and olive oil.

'Oh, they'll sort it all out,' said Stephen, lightly, swilling his wine so that it slid to the lip of his glass and back again. 'Peter, no doubt, will get his cheque book out . . .' He threw back his head and laughed. 'Like he did for me once, remember, when you all thought I was going to expose your mother's affair with Eric in my book?' He shook his head, still chuckling. 'Happy days, eh?'

Cassie laughed, too, but with less certainty. The days to which Stephen referred had been far from happy, not just because they had feared public exposure of something so private but because she had been reeling from the death of her niece and the end of her relationship with Dan. Stephen, rightly, had been disgusted at her brother's attempts to buy his silence. He had withdrawn the offending references from the book anyway, retreating into a hurt silence and the continuing agony of loving her but getting nothing in return.

'It's good that you can laugh about it,' she ventured, after a pause, taking heart suddenly at this simple evidence that even the grimmest things could become amusing, or at least harmless, given a decent passage of time. Maybe it would happen to them, too, she mused, when they looked back on the tensions that seemed to have grown since their engagement. Maybe even, one day, they would be swinging a toddler between them, laughing at the needless to-do that had led up to his or her conception. 'Poor Ed,' she murmured.

Stephen had dropped his head on to her shoulder and was basking in the brief respite the day had offered from the treadmill of his anxieties: an appointment with a woman in Clapham, trips to a couple of fabric shops, a phone call to him while she ate her sandwich on a bench in Grosvenor Gardens; saying he was on the way to the butcher's had meant that he had had to race there *en route* home afterwards, but all in all it had been a good day, another building block in the still delicate wall of his trust. Soon they would be in Italy, rubbing sun-cream into each other's back and strolling through olive groves.

'Don't you feel sorry for him?' Cassie pressed.

Stephen snorted and said that as far as he was concerned both Ed and the girl had behaved like idiots. Cassie murmured agreement and sipped her wine. While irrefutable, it wasn't the sympathetic response she had been looking for. But, then, she was learning the danger in demanding responses, just as she was learning to make the most of tranquil evenings. It was a juggling act but, then, what wasn't? Like Stephen, she was hanging on now for the holiday, certain that relaxing in a warm climate would ease the tension between them and within the mysterious labyrinth of her reproductive system.

August

The villa was, if anything, even more perfect than the glossy images in the brochure had suggested. It sat at the end of an avenue of poplars, surrounded by sloping terraces of olive groves, its white stucco walls, blue shutters and red-tiled roof brilliant in the sunshine. In the distance, shimmering like a mirage between two folds of undulating countryside, lay the town of Todi, the small dome of its cathedral glinting like a crown jewel on a velvet cushion. The swimming-pool, lined with mosaic tiles of blue and white, was tucked away discreetly at the back of the villa, and landscaped so cleverly that it only became visible from the dining terrace that overlooked it. It was a decent pool, too, equipped with a diving-board and a crescent of little steps for less adventurous participants. Parked round it at angles under striped parasols were a dozen sun-beds and several small tables. Two symmetrical flights of steps linked this area to the terrace above, curling round a vast rockery that played host to some fierce-looking cacti and scores of exotic flowers with flamboyant petals and colours so vivid that little Genevieve wasn't the only one who couldn't resist reaching out to touch one every time she passed. No one else tugged them quite so hard or made a small store of broken petals behind one of the giant earthenware pots that decorated the terrace.

Although Helen and Peter were due to stay for the full four weeks, the departure dates of the other members of the family were sufficiently complicated for Helen to have felt justified in transposing them on to a chart, which she had stuck on the fridge door. Organizing the sleeping arrangements proved even more taxing, since all of the seven bedrooms were doubles and they would, at maximum capacity, be fourteen. The children would share, obviously, but when they were consulted mayhem broke out, largely thanks to Chloë, who said that she would rather be roasted alive than sleep in a room with her little sister. Gathering that she was not wanted, and exhausted from the journey, Genevieve sobbed until Roland scooped her up and said he'd like her as his room-mate if she'd have him. Whereupon Helen suggested that Ed and Theo go together, only to be informed by her nephew, far too curtly, she felt, that he had already struck a deal to share with Clem. At which point Chloë said that she, too, had been hoping to share with Clem and that she didn't want to be in the same room as her brother.

'You shouldn't have consulted them,' said Peter, laughing, when Helen stormed out to join him by the swimming-pool, hurling her book and her towel on to a sun-bed in a state of such frustration that a rash of angry red heat-spots had broken out across her chest. 'Giving people a choice is always fatal.' He smiled, peering at his wife over his sunglasses. 'Children and adults alike respond far better to orders.'

Peter was feeling good. He had already had a swim. Ploughing through the water for several lengths with his steady, stylish crawl, he had been vividly aware of the strength in his limbs and the life-affirming warmth of the sun on his back. I can do this, he had thought, smoothly turning his head to gulp air, then plunging his face back into the water, a few seconds in between, finding the rhythm. I can have a lover, come on holiday with my family and be happy. Life is a house of many mansions and I can occupy them all. It's just a question of having broad enough shoulders, of being in one room and closing the door on the other . . . *Compartments*. Delia in one, Helen and the children in another. It was easy. 'I'll sort them out,' he promised, reaching for the sun-cream Helen had brought and squirting some on to his tummy and legs even though the hairs were still matted and thick with pool water. 'I'll *command* them into submission, you just watch.'

'And Elizabeth will have to move in with your mother when Stephen and Cassie arrive,' said Helen, with a sigh, perching on his sun-bed so he could rub some cream into her back. 'I hope they'll be okay about that – with Pamela so in need of a lie-down and Elizabeth busily unpacking I didn't have the heart to mention it just now.'

'They'll be fine about it. Stop worrying.'

'I know. Sorry.' She lay down and closed her eyes, then opened one a second later to remark, 'Don't forget your bald patch.'

'Aye aye, Captain,' Peter muttered, his spirits deflating at this small wifely reminder of the one physical deterioration that eating well and keeping fit had no power to amend. Delia, he recalled happily, had said she found bald men immensely attractive. As if to curb any doubts on the subject, she had pressed his face between her breasts as she delivered the reassurance and kissed the naked top of his head with eager lips. The memory was vivid and caused Peter to feel a heat that had nothing to do with the ferocity of the sun. He turned on to his stomach to conceal the fact and closed his eyes, pretending to doze. A wife and a lover might occupy different compartments but he was finding that the doors between the two could slide open at the most inappropriate times.

A few minutes later the rest of the party arrived at the poolside. Charlie and Serena led the way, looking white and distinctly British in their sun-hats and swimsuits. Theo, his handsome rower's physique somewhat undermined by the vivid T-shirt and shorts marks on his arms and legs, overtook them and sprang off the diving-board into the water, followed, amid much shrieking, by Chloë. Roland, in a pair of voluminous green trunks, which Elizabeth had bought in a sale the week before, bombed in between them, creating a nuclear explosion of a splash of which Clem, preparing to enter the water at the shallow end, received the worst. As her cousin surfaced, laughing, shaking the hair out of his eyes, she stuck out her tongue, then slipped under the water, eel-like, with no splash, to see if she could manage a length without breathing.

Ed, meanwhile, kept at a distance from all the horseplay, first strolling to inspect the low wooden fence separating the pool area from the olive orchards, then going to sit on the edge with his feet dangling in the water. He was joined a few minutes later by Genevieve, who, sensing her cousin's isolation but with no concept of its origin, squatted next to him with an earnest expression on her freckled face, saying that if he couldn't swim either they could take it in turns with her armbands. Ed tried to ignore her, but couldn't resist grabbing her, holding her out over the water and snarling that all bad pirates had to be fed to the crocodiles.

'Lovely to see them all enjoying themselves,' said Serena, pulling her sun-bed alongside her brother and sister-in-law. 'Thank you, you two, for organizing it and insisting that we come in spite of . . . everything. It is *so* what we all needed.' She glanced a little anxiously at Charlie, wondering how anyone could not guess at the new and terrible tension between them, as impossible to ignore as clashing cymbals. Since the fruitless trip to Wandsworth they had, in the tense, whispered privacy of their bedroom, said terrible things. She had claimed that he lacked compassion and wanted a quick-fix solution. He said that Jessica's determination to have the baby was absurd and destructive, and she had encouraged it. She said his silent hostility towards Ed was making the boy wonder why he had bothered to return home. He said that her compassion was nothing more than cowardice about facing the issues. Going upstairs to pack the night before, tensing at the sound of Charlie's footsteps on the stairs behind her, it had occurred to Serena that their bedroom felt more like a battleground now than a sanctuary. 'Charlie, darling, we must *unite*,' she had pleaded, wringing her hands as he closed the door. 'We want the same things, surely? Happiness for our son, the safe upbringing of this unlooked-for child . . .'

Instead of responding as she had hoped, Charlie had folded his arms and said, no, he wasn't sure they did want the same things and where were his swimming trunks? She had plucked them from the pile of clothes on the bed, then hugged them to her chest, asking him what he meant by saying such a thing. He had gone red, blown out his cheeks and said, on a gasp of rushed angry air, that maybe she wanted Ed and Jessica's baby for herself, to fill the gap. Serena, feeling as if she was uncoiling like a too-tight spring, had flung his trunks across the room. How dare he and what gap – what fucking gap? Her voice had been whispery and high. If anyone had a gap it was him, she said, a gap where his heart should be. Charlie had studied her with dark, sad, accusing eyes, then taken himself into the spare room.

They had argued before, of course, during two decades of marriage, but never so nakedly. Even in the thick of the Tina crisis they had mostly left their worst thoughts unsaid, thereby allowing them to be defused by time or a good night's sleep or the simple fact of loving each other. What could they do now with these *said* things? Serena wondered. They were like exploded bombs, the debris spread far and wide, coating all that had been good with ugliness. How, with so much damage, could they ever claw their way back to the state of not-saying – of not-knowing – necessary to love?

Other than the holiday there was no respite in sight: Jessica, as reported by an increasingly desperate Maureen, was sticking to her guns. The remaining months of the pregnancy stretched ahead like a path no one wished to tread, with the unimaginable prospect of the baby at the end of it – their *son's* baby, their *grandchild*. It was due in January, they had calculated, with some wretchedness, in the same week that Cassie and Stephen were getting married. The one good thing on the horizon – and now that would be ruined too, Charlie had thundered, just as Ed's life would be ruined and theirs, too, through having to pick up the pieces.

Serena remained incapable of seeing everything quite so bleakly, not just because of her continuing joy at Ed's safe return and a knee-jerk compulsion to provide some sort of ballast to her husband's negativity, but also because it seemed inherently wrong to bewail the prospect of a newborn baby, no matter how dire the circumstances of its conception. They would have to find the funds to help provide for it until Ed was old enough to assume the responsibility. It was a terrifying prospect but one that Serena believed could be okay, if they handled it right. It might even be . . . but here Serena stopped herself, not wanting to nurture the tendril of fear that Charlie's most hurtful accusation contained an element of truth. Was that nerve still too raw? Was there a *gap* still at the heart of her? Was her compassion for the hapless Jessica's position connected to it?

'Cream?'

'Oh, no, thanks, Helen, I've got my own . . . Boots' special offer,' she added, producing a cumbersome orange plastic bottle and waving it to attract the attention of her son and daughter, whose skin was as porcelain pale as her own.

'In a minute,' shouted Clem, who had been diverted from her underwater swimming to pose with Roland as a marauding crocodile.

'Clem looks *so* well,' said Helen, kindly, following Serena's gaze as it lingered on her still skinny but radiant daughter. 'Whatever she's getting up to in London clearly suits her. And have you heard about Theo's film plans, with her as the lead? It's really very sweet, if you think about it – all their childhood games blossoming into grand projects . . . and with Clem, too, who was always the shy one, wasn't she? Talking of which, is Maisie still having a lovely time?'

'Oh, I think so,' replied Serena, cowering under so much questioning and rather wishing she had parked her sun-bed a little further away. During visits to Ashley House Helen was rarely so keen to talk, her discomfort at being a visitor in the family home often evident to the point of embarrassment. Being on holiday had put her in a different frame of mind, no doubt because the idea and planning of the venture had been hers and Peter's. That her brother- and sister-in-law were the uncontested masters of the villa had been obvious from the moment they all crossed the threshold. When they had parked their bags in the biggest bedroom with the best view she and Charlie had agreed without so much as an exchanged glance. Peter and Helen's suggestions ever since, about sleeping arrangements, food, the pattern of the day, already had the weight of an authority that Serena felt little inclination to resist. In fact, after all the subtle power-play overshadowing the management of Ashley House, it was almost a relief to let them take charge.

'We haven't heard from her for a while, which is a sure sign she's enjoying herself,' she replied. 'We've not yet told her about the Ed business, by the way. She'll hear it all soon enough and we didn't see any point in ruining her last few weeks. She's due to head back soon – via a friend in Seattle and another in New York – so we're not expecting her home until the middle of September when, of course, she'll have to start getting ready for Bristol.'

'I know Theo would have liked Maisie here.'

'We would all have liked Maisie here,' murmured Serena, glancing at Ed who was lying on his stomach on the diving-board, trailing his arms in the water.

'I just wish Ed would forgive Theo, or at least *talk* to him.'

'He's not really talking to anyone at the moment.' Serena

turned on to her side with her head towards Charlie, wishing he would lower his thriller so that she could see his face.

'No change, then, on the Jessica front?' pressed Helen.

Serena shook her head absently, her focus still on the peppered mop of her husband's bowed head. Normally he would have plunged into the pool with the children, raced with Ed and been a crocodile for Genevieve. He looked too hot and wasn't enjoying his book, she could tell, from the way he was tugging at his ear-lobe and chewing his lip. 'She's determined to have the baby,' she continued, wresting her eyes away from Charlie, suddenly disliking how well she knew him, how impossible it made it not to care. 'We're just going to have to find a way of dealing with it . . . a way of helping Ed through, financially and emotionally. I'm still just so glad he's *safe*.'

'Of course you are.' Helen squinted into the distance beyond the olive groves where the dome and the cluster of buildings surrounding it had turned a blue-grey in the heat-haze of the afternoon. She had looked up the cathedral in her guidebook. It had taken a hundred and fifty years to build and cost the lives of scores of local craftsmen. 'What about a trip to Todi this week? We could leave the men in charge.'

'I'd like that, Helen.' Serena's patience with the interrogation was at breaking-point. She made a big production of opening her book: a hilarious account of a woman trying to have it all, the blurb said – career, family, husband – and struggling on all fronts. She started to read, with a fake frown of concentration, wondering how trying to 'have it all' could be *hilarious*, when in reality it was heartrending and hard even for women like her, whose nod at work had never got beyond misshapen pieces of pottery and padded picture frames.

'It goes without saying,' continued Helen, 'that if there is anything further Peter and I can do – *anything* – you and Charlie have only to ask.'

Serena stopped this last outburst with a hasty, desperate

expression of gratitude, then hid her face behind her novel. Worse than being pitied was the underlying note of smugness in her sister-in-law's tone. Life in Barnes had always run like a well-oiled machine, all the cogs interlocking smoothly. Chloë had yet to test either of her parents while Theo would never have slept with a girl like Jessica in a million years, let alone without taking precautions. The way he had behaved in bringing the details of the crisis to their attention summed it all up. She and Charlie remained indebted to him, just as they did to Peter, for his willingness to offer advice and be involved. Yet it irked Serena, too, to feel they had given her husband's brother yet another opportunity to parade his superiority, to tell them how things should be done, in exactly the manner that he liked to interfere with Ashley House. Charlie couldn't see it, of course. But at the moment Charlie couldn't see anything.

Elizabeth arrived at the top of the steps in a turquoise bikini, which fitted well but left no room for charitable guesses as to the extent of her stomach, and hesitated at the sight of her family scattered before her round the pool. She was recovering from a mildly embarrassing encounter with the housekeeper, whom she had run into in the kitchen while on a quest to make Pamela a cup of tea. The woman, whose name was Maria, had been busy at a chopping-board, her knife flashing through onions and tomatoes the size of cooking apples and aubergines with skins as glossy as polished mahogany. Clearly of a similar age, but attired in a sensible grey dress and white apron, the sight of her had made Elizabeth feel both large and exposed. Clasping her towel to her chest, she had explained, in rusty O-level Italian, about the tea, then backed out with as much dignity as the circumstances allowed.

Standing on the terrace now, she attempted to tie the towel in something pertaining to elegance round her chest but then thought, What the hell?, and slung it over one shoulder before setting off down the steps. She loved the bikini in a way she would have found hard to explain. It was fashioned with large bows at the cleavage and the sides of the bottoms and had cost an amount of money entirely disproportionate to its size, even though it was in the sale. Staring at her reflection in the cramped changing room of the department store, Elizabeth had been unable to see beyond the bold display of her ample stomach and the bulge of her thighs. Then she had thought of Keith, recalling the eager affection with which he had explored the same terrain, and the beauty of the bikini had come into her sights at last – the magnificent way its lavish colour cupped her curves – and the purchase had become irresistible.

After the drama of her nephew's reappearance Elizabeth had broken her word and phoned Keith on his mobile. He had told her off – and not to do it again – but sounded pleased. She had jabbered like a teenager, loving the sound of his deep voice, full of common sense, loving the simple verification of his existence. He was still job-hunting but seeing a lot of his boys, he said. He was thinking of doing a computer course. He missed her but he was fine. She had promised not to call again, then longed to break her word the moment their conversation ended.

He is with me, she thought happily, as she trotted towards the pool. Loving him has changed me and made me strong. I have a guiding light at last, no less vivid for being invisible.

'Elizabeth . . . everything okay?'

'Oh, everything's wonderful. I've met our slave – she's called Maria and she's making Mum a cup of tea and all of us some ratatouille for supper. Make way, you lot, I'm coming in.' Dropping her towel, she strode over to the diving-board, bounced once with one leg raised, then swallow-dived into the pool.

'Go for it, Lizzy,' yelled Peter, clapping his hands. 'I'd forgotten she was so good, hadn't you, Charlie?'

His younger brother, who had lowered his book to watch,

nodded and smiled, then let his gaze drift towards the valley. He didn't have to put on a show. He was preoccupied and had every reason to be. His siblings understood that better, apparently, than Serena, who had spent half the day shooting scolding glances at him for being miserable. As if she really believed that changing the geography of their surroundings could change other things too. Move from the drizzling greys of England to the sultry pastels of Umbria, spread around them like a banquet, and hey presto! All would be well.

Except, of course, it wouldn't. It was only a view, after all, and had no power to change anything, least of all the increasingly bleak landscape of his marriage and the future now facing his son. How could Ed be a father? That such a thing was possible struck Charlie more and more as some kind of biological joke. The boy could barely tie his own shoelaces. He liked kicking a ball and watching television. During his first driving lesson he had, apparently, come close to colliding with a lorry. He was an unformed bundle of irresponsibility. Just the thought of this beloved, hopeless creature entering even the most removed version of parenthood made Charlie want to weep. It made him feel, too, that all Serena's panic-induced talk of failure during their recent terrible row had been spot on. She was right: they had failed as parents, as a family. So doggedly upbeat now, with a new, unacknowledged agenda of her own, Serena refused to admit it. But, looking ahead, Charlie could not see beyond the fact that everything he had fought for and believed seemed to be slipping from his grasp.

Closing his book and pretending to sleep, Charlie let his thoughts drift to the increasingly appealing option of handing back the title deeds of the family home to his elder brother. His and Serena's stewardship of Ashley House had brought nothing but unhappiness on all sides. His wife, he reflected fiercely, had been right to accuse his brother of being superior. Peter *was* superior – in every way. Far better to step back and let him take over, as their father had originally planned. The house, which was eating into their savings, would be better cared for, Pamela would almost certainly be happier, and it would allow him and Serena to concentrate on the mess that had overtaken their own lives, a mess that Charlie was sure they would have a far better chance of sorting out if they were beyond the spotlight of family attention, instead of living at its heart.

Long after everyone had gone to bed Pamela lay awake, listening to the whir of the air-conditioning and wishing, every time she rolled over, that she had had the foresight to bring a pillow from her bed at home. The coolness of the air was too sharp, yet if she pulled the covers up to her chin she quickly grew too hot. She longed to turn off the machine and throw open the shutters to the night air. At Ashley House she always slept with a window open, but here she felt too intimidated by the panel of buttons responsible for controlling the cooling system and the worry that every passing insect might spot the chink in the sealed armoury of the villa and swarm into her room to celebrate. As it happened, Pamela was good with insects. She rather liked fishing leggy spiders out of shower-heads and plug-holes to deposit them on windowsills. Moths held no fear for her either – they were always fluttering in and out of her bedroom window at home. Even when John was alive it had been her duty to chase them round the lampshades and cup them in her palms to release them into the night. With the lake being so near, they always had more than their fair share of mosquitoes too; quite often in the summer she would light a coil and place it on the windowsill to keep them at bay. The smell didn't bother her and she liked staring at its red torch-tip burning a hole in the dark.

Twisting and turning in the unfamiliar bed, Pamela became aware that she was worn out less from the journey – which, in spite of the attentive concern of her family, had been arduous – than from being so surrounded by her loved ones. Dear though they all were, their endless talking and plans, the complications of their lives, the sheer *noise* they made was exhausting. At Ashley House it was easier to withdraw, to dip in and out, according to her energy levels; but here with only her bedroom – soon, apparently, to be shared with Elizabeth – to retreat to, with no Poppy to walk or telephone to pick up, and the heat so imprisoning, the pressure was already, even after one day, quite draining.

I've rather had enough of them all, she confessed to John, moving her lips round the words but making no sound. *I think I'm ready for something else . . . not to come to you, dear, not yet, but to find a space that is more my own. You know how I love them and, goodness knows, they need loving, with the mess they're in . . . Dear Edward, it's still hard to believe, but what can I do, after all, other than watch it unfold? And I'm beginning to think I'd prefer to watch from a greater distance. Marjorie says Crayshott Manor takes dogs. I know that, to anyone else, that might sound a silly consideration, but you will understand that I couldn't think of leaving Poppy. And she'd like it there too – the grounds are so large, plenty of new places for her to explore, and so long as I was there I know she'd be happy. As for leaving Ashley House . . . well, even a few months ago I couldn't have imagined it, but now it seems not only possible but also rather appealing. I lived there with you, didn't I, my darling? It was our home. Now it is Charlie and Serena's, and with me gone they might feel that rather more than they do at the moment. They are at such sixes and sevens, the poor loves, tying themselves in knots because of Ed and this baby, which no one can bring themselves to imagine. They'll find a way through, I know they will. There's always a way through, if one looks, isn't there, my sweet? I will become a great-grandmother – can you imagine? An honour I had not thought could possibly be mine, what with the independence of all the young ones today, girls wanting careers before families and so on . . . I'm sure it will be years before either of the twins gets round to it, or Theo, for that matter*

. . . though he is coming along nicely, that one, so self-assured and hand-some, not at all the gawky creature with bumps on his face that you knew. Anyway . . . where was I? Oh, yes . . . hardly ideal circumstances, of course, but there we are, a baby is a baby, and I can't help feeling a little bit curious about getting to know this one in spite of the pitiful Jessica being its mother. I can't say that to them, of course. They all think the world has ended and must conclude for themselves that it hasn't.

If there is a God and He's with you, could you say hello? Could you say, too, that some of the Harrisons could do with a helping hand? Could you ask Him to be ready for me when I come? Oh, and thank Him for pushing Marjorie my way – she's such a solid jolly creature, so exactly what I needed. It's largely thanks to her that I realized my world hadn't ended either. Funny business, living, isn't it? Complicated to the end . . .

As Pamela's eyes grew heavy an Umbrian relative of a May-bug appeared from nowhere and began to bounce noisily against the ceiling. 'Shoo, silly thing, you don't scare me,' she murmured, batting one hand in its direction as she turned and sank her head into a cool fresh section of her pillow, knowing as she closed her eyes that they wouldn't open again until morning.

A week later, Stephen and Cassie arrived at Rome airport and lugged their bags to the car-rental desk only to find there had been a cock-up over their booking. Instead of the economy five-door they had been promised the only available vehicles were a seven-seater Ford Galaxy or something in the luxury sports-car range and, no, a discount wouldn't be available on either.

'For Christ's sake, look – our booking's here. We booked *this* car,' insisted Stephen, waving the documentation he had printed off the Internet.

'I know, Mr Smith, and I am most sorry for the inconveni-ence, but this is our holiday season so we are very busy at this time.'

'Don't tell me it's the holiday season, I *know* it is. That is precisely why we are visiting your country.'

'A sports car might be nice,' ventured Cassie, tired of the wait, and the debate, which was clearly going nowhere.

'Yes, but that's not the point, is it?' Stephen waved his piece of paper again, earning a glare from the weary-faced couple who were standing in the queue behind them, knee-deep in luggage and small children.

It was quite clear to whom the Ford Galaxy should go, Cassie mused, offering a tight smile of apology to the couple, then grinning at the smallest child, who was sitting cross-legged on the floor, sucking disconsolately at the beak of a fluffy orange duck and several strands of her own hair. She had a tangle of corkscrew curls, matted so badly across the crown that Cassie wondered how on earth a comb would ever tease it free. When she was little her hair had performed similar feats of rebellion. Pamela would lift her on to her dressing-table stool to attend to it, promising a rummage through her jewel-box if she withstood the eye-watering pain without too much yelping. After the ordeal, hair shining, scalp tingling, Cassie would plunge her hands into the trinkets, draping herself in necklaces and bangles and trying clip-on earrings till her ear-lobes throbbed. 'I am a princess,' she would say, swivelling her head and swinging her arms.

'For that you'll have to marry a prince,' Pamela would reply, shaking her head and smiling mysteriously.

And here he is, thought Cassie, returning her attention to Stephen, who was busy now writing down the name of the local manager of the car-hire firm and promising to take the matter further. Her prince, without a crown, but with lips that begged for a smile and a claim that he loved her enough to want to die without her. He wasn't what she *thought* she had been looking for but, then, fairy-tales were all about the answers to life's desires arriving in unexpected packages. And he was certainly full of the unexpected: that week there had been tickets to the Royal Opera House one night and a surprise lunch the following day. Leaving Frank's house in Ebury Street, she had literally bumped into him at the bottom of the steps, leaning against the railings reading a newspaper. 'Surprise,' he had said. 'Surprise lunch at Ken Lo's – we haven't had a Chinese in ages.' She had wanted to say she was too busy, that she had calls to make and bills to tot up, but had stopped herself, wary of disappointing him and behaving like a spoilsport. Most women, she had reminded herself, would give anything for a man to behave so spontaneously, so romantically. So she had said yes, what a treat, and tucked her bulging bag of paperwork under her arm for the walk to the restaurant. They had had a wonderful lunch, drinking more than they should have and laughing in happy, covert union at a neighbouring couple, who looked smart and bored and asked for cutlery instead of chopsticks.

The sports car worked a sort of magic. Even before they had negotiated their way out of the hiss and hoot of Rome, a reckless, binding sense of fun arose between them, like a genie released from a bottle. They lowered the windows and the roof, put on their sunglasses and took it in turns to try every one of the buttons on the dashboard, squealing like delighted children at the results. Between Cassie's faltering efforts at map-reading, Stephen sang 'King Of The Road', using the many traffic standstills as an opportunity to beat out a rhythm section on the steering-wheel. And then, just as the fun and Stephen's voice were in danger of wearing out, they found themselves on the right road sweeping north, with the dusty greens and yellows of rural Italy in high summer unrolling before them like a new carpet. With the warm wind blasting in their faces and roaring in their ears, there was too much noise to talk. Yet within it a happy silence reigned – a silence Cassie would have bottled and stoppered if she could. It was such a far cry from the mute tension of other recent car journeys that after a while she shouted, 'I love you, Stephen Smith.'

'And I love you, Cassie Harrison,' Stephen yelled back, recklessly taking his eye off the road to plant a kiss on her cheek.

They arrived at the villa a couple of hours later, windswept and dry-mouthed but still glowing with a rediscovered sense of intimacy. Peter skipped out to the car to help them with their bags, proudly listing the villa's many virtues as he led the way through its porticoed entrance and into the wide, marble-floored hall. Everyone was either on the tennis court or round the pool, he said. They had barely moved all week. Helen and Serena kept talking about a trip to Todi but had yet to get round to it. Thanks to Maria's impressive catering, they were eating and drinking like lords and waistlines were expanding, although there was an impressive air-conditioned gym in the basement for those willing to make the effort.

'But I'm not allowed to go in there,' whined Genevieve, who had appeared, shivering in a wet swimsuit, through one of the arched doorways leading off the hall, 'not even to sit on the bicycle.' Having delivered this information, she skidded out of sight, while Peter shouted after her about drying her feet before coming into the villa. 'Little monkey.' He grinned at Cassie and Stephen, gesturing for them to follow him through one of the other arches. 'We've put you in here,' he announced, pushing open a door at the end of the corridor, 'because we thought it would be nice and quiet. There's an *en suite*, of course. All you can see is the tennis court, but that's not such a bad view, is it?'

'It's lovely,' murmured Cassie, strolling to the window to watch Theo serve to Clem, who swung and missed, then ducked as Chloë, clearly commandeered to man the base line, managed a neat lob back over the net. 'American doubles . . . We used to play that, do you remember, Peter?' She turned to smile at her brother. 'Because Elizabeth always said she was too useless to play.'

Peter rolled his eyes. 'Certainly do. You should see her in the pool, though. She's a hell of a swimmer – I'd quite forgotten.'

'Where's Ed? More to the point, *how* is Ed?' added Cassie, leaving the window and peering round the bathroom door. 'Such an appalling situation it's hard to know what to say to them all, isn't it, darling?'

'Impossible,' agreed Stephen, who had little desire to dampen his spirits by dwelling on the new predicament facing his fiancée's family. Ed's stupidity remained beyond words, but within that lurked the infinitely more irksome fact, so blithely pointed out by Cassie, that his soon-to-be nephew had haplessly conceived a child during the course of one coupling, while he and his fiancée had waged almost a year's campaign of unprotected sex with no result. Stephen's qualms about fatherhood remained as strong as ever, yet within that there now existed a ring-fenced sense of failure. Not truly wanting a child was one thing, but Stephen was beginning to see that not being *able* to have one was another matter. The paradox annoyed him almost more than the see-saw of emotions it invoked. He hated, too, the compulsion to resist voicing such dilemmas aloud. Increasingly, it seemed, all his most serious preoccupations – making certain of Cassie, getting nowhere with his work, not to mention the possibility that he was *firing blanks* – were things he had to keep to himself. Stephen's brain bulged sometimes from the sheer pressure of it, especially when he made mistakes, like hovering too near the Ebury Street house and having to think on the spot. He'd got away with it, but for hours afterwards – during the Chinese meal and throughout the journey home – he had been aware of a trembling all over his body, as if he was suppressing too much, as if something had exploded inside and all the aftershocks of energy were rippling up and down his limbs, looking for a way out.

After such tensions Stephen was in a state close to euphoria at having arrived on a fresh wave of intimacy at the villa – somewhere he could enjoy his fiancée instead of watching her, where maybe he would feel sufficiently inspired to add some readable paragraphs to his manuscript, where even, as Cassie herself clearly hoped so desperately, Fate might step in on the pregnancy front and they'd have their own baby to worry about instead of their nephew's.

'I thought this was to be a work-free two weeks,' exclaimed Cassie, after Peter had left them and Stephen had pulled out his laptop from inside a folded towel in his suitcase. 'You'll need an adaptor anyway, won't you?'

'Not by the look of it,' grunted Stephen, squatting down to examine the wall space under one of the bedside tables. 'There are sockets for every kind of plug . . . Blimey, this place is something else, isn't it?'

'But having that thing means you're going to *work*,' complained Cassie, sufficiently confident of their new-found closeness to put on a display of genuine petulance. Stephen, she reminded herself, had been madly keen for her to take a break from *her* work.

'One never knows when the muse might strike.' He peered out from under the bedside table, then glanced quickly away as the real reason for his recent pitiful lack of literary output gusted across his mind. With the holiday having started so well, he was aware suddenly of all his recent vigilance as both uncouth and unjustified. Maybe he would tell her about it one day, Stephen thought, struggling to his feet and putting his arms round her. Maybe when they were old and in armchairs by a fireside, as solid and indestructible as her own dear parents had been when he'd first met them at Ashley House, he would confess it and make her laugh. '*You* are my first priority,' he said gently, 'and always will be.'

When Roland put his head round the door a few minutes later they were kissing. 'Oh – sorry.'

'Don't be silly,' said Cassie, pulling free and planting a kiss on each of her godson's burning cheeks. 'How lovely to see you – and looking *so* well. I'd give anything for a tan like that. What's your secret, other than swimming and tennis?'

'I don't play tennis,' muttered Roland, fiddling with the hem of his T-shirt. 'But I've been drawing quite a bit . . . the views and so on.'

'Of course you have, you *artist* you.'

Roland looked at his feet, contemplating how hopeless adults could be at knowing what to say and abandoning any idea of expanding now on his one and only talent. Much of his eagerness with his sketchbook stemmed from Clem's nonchalant announcement at the start of the holiday that she had not – as he had supposed – forgotten about his paintings but had delivered them to her artist friend for comment. Delighted, he had begged her not to tell anyone, then promptly blurted out the news to his mother, who had hugged him and said she'd keep her fingers crossed; though quite what for Roland was unclear. He was increasingly aware that someone liking or not liking his work didn't matter. He painted because he *had* to, because it gave a shape to things and made him feel better.

Meanwhile Cassie's gaze had followed her godson's to his bare feet, with their too-long nails and tide mark of dirt round the heel. 'I so enjoyed our shopping trip, didn't you?'

'Uh . . . yeah . . . Thanks again for the jeans and the shoes,' muttered Roland, dutifully, trying not to squirm at the thought of the dusty shoebox in the bottom of his wardrobe and his recollection of the man they had met in the shop, the gay man, who had looked at him in that unforgettable way, as if he knew the very thing about which Roland himself remained so curious yet so uncertain. One of the more excruciating consequences of his cousin's recent misfortune had been a talk from his mother on the dangers of unprotected sex. Roland had endured it with pink-faced stoicism, knowing she was trying to be helpful but wondering how she would feel if he confessed that the good sense of using condoms was for him beginning to have other implications. He had thought, too, wickedly, that if Carl called him, as his request for Roland's telephone number at the end of term suggested he might, the last anxiety on his mind would be an unwanted pregnancy. There would be other terrors – hordes of them – but not that. 'I just came to say,' he stammered now, 'that Uncle Peter told me to tell you he's serving cocktails on the terrace.'

'*Cocktails* on the *terrace*?' squealed Cassie. 'Is he now? Give us a minute to change and we'll be right there. Oh, Stephen,' she murmured, after Roland had closed the door, 'I'm so happy I could burst. I wish we could get married *now*, this minute, while everything feels so beautiful and right . . . on the terrace with a few bougainvillaeas in my hair, surrounded by my family. Of course I still want the big wedding and everything, but I had no idea that planning it would be quite such an ordeal. Forgive me, darling, please, for getting so stressed out. I'm going to try harder from now on, I promise, not to let it get on top of me, to make sure that the next five months are plain-sailing, to remember that all that matters is us standing side by side in St Margaret's and saying our vows . . . Oh, Stephen . . .' She put her hands to her face and began to cry quietly. 'Sorry,' she sobbed, 'I'm just so *happy*.'

'Hey, hey there . . . you funny old thing! If this is happiness what do you do when you're sad?' Stephen pulled her close, cradling the curve of her head with one hand and pressing her to him. She stopped crying and nestled into him, so snugly he could feel the squash of her breasts against his chest and the rise and fall of her breathing. Aroused by the embrace and his own restored sense of happiness, Stephen was dismayed to note that the many luxurious touches in the villa did not include a lock on their bedroom door. Sex would have to wait until darkness protected them. No matter. He was good at waiting, after all, he reflected ruefully, not just in bus shelters and behind lampposts but in the wider scheme of things. Hadn't he waited all those years for Cassie to reciprocate his love? And in the last few months, too, hadn't he been biding his time, not panicking, doing what he could? And here it was, the reward, the *reciprocated* love, just as in the early, heady days but better, somehow, for the intervening patch of terror that it might all be slipping away.

'Roll on January,' he whispered, groaning softly as he nuzzled her neck, inhaling the musky scent, loving the way she pressed against him in response, loving, above all, the certainty that he was wanted.

Two days later Helen and Serena set off on their long-postponed trip to Todi. After endless discussions as to who should go and which car to use, the only person who decided to accompany them was Cassie. The younger members of the group, hearing talk of palazzos and duomos, had backed off with various excuses, except Theo who, having discovered from his mother's guidebook that the main piazza had been used as a location in several famous films, was sorely tempted to go along for the ride. What prevented him was a sudden enthusiastic offer of Clem's to have a proper readthrough of his script. The offer, which took place during breakfast, had raised the question Theo had been hoping to defer about how he planned to fund the project. At mention of his trust fund, Ed scraped back his chair and left the table, while his parents exchanged a glance and swiped butter across their toast. 'We'll talk about it later,' Peter had said finally, 'when we've all had more time to consider.' Theo had let the moment pass, though inwardly his resolve to fulfil his project had hardened, making it all the easier to put his script before the option of sightseeing.

Among the grown-ups, decisions about how to spend the day had been no less complicated. Pamela could see the glinting sixteenth-century dome from her window and longed to go, but feared for her stamina in the heat, which had been gathering weight all week, swelling round the villa as if it might crush it out of existence. She would let the other women down, she was sure, needing rests and cups of tea while they were still eager to explore side-streets and click their cameras. Even in her hat and thinnest frock, sitting on a chair in the shade of the orange trees clustered between the pool and the tennis court, she had found she could only last half an hour or so before a dizzying urge overtook her to escape into the synthetic cool of the villa's interior. In spite of gentle encouragement, she had so far resisted swimming as a mode of refreshment. They were all so young and sturdy-limbed that the thought of revealing her flimsy flesh, as white and blue-veined as French cheese, was faintly repulsive, even to her. Yet beneath that there lurked a deeper reserve, about how it might feel to have cold water sliding over her limbs, whether it would make her mad again and needing pills. She hadn't renewed her prescription for several weeks and wanted to keep things that way.

'I'll save Todi for another day, I think,' she had said at last, busying herself with washing the breakfast dishes, although Helen had instructed her not to. She worked slowly, watching her hands swell in the heat of the water, and thinking, with sudden longing, of the inoffensive grey drizzle through which the plane had ascended as they left Heathrow.

'And I'm going to stick with this, thanks,' grunted Charlie, patting another of the fat bestsellers he had bought at the airport, as if the decision arose from a new passion for detective stories rather than lingering low spirits. 'Like Mum says, maybe another day.'

'Same for me,' said Peter, whose mind had fast-forwarded to the irresistible notion that his wife's absence might allow him to put through a call to Delia. 'And, of course, someone should keep an eye on our youngest,' he added quickly, seeking refuge from his guilt in the obvious virtue of the observation.

'But I can do that,' protested Elizabeth. 'I don't want to sightsee. It's far too hot. And, anyway, Genny and I already have plans, don't we, poppet?' She winked at her youngest niece, who was sitting cross-legged on the floor in her swimsuit, her face and limbs already glowing a luminous white from Helen's lavish applications of sun-block.

'I'm going to learn to *swim*,' explained Genevieve, solemnly, 'not using armbands. When I do it I will get an ice-cream.'

Helen laughed. 'Oh, Lizzy, thank you – what a wonderful idea. So you could come, Peter, darling,' she added, returning her attention to her husband. 'We'd love you to, wouldn't we, ladies?'

Peter frowned, pretending to think. 'No, I'll pass all the same.'

'But, darling, you'd *love* it,' exclaimed Helen, genuinely baffled. Peter was the biggest culture-vulture of the family. 'The cathedral's called Santa Maria della Consolazione, it's early sixteenth-century and there are at least three other churches, the ruins of a medieval fortress and a Roman amphitheatre.'

Peter shook his head. 'Maybe another day – we could do a *boys'* trip, eh, Charlie?' he joked, glancing at his brother and Stephen, who had excused himself on the grounds of doing some work on his book. 'I tell you what, though, I'd love a newspaper if you can find one – anything in English, but preferably the *Financial Times*.'

'A *newspaper*, honestly,' scoffed Helen, grinding the unfamiliar gear-box of their hired car as they set off down the dusty drive at last; 'they say they want to get away from it all but they don't, really.'

'Like Stephen,' agreed Cassie, who was sitting in the back, 'scuttling off to *work*.'

'And Charlie saying he wanted *proper* bacon with his eggs,' put in Serena, wanting to join in the merriment and trying not to reflect on the fact that this was virtually all her husband had said to her for almost twenty-four hours. Rather than exposing their problems, as she had at first feared, being so surrounded was helping to mask them. There was always a conversation going on, someone or something to respond to. No one could have guessed at the guillotine of silence that now descended at every moment they were alone.

'Ed seems to be doing okay,' ventured Cassie, a few minutes later, seizing on her first opportunity to refer to the crisis.

'Oh, he's fine,' said Serena, her voice hollow and bright, 'living in the moment, as they do at that age, not thinking ahead. His A-level results are being phoned through tomorrow – I truly think he's more worried about those.'

'He's sweet with Genny,' put in Helen.

'Maybe,' suggested Cassie, in a small voice, 'that means he'll be a good father . . .'

'Maybe,' agreed Serena, grimly. 'I find it hard to think about. I mean it's all just going to *happen*, so there's nothing any of us can do about it, is there? Actually – and don't take this the wrong way – just for today I'd rather like to stick to the glories of the Renaissance . . . an Ed-free zone.' She laughed sharply. 'Would you two mind?'

'Of course not,' they muttered, exchanging a glance of mutual compassion in the rear-view mirror while Serena pressed the creases out of the road map.

'We want the next left, second right, and then it will be a question of finding somewhere to park.'

'Well, that sounds easy enough,' said Helen.

'A piece of cake,' agreed Serena, privately wishing she had a set of comparably easy instructions for negotiating the months ahead.

An hour later, sipping cold drinks at a café on the edge of Todi's main square (the Palazzo del Popolo, Helen had informed them, putting on her glasses for yet another forage in her guide-book), Serena recalled that she had never got round to responding to Cassie's phone message. 'I'm so sorry, I've been so distracted,' she said. 'I expect it was something about the wedding, wasn't it? I can't tell you how much we're looking forward to it – the one bright spot on the horizon, frankly.'

'Oh, no . . . It wasn't about the wedding. It was . . .' Cassie sucked at the straw in her Diet Coke, struggling, with the sunburnished beauty of their surroundings – given a sharp blue tinge by her sunglasses – and the pleasant pulse of heat on her bare shoulders, to recall the particular misery of that rain-soaked June day: how pinched she had felt in her wedding dress, how the sight of the chubby-limbed Noah had reached out to her and strangled her heart. 'Stephen and I were going through a bit of a bad patch . . . It was getting me down. I needed to talk to someone . . . but I – we – are *fine* now,' she added, seeing the stricken expression on Serena's face. 'Please, don't feel bad. You've had plenty of other far more important things to worry about and, anyway, every couple has bad patches, don't they?' she urged, curiosity seeping into her tone. These women were the wives of her brothers after all, with over forty years of marriage between them.

Helen, aware of this and rather taken with the licence it gave her to impart wisdom, lowered the guidebook and took off her sunglasses. 'I think we'd agree with that, wouldn't we, Serena?' She laughed with a confidence born of her own husband's recent ebullience and keenness to please. They had had their hard times, all right, most notably when it dawned on her that having Genevieve hadn't caused a seismic shift in the balance of things, as Peter had promised, that it would be up to her – as it always had been – to keep the show on the road. She had been very tense then, resentful, even. But now . . . it was a doddle. 'Ups and downs, for better for worse and so on – it's all true.'

'And you just have to stick with it,' put in Serena, fiercely, talking as much to herself as to Cassie. 'You have to listen and forgive, then listen and forgive again and grope your way along, and sometimes it seems bloody hard, so hard it's almost like a faith, like trying to believe in a God you can't see but whom you have to take on trust, who you know will appear in some form when you need Him most . . . not that I believe in God,' she faltered, picking up her glass and rattling what remained of the ice-cubes, 'but I think they're similar – marriage and faith – believing when sometimes there seems no reason to.'

'I've had a go at believing in God recently,' remarked Helen, as if referring to a sample one might pick up at a supermarket. 'It's been going rather well, actually.'

'Right.' Cassie looked from one to the other, at a loss as to how to respond. Serena was clearly feeling too emotional to talk sensibly about anything, and she had no desire to engage the formidable Helen in a discussion about religion. She had observed the piety in her sister-in-law's eyes as they approached the altar in the cathedral – the quick, fervent crossing of her chest – and not liked it very much. Where had such zeal come from and why did she have to parade it? All Cassie's own wavering faith had died with her niece. Churches for her were now solely about architectural beauty, tradition and public ceremony; rituals for humans rather than gods.

'My dear, marriage is fun,' continued Helen, warmly, reaching across the table and patting Cassie's hand. 'Pre-wedding nerves are perfectly understandable. You and Stephen were *made* for each other – both Peter and I have always thought so,' she declared grandly, even though neither of them had ever said any such thing.

'Have you? Oh, that's nice . . . thanks.' Cassie sighed and smiled, tempted to add that if she could only be pregnant she would be the happiest woman in the world. But then she looked at Serena, still tight-lipped and sombre from her outburst, and pushed the thought away. Given the situation facing Ed, talk of wanting babies was hardly appropriate. 'A newspaper,' she exclaimed instead. 'We mustn't forget to look for one.'

'But only after we've seen the Rocca and the Nicchione,' countered Helen, rolling her vowels in a way that she hoped sounded Italian. 'Come on, let's pay the bill and I'll tell you all about them as we walk.'

A few minutes later the trio set off across the cobbled stones of the piazza, progressing slowly, thanks to Helen's insistence that no detail from her guidebook should go undisclosed. They had reached the cooler, shaded corner of the piazza, when a voice, female and high-pitched, rang out behind them. Serena turned first, seeing an unfamiliar, deeply tanned creature with braided hair in combat trousers and a skimpy vest-top running towards them, a bulging rucksack bumping awkwardly against her back.

'Mum!' screeched Maisie, waving both arms in frustration that she hadn't been recognized.

'Oh, look! Oh, Helen! Cassie! *Look!*' A moment later Serena was hugging her daughter and the rucksack, not knowing whether to laugh or cry, asking if she was all right and what was she doing in Italy instead of America, and why hadn't she told them?

'I wanted to surprise you,' squealed Maisie, crying a little herself. 'I changed my plans – decided to come back through Europe and hook up with you lot, only I didn't have the address so I thought I'll get to this Todi place, then call you on your mobile. I got off the bus literally *five* minutes ago and here you are! It's unbelievable, isn't it?'

'Yes,' gasped Serena, who was crying in earnest, reaching out between sobs to stroke her daughter's freckled brown arms and curious tight plaits, as if to reassure herself that she wasn't an apparition. 'I must tell Dad,' she said, struggling through her blur of tears to find her phone.

'No! Let's surprise him.'

'Yes, let's,' agreed Cassie and Helen, thinking how delighted Charlie would be. The same thought crossed Serena's mind, only to be darkened by the realization that Maisie needed to be brought up to speed with regard to the antics of her brother. She was taking a deep breath, wondering when – how – to start, when Maisie said, 'I know about Ed and Jessica, by the way. Don't be cross,' she added, glancing at their three astonished expressions, 'but Clem told me and I'm bloody glad she did. It's one of the reasons I changed my plans.' She swung her rucksack off her back, rolled her shoulders and stretched her arms. 'The total twit! I mean, what was he *thinking*? And poor you, Mum – and Dad, poor *everyone*. Making me and Clem *aunts*, at our age.' She giggled and clapped her hand to her mouth. 'Sorry, but I still can't believe it and I'm just so *pleased* to see you.' She hugged Serena again, saying, 'He's been a twit but he's still Ed, isn't he?'

'Yes,' murmured Serena, feeling a huge comfort at this small, obvious piece of wisdom and managing to laugh a little herself, 'he's still Ed, all right.'

'Well, we saw the Duomo anyway,' remarked Helen wryly, as they set off back in the direction of the street where they had parked the car.

Serena and Maisie had fallen behind, linking arms. 'Is this to be a permanent style?' teased Serena, tugging at one of the braids and thinking that Maisie could have shaved her head and she wouldn't mind.

'No, just helps keep it clean. I'll take them out tonight. God, I can't wait for a *bath* – it does have baths, this place, does it?'

'It has *everything*,' replied her mother, 'and *everybody*, come to that.'

'Ashley House but in Italy,' exclaimed Maisie happily, tightening her grip on her mother's arm, unable to explain how much she had missed them all, how magical it was to have stretched her wings but to have her family still there, awaiting her return.

It was Cassie who remembered the newspaper again, darting into a shop just before they reached the car. 'It's only a *Daily Mail* and it's yesterday's, but better than nothing. Look,' she continued, as Helen manoeuvred out of the space, edging past the wheel of a large motorbike, 'there's a new terrorist alert in London, the worst since September the eleventh.'

'Well, thank God we're all out here,' said Serena, too giddy with delight to care about bombs. She patted her daughter's bare leg, certain suddenly that her arrival marked the turning point they so badly needed, that everything now would get better.

Shortly after the women's departure Charlie strolled over to Peter's sun-bed and challenged him to a game of tennis.

'Bit hot, isn't it, old man?'

'Don't be a wimp. It'll do us good.'

'Perhaps I could play the winner,' ventured Stephen, who had deferred his good intentions about work in favour of a swim. He swung his towel across his shoulders, keen suddenly to be fully accepted by the brothers. He would be a member of the family soon, after all, and wanted it to be on the best possible terms.

'Okay, then,' said Peter, not really liking Stephen's obvious eagerness, but unable to resist the harder challenge of beating both of them. 'I've, er, just got to put a call in to work, then I'll be with you.'

'Give me a shout when you've finished,' Stephen called, trotting up the steps. 'I'll be in my room.'

'You've got to call work?' Charlie snorted. 'Whatever for? I thought you had a team of underlings, these days?'

'But the buck still stops with me,' replied Peter, glibly, following Stephen up the steps to the terrace. 'I need to put my trainers on anyway. Won't be long.'

In his bedroom, he took his phone into the *en suite* and locked the door. Delia answered when he was on the point of giving up. 'I'm with a patient.'

'Sorry . . . Just wanted to hear your voice . . . to tell you that I miss you all the time, that I can't stop thinking about you – that I love you.' It was the first time Peter had uttered such words to anyone but his wife, and he caught his breath, trembling with shock both at their truth and his own daring in voicing it.

At the other end of the line there was a rustle and a muffled thump, then Delia's voice, hushed but more relaxed. 'I've got two minutes. I wanted to talk to you too.'

Peter laughed. 'Well, thank God for that.'

'My son has met your niece, did you know that?'

'What?'

'On their travels. They bumped into each other, took the same flight to Europe. Julian got back this morning – he's been full of it.'

Peter, perching on the edge of the bath, reached out a hand to the shining wall of white tiles to steady himself. 'That's not possible.'

'You think not? How many Maisie Harrisons aged twenty and living in west Sussex can there be?'

'Christ! I don't believe it! Are they – Is something going on between them?'

'I don't know, but it changes things, doesn't it? Even if they're just friends.'

'No,' said Peter, firmly, desperation surging inside. 'It's just important that we know, that's all. It means we can deal with it . . . work our way round it . . .'

There was a sigh. 'I can't talk now, Peter, I've left my patient waiting.'

'You are glad I rang, aren't you?'

'Of course I am.'

'And you want to see me again?'

'And I want to see you again,' she echoed, 'but . . .'

'Oh, here we go, the big "but",' interjected Peter, trying to sound teasing rather than terrified.

'You know the "but", my darling,' she said softly, so softly that all the terror melted to sheer desire. 'You know it, don't you?'

'Yes. You don't want to jeopardize either of our marriages. You want to carry on seeing me but to stay with your husband. That's fine. That's what I want too.' Peter recalled his confession of love and wished she would offer some similar endearment in return. She had had other lovers, he knew that. She needed more than her husband, she said. She was sure he saw other women, but exercised similar discretion. They had a good, solid, shared history, a son they adored, considerable wealth, security – too much for either of them to countenance giving up the marriage. It had sounded ideal. It *was* ideal, Peter reminded himself now, sliding along the bath to lean more firmly against the wall. No demands, no hysterics, just closeness and sex . . . Millions of married men would give body-parts for such an arrangement. He was lucky beyond words. But sitting there, with his forehead pressing against the cool hardness of the tiles, Peter didn't feel lucky so much as desolate. He wanted her to say she loved him, too. He wanted her to say that they would carry on seeing each other, no matter what. He hated it suddenly that she had had other lovers, that she had dipped in and out of such passions, while what he was experiencing was so new, so overwhelming. 'I want you now,' he said huskily, pressing his palm against the swell in his shorts. In the same instant he heard the bedroom door open and Charlie calling his name. 'I've got to go. I'll call again soon.'

A moment later the bathroom door handle rattled. 'Are you in there?'

'Christ, can a man get no peace?' Peter shouted, stuffing the phone into his shorts pocket and pressing the flush on the lavatory.

'It's getting hotter, that's all. We should hurry up – maybe play just one set.' Charlie folded his arms and stepped aside as Peter emerged. 'Often make your business calls on the throne, do you?'

'Only when nature calls at the same time, old chap,' replied Peter, thinking fast – Charlie must have heard him speaking. 'I say, you've perked up a bit haven't you? Getting at me – that's a sure sign.'

'Ed's school secretary just phoned with his exam results – two As and a B. Remarkable, given the circumstances.'

'It certainly is. Excellent – well done.' Peter shook his brother's hand, as if the achievement had been his rather than his nephew's. 'I thought they were due tomorrow.'

'So did we – so did Ed. Can you imagine? Something so important and he doesn't even know the *day*.' Charlie shook his head, lost in exasperated affection. 'Not that it matters. His life's still a fuck-up,' he said glumly, sitting on the bed and performing a desultory swing with his tennis racket.

'No, it *isn't*. I never heard such nonsense. He's bright, your boy, and he'll do well in spite of this wretched business. It's up to you to be strong, to help show him the way to –'

'I've decided you should take over at Ashley House.' Charlie spoke loudly to prevent the words sticking in his throat.

'What?' One trainer on and the other in his hand, Peter hobbled towards his younger brother. '*What* did you say?'

'You heard.'

'Why?' gasped Peter, then thought he should really have said, 'No,' or 'Don't be stupid.'

Charlie shrugged. 'We . . . Serena and I, we're not . . . coping. Being there doesn't *feel* right. It never has, to be honest. Mum would prefer you there – you know she would. Christ, in her own sweet way she's made it clear enough, hasn't she?'

'Now you're being ridiculous.'

Charlie shook his head wretchedly. 'This year, it's all gone wrong and it feels connected to our being there.' He held up his racket, peering first at its criss-crossed face, then through it towards the window and the unreal blue of the sky. It was like staring at something unreachable through the bars of a cage.

'Does Serena know you feel like this?' pressed Peter, trying harder now to say the right thing, trying, above all, to disguise the irrepressible bubble of excitement mushrooming inside. Ashley House . . . Christ, he'd handed it over willingly enough, had not subsequently wanted it – had never *let* himself want it – but now, here, with such an offer slung at him from nowhere, a terrible hope had taken hold. His mind was racing already – Helen would need persuading but how wonderful it would be to live in the beloved place, how perfectly he would run it, how fine it would feel to sit at the big desk in his father's old study surrounded by his books, how – his thoughts galloped faster – he could keep a flat in London, stay there a night or two each week . . . see Delia.

Charlie laughed darkly. 'Oh, I think so. Serena was the first to mention it.' He lowered the racket and looked at Peter properly for the first time. 'We're not . . . happy . . . together.'

For a moment Peter was almost more astounded by this than the proposition about the house. 'What are you talking about? You and Serena have always been stupendously happy – an example to us all,' he added, as a little eddy of shame surged and retreated inside.

'This Ed business, it's driven us apart. She *wanted* that loathsome girl to have the baby – right from the start . . . because . . .' But there Charlie stopped, driven by some deep, lodged loyalty not to convey his darkest suspicions even to his brother. He slapped his knees and stood up. 'There! So now you know. Think about it, would you? We'll need more money, you see,' he added, watching as Peter crouched with fumbling hands to tie his laces. 'Another child to raise, educate . . . It will be years before Ed has the finances for such things. All our savings from the sale of the Wimbledon house are being gobbled up as it is, far faster than I'd anticipated. Frankly, we're going to need every penny we can get, particularly –' Charlie broke off, as another portcullis clanged shut in his mind – nothing to do with loyalty this time so much as the still impossible notion of separating from Serena. He might think it, but saying it – giving it the legitimacy of articulation – was still too hard. 'Like I said, just think about it, okay? And now we'd better get a move on before our resident novelist starts pacing the tramlines. Is he any good, do you know?'

'Soon see, won't we? You've got me to worry about first.'

'Shoulder okay?' countered Charlie, rising, in spite of everything, to the easy, pleasurable business of sibling competition, as familiar and comforting as a pair of old shoes.

'Never better.' Peter flexed his arms, feeling a rush of joy and certainty about Delia – she might have complicated his life but she had energized it too. It was through his sore shoulder that he had found her, after all, he mused exultantly, following Charlie out of the room. She had brought his body into line, given him the focus he hadn't even known he craved, restored a love of living that had been in danger of growing stale. And now Ashley House was his for the taking too – another joy landing in his lap when he had least expected it.

Stephen kept an eye on the tennis through his window, weighing up his opponents. Charlie was imaginative but slow, while Peter had more power and a darting speed that was truly impressive, given his broad frame and relatively advanced years. Watching him, Stephen began to doubt whether his own unorthodox but hard-hitting style, acquired on ex-pat tennis courts during his years of teaching in South America, would be up to the challenge. Peter was winning, it was clear, but with the inter-mittent bursts of concentration Stephen was giving his manuscript, it was hard to be sure by how much.

In spite of the distraction, his writing and Jack Connolly were having a good day. The detective's self-doubt and binge-drinking were on hold for once, while the pieces of his case were fitting more snugly. It was becoming evident that his pro-tagonist might not only solve the murders of several lap-dancers but sort out some of the muddle in his private life too.

On the way to the tennis court Stephen passed Clem lying on the sofa studying a wad of papers. She glanced at him and flicked her eyes back to the text.

'What are you reading?'

'Theo's script,' she muttered.

Clearly she didn't want to talk, but Stephen did. And he had time, too, since the match had only just ended and both Charlie and Peter had disappeared in the direction of the pool.

'I've been meaning to ask, how is *your* writing going, these days?'

Clem studied a fingernail. 'I haven't done much since . . . Thanks, by the way, for that writers' book you sent.'

'I was thinking,' interjected Stephen, feeling bad at his flimsy response to the child's request for help, aware that even if she had felt its inadequacy she would have been too full of youthful timidity to say so, 'I could show your manuscript to my editor – ask for a few comments. Would you like that?'

Clem lowered the script and levered herself upright, giving him her full attention at last. 'But it's not good enough for that. Is it?'

'It might be.' Stephen smiled, enjoying this new generosity of spirit, aware that it reflected a surge of confidence in his own writing rather than hers. 'I'll give you her name and write a covering letter so you can send it yourself when you're ready. Okay?'

'That would be brilliant. Thanks, Stephen. And . . . er . . . have you had a good morning on your book?' Clem inquired shyly.

'Fantastic, thanks. As of about five minutes ago I've got a title.' Stephen rubbed his hands together in happy recollection of the moment, which, historically, had always been a turning-point when he was working on a manuscript.

'Oh, that's good. What is it?'

'*The Lap-dancer*, which probably doesn't sound much to you but makes a lot of sense, given my plot.'

Clem frowned, then smiled impishly. 'Sounds sort of . . . *rude*.'

Stephen laughed. 'I suppose it does. I have all these lap-dancers, you see, who get killed one by one, all from the same club . . . Anyway,' he sensed she would be bored if he continued, 'I'm about to play your uncle at tennis. I'm pretty sure he's beaten your dad.'

Clem groaned. 'I wish he wouldn't. Dad's in *such* a grump as it is.'

'Is he? Oh, because of your brother, you mean?'

Clem made a face. 'Yup . . . At least, I suppose it's that. It's pretty ghastly, after all. Poor Ed . . . He got his results just now – they're really good too. Dad was pleased for about a nanosecond, then exploded about how his education had been a waste of time. He thinks that about me, too, you know,' she added, with a scowl.

'I'm sure he doesn't.'

Clem nodded sadly. 'He does.'

'Well, when I was your age I got lousy grades and didn't know what to do with my life and then . . . well, things sort of fell into place.' Stephen smiled again, feeling strong and avuncular. 'So don't worry.'

'Thanks . . . and showing my stuff to your editor – that would be *fantastic*.'

'No problem.' Stephen sauntered into the kitchen, took a bottle of mineral water from the fridge, drank half and took the rest with him to the tennis court which was deserted. A few minutes later Peter joined him, wearing a pair of shorts, the grey hairs on his chest glistening from his swim.

'Just one set, then, given the heat?'

'Suits me,' replied Stephen, glad of all the hours on the baked-clay courts of his ex-pat friends, quietly confident that the experience of playing in such heat would give him something of a head start.

They were at two games apiece when the women returned and too absorbed in the match to think the shrieks from the pool indicated anything that warranted investigation. When Cassie signalled madly from their bedroom window Stephen, swiping the sweat from his eyes, offered a brief wave in return. Peter, not surprisingly, was tiring. He had held his second service game with difficulty. It was Stephen's turn now and he had every intention of capitalizing on this slim advantage: angled serves, drop-shots, lobs, he would be ruthless. Seeing Cassie wave again, he raised his racket at her before tossing the ball up to serve. He liked it that she was watching. It made him feel more inspired, more eager than ever to assert himself.

Cassie, who had been trying to tell him that something momentous enough to interrupt the match had occurred, shook her head in amused despair as she turned away. From down the hallway she could hear the hubbub that had been triggered among the rest of the party by Maisie's appearance: Charlie's booming laugh, Clem's squeals of disbelief, Pamela offering, with sweet inevitability, to make a pot of tea. Peter and Stephen would pick up on what was going on soon enough. Someone would run out there and tell them – probably Genevieve, who was leaping around in a state of high excitement not so much at the appearance of her cousin as the discovery, made in the pool earlier, that while swimming remained beyond her she could *float* without her armbands. Maria, appearing with an armful of groceries, had gathered the mood of family celebration and promised a splendid feast for the evening, out on the terrace under the stars. The villa was pulsing with joy, like a creature brought to life.

Stepping back from the window, Cassie began to peel off her clothes and reached for her bikini. As she did so she noticed that Stephen had left his laptop on. Wondering if he had managed to do some work, she glanced at the screen, recalling fondly how he had once gone through the motions of seeking her opinion on his writing. She rather missed that, she decided, even though she had almost certainly been of little use, too unsure of her own literary judgement to offer anything but praise. What was Jack Connolly up to now? She idly scanned the icons, looking for a title that might indicate work in progress, half her attention on the clasp of her bikini, which was like one of the puzzle rings she had owned as a teenager, which only worked if slotted together in a certain way. Out of the corner of her eye she was aware of a little troupe now approaching the tennis duo – Charlie, Serena, Clem, and Maisie, led by Genevieve, skipping and tugging at her arm. Given the natural screen of the window, it was like watching an old silent movie: Stephen throwing up the ball, then catching it, looking at the group, doing a double-take, while Peter bounced on his toes to receive the serve, moving from eagerness to impatience to puzzlement, until the situation finally dawned.

It would be wrong to sneak a look at his work, Cassie decided, and anyway, there wasn't time. But then her attention was caught by a small icon in the middle of the others: a tiny shimmering red flag, under the initial C . . . her initial. Though it could have a million other meanings too, of course, Cassie reminded herself, withdrawing her finger with a frown. Years before, Stephen had inscribed 'for C' on his first book, the one that had recounted the war exploits of her uncle Eric. She had stumbled on the dedication by accident, seeing it as an endearing mystery, and thoroughly enjoyed Stephen's stammering confession, delivered months later, that it did indeed refer to her. Could this C be her too? If so, what unexpected sweetness might such a file contain? One of his love poems, maybe, or ideas for a wedding gift, or the oh-so-secret plans for their honeymoon on which hours of quizzing had got her nowhere.

Feeling wicked, and a little excited, Cassie double-clicked on the icon. The screen sprang to a page – not of loving words, or flight details, or gift lists, but a sort of spreadsheet . . . a calendar with dates and notes under each one . . . notes about *her*. Cassie studied it with mounting incredulity, her mind flailing for reasonable explanations. *Lombard Street – fifty-five minutes. Coffee and sandwich in La Cave. To O&L King's Road for samples. Two phone calls. Home at six.* Her eyes flicked down the dates, coming to rest on one of the most recent entries. *Ebury Street . . . whoops!*

Cassie looked out of the window. The tennis court was empty now, apart from a water bottle lying between the bench and the tramline. As she watched, it was caught on a light breeze and rolled towards the line, then back again, as if it had a mind of its own but couldn't decide where to settle. Cassie stood up and pulled on her bikini bottoms. She moved slowly, entranced by the small word Stephen had used for the day of her appointment at Frank's. Such a slight, silly word, redolent of determined cheerfulness, of adult effort to underplay disaster: spilt milk, a tumble, a childish mistake. *Whoops!* During her childhood Pamela had said it all the time, to defuse a variety of domestic crises. It seemed wrong, somehow, that such an innocent item of vocabulary should be capable of containing horror, let alone in sufficient quantities to alter the course of a life. But, then, life changed quickly – her niece being hit by the motorbike, the conception of her nephew's child, Keith wrenching her mother from the lake: all of these momentous things had happened in an instant. It was the consequences that reverberated like echoes across the years.

Cassie returned the computer to its main screen and reached for her sunglasses. She breathed deeply before she put them on, feeling, as she ventured out into the corridor, like a film star about to confront a pack of flashing paparazzi. Her moment, her pivotal crisis, had just occurred but none must know of it. Not yet, not until she knew what she felt, what she would do. She hurried down the corridor towards the sounds of merriment, her bare feet squeaking on the marble floor, her heart ticking too fast, like an invisible bomb. Approaching the doorway and hearing Stephen's voice, she pressed her hand to her chest to slow it down, telling herself not to panic, not to rush to hasty decisions. In the same instant it occurred to her how badly she wanted to be married and how, with the other unfolding dramas of the year, her and Stephen's wedding had taken on a significance beyond their exchange of vows. It sat on the horizon like a beacon of hope, a milestone for the future of the family – Serena had said as much only that morning. The thought of pulling out was nothing short of terrifying.

Then there was Stephen. Cassie pressed her palm harder against her chest. If she left him he would be devastated. She was more sure of that than anything. But could she marry a liar and a spy? Did spying and lying out of love make it okay?

'How come the stars look better abroad?' exclaimed Peter, tipping his head to examine the glittering black canopy above the terrace. The rest of the family followed suit, fifteen of them, now that Maisie had unexpectedly joined them, which made for such a striking sight that Maria, arriving to clear away the plates from the seafood salad she had served as a starter, couldn't resist looking up as well, wondering if they had seen a UFO or a shooting star. 'We should eat outside more often at home,' Peter added, 'in the cloisters, for example. We could set up a long refectory table and a couple of those free-standing heaters.' He continued to describe his vision in more detail, too absorbed by the image to notice that he had used the word 'home' in reference to Ashley House, or to register the dismay that flickered across his wife and sister-in-law's expressions. 'Being outside is such a *pleasure*.' He beamed at them all, their tanned faces glowing under the pretty line of scented candles Maria had placed among the crockery: his family, so huge and fantastic, so impossible to give up. Charlie, in spite of his earlier remarks, looked comfortable next to Serena, their elbows brushing as they ate. His brother had been exaggerating his marital woes, Peter was sure, thinking the worst because of the predicament they faced with Ed. That they would need more money, however, was certainly true, and if leaving Ashley House would ease that pressure, who was he to argue?

Ed, seated among Clem, Maisie and Theo, was looking more relaxed too, drinking wine for the first time since they had arrived, albeit with wary glances at his father between sips. Studying them all, Peter was aware suddenly of how *large* all the children had grown, how much room they took up, how much energy they exuded. A lively discussion over the starter about terrorism, triggered by the headlines in Cassie's *Daily Mail*, had been entirely dominated by Theo and Maisie, taking opposite sides over the home secretary's new house-arrest plans and whether to reintroduce the death penalty. Peter had listened proudly to them, thinking, I want all of this and I want Delia, and both are possible and not at all bad. And if Charlie wants me to have the house, to lead from the front, I'll do that too. I'll do whatever it takes to keep all that I now have, all that I cannot live without. It was a question of keeping his head, keeping perspective.

'I think a few toasts are called for, don't you?' he said, once the stars had been admired and they had all tired of trying to point out the Plough to a sleepy Genevieve. There were groans round the table. 'Now, come on,' he insisted, 'we've got Maisie here for a start, safely back in the fold from her travels, gracing this gathering with her presence.' He grinned at his niece who rolled her eyes but looked pleased. 'And then there are Ed's A-level results – excellent, truly excellent.' Peter raised his glass. 'Whatever happens, mate, no one can take those away from you.'

His remark was followed by a brief, intense silence. Peter took a sip of wine, irritated with himself for having referred to the only subject that could darken the atmosphere. 'And this film of yours,' Peter went on quickly, turning his attention to his son, 'you use your trust fund, Theo, if you want to.' He glanced at Helen, whose eyebrows were working in agile and not altogether approving surprise. 'He's old enough to decide for himself, surely? When it's gone it's gone.'

'Thanks, Dad – good news, eh, Clem?' muttered Theo, dimly aware that his father's public relenting was connected to a desire to keep the conversation on safe ground rather than because of a sudden faith in his abilities behind a camera. He tried to smile at Ed, who still wasn't talking to him, but then Clem said something and he had to turn to her instead.

Serena, equally anxious to keep off difficult subjects, chose the same moment to ask Stephen if he had any hopes of seeing his work on the big screen. He was on the point of answering when Maisie, brimming with all the boldness of having fended for herself for nine months, leant across the table to ask her brother, in a loud, ringing voice, if he had considered a paternity test. 'Are you *sure* you're the father of this baby?'

'Maisie, darling, I hardly think this is the time . . .' murmured Serena, casting a worried look at Charlie, who was clenching his jaw as if trying to contain the release of something demonic.

'No, but are you sure, Ed?' persisted Maisie. 'I mean . . .' She looked round the table, tossing her hair, which, washed

334

and out of the braids, had expanded to a soft hedge of glossy chestnut. 'What's the point in not talking about it? It's like you're all pretending it's not going on.' She laughed uncertainly, searching their faces for evidence of support and settling on her sister, who was staring at her with wide, admiring eyes.

'We've been through all this, Maisie,' Clem explained quietly. 'Apparently there's no doubt, is there, Ed?' Clem glanced at their crimson-faced brother, then back at her twin, wondering, for the umpteenth time that day, how she could ever have imagined life was more enjoyable without the companionship of her sister. Within minutes of finding themselves alone Maisie had exploded with renewed apologies about Jonny Cottrall, reiterating that it had been ancient history and rushing on with news of a new man in her sights called Julian, with whom she had travelled from Mexico to Europe. Clem had responded with a blurting confession about Nathan Chalmer, the weirdness of fancying an older man, the disappointment when he had ended their final session without so much as a kiss, how she felt sort of relieved but also totally dumb. Maisie had hugged her and said wasn't wanting sex peculiar and how it didn't necessarily seem connected to love and no wonder daft old Ed had made such a balls-up. They had had a good laugh, then a swim and then lain on sun-beds talking until their throats were dry, each feeling as if seconds rather than months had elapsed since their parting.

All eyes had turned now to Ed. 'That's right . . . no doubt . . . unfortunately,' he growled, rolling a thicket of pasta on to his fork, but feeling too much under scrutiny to place it in his mouth. 'She . . . er . . . There was just me.'

'That's what *she* says, is it?' sneered Maisie, her mouth crammed with food.

'Your sister is quite right,' said Peter, who had been listening attentively, inwardly wondering why he had not pressed this point more thoroughly. The question had been asked, of course, but had received such irrefutable answers on all fronts that he had not pursued it. His nephew had been so sure, so ready to despair. 'A paternity test is definitely called for. We should see to it, Charlie, the moment we get back.'

Charlie was already nodding vigorously. Serena, sitting next to him, seemed less sure. 'Can they do that *before* a child is born?'

'Oh, they can,' put in Stephen, who had researched the matter for one of his plots. 'They can either do an early sample from the placenta, look at what's called the chorionic villus, or by amniocentesis later with a needle through the abdomen. They'll take a sample of the father's blood and analyse it in conjunction with the foetal test. It costs, of course, and the NHS would only agree to such a procedure on medical grounds. If you have it done privately you'll pay around eight or nine hundred pounds.'

'Really?' murmured Cassie, torn between astonishment and the unnerving sensation, building inside her all afternoon, that she had been sharing her life with a virtual stranger. It occurred to her in the same instant that getting to know someone was not about what they told you so much as what they held back. Stephen had never made any secret of his rotten childhood. His father had hit him with a belt. His mother had watched. Cassie had loved him for revealing such things, felt tender, understood better why he should be so drawn to her and the solidity of her own upbringing. What he had never described to her, however – except, perhaps, through his vacillating reservations about becoming a father – was the *effect* of this treatment: possessiveness, insecurity, lack of self-esteem, deceitfulness . . . It had been up to her to find out such things and now that she had . . . Cassie blinked at her fiancé's profile, astonished that such easy good looks, such articulation could conceal so much mess. Was love about discovering a mess and forgiving it? Could she do that? Did she have a big enough heart?

Peter was saying that the cost of the process surely didn't matter. 'Worth every penny, wouldn't you say? The more I think about it, the more insane it would be to take the girl's word . . . Oh, well done, Maisie, well done indeed.'

'It does seem sensible, dear,' agreed Elizabeth, who had been helping Maria clear the plates in spite of their employee's tutting efforts to persuade her to remain in her seat. Since their first unpromising encounter the pair had struck up a bit of a friendship, aided by Elizabeth's willingness to try out her creaky O-level Italian and the discovery that Maria, too, was a single mother with a teenaged son. He was called Roberto and had been brought along that evening, though whether for company or to help in the kitchen remained unclear: the boy had spent most of the time slouched at the kitchen table, either receiving kisses on his head or having his knuckles slapped when he picked at the food. As Maria stepped out on to the terrace now, though, bearing a freshly made *panna cotta* as if it were a crown on a velvet cushion, Roberto appeared behind her, cradling a huge plate of fresh fruit – figs, peaches, strawberries, melon and grapes, all sliced and arranged in a rainbow of shapes and colours.

'It's like a painting,' murmured Roland, leaning towards his grandmother so that the plate could find safe passage to the table.

'*Come?*' said Roberto, hesitating and looking anxious.

'*Pulchrissima!*' interjected Elizabeth, pointing at the plate.

The boy's face broke into a grin. He said something else, a long, incomprehensible sentence, which he directed at Roland before he was commanded back inside by his mother.

'It *is* like a painting, Roland, darling,' whispered Pamela. 'How right you are.' She pressed his hand, feeling, as always, a great affinity with this particular grandson, so much more alone always than the others, so encased – as, indeed, she was, these days – in his own world.

337

'Talking of drawing,' boomed Peter, on the prowl for happy subjects now, 'how's it going, Roland? All that sketching you've been doing, when do we get to see any of it?'

'I'm not sure . . . I . . .' Roland faltered, quavering both from the attention and a lingering awareness of the Italian boy's beauty, the thick, ink-black hair, the lithe, compact body sliding beneath his clothes. It felt wrong to notice such things, but unavoidable too. Like feelings, the thoughts just came. It wasn't like he *chose* them.

'Clem has shown his work to her painter friend, haven't you, Clem?' blurted Elizabeth, clapping her hand to her mouth as she remembered she wasn't supposed to say anything. She had been thinking of Keith, trying and failing to imagine him at such a gathering, missing him. She mouthed an apology at Roland, who shrugged and smiled with such obvious, disarming forgiveness that she felt even worse.

The spotlight of the conversation, meanwhile, had shifted to Clem. 'What painter friend?' asked several people at once.

'Oh . . . just someone who . . . A regular in the wine bar, a man called Nathan Chalmer,' Clem answered, as breezily as she could, trying not to look at Maisie, or Theo, who was leaning back in his chair and smirking.

'Nathan Chalmer? But I've heard of him,' exclaimed Peter, clearly impressed. 'He's American, isn't he? Figurative portraits. Had an exhibition somewhere a couple of years ago. Blimey, Clem, now that's what I call networking.'

Clem nodded, pink-faced and hollow with terror at the thought of her family ever clapping eyes on Nathan's now completed image of her: tousled raven hair, pearly white skin, the pink slit like a jewel in the dark triangle between her legs, the blue silk flowing like water round her limbs. Staring at it, even with him, she had felt embarrassed. The body, painted in odd wavering lines, could have belonged to any skinny girl, but the set of her face, with its wide, high cheekbones, round dark eyes and full red lips, the upper one protruding in its annoying inimitable way, were unmistakable.

'Well, there's another cause for celebration,' declared Peter, raising his glass yet again, aware that he was sliding towards a pleasing state of inebriation. 'Bravo.'

After the *panna cotta* had been demolished and only a sliver of melon remained on the fruit plate Chloë asked if they could have a midnight swim.

'Is it midnight?' whispered Genevieve, awestruck at having been allowed to stay up so late and staring with wide owl-eyes at her mother.

'Not quite.' Helen pulled her youngest on to her lap and kissed her hair. 'But it is very late . . . far *too* late for a swim.'

'I disagree,' cut in Peter, glancing with some longing at the shimmering dark rectangle of the pool on the terrace below. 'What do you say, Charlie? Remember that time we sneaked down to the copse?'

'*I* remember it,' said Pamela, wanting to respond to the mention of the copse before anyone had time to feel awkward. 'It was October and you both caught a chill.'

Laughter rippled round the table, drawing them all together, making the notion of swimming in August under an Italian night sky irresistible. The elder children were already pushing back their chairs. A moment later Theo, scrabbling in the corner of the terrace, found a switch that turned on the underwater lights. The pool lit up with instant, mesmerizing beauty, a glassy blue square of perfection, a portal to another world.

Pamela stood above the rockery and watched the scene unfolding on the terrace below. A scene as pieced and colourful as one of the Roman mosaics featured in Helen's guidebook, she decided, except that this one was alive and changing every second. The boy, Roberto, had been persuaded to join the fun, in a pair of Roland's shorts, which ballooned round his thighs as he swam. Someone had produced a tennis ball, which they threw to each other between ducking and diving; everyone was included in the game, even Genevieve, who paddled and squealed at the shallow end, armbands firmly back in place.

Maria, loading the last of the dinner plates on to a tray, paused to sigh wistfully at the sight, pressing one hand to her ample chest and whispering, '*Bella famiglia*.'

'*Bella* indeed,' murmured Pamela. The pleasure of seeing her family enjoy themselves was immense, impossible to put into words. Troubled times lay ahead – they always did – and such a romp as this, not to mention the holiday as a whole, would help them all immeasurably, she knew. Yet the longing to get home was pushing inside her all the time now, tightening the back of her throat like thirst. She couldn't wait to rescue Poppy from the kennels, to have a proper chat with Marjorie, to make inquiries about a vacancy at Crayshott Manor.

It wasn't until much later that night, when Elizabeth was asleep and the villa quiet, apart from the quiet grumbles of Peter's snores, that Pamela put on her dressing-gown and tip-toed along the hallway, through the kitchen and on to the terrace. Moving carefully in her bare feet, not wanting to trip or tread on anything unpleasant, she made her way down the steps, past the rockery to the poolside.

The water without its clever lights was like treacle, but the moon was bright and its reflection shone in the middle like a penny in need of retrieval. It was on this that Pamela focused as she peeled off her dressing-gown and stood naked in the dark. Skinny-dipping, that's all it was. She had done it with John once, not in the copse, which was always too cold, but in the sea at Biarritz on their honeymoon. She dipped a toe in and shrank back at a sudden injection of icy fear. Maybe it was too soon, after all, to expect so much of herself. But then she heard John telling her not to be silly, telling her how good it would feel, and she went in, not diving or jumping, but simply taking a step, like walking off a cliff. And there was a falling, of her body and her heart, and then a surge of joyous energy as she surfaced, nose pointed to the stars, hair sleek, mouth open and ready for air.

September

Back in England an Indian summer lay in wait, each day a hot, sultry package encased in the freshness of dawn and dusk. Unattended for four weeks and fed by rain, the garden at Ashley House had swelled to the point where the house itself seemed to be sinking among the tidal waves of verdure and colour that surrounded it. Butterflies and insects bobbed lazily at the full fat flowers, splayed among the beds and bushes like the basking populace of a crowded beach, all heedless of the shortening days and the occasional tugging breeze that warned of change.

Serena, tracing the particularly busy traffic of bees to a crack in the lintel above the front door, thought of calling Sid, or a pest-control company from the *Yellow Pages* but didn't have the heart. The weather would turn eventually and the bees would disappear. They were living on borrowed time, on borrowed hope, clinging to the coat-tails of summer, just as she, Charlie and Ed were clinging to the feel-good shreds of the holiday and the new, desperate hope about the paternity test. Change, and reaction to it, would be forced upon them all soon enough. She only wished she knew where it would lead. The natural world might have its patterns, its enviable seasonal grand design, but she was losing faith in the notion that the existence of humans could relate to anything so comfortingly certain.

As she turned towards the garden, Serena experienced a reflex of pleasure at the sight of it, so gloriously abandoned and rampant, so oblivious to its own imminent demise. At least all her loved ones were in good health, she reminded herself, and if Helen's God existed, He would surely see to it that the paternity test proved negative. Then, with time, she and Charlie could emerge from the separate corners into which Ed's crisis had propelled them and start to talk – to love – properly again. The terrible said things would be forgotten. The future would beckon, as it once had, so effortlessly.

And if the test was positive? Ed had been so certain, after all, so unquestioning of his culpability. Serena moved closer to the flowerbeds, humming to herself, aware that the prospect of an even so clumsily conceived grandchild still filled her with a sort of excitement. A dreadful thing, maybe, which Charlie had every right to distrust, but as solid and undeniable as the old walls of the house towering over her, soaking up the sunshine. She began to hum louder, picking flowers now, even those that were too full-blown to last more than a couple of days, dipping her hands carefully among the insects to preclude the possibility of being stung.

In London Cassie was waiting for the arrival of her period and the state of clear-headedness that she was sure would accompany it. As the heat ballooned and retreated with its new diurnal rhythm, she felt as if the world and the weather had stopped moving, suspending her in some timeless limbo in which there was no sense of where she had come from or where she might be heading. She sought refuge instead in the immediate demands of each day, working hard, a wary eye over her shoulder as she moved between appointments, and overseeing wedding preparations in the evening. While Stephen ploughed through the pile of invitations, complaining merrily about his aching fingers and the taste of the envelope glue, she sewed the finishing touches to Sylvie's bridesmaid dresses herself, closing her mind to everything but the challenge of attaching a lace trim to a velvet yoke, forcing the squeaking, reluctant needle through and out again, gripping ever tighter as her hot fingers slipped on the metal.

In a hotel bedroom near the Aldwych Peter, too, was learning to lose himself to the precious ticking of the present. The world of his family, his work, his guilt, his brother's troubles remained outside, in a parallel universe. When Delia had tried to talk of Julian and Maisie, in regular phone contact, apparently, since the family's return, he hushed her with a kiss. 'Not now,' he said. 'Now there is only us.' When, complaining of the heat, she tried to open a window, he prevented that too, not wanting even the toot of a horn to remind him of any reality other than the one at hand. 'You are the love of my life,' he said. 'Let me enjoy this little piece of you.' She tugged at the curtains but he pulled them back again. 'I want to see you . . . all of you.' She laughed and said he was impossible, while he peeled off first her clothes and then his own, touching and kissing her with precisely the reverence she sought, which kept her hungering for lovers as well as a husband. In the heat their bodies slid against each other making unseemly noises and moving in ungainly ways, watched only by the glaring eye of the sun and a pigeon, which landed briefly on the windowsill before taking off in search of shade.

A few miles south Nathan Chalmer peered out of the window of his studio flat until Clem had emerged safely on to the pavement below. By the time she looked up he had already stepped out of sight, nearer the whirring blades of a recently purchased fan, which moved the air but did not cool it. Nathan sighed and ran his hands over his face. He had seen the sadness lurking in the child's expression and known that it was because of him. He liked his subjects to fall a little in love with him, and he with them. He knew how to do it too, how to open them up so that their vulnerability, their *essence* could find its way on to the tip of his pencil. With Clem it had been more intense than usual, so intense, indeed, that he had been half tempted to cross the line. Even that day, recognizing the care with which she had dressed, the thin white cotton T-shirt (no bra), the flimsy silk skirt, all showing off to him the alluring, toffee glow of her Italian tan, he had toyed with the idea of pursuing the seduction for which she so clearly yearned. It hadn't helped that she had been full of breathless, endearing talk, spilling the ups and downs of her holiday – the appearance of her beloved twin sister, the uncle's promise about her manuscript, her cousin's film script, the paternity test for her hapless brother. Listening to it all, Nathan had come closer than he cared to admit to scooping her up in his arms and feasting on the sheer energy of her, so young and pretty, a bud half burst.

But he had feasted enough, he knew: Clem's fragility and strength, that poised state between girlishness and womanhood, shone out of his finished painting, making it alive and good. He had a new subject now, Nathan reminded himself, a petite chocolate-skinned girl with full lips and enormous slanted brown eyes. He had found her on the tube, little cream headphones nestling in her ears, her beautiful mouth silently shaping the words of the tunes.

Nathan returned to the window to check on Clem's progress. She had stopped on the corner of the street and was talking animatedly into her phone. He hoped she was telling the cousin about his offer. He watched, pleased that he had given her something to take away, after all. And it hadn't been out of charity either: the boy could paint, that was plain. Although the product was still raw and untamed, talent blazed from every stroke. And where would he have been, Nathan mused, without his own first chance to exhibit? He'd have to swing it with his agent, of course, but that wouldn't be hard, not these days, with the prices he could command.

Clem had been so delighted that he thought for a moment

she might bust out of her delicious shyness and kiss him. But an instant later she was grave-faced, eliciting a promise that her portrait wouldn't be exhibited at the same time. Nathan, not liking the demand, had prevaricated, muttering that the exhibition wasn't until December and she might have changed her mind by then. But Clem was adamant. Only her sister knew she had posed nude and she wanted to keep it that way. Her family had had a tough year and she didn't want to round it off by giving them any further shocks. When still he hesitated she threatened, with a cheek that astonished him, to walk away with Roland's paintings and forget the whole deal.

'You could be walking away with his future under your arm,' Nathan had pointed out, laughing.

'Well, it's my future too and I want to be in control of it,' she snapped, so strong and grown-up, so unlike the starving waitress he had first propositioned, that he had held up his hands in surrender.

Clem waited at the bus stop for a few minutes, enjoying the sight of everybody dawdling on doorsteps and the heat pulsing up from the pavement, caressing her bare legs. She was thrilled with herself about Roland. The most she had expected of Nathan was a few comments, or maybe, at very best, a suggestion that he meet her cousin to talk stuff through. But to offer to hang Roland's two weird swirling oil paintings in one of his own exhibitions had never entered her wildest imaginings – or Roland's, from the sound of the unRoland-like shriek that had pierced her ear on the telephone.

As a bus lumbered into sight Clem turned her back on it and began to walk, in no mood to be cooped up among the crush of body smells and people with desperate expressions on their faces. Sadness was seeping back into her, riding in on the knowledge that she had probably seen Nathan Chalmer for the last time. He had asked for Roland's address, so he could send details about the exhibition, he said, and also arrange to have the pictures returned to him afterwards. Clem jotted it down for him on a piece of paper, aware of the gentle rejection the request entailed. 'You were great, Clementine Harrison,' he said, when she had finished. Waiting with her for the lift to arrive, he had repeated the compliment, planting a fatherly kiss on the top of her head. 'You *are* great, never forget that.'

Clem took a detour into a park and sat on a bench, telling herself to have a little cry, if she wanted to, to get it out of her system. But then she spotted a kiosk and bought herself an ice-cream instead, a plain orange one that melted almost faster than she could eat it. She wasn't *that* sad, she decided, licking her fingers afterwards. He was so *old*, after all, the whole thing would have been totally weird; not exactly the sort of boyfriend one would want to shout about, even if he was as famous as her uncle had suggested.

Clem left the bench and began to walk with more purpose towards the street. She was getting used to the situation already, she mused, just like she got used to almost anything with time. Like the Ed and Jessica fiasco, the whole notion of her brother fathering a baby. Back at Ashley House for a brief spell after the holiday, she and Maisie had even had a giggling conversation about names and whether, if there was a christening, they would want to attend. 'We could cut off the hems of our bridesmaid dresses and wear those,' Maisie had shrieked, leaping in front of her bedroom mirror to perform her best rendition of a simpering aunt. Clem had laughed till her eyes streamed, squawking admonitions but loving every moment, loving how they understood one another.

Maisie was coming to supper that night with her new boyfriend. Clem had phoned her mother to ask how to cook *coq au vin*. She had a list in her pocket of what to buy and how long to fry the meat and onions. And the bacon, too, she mustn't forget that. And garlic. Two cloves at least, her mother had said, clearly delighted to have been consulted. They had had a lovely talk, Clem disclosing that she had packed in the wine bar and applied for a couple of jobs on the Internet – one as a junior press officer for Southwark borough council and the other as a publicity assistant in a small publishing house. Serena had sounded so pleased, so *interested*, that Clem had almost told her about her manuscript. Then she had pictured it sitting in a dusty, untouched pile on Stephen's editor's desk and switched to the subject of her and Maisie's bridesmaid dresses instead. Her aunt was planning a final fitting for them at Ashley House the following month before Maisie started at Bristol, the idea being that the dresses could be stowed there afterwards, ready for the big day. They were worried, Clem confided to her mother because, since giving their measurements, she had put on weight and Maisie had lost some. Serena had laughed – a wild, exultant laugh which, Clem knew, was because she had managed to talk, like it was no big deal, about having got a bit fatter. Cassie was a wizard with a needle, Serena had assured her happily, and Granny too. Hems and seams could be altered. It didn't matter a jot.

Clem had saved inquiries about her brother till last, fearful that so dark a subject might somehow shatter this new ability to report and share things about her life without the sense that they were being offered up for parental approval. But Serena had been upbeat about Ed, too. After initial resistance Jessica had co-operated with the test and the result was due any day, she said. 'Keep your fingers crossed,' she added, 'but I have a good feeling that everything will be fine.'

Back at the flat, Flora and Daisy were busy in their rooms, practising for an evening concert. Clem had shut herself into the kitchen and was studying the heap of half-frozen chicken thighs she had bought at the supermarket when Daisy's head appeared round the door.

'Two messages. Can you ring Theo? He wants to shoot your scenes before he goes back to uni and . . .' She stopped, looking bashful and then hopeful, as Flora appeared beside her.

'Jonny came round,' said Flora, stoutly. 'He wants you to help out with a gig this weekend.'

'Does he now?' Clem measured a careful tablespoon of oil into a frying-pan.

'Well?' said both her flatmates at once. 'What are you going to do?'

'I have no idea,' replied Clem, haughtily.

'Well, we are cool, aren't we?' remarked Flora, folding her arms and giving Daisy a nudge with her elbow. 'Should we have told him to fuck off?'

Clem took a step back from the frying-pan, which was spitting. 'I don't think so. I might do the gig . . .' She frowned. 'But only because it would be fun to sing again. So don't go getting any ideas.'

'Wouldn't *dream* of it,' they chanted, laughing.

'Oh, bugger off,' retorted Clem, laughing too. She returned her attention to the preparation of her meal, unaware until she placed the lid on a passably appealing mixture of meat and sauce that she hadn't thought about Nathan for almost two hours. It was just something that had happened, she mused, something that had kept her going when she needed it and was now going to help Roland. And as for Jonny . . . All she knew was that she wanted to sing, that she felt *ready* to sing, ready to reconnect with the joy that for her was integral to the business of opening her lungs. Life, in its mysterious, complicated way, was getting good again. All that was required to make it perfect was the right result on Ed's horrible test. Remembering her mother's words on the phone, Clem crossed her fingers and managed, with considerable difficulty, to keep them that way all through running a bath and getting her clothes off. Flexing them free in the water, she began to sing, so lustily that

Daisy and Flora, tying black velvet ribbons in each other's hair, did a couple of high fives.

Sitting in line with the other interviewees, Keith ran his finger round the inside of his shirt collar, wishing he had picked a seat away from the windows where the glare of the afternoon sun was less intense. On the wall to his left was a poster entitled, *Hull: Regeneration & Vision: A City of the Future*. He had read this and the text underneath it so many times that he could have recited whole sections with his eyes closed.

Hull is fast turning from a hopeless, end-of-the-line town to the youngest, most exciting waterfront city in Europe. 'On a sunny day you could be anywhere in the world,' says Bill Crowley, development manager of Cityscape, Hull's urban regeneration company. Island Wharf, the first phase of the Humber Quays development, has a panoramic view of the Humber. The Fruit Market on the other side of the marina brims with old town charm. The East Bank of the river Hull is being transformed by riverside apartments and lies within walking distance of the city centre, connected by several new foot and cycle bridges. Projects at Albion Square and Quay West will improve shopping and a transport interchange at the £165-million St Stephen's development will be enhanced. Redeveloped residential properties are available at well below the national average while Humber Bridgehead and Willerby Hill offer state-of-the-art leisure facilities. With several luxury hotel developments in progress and a Michelin starred restaurant in the historic old town, Hull is bringing its vision of a new city to life.

Keith wished there was something else to look at, something that bore a closer, less ironic relationship to the tense, brooding atmosphere in the room. One job and a score of candidates. A couple looked older but most were definitely younger than him. All were men and not one seemed nearly as uncomfortable as Keith felt, strapped into the uncustomary uniform of a suit and tie. A project manager on a rural housing development – who was he kidding? Worse still, he was only there because Barry had mentioned it to June, who had mentioned it to him. No harm in trying, she had said, having gathered through their snippets of doorstep conversation that Irene wanted him out and he had nowhere to go.

But maybe there was harm in trying, Keith decided now, when failure was so certain, when his inner battery of determination and self-esteem was so close to empty. He glanced nervously at the door to the interview room. Lately, the thought of the kids was about all that got him off the sofa-bed – that and Irene banging the breakfast things, saying, with each clash of metal and china, *'Get out, get a life, FUCK off.'*

The door opened and the young man with the neat blond crew-cut and shiny suit who had entered twenty minutes before bounced out, looking pleased. Keith ran his damp palms up and down his trousers, trying to focus on what he would say, how he could possibly package his years of building-site experience into a convincing presentation of the possibility that he was ready to run a project of his own. He was getting nowhere when the quiet buzz of his phone sounded in his pocket.

'Keith – it's Stephen.'

'Can't talk now, mate,' Keith muttered, swivelling towards the blinding heat of the window to avoid being overheard. He had only kept the phone on because there was a faint chance of three tickets to see Hull City play at the new stadium that evening. He'd cleared it with June already, just in case, but instructed her not to get Craig and Neil's hopes up.

'It won't take long, I promise. I've got a request.'

'Not like the last one, I hope,' growled Keith, their unpleasant conversation of two months before flaring in his mind.

'No . . . I'm so sorry about that. You were quite right. I felt really bad afterwards. Cassie and I . . . we're fine now – *great*, in fact. It's all systems go for the wedding – and that's why I'm ringing. I'd like you to be my best man. Would you do that for me, Keith, as my oldest friend? There's no one else who fits the bill.'

'Blimey, Steve . . . I don't know.'

Stephen laughed, undeterred. 'I'll take that as a yes, shall I? And don't worry about the speech. Just tell a few of your old jokes, nothing too blue – not that one about the snake-bite anyway – thank the bridesmaids, usual stuff.' He talked on, irrepressible, ebullient, almost manically so, Keith decided afterwards, as he reflected with deepening gloom on the implications of the commitment. It would be huge and grand, morning suits, microphones, marquees. But I would see Elizabeth, he thought suddenly, and stood up as his name was called. Elizabeth and all the rest of them, the old bird, sweet, porcelain-faced Serena, bumbling, cheerful Charlie and their messed-up son . . . Warmth, an entirely pleasant sensation that had nothing to do with the heat of the day, spread through Keith as he stepped into the interview room. How were they all? How would they deal with this bastard grandchild? Who had they got to take his place helping the doddery Sid with replastering damp walls and managing the rebellious glories of the grounds?

Even as he shook the hands of the interviewers – three, in an imposing line behind a long desk – memories of his spring at Ashley House flooded Keith's mind. Leaving had been the right thing to do, but so hard – one of the hardest things he had ever done. No wonder, then, that his heart should soar at this legitimate, unexpected pretext to return. It would be brief but beautiful, as brief things often were. It would be good to see them all, to squeeze Elizabeth's hand and tell her that, while not in his life, she remained in his head and would do so until the day he died.

'Good afternoon, Mr Holmes. Please, sit down.'

Keith sat in the chair opposite the desk and folded his hands in his lap to conceal how they trembled.

'Perhaps you could begin by telling us why you think your experience makes you suitable for this job?'

'Hull has a vision for the future and I want to be part of it.' Keith unlaced his hands and leant towards them, making eye-contact, resting his elbows on his knees. 'I've managed teams on site for twenty years and am ready to take the next step up.' June was right: there *was* no harm in trying. What else was there to do, after all?

That evening Peter bought flowers from the stall near his chambers, three extravagant bunches, two because they had dinner guests, 'And one just for you,' he told Helen, thrusting them into her arms, then running upstairs to shower and change.

'They're not due for an hour, you know,' Helen called after him, then returned to the kitchen to check on the meal, all three courses of which she had prepared the weekend before and pulled out of the deep freeze that morning. She arranged the flowers in vases, placing one on the dining-table in the conservatory, one on the mantelpiece in the sitting room and one on the table in the hall, brushing off the dusting of pollen that fell on to the polished wood as she turned to check her appearance in the mirror. She had had her hair cut and coloured in her lunch hour. In the heat of the afternoon it had lost some of its buoyancy, but still looked almost too good for the dinner, which was merely a pay-back for a couple of sets of neighbours. The Wilsons and the Burridges would talk of mortgages, no doubt, and schools and what everyone was doing for half-term. Helen yawned, bored at the prospect, and decided that with her coiffure on such top form she could get away with her comfy black trousers instead of a dress.

On the way upstairs she glanced in at Genevieve, who was in bed cuddling her favourite doll and listening to her tape of *The Little Mermaid*, eyes glassy. She popped into Chloë's room too, even though Chloë was on a school outing to the theatre.

In her own bedroom, she stepped out of her work clothes and laid them carefully over the back of the chair. Peter was still in the shower, not singing for once. Helen lay on the bed in her bra and pants and closed her eyes. The blast of the shower was soon replaced by the sounds of running taps, brushing teeth and then the buzz of the electric razor, which Peter only ever used for an evening shave. In the mornings he ran a basin of water and indulged in the ritual of a blade and a badger brush, just as John Harrison had and his father before him. Familiar sounds were comforting, Helen mused, too pleasantly cool in her underwear to feel any urgency to get on with the business of dressing. The meal was ready, her makeup was fine; there was, as she had said to Peter, no hurry.

He emerged from the bathroom naked but for a pair of boxers, rubbing the sparse strands of his hair with a hand towel.

Helen patted the bed. 'Come here a minute.'

'Hadn't we better get dressed?'

'We've ages yet.'

'Where are the girls?'

'Genevieve's almost asleep and Chloë's out. *My Fair Lady*, remember?'

'Of course she is.' Peter rubbed again at his hair, even though it was quite dry. He opened the wardrobe and began to riffle through his shirts.

'Peter? Is something the matter?'

'Of course not.' He spun round with an amazed smile. 'Whyever would anything be the matter?'

'Come here, then.' It was Helen's turn to smile, not amazed at all, but full of sweet, obvious intention.

Carefully Peter hung the shirt he had chosen – salmon pink with double cuffs and a button-down collar – back in the wardrobe before moving towards the bed, trying to muster the right facial expression, trying to act the part – to be the thing he had been so effortlessly for twenty-five years. It was

Helen, he reminded himself, Helen, his wife, to whom he had made love thousands of times. Helen, who asked for sex so seldom that it would be inexplicably unkind to turn her down and yet towards whom, as she lay there in her familiar faded bra and pants, he could muster nothing more than brotherly affection.

'We haven't done it for ages,' she whispered, stroking his arm as he stretched out next to her.

'That's not true.'

'Yes, it is. Twice in Umbria and not since we got back.'

'Well, we're both so busy and tired,' Peter muttered, stroking a loose thread of hair off her face.

'Do you like it? My hair? I had it done today.'

'Yes, it's nice . . . very nice.'

'Not that the Wilsons and the Burridges are worth ninety-five pounds.'

'Bloody hell! Is that what it cost?' Peter cried, glad of something to latch on to, some distraction from the sheer awfulness of not desiring her. He *liked* her, God, he liked her – it was impossible not to: she was kind and clever and organized and undemanding and –

'Mummy – Daddy – is it your bedtime too?'

'Genevieve, darling . . .' There was a catch of gratitude in Peter's voice. 'Shouldn't you be asleep?'

Helen, less delighted, told their daughter to go back to bed.

'*You* come with me,' replied Genevieve, folding her arms in the manner of someone well beyond her years, someone with all the time in the world to negotiate.

'I'll come in a minute,' insisted Helen, firmly.

'Can I have a story?'

'Maybe . . . yes . . . Yes, you can have a story, if you go *now*.'

Peter put his arms round his wife and kissed her tenderly on the lips. 'She's awesome, isn't she?' he murmured. 'Just like her mother.'

Helen wriggled upright. 'You didn't want to anyway, did you? I could tell, so don't deny it.'

Peter opened his mouth to attempt a denial, but faltered under the honest inquiry of her gaze. She knew him so well, too bloody well. 'No, I guess I wasn't totally . . . er . . . The truth is, there *is* something on my mind.'

'I knew it,' Helen snapped, managing to look at once triumphant and hurt.

'The fact is, this paternity test of Edward's . . . More is hanging on it than you realize.'

'Really?' She sounded insulted now, as if he had accused her of not caring enough about the woeful position of their nephew.

'If the baby proves to be his,' explained Peter, in a rush, anxious not to lose her sympathy before he had started, 'then . . . well . . . Charlie is worried, among other things, about their financial position, supporting it, education and so on . . . so much so that he has asked me if I would consider taking over Ashley House.'

Helen laughed, astonished and disbelieving. 'For goodness' sake, they're not that broke, are they? And, anyway, it's out of the question, isn't it? Peter, you told him it was out of the question, didn't you?'

'No, I didn't,' admitted Peter, wearily, 'at least, not exactly. You see, there are other considerations too . . . Running the place, he's found it hard. He says he and Serena have not been at all happy there. He seems to think they need a fresh start.'

'Fresh start?' Helen sneered. 'You – we – *gave* them a fresh start. They live in one of the most beautiful houses in southern England, they have *everything* they ever wanted.'

'That's not strictly true, is it? I mean . . .'

'You mean Tina, which was several years ago and which, if you recall, was one of the reasons you felt moved to hand over the bloody house in the first place.'

'Yes, Tina, but also, what with Mum . . .' Peter ploughed on, thinking bleakly of how contrastingly well Delia had understood and sympathized with the situation, how, in spite of all the difficulties facing them, she, too, had been excited at the notion of his acquiring a *pied-à-terre* in town. 'And now this business with Ed . . .'

'What's that got to do with the *house*?' wailed Helen, getting off the bed and starting to pull on her dress, then remembering her decision about the trousers and taking it off again, messing up her hair in the process. 'The whole thing sounds mad to me, totally mad.' She turned to him, trousers in one hand and hairbrush in the other. 'As you well know, I have never had a strong desire to live in the country. I do not want either to give up my job or to spend fifteen hours a week on a train. In addition, Genevieve has only just settled into her school and Chloë would hate the disruption of leaving hers. Your brother is clearly in a state of utter panic even to have suggested such a thing, which in the circumstances is understandable. What is *not* understandable is that you not only failed to recognize that but have, without telling me, agreed to the whole insane plan.'

'I have not agreed,' protested Peter, weakly, wishing with all his heart that he had undone her bra strap and kept his mouth shut.

'Really? Oh, good! Well, in that case we don't have a problem, do we?' At which point a squeal of 'Mummeee' floated to them from along the corridor. Helen, still glaring, set off to respond to it, but then paused in the doorway, sighing heavily. 'Charlie is all cut up about Ed and looking for things to blame,' she said, sounding much more conciliatory. 'It's clearly bonkers.'

Peter remained on the bed after she had gone, in despair over his own ineptitude. Of course it was bonkers. Helen was right – she was always fucking right. Hadn't he been aware, even as he responded to Charlie's initial cry for help in Italy, that his perspective had been warped by his feelings for Delia, together with the unforeseen, alluring prospect of being given a second chance to assert his claim to the family home? It wasn't helping Charlie he had been interested in, so much as helping himself.

Applying his intelligent, logical mind to the situation, Peter studied his own selfishness as if it were a specimen under glass – closely but at a clinical distance. How he *felt* about it all remained unchanged. He simply could not countenance either giving up Delia or turning his back on the possibility of taking over Ashley House. Everything seemed to hang on the result of the paternity test. If the baby turned out to be Ed's and Charlie really couldn't manage financially, there was a case to be made for the proposition of moving there. Helen would see that. She, too, was logical, good at weighing arguments: it was one of the many traits he valued in her.

Peter pulled the shirt back out of the cupboard, then swapped it for a plain white one. To wear pink required a certain exuberance and the argument, with the contemplation of his various dilemmas, had robbed him of that. White showed off his still striking tan, and was the colour of innocence, he mused bitterly, studying his reflection in the mirror but avoiding his own eyes.

In the Arndale Centre a poster advertising vitamins featured a pregnant woman with long, glossy auburn hair and a toothpaste smile. She was lying in a bikini on a beach between two palm trees, her belly a beautiful smooth olive slope, rising in the space between her hips and her ribcage with all the grace of an exotic sculpture. Next to her lay a handsome blond-haired man, smiling adoringly, one arm on hers, the other round a chubby-legged toddler, who was squatting beside a sandcastle.

Jessica stopped to look at the poster whenever she wandered through the arcade, feeling each time a little angrier, a little more despairing of her own ugly state, not just without a man but with a belly that had swelled sideways as much as outwards, mysteriously taking with it any shape her thighs had once possessed. Her bum, too, had inflated, then collapsed, like a punctured beach-ball, while her bust was so big she had had to buy several bras.

The poster was outside Mothercare where Jessica found herself drifting most days. She'd pick things up and put them down, browse through the rails of miniature outfits, trying to equate them with the kicking creature clearly bent on destroying her body as well as her life. It was wrong to feel like that, she knew, and not what she had planned or imagined. Bella, the girl she'd mentioned to Ed who'd had a baby, had spent her pregnancy preening and boasting, relishing the attention and the excuse to give up school. Jessica had seen her a couple of times since, proudly pushing her pink buggy, with bags and baby toys dangling off it like decorations on a tree, her mum in tow, spewing to anyone who would listen about how emotionally mature Bella was and how great to be a grandmother at thirty-nine. It was shite, all of it, of course, but better than having a mother who didn't speak at all except to yell about the flat being a tip and how she had the dumbest daughter in the world – dumb enough to turn down Jerry's offer of a full-time job and to agree, like some brainless cow, to the Harrisons' bee in their bonnet about a paternity test. If Jessica was so bent on having the kid, she said, she should have made the Harrisons hang on, got some money first, played the thing out.

Jessica hadn't liked the test. Amniocentesis, they called it; a long word for a long needle. She hadn't watched – kept her eyes tight shut – trying to keep the doubts out. Of course it was Ed's. The Jason thing had been months and months before and on the couple of times they'd gone all the way he'd pulled out, spilling his come on her belly. Of more concern was the time with Jerry; but he'd been inside her so briefly – just as long as it took for her to scramble to her senses and use her hand instead . . . Surely no baby could have resulted from that.

Behind her squeezed eyes Jessica had nevertheless found herself imagining a single sperm – fat, stubborn and goofy-faced, like its producer, swimming up the tube towards her womb, like some gross, burrowing worm. Not having even entertained such a possibility before she agreed to the test, it now haunted her. Jerry himself didn't even know she was pregnant, since she'd left the salon before it had got obvious. When he called, out of the blue, to offer her the full-time slot, she'd been as sharp and unfriendly as she could manage without actually telling him to fuck off. He'd tried to chat anyway, asking about her rubbish GCSE grades and plans for the future, wheedling as he always had for her to like him. Jessica, looking at the handset resting on her bloated belly, had had to suppress a sudden, vicious urge to tell him everything – give him some of the worry that she now dragged around like a ball and chain. But she'd known there was no point. If by some sick fluke the kid *was* his, she'd die rather than confess it, to him or anyone else. She'd rather chuck the thing in the canal.

'Can I help you?' asked a shop assistant, nosing in like they always did the moment she touched anything. 'Can't be long now,' the woman added, nodding at the bare bump protruding between Jessica's T-shirt and stretch-waist jeans. 'How many weeks?'

'Not enough,' snapped Jessica. 'Not bloody enough.' She thrust the little yellow and green vest she had been holding into the woman's hands and ran out of the shop, her belly straining as if it was trying to break free. By the time she got to the poster she was breathless, sweating hard and close to tears. She didn't want the stupid baby, Ed's or anyone else's. Her mother – all of them – had been right. She had not thought it through, the *grossness* of it, the sheer impossibility of things working out well. Ed had phoned just once since he'd got back from his swanky family holiday to say that if the kid did turn out to be his he didn't want anything to do with it. She would get money and that was it. Nothing more. EVER. He had shouted the last word, his voice cracking like he wanted to cry.

Jessica began to weep in earnest, sinking to her knees under the poster, as if prostrating herself before an altar. What an idiot she had been and all because of some dim hope about keeping Ed and not liking being told what to do – not by the stupid, pompous judge of an uncle, or Ed's goggle-eyed parents, or her mum, being smarmy and grasping after cash as usual. If they'd begged her to keep it she'd have probably flounced off to the abortion clinic that minute. What a cretin she'd been – what a fucking cretin.

'Are you all right, dearie?'

Jessica shook her head, unable to speak.

'Oh, and look at you, *expecting* and all . . . Poor love. Let's get you up. There we are, that's better. You look like you could do with a nice cuppa.'

'No, I'm all right, honest.' Jessica wiped away her tears, managing a weak smile for her rescuer, a tiny, shrivelled lady with a beaky nose and legs like pencils. 'I just . . .'

'I know, I know . . . Cried my eyes out when I was expecting mine. Lovely, though, when they come – you'll see.' The woman patted Jessica's arm, then launched herself back at the crowds of shoppers.

For a moment Jessica was tempted to run after her, take up the offer of tea, see what the old dear said when she explained that her baby was the biggest mistake of her life, too unwanted to be lovely to anyone. But when she looked again, the tottering spindly figure had disappeared, swallowed up in the busy tunnel of the arcade.

The result of the paternity test arrived the next morning, a slim white envelope with the name of the hospital printed on the back. Pamela, standing in the hall, tying her headscarf in preparation for a visit to Marjorie, with Poppy springing at her heels, heard the postman come down the steps, whistling one of his tuneless tunes, and saw the envelope land on the doormat. With her long-sighted eyes, she spotted the official stamp of the hospital and knew at once what it contained. Excited as always by the postman, who sometimes gave her a biscuit, Poppy sniffed it once, then put her nose to the crack under the door and whined softly.

'Not today, darling,' murmured Pamela, approaching the mat, then glancing over her shoulder along the hallway to the half-open kitchen door where her grandson and his parents were enjoying the mindless, comforting ritual of family breakfast. She should pick it up, of course, bending carefully as she had to, these days, especially in the mornings when her bones felt stiff and unwieldy as if a night's repose had glued the joints. Instead, staring down at the envelope, Pamela thought of all the bomb talk on the radio that morning, the home secretary's plea for public vigilance, how any odd behaviour, any odd packages were immediately to be reported to the appropriate authorities. Here was an explosive package, all right, she reflected sadly, but not one that could be defused or taken away.

Poppy was whining more insistently now and scratching at the door. Pamela hesitated for a couple more moments, then reached across the dog and unlocked the door. Poppy bounced through the gap and Pamela, careful not to tread on the envelope, followed her. It was their bomb, after all, not hers, and if she delivered it to the table she would be forced to wait and deal with the fallout. She would deal with it anyway, of course – the news, good or bad, would be forced upon the entire family soon enough – but for now her own future beckoned: coffee with her old friend and a tour round Crayshott Manor. Even Poppy, frisky as in her puppy days, had sensed all morning that something exciting was going on, something beyond their usual stroll down the lane.

She trilled a goodbye, closed the door and wondered what state she would find them all in when she returned.

A little over an hour later, Ed slammed the same door behind him and ran up the steps to the drive. Unaware of his mother watching from an upstairs window, her heart bursting, he looked about him, at the silver birches, at the lane, at the path leading round the far side of the house, trying with almost comical obviousness to decide which way to go.

'You don't suppose he'll run away again?' said Serena, dropping the curtain.

'No.'

She approached Ed's bed, where Charlie was still sitting, arms dangling open and useless, head bent. She looked about her, at the framed photographs of Ed posing with school football teams, at the Airfix models and plastic trophies on the shelves, at the two moth-eaten teddy bears abandoned on top of the wardrobe. 'We'd all got our hopes up. Now we must be strong for Ed.'

'Strong . . . for Ed . . . yup.'

'Charlie, this isn't the worst thing that could have happened.'

'Isn't it? Really? And what would have been the *worst* thing?'

'You know what.'

He frowned, tapping his temple with his index finger, as if to encourage his brain to embark on the retrieval of an important fact. 'Ah, yes . . . something *happening* to Ed. That would have been worse, wouldn't it? Because of what *happened* to Tina.'

'Charlie, don't, please.'

'The fact is,' he continued, ignoring her, 'something *has* happened to Ed, something pretty fucking terrible, and I reserve the right to say that, at the top of my voice, if I want to. Just as you have the right, Serena, darling, to pretend that you're upset when in fact you're rubbing your hands with glee at the prospect of getting your hands on –'

Serena let out a small cry, raising her palms as if to defend herself from a physical blow.

Charlie stood up, tugging at his shorts where they had hitched up round his crotch. 'Sorry, that was too harsh. I'm upset, forgive me.' He crossed the room to look out at the now empty drive. A wind had picked up and was raking through the branches of the silver birches, sending a scattering of leaves on to the grass below. 'Do you know?' he added, putting his hands into his shorts pockets, his voice matter-of-fact. 'I really thought it was going to be okay . . . the test. I really thought it would be okay.'

'Things still can be okay,' whispered Serena, hugging herself. She was still reeling from the sting of his words. *Rubbing your hands with glee* – of course she wasn't. She just couldn't help loving the idea of Ed's child. Even if she never met it, she'd love it. That was all.

Charlie shook his head. 'No, no, they can't, not for Ed, not for any of us . . . not really.'

'That's nonsense. You're talking nonsense.'

But Charlie was in his own dark world. 'I realized, thinking about it all in Umbria, that our time here, at Ashley House, has been jinxed from the start. It was never meant to *be*. Accepting Peter's offer, coming to live here, has been a hideous mistake. Deep down you've been feeling as much yourself all year – you can't deny it. "We have *failed* as a family." Those were your exact words . . .'

'It's been difficult lately, I admit, but when I said that I never meant –'

'No, you were right. It's time we both recognized it . . . recognized it and moved on. My mother has certainly recognized it . . .' Charlie laughed darkly. 'She's planning on leaving us, did you know? I saw the form – an application for a place called Crayshott Manor. She'd put in Poppy's details and everything. Christ, Dad must be spinning in his grave. The deal was that we looked after her, do you remember? Talk about a botched job . . . Jesus.'

'No, I didn't know that,' said Serena quietly. She had gone to sit on the bed in the indentation left by Charlie. She could feel his warmth still on the linen. It made the coldness of his voice almost impossible to bear. 'I'll talk to her.'

Charlie shrugged, thrusting his hands deeper into his pockets. 'Nah . . . I shouldn't bother. She'll tell us in her own good time. Anyway, she might change her mind when she hears Peter's taking over.'

'Peter?'

'I asked him, in Umbria, explained the position, said the way things were looking it would be money we needed rather than this roof over our heads. If Peter takes it we can revert to the original plan of whatever cash Mum leaves being split between me, Cassie and Elizabeth. The last thing Peter needs is more money – he's drowning in it.'

'We need more money?' Serena gripped the edges of the bed, feeling, even though her feet were planted firmly on the carpet, as if she might fall off it.

'To – pay – for – the – child,' said Charlie, giving equal accent to each word, as if he was spelling out a difficult sentence for a foreigner. 'I presume you had thought about that, hadn't you, in all your secret plotting to get the thing born?'

'I don't need . . . I don't deserve this.' Serena stood up very slowly, fighting the dizziness that threatened to topple her to the floor. 'This – this is not how it should be,' she faltered, trying, in spite of everything, to cling to her knowledge of the fact that somewhere behind this cold, accusatory voice was the kind man she had married. Distress had warped him . . . warped them all.

'No, you're right there. This is not how it should be. We'll see Cass through her wedding, then move out, further east, near Brighton, maybe. It's well in the commuting belt, these days.'

Serena had put her hands to her ears. 'Stop this, Charlie. You're not making any sense. I don't want to leave Ashley House. Giving it back to Peter would break my heart.'

He laughed, a hard, sharp noise, like a gunshot. 'Would it, now? Well, that means we'd still have one thing in common anyway. Mine snapped months ago when our son committed the worst error of his life and you took his side instead of mine, when it struck me that you're not over Tina and never will be –' He broke off, as the room and his wife's ashen face came back into focus. 'Sorry, I –'

'No. Never mind. It's what you feel.' Serena began to move towards the door. Her breath was coming in odd, heavy spasms, making it hard to talk. 'You're right. I'm not over Tina. I never will be. The love I have for her sits here . . .' She pressed her knuckles into her ribcage. 'It will never go and I don't want it to. My love for Ed is like that too and –'

'And me? Where is your love for me, Serena?' Charlie knew the question sounded ugly. He knew, too, that with his own feelings in such disarray and the extent to which in recent weeks at least, he had been *unlovable*, he had no right to ask such a thing. 'Where do I fit in?'

Serena stopped with her hand on the door. 'You are my husband,' she said simply, giving him a sad smile, then leaving the room.

Charlie looked out of the window through a blur of tears. On the windowsill was a photograph of his father with Ed, aged about five, on his lap. His father was pointing at the camera with his pipe, and saying something into his grandson's ear, something compelling, clearly, judging by the alert expression on Ed's face. Thinking of his son's glazed misery as he scanned the letter that morning, Charlie began to sob. Serena, with all her talk of love, was missing the point. He loved Ed beyond words, of course. And he loved her too, still, somewhere within the deep, dark anger that had overtaken his heart. But it wasn't enough, not when it was pitted against his now permanent sense of failure, not just as a parent and a husband but as a custodian of the beloved family home. How had he ever imagined he could do a better job than Peter? How had he thought he and Serena were strong enough? They were flimsy and hopeless, their stewardship doomed from the start. The sooner they got out the better.

Charlie pulled out his handkerchief and wiped the tracing of dust off the photo before blowing his nose. He wouldn't go to work that day. There was too much on his mind, too many phone calls to make – to the Blake family, to Peter, of course, maybe to an estate agent or two. It was never too early to start. And, badly as he had handled living at the place, Charlie wanted to manage the leaving of it as well as he could. There could be grace in failure, after all. Strengthened a little by the thought, he turned the photo face downwards before he left his post by the window, unable to bear the thought of the two alert pairs of eyes, his father's and his son's, watching him retreat from the room.

Ed found the key to the barn in its usual place above the lintel. Inside, it was hot and airless. Dead flies were scattered on the windowsills. In one corner the crisp white tendrils of a dead spider plant trailed over the sides of a ceramic pot. He went into the kitchen and ran himself a glass of water. Hearing the hum of the fridge, he looked inside and saw several cans of lager. Taking one, and another glass of water, he returned to the sitting room, levered open a couple of windows and sank heavily into an armchair. Lighting a cigarette, he inhaled slowly and deeply, surveying the empty room through a thickening, pungent grey mist and thinking of Keith's brief but intense tenure as the family handyman – the countless offers of friendship, his obvious keenness on Aunt Elizabeth, the extraordinary rescue of his grandmother. It was a total shame the guy had left, Ed reflected, wishing suddenly that Keith was parked opposite him with that open, unjudging look he had, like he knew something was wrong and wanted to help.

Ed belched, thought about getting a second can but drank some water instead. He needed to talk to *someone*. Not about the bloody baby – he'd known all along that it was his, that the stupid paternity test was a red herring. He had been even more sure when Jessica had agreed to the test, as if she had nothing to be afraid of. No, what was burning inside Ed now was the new knowledge that the mess he had got into wasn't just *his* mess, that there was a bigger picture, which involved his parents and what he had once regarded as the solid future of his family.

After hanging around in the drive he had gone back inside, seeking the sanctuary of his bedroom, never imagining that his parents, who had raced after him when he left the breakfast table, would still be there. Hearing voices, he had stopped at the door, pressing first one eye and then his ear to the crack, his heart galloping. That they were arguing was nothing new, although since the holiday he had thought they were getting on better. But with his ear glued to the crack, taking in all the stuff about failing and being jinxed and money and *moving*, Ed had realized not only that they weren't getting on at all but also the extent to which he had been seeing everything solely from his own point of view. Of course he had recognized the strain of his predicament for them too, but not the hugeness of it.

Standing, shaking, in the corridor for those few minutes, Ed felt as if his life was fast-forwarding towards a living nightmare, taking the last shreds of his pathetic, youthful innocence with it. How could his parents think of handing Ashley House back to his uncle and aunt, to Chloë and Theo? It was *their* home, not his cousins'. Even if his grandmother chose to leave, it would still be their home. Such was Ed's conviction that he had almost burst into the room to exclaim it to them; but then his father said the stuff about his mother not being over the death of his little sister and he had backed away towards the landing, heart quailing at how complicated everything was, how *connected*, and how thick he had been not to see it that way before.

Sitting in the barn now, going over it all, Ed's thoughts kept returning to the subject of money. For all his father's wild talk about failure and jinxing, money seemed, as ever, to lie at the heart of everything. In all their various stilted conversations about supporting the baby, both parents had only ever said that they would foot the bill until he was ready to assume the responsibility himself. So much so that Ed had begun to take this aspect of the situation for granted. In addition to which, he had only ever thought in terms of weekly or monthly amounts, what it would take to keep Jessica and the child out of his life. It had never occurred to him that such amounts could build to the sort of total that might cause his father to move them all to some poky house in Brighton. In truth, he had been fixing his hopes on going away at the first moment he decently could, after the dreaded birth – and his aunt's wedding, of course, he'd have to hang around for that. He had been planning a year out at least, funded, with any luck, via a job at the Rising Sun, washing up or serving tables, five quid an hour plus tips. But now Ed could see that this wouldn't do, not just the five quid but the whole idea of going away. He needed to be around, to earn proper money, take what pressure he could off his parents. He had good A levels, after all – there must be something he could do to earn a decent wage. And he could use his five thousand to kick-start things. He'd get on the Internet that afternoon, Ed decided now, squeezing his empty beer can till it collapsed, start filling in applications. Jessica deciding to keep the baby was a disaster, but he could see now that it was *his* disaster, not anyone else's. If his parents left Ashley House it wasn't going to be because of him.

Lost to such thoughts, Ed didn't hear the creak of the stairs or Roland pushing open the door. At the sound of his cousin's shy 'Hello,' he jumped as if he had been shot. 'Christ, you gave me a fright.'

'Sorry.' Roland hovered uncertainly by the door, still gripping the handle. 'Thought I'd find you here.'

'Did you? And why was that?'

'You left the front door open downstairs. It was banging. Sorry about the test result, by the way. That's really tough.'

'Yeah, it's a fucker, all right. Do you want a beer? Keith left a load of cans in the fridge. Help yourself. Why did the guy leave, by the way? Was it some falling-out with your mum?'

'How should I know?' Roland muttered, unwilling to discuss a subject he had pondered, with some embarrassment, himself.

'Because I sometimes got the impression that the two of them . . .'

'Yeah, but they're not now, are they?' interjected Roland in a tone curt enough to indicate that he considered the matter closed. He fetched himself a beer and went to sit on the sofa, all the while keeping a wary eye on his cousin, who had lit a new cigarette from the stub of the last and was smoking with the glazed intensity of one lost in true crisis. Roland, who had come up to the barn with the intention of saying all sorts of mundane, comforting things, could not think now where or how to start.

'Well done on your paintings, by the way,' Ed burst out, 'getting into a proper exhibition. Bloody fantastic. Cheers.' He raised his crushed can.

'Thanks.'

'You just do your own thing, don't you, Roland, mate? Always have, I suppose.'

'Have I?' Roland frowned, uncertain as to whether he was being criticized or congratulated. 'I guess I learnt to cope on my own pretty early on . . . what with Mum and Dad splitting up and so on, and then Mum, well, she's never been that *sorted*, if you know what I mean, though I have to say recently she –'

'Bloody right! We – all of us on the fucking planet – are *alone*,' agreed Ed, eagerly, leaping up from his chair to fetch two more cans of beer and dropping one into Roland's lap. 'It's only just dawned on me . . . I mean, take this whole sick situation I'm in, it's like all along I've been waiting for something to happen that will fix it, like it might *go away*, when of course it's not fucking going to.' He slumped back into his chair and sighed heavily, as if the outburst had exhausted him.

'I know this might not be a totally helpful thing to say,' ventured Roland, after a few moments, 'but . . . I never liked Jessica. Even when we were kids I used to think there was something . . . not right about her.'

'Yeah, I never liked her either,' Ed muttered. 'Felt *sorry* for her sometimes, though that's hard to imagine now. Amazing what lust can make you do,' he added, managing a ghoulish smile.

'Amazing,' agreed Roland, dropping his gaze as he recalled the flick of Carl's tongue between his teeth, the gentle pressure of his palm pushing against his lower back, pressing their hips so perfectly together, like two interlocking pieces of a puzzle.

'But I've decided I'm not going to let it ruin everything,' continued Ed, talking fast again, his voice filled with fresh conviction. 'I'm going to start looking for a proper job so Mum and Dad don't have to worry about bailing me out . . . Do you know? They're so worried about money that they're thinking of handing this place back to Uncle Peter. Can you believe it?'

'Blimey! That's drastic.'

'Fucking right it's drastic. It's also stupid and just not going to happen, not if I have anything to do with it.'

'Theo would be pleased, though,' said Roland, absently. 'He always minded, you know, about his dad handing this place over to yours.'

'Did he, now? Bloody Theo, I might have guessed. I can just see him playing lord of the manor, can't you, with all his snotty Oxford ways?'

'I like Theo.'

Ed made a growling sound. 'So did I, once upon a time.'

'What he did,' Roland pressed on, 'phoning his dad when you turned up at Clem's, he only meant for the best.'

'Yeah, yeah, I know he did.' Ed sighed, then drained the contents of the second can. 'And having a father who gives away somewhere like Ashley House . . . I guess I'd have been pretty pissed off too. But we're not giving it back,' he added hastily, 'I can tell you that for nothing. What's done is done. Like Uncle Eric handing the place over to Granddad – that was never a problem, was it?' He leant forwards, rubbing his palms together. 'Ready for another beer, old chap?'

'No, thanks. And I don't think you should either, Ed.'

'Don't you now?' said Ed, nastily. 'I'd have thought you of all people would be used to a spot of *excess* drinking, what with the amount your mother puts away.'

Roland went red.

'Sorry, mate, below the belt.' Ed struggled to his feet, aware that he was hot and giddy.

'Actually she's not drinking much at the moment. She's better.'

'Good . . . really pleased.'

'You're not the only one with bloody troubles, you know, Ed.'

Ed sat back down. 'I know that.'

'Well, you don't behave like it.'

'You have to admit I've got more than my fair share at the moment.'

'Well, I'm gay,' said Roland, glaring at him. 'Go on – laugh. You clearly want to.'

'No, I don't . . . Christ, that's a bit heavy . . . Fuck . . . Are you sure?'

Roland remembered again his recent encounter with Carl and experienced a reflex of recollected pleasure, like being stabbed in the gut, but nice . . . really nice. 'Unfortunately, yes.'

'But I thought you and Polly, that girl . . .'

'We went to primary school together. We were always just friends. It was when she wanted more that I began to see it wasn't for me.'

'Right . . . I see . . .' Ed left his chair and went to open another window. 'And is there . . . ?'

'Yes, but don't ask because I won't tell you.'

'Of course . . . I . . . That's fine, of course.' Ed continued to fiddle with the window latch, fighting both astonishment and groping for the correct response. He might have laughed once, he knew, not that long ago either, when the world had still been a benign black-and-white place, something he imagined he might command instead of something that had the power to kick him in the teeth. 'Well . . . er, thanks for telling me.'

'Thanks for being okay about it.' Roland stood up. 'I'd better be going. Mum will wonder where I am. Shall I say I haven't seen you?'

Ed shrugged. 'It doesn't matter . . . Say what you like. Your mum, does she know about . . . what you just told me?'

Roland shook his head. 'Not yet. I – I don't think she'll be too pleased. She wants grandchildren and stuff.' He smiled, managing a show of bravery he did not feel. 'And as for my dad . . .' The smile crumpled. 'He'll go ape-shit, and it's not like we've ever got on that well anyway. He's supposed to be coming over at Christmas . . . Guess I'll have to break it to him then.'

'But surely you don't have to *break it* to either of them,' exclaimed Ed, grimacing with horror on his cousin's behalf, quite forgetting, for a few lovely moments, all his own worries. 'I mean, you don't have to tell anyone, do you?'

Roland straightened his shoulders, raising himself to his full, impressive height, managing to look manly in spite of his still milky skin and the glint of fear in his wide brown eyes. 'But then I'd be living a lie, wouldn't I?'

'Yes,' conceded Ed. 'I suppose you would.'

'I was thinking of a letter – to my dad – to sort of ease the blow. What do you think?'

'A letter . . . Maybe . . . Yup, letters can be good. Best of luck with it, anyway,' concluded Ed, awkwardly. 'And I won't breathe a word, I promise. You can trust me on that . . . unlike *Theo*.' He pulled a funny face and they both laughed.

Ed waited until Roland had gone before he closed the windows and gathered up the empty cans. His cousin's confession had made him feel better about his own woes: it had helped him to see that life was complicated and difficult for everyone. Gay! Christ, poor bastard. It occurred to Ed in the same instant that Roland's decision to tell him might have been an act of generosity rather than personal release, that he had guessed somehow it would make his cousin feel better.

'Impressive,' muttered Ed, as he closed the barn door. And the idea of a letter wasn't bad either, he mused, slipping the key back on top of the lintel, then setting off up the path towards the house. With a paper and pen he might be able to set out his own thoughts clearly, explain to his parents how he planned to handle things from now on, how he had never meant to muck everything up for everyone else, how . . . how he was sorry. Ed stopped on the path, swiping angrily at a fat horsefly as he absorbed this small but awesome oversight. He had not apologized. He had been too full of self-pity even to consider it. It was several minutes before he began to walk on, striding through the overgrown tangle of blackberry briars and long grass, his gaze fixed on the slates of Ashley House.

'Okay,' said Theo, scratching the now substantial thicket of his beard, and gesturing with his arms. 'I want you, Ben, to get up from the bench first and then, Clem, you stay where you are, your eyes following him. You don't move, but your whole body is, like, full of the desire to, and then just when it looks like you're going to give in to it you reach out and touch the brief-case to remind yourself of your other destiny.'

'I wish she *could* follow him,' said Clem. 'I mean, he's sup-posed to be her soul-mate, isn't he?' She pulled a face at the boy sitting next to her, one of Theo's university friends and actually called Ben in real life. Under Theo's direction they had already kissed and had a blazing row, an ordeal that Clem, to her amazement, had found rather easy. Although Ben, arriving that morning with lanky·hair and sleep in his eyes, wedged among the camera equipment in the car Theo had borrowed for the trip, had hardly looked the ideal leading man, he had proved to be – instantly and obviously – a tremendous actor. Subsequent exchanges had revealed that he had played Romeo for the National Youth Theatre in his gap year and was shortly due to appear as Hamlet in a student production at the Oxford Playhouse. He had the ability to speak his lines as if they had only just occurred to him, as if they really were his own words. And when it came to kissing he had been so immediately intense and assured that Clem might have thought he was trying to tell her something, had he not subsided into his lanky, quiet self the moment Theo shouted, 'Cut,' and stepped out from behind the camera.

'The bomb in the briefcase is already ticking,' Theo reminded her. 'It's going to go off anyway, so she might as well get it to the right place.'

'Victoria station.'

'Yup – at least, *a* station, I haven't decided which.' They were in a small, wrought-iron-fenced garden that Ben had suggested, not far from Chancery Lane tube station, ideal because it was open to the public, yet not widely used.

'And I – she is definitely going to die?'

'Yes, she is . . . Clem, I don't have time for this, we've got a lot to get through.'

'Couldn't she leave the case and race off in time to avoid getting killed and catch up with lover-boy instead?' They all turned to see Jonny strolling towards them, a packet of biscuits tucked under his arm and four paper cups of coffee pressed between his hands.

'Oh, Jonny, good man.' Theo glanced at his watch, wondering at how the time was racing and whether he had been wise to let Jonny Cottrall in on things, particularly given that he and Clem were clearly back together. When he had arrived at his cousin's flat that morning, it had been Jonny who answered the door, still pulling on a T-shirt, an impish grin on his face. 'He's just going, aren't you?' Clem had declared, emerging, noticeably pink-cheeked, from her room. At which point Jonny had asked Theo, in his direct, inoffensive way, if he could offer his services to the film project as an odd-job man and, more significantly as far as Theo was concerned, by having a go at composing a soundtrack. Tone deaf himself, unable to remember the sound or names of tunes, Theo had been wondering what to do about this very thing, so essential to a good, finished film. 'And we could use my van,' Jonny had added slyly, as if he knew about the little car Theo had borrowed, in which Clem would have to sit on Ben's lap to travel between locations.

'Seriously, mate,' Jonny continued now, handing out the coffees and tearing open the biscuit packet with his teeth, 'I love a bit of drama as much as the next man, but if you want to make it on the big screen, these days, you have to have a happy ending, don't you? Clem could uphold her cause *and* get her man, couldn't you, babe?' he said, giving her a nudge as she took a biscuit.

Clem nodded but then, fearful of pissing off her cousin, said she was only there to follow instructions and would do whatever Theo thought best.

'I'll shoot it both ways,' said Theo, at length, 'make my final decision when I edit. Are you happy with that, Ben?'

'Your call, man.' Ben lit a cigarette and moved away from them.

'Boy, have I missed you,' murmured Jonny, pressing himself closer to Clem and giving her a dreamy look. 'Nothing was the same – the band, life, nothing.'

'I missed you too,' admitted Clem, dunking her biscuit in her coffee, then quickly getting her lips round it before it fell apart.

'You didn't *enjoy* that snog, did you?' muttered Jonny next, scowling at Ben, now deep in conversation with Theo.

'Yuk! No way – just *acting*.' Clem giggled, enjoying the new sense of power she had in the relationship, so unlike her hangdog approach before the split. She had enjoyed, too, sharing with Jonny the million things that had happened since they had seen each other, all the ups and downs, astounded that she could ever have imagined a life lived alone was better than one with its doors open to other people. When she had heard the result of Ed's paternity test, via Maisie, it was Jonny she had phoned. He had come round at once and they had sat up half the night talking it through, not making love until the sky was grey with the promise of morning, when touching each other felt like an expression of how close they were already instead of a way of *getting* close. They had put the Durex on carefully, though, together, rolling it right down, each aware in a new way of the magnitude of what they were doing, of the life-force behind the pleasure.

'By the way,' said Jonny, linking arms with her while they finished the dregs of their coffee, 'I saw your uncle just now.'

'Peter?'

'That's the one.'

'But you don't know him, do you?'

Jonny looked hurt. 'Last summer, remember, when I came for that day and half your family were there and –'

'Oh, yes,' Clem interjected, a little sharply, remembering the day only too well. It had marked the start of her suspicion that Jonny and her sister had shared rather more than the same biology teacher.

'The thing is . . .' Jonny glanced at Theo, who was getting ready to get going again '. . . he was with a woman.'

Clem laughed. 'Oooh! A *woman* – you don't say.'

'Not your aunt Helen.'

'Yeah, like a client or a colleague or . . . We're not far from all the law courts and stuff where he works.'

'They were holding hands.'

Clem turned to look at him, still more disbelieving than astonished. 'That's impossible. My uncle *Peter*? He just . . . well, he just *wouldn't*.' She laughed. 'He's about the most old-fashioned, upright, *boring* adult I know.'

'That may be true, but he has a bird,' declared Jonny, taking her empty cup and dropping it into the bin next to the bench. 'Being boring doesn't mean you don't want a screw on the side. He's probably been at it for years.'

Seeing Theo approach, Clem tugged at Jonny's arm.

Observing something conspiratorial in their manner and sensing it was connected to him, Theo said, 'Look, I can't have any plotting, you two. If you're not on board, Jonny, if both of you aren't totally up front with me about any issues . . .'

'No, we're not – I mean, we *are*, totally on board,' Clem assured him.

'I don't want any funny business, okay? Music or no music, Jonny, we've all got to behave like professionals, okay?'

Jonny saluted, then winked at Clem and trotted off to ask a

couple of new entrants to the little park if they would mind skirting round the area that was being used for shooting. Returning to the scene, he sat carefully out of everybody's way in a patch of dappled shade and watched all that Clem did with a singing heart, wanting, every time Theo asked for another take, to yell that she was perfect. As the heat intensified he slipped closer to the tree under which he had sought protection and began to think about tunes, trying to feel the right pulse for the scene, how and with what instruments he might communicate the parallel tensions of a broken heart and a ticking bomb.

Later that day, mulling over lists of possible hymns for the wedding, to the background accompaniment of the last night of the Proms, Stephen and Cassie, too, were immersed in contemplation of the stirring power of music. Having said he knew very few hymns and would go along with anything she suggested, Stephen turned out to be full of controversial opinions. 'Love Divine' was too dirge-like, he said, and, no, he had never been keen on 'Dear Lord and Father of Mankind' and what about 'He Who Would Valiant Be'?

'"'Gainst all disaster" . . . I've never really liked it much.'

'But it's such a jolly tune.'

'Okay, but only if I can have "Love Divine" and "O Jesus I Have Promised" . . .'

'I don't even know that one. How does it go?'

'Well, it's got several versions but the one I like best is . . .' Cassie started to hum, just as the strains of 'Jerusalem' began to flow from the television. She reached for the remote but Stephen put out a hand to stop her.

'Look at that,' he murmured, evidently transfixed by the television cameras pulling back out of the Albert Hall to reveal the sea of people in the park, old and young, babes in arms, Union flags fluttering, swaying as one before the big screens

379

relaying the concert to the open air. 'Quite a sight,' he breathed.

Cassie looked first at the screen and then at her husband-to-be. He was close to tears, she saw suddenly, and with some amazement. His Adam's apple was bobbing furiously and he was clenching his jaw to control the tremors in his cheeks. 'Can we have this one too . . . "Jerusalem"?'

'Sure, why not?' Cassie said lightly, aware all the while of a coldness creeping round her heart. She wasn't keen on the Proms, all that grand, sentimental emotion, cheap, somehow, too easily tapped, too *unearned*. I should love him for this, she thought, for being so easily distracted from my little effort at singing, for being sentimental enough to weep at the Proms. It should be endearing. But, glancing again at his twitching face, she felt only pity and a faint repugnance. Love is hard work, Cassie reminded herself, clenching her own jaw in recognition of the fact; all veterans of the science agreed it needed working at, compassion, understanding, forgiveness . . . and, my goodness, hadn't she tried all of that? Especially lately, fighting her knowledge of how he had tailed her, like a stalker, fighting her disappointment at the red streak in her pants and the rising suffocating sensation that no haphazard natural methods would get her what she wanted, and that if she decided to pull out all the stops on the long, arduous quest to have a child, the man she was to marry was not the strong, willing companion she needed to see it through.

I don't love him, she thought, the screen blurring as the horrible enormity of this admission sank in. And we're not yet married so I don't have to carry on *trying* to love him. Her own throat was working now as the implications of this – held in check for so long – stormed her consciousness: caterers, present lists, flowers, the photographer, the wedding cars – all would have to be cancelled in gruelling letters and phone calls. And then there would be the ordeal of telling her family, letting them all down too, although in the few weeks since Italy, when she had been removed once more from their immediate orbit, this aspect of her situation seemed, for those instants at least, marginally more manageable. It was her life, after all, Cassie reflected bleakly, looking at the still fresh decoration of her and Stephen's sitting room and longing suddenly for the chance to occupy it – to occupy any room – without the pressure of his swinging moods dominating the atmosphere. She couldn't handle him any more, carefully or otherwise: it was destroying her.

'It is moving, isn't it?' said Stephen, seeing her glassy-eyed expression and misinterpreting its origin. 'It was the one event that used to make my dad cry, stupid bastard. He'd sit watching it each year over his can of Guinness, snivelling like a three-year-old. Funny, isn't it? I can actually think of that now and feel sort of fond of him – glad it gets me by throat, too, like it's some small daft thing we have in common.' He switched off the television. 'They wouldn't bother to reply to an invitation, by the way, I can tell you that now. They'll turn up or not, depending on their mood and whether they feel up to the journey . . . Hey, cheer up, love, you look quite cut-up.'

'Do I? Sorry, I'm fine.' Cassie stood up quickly and went into the kitchen, where the remains of their supper needed clearing away. With trembling hands she set about scraping soggy lettuce leaves and abandoned Bolognese into the bin. She crossed to the sink, ran her hands and as much of her arms as she could under the cold tap, then flicked water at her face. Now was not the moment to say anything. She was too unsteady, still too caught off-guard by the rush of her own emotions, the awful certainty as to what had to be done.

'Hey,' Stephen called from the sitting room, his voice low and lazy, sickeningly confident, 'had any thoughts about next Monday?'

Next Monday . . . next Monday . . . Cassie's mind raced, her sole concern being to remove the need for him to enter the kitchen, to stop him seeing her before she had composed herself. 'Your birthday?'

'Ten out of ten. That new Thai restaurant I was telling you about the other day, do you mind if I book it?' His voice was closer.

'Lovely,' Cassie almost shrieked. 'Go right ahead.'

'Not your favourite food, I know, but, then, it is *my* birthday.'

She heard him laugh, then the thump of his feet on the stairs. Cassie remained motionless, staring at her reflection in the kettle, a warped, Disney version of her face. She had made him happy and now she was going to destroy him. She clenched her face, making her reflection still more distorted, more akin to the ugliness swelling inside. All her love for him had turned to pity; all her kindness had become calculated, cautious. There was no true reciprocity, no balance, no trust. The knowledge that a lot of his problems stemmed from his difficult childhood made no difference. She had wanted to be his wife, not his healer.

She would, however, be kind, Cassie decided, dabbing her wet face on a tea-towel, at least more so than he had been with her. She would make no mention of the pathetic spying, simply explain the central, more important truth that the form of love he sought from her was too cloying, too oppressive. She would explain that she could no longer play down her desperation to have a child, that she would prefer to take the medical route alone, than with him as a reluctant partner.

Cassie filled a saucepan with milk and scoured the back of a cupboard until she found a jar of hot chocolate, a sticky, dusty old thing that dated back to her days of living alone. She hugged herself while she watched the milk bubble and heave, shivery suddenly with cold, while inside a new loneliness took shape, worse than anything she had known during her singleton spells, worse, even, than all her longing for Dan Lambert, borne as it was on a sense of immeasurable sepa-

382

ration from the man now creaking round the bedroom floorboards overhead.

A moment later the milk had boiled over, producing an acrid smell and thick brown stains round the ring. Cassie sat at the table to drink it, gripping the hot mug in both palms.

Ed stayed up most of that night composing his letter, first on his laptop and then, wanting to make it as personal and immediate as he could, copying it out by hand. He laboured slowly, trying to make his famously scruffy writing look neat, only noticing when he got to the bottom of the page that all the lines sloped at a childish angle, as if the words were trying to run off the page. He struggled, too, over how much to say, to what extent he should reveal his eavesdropping that morning. In the end he decided it didn't matter, that the prospect of being responsible for the implosion of his family's entire and lovely way of life was too important to worry about such niceties.

The point is, I am the one who has made a mess of everything, so please don't let it muck up the whole family as well. If you decided to leave Ashley House all because of me and the money worries I have caused then I would never forgive myself. So, please, let me use my trust money to pay whatever Jessica will need to start off with. In the meantime I am going to begin some serious job hunting so that I can continue to make whatever monthly payments are decided. I'm not saying I think it's going to be easy but please let me try. I'm afraid it will mean me living at home for a while yet to save on rent etc.! But in time hopefully I'll be able to set up somewhere on my own. One thing I am also sure of is that I don't want to be involved with Jessica or the child beyond giving them money. I'll pay – literally – for my mistake, but I don't feel up to doing any more. Jessica knows this already.

Lastly, I want to say that I am SORRY for all the worry I have caused you when you have both been so decent and didn't deserve it.

Love Ed

It was by no means a perfect letter, but as the night wore on Ed lost the clear-headedness required to improve on it. The next morning he woke early and stole downstairs to leave it on the doormat for his parents to find under the morning post.

He was hurrying through a bowl of cereal, wanting to be gone before anyone else came down, when his grandmother, silent in her slippers, came shuffling into the kitchen. 'Darling, this is early for you, isn't it?'

'I couldn't sleep,' Ed muttered, his mouth full of cornflakes.

Pamela sighed, folding her arms and looking at him fondly. 'Well, you do have a lot on your plate, after all.'

Ed nodded warily, loath to be drawn into analysis of his situation. The letter had got a lot of stuff out of his system, cleared his head, and he didn't want to go over it again, least of all with his grandmother. But Pamela seemed in no mood to press the matter and merely asked if he wanted a cup of tea.

In fact, the old stick was good at not saying anything, Ed mused, watching her fill the kettle and make a fuss of Poppy and Samson, who were twining themselves round her legs in the hope of breakfast. She had had her own low spots during the year, he reminded himself, wondering suddenly, with his new awareness of perspectives other than his own, how on earth she had pulled herself together, wondering *where*, literally, her delicate birdcage of a frame had accommodated the unhappiness that, just a few months ago, had driven her to the point of suicide.

'You're not really going to leave Ashley House, are you, Gran?' he blurted, forgetting he wasn't supposed to know, forgetting anything, indeed, but his new, overwhelming desire to keep the world he knew and loved from pulling apart.

Instead of asking how he had found out or telling him off for being nosy she laughed softly, pushing a thin straggle of her loose, silvery hair off her face. 'That's the last thing you should be worrying about right now, young man.' She took Ed's empty bowl and put it in the dishwasher. 'The fact is, dear, I rather want to leave. I've been a lodger here for a while now. Poppy and I want our own little nest, don't we, darling?' she murmured, putting out her hand, which the dog nuzzled dutifully and then, smelling a trace of Ed's cereal milk, licked. 'Do Mum and Dad know my plans, then?'

Ed nodded meekly.

'Well, thank you for telling me, dear,' she replied, stirring as she poured water into the teapot. 'I shall talk to them about it. You see, I'm still only on the waiting list,' she added brightly, undeterred by Ed's blank expression, 'so nothing is likely to happen for a while yet, not till after the wedding anyway.'

Hearing someone coming downstairs Ed, muttering about having things to do, let himself out of the back door and ran round the side of the house towards the garden.

'It changes nothing,' said Charlie, slapping the letter with the back of his hand, some ten minutes later. 'Good of him to write it, a good effort, but out of the question, of course.'

Serena, who had read the letter first, amid murmurings of surprise and admiration, stared at her husband in disappointment. 'Is it?'

'Of course. He needs more education, not a job. It's up to us to support him – any decent parent would do the same.'

'But we let Clem –'

'Yes, and we shouldn't have done. Clem is *wasting* herself. She's not even working in that wine bar any more, is she? Which rather begs the question, what the hell *is* she doing? Christ . . .' Charlie shook his head.

Serena took a deep breath and tried again, resisting the temptation to be side-tracked by an attempt to defend their daughter. 'But Ed's trying so hard. He must have overheard us yesterday, poor love. It's made him finally grasp what's at stake and he wants to prevent it. Surely, if we *did* let him get a job it would –'

'– mean we can all stay here?' Charlie snapped, using the new armour of steeliness with which he now seemed to approach everything, good or bad. 'I don't think so.'

Serena, who had been clutching a pot of coffee, set it down carefully in the middle of the table, exactly half-way between her plate of toast and her husband's. She felt she was at some half-way point herself, that if she moved too suddenly in either direction, some vital, indefinable balance would be lost for good. 'So, leaving here . . . it isn't just about money, then?'

Charlie made a sort of hissing sound through his teeth. 'Money's part of it, all right, but you know bloody well that it's about many other things, too, so please don't demean yourself by pretending otherwise.' Hearing her gasp at his harshness, he drummed his fingers on the table and stared up at the kitchen ceiling, as if some wisdom or patience might be retrieved from the strings of garlic and dried flowers suspended above them. 'I tell you what, we'll put the whole matter of the house on hold till after the wedding, okay? I'll talk to Peter today – explain that the proposal stands but we're sitting tight until the end of January. Okay?' he repeated, using the tone of one acquiescing to the demands of an unreasonable child.

'What's on hold till January?' inquired Pamela, who had been upstairs to get dressed and do her hair.

'Oh, all sorts of things.' Charlie abandoned his half-eaten toast and reached for his briefcase.

'Are you in a rush, dear?' asked Pamela, feigning innocence when she knew, from the atmosphere – like walking into a wall – that they had been arguing again. No doubt because of the test result, which, with set, grim faces, they had told her about on her return from Crayshott the day before. And now the bomb is exploding, she thought, feeling a fresh swell of pity for them, so neck-deep still in the crisis. 'You've ages yet, haven't you, Charlie dear, unless you're catching an earlier train?'

Charlie looked at his watch. 'Do you know? I think I shall.'

'Well, take your brolly, won't you? The weather's going to break today, they said so on the radio.'

'Did they? Right. Brolly . . . good idea.' He looked round the kitchen, a little desperately, as if lost suddenly as to the best way of leaving it.

'Charlie, darling, Serena, this might not be the best moment but . . .' Pamela patted her bun, as she always did when she was nervous, finding comfort in its silky tightness '. . . I gather from Ed that you know, anyway, about me wanting to move to Crayshott Manor. I just wanted to . . .'

Charlie put his briefcase on the kitchen table and turned to his mother, smiling brilliantly. 'There will be no need for that, Mum, no need at all.'

Pamela wrung her hands, looking anxiously from Serena's soft, concerned expression to her son's tight smile. 'But I want to go, dears, really, I –'

'There is no *question*,' repeated Charlie, almost savagely.

'Charles,' replied Pamela, her voice wavering but imperious, 'you will not tell me what to do.'

Charlie groaned. 'Mum, the fact is, you want to leave Ashley House because, what with one thing and another, it's been a stinking year.' He cast a dark look at the old yellow sofa to which Serena had decamped, curling herself into a tight ball. 'And because Serena and I have not been the custodians any of us had hoped we would be.' He cleared his throat, proud suddenly of what he was about to say. 'Peter and I have all but agreed that next year he will move in here instead. Peter and Helen,' he repeated, prompted by the bafflement on his mother's face to wonder if she had chosen that moment to have one of her absent spells. 'Once Cassie is married, Peter and Helen are going to live here instead. They'll manage it a whole lot better. It will be marvellous for everyone, especially you.'

'Marvellous for me?' echoed Pamela, her expression switching from bemusement to irritation. 'But I've told you, I'm going to Crayshott. I'm on the waiting list –'

'But that's silly. You'll be much happier here with Peter in charge, you know you will. He's so much more like Dad.'

Pamela's normally pale face had blanched to sheet white. She glared at Charlie and then at Serena, who was still curled up in the far corner of the sofa, as if she were attempting to disown the proceedings. 'Do *not* call me silly, Charles Harrison, and do not drag me into whatever plots you're hatching with your brother. I will *not* be happier with him, as you so crudely put it. Nor do I consider it relevant that he bears more than a passing resemblance to your father. You're like him, too, you know, especially when you're being obstinate and arrogant. But your father himself is *irreplaceable*. That I ever allowed that fact to make me desperate – to put you two through so much – is something for which I will never forgive myself.'

'Pamela, really, there's nothing to forgive,' murmured Serena, unfolding her legs and starting to listen intently.

'A stinking year it may have been,' continued Pamela, 'but some years are like that. When you've lived almost eighty of them you get to know it, believe me. The fact remains that I *want* to move to Crayshott Manor. I shall be able to take all my favourite things, including Poppy. I know I shall be very happy there. I *want* to go,' she repeated, 'and will be most displeased if you start ascribing motives for my departure that do not exist. Now, you'd better go or you'll miss your train.'

Following Charlie out to the drive, Serena was almost exultant. 'You see? It's not us – she wanted to go anyway.'

'It doesn't change anything,' Charlie muttered, casting a forlorn glance at the house, as if he were saying farewell to it already.

'Look, take the day off,' Serena pleaded. 'Talk to Ed with me – about his dear letter.'

'I'll see him tonight,' snapped Charlie. 'I'll explain that moving isn't really his fault, that deep down I'd always felt it was wrong to let Peter give me this place.'

Watching him open the car door and slide into the seat, Serena had the strong, sudden sensation of him sinking away from her, like someone in the last stages of drowning after they have given up the fight. It struck her in the same instant that, despite his solidity and wide, warm, elastic face, he was as delicate as she was, as damaged by all that they had been through. Yet the emphasis of concern had always been for her – from him, from everybody.

'Charlie . . .' She reached into the car to touch his shoulder, aware that she was reaching across a far bigger and more difficult divide than the car door. Hadn't he reached for her many times? Wasn't that what strong couples did, grabbing each other, going up and down, like a pair of self-balancing scales? Serena found his shoulder and squeezed it, thinking suddenly of Keith lunging for Pamela in the blinding cold of the lake. Wasn't that what love was? Being prepared to reach for someone in hopeless dark?

'I'm late,' said Charlie, removing her arm and pulling the door shut. A moment later he was swinging out of the drive and down the lane, driving so fast that Serena could hear the clunk of metal as the car pitched and rolled among the sharp, stony edges of the pot-holes. By the time she arrived back at the gate a few drops of rain had landed on her cheeks and bare forearms, and a sharp wind was tugging the now flowerless clematis loose from its moorings round the front door.

'He never took his umbrella,' remarked Pamela, watching her daughter-in-law closely, as she came back into the kitchen.

'No. And now it's raining.'

'He needs you, dear,' said her mother-in-law, softly, 'now more than ever.'

'Yup.' Serena bit her lip, resisting the urge to say that being needed wasn't enough, not if the person in need had decided to give up. She picked up Ed's letter and carefully folded it back into its envelope. 'I must talk to Ed.'

Pamela pointed at the back door. 'He wolfed his breakfast and then –'

But Serena was already outside, feeling, as she called Ed's name, as if she was darting between spinning plates, each one losing its momentum and in danger of toppling to the ground.

She found him, to her intense surprise, in her studio, fiddling with something on one of her shelves. 'Darling . . .'

He spun round as she entered, holding something behind his back.

Serena, all set to talk about the letter, to say how brave it was, how much it meant to them, was momentarily alarmed. 'Ed, what were you doing? What are you hiding?'

Ed blushed and hesitated. Then, slowly and with huge reluctance, he pulled his arm from behind his back.

'A *duster*?'

'I – I was . . . cleaning.' He dropped his gaze to the floor. 'It had all got a bit messy in here and I just thought, well, I guess I thought that if I cleaned it up you might feel more like coming in here and doing . . . what you do.'

'Oh, Ed, oh, darling . . .'

'Have you read it?'

'Your lovely letter? Yes, Dad and I have both read it – thank you, darling, so much – but . . .' He was staring at her so eagerly she had to look away. 'But we both feel your education is more important and –'

'We can't give this place back to Uncle Peter, we simply *can't*,' Ed wailed. 'At least, not because of me. Yesterday, when I heard you and Dad talking, I couldn't believe it. I mean, all that stuff Dad said, he doesn't really mean it, does he?'

'I'm not sure your father knows what he feels about anything at the moment,' Serena murmured, unsurprised to hear confirmation that Ed had eavesdropped on their ugly conversation. Glancing at her worktop, she noticed, with a wrench, that it had been tidied to a state of geometrical order that bore no resemblance to the treatment of any workspace Ed had ever occupied. 'Oh, sweetheart, you've made it so nice in here. Thank you.'

'But from what you've just said it's all pointless, isn't it? I thought my letter would help, make things better . . .'

'Your letter was wonderful –'

'I *meant* it, you know,' he said bitterly. 'Every word. I've applied for two jobs already – one at an estate agent's, offering *fifteen thousand* a year. That should be enough, shouldn't it? If I live here and don't have bills and –'

'Ed, darling, we know you mean well but –' Serena tried to hug him but he fought her off, stumbling against the shelves and knocking over a vase.

'Shit.'

'It doesn't matter. Leave it.'

'You can't have it both ways, you know,' he said viciously, catching the vase before it rolled off the shelf and looking for a moment as if he might hurl it to the floor anyway. 'It's, like, you and Dad, for years you've hated me for being irresponsible and yet now, when I try, you won't let me take any responsibility either. It's fucking not fair.'

'*Hate* you? How can you think such a thing?' Serena took a step away from him, reeling. 'We love you. We just want what's best for you.'

'Well, let *me* deal with it, then.' He glared at her and then, with no warning, burst into tears, trying vainly to conceal it with the aid of the duster.

'You're right,' Serena muttered, after a pause, close to tears herself, exhausted by the traumas of the morning and her growing sense of powerlessness over the abhorrent prospect of her brother-in-law taking over their home. 'We should let you deal with it, but . . . no one has to make any big decision today, or tomorrow, for that matter – even Dad can see that. There's months to go before the baby's due. Anything could happen. We'll work it out *together*. Okay?'

She had slipped her arms round him as she spoke and he didn't resist. Now, in spite of being so much taller, he was clinging to her, crying too hard to speak. Her son in her arms – in spite of the dire circumstances Serena felt a huge gratitude for the simple beauty of the fact. But he was right. He was eighteen, a grown-up, trying to do the right thing, and he deserved their support.

'Everything's changing,' he muttered, pulling free and blowing his nose on the duster. 'Everything's changing, and it's all my fault.'

'It's not your fault,' she said softly, handing him a tissue and tucking the duster into her pocket. 'Things were changing anyway.' She frowned as her thoughts drifted back to Charlie, to all the battles still to be fought, and the realization that most of them were probably related, still, to the chasm left by their little daughter. 'Life always changes,' she added sadly. 'It's one of the few things you can count on.'

Outside the rain was falling more thickly. Serena let out a small cry of dismay, then took Ed's arm. She leant into him for the walk back to the house, fighting the unsettling notion that her love for her son and her husband occupied two worlds, and that she was stretched to breaking-point between them.

In the taxi on the way back from the theatre that night, Helen snuggled against Peter, resting her head on his shoulder, seeking intimacy in the way she had seemed to do lately at every opportunity – almost, Peter couldn't help thinking, as if her tracker-dog instincts had sniffed out his reticence and wanted to expose it.

'So this wretched baby *is* Ed's, but the Ashley House business is all on hold.'

'Yes and yes . . . at least till after the wedding, Charlie said.' Peter's tone was guarded. His brother had called just before curtain-up, sounding angry and bewildered. In the company of friends all evening, there had been no time to sound out Helen on the matter. Since their argument she had gone out of her way not to mention the subject, a sure sign that she was mulling things over and coming to a view.

'So we're to become a great-aunt and -uncle after all. Poor Ed, poor all of them. Do you think,' she continued, after a pause, still, maddeningly, giving no indication of where she thought the new position left them, 'that some people attract bad luck? I mean, like Charlie and Serena . . . After all they've been through and now *this*. It doesn't seem fair. I thank the Lord we're not in their shoes.'

Peter nodded, gritting his teeth. She said things like 'thank the Lord' a lot, these days, not in a normal swearing-adult way but as if she really was making a statement of gratitude to her Maker. It annoyed him intensely.

Helen snuggled closer to him, not seeming to mind his silence or the wetness of his coat, which had received a thorough soaking in their quest for a taxi. 'We must do what we can to help, I suppose, even if that means . . . I'm not saying I desperately want to go and live there, but if it comes to that, if Charlie and Serena really cannot manage financially then I can see it would be our duty to step in and help.' Surprised that the comment, which she had been steeling herself to make for days, should have prompted no response, Helen lifted her head and looked at him. 'Peter? Did you hear what I said?'

'Yes . . . of course,' he replied hastily. 'Of course, and thank you. I knew you'd understand. We're in a difficult position . . . very difficult.' Peter returned his gaze to the rain-streaked window, thinking, as he had been all evening, not of the multifarious dilemmas facing his younger brother or his wife but of Delia, whom he had met briefly that morning. Just for coffee and a walk. Better than sex, he had told her, during the precious moments she had allowed him to hold her hand. The rest of their time together had been rather more fraught. They had to stop, she had insisted, because of Julian and Maisie. His niece had actually been to her house – sat on the leather sofa and drunk her tea. It was all too dangerous, too close. It broke all her rules. One last time, he had begged her. Could they meet for one last time at their place near the Aldwych – so easy to get to from his chambers – or anywhere she liked? He would meet her anywhere, for one last time. She had agreed eventually and his heart had soared. Another meeting meant there was hope. She might not love him quite as he loved her, but she did like him, he was certain, and hated, as he did, the thought of giving it all up. The Aldwych place, the week after next, just . . . Peter pressed each finger in turn against his knees, as he counted . . . nine days. Two hundred and sixteen hours. Not so long to wait, he reasoned, although as he sat with his loyal wife in the taxi, it felt like an eternity.

By the time they got to Barnes Helen had fallen asleep. When he nudged her she woke like a drunk from a stupor, so reluctant to leave her dreams that he had to shake her almost violently. 'Oh . . . Peter,' she muttered, clinging to him, her voice drowsy, 'I dreamt you'd gone . . . that I'd lost you.' She opened her eyes properly and smiled. 'But here you are, all safe and sound.'

'Of course I'm here,' Peter growled, rummaging in his wallet for notes. 'Where else would I be?'

October

It is a bright crisp autumnal day. She goes to sit on the bench in the park before making her way to the station. As she walks things keep cutting across her path – a girl on rollerblades, a kid with a football, a father flying a kite. The streets, too, are busy; a tourist tries to ask her directions, a businessman on his phone bumps into her. She grips the briefcase more tightly, checking her watch and then her phone for messages. There is one from her lover saying: pls call. She looks at it as she walks and then throws the phone in a bin. The station is in sight now, its Victorian arches rising behind the steady morning rush-hour flow of taxis and people and buses. She notices a flock of birds flying in an arrow across the sky, geese of some kind, necks stretched, moving as one towards their winter home.

Charlie woke early with a sore throat. Lying in bed, watching the sun light the room, he fought the temptation to wake Serena, part of him longing for the touch of her cool fingers on his tender glands, the motherly announcement that he was ill and not to move from the bedroom. He felt his glands himself, noting with some satisfaction that the one on the left was almost the size of a golfball.

When the alarm went off he took a couple of aspirins and fell back into a fitful sleep. An hour later, feeling much worse, he forced himself out of bed and stepped under the shower. Planting both hands on the wall, he leant forwards and let the hot water drill into the top of his head, doing his best to ignore the fact that every time he swallowed it felt as if concrete blocks were being forced past his tonsils.

It was probably mad to go to work, Charlie knew, but he had no desire to stay at home. In recent weeks Ashley House had felt almost hostile, perhaps because he was steeling himself to leave it, perhaps because his wife, his son, his mother seemed, in various ways, to be ranged against him. None of them was talking much about anything: it was all, as Charlie had said, *on hold* till they had got January out of the way. Yet the pressure of what they were *not* talking about remained intense to the point of intolerability.

If he did take the day off he'd have to start looking at the growing pile of estate-agent specifications on the hall table, which Pamela ignored and Serena refused to open. He'd have to face Ed, too, suffer the ignominy of the boy's disappointment when he crept downstairs mid-morning and discovered his father hadn't left for London. Ed would make himself scarce, no doubt, Charlie mused grimly, until it was time to set off for his washing-up job at the Rising Sun, which kept him out of the house most evenings, too, now. If they ever attempted a conversation it usually ended in an argument – sport, the weather, any subject, no matter how innocuous, had become a minefield. No, Ed didn't think Arsenal had a chance in the Premiership, no, Ed didn't think the sunshine would last . . . If each trivial disagreement hadn't hurt so much Charlie might almost have found it funny. Yet it wasn't funny, it was punishing. He was being *punished*, Charlie reflected bleakly, and all because the stupid boy wanted the right to be enslaved prematurely in some dead-end job to pay half his wages to the adolescent mother of his child.

'Ha.' Charlie spat out a mouthful of shower water, feeling for the millionth time the injustice of his position. And as for Serena – he spat again, hurting his tender throat – she was on Ed's side and always would be. While his mother was playing some sort of insane charade of her own, pretending still that she *wanted* to leave, when it was perfectly obvious that if she ever went to the Crayshott place she'd last as long as it took Peter and Helen to swing into the drive and unpack their suitcases.

Charlie turned off the taps and used a flannel to wipe a path through the steam in the mirror over the basin. Even he had to admit that he didn't look good: pasty face, red-rimmed eyes, jaw sagging instead of round. Not that anyone else would notice, he decided, spraying a mound of foam into his palm, then starting to swipe his razor across his cheeks.

'You're not well,' declared Serena, the moment he sat down at the kitchen table.

'I'm fine.'

'No, you're not. You look terrible. Have you taken anything?'

Charlie nodded, scowling as he attempted to swallow a mouthful of toast. Having longed for her attention, his instinctive response was to reject it.

'You shouldn't go to work. You're very late anyway. Why not take the day off?'

'I'm perfectly all right.'

'You'll give it to everyone else.'

'I'll wear a bag over my head,' he snapped, seizing his car keys and leaving the table.

Inspired thus by a sort of rage, it wasn't until Charlie had parked the car and was trying, unwisely as it turned out, to run up the steps to the station platform, that he discovered he was truly unwell. He leant against the damp wall of the tunnel that connected the two sides of Barham's small station, breathing heavily, his head throbbing, close for a few moments to throwing up.

'All right, Guv?' inquired the station-master, hurrying past to greet the London train.

'Yes . . . That is, no. Think I might be going down with something.'

'Lot of flu about – I should get back home if I was you. There's chaos in town, anyway, by the sound of things.'

'Is there?' asked Charlie, weakly, dabbing his face, which was pouring with sweat. 'Why?'

'Some sort of explosion – a mate of mine just phoned. It's not even on the news yet.' Charlie watched the man race on up the steps. There seemed nothing for it but to go home. The guy was right. There'd been such sensitivity about terrorism recently that even the most minor incident was bound to cause havoc. He turned and shuffled back to the car park, but then drove left, not right, out of the station with the aim of scrounging some antibiotics out of Dr Lazard.

'It's a lovely day, isn't it?'

Elizabeth looked up from her marking to see the new business-studies teacher, Bill Jackson, offering her a friendly smile.

'Yes.' She glanced out of the staff-room window, which overlooked the playground. Bordered on two sides by farmland, she sometimes thought its Tarmac surface resembled a harsh black footstep on the countryside. That morning, however, thanks to the three giant oaks at the top of the nearest field and the buffeting winds of the weekend, it was a tapestry of leaves, the gold ones shining like sovereigns among the red and brown.

'Someone said you had a son. Is he at the school?'

'No, the college down the road – first-year sixth.'

'That's nice.' Bill flexed his fingers, making the joints click. 'Mine have long since flown the nest. Like their mother.' He made a face.

'I'm sorry,' murmured Elizabeth, picking up her pen. She made a comic face of her own, gesturing at her pile of work.

'Would you . . . that is, after school one day . . . I was wondering if you were free . . . if perhaps you'd care for a drink?' He had taken off his glasses and was chewing one end, clearly needing assistance to get the words out.

'How kind. I . . .' Elizabeth faltered, wondering if indeed she was free, not in the immediate do-I-have-a-spare-evening sense – she had seven of those each week – but in the not-being-committed-elsewhere sense. She wasn't committed, of course. She hadn't spoken to Keith for weeks. The one time recently she had cracked and dialled his number she had got a recorded message. *The person you are calling is not available* . . . Not available, no, but *there*. Alive. On the planet. This fact, which had once felt empowering, like a secret weapon, was beginning to wear Elizabeth down. Yet her memories of their brief time together were still so sweet that she couldn't bring herself to give up on them. 'But I'm afraid I'm not free,' she said at length, offering her would-be suitor a smile of apology.

'Fine. Okay.' The glasses were on again, settled back into the small furrow at the top of his nose. 'If you change your mind . . .' He blinked at her, his brown eyes, large behind his lenses, full of meaning.

Nice eyes, Elizabeth decided. She picked up her pen and tried to work, aware still, in spite of Bill's own pose of concentration and the other members of staff milling round the room, of his attention, beaming across the room with all the intensity of a door-stepping salesman looking to get a foot in a closing door.

At break, standing near the oak trees on playground duty, she broke the rules again and tried Keith's number. I'm in demand, she wanted to say, and what are you going to do about it? But all she got was the same dispiriting message confirming his unavailability. Elizabeth tipped her head back and looked at the sky. It was a beautiful morning but very cold, particularly when the sun lost out in its battle for space between the huge clouds bulging on either side of it. Like giant ocean liners swamping a tiny sea, she decided dreamily, solid and slow. But as she looked, blinking away the tears teased from her eyes by the wind, she saw that these liner-clouds were moving at great speed and also changing shape every second, from ships, to dragons, to mountains, to the profile of an old lady to . . . Elizabeth dropped her gaze, giddy suddenly with the unsettling sense of being a pinprick on the face of the world, small and left behind.

Keith was clearly moving on, and so must she. If Bill asked again she would respond differently. She needed a companion. She was that sort of person – simply no good on her own. And it wasn't fair to rely on Roland: she had done too much of that already. And it was no longer possible anyway, given that her son's social life had recently taken off. In retrospect, it was the news about exhibiting his paintings that had clearly been the turning-point. Ever since, he had been out so much and so late that Elizabeth had felt duty-bound to deliver one of her rare parental lectures, warning that one unplanned baby in the family was quite enough and receiving a squirming scowl for her pains.

Dutiful lectures aside, Elizabeth was thrilled for the most part that her quiet son had found a reason to stop spending quite so many hours locked in his bedroom with his music and his easel. The old selfish sadness at the prospect of losing him was still there, beckoning like a hag with a crooked finger, but she had discovered lately that keeping busy rather than reaching for a wine bottle was the best way to combat it. She didn't drink at all during the week now. She went swimming instead. And she had started an evening class to freshen up her Italian. When the practice tapes bored her she wrote emails to Maria, who replied in comparably broken English, full of pleas for her and Roland to return to Umbria, as guests in her own house this time. *No swimming-pool but plenty eating and horses to ride – you come quickly!*

It took Elizabeth several minutes to absorb that something unusual was happening in the playground. Although there were still ten minutes left of break, the football had stopped. Several children, in defiance of school rules, had got out their mobiles and were huddling in groups.

'Jimmy, Colleen, put those away. You know you're not sup-posed to –'

'But, Miss, haven't you heard?'

'Heard what? Colleen, if you don't put that away I'm going to have to confiscate –'

'There's been a bomb, Miss.'

'A bomb? What sort of bomb?'

'In London. At a station. Loads of people killed, apparently. Jimmy's worried, aren't you, Jimmy? His dad works in London – catches the train every day. He's trying to call his mum, aren't you, Jimmy?'

Soon children were clustered around her, all talking at once. Between trying to find out what they knew and offering reassurance, Elizabeth thought, with a leap of the heart, of her younger brother. On the far side of the playground several members of staff had appeared, the head and Bill Jackson among them. She hurried over to them.

'It's Charing Cross,' said Bill, before she could ask anything. 'The bastards have blown up Charing Cross. Morning rush-hour, bloody carnage. The head's thinking of letting the kids go home.'

'I don't think he should do that. We should carry on, shouldn't we?' Elizabeth glanced back anxiously at Jimmy and then at the scores of other children now talking into their phones and putting their arms round each other. A couple of girls were crying. She felt in her pocket for her own telephone, torn between calling Serena and the more immediate need to do something to assuage the hysteria growing in the playground. Charing Cross was safe, after all, at least as far as Charlie was concerned. He caught the train to Victoria and then . . . Which tube did he take? Oh, God, her own brother, and she didn't even know which tube line he took to work, where his office was. And there was Peter, too, of course. Elizabeth's stomach knotted again. How had she not thought of Peter? He was near Charing Cross, near the law courts, which were by the Aldwych, which was just along from the Strand, which –

'How big was it, the explosion? Do you know?'

Bill shook his head. 'Big enough. Like Madrid, they're saying.' Next to him the head blew a whistle and the children froze, like a film freezing mid-frame.

'Into the hall, everybody, please. I need to talk to you. In an orderly way, please, no running.'

Elizabeth, trying not to run herself, started a text to Roland, then didn't know what to say. She settled in the end for 'Call me, luv Mum', wanting just the simple reassurance of contact even though she knew he was safe and sound a couple of miles down the road. It crossed her mind to call Peter but she didn't have his number on her phone. She'd check with Serena, she decided, the moment everybody was back at their desks.

Peter parked in the furthest, most discreet corner of the car-park and peered gingerly at the hotel entrance. Comfort Lodge, it was called, a nowhere place on a nowhere stretch of road, one of those he had driven past a thousand times with no thought other than what sort of travelling salesmen might be desperate enough to stay there. He looked again at the building. Paint was peeling off the window-frames. On the billboard advertising its name the L of 'Lodge' was hanging at an angle under a spattering of bird excrement.

I'm not desperate, he told himself, knowing even as the thought crossed his mind that it was untrue. He *was* desperate, but only because he was in love. For the first time in his life, precipitously, madly, excitingly, Peter reminded himself, deliberately averting his eyes from the sign, not wanting its seediness to sully the energy – the purity – of the emotions that had impelled him to park under its shadow.

For a brief, dreadful time the previous evening it had looked as if the whole thing was off, a crisis made all the more difficult because it had blown up after he had got home, via a long, frantic text from Delia. She couldn't make lunch, after all. Something had come up. If they met it had to be much earlier, much closer to home. Peter had despaired, then checked his emails on his Blackberry only to discover that, due to the fabulous coincidence of both a client and a solicitor going down with flu, his meeting the following morning had been cancelled. He had a free morning! He could meet her anywhere she wanted. It was all falling back into place, as if it was meant to be.

Exultation had bubbled out of him for the rest of the evening. He had bounced Genevieve on his lap till she squealed, lounged with Chloë in the den, then fussed round Helen during dinner like a waiter at an exclusive restaurant. More wine? A little more salad? Should he wash up or dry? In the bathroom later, while she was safely dozing over her book in bed, he had got out his special little scissors and clipped the hair sprouting from his nostrils and his ears, then thumped his palm against his chest, not caring that he was behaving like some sort of sad, mad Tarzan, feeling only *alive* – vibrantly so, as if his system had been charged with chemicals.

He had left that morning before Helen (a goodbye peck on the cheek, a ruffle of his daughters' heads – it was so *easy!*) playing his Vivaldi tape instead of listening to the news. The opening movement of the *Four Seasons* matched his mood perfectly. The calendar might say it was autumn but it felt and looked to Peter like spring. He had opened the sun-roof and hummed along to the music, feeling the warm kiss of the heat on his bald patch as some sort of a benediction, a sign that whatever deity Helen had taken to conversing with was somehow smiling upon him too, for all his wickedness. Yet as he moved past the dilapidated hotel sign and up the entrance steps, Peter did not feel wicked. How could love be wicked? How could anything that felt so good be bad?

* * *

Jessica watched the events unfolding on television with a can of Fanta and a bag of plain crisps. There were bodies everywhere, bits of bodies too, though the cameras tended not to linger on those, focusing instead on the piles of twisted, smoking wreckage, interviews with not too gruesomely wounded survivors and accounts of the efforts of the rescue teams. It was awful, of course, but also, Jessica couldn't help thinking, very *interesting*. It made her feel as if she had something to do at last, something almost important. When one channel took a break from covering the atrocity she flicked to another, so she received all the statistics as they unfolded and had even seen some of the interviews several times. There had been, as far as the authorities could gather, a total of six bombs, two on an arriving mainline train, one on an underground platform and three at the station, designed, apparently, to go off as the rescue teams arrived. All the devices appeared to have been stuffed into backpacks; a substance called tidadine – a compressed form of dynamite – was thought to have been used, along, of course, with detonators. No organization had yet claimed responsibility but the view seemed to be that a shadowy group linked to Al Qaeda was behind it. Between reports on the carnage, there were statements from the prime minister, the leaders of the opposition parties and the home secretary who, trying to speak as he arrived at the scene, looked as if he might actually puke up his breakfast in front of the cameras.

By late morning, Jessica felt quite the expert.

'Fucking nutters,' said Maureen, arriving back from a morning job and dropping into the chair next to the sofa.

'There was this gross bit with a woman screaming,' said Jessica, prompted by the scale of the proceedings temporarily to overlook the recent state of deadlock between them. 'There was, like, part of her arm missing. It was *gross*. I mean, how much would that hurt, having your arm blown off?'

Maureen gave an exaggerated shudder, offered her daughter a cigarette, then snatched the packet out of her reach. 'Oy, not you. I forgot.'

'I bet you smoked when I was inside you,' said Jessica, viciously.

'I did *not*,' she retorted, inhaling fiercely – gloatingly, it seemed to her daughter, as if she was sucking the last drops of a delicious drink through a straw. 'At least, hardly at all.'

'Oh, sure, like I'm going to believe that. I bet you puffed your head off all the way through. It's probably why I like it so much – I was probably *born* addicted.'

'That's it, blame me, like you always do.'

'Blame *you*? I like that. Oh, fuck, I can't be arsed with this, I really can't.' Jessica snatched up the dog-eared paperback lying on the sofa cushion next to her and opened it. She wouldn't be able to read properly, she knew, not with her mum chugging in the chair next to her and the TV on. But she couldn't quite bring herself to retreat to her bedroom either, not with all that was happening. There might be other bombs, they had said, that hadn't gone off yet. As it was, a hundred and eighty people were already known to have died. A hundred and eighty. Whichever way you looked at it that was a fuck of a lot of bodies.

'What are you reading *now*, bookworm?'

'None of your business.' Jessica flattened the book to hide the cover. It was called *A Passage to India* and she was well over half-way through. The woman at the library had recommended it. Jessica liked the story – a lot easier than the Virginia Woolf stuff – but was also finding it a bit old-fashioned: posh Brits with parasols and servants, worried about showing their legs or catching the sun. It was like reading about dinosaurs.

'Well, you make the most of it, my girl, that's all I can say – lounging about with nothing to do but read, eating me out of house and home. You just wait. When that kid of yours arrives you won't know what's hit you. Hey, have you been to that solicitor Dot told us about yet?'

On the television a man in a yellow plastic coat was carrying a baby. It had blood on its face and lay very still in his arms. The man was crying.

'I've told you, I don't need no solicitor.'

'And I've told you you bloody do, to get down in black and white exactly what those Harrisons are going to pay you so they can't try and weasel out of it again. Not *ever*. And you could do well by it, you know, girl, very well, if you play your cards right.'

'And still the death toll rises,' said a ginger-haired Scottish journalist, pressing nervously at the hard hat perched on his head. 'One hundred and ninety-six, and well over a thousand injured. The scene here is almost beyond description: the smell of blood, of death, of burnt metal and smoke, a body-blow to the infrastructure of our society, exactly the sort of atrocity the government had feared.'

'I don't suppose any of them Harrisons would have been in that part of town, would they?'

Jessica shrugged. 'How should I know?'

'Hey, make us a sarnie, there's a love.'

'Make it yourself.'

'All right, I bloody will. Don't know why I bothered asking.'

Jessica watched from under lowered lids as her mother stomped out into the kitchen, then slipped with her book into her bedroom. All the death and blood had got to her a bit. She felt kind of queasy, like if she saw one more sobbing person or twisted bit of railtrack she might revert to her old trick of throwing up. And her mum made her feel sick too. All that she said and did, it was like living with a CD that had got stuck and kept repeating itself. Maybe she should see that solicitor after all. Maybe, with professional help, Ed's parents could be persuaded to cough up enough money for her to set herself up in her own place, so she'd never have to put up with her mum's needling and whining ever again. Maybe . . . Jessica sighed and opened her book. The truth was she'd be scared to look after the baby without her mum around. She was a cow half the time but at least she'd know how to change a nappy and what to do when the thing bawled its eyes out.

A few moments later Jessica sighed again, but more peacefully this time. Aziz was leading Miss Quested into the Marabar caves, holding her hand, all excited and keen to please. Jessica found herself hoping that the story wasn't too old-fashioned for them to have a snog. Maybe even fall in love. That would be nice, even though Miss Quested was supposed to love someone else. It was obvious she didn't, really. She couldn't: the guy was a jerk.

Jessica riffled through the remaining pages, half tempted to skim-read ahead and find out what happened. As she did so it occurred to her that at least Aziz' and Miss Quested's lives *would* be sorted out; that there existed an answer to their tangle, even if it took a little patience to get to it. Unlike real life, which seemed to get knottier and messier, with mums and terrorists out for themselves, with people like her and that poor screaming woman with half an arm caught in the middle. 'Hey, turn it down, can't you?' she yelled at the door, then settled the book on the bulge of her belly and half closed her eyes to read, so that there was nothing in her line of vision but the words on the page.

Serena had put the finishing touches to the new frames on the photo collages and was varnishing a pot when she heard the crunch of footsteps on the path outside. She held her breath, hoping that whoever it was would leave her in peace. Lately she had sought refuge in her studio more and more often, finding comfort in its cosy quietness and the simple pleasure of making things, of creating order on a small scale, even though she might remain powerless on the bigger stage beyond its creaky wooden door.

A moment later all such hopes of peace were shattered as the door swung open with its customary squeak of resistance, letting in a gust of cold air and her mother-in-law, full of the grisly news from London. 'I only just heard, dear, I thought you'd want to know. It sounds horrific – I put the television on but then couldn't bear to watch. Charlie doesn't go near there, does he?'

'No, but . . . I suppose . . .'

'Peter,' said Pamela, already well advanced along all the obvious lines of concern. 'I know, I've already tried him. There's no reply from his chambers and his mobile isn't switched on. I thought maybe we should ring Helen. What do you think? One doesn't want to be alarmist about these things but . . .'

Serena was already out of her chair, pushing the pot and the frames out of the way, disrupting the tidiness Ed had so carefully created among her pads and pencils. 'I'll do it. And Charlie – I must call him too. If only he hadn't gone to work – he *shouldn't* have gone to work. I told him not to. How many did you say?'

'How many what, dear?'

'How many people dead?'

Pamela hesitated, wringing her hands, the old blankness threatening to fog her mind as it often did when she felt under pressure and in most need of lucidity. 'Nearly two hundred, I think, but it keeps going up.' She pressed her hand to her heart, winded suddenly at the prospect of her family being caught up in the disaster. For all her recent brave show to Charlie, she knew that there was just so much one could take, after all, just so many times one could pick up the pieces. 'I'm sure Peter is fine,' she said firmly, 'but one can't help worrying, can one?'

'No, one can't,' Serena agreed gently, putting her arm round her mother-in-law's frail shoulders in a way that she hoped betrayed little of the anxiety storming her own heart. To think the worst was natural, she reminded herself, only human, especially for those already too well acquainted with misfortune. 'I'll call Helen, Peter, Charlie . . . *everybody*,' she promised, a little wildly, steering Pamela towards the door.

As Charlie negotiated the dips of the lane half an hour later, a bottle of amoxycillin tablets on the seat next to him, he was surprised to see his wife's Mondeo heading at speed towards him. He beeped once, then flashed his lights, expecting her to reverse back into the wider section of road just behind her. The next thing he knew they were bumper to bumper and Serena was leaping out of the car, waving her arms and shouting.

Charlie wound down the window. 'What the hell –' She was flinging words at him, hair sticking to her mouth, eyes popping. In spite of the cold wind she wore only a flimsy pink shirt, which billowed round the waist of her jeans like a life-belt.

'The bomb – in London – I thought you – I thought –'

'I never went to London,' said Charlie, rather obviously. 'I went to the doctor.'

'You never *called*,' she shrieked, thumping the car roof so hard he could hear the smack as her rings hit the metal. 'They said there might be more bombs and you never *called* – I tried and tried your phone. How the *fuck* could you not call me? How *could* you?'

'I'm sorry, I –'

'Don't *ever* do that! Okay? Don't *ever*, ever do that!'

Charlie tried to get out of the car but she had blocked the door with her body and was thrusting her head in through the open window. 'Ignore me, shout at me, move us all to Brighton, let Peter and Helen take over our lives – do anything but *not call* when I need to know where you are. And I'll tell you something else, Charles Harrison,' she hissed, 'you can try all you like to piss me off, but I'm never giving up on you – on us! Do you understand? *Never.*'

It took Charlie a moment to absorb that these last words, in spite of being released like missiles from between her clenched teeth, were not hostile. On the contrary. 'I'll try to bear that in mind,' he growled, thinking how typical it was that she couldn't even say something nice *nicely* – what an indictment it was of the sorry level to which they had sunk. Besides, he was ill. He needed sympathy, not a telling-off. 'Look,' he said wearily, 'I'm sorry I didn't phone. I knew there'd been some sort of explosion, but I've been at the doctor's –'

'Some sort of *explosion*?' She was screeching again. 'Six bombs – Charing Cross – two hundred dead, thousands injured and we can't get hold of Peter. No one can get hold of Peter! Helen's going out of her mind.'

Charlie gaped at her, shocked into silence, uncertain, through the throb of his head and throat, whether he was up to mustering the level of panic she seemed to think the situation warranted. He had a nasty suspicion, too, that part of her was enjoying the drama, a fresh opportunity to make him feel bad. 'Serena, honestly, I had no idea. I see now why you were so worried. Of course I would have phoned – of course – and as for Peter, his chambers are two miles at least from Charing Cross. At worst they'll have had their windows blown out.' Charlie stared out of the windscreen, gripping the steering-wheel as if the car was on the verge of going out of control rather than stationary in the lane. 'Let's get home,' he muttered, as a large lorry appeared in his rear-view mirror, knocking branches off as it lumbered down the lane. 'Can you reverse?'

'Of course I can,' she snapped, turning towards her own car.

'Where were you going anyway?' Charlie called after her, sticking his head out of the window.

Serena stopped and shrugged, looking lost. 'I'm not sure. I – to find you, I think. I . . .' She couldn't articulate the sixth

sense that had made her grab her car keys, the conviction, somewhere deep inside her, that her husband, geographically at least,
was still within reach.

As the two cars turned into the drive Pamela came hurrying
to the gate to greet them. Poppy, incorrectly scenting the chance
of a second morning walk, was yelping at her heels.

'He had gone to the doctor's,' said Serena, flinging an arm
in the direction of Charlie, who had returned to the Volvo to
fetch his pills. 'He didn't know how serious the bombings were
or he would have called.'

'Since you left the phone hasn't stopped,' gasped Pamela,
gripping the gate, as Charlie hobbled up to join them clutching
his briefcase, the pills rattling in his pocket. 'There's news!'

'News?' Forgetting her fury, Serena reached for Charlie's arm.

'Peter is fine . . .'

'Thank God for that.' Serena blew out her cheeks, smiling
with relief.

'I thought so,' muttered Charlie, wishing his mother would
move so that he could get through the gate and crawl, with his
sore throat and misery, into bed.

'But Cassie –'

Charlie and Serena looked at each other, their expressions
freezing. 'Cassie?' prompted Charlie.

'No, no . . . That is . . .' Pamela knew she was making a hash
of everything but there had been so much to take in. Her mind
felt scattered, full of facts that no longer joined up or made
sense. 'No, my dears, Cassie is all right . . . in a manner of
speaking.'

'Mum, for Christ's sake, spit it out. Was she there? Has she
been injured?'

'No, she's called off the wedding and she's on the way down
here. And Stephen has gone missing. And she . . .' Pamela
faltered, trying to recall her youngest daughter's exact words
'. . . she fears the worst.'

Charlie groaned. 'Dear God.'

'Pamela, you're cold,' said Serena, gently. 'We should go inside.'

'Yes, I am rather,' she admitted weakly, tugging her thin cardigan across her chest as she turned to walk down the steps. At the bottom Charlie and Serena caught up with her and tried to take her elbows but Pamela deftly avoided them by bending down to make a fuss of Poppy. She might be unsteady and woolly-headed on occasion but she didn't want their help. She didn't want to be so in the *thick* of everything either – she had done her time on that score. It was their turn now, Charlie, Serena, Peter, all of them. If they wanted her she would be there, until her last breath. When Cassie arrived, she would offer what counsel she could. But at the same time Pamela was aware that the impatience she had felt in Italy was stirring again. It had nothing to do with love. She adored them all – but was growing increasingly fond of the revelation that, at the ripe old age of eighty, it was no longer her duty to prop everyone up, that she had earned the right to remain on the sidelines, the right to a little peace.

'What exactly does Cassie think has happened?' ventured Charlie, once the three of them had assembled in the kitchen. He pressed his fingers to his temples and leant against the Aga, relishing the feel of its sharp warmth through his trousers. Serena bustled between them, fetching teabags and filling the kettle, then handing him a glass of water for his pills.

Pamela lowered herself into one of the kitchen chairs, moving stiffly, gingerly, almost as if she doubted its capacity to hold her safely. 'She just said what I told you . . . and that she couldn't marry Stephen because she didn't love him.'

Charlie groaned. 'That bloody girl! I might have known we weren't going to get to January without something like this – pre-wedding histrionics. Of course she loves him, she's just got the jitters.'

'And Stephen has run off, has he?' probed Serena, handing Pamela a cup of tea.

'I suppose that's it.' Pamela shook her head. 'She'll be here soon – you can ask her yourselves. Goodness, what a morning. I think I might go for a lie-down.'

'It's clearly ridiculous,' said Charlie, after his mother had left. 'They were fine in Umbria, weren't they? More than fine – like a couple of love-birds.' He placed a pill on his tongue, grimacing with pain as he swallowed. 'Pre-wedding nerves. A bride's prerogative.'

'I never had any.' Serena had taken up her customary pose in the corner of the sofa and was staring into her tea. 'Marrying you, I was never more sure of anything in my life.'

Charlie, forcing down the second pill, eyed her suspiciously. 'A few doubts now, though, eh?'

Serena continued to stare at her tea. She had put in too much milk and there was an oily sheen on the surface. Her husband was ill, she reminded herself, ill and blind. He would get better. They would get better. She had to believe it. As she had tried to explain to Cassie in Italy, marriage was like faith sometimes, believing when there seemed nothing to believe in, when there was no reason to carry on. 'Poor Cassie.'

'Poor Stephen.'

'Yes, poor Stephen.'

'So . . .' Charlie picked up his own mug of tea and pushed himself off the Aga. 'Maybe that's it, then.' He was burning up now, he could feel it, as if fire, not blood, was pumping through his veins.

'What is?'

'Cassie's wedding. It's like the last brick in the wall, the one decent thing left, and now that's a mess too. A bad end to a thoroughly bad year. Christ, I'll be glad to see the back of it.'

'Go to bed.' Serena spoke harshly. As so often, these days, anger seemed the only safe emotion, the only way of not giving up. Where was his relief about Peter? Where was his compassion for his sister? Where was *he*? She was on the verge of pointing this out – of shouting at him – when she was struck by the humbling thought that maybe this was exactly how she had behaved after Tina, withdrawing into the selfishness of grief, immune to efforts at kindness from her husband or anyone else. Charlie, she knew, had almost given up on her. And it had been a see-saw ever since, she reflected sadly, one up, the other down, no balance. 'I'll deal with Cassie,' she said, much more softly. 'She tried to talk to me once before, when things between her and Stephen were bad, and I never called her back.'

'Did she?' Half-way out of the door, Charlie hesitated, a glimmer of surprise surfacing through his self-pity. Serena appeared very small on the sofa, her long legs coiled under her, her arms hugging her chest, her silky hair falling across her face. She looked frail but very beautiful, almost as if adversity suited her. Yet she wasn't frail, she was strong, Charlie reminded himself, the kind of woman whom others liked to lean on. Like Cassie, tearing down from London to cry on her shoulder. Climbing the stairs a few moments later, it occurred to him that he had leant on her too, once upon a time, before grief had upset the applecart, making him afraid to lean on anything.

Speeding past flashing grey box cameras on the M3, Peter felt as if he had slipped into someone else's dream, a terrible dream, full of unfamiliar faces and crises that had no business to be there. He had listened to the news, then switched it off, appalled not so much by the still-breaking coverage of the Charing Cross bomb so much as the realization that he had been one touch away from averting the personal disaster into which the atrocity had pitched him. One touch and the radio would have been on, instead of Vivaldi. One touch and he would have known that the Strand was sealed off, that Waterloo Bridge was closed,

that those whose buildings remained out of the fray had had
their morning shattered by the screech of sirens and the smell
of smoke wafting across the city like a cloud of poison.

But he hadn't known. Delia had been in the poky hotel bathroom redoing her hair. He had been lying on the bed, still dazed
by her insistence that she would not meet him again, that they
had made love for the last time. Reaching for his trousers, his
phone had fallen out of his pocket. Not thinking, more for
distraction than anything, he had switched it on, only to find
a stack of messages from Helen. He had been puzzling over
whether to examine them when the phone had pulsed into life.
Helen's mobile number had lit up the screen. She was ringing
him. Peter had stared at the digits, fighting conflicting impulses
of deep habit and deep fear.

When he answered, Helen sounded so joyful that he almost
relaxed.

'Peter . . . thank God.'

'Hello, darling.'

'Where are you?'

'Where am I?' He had managed a laugh. Where indeed was
he? Bloody good question. 'I'm just heading out of the office
. . . for a meeting.'

'So the bomb –'

Her voice caught, and instead of waiting, instead of thinking,
he said, 'What bomb?'

Looking back, Peter wondered if those two words would
have been inflammatory enough. As it was, Delia chose that
moment to emerge from the bathroom and say, in her strong,
lovely voice, 'Is one of my earrings in the bed?'

As the car gobbled up the motorway, Peter contemplated the
ruin and couldn't help wondering still if there was anything he
could have said, even then, to avert the disaster. A passer-by
might have lost an earring. He could have pretended the passer-
by was referring to a flowerbed. Yes, he could have pulled that

off, surely. He should at least have tried. He was good at that sort of thing – being persuasive when he was on shaky ground: it was how he made a living. Instead, he had said, 'Oh, Helen.'

'You're with someone,' she whispered. 'You're nowhere near work. If you were you'd know about the bomb. You're with someone.'

'Helen . . . I can explain . . .' But it was too late. He could hear the defeat – the guilt – in his voice.

'Don't come home,' she said at once, her voice breathy with shock but also hard, very hard. 'Don't come home. I won't let you in. Don't try to call me. I don't want to talk to you. I need to think.'

'Oh dear,' said Delia. She was standing next to the bed, holding up the lost earring. 'Peter, I'm *so* sorry.' Her voice was kind, but she was already – with bruising, businesslike movements – pinning the offending article into her ear-lobe and slipping on her shoes. 'I thought your phone was off.'

'It was. I . . .' Peter looked at the mobile in the palm of his hand. 'I just put it on for a moment. I . . . She called. There's been a bomb of some kind . . . She was worried . . . She – Oh, dear God, what am I going to do?'

'She'll come round. This sort of thing happens all the time.' Delia tied a little grey silk scarf round her neck as she talked. 'Of course, it seems terrible now but . . .'

Peter stared at her, aghast at the insouciance of her tone and the severity of the pain it caused him. 'Does it happen all the time?' he gasped. 'Who to? To *whom* does this happen all the time?' She neither answered nor looked at him, continuing instead, with her slim, deft fingers and pearly-painted nails, to arrange the scarf. Peter watched as if in a trance, recalling how he had untied the very same item of clothing just an hour before, remarking on its prettiness as his fingers trembled at her throat and his heart pounded. 'You never loved me,' he said.

Delia dropped her hands to her sides with a heavy sigh. 'Peter, darling, you know I love you – I shall always love you – but, as I made clear from the start, I was never in the business of busting up our marriages. You *knew* that. Of course I never meant for it to end this way . . . all such a mess now. It's horrible that it has and I wish there was something I could do. But, as I say, I'm sure Helen will forgive you – most wives do, you know. Just give her time. Didn't you say she's gone all churchy recently? I'm sure that will help her, you know, to *forgive*.'

'Stop it,' Peter groaned, feeling more wounded with each word. Her matter-of-factness, her pragmatism, telling him what *Helen* would think – it was too much to bear. 'You're not going to miss me at all, are you?' He seized one of her hands and pressed it to his mouth. 'Delia . . .'

'Don't be silly! Of course I'm going to miss you. But you've got three lovely children to think of and –'

'Don't tell me what I've got,' he shouted, throwing her hand back at her, then trying to seize it again. 'I'm sorry, my sweetheart, I'm sorry, it's just that I know what I've got – or, rather, what I had – but I fell in love with you, didn't I? I fell in love with you.' He dropped his face into his hands and wept.

'Darling, calm down.' Holding her car keys now, her handbag over her shoulder, Delia came to sit next to him on the bed. 'We had agreed to end it anyway, hadn't we? Just tell her that – that it was over.'

She tried to stroke his head but Peter ducked out of reach, pressing his palms to his ears, like a little boy trying not to hear a telling-off.

'Darling, I'm sorry, but I've *got* to go . . . I'm late as it is.' She leant forward and planted a kiss on his head. 'It was lovely, what we had, I wouldn't have missed it for the world. There'll always be a special place for you in my heart, Peter Harrison. Darling, just one more thing . . .' She waited, with her fingers round the door handle, until Peter had lowered his hands from his ears. 'It's just that, well, darling, you won't be silly and try to call me, will you? I mean, no point in making a bad situation worse . . . One collapsed house of cards is quite enough, don't you think?'

Peter had studied her through a mist of tears, trying to equate the audacious, lovable woman who had stolen his heart with this clumsy, cowardly request for his discretion. 'Don't worry, Delia. I won't tell Geoffrey.'

'Thank you, darling. I knew you'd understand.' She blew him a kiss and was gone.

Although she closed the door lightly, it felt to Peter as if it had been slammed in his face. Moving slowly, drugged with shock, he had gathered up his things, settled the bill and walked back down the steps, past the sign with the hanging L, to his car. Once behind the wheel, he tried Helen's landline and mobile numbers, but was almost relieved when she didn't answer. He should beg forgiveness, he knew, plead to be taken back. But Peter didn't feel ready for that, not yet. Delia, for all the clumsy brusqueness of her departure, still owned his heart. He had never, in all his fifty-five years, loved so madly, so absolutely. Giving up on it felt like giving up on part of himself. He needed time to adjust his focus, to steel himself for the inevitable onslaught of interrogation and outrage from Helen, to prepare what defences he could. So Peter had headed south, to the only refuge he could think of. After the M3 he cut east along the M25 taking the slip-road on to the A3. When he stopped for petrol, he managed to muster the wherewithal to phone his chambers and report that he was going down with flu. Afterwards he felt calmer. He had bought a little time. He would try Helen again after he got to Ashley House, start the ball rolling. She couldn't not talk to him indefinitely.

It was only as Peter drove past the Rising Sun and caught sight of his nephew leaning against the wall smoking a cigarette that the panic returned in earnest, borne on a chilling, reluctant recognition of the wider implications of his fall from grace. Once, only a few hours ago, he had pitied his brother's family for what the boy was putting them through. Yet now, in the light of his own behaviour, Ed's crime did not seem so bad. The boy was still only eighteen, an age at which the boundaries of morality were blurred and getting things wrong was allowed. Furthermore, seeing him in his casual pose against the pub wall, so slim and tall and young, his hair standing to attention in its habitual gelled spikes, his jeans torn and belted round his underpants, caused Peter to think properly for the first time about his own children, of Genevieve's heart-aching innocence, of Chloë, such a tangle of adolescent contradictions, of Theo . . . oh, dear God, Theo. Peter felt his mouth go dry. He had let Helen down, of course, but only now, as he headed up the rutted lane leading to Ashley House, did he experience the first real, terrifying rush of shame as a father. Theo, thank God, had gone back to university a week early. And as for the girls, Helen wouldn't tell them, would she? At least, not until they had talked, decided what to do . . . Peter's hands slid on the steering-wheel. He had no control over what Helen did. He had lost all such rights by betraying her.

As he turned the final bend in the lane Peter was almost blinded by the flash of the high bright sun bouncing like a salutation off Ashley House's top-storey windows and sloping silvery slates. At the sight Peter let out a choke of relief. And the place was his now, he reminded himself, leaping on the recollection of Charlie's recent dramatic decision, like a tired swimmer lunging for a life-raft, not caring – not even thinking – of the distressing conditions that had prompted it. Ashley House was his. Helen could kick him out – rip him to shreds – but at least he had this. Let her stay in London, as she had wanted to all along. He would seek solace in the stewardship of the family home, exactly as his dear father had once intended.

* * *

419

Charlie heard the crunch of wheels on gravel as he made his way upstairs and peered in some astonishment through the first-floor landing window. 'I thought you said Cassie was coming.'

'She is.' A few steps behind him, Pamela peered over his shoulder.

'When Helen called, what did she say?'

'Nothing, except that Peter was all right – nowhere near the bomb, she said.'

Serena, appearing along the corridor with an armful of fresh sheets to make up a bed for her sister-in-law, stopped to see what they were looking at. '*Peter?* Oh . . . and, look, Charlie, he's . . . he's . . .'

'He's crying,' Charlie whispered. For a few moments all three were too stunned to speak. Below them Peter, oblivious to an audience, was standing next to his open car door, head bowed, shoulders shaking, almost comically, as if some invisible puppeteer was pulling strings.

'Maybe someone he knew was killed by the bomb?' suggested Serena.

'Whatever it is,' said Pamela, 'he'll want you, Charlie dear.'

But Charlie was already plunging down the stairs, taking them two at a time, sick at heart in a way that far outstripped his illness or his anxiety about the whereabouts of his sister's jilted fiancé. Peter never cried. Even when they were boys, he had never cried. Charlie had been the baby, seeking out Pamela's lap for bruises and scrapes, often earning his brother's contempt. Such images flashed across Charlie's mind with the feverish lucidity of delirium as he tore across the hall and tugged open the front door. For the first time in his life Peter, his rock, needed him, and he would be there – by God, he would be there. At the bottom of the steps up to the drive Charlie hesitated, made timid suddenly by his brother's grief and that Peter didn't even know he was at home. Then the wind caught the front door, slamming it with a violence that set the bell jangling and the dried twines of clematis hissing in protest. Like a runner responding a little too late to a starter gun, Charlie took a deep breath and raced on up to the gate.

'So I won't need my shoes, then?'

'Your shoes?'

'The ones Cassie bought me for the wedding, the horrible fancy leather ones with slippery soles.'

Elizabeth couldn't help laughing. 'Well, that's one way of looking at it, I suppose.' She had picked Roland up from school and taken him straight to their favourite pizza parlour. He had subsequently demolished a heap of garlic bread, while Elizabeth worked her way, as slowly as she could, through a packet of breadsticks.

'Funny, isn't it,' Roland continued, reaching for the last breadstick and breaking it in two, 'how, like, nothing happens for days and days and then loads of stuff happens all at once, like it's suddenly reached bursting-point?'

'Today has certainly been one of those,' Elizabeth murmured, pushing his napkin at him as the waiter delivered their plates of food – a salad for her and an extra large American for her son. She was still absorbing the news from Ashley House. It was like a field hospital, Serena had said, with Charlie, Peter and Cassie huddling in their bedrooms like invalids, and her and Pamela rushing between them with bowls of soup and sympathy. The victims of the bomb who wouldn't make it into the newspapers, Serena had added, sounding so on top of it all that Elizabeth hadn't argued with her insistence that she could manage the situation alone.

'Is that what Dad did?' asked Roland, suddenly, his mouth crammed.

'What?'

'Have another woman on the side. Is that why you left him?'

'No . . . That is, there was someone else, yes, but I left him for a million other reasons. We never really got on that well, not like Peter and Helen . . . I still can't believe it, I really can't.'

'And Aunt Cass, what's going on there, do you think?'

'Oh, Roland, I don't know. Relationships – *all* relationships – are such complicated things. Who's to know what really goes on anywhere behind closed doors? All I can say is that if Cassie was having doubts she was right to call the thing off. It's just too tragic that it should all have blown up – so to speak – on such a day, because now, according to Serena, Cassie has convinced herself that Stephen might have got caught up in the bombs.' Elizabeth stopped, aware that she had lost her son's attention. He had lowered his forkful of pizza and was staring at his plate. 'Darling, what is it? Do you feel ill?'

'No. I – It's just that . . . I mean, it's probably not the time and all that, but this is, like, one of those days when the crap is flying around and I've just got to the point where I hate you not knowing – I can't handle it.'

'Can't handle what? Roland, what are you saying?'

'I'm gay, Mum. I didn't know how to tell you,' he raced on, wanting to explain, but also to delay the moment of her response. 'I knew you'd be, like, really upset and stuff, but that's how it is and there's nothing I can do about it and I thought of not telling you but that's been, like, crap . . . you know, like I'm *lying* the whole time and now, whatever you say, I feel better, I really do, because it's out there and not eating me up inside. And don't ask me if I'm sure or any bollocks like that because it's not like something I've chosen, just how I am,' he finished, dropping his gaze to a piece of wilted pepperoni hanging over the edge of his plate. 'Sorry,' he muttered, picking at it.

'Don't say sorry. There's nothing to be *sorry* for.'

'You mean you don't mind?'

'Of course I *mind*. But only because . . . because . . .' Elizabeth groped for the right words '. . . because it will make your life harder than I want it to be. It will make it harder for you to be happy and all I want, darling, is for you to be happy.'

'But I am,' Roland insisted, his eyes shining. 'I've met . . . There's someone . . .' Hearing his mother's sharp intake of breath, he stopped. 'Well, anyway, now you know, that's the main thing.'

'Now I know,' echoed Elizabeth, unable to keep the shock from her voice, but thinking, too, that somewhere in her heart she had probably always known. 'Hey, telling me was good, really . . . brave.' She reached across her salad and patted his hand.

'It felt like a day for truth,' said Roland, simply, offering her a wan smile, then returning to his pizza.

Recalling the phrase as she lay in bed later that night, Elizabeth marvelled at her son's capacity to see to the heart of things, how he managed to combine the innocent honesty of a child with the maturity that had always been beyond his years. It made her think she had done something right, after all, something truly good. His life would be burdened – defined, even – by his sexuality, but so were all lives. It took courage, that was all, and Roland had that in bucketfuls.

Elizabeth levered herself upright and switched on her bedside light. Her head was too full for sleep. Her son was gay. Her sister had broken off her engagement. Her brother had been unfaithful to his wife. And she was in love with someone she couldn't have. Muttering at the madness of it all, she threw off the bedclothes and tiptoed down to the kitchen. Or maybe it wasn't mad, she mused, unclipping her handbag and pulling out her mobile phone. Maybe it was just *life*. Everybody struggled. It was only the visibility of the struggle that varied.

She pulled on a fleece for warmth, and sat at her small kitchen table to compose a long text to Cassie, saying she hoped she was all right and promising to call round at Ashley House the following evening. She then checked her in-box, even though she knew it contained nothing new. As the events of the week had unfolded, her urge to talk to Keith had grown stronger. Yet chasing him, she knew, wasn't fair. He was under enough pressure trying to find work and be with his children; not to mention the other thing, the one that sat like the final trip-wire to all Elizabeth's attempts to rationalize why they should have to lead separate lives. The little Pakistani girl: Elizabeth imagined her sometimes, glossy black hair, wide brown eyes and skinny limbs, a satchel over her shoulder, maybe, and long socks, white against her skin, a striking but slight creature, no match for the bumper of a speeding car.

As the clock ticked and the silence continued, Elizabeth's gaze drifted to the wine rack. It was empty, apart from a bottle of whisky someone at work had given her for her birthday. She had watched, with mounting satisfaction, the dust gathering on it ever since. Yet whisky would help her sleep, she reasoned now. It had been a tough week, after all. And even on normal days people all over the world used the tonic of a nightcap to get their eyes closed. Why should she be any different? Why should she be 'good' when there was nothing – no one – to be good for? What did it matter? Who would care?

Elizabeth looked hard at the phone, lying so still and quiet, and then at the bottle, wondering which to choose.

'Are you sure they won't mind?'

'Their lovely daughters-whom-they-never-see arriving a day early for their dress fittings with their equally lovely boyfriends, of course they won't mind, will they, Clem?' Maisie grinned at her sister and Jonny, framed in the rear-view mirror, cheek to cheek, like one of the snaps they had posed for in photo booths as kids. 'And I'm skipping freshers' week so I've got a few days more freedom before Bristol, and I want to make the most of you, Julian, don't I? And as for those two, they're, like, *glued.*' She ducked as her sister tried to cuff her.

'And me?' ventured Theo. 'Will they be pleased to see me?'

'*Star* nephew – doh – I think so.' Maisie tapped her temple, then opened the glove compartment, spilling a pile of tapes on to her lap. 'Rod Stewart, anyone?'

'So, how come you get to drive this swanky car, anyway, Julian?' put in Clem, nestling against Jonny.

'It's my mum's. I'm an only child, I get spoilt, it goes with the territory – you lot don't know what you're missing.'

'I still can't believe it,' muttered Theo, so cramped between Jonny and the door handle that he was beginning to wish he hadn't come. He had hitched a ride to London with a friend the night before for what had turned out to be such a damp squib of a party that he had left early and presented himself on Clem's doorstep.

'Can't believe what?' asked Jonny, raising his voice against 'Maggie May' and beating out the rhythm on his thighs.

'That bloody bomb. I *wrote* it and then it happened. Can you believe that?'

'Spooky,' said Maisie, rolling her eyes.

'It's bloody annoying, that's what it is,' persisted Theo. 'Now it will look like I stole the idea – can't you see? It removes all the originality from my work.'

'Don't be an arse. Your work will be *very* original – especially with Clemmy in it, groping your friend. Oh, I can't wait for the première – I just can't.'

'Ben isn't just a friend, he's an actor who, one day, I promise, will appear on a West End stage, and the scene to which I believe you're referring was superbly acted by your sister – when she'd stopped blushing like a beetroot, that is,' Theo teased, deliberately lightening his tone, having learnt the wisdom of keeping his natural arrogance in check.

'I did *not* blush.'

'You did, babe, just a tiny bit,' put in Jonny, poking her in the ribs.

'Supermarket!' shrieked Maisie, pointing ahead. 'We must stop and buy loads of food. Then Mum can't mind us coming, can she?'

'Oh, God, so she *is* going to mind,' groaned Julian, the tyres squeaking as he swerved across the road towards the entrance.

Half an hour later the five, laden with bulging plastic bags, stood gazing disconsolately into the boot, which was small and already crammed with their luggage. 'We'll have to keep this stuff on our laps,' declared Maisie, over her companions' groans. 'It's not far now and Julian's going to drive really fast, aren't you, Jules?'

'Yeah. Anything for you, girl,' murmured Julian, bending down to kiss her lips, his floppy fair hair falling into her eyes.

'Blimey, who's *glued* now?' moaned Clem. 'Cut it out, you two, or we'll never get there.'

'Hear hear,' added Theo. The circulation had returned to his legs but he was feeling more and more like the proverbial gooseberry. So much so that even the thought of seeing the hapless and still resentful Ed was comforting. 'Speaking as a director, you two would only get five out of ten for that effort anyway – not enough *passion.*'

'Fuck off, Theo,' said Maisie, happily, disentangling herself. 'Here, give me some of those bags – I can wedge them round my feet.'

'Maybe we should call,' ventured Julian, once they were on their way again, 'I mean, you've seen *Meet the Parents*, haven't you?'

'Oh, shut up and drive. You'll love them. They'll love you. I want to surprise them – like I did in Italy. That was *so* cool. They were expecting us tomorrow anyway for the dress fittings, remember, so it's not like they're going to *die* of shock.'

If Ed hadn't been parking his bike in the side alley between the Rising Sun and the cottage next door, he might, had he recognized the heads in the car, have been able to flag the party down and offer a warning as to the number and precarious mental states of the adults on whom they were about to descend. As it was, Julian was soon bumping too fast over the pot-holes in the lane, denting the car's undercarriage in several places, then turning into the drive and asking where on earth he was supposed to park among so many vehicles.

'Blimey! Everybody's here,' exclaimed Clem, as they all peered out of their windows. 'Aunt Cassie must have come early too. And that's your dad's car, isn't it, Theo? I didn't know *he* needed a dress fitting.'

Having observed the arrival through the kitchen window, Pamela hurried off in search of Serena, trying first her studio and then the bottom section of the garden, where she found her daughter-in-law wielding shears among the thickets of brambles that – thanks to Sid's increasing absenteeism – were now invading several of the perimeter flowerbeds.

'The girls – really? How lovely,' exclaimed Serena, putting down the shears and pulling off her gardening gloves.

'Yes, dear, but none of them *knows*, do they? And Theo is with them and he doesn't *know* either – and Peter is here, after all, isn't he? And there are two young men with them as well.'

'Peter is out for a walk,' said Serena, paling as the gravity of the situation dawned. 'He took Poppy down to the copse.' She squinted across the field where the cluster of trees were more purple than grey in the sharp autumn light. 'And as for the girls – oh, no.' She slapped her hand to her mouth. 'It's Thursday, isn't it?'

'Yes, dear, why?'

'They were due tomorrow anyway for their fittings – the bridesmaid dresses.' She stuffed the gloves into the pocket of her anorak and began to run, calling over her shoulder, 'I must get to them before they see Cassie – warn them.'

She was within yards of the house when the group appeared

427

round the corner, clutching holdalls and plastic bags, all jostling each other, laughing, exuberant and beautiful. Serena paused to consider what a welcome sight they were: the house, like a morgue for two days, would come alive in a way that it hadn't for months. As she opened her mouth to greet them, Cassie stepped out from the drawing room into the cloisters. In that instant, as if in a clumsily staged drama, Poppy appeared and bounced up to them, followed, rather less enthusiastically, by Peter, who stopped and did not speak.

'Dad.' Theo smiled uncertainly. There was something untoward in the weird state of suspension that had overcome the household.

'I told you,' hissed Julian, nudging Maisie with one of the bags.

'Hi, everyone,' said Maisie, her voice a little shrill. 'We thought we'd surprise you . . . You wanted us tomorrow anyway to try on the dresses, didn't you?' She had addressed Cassie, but looked in some perplexity at her mother. 'And this is Julian, and, well, you know Jonny, don't you, and Theo was at a loose end and – Mum, is everything okay?'

'Of course, darling,' murmured Serena, coming to her senses and hurrying towards her.

'The thing is, girls,' said Cassie, too loudly, 'I'm not getting married any more. And I don't know if Stephen is alive.' She burst into tears and stumbled back into the house.

'And I,' said Peter, his voice thick, 'need to talk to you alone for a moment, Theo – that is, if you wouldn't mind.'

'Of course, Dad,' said Theo, 'I'll just put these bags –'

'I'll take them,' offered Jonny, looping them on to his already laden arms and whispering a quick, 'Good luck, mate,' as Theo moved towards his father.

'Use my studio, if you like, Peter,' Serena called after them. 'Pamela, could you go up to Cassie? I'll be there myself in a minute.' She turned to her daughters. 'Clem, Maisie, darlings, perhaps you could put the kettle on. Oh, and Dad's upstairs, ill. We've had a bit of a week.'

'I think we should go home,' whispered Julian, dropping into a chair, with a groan, once the four of them were in the kitchen.

'Good plan,' agreed Jonny, tugging at a string of garlic, then going to inspect the photographs Serena had recently hung on the walls. 'Jeez, there are a lot of you Harrisons, aren't there?'

'None of us is going anywhere,' said Maisie, firmly. 'We're going to deal with this lot and make tea. In fact, why don't we offer to do supper? Mum would love that, wouldn't she, Clem?'

'Probably,' her sister muttered, on her knees, unloading food into the fridge. 'Poor Aunt Cass – and what's Theo done? That's what I want to know – I've never seen Uncle Peter look quite so storming.'

'Yeah, I thought he was going to shout at *me*,' chuckled Julian, tickling Maisie as she tried to empty the bags, then hurriedly straightening as Serena stepped into the room.

'Hi, everyone.' Serena hugged her daughters.

'Mum, I'm so sorry – we had no idea.'

'It's all right, darlings, of course you didn't. Is that tea ready? I've got rather a lot to tell you . . . You poor boys,' she said, to Jonny and Julian, 'arriving in the midst of such chaos, I'm so sorry. We're not always like this, you know. As a family, we're usually pretty welcoming to our guests. And, believe it or not, I'm delighted to see you all – it's exactly what this madhouse needed.' She glanced out of the kitchen window towards her studio as she spoke, feeling, as she had said to Elizabeth, as if she was manning some makeshift hospital with bombs landing on all sides. 'I'm afraid Theo's in for some rather shocking news,' she began, taking the tea Clem handed her, aware that for the first time in years she was more worried about other branches of the family than her own. Which was rather refreshing.

* * *

429

Cassie sat on the wooden seat under her bedroom window and gazed out towards the downs, as she had so many times before, in so many different states of mind. It was almost as though they were companions whose rolling grey-green slopes had shared every one of her ups and downs.

It was a comfort to be at Ashley House. It always was. How did people manage without families? she wondered. What were their safety-nets? Her mother, Serena, all of them, couldn't have been kinder, yet she could tell they thought she was over-reacting. Cassie wasn't sure what had happened to Stephen. She was simply certain that with all that had happened that year – Pamela, Ed's disappearing act – he would have contacted her if he could. In spite of everything. Her family couldn't under-stand, and she could not explain, the set of Stephen's face when he had walked out of the door. Ever since her frightening moment of revelation, scraping their dinner plates in the kitchen, Cassie had hoped that her feelings might pass, like a sickness, that she would wake one morning and find that she loved him after all, that it was just 'jitters', as Charlie had sweetly suggested. Instead it had got worse, the knowledge that she did not love him coiling inside her, like a tightening spring, until – beyond her control – it had burst out, with dreadful timing, after his birthday dinner. 'I don't love you enough to marry you, Stephen. I'm so sorry. I don't love you enough.' At first he had been kind – almost reassuring – trying to cajole her into a rethink. He loved her, he insisted, more than his own life: he had enough love for the two of them. It had taken him all night to accept that it was hopeless. 'I don't like the way you love me,' Cassie had confessed eventually. 'It's not what I want. It *compresses* me.'

Some deep inner scaffolding in Stephen's face had col-lapsed. 'Okay,' he had said, savagely, 'have it your way, but you should be careful what you wish for. Remember that, Cassie Harrison.' Panic had seized her then, riding in on memories of his reaction to her mother's breakdown. *If I lost you I would kill myself.* She had rushed after him to the front door, asking him what he meant, what he planned to do. 'What do you care?' he had snarled.

So many years together, such closeness, such heartache, such *trying*, and those had been his last words. Of course she cared – she cared so much it was like she was bleeding inside. It might be the end of his dream but it was the end of hers too.

Since then there had been no word. Most alarming of all, Stephen's mobile had eventually been answered by a stranger, claiming to have found it on the wall outside Camden Town tube station, a mere seven stops from Charing Cross, and it was early morning when he had left, a mere half-hour before the first of the stuffed rucksacks had exploded. Cassie wept whenever she thought about it, not just for Stephen but for the awfulness of not knowing – of maybe never knowing what had happened.

Her family's refusal to think along such lines was, she knew, in part an attempt at comfort. The police, too, on hearing of the circumstances, had said maybe it was too soon to put him on their missing list. He would be in touch when he was ready, they all assured her. Like Helen would with him, Peter had grunted, teasing a smile out of her, apparently so on top of things that Cassie had barely believed Serena's account of how they had witnessed him weeping in the drive.

Arriving at Ashley House hot on the heels of her elder brother had been far from ideal. Cassie had walked in, full of her woes, to find Peter standing by the fireplace in the sitting room, delivering a grim-faced confession of his situation in a strong imperious monotone, almost as if he was holding court. They had all hugged her and said how sorry they were, and how they were sure things would work out in time, then allowed Peter's shameful predicament to resume centre-stage. Cassie, hearing the sordid details, had been amazed by her brother's composure, how he could brief them so dispassionately on something so passionate, almost as if he was relaying an account of something that had happened to someone else. He used platitudes too – scores of them – he laced 'time would tell', 'not counting chickens' and 'coming to terms' with absurdly formal expostulations of gratitude that he had Ashley House as a refuge.

Sitting on the windowseat, Cassie was aware that she, in contrast, remained in a state of almost total incoherence. It seemed incredible that the only thing once clouding her life had been the desire to have a child. What did such things matter when a man's life hung in the balance – a troubled, impossible-to-love man, but one for whom she still cared deeply? The tears came again, misting the downs and the wide blue sky to a blur of green and blue. If Stephen had died, how would she live with the guilt? How, for instance, would she ever explain herself to his parents? His parents. Cassie stood up, her head clearing for the first time in forty-eight hours. She should tell them, of course. And not by phone. All that had happened – all that *might* have happened – was simply too serious. Stephen had not wanted her to meet them, had been deliberately dismissive of the significance of their presence at the wedding, but any parents, Cassie reasoned, no matter how imperfect, deserved to know if something had happened to their child.

She breathed deeply as she stared out of the window. The view was clearer now but the sun was losing its force. Shortening days, longer nights . . . Cassie shivered, wondering what lay in store for her, what new map the future might hold.

'Aunt Cassie?'

'Ed, darling, drop the "aunt" – it makes me feel so old,' she cried, managing a smile at the sight of her nephew's face bobbing round the door.

'Right . . . okay . . . cool. Er, we're all doing dinner and just wondered – someone said you don't like walnuts and Maisie wants to do this salad thing and I've been despatched to ask how you feel about it.'

'Oh, Ed, how sweet! You children are all cooking dinner, are you?'

He nodded, so cheerful that Cassie couldn't help thinking what a relief it must be for him not to be the main focus of concern for once. 'I hate walnuts, it's true. But don't mind me, I'll pick them out – don't do anything special, for heaven's sake.' But he had already gone, bounding along the corridor as if the components of a Waldorf salad were his only care in the world.

'The children have been fantastic,' Serena reported, later that night, in the spare room where Charlie had quarantined himself and his now streaming cold. 'You would have been so proud. I've brought you a Lemsip and more tissues.' She sat on the bed and pressed her palm to his forehead.

'What time is it?' he croaked.

'Just gone midnight. Sorry if I woke you.'

'Fat chance. Can't sleep – too bunged up.'

'Poor you.' She pushed a strand of hair off his face and kissed his forehead.

'Mad woman.'

'Mad? Why?'

'You'll catch whatever it is I've got.'

'I don't care. In fact . . .' She was peeling off her jumper.

'What are you doing?'

'I'm going to sleep here with you.'

'Don't be ridiculous.'

'I'm not – ow! My jumper's caught on my necklace.'

'Let me see,' muttered Charlie, scowling as he switched on the light. 'Your hair's in the way.'

'There – is that better?'

'Yes, don't move.' Charlie breathed heavily, moved in a way he could not have described by the white curve of his wife's

433

bare neck, exposed in all its vulnerable perfection as she lifted her hair. 'Got it.' Serena remained sitting on the bed, so still that for a moment he feared she had changed her mind. 'What do you mean, the children were fantastic?' he asked, more to keep her there than because he really wanted to know. He was too ill to eat, but supper had drifted up to him in the form of voices and clatter, intensifying his sense of isolation. Whatever grand bonding he had hoped for with Peter hadn't happened. On seeing Charlie stride towards him across the drive, his brother had put out a hand, not in welcome but to keep him at bay. Once they were all gathered in the drawing room, he had delivered the facts of his downfall with almost chilling buoyancy, giving no visible indication of shame, regret or, indeed, of any emotion. Serena said it was probably shock, but Charlie wasn't sure. Traipsing upstairs afterwards, his head pulsing and his distraught sister in the more capable hands of his wife, Charlie had found himself wondering what sort of man his brother was; whether Peter had worked so hard at out-ward appearances that something vital had been lost along the way, something with which – for all their chaos – he and Serena were at least still battling.

'The children were splendid,' said Serena, kicking off her shoes and stretching out along the end of the bed. 'They just took charge – cooked, served, washed up, everything. There were three courses – Maisie did the starter and Clem made a huge trifle. Jonny and Julian produced the main course – steak with a delicious peppery sauce. Theo and Ed laid the dining-table – candles, napkins, the works – and during dinner *they* were the ones who kept it all going. Theo, especially, was magnificent, not letting any silence get too awkward, making sure everyone was included. Given what the poor boy has had thrown at him today, he was truly remarkable. Goodness knows what was going on in his mind. Peter was a bit subdued and – please don't misunderstand this, Charlie, I know he's having a

434

terrible time, but he has brought it on himself – well, it was almost *nice* to see him in a back seat for once, letting the young take the lead. Which they did so well that –'

'That what?'

'Well, it made me think.' Serena had sat up and was peeling off her socks. 'All this time we've thought we were protecting the children, but in so many ways *they* protect *us*. At least, they did tonight.' When Charlie, who was watching the socks, said nothing, she continued, 'It also occurred to me that, during this terrible, difficult week, everybody has come running to *us*. Has that occurred to you, Charlie?'

'No, I . . .' She was pulling off her shirt now, undoing the zipper on her jeans.

'Don't you see?' she cried, flinging the jeans at the bedroom chair, 'Cassie, Peter . . . They're here because they need our support. And Ed is picking himself up, doing what he can, and the girls, pitching up with their boyfriends, all doing their best to help. It's fantastic. Like a miracle. We thought we were falling apart but we're not. We're the strong ones, we –'

'It's just the house,' Charlie croaked. 'It's a big house . . . There's room –'

'No, it's not just the house, it's us – it's –'

'Serena . . . darling . . . what are you doing?'

Serena, standing next to the bed now in just her bra and pants, went very still. 'Say that again.'

'What are you doing?' Charlie repeated, swallowing to clear the thickness from his voice. 'It wouldn't be wise to sleep here. You'll catch my germs.'

'No, silly . . .' Serena whispered, crouching next to him, and pressing her face so close that Charlie could feel the warmth of her breath on his mouth. 'The other thing you said . . . the *darling*. Say it again.'

'Darling . . .'

'Again.'

'Darling . . . Serena . . . I don't know what to do about anything . . . I . . .' Charlie faltered, defeated by a swelling at the back of his still tender throat that had nothing to do with his tonsils. He tried to speak again but his wife was kissing him, despite the germs, and soon he was kissing her back in a way he hadn't for months, revelling in the wonderful obstinacy of her hope.

Padding along the corridor half an hour later, Theo was stopped in his tracks by the sight of Julian, clad only in boxers, balancing on the balls of his feet a few yards short of Maisie's bedroom. On seeing Theo, he raised his finger to his lips, then pointed at the floor in reference to the inconvenience of creaking floorboards.

Theo felt a momentary pang of envy. What a bloody great idea. Good luck to them. He gave Julian a smile of encouragement and headed, floorboards groaning, for the stairs. He needed a drink. Brandy or Scotch. The effects of the wine, which had helped him through the ordeal of dinner, had almost worn off. Now he needed something to allay his anger. His father . . . his *bloody* father.

Theo went to the drinks cabinet in the dining room and poured himself three inches of Cognac. Spotting a pack of Havanas at the back of a shelf, he unwrapped one and stuck it into his mouth. His poor mother . . . his *poor* mother. Theo rolled the cigar across his lips as he recalled their phone conversation that afternoon, the most difficult of his life. She didn't know what she thought, she said. She couldn't speak to his father until she did. She was sorry, she hoped Theo was okay, that he wouldn't let it get him down.

Get him down? Theo smacked his hand against the drinks cabinet, causing such an orchestra of rattling among the decanters and glasses that Poppy trotted in to investigate. Theo turned his back on her, shamed somehow by her inquisitive face, and took a swig of his drink, then topped up his glass. He didn't feel *got down* so much as *stupid*. His father annoyed him – more and more over the years – but he had always trusted his judgement. Now Theo felt as if he had been leaning against a wall that wasn't there. It made him wonder, too, about all the things he had done in pursuit of paternal approval – like not properly considering film school, like choosing to read politics and philosophy when history was much more of a passion, like . . .

'Theo?'

'Ed . . . I . . .'

'You need a light by the look of it,' declared his cousin. 'Come on, I've got one in the kitchen. Clem and Jonny are there too. We've opened a bottle of wine – though you look pretty sorted on that front. Poppy got into the pantry and ate what was left of the trifle so we're waiting for her to throw it up, aren't we?' He slapped the dog, who nuzzled him.

'Welcome to the party,' announced Jonny, raising his glass as the two young men entered the kitchen. He sidled closer to Clem on the big old yellow sofa while Ed produced a lighter for Theo's cigar. 'We're on ice-cream,' he explained, tapping the plastic tub on Clem's lap and offering Theo a spoon. 'Raspberry ripple. Finished the chocolate fudge, I'm afraid.'

'Nah.' Theo held up his cigar and brandy. 'I'm all right with these, thanks.'

'We were discussing your family,' continued Jonny, brightly, 'and how exciting it is. I've only got a boring geeky sister, a cousin I barely see and a father who's never quite grown out of being a hippie – long hair, flared trousers. I can't take him anywhere.'

'We sort of knew,' ventured Clem meekly, 'about your dad and his . . . friend. Jonny saw them that day we were shooting in the park. I told him not to say anything but now I wish I had.'

437

Theo shrugged. 'Don't worry about it. I probably wouldn't have believed you anyway.'

'Are they going to split up, do you think?'

'God knows. It's up to Mum, I suppose. Dad . . .' Theo paused, momentarily reliving the horror in his aunt's studio that afternoon, the sun shining in squares on the desk, the winded feeling in his stomach, as if a heavy boot had landed under his ribcage. 'Dad said time would sort it out. He said . . .' Theo scowled '. . . he fell in *love*.' There was a silence, while they all absorbed the implications of this. Theo got up from the sofa, ran the tip of his cigar under the tap, then dropped it into the bin, almost regretful that, even in a state of such extremity, he couldn't enjoy it enough to smoke it. He took another swig of brandy by way of consolation, noting with some disappointment that his glass was almost empty.

'Did he say he was sorry?' ventured Ed.

'I don't think so, although I suppose he must be.' Theo walked back to the sofa, draining his glass and filling it with wine on the way. 'He seems to be planning on staying down here for the time being, commuting to work. He said there was some sort of new arrangement about this place, anyway, that your father asked him to move in and take over.' Theo was aware that the alcohol had loosened his tongue to the point at which consonants were slipping out of reach. 'He seemed to think,' he continued carefully, 'that the idea would give me some sort of pleasure.'

Ed glanced at Clem. During the evening he had told both his sisters every sad twist of what had been going on at home. He hadn't planned to. Not long ago he would have avoided telling them, especially Clem, what time it was. But Clem had apologized several times now for her behaviour earlier in the year, and both his sisters had been so open and concerned, so aware of what a vile time he was having, that as they all bustled round with cutlery and crockery, chopping vegetables and stirring saucepans, the confidences couldn't slip out fast enough. They were on his side, he had realized, not just about the bloody baby but all the other stuff he had been trying to deal with as well.

'And does it give you pleasure?' asked Ed, now, watching Theo, remembering what Roland had said about his cousin's resentment and wondering whether to mention it. The wine had left little pink stains on his cousin's lips, he noticed, like smudges of lipstick.

'No,' Theo snapped. 'It fucking doesn't. Maybe once . . . but now it doesn't seem important. You guys . . . you're good here. It's *your* place now. I just want things back as they were,' he finished, slamming his glass down and standing up. 'Good chat . . . thanks.' He took a step and fell against the table. 'In a way, all that's happened is good,' he mumbled, studying their concerned faces through bleary eyes. 'Bloody parents off the fucking pedestal at last. Lets me – lets us – off too, doesn't it? Freedom.' He flung out his hands to emphasize the point only to fall back against the table.

'My hippie dad is happier without my mum,' said Jonny, quietly. 'A good divorce is better than a bad marriage and all that.'

'Yeah . . . whatever.' Theo tried again to stand alone, to be caught this time by Ed.

'I'll take you upstairs, mate, shall I? I'm going anyway.' He put an arm round his cousin's back.

'Most grateful. Thanks,' muttered Theo, too tired and loose-limbed to resist. At the stairs he gripped Ed's arm more tightly, whispering with sudden urgency, 'You run into any more problems and I'm your man, okay? The Jessica thing . . . I should have kept my word. Next time I won't tell a *soul*. Do you read me, Ed?'

He continued to tug hard at Ed's arm, refusing to move until his cousin had agreed to consult him about any more unplanned pregnancies or crises that might require discretion.

* * *

439

The next morning Charlie woke to find he was alone. Disappointed, he hugged one of the pillows Serena had used, wishing he could detect a trace of her scent through his blocked nose.

He had almost fallen asleep again when the door opened and his twin daughters processed into the room, Maisie carrying a tray and Clem the newspaper.

'Mum said she thought you'd be up to a little breakfast.'

'Did she now?'

'She said you'd be feeling better,' announced Maisie, setting down the tray and pulling back the curtains to reveal another sparkling day, 'but that we probably shouldn't kiss you because she doesn't want me getting ill before uni.'

'Or me before my job interview,' put in Clem, 'to be a junior press officer.'

'A press officer!' exclaimed Charlie, hunting for a clean spot on his handkerchief. 'I didn't even know you were looking for a job.'

'There are a lot of things you don't know, Dad,' declared Maisie, stepping away from the window, arms folded.

'Indeed?' Charlie murmured, too pleased at the sight of his boiled egg and toast to mind the archness in his daughter's tone. 'And what would they be?'

'Ed should be allowed to get a job instead of going to uni, if that's what he wants to do.'

'You let me,' Clem pointed out, 'and I didn't even have a baby to worry about.' She had gone to stand next to her sister. Charlie was struck afresh by how different they were for twins, yet how united – defiant too, standing there, feet planted, arms crossed, like two buddies squaring up for a fight. 'Or do boys get different treatment in this family?'

'And,' continued Maisie, before he could respond, 'we all think it's totally unfair that you should decide we leave Ashley House.' She looked at her sister. 'We think it should be a *family*

440

decision. And if it's because Ed's baby is going to cost so much money it's totally unreasonable not to let Ed try to do something about it.'

'And Theo doesn't want to live here anyway,' added Clem. 'We talked to him about it last night. He wants his mum and dad to patch things up and stay in London.'

Charlie, too, had folded his arms in an attempt to seem resilient rather than disarmed. 'I see. Anything else?'

The girls exchanged a glance, then shook their heads. 'No, that's about it. Oh, except Mum asked us to tell you that Aunt Cassie has left to see Stephen's parents in Hull, but not to worry as Aunt Elizabeth has gone with her.'

They were sidling towards the door now, their composure gone. Maisie lunged for the handle first and there was a tangle of elbows before they got themselves out on to the landing. In their haste, they failed to close the door properly, allowing their father, gazing in some bewilderment now at the freckled crown of his egg, to hear their excited whispers as they retreated to the stairs.

'Ladies and gentlemen, I was chuffed to bits . . . er . . .' Keith frowned at himself in the bathroom mirror and tried again. 'I was very honoured . . .' A lot better. 'I was very *honoured* when Stephen asked me to be his best man because he and I go back a long way and, well, that means there are things I know about him that I probably ought to keep to myself.' Pause for laughter. Or maybe they wouldn't laugh. Maybe there would be one of those awkward silences while Stephen looked at him in open horror as to what he might reveal of their ugly childhood alliance, driven as it had often been by a mutual desire to survive rather than pleasure. 'Our lives were pretty tough but we saw each other through – looked out for each other.' No, he couldn't say that. He needed a different tack altogether. One about the Harrisons maybe – yes, that would do. 'It's all thanks to Steve that I got to know –'

Keith was interrupted by a loud rap, followed by his sister's strident voice asking who the hell he was talking to. 'No one.' He unlocked the door and blushed as she scoured her small bathroom for evidence of another occupant. 'I was . . . practising for the best-man speech.'

'But that's months away, you berk.'

'Well, I need months, don't I?' Keith muttered unhappily.

'You'd be better off getting down that job agency.'

'Don't start, Irene, okay? Just don't start. I'm doing what I can. I so nearly got that last one – down to the final three, they said.'

'Yeah, I know.' His sister sighed. 'You'll find something soon, I'm sure, just don't give up, okay? Anyway,' she continued, straightening the bathroom mat with her foot, 'there's someone downstairs to see you. A woman. I showed her into the lounge. I'm off out now so I'll leave you to it,' she added, giving him a sly look before she skipped down the stairs.

'Is this where you sleep?' asked Elizabeth, nodding at the pillow and sleeping-bag folded at one end of the sofa. She had her hair in a high ponytail that tightened her features, and was wearing a long dark overcoat and heavy-soled brown boots that looked ungainly but soft as weathered slippers.

Keith nodded. He had known somehow that it was her, not just because of the funny look on his sister's face but because of the unsteadiness in his legs as he hurried downstairs. 'How are you?'

Elizabeth laughed, throwing back her head so that her hair swung across her shoulder. 'Fucking awful, thank you.'

'Oh dear.'

'And how are you?'

'Awful.'

They grinned at each other.

'I came up by train with Cassie. She's gone to see – Oh

442

dear, there's a lot I need to tell you and I hardly know where to start.'

'Would a cup of tea help? Or something stronger?'

'Shall we settle for strong tea? You'll need it, I warn you.'

'Oh, blimey . . . I might have known. Have I done something wrong?'

'Yes, but so have I, and we're going to put it right.'

Keith let out a low whistle. 'Now you've got me really worried. Hey, you look different.'

Elizabeth scowled. 'You mean thinner?'

'I suppose . . . but not just that. You look well.'

'Maybe I am.' She wondered when on earth he was going to touch her, then issued a warning to herself: maybe things had changed, maybe the female equivalent of Bill Jackson had got her hooks into him.

'Strong tea it is, then,' Keith said, nodding at her to follow him into the kitchen. When she didn't move he crossed the room and took her hand. He studied it as he led her round the sofa and out of the room, as if the course of both their lives might be legible in the faint lines crossing her palm.

After the taxi had gone Cassie walked down the road away from the house. She felt hollow with fear but calm too. Talking to Elizabeth on the train had helped enormously. She was touched by how her elder sister seemed to think she had been neglecting her. 'It's my fault,' Cassie had insisted. 'When you're unhappy you lock it away, especially if everyone is busily assuming you're euphoric.' Elizabeth had nodded eagerly, and went on to explain in more detail than she ever had before what it had been like living with Colin while her marriage slowly disintegrated, how an engagement unhinging had to be exactly the same, but with even more pressure. They had shared a packet of sandwiches and drunk several cups of coffee, letting the conversation spill out at its own rhythm, soothed by the rumble of the train and the changing landscape zipping past the window.

'If Stephen has died,' Elizabeth said, 'in whatever way, it's not your fault. You've done everything you can – telling the police, deciding to see his parents. There is nothing more you *can* do. Your only crime, Cass,' she added, reaching between the Styrofoam cups and stroking her sister's hand, 'was to tell a man you no longer wanted to marry him. That's hard, but not *illegal*. Frankly, Helen has more reason to go storming off than Stephen. You were *honest*, which I'm beginning to recognize is about the only thing in this world that matters.'

It was only as the train was crawling into the station, and Cassie insisted apologetically that she wished to make her difficult visit alone, that Elizabeth revealed she, too, had someone to see.

'Keith?' Cassie exclaimed, so loudly that the elderly gentleman occupying the seat across the aisle peered over his book of crosswords. 'I thought you'd go shopping or something. Keith? Whatever for?'

'We . . . for a time . . . while he was at Ashley House . . .'

'Bloody hell, you kept that quiet.'

Elizabeth smiled. 'Oh, I think one or two people guessed . . . I'm pretty sure Roland did.'

'Well, Stephen didn't – or he would have told me. That is, I think he would.' Cassie frowned, all her surprise shrinking at the recollection of the confusingly layered personality of the man she had once loved, how she had ended up believing she knew almost nothing about him. She thought, too, how odd it was that two such old friends, from such different backgrounds, should have become ensnared in her and her sister's lives without either side knowing about it. 'So you two fell out, too, did you?'

'Oh, no, not at all.' The train had come to a stop and was hissing loudly. Elizabeth was busy buttoning her coat and tightening her ponytail. 'It was all too . . . complicated. But,' she continued, 'since you're determined to manage alone, I'm sure he won't mind giving me a cup of tea.'

Hovering outside the gate that led to a brown front door, Cassie wished very much that her sister was at her side, if only to push her physically in the right direction. Then, when she had plucked up courage to open the gate, the latch was stuck. She was tugging at it with both hands when the front door opened and a heavy-figured woman with short white hair and a large mole on one cheek said that if she was Jehovah's the answer was no.

'I'm not. I – I'm a friend of Stephen's,' Cassie faltered, moving rather faster than she had intended towards the door as the gate finally let her through.

'Are you now?' The woman narrowed her eyes and folded her arms.

'Yes. In fact, I'm Cassie Harrison. His fiancée?' Cassie was unnerved by the elder woman's still hostile gaze. 'The fact is . . . Really, this is very difficult . . .' At which point Stephen's father – unmistakable with the same high forehead and full lips, the identical wide brown eyes, the same long nose – nudged his way on to the doorstep.

'She says she's Stephen's fiancée,' exclaimed the woman, keeping her eyes on Cassie.

'Well, I *was* . . .' Cassie faltered, taking another step towards them, uncomfortably aware of how their square, heavy frames filled the doorway, as if they were determined to prevent her crossing the threshold. They looked older than she had expected, and also curiously similar, as some couples did after decades of shared living.

'Well, he never told us, did he, Den?'

'He never . . .' Cassie left the sentence hanging. She gripped the strap of her handbag, trying to focus on why she had come. It didn't matter that Stephen had never mentioned her, she

445

decided quickly. It was hardly surprising. He had lied about so much. It was one of the many reasons he had become unlovable. 'Look, I'm sorry to barge in on you like this, but I'm afraid I have some very *difficult* news . . .' They exchanged a glance, pressing their lips together and tightening their folded arms. 'The fact is, I'm afraid something might have happened to Stephen.'

'This morning?' they exclaimed, eyes widening in alarm.

'No, not this morning, no . . . I . . .' Cassie looked up at the sky, considering the naïvety with which she had set out on her mission. She had pictured tears, poignancy, anger, even, not an exchange so banal that it felt as if they were communicating in different languages. 'No, earlier this week, when . . .' Cassie stopped, not out of timidity but because their steely expressions had melted into smug amusement.

'Here he comes now,' chuckled Stephen's father, pointing over her shoulder, 'and he looks in one piece to me.'

Cassie turned slowly, aware of the need to keep her balance. Even so, the little garden with its low stone wall and single tired rosebush spun as if she was on a carousel. Stephen was walking down the street towards them, wearing his old jeans with the slit in the knee and the blue jumper she had bought him from a catalogue.

'Oy, Stevie,' the older man shouted, pointing at Cassie as if she was an interesting landmark, 'this girl here says she's your fiancée.'

Stephen stopped, but only briefly. He looked at Cassie and then at his parents, frowning. At the gate he paused again, but only to put his head on one side in such a perfect rendition of bafflement that Cassie almost believed in it. 'Does she now?' he said. 'Well, that's odd, because I've never seen her in my life.' He stared at her, so blankly, so clearly *not* looking, that for a moment Cassie even wondered if this show of amnesia was genuine, whether a strong drug or state of shock had induced it. But then there was a flicker – of pain or malice, she couldn't tell which – and she felt her hand leave her side, involuntarily, the palm ready to slam, with all the impact she could manage, across his cheek. He caught her wrist, so tightly that she gasped. Next to them his parents shuffled but said nothing. 'You are clearly upset, Miss,' said Stephen, 'but I'm afraid we can't help you, can we, Mum and Dad?'

They shook their heads, their faces as closed as masks. 'We tried to tell her, Stevie,' muttered his mother. 'We tried to tell her she had the wrong house.'

'The wrong house,' repeated Stephen, releasing Cassie's wrist and stepping past her to herd his parents inside.

November

Two weeks after the explosions, the debris from the bombs had been cleared, exposing a dramatic tableau of blackened stone that rose in spikes and crags from the cratered ground, like the remains of a giant rotten tooth. The orange tape surrounding it, fluttering like striped bunting in the wintry breeze, seemed too flimsy and too festive for the containment of such ruin, as inappropriate as the steady stream of tourists wandering along its perimeters, pointing and clicking cameras under the watchful eyes of the policemen assigned to guard the site.

Stephen, in London on a mission to retrieve his passport and laptop, could not resist taking a detour to see it for himself. He moved slowly along the line, between two Swedish girls, giggling and posing for snapshots with their phones, and a couple walking in more mute appreciation behind, so absorbed by the scene that one kept stepping on his heels. In spite of such irritations, Stephen found the dark, Gothic remains of charred stone both compelling and oddly comforting. The world had changed, the papers said, and how right they were.

Arriving at the house that morning, checking for the absence of Cassie's car, he had been reminded of the vigilance with which he had watched his fiancée a few months, and a lifetime, before. To guard something one cared for had seemed so natural that Stephen still couldn't quite believe that, in the end, it had offered no protection against losing it. No one could have loved anything more absolutely or wanted to keep it so much. Yet it had not been enough. Cassie did not love him.

She had said so, several times during the long, dreadful night after his birthday meal, each repetition landing like a hammer-blow on a spreading bruise.

Cassie had been right to fear the set of his face as he left the house. Staggering towards the tube station, it had been all Stephen could do to remain upright. When his phone rang, pulsing in his breast pocket like a phoney heart, he had hurled it in the direction of a bin, not caring when it hit the ground and skidded several yards short. In his mind's eye he was already standing on the station platform by the dark mouth of the tunnel, waiting for the tingle of cold air on his scalp that would presage the approach of a train.

He did not think of Pamela's brush with death, or Ed's disappearance, or even of Cassie. The task at hand was too huge, too in need of the self-focus that constitutes despair. It was several minutes before he realized that the platform was unusually full, that those pressing into his space by the tunnel entrance were as concerned as he was that nothing had yet emerged from its dark centre. A woman to his right asked if he knew the time. A man next to him had said it was eight o'clock and a bloody outrage. The whole network, a bloody outrage, he had repeated, looking at Stephen for support. Stephen had returned his gaze to the tunnel, doing his best to shut out the hubbub, willing himself to have the courage to let go when the moment came.

He shuffled nearer the track, until the tips of his shoes were over the edge. *I am dead anyway. I have lost her. I am nothing.* He bent his knees slightly, aware, as he braced himself, of a rush of adrenaline so massive that he could have launched his body into the tunnel itself had he wanted. As he continued to wait, however, poised like a diver on the edge of a board, the adrenaline, with nowhere to go, seemed to turn against him, liquefying the muscles that, instants before, had felt so strong. Where was the train? He needed the fucking train *now*, before it was too late, before the moment – the sticking point – passed.

'We are sorry to inform passengers that an incident at Charing Cross has caused serious delays to the Underground network.'

The announcement burst through Stephen's concentration, bringing with it the groans of the waiting crowd and a renewed sense of his now shivering body, so feeble and debilitated that it felt as if he had annihilated himself anyway.

Outside, the punching glare of the autumn sunlight made him weep. Turning his back on his street – on Cassie, on his life of the last seven years – he walked until his hips ached, stopping every so often to watch the events unfolding in the city over the rim of a beer glass. Only then, as a sense of the world returned, did it occur to Stephen that Cassie might wonder what had happened to him. A body on a track, credit cards handy for ID, would have left no room for doubt, but this new catastrophe, with all the talk of charred remains and dental records, was another matter. There was almost something fitting about it, he had decided, even then. Mayhem inside and out. People used such disasters all the time for their own purposes. When the towers went down, several bankrupts sank conveniently from view. After the Asian tsunami, the papers had been full of grisly stories about paedophiles trawling the chaos for orphans. Atrocities threw up opportunities. Cassie was lost to him and he to her. Why not let her assume he had died? The more he thought about it, the more it seemed to Stephen that to allow such an assumption would be both apt and convenient. The idea of punishing her, too, was irresistible. He was suffering so much, why shouldn't she?

When he had seen her on the doorstep at his parents' house a few days later, so drawn and pale, so uncertain, his conviction had faltered. Stephen had slowed his pace, needing time to think. He had never imagined she would look for him, least of all in a quarter he had so openly despised and from which he had spent two decades trying to escape. He could hardly believe he had come there himself, except that, given his desire to disappear, there had simply been nowhere else to go.

But the panic lasted only a moment. He had resumed his casual pace, swinging his arms, tempted even to whistle. It didn't matter that Cassie was there or what she had said. His parents knew nothing, and such ignorance, Stephen had seen suddenly, offered protection. In responding to their inquiries with the announcement that he had never seen Cassie before, he had felt almost exultant. The statement felt so simple, so *true*. The woman with whom he had fallen so passionately in love *had* gone, eradicated by the loss of her capacity to reciprocate his feelings.

His parents had asked no questions. He had known they wouldn't. When he had arrived without so much as a toothbrush earlier in the week they hadn't asked anything either, except how long he would be staying and whether he wanted beans or peas with his tea. They seemed to know that they had long since lost the right to ask how he felt about anything; poor recompense, perhaps, for the infliction of physical injury that had passed for parenting, yet it suited Stephen now. If anything, they were scared of him, these days, of the simmering anger in his moods, and the powerlessness inherent in their reluctance to know whence it came or where it might lead.

Easing open the front door of the Camden house that morning, seeing the coatstand and the small, gilt-framed mirror, the still gleaming paintwork, Stephen had been half afraid of what he might do. He was, after all, his father's son: violence was in the vocabulary of his upbringing. It was tempting to give in to it. Yet to trash the place would somehow have been too obvious. To maintain the pretence of non-existence was far better, far more chilling too, if hurting Cassie remained his aim. So he had gone upstairs, trailing his fingers along the expensive silky wallpaper, climbing slowly because of the weight of his rucksack tugging on his shoulders. In his study, he had gathered up his things, pausing only to bid a silent farewell to the little tree – as bare as a birdcage – through the window overlooking the garden.

Now, sick of the bombsite, Stephen elbowed his way out of the queue and jumped on to a bus. Forty minutes later he was settled in a corner seat on the Gatwick Express, his cap pulled over his face both to deter would-be conversationalists and in the hope that he might fall asleep. Instead, the past rushed at him from the dark: deserting Hull, his parents, Keith, he had done it all before. Starting over, finding a new context in which to exist – he knew the ropes. Only this time, Stephen consoled himself, he had money – enough not to care what Cassie chose to do with the house, which was in her name anyway – and a career. Jack Connolly, he had decided, would be seconded to a case in South or Central America, possibly even Cuba. Stephen could already picture his big-bellied hero in bright-coloured shirts and a Panama, switching his penchant for whisky and cigarettes to rum and cigars. And there would be women too, of course, full-figured, dark-eyed beauties, purring round his hero like cats, full of breathy hints and secrets.

'Is this seat free?'

Stephen pushed up the rim of his cap and nodded, glad, though he had tried to prevent it, of the intrusion.

The woman gestured at the rucksack as she sat down opposite him. 'Going anywhere nice?'

Stephen noted that his new companion had an ugly beak of a nose but a good figure, displayed to striking effect in a tightly fitting pinstripe jacket and a skirt that made no secret of her long legs. Good ankles, too. Which was important, Stephen decided, taking off his hat and pressing it between his hands. 'South America . . . or possibly Cuba. I'm a writer, you see, looking for inspiration.'

'How wonderful.' She dropped her briefcase on to the floor with a sigh. 'I mean, what a great job, just to be able to go like that while the rest of us are stuck on our treadmills.'

'I know. I'm *very* lucky.' Stephen glanced out of the window, then back at the woman, preferring the beaky nose to the muted browns and greys of the countryside, stripped and ready for winter.

Not many miles further south Ed was staring disconsolately at a similar landscape. In the seat next to him his father was driving in the most annoyingly snail-like fashion, offering a commentary on every touch of the gear-stick and passing road sign. They were in his mother's Mondeo on their way to see a lawyer in Chichester, an appointment Charlie had set up, then suggested they use the journey as a driving lesson. It was kind of him, too, of course – Ed hadn't needed his mother's beady look over the breakfast table to work that one out: his dad had taken the day off specially and spent a good part of the morning testing him on the manual, delighting in offering the most minor corrections to Ed's answers.

'There's the blind spot, of course – have you learnt about that yet?'

'Yes, I –'

'Just over your right shoulder – bloody dangerous. You simply *have* to be aware of it whenever you're pulling out. The mirrors alone are not enough. And also – Ed, are you listening? When you do your test, you must exaggerate every single movement – ham it up almost. Those buggers need to *see* that you're doing all you're supposed to be doing – a flick of the eyes isn't enough. I remember in my test . . .'

Ed let his gaze drift back to the window. His father, he knew, was enjoying the occupation of an arena in which he could still exercise parental authority. Protected by the dos and don'ts of the Highway Code, he was puffing out his fatherly feathers with

453

the sort of aplomb Ed hadn't seen for months. It was sad, but also kind of endearing. And it certainly beat the hell out of the still impossible thorny business of trying to discuss the future. Maisie and Clem's brave intervention – planned and plotted by the three of them – had so far produced no shift in his father's reasoning on any front. What his mother thought about it all remained a mystery. Since the run of family crises after the bombings, she had closed ranks with Charlie in a way that Ed suspected was good, but which left him longing for another chance to press his ear to a half-open door and glean some clue as to what was going on behind the scenes.

Reporting by phone to his sisters, busy once more with the unfurling paths of their own lives (Maisie managing to meet the needs of both Julian and her history course, while Clem was through to a final interview for her press-officer job), Ed couldn't help but be gloomy. No change on the house front was bad, but Charlie taking Ed to see a lawyer was good, they had insisted, using such similar, determined exclamations of hope that Ed was reminded of how alike they were, like two halves of a sandwich, with him in the middle – squashed to death half the time, but glad of their protection. When they had left Ashley House Ed had felt desolate. They were texting him now, though, more than they ever had in the past – mostly in-jokes and nonsense, but each one washed over Ed with the reassuring warmth of conversation.

'We should have done this before.' Charlie had pulled into a lay-by and tugged up the handbrake.

'What? Go driving together?'

'No – well, that too, but the lawyer. I have to confess that I'd been relying on your uncle there.'

A silence followed while father and son contemplated Peter, commuting regularly now to London, filling pockets of the house with his belongings and their once quiet mealtimes with the force of his conversation. Much to everyone's relief, Cassie had gone straight from Hull to Camden Town; but with the increasing likelihood of their own departure from Ashley House, and Pamela sorting through boxes and cupboards in preparation for her move to Crayshott Manor, every aspect of home life was dominated by the disturbing shadows of upheaval.

While drawing comfort from the support of his sisters and knowing that adult lives were in a state of turmoil that matched his own, Ed still ached with regret for the part he had played in the changes. The idea of leaving Ashley House remained abhorrent, especially since the new owner was to be his uncle. The guy had fucked up big-time. It didn't seem right to Ed that he should come out of it all with *their* house. Equally abhorrent was the notion of being forced to continue his education so that his parents could martyr themselves by paying Jessica to look after his child. But, above all, as January loomed, it was Jessica's due date that preoccupied Ed. The fact of fatherhood remained terrifying, no matter at how great a distance he assumed the role. It seemed incredible now that he could ever have imagined nine months as a long time for the evolution of a baby. All year the dreaded deadline had hurtled towards him, as if propelled by its own vicious momentum. Waking to the reality of it now – a little closer each morning – Ed felt increasingly as if he were staring down the barrel of a gun.

'But Peter has worries enough of his own,' muttered Charlie, switching off the engine and handing over the keys.

'You could have left them in the ignition,' Ed pointed out.

'So I could . . .' Charlie was distracted not by his son's logic but the recollection of the firm slap Peter had given the pile of estate agents' correspondence the night before. When, his brother wanted to know, would the house-hunting begin in earnest? There was no wedding to wait for now, only Ed's child and the start of the added financial difficulties that that would entail. Charlie had gripped the linings of his pockets, torn between outrage and sympathy. Peter, he knew, had just concluded yet another difficult conversation with the still intractable Helen and was seeking consolation. Though it was little discussed, the entire family knew that Charlie intended to stand by his decision about Ashley House. True, he and Serena were getting on a lot better, but he still feared it might only be a temporary reconciliation, wrought by the rediscovery of their sex life and having to deal with his siblings' plight. Meanwhile, Ed's baby continued to hang between them, a drain on the future stability of both their bank balance and their marriage. For, deep in his heart, Charlie still nurtured distrust of Serena's attitude to the predicament: from the start she had wanted the baby to be born. She might have worked hard to dress up her reasons as to why, but Charlie could not shake off the suspicion that, beneath it all, his wife was guided by her grief, all the more treacherous for her refusal to admit to it.

And yet . . . and yet . . . Facing his brother in the hall, Charlie's sense of outrage had grown. Although the decision made financial sense, although he still doubted his and Serena's solidity, it was still a huge thing to have offered Ashley House back to his brother – too huge, Charlie felt, for Peter to bully him about it. Nor, now he thought about it, had his brother shown due concern for the circumstances that had prompted the offer. Even with his marriage on the rocks he hadn't asked about Charlie's. The sadness of their sister's situation still didn't seem to have touched him either, let alone the difficult prospect facing his nephew. Tussling with such thoughts during their conversation in the hall, uncertain as always whether to be appalled or admiring, Charlie had found himself latching on to his and Ed's meeting with the lawyer as the main pretext for delay. They needed a clearer idea of the financial position, he explained, patting the house specifications and then they would be able to proceed.

Ed had taken the car keys and was swinging them round his

finger. 'I know a good back route to Chichester, Dad. Shall I show you?'

'If you don't mind, I'd prefer you to keep to the main road,' Charlie muttered, getting out of the car, then succumbing to one of the violent fits of coughing to which he had become prone since his illness.

'I'm not a complete idiot, you know.' Ed strode round to the driver's side, then hung back a little awkwardly until the bout had passed.

'That's reassuring to hear.' Charlie hit his chest only to cough again. 'Go on, then,' he rasped weakly, once they were both back in the car. 'Show me this short-cut, if you're so keen.'

'Great.' Ed grinned and revved the engine.

'Gently now, we're not at Silverstone.' Charlie closed his eyes and gripped the seat then opened them in some surprise a moment later as Ed smoothly manoeuvred the Mondeo back on to the main road, then cut down a narrow, pretty lane of arching trees and high banks.

'It's a question of playing chicken if another car comes, but that's fun, too, isn't it?' Ed, his confidence and spirits rising by the minute – he loved driving and knew he was good at it – grinned cheekily at his father. 'Good route, eh, Dad?'

Charlie smiled encouragingly, his heart full of an extraordinary unexpected joy. He was dreading the meeting with the lawyer – as, no doubt, Ed was too. The future, in whichever direction he looked, was fraught. But for now here he was, chest aching, sinuses blocked, enjoying the simple, novel, unlooked-for pleasure of being driven down a beautiful country lane by his son; impulsive, flawed, irrepressible Ed, in charge and doing well. It was a small reprise, perhaps, but in Charlie's tender state it was like a curtain lifting in the gloom.

Jessica could feel the wind driving against the back of her coat, bowling her along, hurrying her, like the hand of an impatient

457

adult. Her coat didn't do up any more. Her bump stuck out between the panels, like it was bent on being noticed and shaming her. The coat had been her bid to look smart for the lawyer. Underneath she wore the same thing she had all week – a blue corduroy tent of a dress she had bought in the Mothercare sale and extra large tights, which still barely stretched up to the bobble of her tummy button, so ugly that she had cried out at the sight of it, fighting the new thought that the baby was pushing at her innards, trying, literally, to turn her inside out. The skin round her belly-button was ugly too now, thanks to a network of itchy pink lines that had sprung up overnight, surfacing like some ancient map from the buried depths of her womb.

'Stretch marks,' Maureen had declared, catching her daughter studying the damage in her bedroom mirror that morning. She had pointed gleefully at Jessica's stomach with her fag, like a teacher jabbing a piece of chalk at a blackboard. 'There's creams for that now.'

'Whatever.' Jessica had hitched up her voluminous tights and yanked down her dress. Her main aim, these days, was concealment. She was glad it was winter when only total slags showed off their bodies. Thinking back to the times when she had paraded her own curves made her feel not just sad but *jealous*, of the girl she had been, now lost for good. On bad days it felt like she'd mislaid her best friend.

It was also a new and horrible sensation to feel less attractive than her mother – a reversal ensured not just by her pregnancy but by Maureen having spent the last few weeks starving herself to a size twelve. She'd been to Jerry's too, to have her usual peppery tangle cut and coloured into a state that, even Jessica had to admit, made her look nearer thirty than forty. She was also dressing better – pointy heels and tight skirts, even when she was going to work, taking her trainers and apron with her in a plastic bag. All of which meant only one thing. Jessica, having seen it all before, couldn't bring herself to ask. She'd hear soon enough, when the guy wanted to move in and she'd be banished to her bedroom every night so they could touch each other up on the sofa while they watched telly. And with the baby too – Christ, she'd go mad.

Jessica stepped out of the wind into the newsagent's. Staring at the array of brightly coloured sweets, she was momentarily tempted to slip something into her pocket, like she had when she was small, dodging behind her mum's wide bum for protection. But now there was no one to protect her, only her bump, which made it hard to reach. And she shouldn't buy anything anyway, she reminded herself, not after what the lawyer had said. Fucking man with his horrible hairy chest poking through his shirt buttons and his gold necklace – no wonder Dot had recommended him: he was just her sort. What Dot and her mum hadn't known, because they were stupid and only ever thought what they *wanted* to think, was that the man had had nothing to tell her but bad news. So bad that Jessica bought a pack of Camel Lights as well as a bar of fruit-and-nut. She lit one as she left the shop, even though it was a struggle to smoke with the wind blowing ash in her eyes and her fingers stiff with cold. She stubbed it out before she got to the café but her mum, seated in the window with her own fag, saw it anyway.

'You're a bloody idiot, you are.'

'Yeah, and you're Einstein.' Jessica dropped into the empty chair, not bothering to take off her coat.

'Dot's coming in a minute.'

'Hooray.'

'Do you want anything?'

Jessica shook her head and then, more to piss her mother off than anything, lit another Camel.

'Well?' prompted Maureen eagerly, pushing her new ash-blonde fringe out of her eyes. 'How did it go?'

For a moment Jessica toyed with the idea of lying, not to protect Maureen but to hurt her. When the truth had become apparent – that Ed Harrison owed her nothing beyond what he himself could afford, that the wealth of his family was irrelevant – it would be such a fantastic shock, just like the one Jessica had suffered, sitting opposite the hairy chest, eyes stinging, lips all quivery, like they'd taken on a life of their own. It had to be wrong, she had stammered, it had to be. The kid was half Ed Harrison's: surely it was owed all the privileges of its father, surely . . . The lawyer had shaken his head, half smiling, like he was pleased to be cleverer than her. Under the Children Act of 1989, he said, she could apply for maintenance, not capital, and it would be the father's resources that were taken into account, not his family's. If the father had nothing, she got nothing. Later on, maybe, when he . . . But Jessica, with the baby performing cartwheels against her ribcage, like it was celebrating her distress, could not think of 'later on'. There were always benefits, of course, the lawyer had added, like he was trying too late to be kind – no one, these days, was left without help.

When Jessica had finished explaining Maureen slammed her cup down. 'You'd better be bleeding joking.'

Jessica shook her head, biting her lip till she had blood to swallow against the lump rising in her throat. 'Poor you, Mum . . . all your hopes down the drain. What were they, anyway? A better flat, a new bathroom, a bigger telly?'

'You can cut that out for a start,' snapped Maureen, who hadn't known exactly what she had hoped to gain beyond the vague access to a better life – a little of the ease with which people like the Harrisons swept through the world with their big houses, cars and holidays. 'You're a bloody idiot, that's all I know. You got yourself into this. You should have taken that two grand and got rid of it. We tried to tell you, didn't we? But you wouldn't listen.'

'Ed's mum didn't want me to get rid of it,' muttered Jessica, remembering suddenly the kindness in Serena's tone that day when the Harrisons had squashed into their poky sitting room, how it had shone like a ray of light in the dark.

Maureen snorted. 'Yeah . . . Fat lot of good that does you now. I can tell you, girl, the benefits are crap – I know cos that's what I had to manage on, bringing *you* up.'

She was prevented from continuing her usual sad trawl down Memory Lane by the arrival of Dot, who flounced into the café with shopping-bags and her phone to her ear, followed by her daughter, Jade, juggling similar items. With their long, streaked hair, skin-tight jeans and leather jackets, the pair were like sisters, except that Jade had a flat stomach and smooth skin, while Dot's belly bulged over the waistband of her jeans and her skin was saggy, like a piece of leather that had been stretched and let go. Jessica, who had never liked them, ignored her mother's protests and gathered up her things. 'You don't need me here, Mum – in fact, you've never needed me,' she quipped, enjoying the put-down until she got into the street when it occurred to her that with Ed not only distant but *safe*, apparently, from the obligation on which she had been pinning her hopes, it wasn't Maureen's needs that were at issue so much as her own.

Scared, suddenly, at what it meant, Jessica started to run – or *lumber* – her bag thumping against her stomach. She'd have to get a job. Jerry, no doubt, would take her on, once she got her figure back. But how would she work *and* look after the baby? Somehow she couldn't see a pram parked in the salon while she lathered hair and swept up clippings. She'd have to be nice to her mum, Jessica reflected miserably, sweet-talk her into helping out. And as for the pram and all the other gear – nappies, clothes and Christ knows what – she'd have to persuade her to help with that too. Every time Jessica went to Mothercare, her wish-list grew. Sometimes she had even imagined shopping for it all with Ed, like other couples she saw, all cosy and arm in arm, filling baskets to overflowing, then pulling out their credit cards like it was no big deal.

Cantering clumsily down Wandsworth High Street, Jessica felt as if she was running away from her foolish dreams towards a reality that would be unremittingly hard. She didn't stop until she had reached the railings separating their flats from the block next door, by which time a pain had started in her belly, low down and deep, as if a meat hook had snagged her innards. As she gripped the railings the pain changed, spreading into a wider, pulling sensation, as if some extra gravitational force had latched on to her lower belly and was trying to suck it towards the ground. Dizzy, panting hard, Jessica half fell against the cold metal bars. Inside her there were no cartwheels now, no sliding sensation of small bony limbs, just the throb of pain. She clenched the rails harder still, opening her legs and bending her knees, willing the little bastard to do its worst – to tear her open and die on the pavement among its own entrails and the blobs of dirty chewing-gum. No one would give a fuck. And she might as well die too, Jessica decided, from loss of blood or infection or some such thing. Everybody would feel bad and say nice things, like they always did after someone had died – like the Harrisons all had at the funeral of that horse-faced great-aunt . . . all except Ed, she remembered, closing her eyes as the pain in her stomach eased, and the fusty smell of the guests' coats came back to her, mingled with the sharp scent of Ed's aftershave and the excited pulse of her heart.

Peter parked a few yards from his house and watched the minute hand of the dashboard clock edging towards the time at which Helen had asked him to arrive. She liked punctuality, as did he. Turning up early or late, he knew, would get things off to a bad start. Anyway, he needed time to compose his thoughts. In court that day he had performed brilliantly, cross-examining a witness who had had no idea, until the last minute, that he was being outwitted. It had been like watching a small fish swim into the confines of a huge, tightening net, with him pulling the strings. Recalling the scene, the admiring looks of his colleagues, Peter wished he could summon the same focus for his energies now, the same unshakeable conviction as to the best line to take.

He had seen his daughters just once since the appalling, sordid climax of his affair – for a Saturday afternoon. He had taken them for tea at the Ritz, dimly hoping to impress Helen as much as the girls with the lavishness of the treat. Helen herself, having warned that she wouldn't put so much as a fingertip round the door, or let him across the threshold, had stuck to her guns. His daughters had shuffled on to the doorstep like parcels awaiting collection, Chloë displaying a scowl that had stayed rigidly in place all afternoon, while Genevieve had leapt at him like a puppy wanting to play. Even with the tea, it had been hard. Hard and horrible.

But now Helen had agreed to talk – properly, at last. She had phoned back late the previous night, when the rest of the household had gone to bed, and Peter had retreated for some quiet contemplation into the Ashley House study. She had spoken in her new curt voice, the one that had cut off all his attempts at explanation, the one that, beneath all the sorrow, indicated a new sense of power. After work, seven o'clock, Genevieve would be asleep, Chloë at a friend's – would that be convenient? 'Yes, most convenient,' Peter had muttered, pressing one finger to a pulse in his temple, glad that he was seated in the quiet library-hush of his favourite room, with its timeless smell of leather and polished wood, its dark green carpet and velvet curtains, its oak-panelled walls lined with books. The presence of his father was still vivid there, too, thanks not just to the pipestand and the photo of him and Pamela on honeymoon in Biarritz, but something in the atmosphere, an invisible imprint left by the hours John Harrison had spent sitting in the little Jacobean desk chair, feasting on the view through the arched hollows of the cloisters towards the lawns.

After the call Peter had sat in the same chair with a tumbler of whisky, drawing back the curtains so that he could see the shadowy contours of the garden, brightened only by a flash of Samson's yellow eyes and the few brave white roses still clinging to the pergola, like dimming party lights. If anything, Peter's love of these surroundings had grown fiercer during his exile from London. The comfort of Ashley House's easy, grand beauty – its familiarity – soothed his nerves in an immediate sense and as consolation for the very real prospect that his exile would become permanent. He wanted back his marriage – his family – of course. He missed them all terribly. But the fact remained that, in spite of their horrible parting, he missed Delia too. Alone in his big bed, he thought of her all the time, the smell of her skin, the passion she had released, like a genie from a bottle. Each day a tiny ridiculous part of him hoped still that she would call.

None of which had made either for a good night's sleep, or much degree of clarity as Peter – at six fifty-nine exactly – approached his front door. He was wondering whether he could muster the humility necessary to ring the bell, rather than using his keys, when it swung open.

'Thank you for coming.'

'No need for thanks,' he muttered, aware of how she stood back as he stepped inside, precluding physical contact. The way she had dressed looked deliberate too – a black trouser suit that he last remembered her wearing for Alicia's funeral – no makeup and her hair clipped back off her face, revealing the dry thickets of grey that sprouted along her hair-line.

'How are the girls?'

'Great.'

464

'And Theo? Have you heard from him?'

Helen nodded, the impassive mask slipping for a moment. 'He phones every day. He worries about me . . .' She shook her head, smiling absently. 'Funny, to be worried about by one's son. Such a role reversal. I rather like it, if I'm honest.'

'He doesn't call me – which is understandable, of course,' Peter added, knowing that to expect sympathy from her was close to ludicrous. Nor did he want her to know the extent of his pain, which had started with his dreadful mishandling of the conversation in the stuffy too-small space of Serena's studio. He had opted for a man-to-man approach. 'I will honour you with the truth,' he had declared, his heart pumping not only with the obvious shock of seeing Theo but the realization that the blond young man holding his niece's hand had to be Delia's son. 'I fell in love,' he had continued, so eager to explain, so swamped by his own churning emotions, that he had almost overlooked the fact that he was addressing his son. It was only as Theo's grave, solid, wide-eyed face sank into disappointment and disgust that Peter grasped the extent of his misjudgement in attempting to put truth before the parental duty of re-assurance. He had tried to back-pedal, to play it all down, to say it would be fine and to talk about his uncle's exciting new proposition, with regard to Ashley House, but it was too late. Theo's look of disgust remained, heightening the stress of that long afternoon and evening all the more for his impressive ability to behave normally in spite of it. Crushed and silent, Peter had watched the display helplessly, drawing little comfort from the obvious fact that he was being treated to a mirror image of his own strengths.

Perhaps in recognition of the inherent gravity of the meeting, Helen led the way past the kitchen and den and into the formal elegance of the sitting room at the back of the house. Opening the drinks cabinet, she pulled out a bottle of wine and two glasses from the set Charlie and Serena had given them as a wedding present. Watching her place the glasses on the coffee-table, fighting the urge to offer to open the bottle, Peter wondered if the selection of these particular items had been deliberate. It would be typical of Helen to have thought through such a detail.

She filled both glasses and pushed one towards him, saying airily, 'Oh, Theo will come round. Our offspring are so much more adaptable than we think, so much more forgiving.'

Surprised, grateful for the reassurance, Peter dared a half-smile. 'Unlike us, eh?' Her self-control astonished him – impressed him too. What other wife in the world could have sat there so cool-as-you-please, as if the pair of them had nothing more serious to discuss than plans for Christmas and whether to visit the exhibition of their nephew's art in one car or two? For a brief moment, Peter wondered if it was all going to be easier than he had thought, that Delia's remark about forgiving wives had been true and that the only remaining obstacle to his happiness was persuading Helen that they should pick up the pieces of their marriage in Sussex rather than Barnes. He tried another gentle smile, one designed to communicate all the regret he truly felt. He might not be able to *un-wish* Delia but he was certainly sorry for the pain he had caused.

Helen responded with steady, unsmiling eyes, then said, in an equally steady voice, 'I think it's the physiotherapist. I checked your phone bill and looked up the number in your address book . . . So many hours, so many texts. Who would have thought a stiff shoulder could require such a *barrage* of attention?'

Peter blushed violently, cursing himself for having under-estimated her. When he spoke his voice was hoarse. 'As I've tried to tell you several times, Helen, it's over.' He paused, aware that, out of a combination of shame and some dim, protective reflex towards Delia, he could not bring himself either to say his lover's name or to acknowledge the veracity of Helen's statement. 'Over,' he repeated, startled, despite his discomfort, by how she had worked it out. Typical Helen, always right, even about being wronged. Taking a sip of wine to steady himself, he stole a glance at her, noting that her usual string of pearls had been replaced by a small crucifix, which dangled between the buttons of her shirt like a tiny dagger.

She nodded slowly, twirling the delicate stem of her glass. 'So, it's all in the past, then?'

'Yes.' Peter had to force out the word, partly because he wanted the torture to end and partly because, even amid the unspeakable stress of the interrogation, part of him resisted the huge renunciation this small word entailed. Of course it was over, his brain knew that, but his heart continued to put up a fight.

'Your mother has been supportive, I expect.'

'I beg your pardon?' Peter was alarmed by the remark and the new icy calm of her voice.

Carefully, Helen set down her glass on a coaster and interlaced her fingers. 'Well, she had that affair, didn't she, with your uncle Eric? She must understand, presumably, the difficult time you're having. Hey,' she slapped her thigh with a sharp, triumphant laugh, as if she had stumbled upon a universal truth, 'maybe it runs in the genes, *infidelity*, passed down through the great Harrison line like Huntington's or sickle-cell anaemia. What do you think?'

Peter stood up. 'I haven't come here for this.'

'Oh? And what have you come for exactly, Peter? *Forgiveness?*' She had gripped the little cross and was twisting it round her fingers. 'Lucky we're rich, isn't it? What with the girls to educate and two houses to run, you're going to need every penny. Lucky, too, that Serena and Charlie have had such a ghastly year, wanting you to take over the family jewel. It's all so perfect.' She clapped her hands together. 'Really, I couldn't be happier for you.'

'Helen, stop this, please,' Peter muttered, backing behind the sofa.

She laughed wildly. 'Oh, indulge me a little.'

'I came here under the illusion that we were going to have a sensible discussion –'

'Oh, we are, we are,' she exclaimed – clearly, in some hysterical way, enjoying herself. 'I'm good at that, aren't I, being *sensible*? Good old sensible, boring Helen. Let me see . . . What else?' She held up her fingers and began to count. 'Predictable, organized, *loyal* – let's not forget that.'

'I think it would be better if I went.'

'Do you know?' she continued brightly, pointing at him as she advanced upon the sofa. 'I think you might be right. But, please, one more answer before you do. That night, the one of our boring, *sensible* dinner party, when you brought me all those heavenly flowers, when you so clearly didn't want to *fuck* me, was it because you had been *fucking* her? Oh, don't frown, darling, it makes you look *so* old. And, on second thoughts, don't worry about answering because I know . . . I *know*,' she repeated, her voice shrinking to a dry, deathly whisper, her eyes like knives. 'I have a good lawyer. I suggest you get one too. In the meantime you can see the girls whenever you want – just call,' she added, striding towards the hall.

'Helen –'

She kept her back to him as she tussled with the lock and latch on the front door, which had always been stiff. 'Give my love to everyone at the old homestead, won't you? I'd have been no good at it anyway, you know, running that place, playing nursemaid to your dear mother . . .'

'Mum is leaving,' mumbled Peter. 'She's made up her mind to go to some sort of country manor of a home. Which means that once Charlie and Serena go I'll be living there alone . . . unless you . . . we . . .'

'Pamela's leaving Ashley House?' Helen turned to him,

clapping a hand to her mouth in genuine amazement. 'Really? Goodness . . . how *unexpected*. Well, give her my best, anyway,' she continued, resuming a tone of false, belligerent cheerfulness. 'And Charlie and Serena, of course.' She opened the door a little, then paused, leaning on the handle. 'Funny, don't you think, how just a few months ago we actually *pitied* your brother and his wife for the trouble caused by that errant son of theirs, when all the while some equally *puerile*,' she spat the word, 'behaviour was driving our own family to collapse? How did you feel about that, by the way? How did you *really* feel? Did it occur to you to make any sort of *connection* between your nephew's fall from grace and your own?'

Peter stared at the floor, noticing for the first time that, beneath its polished surface, each tile was scored with thousands of little scratches. He wondered idly if there was anything that could be done to get rid of them, whether the guarantee on that particular job had expired. 'A connection?' He frowned, reluctant to engage with so discomforting a line of questioning, wanting only to get out. 'I'm not sure I follow . . .'

'Oh, never mind.' Her voice had found yet another gear – trilling and sing-song. 'It doesn't matter.' She tugged open the door. 'And pass on my best to Cassie, too, when you see her. I know I've never been close to your younger sister, but to pull out of the wedding when she wanted a child so badly, not to mention, one assumes, a husband, means she must have been feeling . . .' Helen found suddenly that she could not complete the sentence. The cold night air was creeping up under her trousers. The word she had wanted to use was 'desolate'. But to release it, she knew, would unleash all that she was trying so hard to hold in check. She jerked her head in the direction of the street, an icy black rectangle framed by the open door between them. ''Bye, then. I'll call you.'

'Helen –'

'Goodbye, Peter.' She dropped her gaze as he stepped past

her. The letters *WELCOME*, etched into the doormat, heaved and blurred. Only when the door was properly closed and bolted, when the sound of the car had receded down the road, did Helen sink to her knees, her mouth opening and closing in a form of weeping that was too deep for sound.

'There we are.' One white wine, one packet of pork scratchings and a list of their bar snacks. Are you sure you wouldn't like to eat somewhere else – somewhere a bit more . . . substantial?' There was a note of pleading in Bill Jackson's voice, as if he sensed Elizabeth's reluctance to commit wholly to the business of sharing her evening.

'Oh, no, I love this sort of food, don't you? One gets so fed up of *square* meals, don't you think?' Elizabeth, aware that she was talking nonsense, that she was struggling with the normally instinctive business of being herself, opened the little packet and offered it across the table.

Bill shook his head ruefully. 'My teeth can't take them these days.'

'Oh, bad luck,' she replied gaily, popping one of the dry, salty nuggets into her mouth and endeavouring to chew it in a way that suggested no comparable fear on her part. Her teeth proved robust enough but the cracking noises did little to ease the lurching progress of their conversation.

'This exhibition of your son's work,' said Bill next, 'it sounds fantastic. You must be very proud.'

'Oh, yes, even though it's only two paintings in someone else's exhibition – someone quite famous, apparently, which, of course, makes it more exciting.' Elizabeth did her best to inject a note of warmth into her voice. He was trying so hard. He had even substituted contact lenses for his thick-framed glasses – to draw attention to the appealing soft brown of his irises, she supposed. Instead she had found her gaze returning again and again to the deep pink ridge on the bridge of his nose and the pouched too-white circles round his eyes. It all looked painfully raw somehow, as if he was exposing things she had no right to see.

'Lovely pubs round here, aren't they?'

'Lovely,' Elizabeth agreed, putting her fingers to her mouth as another scratching exploded – impossibly, absurdly loud – between her teeth. 'Lovely,' she repeated, making a big show of looking appreciatively at the stone walls, the sepia photos of fishing and hunting, the horse brasses studding the dark beams. The pub to which Keith had taken her after their cup of tea had been soulless in comparison, with big modern lights, pot plants and varnished pine tables. Yet as they sat side by side on one of the velveteen banquettes, with their orange juice in front of them, Elizabeth had thought it beautiful. Even after everything had gone so badly wrong, when he had slammed down his empty glass and told her that the business of the little Pakistani girl was *his* history not hers, that she should back off with all her high-flown talk of honesty and leave him to his loser-life, there had seemed to be a trace of magic about the place. It was Keith's local, after all, where he had said he came several times a week to give his sister a bit of space, to sip soft drinks and play darts.

'Do you play darts, Bill?'

Her companion looked over his shoulder, wondering with good reason, what had triggered the inquiry. 'Only very badly. Why? Do you?'

'No. I . . . just wondered.'

'I see.' He smiled and nodded, clearly determined to find such inanity charming. 'What *do* you like doing, other than teaching maths?'

Elizabeth made a renewed effort to focus. Getting to know someone took time, after all, and hard work, she reminded herself. 'I like swimming and I'm learning Italian . . .' She gripped one of the bunches into which she had tied her hair and wound it round her fingers, racking her brains for what else to add to this meagre list but managing only to think of the time in the barn with Keith when, at her suggestion, they had made a similar attempt to short-cut the business of getting to know one another. She had reminded him of it in the pub in Hull, probing gently, doing her best to prepare him for what she had really come to say. She had told him about Cassie and Stephen too, and then about Roland, trying to explain how such brave confessions had made her certain that honesty was the only sure defence against anything.

Keith had been deeply concerned, tender, understanding, until she had reached the heart of her quest. The table had wobbled badly when he slammed down the glass. Outside, parting awkwardly, the wind had lashed at their clothes as if bent on pulling them apart. Next to them a chalkboard, advertising a live band later that night, lay on its side, rocking with each gust. Keith stood facing her, his hands in his pockets, his eyes as full as hers. There was no point, he said, speaking more gently now but with a firmness that put paid to any last faltering hope she might have had about him changing his mind. There was no point in keeping in contact, no point in dragging Serena and Charlie down, no point in anything. The demands – the geography – of their families meant they had to be apart. There wasn't even the wedding to worry about any more. But even without those things, he said, he would never acquiesce to her suggestion that he tell Charlie and Serena about the little girl. They had thought well of him and he could see no sense in ruining that good opinion along with everything else. He hoped she understood. He was sorry. He would think of her often. Often, he had repeated, stroking the side of her face one last time. Then he righted the board and walked off down the street.

Bill was saying that he spoke Spanish; that he liked swimming too, but only in tropical climates, preferably with a cocktail bar to hand. Elizabeth watched his mouth move, noting the inner pinkness of his lips. Once upon a time, not that long ago, the Keith business would have left her in pieces, she knew. Since her return from Hull, however, there had been a new emptiness to her life but also a new determination. She had phoned him just once to relay the news – reported to her by Cassie soon after Keith had strode down the street – that Stephen had merely been hiding out of embitterment at their broken engagement. For once Elizabeth had been relieved to be greeted by his answering-machine. In the process of trying to accept the reality of her own situation, she had no desire to subject herself to the ordeal of a proper conversation. Then she had got out her current diary and the new one she had bought for the following year. She had riffled through the weeks and months, wanting to remind herself of how much there was to look forward to – the exhibition, the Christmas holidays, a plan to visit Maria in the spring. Turning back to January, seeing the entries referring to Cassie's wedding and the due date of her nephew's baby, Elizabeth had concluded that, for once, her own life was more ordered than her siblings'. Peter's banishment by Helen, all the talk of Charlie and Serena leaving Ashley House, not to mention her mother's continuing resolve to spend her last years alone – it was as if the planets were trying to spin out of their orbits. All except her. She had had her share of shaky times that year, but had come through them, healed by the knowledge that she was lovable, that she had a son who wasn't afraid to tell the truth, that fifty-four was not too old to make new friends . . .

'Can I get you another?' Bill stood up, tweaked his trousers and straightened his jumper.

Elizabeth pushed aside the half-eaten packet of pork scratchings and looked at her still unfinished glass of wine, which had grown warm in the heat of the pub's open fire. She didn't want another drink – nor a man with small, delicate hands and filed nails, who tweaked his clothes into symmetrical angles. Bill was nice, but she didn't *need* him. She smiled as kindly as she could. 'I'd like a glass of water, please. And, Bill . . . I'm not good at this sort of thing, but could we just be friends – not that I want to appear presumptuous?'

'Of course.' He had stood up and was holding their glasses.

'I'm sorry if I . . . only there's a lot going on in my life at the moment, family things, I just don't –'

'Please – no need. Understand. One water coming up.'

He held himself very upright as he walked past the fire and ducked through the low doorway towards the main bar. Watching him, seeing the damaged pride in the rigid set of his back, Elizabeth felt both sad and proud. She would drink the water, then go home. She might be in time to join in with the pasta and salad she had left out for Roland. She would email Maria and catch up on her marking. She would get an early night and think about Keith, remembering his touch, missing him, but drawing comfort from the fact that she had tried her best.

Skirting-boards, Cassie decided, were the most interesting things, when one looked closely enough, covered with flecks of dust, hairs, scuffmarks. A small grey spider had set up home in the corner nearest her nose, stringing out its web across the angle like some busy miniature housewife pegging out a zigzagging clothes line. Normally Cassie didn't like spiders. Years before, on Stephen's first visit to Ashley House, a particularly large, hairy specimen had startled her as she stepped from the cloisters into the music room. Stephen had rushed to tell her how he hated them too, how his sister had planted them in his bed when he was a boy. He had stepped towards her as she ducked under the web, clearly ready to set aside his own fear and leap to her defence, should the creature choose that moment to abseil towards her hair.

Looking back, Cassie could see that this small first exchange encapsulated everything that had brought them together, then driven them apart: the sympathy, the closeness, the illusory sense of being protected, even that first veiled reference to his miserable childhood – every single element, good and bad, had been there. Which was horrible, she decided, as if her life-story had been written before it started; as if each life was just an unravelling ball of string.

Watching the spider now, a few inches from her face, Cassie could muster nothing stronger than indifference. The phobia was still there, all right, she simply couldn't *access* it. Just as she couldn't access other, more obvious things, like feeling sleepy or hungry, or caring who owned Ashley House, or whether Helen forgave Peter for behaving like a middle-aged arse. Checking the finishing touches to her final ongoing job that day, she had felt only relief that, thanks to a deliberate winding down of her commissions in the approach to Christmas and the wedding, nothing else required her attention.

On getting home she had kept her coat on rather than bothering to turn up the heating and then, because it was nearly seven o'clock, had eaten a piece of bread and an apple standing up next to the sink. Afterwards she had stared into space for ten minutes at least, wrestling with whether to watch television or have a bath, only to jettison both options in favour of lying on the sitting-room floor.

She was depressed, of course. That was obvious. Less obvious was why. After all, she had ended the relationship. Stephen had merely denied knowing her. Which was fine, perfectly understandable, in fact; part of her had thought so even as she had endured the drill of his blank gaze on his parents' doorstep and the chilling charade that had followed. It was only later, in the taxi back to the station, getting out her phone to tell Elizabeth that Stephen was alive and well and she would travel back to London alone, that the crushing panic had set in. He had wanted her to think him dead. It was calculating and sick, the behaviour of a monster. She had loved a monster. Her prince had been a frog. Thinking it through, recalling the tension and controlling deceit, it seemed to Cassie that Stephen had deprived her not only of her dreams for the future but, worse still, of what she had believed about the past.

When Serena phoned that evening to ask about the trip, Cassie had done her best to sound upbeat, taking refuge in exclamations of relief and gladly switching subjects to satisfy her sister-in-law's curiosity about Elizabeth and Keith. There had been something between the two but now they were just friends. Wasn't life extraordinary with its twists and turns? She had then shifted to the logistics of dismantling the wedding, insisting that she would handle it herself and joking that the bridesmaid dresses might make a luxury bed for Poppy. Afterwards she had rushed up to her computer and – within ten minutes – printed out a hundred and fifty copies of the words 'This is to inform you that the wedding between Cassandra Harrison and Stephen Smith will now not take place. All gifts will be returned to John Lewis. Thank you for your patience.' The envelopes had taken far longer, but she had stuck at it until they were done, aware all the while that, while her right hand might continue to steer the pen, a paralysing numbness was creeping round her heart.

The web looked finished but the spider still hadn't settled. Cassie rolled on to her stomach to watch, resting her chin on her fists. Closing her eyes, she became aware of her hip-bones pressing into the carpet and the taut emptiness stretching between. She remembered suddenly that she had been lying in a similar position, sketching dress designs when her period had started, and Keith asked if she liked grilled tomatoes. She had felt so desolate and he had been so kind that she had found herself explaining how the desire to become a mother had blossomed out of the tragedy of her niece. Darling little Tina . . . Cassie dropped her forehead to the ground as the waves of loss rippled through her, not for her niece but for her own never-to-be child. On the carpet last time there had been hope. Now there was nothing, nor ever would be again.

Cassie staggered to her feet, clutching her stomach, then fell against the wall, crushing the web and, for all she knew or cared, the little spider with it. She had hated the numbness but wished now that it would return. Instead there was pain, not just in her stomach but in her back, her legs, her heart, her mind. She reeled round the room, wanting but not managing to cry, while a lucid part of her wondered if the celebrated agony of childbirth could hurt as much as this small private agony of her own bereavement.

As the gleaming walls of the sitting room closed in, Cassie fled upstairs, across the landing, past the mess of her unmade bed and into the bathroom. Opening the cabinet above the basin, she pulled out the little gadget for testing her fertility and dropped it into the bin. Catching sight of herself in the mirror, she was appalled to see that she looked *well* – face flushed, eyes shining, long hair tumbling down to her shoulders in its pretty white-blonde curls. Cassie leant closer to the mirror, tugging at the skin on her face, seeking evidence of the ugliness exploding inside. It was wrong, surely, to look so good and feel so bad? Furious suddenly, forgetting the pain, she lunged into the cabinet for her nail scissors and hacked at her hair until the basin was full of long tresses and the sharp pink triangle of her face at last had nowhere to hide.

When the doorbell rang she dropped the scissors and stumbled out of the bathroom. Not Stephen, surely? Please let it not be Stephen. Ducking past the window, Cassie tiptoed out on to the landing and leant over the banisters. The bell rang again, more insistently. Reminding herself that Stephen had keys, should he choose to use them, Cassie backed along the landing and into the study, vowing silently to change the locks or maybe, better still, to move. Living here was part of the problem, she saw suddenly, the reason she had got into such a state.

Stephen's study was cold and quiet. Cassie leant against the window to catch her breath. In the garden she could make out the skeleton of the tree, its bare skirt of branches trembling in the wind. Sidling away from it, feeling calmer, she eased herself into the desk chair to wait a little longer. Sitting thus in the dark, with only the rush of her own breath for company, it was a few moments before she noticed that the desk had been cleared. No notebooks, no laptop, no pens or pencils. Turning her head slowly, as if fearful of frightening herself with any sudden movement, Cassie noticed that the desk drawer was open. Open and empty. So he had been to the house. But when? That day? A week ago? Cassie started to shake. Maybe it had been that day. Maybe he was still there.

When the phone on the desk rang Cassie lunged for it with both hands.

'Darling, I'm freezing my bollocks off on your doorstep – are you going to let me in?'

'Frank?'

'Who else, sweetie? We agreed, remember, however many days ago it was, that I would call by for a spot of tea and sympathy. Except I've brought champagne and smoked salmon instead . . . Open the door, there's a good girl.'

'No, Frank. I'm not feeling well.'

'You gave that fiancé of yours the boot – of *course* you're not feeling well. When I broke up with Clive I cried solidly for six months. I know it was a long time ago but I still remember it as if it was yesterday. Breaking up is *ghastly*, darling, however it happens. Now, do let me in before I catch pneumonia.'

To Frank's credit, he let out only the briefest cry of horror at the sight of her. The next minute Cassie found herself being pulled against the soft wool of his overcoat while he issued clucking reprimands about the sieve-like state of her brain.

Feeling safe at last, as if she had thrashed her way through a state of near-drowning to an unlooked-for shore, Cassie clung to him, weeping properly at last and wailing thank-yous. Frank steered her into the sitting room, eased her into a chair and told her to cry her heart out while he found some glasses.

By the time he returned Cassie had found a box of tissues and was sufficiently composed to apologize. 'It just . . . all of it . . . tonight . . . on top of me.' She patted her chest. 'Couldn't breathe.'

'Of course you couldn't. Horrid business – *horrid*. Don't speak, darling, just *drink*.'

'Frank, I will drink – but first could you, would you mind – I know I sound mad but would you search the house for me?'

He raised two symmetrically plucked eyebrows, genuinely perplexed. '*Search* it? What for, exactly?'

'Stephen,' Cassie whispered, flicking her eyes over her shoulder. 'I think he might have been here, maybe even today. I can't help being afraid that –'

Frank set his glass down and stood up. 'Say no more. You blow that pretty nose and I'll take care of everything.' He took of his jacket and rolled up his sleeves. 'Though could I perhaps ask a favour in return?'

'Of course,' Cassie murmured, dizzy with exhaustion.

'Could I have a go at your hair?'

'My –' Cassie let out a cry. She had forgotten it. She put her hands to her head, feeling air and then the shredded ends of her handiwork with the scissors. Her princess tresses, her *crowning glory*. 'I don't know why, I just wanted –' She broke off, still too close to the distress to explain it.

Frank crossed the room and patted her head. 'Now, I'm going to tell you a secret, but you have to promise to keep it until you die. And that is,' he took a deep breath, 'in my other life, before Rupert, before Clive, before all of them, I was a hairdresser. A bloody good one, though I say it myself. So let

479

me sort this lot out, okay, darling? We'll aim for Mia Farrow in the seventies – deliciously *gamine*, okay?'

Ten minutes later he returned, declaring that he had checked under every bed and behind every door and brandishing a pair of kitchen scissors, a bowl of water and a towel, draped waiter-style across his forearm. 'No vermin of any kind – I've looked everywhere. And now to work.' He set down the bowl and pulled out a small tortoiseshell comb from his back trouser pocket. 'And while I work we're going to talk about where you'll go to get away from all this. It's perfectly clear to me that you can't stay here, not if you're going to chop your hair off every time you think that man of yours is coming back to get you.'

'He's not my man,' murmured Cassie, smiling weakly as her improbable saviour danced round her shorn head, making appalled faces and waving his comb. 'Nobody is anybody's, not really.'

Purring through the muddy darkness in the heated cocoon of his car, Peter allowed himself to think about Delia, constructing a tantalizing, wonderful fantasy in which she announced that a *pied-à-terre* simply wasn't enough and moved herself and her physiotherapy practice to Ashley House. During their affair he had talked to her often and lovingly of the family home, wanting her to know and love it too, lamenting on several occasions the impossibility of taking her there. He pictured her now, waking and stretching in the big four-poster, or subsiding into one of the glorious lion-footed cast-iron baths, or strolling through the garden, her green almond eyes wide with pleasure and admiration as he pointed out the broad, beautiful boundaries of the surrounding land.

Coming up behind a lorry, Peter took his foot off the accelerator with a tut of impatience and glanced into the rear-view mirror. As it was so late, the motorway had been pleasantly clear ever since he left London. It had made him wonder whether he shouldn't drive the commute more often. The soft bounce of the car wheels flying along the smooth Tarmac had soothed him, easing him away from painful flashbacks of his meeting with Helen to the infinitely more appealing vision of a life with his lover. But maybe more than a vision, decided Peter, fiercely, pulling out to overtake the lorry. If one wanted something badly enough, one got it – he had always believed that. So surely – The hoot of the car horn was so sudden and loud that Peter reacted instantly, swerving back inside his lane. His car, for a few brief, terrifying seconds, tipped on to two wheels, then righted itself. The other car, which he had not seen and which had hooted, tore on past up the dark streak of roadway. Peter, his heart thundering, hands sliding on the wheel, slowed again to catch his breath. He was tired, distracted. He needed a break. Seeing the neon sign of an eatery – one of the modern concrete boxes he normally despised – he signalled carefully and turned off the motorway.

Five minutes later, nursing a strong, bitter coffee at a small Formica table in the over-lit glare of the café, still trembling a little from his misjudgement, Peter felt as if he had been rudely awoken from a dream. Delia had not called and never would. She had not loved him and never would. For understandable reasons, Helen did not love him either. Peter folded a little paper napkin while he allowed his thoughts to return to their encounter that evening, pressing tidy creases with his fingertips as the square grew smaller and fatter. Helen's sneering savagery had been shocking but, most unpleasant of all to Peter, he had been outwitted. He should have expected such a response, been more *prepared* for it, instead of backing out of the house like a stranger – like one of the sad creatures he saw so often in court, rolling over to let life crush them, born *victims*. He looked about him, taking in his surroundings properly, noting the thin scattering of tired, hunched figures at the other tables. The place was vile. The coffee was disgusting. He did not belong there.

Peter screwed up his napkin, dropped it into his coffee and strode out into the night. He belonged to a better world, a better life. There were worse things, after all, than failed marriages. He would be fair to Helen, but he wouldn't let her walk all over him. He was stronger, worth more, than that. He had status and, thanks to hard work and astute investments, he had wealth – more than even Helen knew. And then, of course, there was the house, the jewel in the crown, as Helen had called it, which he had resisted once but which he could see now had always been *meant* for him. It was almost, he mused, pulling cautiously on to the motorway, as if Fate had intervened. Serena's grand design again. Well, maybe she had a point. An hour before a car might have killed him, but it hadn't. Nor would a messy personal life get the better of him either. Chaos was for other people – for Charlie, Serena, the hapless Ed, Cassie, Elizabeth, stumbling around as they always had. His destiny was different, *better*. He could feel it now, pulling him south, pulling him *home*. Commuting, having the girls at weekends, forging a peace with his son, visiting his mother, it wouldn't be so bad.

By the time he had embarked on negotiating the deepening pot-holes in the lane leading to Ashley House, Peter felt sufficiently – defiantly – *reassembled* to resolve that his first act on resuming ownership of the estate would be to get the lane properly resurfaced. It was ridiculous, after all, to risk gashing the undercarriage of expensive vehicles every time one undertook a journey, and all for the sake of some quaint notion of rural beauty. There was nothing particularly rural or beautiful about mud and ruts. And the trees and hedges on either side needed a good pruning too, he decided, hating how the trailing branches clawed at the windows, like scaly fingers on scaly hands, trying to pull him into the murky dark.

Given the lateness of the hour, Peter was surprised to see a light on in the drawing room. Surprised and pleased. A nightcap, the solace of company – it was exactly what he needed. His pleasure increased at the sight of Charlie lying on the sofa, propped up by several cushions, a glass of Scotch in one hand and a book in the other. 'I've been waiting up for you,' he said, putting down the book and sitting up.

'Have you? My goodness! Well, thank you . . . thank you very much.'

'How did it go?'

'Hang on, I'll fix myself one of those.'

'So it went well, then?' Charlie called after him. When there was no reply he set down his glass and ran his hands over his face. It had been a long day. Waiting on the sofa with his book he had fallen asleep several times. Once, he had woken to find his mother standing next to him in her worn yellow dressing-gown with her hair loose. She had smiled tenderly and ruffled his head as if he were a little boy, as if she still knew all of his churning thoughts. Maybe she did. It was hard to tell, these days: she seemed contented enough, but said little, almost as if she was deliberately withdrawing from them in preparation, perhaps, for the real leave-taking, now a few weeks away. Peter had been too distracted to do a proper job of talking her round, and now it was too late. She had waved the piece of paper at him and Serena that afternoon, the ink of her signature still glistening. A colonel had died and his rooms were hers, if she wanted them. They were being redecorated and would be ready for occupation in January. Heady still from his and Ed's visit to the lawyer, Charlie could think of no better response than an encouraging hug, much as he had given each of his daughters when they had launched themselves back into their lives the month before.

Peter came back in with a large glass of malt, which he set down on the mantelpiece. Turning his back to Charlie, humming quietly, he extracted the largest of the pokers from the set of brass fire irons parked on the hearth and began to stoke a glow from the smoking pile of ash. 'That lane needs cutting back, you know. If it had been done a couple of weeks ago we could have used the brushwood for a bonfire. Do you remember the November bonfires we used to have?' He put the poker back in its slot and turned to smile at his brother. 'Old Sid took such pride in building them, each year's bigger than the last. Dad was like a kid with the fireworks. Do you remember, Charlie?'

'Of course,' said Charlie, softly, delighted at this evidence of such high, positive spirits. 'And Helen?' he pressed. 'How was she?'

Peter picked up his glass and swilled the whisky, which gleamed like molten honey. 'Helen was . . . *well*, very well indeed.' He nodded to himself, took a sip from his glass and let out a loud, satisfied sigh. 'And what about you? Did the lawyer earn his or her hourly fee?'

Charlie wished he could borrow some of his brother's easy manner. He cleared his throat. 'Yes, he did.' He coughed. 'It turns out that only Ed is financially liable for his predicament. That is to say, the assets of the family are irrelevant. Jessica is entitled to nothing beyond what Ed can afford – in other words, some of that five grand Dad left him. I suppose neither you nor Helen could possibly have known – family law isn't your field, is it?' Charlie had clasped his hands together and was staring hard at Peter, willing him to guess the direction in which this new information had taken him and Serena that afternoon, talking it over with Ed, some of Pamela's flapjacks and cups of tea. His brother remained poised, one elbow on the mantelpiece, his face set in unwitting yet comical likeness to the sombre expression on the face of John Harrison in the portrait above. He looked at Charlie at last, smiling absently. 'Good. That will take the pressure off, then.'

'Yes, indeed.' Charlie stood up, responding to a dim need to be more on a par with Peter's tall, imposing frame. He felt too short – too wide – next to his brother. He always had. 'It's allowing Ed to have a complete rethink about university and so on. To put it crudely, the longer he defers getting a job the less he will have to shell out, and whatever he can provide will be purely as maintenance for the child. When it turns eighteen he'll be off the hook. Jessica herself is entitled to nothing. I know I sound callous – obviously we'll make sure the baby is provided for – but my first priority has to be Ed. The point is, Peter, this new understanding of our position, you must see that it changes everything.' Charlie watched his brother carefully, aware all the while of the cool stare of their father blazing from the wall.

'Everything,' echoed Peter, warmly. 'Excellent.'

'Peter,' Charlie blurted, 'we want to stay here. Serena and I, the children, we want to stay. It will still be difficult, of course, but I think now we can make a go of it. And I'm sorry, obviously, for mucking you around. But Helen has never been keen to live here, has she? And if you two are going to work things out, then I can only assume that this change of plan will help –'

'Charles . . .' It was more an exhalation of breath than a word. 'Charlie . . .' Peter tried to smile. 'You cannot mean this. I refuse to believe that you *mean* this.' He gripped his glass, pressing it into the mantelpiece.

'Look, I'm sorry if –'

'*Sorry?*' Peter let out a wild laugh. 'Sorry, isn't good enough, old chap. Sorry really doesn't cut the mustard. I urge you –' he was aware of his arm throbbing against the hard edge of the marble '– I *urge* you to rethink.'

'I have rethought. I have done nothing but rethink for weeks. Serena and the children have begged to stay here. And Mum . . . Well, she hasn't done any begging, but she has made it clear that she has no desire to see us move out. Looking back, I can see that I only asked you to take over because I allowed all that had happened, with Mum and Ed and so on, to get on top of me. I wasn't *coping* and neither was Serena because she's still – we're still . . .' Charlie paused, unwilling to confess to his darkest fears and not wanting to confuse a situation that was already so delicate and complicated. 'The point is, I convinced myself that we were a pair of failures, while you, in contrast . . . but now . . .'

'Now, I'm a failure too, is that it?'

'Don't be absurd.' Charlie shook his head unhappily. Gross as the oversimplification was, it contained a dim echo of truth. One of the weirdly heartening things to emerge from the rubble of the last few weeks was the knowledge that his brother was not the solid, perfect, superior being he had always assumed. Serena had been trying to tell him as much for years but he hadn't listened. Accepting it even now felt hard. For almost half a century he had been content to live in Peter's shadow, deferring to him, trusting his judgement and instincts. It had been comfortable to do so, Charlie could see that now, because at some deep level it had allowed him to shirk responsibility. Letting it go felt sad and hard, as if he was releasing some integral part of his own innocence. 'So, you see,' he continued, 'paying for the baby is not going to be the issue I had imagined. Serena and I, we're a bit stronger too – not right yet but –'

'Oh, so the pair of you are all tickety-boo now, are you?' snapped Peter, in such a catty, unPeter-like way that Charlie's jaw dropped. 'You won't be needing me to bail you out. Well, bully for you. Thanks for keeping me posted.'

'Look, I can understand why you're upset,' Charlie had crept back to the sofa and dropped his head into his hands, 'but surely, right now, you have more important things to worry about. All I'm saying is that Serena and I want to have another shot at making this place – everything – work. Just as you and Helen want to have another go . . .'

Charlie was labouring to finish the sentence when the glass Peter had been clutching so tightly somehow broke free of his fingers and skidded towards the edge of the mantelpiece. They both watched as it teetered, then fell, the whisky making a yellow arc across the carpet while the crystal smashed like exploding diamonds on the stone hearth below.

Serena, sitting at her dressing-table, pen poised over a couple of notelets to the girls, looked up sharply at the distant sound of breaking glass. She tiptoed to the bedroom door, wondering what was going on, certain suddenly that Charlie, when the moment came, would not be up to the task. She hung on to the door, quelling the urge to run downstairs and help him fight his corner – *their* corner. She had known better than Charlie how difficult it would be. She had seen only too clearly how ready Peter had been to settle into the house, how eagerly – arrogantly – he had occupied the space, letting the habitual assertiveness show through. As she had pushed Peter's shirts into the washing-machine, served him meals like a housekeeper, seen his smart car parked in the middle of the drive, she had wondered often why she and Charlie were bothering to hang around.

After the smash there was silence, then the murmur of voices and then something else, a noise, like crying. There was crying. Not Charlie, she knew the sounds Charlie made. Peter. Peter was crying – not the shoulder-jerking puppetry of the time he arrived in the drive either, but properly, volubly, wildly. Dear God. Serena closed the door and leant against it, closing her eyes. Charlie would cave in. That heart of his, softening slowly, tentatively in the weeks since the bombings, like a creature coming out of long hibernation, wouldn't be able to stand it. She could hardly stand it and she had the door, the stairs and several walls to protect her. They would move to Brighton, dragging the shadow of the year's failures with them. Their marriage at least was better, safer, *functioning* again. Serena had seen to that and would continue to do so, masking her fears for the future as she knew Charlie was masking his. All the horrible things he had said – about the *gap*, about putting her needs before Ed's – were still there, still to be dealt with, but not now . . .

Serena briskly sealed each card into its envelope. She could feel her thoughts slipping, as they tended to during any unguarded moment, towards the coop of a flat in Wandsworth. It was unwise, she knew, to think of Jessica or the baby. Not thinking about such things had helped her and Charlie to recover some of their equilibrium. With all the dramas since the Charing Cross bombing, it had been almost easy. When Charlie and Ed had bounced back from their visit to the lawyer that afternoon, she had rejoiced with them, suppressing her own qualms over such an apparently easy reduction of their responsibilities. Getting on so well and after a *driving* lesson, she had teased, was close to miraculous. And when Charlie gripped her hand and said that maybe they didn't have to leave Ashley House after all, she had felt as if her heart might burst with happiness. The co-operation, the cohesion, the sense of a shared future, after so many uncertain months, was like oxygen. They had hugged and wept, talking like conspirators, about how to break the news to Peter.

It was only later on when Pamela, preparing for her departure in an endless sorting of spare-room cupboards and tea-chests, had thrust – with a beady look – a bag of baby clothes into Serena's hands that the doubts, old and new, had come crashing back. The bag was with her now, next to one of the spindly legs of the dressing-table. Sticking out of it was a sailor suit, impractical and expensive, which Cassie had bought for Ed, and a pair of pink booties with silk ribbons that Pamela had knitted for one of the twins. Or had it been Tina? Serena sat very still while, inside her, the hollowness swelled like a dark sea. Charlie was right: this baby, which was half Ed – right from the start, she had wanted it to be made real. All the other considerations – morality, the confusion of two teenagers, money – had been nothing but pretence, a flimsy camouflage for that desire.

Breathing slowly, Serena reached for a fresh card.

Dear Jessica,

I hope these clothes come in useful. I hope, too, that you are all right and looking after yourself. Charlie and Ed have seen a lawyer who will be in touch with you shortly. Good luck with the birth and if you ever need anything – anything at all – please just call me on this number . . .

Hearing footsteps on the landing Serena pushed the card under the two envelopes she had addressed to the girls. A moment later Charlie came into the bedroom, his thick hair lank and dishevelled, his eyes glassy. He crossed at once to the dressing-table, pressing his hands on to her shoulders as their eyes met in the mirror.

Serena tipped her head to one side until her cheek was brushing his fingers. 'It's okay. I know what happened. It was obvious that Peter always regretted giving us the place anyway. He was never going to give up a chance to get it back. It's okay.'

Charlie dropped his head. 'When I told him he just sort of . . . collapsed. He said that Helen isn't interested in reconciliation, that Ashley House is all he has left. He also said . . .' Charlie paused '. . . that he had always envied us.'

'Us?'

'Our – our *passion*. That was the word he used. He said he thought he'd found something similar with this woman. He said . . .' Charlie swallowed hard, grimacing at the recollection of Peter kneeling among the broken crystal, moaning like a wounded child. 'He said that when I told him, in Umbria, that we were having difficulties part of him was glad.'

'But that's horrible.' Serena swivelled to look at him, not glancing down as her leg brushed the bag of baby clothes.

'I told him love was what you arrived at, not what you started with.'

Serena caught her breath. 'Did you? Oh, Charlie . . .' She leant back against him, half closing her eyes, too moved to say more. On the dressing-table she could see the small white point of her letter to Jessica sticking out from under the other cards. She would not send it, or the stained little outfits. It was Ed's child, after all, she reminded herself, to ignore or accept as he chose. Her sense of connection to it was undeniably dubious – certainly too dubious to expect any more such breathtaking declarations from her husband if he ever found evidence of it.

'Peter believes that to live at Ashley House is his destiny,' continued Charlie, doggedly. 'He kept saying so – I've never seen him so desperate.'

Serena waited, steeling herself for what was coming next. 'And I suppose you *had* said he could have it,' she ventured at last, inwardly preparing to cope with the disappointment, thinking that a house was only a house, a mere ornament compared to all the other issues of life, loss and love waging war on their hearts.

Charlie straightened himself and took a step back from her. 'I told him no.'

'No?'

'I said Ashley House was ours, that Dad had sanctioned the arrangement and I had been wrong to consider giving up on it. I said I was sorry too, of course,' he muttered, 'fucking sorry.'

'Charlie! That's *amazing*.' Serena tried to put her arms round him, but he staggered back to sit on the bed. 'He wept, Serena . . . He *wept*. He said he had lost everything – *everything*. It was the most terrible thing.'

490

'Maybe because he's only just beginning to see what he *has* lost. I don't mean the house, I mean Helen, wrecking twenty-five years of trust, shattering the children. Maybe it's only just sinking in. It can take time, after all, can't it,' she whispered, 'to recognize loss?'

They remained side by side for a long time, not touching but close enough to be aware of the warmth of each other's bodies, the rise and fall of their chests as they breathed.

Early the following Saturday, Ed slipped out of the house to look for Samson who, for the first time anyone could remember, had failed to present his whiskery tiger-face for breakfast. His grandmother, shaking her head over a cup of tea like an ancient sage, sounded almost satisfied, rather than sad, when she announced that the animal knew she was leaving and had probably taken himself off to die. Cats were wise and had impeccable timing, she said, better than humans, half the time. Annoyed by these observations, half suspicious that they contained some veiled reprimand, Ed had grabbed a walking-stick and an anorak and left the house by the utility room.

Outside the air was raw and the clouds like bunches of steel wool. He walked briskly round the main lawn and down through the pergola, scanning every flowerbed and clump of dark foliage for a streak of orangy gold. Once he was out of sight of the house, behind the wintry dark towers of the rhododendrons, which separated the furthest of the garden fences from the fields, he lit a cigarette and ran the back of his hand across the drip on his nose. Looking at the colourless perimeter of the garden, and the field rolling down towards the copse, Ed felt, for the first time, a grateful, integral sense of belonging; of *wanting* to belong. As children, he and the others had taken Ashley House for granted. Even when his own family had moved in, Ed had been too young to appreciate the magnitude of the arrangement. That had only come in the last few months, with the understanding that it might all be lost.

But now that wouldn't happen. Ashley House was theirs – his mum and dad's, his, Maisie's and Clem's – for ever. There had been a sort of showdown. His father had insisted, and his uncle had backed down. Ed still felt a swell of pride when he thought about it. His uncle, normally so in-your-face, had been like a ghost ever since, tiptoeing about the place with his head down, backing against walls to let people by, missing meals and burying himself in his room. And now he was leaving, that morning, moving, apparently, to a flat near Barons Court. Avoiding the awkwardness of the goodbye had lent added appeal to Ed's hunt for Samson.

He tossed away his cigarette and began to call the cat, doing his best to reproduce the soft, high tones his grandmother adopted. He hoped the creature hadn't died. Ed was eighteen, too, and didn't feel remotely ready to meet his Maker. Scanning the field, beating at any patches of long grass with his stick, Ed set off towards the copse. He moved with a real sense of urgency now, propelled by thoughts of how moth-eaten Samson's glossy coat had looked lately, how long it was since the old cat had performed one of his acrobatic feats between windowsills.

He was almost at the stile, bare feet sliding uncomfortably on the grit in his wellingtons, when he heard a voice calling him. Ed turned to see his uncle, his face a white dot against the dark of his overcoat, signalling to him from the bottom of the garden. Cursing, Ed trudged back up the field.

They shook hands, with some difficulty, over the fence. 'I wanted to say a proper farewell.'

'Yup . . . Sorry, I was looking for Samson.'

'Good man. You'll need another cat soon, though – and a dog, of course. This place needs animals.' Peter turned to the garden and then the view towards the downs, as if imprinting them on his mind.

'Yeah, I guess it does.' Ed kicked at a stone, wondering afresh at this new, subdued version of his uncle and thinking that, in many ways, the old bully had been a lot easier to deal with. Noting the sparse tufts of hair, being blown by the wind round his bald patch, the pouches under his eyes and the sag of his broad shoulders, Ed even felt a bit sorry for him. He was just an old man, after all, a proud old man, who regretted a decision about a house and who had made an ass of himself by screwing a woman who wasn't his wife. In a way Ed didn't blame him, not for the affair anyway: he wouldn't have wanted sex with his aunt Helen in a million years.

He frowned, thinking that he would choose his own mess over his uncle's any day. For one thing he wasn't bald and craggy-faced, and for another, he knew now that the baby didn't have to fuck his life up. As the lawyer had pointed out, it was Jessica who had chosen to have it and Jessica who would be responsible for dealing with the consequences. Apart from handing over a portion of his trust fund, Ed wouldn't have to do anything for years.

'Dad says you've decided to apply to university, after all. That's great. You've got a good brain.'

Ed went pink and dropped his gaze. Their handshake over the fence had left a livid smear of green lichen on the smooth dark arm of his uncle's overcoat. 'See you at Christmas, I expect,' he said, pitching the remark in a way that he hoped would close the proceedings.

Peter sighed heavily. 'I'm not sure, Ed, to be honest . . . It all depends on arrangements.'

'Oh, right, of course.' Ed's blush deepened. 'See you soon, anyway.'

Instead of taking this second hint, his uncle, speaking quickly, gruffly to the muddy tips of his leather shoes, said, 'I'm sorry, Ed, if I was ever too hard on you. What you did with Jessica – the business of the child – it's not your fault.'

Ed gawped, took a step backwards, stumbled on a clod and almost lost his footing.

'I mean it was your fault,' Peter continued, 'but it was also bloody bad luck.'

'Yes,' Ed muttered, 'I suppose it was.'

At last his uncle turned towards the house, then swung round again, so quickly that the panels of his coat flared. 'I was just wondering . . . being close in age, knowing him as you do . . . Any tips on Theo, how I might handle him?'

'Theo?' Out of the corner of his eye Ed saw a blur of orange, moving behind a tree.

'He won't talk to me, you see, ever since . . . Oh, never mind. Forget it – foolish to ask. Forgive me, Ed, I'm not myself.' He raised an arm in farewell, then slipped both hands into his pockets and set off back towards the house.

'I –'

'Yes?' Peter stopped.

'I should think – I mean, I don't have a clue, really,' Ed gabbled, 'but you can only sort of say sorry, can't you? I mean, that's all anyone can do, isn't it?' He shrugged and pulled a face. 'What do I know?' The blur of orange was there again, closer now, among the lower black trunks of the rhododendrons. His uncle was trudging away, taking each step slowly and heavily, as if some huge invisible weight had been strapped to his back. Ed wasn't even sure whether his pathetic pearl of wisdom had been heard. He wished now he hadn't said anything. For all he knew, his uncle had been on bended knee saying sorry to his aunt and cousins since day one.

Ed threw himself on to the grass and rolled under the fence into the inner tangle of the flowerbed. Samson was crouching next to a heap of wet leaves, ruffled but healthy enough. At the sight of Ed, cursing and brushing dirt and twigs out of his hair, the cat tensed and widened his yellow eyes, clearly resenting the intrusion into his private world.

'Silly cat, it's only me. You're a bad puss, you are.' Ed held out his hand, which Samson sniffed before nuzzling his fingertips and starting to purr. 'Not dead yet then, you great sissy,' Ed murmured, glad that only Samson, two woodlice and a slimy pink worm were there to see his tears.

December

Theo wondered that a journey could take so long: Oxford to Paddington, then thirteen stops on the District Line – it felt as if he was crawling across the world. At Paddington carol-singers had been clustered round a flashing tree, jangling money-boxes at anyone who looked like stopping, and a grizzled man with a sandwich board had paraded the words, *Sinners Repent Judgement Is Nigh*. As Theo hurried past, giving it all a wide berth, he had heard the man shouting above the strains of 'Silent Night', 'Who is without sin? Who is pure? Who will be saved?'

No one, probably, Theo reflected, leaping through the closing doors of a tube and fighting his way to a seat. Morality was a minefield – rules and trip-wires – with God, as far as he could see, offering little guidance to either the sinners or those they had wronged. On the phone, these days, his mother sounded lost, like some dazed little girl, going through the motions of saying everything was all right because she believed it was expected of her. Lending what support he could, Theo felt not only fiercely protective but *ancient*, as if the events of the last few weeks had aged him a thousand years.

But, above all, he was angry. Not just with his father for behaving like a selfish, destructive, blind dickhead of a teenager, but with the way everything had subsequently folded like a pack of cards. His parents had separated. Barnes and Barons Court: two homes, two half-families, two loyalties, leaving him, Genevieve and Chloë with the new, horrible job of having to slice themselves down the middle to accommodate it all. He felt especially bad for Chloë: he, at least, had the undiminished pleasures of university life to offer solace, but his sister was fourteen, stubborn, argumentative and caught in the thick of it. Every protective urge in that direction, however, had so far met with a sharp rebuff. She was fine, Chloë insisted, on the rare occasions Theo had managed to corner her on the phone, always adding – if pressed – that loads of her friends' parents had split up and she didn't care.

It was detestable, all of it, and ruthless, Theo had discovered, in its power to contaminate the simplest things. Even this trip to see Roland's paintings – the family were meeting for a grand viewing at a place called the Shaw Gallery near London Bridge that evening – had been absurdly torturous to arrange. Having declared that he would spend the night in London, Theo had found himself so torn between where to stay (so pressurized by both parents' insistence that there was no pressure) that he had asked Clem if he could sleep on her sofa. And then there had been the endless debates as to how the exhibition would be attended – whether Helen and Peter should arrive simultaneously or at different times and with which children. It was like some badly written farce. In dealing with the muddles, it had seemed increasingly to Theo as if no one on either side had put up a fight, or been called to account, or attempted, however remotely, to make sense of any of what was going on.

Hence this private early pilgrimage from Oxford to west London, not to Barnes – the house would be empty until the afternoon anyway – but to Richmond. To Delia Goddard, the physiotherapist. His mother, in surrendering the identity of his father's lover, had released the name like a curse, and Theo didn't blame her. It was ironic to think how concerned they had all been for the wrenched shoulder, how his mother had begged his father to get it treated, how Theo himself had eased off on the squash court all those months ago out of some kind of perverse pity . . . Christ. And what a cliché, too, to take one's *physio* as a lover – or *ex*-lover, Theo reminded himself, as the tube rumbled to a halt at Barons Court. Some of Peter's pleading explanations and apologies pushed their way back into his mind. Theo had cringed under each assault, so many sorrys, not just for the affair but for giving away Ashley House – as if any of that mattered now. And what good were apologies? They were just words that had arrived too late. It was what you *did* that counted, not what spilled out of your mouth.

The train seemed to stay at Barons Court for ever, as if some meddling cog in its engine was trying to tempt Theo to get off and seek out his father's address, instead of Delia's. He clung to his small holdall, trying not to look at his watch as the seconds dragged by. A couple of sparse, unhomely rooms, an unmade bed, some dirty saucepans, no, thank you. No bloody way. Betrayal might deserve punishment, but Theo had no desire to witness any more of it than he had to at first hand. Instead, he tried to focus on his film, which, thanks to an expensive but fantastic piece of software called LastCutPro, was now edited and copied on to several DVDs. He had brought one with him in the hope of finding a moment to show Clem the quiet, electrifying wonder of her performance beside which even the great Ben paled almost to ordinariness. He also wanted to test her reaction to the ending, which, with his own anxious state of mind and the two options he had left himself, had caused many hours of heartache.

The train edged forward at last, although with Richmond approaching, Theo's sense of relief was short-lived. What was he pursuing after all, he wondered, other than a dim, instinctive urge to confront the enemy? *You should know what you have done.* Yes, he would say that, he decided, latching on to the words to stop his courage back-sliding any further. He would look her in the eye and announce his identity; he would tell her that the Charing Cross bombings were nothing compared to the devastation wrought by the impact of her interference in his family, that . . .

Theo moved through the ticket barrier and along the street in a kind of trance, following the route he had memorized from the *A–Z* that morning: third left, second right, first left, fourth right. At the entrance to the neat, semi-circular drive he stopped, taking in the presence of the silver soft-topped Saab and the wide handsome house. Money, then, lots of it; smart cars, lovers – a cushy life . . . cushy enough for him to feel more than justified in throwing a few stones. Redress, accountability. His mission was coming back into focus. Theo took the steps up to the front door three at a time and fired his index finger at the bell before he had time to catch his breath.

A minute later a woman opened the door, an ordinary-looking middle-aged woman with artificially streaked hair and the kind of slim face you could tell had once been quite pretty. She was wearing a green mohair jumper, a black skirt and flat shoes. She appeared, more than anything, impatient.

'Yes?'

Theo said, 'I am . . .' then closed his mouth.

'You are?' she prompted.

But Theo was gazing over her shoulder at a figure standing with his back to them, a tall, fair-haired figure riffling through some letters. Theo blinked, repeating, hoarsely this time, 'I am . . .'

'A friend of my son's?' she finished, smiling encouragingly now, as if to say that such gormless behaviour was both familiar and forgivable. 'Jules, darling, there's someone here for you.' She stepped to one side. Julian glanced round and dropped the letters, his face breaking into a grin of astonished recognition. 'Theo – bloody hell!' He strode towards the door, laughing, his hand outstretched.

Even then it would have been possible to continue. For, as the scene unfolded, in the inexorable slow motion that is the hallmark of pure crisis, Theo felt curiously in command, almost as if he was behind one of his lenses with a finger poised over a button. He could stop it, if he wanted. Or speed it up. Or reshape it into the unsightly thing he had envisaged. Within the constraints of those smooth, sliding seconds, Theo's able brain raced, weighing up the decision. It was a question of right and wrong, and of loyalties, he saw, and between generations too, just as it had been when he had made that promise to Ed, then gone back on it. Julian, surely, deserved to know the truth about his mother. Just as Delia had no right to be cushioned from the knowledge that her behaviour had blown a gaping hole through a family – blasted it to pieces. Theo braced himself, aware that this moment was about meeting his own needs too, seeking the solace of *action* against all the depressing, tail-chasing pointlessness of the last few weeks.

Julian was still talking. He said 'unbelievable', and 'how cool', and then, 'Mum, this is Theo Harrison, Maisie's cousin – remember I told you about him?' And Theo saw at once, in the sharp swivel of her head, the tightening of her thin face, the way her fingers gripped her elbows, that his name had triggered recognition. He saw, too, with almost visionary intensity, that she was suffering already – for whatever reason, fear, regret, it hardly mattered – and understood in the same instant that, with or without a religious framework, there was always a price to be paid for the awareness of wrongdoing.

'Mrs Goddard. A pleasure to meet you.' He managed a smile, safe in the knowledge that she did not – and would never – know for certain what had brought him to her doorstep on a cold December afternoon. Maybe she would wonder; maybe that wondering would be part of her suffering. In the meantime, no more harm had been done, at least not to Julian, whom Theo liked even though he had not got as far as knowing his surname. And the harm had to stop, Theo recognized suddenly, even if it meant that some truths remained buried. It could not be allowed to go on spreading, like a cancer, souring the good and the bad. 'I was paying a visit to my mother,' he lied. 'She lives in Barnes, and I had some time, remembered you lived in these parts and thought I'd look you up – check out what *your* family was like at surprise visits. How've you been?'

'Fine, fine.' Julian was ushering him in. 'Coffee, beer? You're in London for that art thing of your cousin's, aren't you? Maisie told me about it. She also told me about your parents – I'm so sorry. Tough all round.' He touched Theo's arm, coughed. 'Look, about this evening, I was hoping to persuade Maisie to come here afterwards. How do you rate my chances?' He steered Theo down the corridor as he talked. Theo kept pace, nodding, aware of Delia watching him, statue-still and white, as if she had allowed a spectre into her home.

Serena knocked on the barn door and waited, stamping her feet, which were cold, and watching her breath puff out like smoke, misting the wintry grey seascape of the sky and the remote dull ridge of the downs. She was on the point of knocking again when Cassie tapped on a window and shouted down that the door was open and she was to come on up. 'We're almost ready to go,' Serena called, scowling at the smell of stale smoke as she made her way up the little wooden staircase. It was remarkable that this sole unwelcome imprint of the otherwise wonderful Keith's brief occupation of the property should have lingered so long. 'That is to say, your mother is pacing the hall in her best hat, gloves, scarf and overcoat, Elizabeth has made herself a coffee, Roland is having an intense conversation with someone on his mobile and Ed has only just got back from his lunch shift and has rushed upstairs to change. We should go – driving in convoy always takes longer and we've no idea where we're going to park when we get there. I say, you haven't taken up smoking again, have you?'

'No,' Cassie called, emerging a moment later from the

bathroom, fully dressed but patting at her wet hair with a towel. 'Though I've been tempted, I can tell you.'

'I'm sure,' Serena murmured, inwardly reabsorbing, as she still did each time she saw her sister-in-law, the shock of the brutally cropped hair. It had grown considerably in the two weeks since her arrival, but still looked too short rather than chic, like regrowth after trauma. Which was exactly what it was, Serena reminded herself, pressing her cold hands against one of the barn's little radiators and inwardly lamenting her failure to understand that ending a relationship could be as hard as wading through a bad patch. She would never forget watching Frank help Cassie out of the car, the old-lady headscarf designed to hide the assault on her head, flapping in the wind, her face grey, her petite frame not just thinner but shorter, as if she had shrunk to a version of herself that lay three decades ahead.

'I was thinking a hat,' said Cassie now, slinging the towel round her neck so that there was no camouflage for the spiky tufts that still barely concealed her scalp.

'Yes, definitely,' Serena agreed, 'because it's bloody cold.'

'Because I look a sight,' Cassie corrected her, 'and I don't want to scare those members of the family who haven't yet seen me.' She smiled, drawing Serena's attention to the fact that her dimples had returned, along with a faint but discernible glow of good health. 'When Frank was down the other day he gave me this rather fetching red beret – I might wear that.'

'He's been amazing, hasn't he?'

'Totally,' Cassie murmured, shaking her head in wonderment at how things were slowly working out. She felt sad, bereft, *robbed*, ugly, but no longer alone. Frank had seen to that, leading her gently to the idea of calling more permanently on the hospitality of her dear brother and his kind wife, helping her put the Camden house on the market, even giving her the name of a friend who needed help in doing up a cottage on the south coast so that she had some focus for the long days of convalescence. 'I called a couple of estate agents this morning – apparently something's come up in Barham itself – that lovely stone cottage between the almshouses and the old rectory. I thought I might take a look – so long as you're okay with the idea.'

'Whyever wouldn't I be?' cried Serena, pushing herself off the radiator, alarmed that such a consideration should have crossed Cassie's mind. 'But there's no rush to move anywhere. The doors of Ashley House are always open to you – you know that. It was the deal from the start. I'm only sorry I haven't been better at demonstrating it.'

'Better?' Trying to stab some shape into her hair with her fingertips, in front of the mirror Keith had hung on the wall by the door, Cassie let out an incredulous laugh. 'But you've been amazing. We barge in all the time, all of us, like bloody homing pigeons. And I can tell you now that if Charlie had handed the reins back to Peter that would have changed overnight, even if Helen *had* still been around,' she added, waving her towel in protest as Serena tried to interrupt. 'I admit I'm cross with Peter at the moment, not just because he's behaved abominably but because he had everything anyone could want – *everything* . . .' Cassie bit her lip, then continued more steadily, 'The point is, Peter and Helen would never have been so welcoming – they're just not *like* that. They would have run Ashley House like some kind of modern battleship, all guns polished and at the ready, but this place needs more than that. It needs . . . oh, I don't know. Warmth and love and all those things that you and Charlie have always had in spades.'

'Stop, Cassie, please.' Serena gently relieved her of the towel and folded it across the back of a chair. It was impossible to enjoy such praises. The precipice – the knowledge that all the things to which Cassie was so generously and ignorantly referring had nearly been lost for good – was still too close. She also felt bad for having once resented the constant intrusion of the Harrisons and their dramas. Recent events had helped her see that not only she and Charlie but the big old house itself thrived at the centre of things. In being called upon to support the family they had somehow begun to find a way back to each other. It was because of that, she knew, that her husband had been able, properly, for the first time in five decades, to stand up to his brother. Being more certain of her had made him more certain of himself. The interconnection was endless and complicated; symbiosis on the grandest, most fundamental scale.

'You'll be needing this place soon anyway,' continued Cassie, now trying on the beret, which was the colour of redcurrants and sat prettily on the crown of her head, 'for whoever you get to replace Keith. Charlie told me you'd put an advert in the local paper.'

Serena made a face. 'But no one suitable has answered it and everything's so dead at this time of year it hardly matters. And there's Sid to consider – he still comes most days, you know, even when he's not being paid. Sometimes, seeing him sitting on that old tree-stump by the copse, puffing at one of his roll-ups, he reminds of me your father. John loved pottering around, didn't he, his head in a cloud of pipesmoke, just *being* in a way that the rest of us never seem to manage?'

Cassie pulled off the beret with a heavy sigh. 'That's so true and I miss him, but I can't help being glad he was spared the mess of the last few months. The disappointment he would have felt in Peter doesn't bear thinking about. Although,' she frowned, 'I can't help thinking that if Dad had been alive Peter wouldn't have done what he did. Losing a parent, at whatever age, changes things,' she continued thoughtfully. 'It removes a level of authority, a cornerstone. I've even wondered if Peter wasn't having some kind of delayed teenage rebellion. He was always so *good*. Maybe the pressure of it got too much.'

'And was your withdrawal from the wedding a rebellion too?' asked Serena, carefully, flexing her fingers, which were now pulsing and pink from the sharp heat of the radiator.

'God, no.' Cassie sank down on the oatmeal sofa that separated the kitchen area from the barn's spacious living room. 'It was waking up. Reality versus fantasy.' She sliced the air with her hands. 'Stephen wasn't what I thought . . . what I wanted. We both had dreams, but they didn't coincide.'

Serena hesitated, not wanting to press her too hard. 'Have you heard from him?'

Cassie shook her head glumly. 'I'm not sure I ever will. That time he came to the house, I'm pretty sure he took his passport, so I think – I rather hope – he's gone abroad.' She scowled, muttering, half to herself, 'Sometimes I think maybe it was kind of him to remove himself so completely, and that instead of being upset by having my existence denied I should be grateful. I mean, not many relationships manage quite such a clean break, do they?'

A silence followed, while both women thought but chose not to speak of the sad, ragged ending they were witnessing between Peter and Helen: under separate roofs, instructing lawyers, twenty-five years of communication reduced to discussions about logistics – parents' evenings, birthdays, viewing a nephew's artwork. Nothing would ever be the same again.

Serena was moving quietly round the room, examining the meagre selection of ornaments and pictures that Cassie had selected from the packing cases now stacked at one end of the garage.

'Did I tell you I've had a good offer on the house?' Cassie ventured at length. 'Frank has suggested I put aside some of the money in case Stephen returns one day for his share and the clean break turns out not to be so clean, after all.'

'Good. That sounds sensible.' Serena had come to a halt in front of a photograph taken at Roland's christening. He had been placed on his godmother's lap for the shot, a fat, placid, eight-month-old, his big eyes and pale round face like the heart of a flower amid the lacy froth of the ancient, yellowing Harrison christening gown. Cassie had him perched at a lopsided angle on one knee and was smiling a little anxiously at whoever was taking the picture. Serena reached out to touch the frame, thinking not of Cassie but of Ed, testing herself with the now imminent reality of the grandchild who would never be seen, or held at a christening, or patted for burps, sore gums or love.

She had sent the clothes. Of *course* she had sent the clothes, and the note, scurrying into the post office clutching them to her chest like an inept thief. Afterwards she had sat in a coffee shop, weighing up the crime – the betrayal of Charlie's precious, faltering trust in her mental strength – against the sharp joy of having allowed herself one small step in the direction her heart so longed to go. Longed to, but would not.

Serena released the frame. Another small test was over and she had passed. She felt fine about it. Charlie was right to trust her. She trusted herself. Buoyed up, secure again, she remarked breezily, 'It's as well you *didn't* get pregnant, you know, Cass. Just think how it would have complicated things.'

'Oh, yes! Yes, indeed!' cried Cassie, launching into a frenzied search for her coat, reminding herself that Serena had every right to say such things. They made perfect sense. She had encouraged everyone to believe her hair-hacking had been about Stephen, and had no intention of disillusioning them. Her sister-in-law was a bereaved mother, after all, she reminded herself – the real thing – not some spinster-imposter whose hopes had been dashed.

It was a relief, none the less, to hear footsteps on the path and Pamela calling urgently up the stairs, 'My dears, we *must* go.' A couple of minutes later she pushed open the door and tottered into the room in her smart, too-tight shoes. 'Even

Edward is ready now.' She turned somewhat sharply to Serena, the pheasant feather in her hat pointing like an accusing finger. 'I thought you'd come to *fetch* her, not *talk* to her.'

'It's my fault, Mum,' interjected Cassie. 'I've been trying to decide how to hide my horrid hair.'

'It *is* horrid, you foolish child,' agreed Pamela, 'but nothing that nature won't put right in a few weeks. I still don't know what you were thinking.' She spoke briskly, but gently. There was more, obviously, to the episode: a jilted bride might, conceivably, *shear* herself, but surely not one who had done the jilting, especially not one as pretty as her youngest. But Cassie clearly had no desire to talk about it and Pamela had never held any truck with the modern way of getting everyone to bare their souls. In her view each inner life was secret and sacrosanct, not something to be picked at like a plate of finger food. It wasn't something that warranted judgement either, not if you were eighty and had done your own share of sinning. For similar reasons she had kept well clear of Peter and his turmoil; and when Dr Lazard, during a recent check-up, had suggested, in his gentle, circumspect way, some counselling as a follow-up to the pills, she had said no, and perish the thought, and what were his plans for Christmas.

While the good doctor chuckled and answered the question, Pamela had quietly rejoiced in her new ability to keep worries about her offspring and all her own marauding demons at bay. The trick was to distance oneself, to be a little selfish. The dark spaces were there still, but contained, private. All difficult thoughts she now saved for her nightly conversations with John. Only her darling dead husband knew that, much as she was looking forward to Crayshott – seeing more of Marjorie, making new friends, playing a little bridge – when she had inspected the deceased colonel's rooms, the paint still fresh on the walls, she had been overwhelmed by the notion that it would be a good and peaceful place in which to die; easier than Ashley

House, where she would struggle against the pull of so many familiar objects, scents and memories, and the family, no doubt pegged round the bed like guy-ropes, willing her not to let go.

Roland fell back as the rest of the family trooped from the Shaw Gallery's impressive chandeliered foyer into the first room. His mother gave him a look but stayed close to Peter and Genevieve, who was dancing round their legs in what had been proudly described as new pink party shoes. Roland was grateful. Lately his mother had got a lot better at giving him space, reading his moods, instead of it always being the other way round. There had been no third degrees on the gay business either; in fact, it was like nothing had happened, which it hadn't, really, Roland mused. He was who he was. She was who she was. They annoyed the hell out of each other and loved each other, like any mum and son. When the long-awaited response from his father arrived – 'sorry I shan't be able to come over at Christmas after all . . . but this is clearly some kind of teenage phase . . . you are too young to have decided what you feel about anything . . . I am sure there are some good therapists who could help' – she had laughed and said how American and not to worry because Colin had spent a lifetime trying to mould people in ways that suited his nature rather than their own. When Roland screwed the letter into a ball, however, she had smoothed it out, saying that love could be expressed in many different ways and he wasn't to judge Colin too harshly either. His father only wanted what he thought was best, she had explained, stroking his back so calmly, so soothingly, that Roland had been flooded, briefly but intensely, with some of his old little-boy faith in the adult world.

Genevieve's shoes had pink satin bows on top and hard soles that clacked on the gallery's polished parquet floor. It was a good noise, Roland decided, the one natural thing amid all the awkwardness. Waiting in the street for Helen to arrive with the girls, fielding inane remarks about how he was feeling about the viewing – about the *weather* – he had been resentful of the dark cloud cast by the troubles between his aunt and uncle. It was his big day and he wanted it to burn brightly. Instead there were distractions and difficulties on all sides: Chloë, skulking with her phone, kissing her father but not looking at him, while Theo had shaken Peter's hand – as if his father were some stranger he was meeting for the first time – then stepped firmly to Helen's side where he had stayed ever since, steering her by the arm as if he were suitor rather than son. Muddling along in the middle of it all, like buffers protecting a dangerous space, were his mother, Charlie, Serena and his cousins, nudging each other and laughing in a way that was too jolly to ring true. His godmother, meanwhile, clearly trying to draw attention away from her weird new hair and equally weird red hat, had fussed over his grandmother, inquiring every few seconds if she was cold or tired or in need of anything. When Pamela had said – just after Helen and the girls had arrived and they were all filing inside – that she would like to visit the ladies', Cassie had looked delighted, as if the day had found its focus. 'You go on – we'll catch up,' she chirped, fluttering her fingers in a wave, then feeling for the cherry-red beret in just the way Roland had so often seen his grandmother feel for her bun, like it held the key to an ordered world.

Roland clasped his hands behind his back and stepped towards the first picture, a sketch of an old man on a train. Out of the corner of his eye he could see the family group moving to the far end of the room. He loved it that they were there. He loved, too, their glorious, loud, messed-up Technicolor – the awkwardness, even: it was like a work of art in itself. But he wanted to move through the gallery alone, to experience it like the ivory-skinned girl with the satchel handbag who had come to stand next to him. She was squinting at the picture, flexing her gingery brows, taking in each clever, loose sweep of the artist's pencil. Roland wanted to get as close as he possibly could to experiencing his own two pictures in the same way – to stumble across each one, to absorb that real first shock of a new visual image – see them as the girl with the satchel would see them; only then, he believed, would he truly know whether they were good or bad.

Clem had been upset that the great Nathan Chalmer wasn't there to greet them – tied up with some other commitment, the girl at the desk said, as she inspected their tickets and waved them through. But Roland didn't mind. It would have been yet another distraction – struggling to express gratitude, being tongue-tied, boiled alive in embarrassment. It mattered far more to him that the girl with the satchel bag was there, a businessman too, blowing on his cold hands, dabbing a handkerchief at whiskery nostrils. This first room led into the last, and through the doorway Roland could see several other people shuffling from picture to picture, clearly reluctant to make their exit back into the foyer. His work was in their heads now, he thought – subliminally if no more than that. He had penetrated their lives. One day money – sales – might matter more, but he hoped not. Remember this moment, he told himself, so sustaining, so electrifying. Never let it go.

He turned back to the sketch of the old man. He had seen it before, thanks to a search engine on one of the school computers. *Man on a train*, it was called. It looked a lot better off the screen. The man was very old, wizened and unsmiling, but the rheumy-eyed gaze fixed out of the train window was one of profound contentment. He was wearing a T-shirt and shorts, exposing gnarled hairy knees and thin calves. In one hand he held an open book and in the other a half-eaten apple that displayed the crooked imprint of his teeth. So much story in so few lines; studying them all, scrutinizing each tiny stroke, Roland's exultation faded. His stuff was rubbish in comparison. Rubbish. He stared about him, heart thumping, seeking escape.

The others were in the second room now. Clem was signalling to him, mouthing something, eyes popping with excitement. To his left his aunt and grandmother had emerged from the ladies' and were walking briskly across the foyer, their terrible hats bobbing in unison. Trapped, desperate, Roland backed out of view of both parties and scampered through the doorway into the final room.

Stage-fright, that was all it was. Entirely to be expected – hadn't Carl said as much when he rang to wish him luck that morning? 'They'll all be looking and you'll want to freak out.' He'd said he felt like that on the sports field sometimes, like he just wanted to charge back into the tunnel and put a towel over his head.

Breathing more evenly, wiping his damp palms on his trousers, Roland looked properly about him, half hopeful, half terrified that one of his measly pieces might fall into his line of sight. Several paintings bore coloured stickers, he noticed, to indicate that they had been sold. For thousands and thousands, no doubt, he mused, relaxing a little more and turning to study the wall nearest to him, which contained two small sketches of a dark-skinned girl undressing and a large painted nude of a woman – no, a girl – lying on a blur of blue satin, her breasts pushed up, her tummy button pierced with a gold loop, her legs open. There was something savagely erotic about the pose, but the face of the girl was fresh and innocent – wide, uncertain blue eyes, a full mouth, slightly open like she was about to ask a question, like she had no idea of the other message her body was sending. Interested, forgetting his terror, Roland moved closer, absorbing the richness of the colours, the contradictions, the fearless depiction of the girl's private parts. Would he ever be that good, that brave?

He would work his way in reverse order round the exhibition, Roland decided, take his time, meet the rest of them in the middle. There were only a few rooms, after all, so it wouldn't take long. Strolling towards the doorway, he turned for one last look at the nude; it was even better from a distance – better and *familiar* . . . the eyes, the long, sharp nose, the full mouth. Roland froze, then he out a laugh of astonishment as the brush-strokes merged into an image of his favourite cousin.

Thus absorbed, he failed to notice Clem herself – and Theo and Maisie and Ed – advancing on tiptoe across the room behind him, as if ten years had fallen away and they were all playing Grandmother's Footsteps on the lawn in front of the cloisters.

'Got you,' squealed Maisie, slinging an arm playfully across his chest.

'You're a star, and should be proud,' scolded Clem, 'not hiding. We've seen them both, they're –' She broke off, struck as they all were by the spellbound expression on Roland's face. 'What is it?'

Roland pointed, muttering, 'If I'm a star, Clemmy, what does that make you? It's brilliant by the way, totally brilliant.'

Theo said, 'Fuck,' and clapped his hand to his mouth, while Maisie, releasing her grip on Roland, let out a low groan.

'The bastard,' Clem whimpered. 'The total bastard. He promised – he – oh, Maisie, we've got to stop them – Mum and Dad, *Granny*! We've got to stop them.'

'Stop who doing what?' interjected Charlie, bounding up to the group with Genevieve on his shoulders, the little pink shoes flapping against his chest. 'Peter's buying one of your pictures, Roland, mate. How about that, eh?'

They were all arriving at the same spot now, Helen and Peter, still walking with military stiffness, several feet and several worlds apart, Chloë sauntering nearby, one ear plugged into her iPod, most of her face masked by her hair. Ed was leaning towards her, making teasing swipes at the other earpiece. Cassie and Pamela were, as ever, bringing up the rear, while Serena was deep in conversation with Elizabeth who, encouraged by a general state of over-excitement, had confided the news of Roland's certainty that he was gay.

Such preoccupations might have been sufficient to save the identity of *Girl On Blue* from those whose opinion Clem most feared, had the artist himself not chosen that moment to stride across the room in black jeans and jumper, arms outstretched towards the group in general and Clem in particular. 'Hey, Clementine – and a bunch of Harrisons, I presume.' He kissed Clem, then flung his arm in the direction of the picture. 'So you've seen it already. Isn't she beautiful? And quite the best sitter I ever had.'

Murmurings of polite assent were followed by a stunned silence as every pair of eyes travelled across the room. Someone coughed, feet shuffled. Roland, more embarrassed by the stupefied hush than by the picture – which was obviously spectacular – stepped forward to introduce himself, stammering gratitude and admiration, explaining that he hadn't seen either of his own paintings yet, but his uncle wanted to buy one and how much should he charge.

Nathan's craggy face lit up with delighted surprise. 'You're the man himself, then.' He shook first Roland's and then Elizabeth's hand as she, too, stepped forward, so shyly that for a horrible moment Roland thought she was going to curtsy. 'Let's take a look at your pieces together, shall we?' the painter boomed, adding, 'They're great, really great,' and offering a hasty nod of farewell to the rest of the family as he steered them both away.

'Shall we go with them, Mum?' suggested Cassie, brightly.

Pamela, whose feet were throbbing and whose eyesight was sufficiently poor for her to make out only a blue blur across the room, confessed that she would prefer a cup of tea. Passing closer to the picture *en route* to the café, she paused to study it, narrowing her eyes and tightening her grip on her handbag. 'Well, I don't think it looks in the least like Clem.

Except maybe the nose . . . The nose is very good, don't you think?'

'Marvellous,' muttered Cassie, wondering when, if ever, her mother would stop surprising her.

Behind them the gawping tableau was coming to life. 'Clem, it's you,' murmured Serena. She took a step closer to the picture, then stopped.

Clem buried her face in her sister's shoulder, wondering if it was possible to expire from embarrassment. Maisie was muttering what consolation she could but marring the effect with feeble attempts to suppress giggles. Chloë, too, was laughing, silently, falling against Theo, properly relaxed for the first time that day. Ed growled, 'Nice one, sis,' and then, with genuine curiosity, 'How much did you get paid for *that*?'

Charlie had breathed, 'Blimey,' then started shaking his head. Genevieve, thinking it was some new game, was trying to grab his ears. Helen, faintly disgusted by the portrait and in no mood for an ugly family scene, clapped her hands at her youngest and said it was time to go.

'I'll get her down,' offered Peter. He reached for Genevieve, who wriggled furiously, clamping her hands round her uncle's neck. Peter gripped her round the waist and pulled harder. He was pleased to have something to do, pleased, too, to be able to turn his back on the livid sexuality of his niece. The painting was obviously magnificent, but looking at it felt close to incest. Worse still, it seemed – like everything, these days – to be speaking directly to him, throwing oil on the already raging fire of his remorse. Carnality and innocence. Lust and love. It was all there. Virtue arose from how one chose between them, how one balanced and channelled them. He had known that once, but had lost the power – the will – to implement the knowledge. Had Clem slept with the man? he wondered. And if she had, what right had he to judge her for it?

Genevieve was in his arms now, sobbing quietly. He tried to

comfort her, wanting desperately to wring something good from another difficult day. He hadn't really wanted to own one of the paintings. Much as he admired his nephew, the whole venture – Clem for organizing it – Roland's style was too abstract for his own taste, colours without shape, in heavy dark frames; the picture would do little to alleviate the empty drabness of his new flat. He had made the offer because it had seemed the right – the most noble – thing to do and because he had nursed the dim, foolish hope that the gesture might raise a glimmer of pleasure, approval, in the grey, rigid face of his wife. Or even a flicker of mercy, Peter reflected, setting his squirming daughter on the ground with trembling arms, wanting only to collapse to the gallery's hard, shining floor and howl like a dog.

He had gone mad, that much was clear to him now. His brain had been infected by the virulent strain of infatuation to which the Greeks had given a name and about which poets liked to write. What didn't get such a high-profile mention was the ugly flip-side of the affliction: the loss of civility, the wounding of all that should be held dear, the warping of perspective, the shattering of self-belief and confidence, the heart-shredding regret. In the days and weeks since his shameful, begging showdown with his brother, Peter had felt like a man waking up to the pain of amputation without anaesthetic. Missing Delia was nothing – a mere ache – compared to this new state of suffering. He had no one; he had nowhere; he had nothing. The self-pity was throttling, but above all he missed more and more all the things he had thrown away – the company of his children, his home, his easy relationship with his brother . . . and Helen. Peter missed Helen so much he couldn't breathe sometimes: her intelligence and seriousness, her cool, clear head, her *command* over the grind of life, her *respect* for him . . .

Having issued hasty farewells to the still shell-shocked group, she was now walking with the girls towards the exit sign. Peter loped after them, reaching into his breast pocket for the list he had compiled, groggy with fatigue and unhappiness, at five o'clock that morning. It was an attempt to marshal all the things he wanted to say, all the garbled thoughts of another sleepless night, scrawled with none of his customary tidiness or articulation on the back of an envelope.

Sorry . . . Love is what you arrive at . . . I MISS you . . . need you . . . SORRY . . .

'Helen.' He was plucking things from his pocket – his cheque book, his pen.

She gave her watch a fierce glance. 'I've got to go.'

The pen fell from his fingers and bounced on the floor. Peter dropped to his knees to retrieve it, scrabbling round the sharp points of her shoes. 'I wanted to say –' He raised his face, seeking mercy still, clutching the cheque book and pen.

'I don't need money now, Peter,' she hissed. 'I'm making a list – income and outgoings, school fees, Theo's allowance – your lawyers will have it by next week.'

'No – I –' Peter clambered upright. The list was out of his pocket at last, sticking to his hot fingers.

'And we're agreed about Christmas, aren't we? You'll be at Ashley House and I'll send the children down on Boxing Day by train. Theo will look after them. He's going to Clem's now. In fact, I think they all are. Will you go too?'

'I don't know – I – Take this, please.' Peter pressed the crumpled envelope into her hand.

She took it without a word and rammed it into a side pocket of her handbag.

''Bye, darlings.' Peter kissed each of his daughters on the head, smelling, hungrily, the clean soft scent of their hair, the faint sweetness of their skin.

The others had moved closer to the picture now. Clem, still pink-faced, was laughing. Charlie had progressed from 'blimey' to 'bloody hell', while Serena was cocking her head in a brave effort to see art as opposed to her naked daughter. Theo was saying something about Clem being an actress after all. Ed chipped in with a quip about his sister's new job at the press office and what would she give him to keep quiet.

Peter watched it all with a hollow sense of banishment: as well as his wife, his family, he had lost his footing, his place, in the wider world. His glittering career seemed a cheap bauble compared to the riches he had thrown away. He wondered that he had ever prized it so much. And as for Ashley House, trying to wrest back the greatest gift he had ever made, what had he been thinking? Helen had been right – he should have tried to talk Charlie *out* of the scheme, not egged him on. Since the showdown his brother and sister-in-law had, typically, been warm and forgiving, insisting he still join them, with or without the children, for Christmas. But Peter, watching the animated group now clustered round the portrait of Clem, wasn't sure that he could stand to be there, bearing witness to all that had become irretrievable.

Keith liked having a desk, even though it was in a dingy room on the lower ground floor with two small windows so high and narrow that they reminded him of prison. At least people walked past them, shoes and ankles, dogs on leads, toddling children. Keith studied them all day, imagining the heads that went with the legs and the places they might be going.

The boredom was something else; staring at screens all day, watching for suspicious people and packages. The footage, running like some silent black and white movie, all looked suspect if you watched hard enough. No wonder he preferred the legs and the dogs, and the photograph of the boys – he looked at that a lot too. It sat facing him on his desk, a little window into the bit of the world that mattered, a daily reminder of what the drudgery was for. They had a good thing going now, the three of them, regular visits, football matches, mucking around in the park. At the cinema the previous Saturday Craig had held his hand, keeping his eyes fixed on the screen, like he didn't even know the whereabouts of his left arm, but Keith had known, all right – the little fingers gluey with popcorn, he'd wanted to squeeze the life out of them.

Keith had learnt not to look at the clock too much, especially not in the afternoons when time seemed to enter some slowed-down third dimension of its own. He wasn't supposed to smoke, but often did anyway, in the loos or perched near an open window, or to read anything but newspapers, so he had taken to doing crosswords and sudokus, saving them for the long haul after lunch. That day he had already filled in every grid on the coffee-break page and it was only four o'clock. Two sluggish hours remained till he knocked off; it was already so dark outside that the legs passing the window were a blur. The screens were lifeless too; the receptionist, the pot plant, the double doors, the lifts. It was enough to make anyone long for an armed robbery.

Then, suddenly, someone was on the screen, and not just someone either, but June, of all people, dolled up with her new platinum hair and a fur coat. Keith saw her stop and talk to the receptionist, and the next moment he could hear the clack of her heels on the stairs. He ran a hand through his straggly hair, straightened his desk, dropped the newspaper into the bin and reached for a pad of paper and a pen. By the time his ex-wife stuck her head round the door he was as poised and studious as an academic putting the finishing touches to a submission for the Nobel Prize.

'Hey, there, can I barge in?'

'June! This is a surprise.'

'Well, presumably you saw me on one of those,' she said, jerking a thumb at the three screens above his desk.

'Yes, but it's still a surprise, isn't it?' he snapped, not liking her point-scoring tone or that she had to see him cooped up in his miserable hole of a job.

'Nice uniform.'

'If you've come here to be rude you can fuck off right back up those stairs.'

'No, I meant it – you look good.' She wiped some invisible dust off a chair and sat down. 'Can I smoke in here?'

Keith shook his head, rather relishing her disappointment. 'What do you want, anyway?' He tipped his chair back, interlacing his hands behind his head and thinking, as he studied her heavily made-up face, that going up in the world didn't necessarily mean getting better-looking or more nicely behaved. 'It hope it's not about Saturday – I've got the tickets now and I can't do the following weekend because I'm moving out of Irene's . . . Hey!' He slammed the chair back to the ground and gripped the edge of the desk. 'The boys are all right, aren't they?'

'Yeah, they're fine.' June shifted in her seat, pulling her coat more tightly round her, as if the place was cold instead of overheated. 'Look, I won't muck you around, Keith. The fact is, I've got some news that you're not going to like. I don't like it much myself, to be honest. Are you sure I can't have a fag?'

He shook his head again and folded his arms, keeping his eyes fixed on her. 'What sort of *bad* news?'

'We're moving. Barry and I –'

He laughed. 'What – to some fancy penthouse on the wharf?'

'No, to Surrey.' She tapped a cigarette out of a packet and rolled it between her fingers.

'Surrey?'

'Look, I know this is hard on you – you've just got settled with this job and the kids love having you around, but Barry's got this new investment and he needs to be there, and I've just found out I'm expecting, and you know how sick I get, and I just want to be settled as soon as I can.' She put the cigarette into her mouth and took it out again. 'There's a house going up every minute down there, Barry says. He's got in on this really big project. He says it's his big break.'

'Barry's big break, is it? Well, good for Barry.'

'I knew you'd be like that.' She rammed the cigarette back into the packet and snapped her handbag shut.

'Well, how the fuck did you expect me to be?'

'You could be more positive for a start. It's not like we're leaving the country. You can see the kids whenever you want – Mum and Dad will want them too. I expect they'll spend half their holidays up here. Or . . .' she hesitated '. . . I suppose you could try your luck again down south.'

Keith was pressing his jaws together so hard that he could feel tiny vibrations shooting up and down his teeth. 'I will NOT –' he hit the desk as the word exploded out of him, like a gun going off '– spend the rest of my life following you and Barry around the fucking country like some rejected dog. I,' he sat up straighter, tugging down his horrible stiff blue shirt, speaking calmly again, 'am better than that.'

June was studying the nails on her right hand, raising her eyebrows as if she was seeing something extraordinary for the first time. 'I know we had a . . . bad time down there what with the – your – but that was London and a long time ago and . . . well, Surrey wouldn't be too far from that woman you were keen on, would it?'

Keith breathed in and out very quickly. 'What woman?'

'Irene told me . . . not that it's my business.'

'No, it's not your business.'

She stood up, smoothing down the glossy panels of her coat. 'About me expecting, you don't mind, do you?'

'Of course not. I'm pleased for you.' He smiled wearily.

'Keith, I don't want to move,' she wailed suddenly, slumping down in the chair. 'I love it up here, but I love Barry too, and he's not one to have his mind changed. In fact, I'm worried sick, if you must know, about starting somewhere new, getting the boys sorted into schools, having another kid. I'm so much older this time and I wasn't good, was I, at that early bit, all that crying and feeding – I got wrung out, didn't I?'

'You'll be fine.'

For a few moments neither of them spoke. June looked at the floor, poking the point of her shoe at a ball of fluff. 'You can have Craig and Neil to stay whenever you want. It'll be a help.'

'I could take you to court, you know,' Keith muttered. 'I could claim my rights, sue for custody.'

'Yeah,' she replied softly, 'but you won't, will you? Because you can't afford it and you'd lose, and you wouldn't want to put the kids through it. You've fucked up in many ways, Keith, but I know you love them.'

Keith walked home kicking at litter, blown from gutters and bins by strong winds, which had descended on the city like a sudden storm. He strode through the middle of it, his chin tucked into his jacket, feeling with each punch of cold air against his body as if his entire life was blowing off-course. To be whirled back down south, like a feather in a hurricane, spend another seven months looking for work, borrow money for a deposit on some poxy flat and without Irene to tide him over – he couldn't do it, he just couldn't. Soul-destroying though the security job was, it paid pretty well. The girl on Reception was nice too – that week she'd even found some pretext for giving him her phone number. The flat he was moving to was lovely – on the ground floor with a small back garden and a second bedroom, which had a bunk-bed and a bean-bag and plenty of wall space for football posters and its own basin on a pedestal in the corner. The boys had been especially excited about the basin, like it bestowed on the place the five-star status of a grand hotel. But even without that Keith was confident that his sons would want to come and stay, that the months of spending time together had paid off. Weekends, half-terms and holidays . . . He'd get his fair share. It wasn't ideal but, then, what was?

Keith aimed his toe at an empty can, sending it noisily into the gutter. Only a sad sheep of a man would choose the option of heading back down south; a man who couldn't forge his own way; a man who said one thing but meant another, who tried to close doors only to go knocking at them five minutes later, like some loser who'd changed his mind. Keith dug the can out of the gutter and kicked it again, harder, further away. His bloody sister! Bloody women, yakking to each other, running their own private grapevine as always.

Keith looked round for something else to kick, but the pavement was empty. He began to walk even faster, dimly seeking escape from the images now flooding his mind: his raised voice to Elizabeth in the pub all those weeks ago – *my history not yours* – and the unflinching gaze of those bottomless blue Harrison eyes, all sad and unafraid, like she knew the anger was about his own lack of courage more than the misery of letting her go.

Irene had made shepherd's pie for tea, with peas and carrots. She had set the table nicely with mats and two bottles of Coke, caps off and ready next to the ketchup. Since he had found the flat she had been a lot kinder, showing more care, like she could manage affection now that the end of the need to show it was in sight.

Having served the pie, Irene reached for a small pile of envelopes and dropped them on Keith's side-plate. 'There's a card from your pal Stephen – palm trees and that. He's landed on his feet.'

Keith glanced at the post, too glum still to be curious.

'You'll have to fill in one of those forms for the post office, tell them your new address.'

'Yeah, I guess.' Keith ate steadily. The pie was good, the mince soft and tasty.

'Aren't you going to read it?'

'I presume you have already.'

'I have not,' Irene cried, her voice flaring with triumph and indignation. After all she had eked out of him about the shenanigans of his old schoolfriend's private life it had taken considerable self-restraint to shuffle the postcard back into the pile. 'Go on, you pillock, look at the bloody thing, won't you? There was an interesting letter too,' she added slyly, 'hand-written, with a Sussex postcode.'

'Quite the Sherlock Holmes, aren't we?' said Keith, testily, setting down his cutlery and picking up the letters. He found the postcard first. The picture was, as his sister had remarked, of the archetypal beach – two palm trees on white sand that curled towards a turquoise sea. The writing was crammed and small, so smudged in places that it was hard to read.

> Keith, as I expect you've heard by now, the wedding's off. Sorry for not telling you myself – had a lot to sort out. Main feeling now is good riddance – those bloody Harrisons, how they love getting under people's skins. We're well out of it, believe me. Have everything here a man could wish for – sun, sand, sea, great sex – apart, that is, from a good mate. Am researching a new book and making arrangements to stay a while. Why not come and join me? If money's a problem, I'd be happy to help out. We'd have a laugh. Life isn't a dress rehearsal, is it? Give me a call (have put number at top). Best, Steve. PS Bring teabags, and the odd tin of baked beans wouldn't go amiss either.

'What does he say?'

Keith shrugged and handed the card to his sister. 'Wants me to go and stay with him – says he'll pay.'

'Bloody hell! You jammy thing – how fantastic! Let's see.'

523

Irene scanned the postcard greedily while Keith, with as much insouciance as he could manage, rummaged for the other letter, the one with the Sussex postmark. He had to look twice, as it was in a brown envelope, like everything else in the pile, and addressed in such small, tidy block capitals that at first glance it looked printed.

Watching him, Irene groaned. 'You drive me mad, do you know that? Open the bloody thing or I'll do it for you.'

'Go on, then.' He offered her the envelope.

'Don't be like that.' She made a face, uncertain whether he was teasing or cross. He had been so moody lately it was hard to tell.

'You obviously think my life is an open book, so go on, take it, read it, tell me what it says.' He thrust the envelope under her chin.

Ignoring the gesture, Irene dropped her cutlery and folded her arms. 'And what's that supposed to mean exactly?'

'Gossiping with June . . . I tell you, Irene, I don't need it.' Keith withdrew the envelope.

Irene rammed the lid back on to the ketchup bottle and stood up, venting her anger in the screech of her chair on the kitchen floor. 'Yeah, I talk to June a bit. So what? She's all right, is June. She put up with – with a lot, after all, didn't she?' She paused, pursing her lips as her brother flinched. The accident and its consequences were a no-go area and, in a balanced frame of mind, she respected that. Keith had paid his dues, after all – two years inside, losing everything, having to start from scratch. 'You and June might have gone your separate ways,' she continued steadily, 'but I still like her and, believe it or not, I still like you. All I want is for both of you to sort yourselves out and move on . . . to be *happy*,' she snarled, seizing her plate and dumping it with a clatter in the sink as she stomped out of the room.

Keith moaned softly to himself. The little brown letter had

a smear of tomato sauce on it now, like blood from a pricked finger. Wearily, he tore open the flap and peered inside. It wasn't a letter, just a newspaper cutting with messy, jagged edges and a ring of red felt-tip highlighting a couple of lines:

> Full-time gardener and handyman required for local country house with 15 acres. Accommodation provided. Non-smoker preferred. Excellent references essential.

Having thundered up the stairs, Irene was now thundering down them and along the hall. A moment later the front door slammed, making the pots and pans jangle on their hooks above the stove. Carefully Keith picked up the postcard and laid it next to the advert, which he had known at once was for Ashley House. Walking home he had felt bludgeoned and powerless. Now, with his head still full of June's news and these two items of post laid before him, Keith experienced the even more daunting sensation of a man standing at a crossroads, staring up at the dark arms of a signpost. He wasn't powerless: he had choices, which was good in a way, but also very bad, since each option was so different and so certain to cause him pain.

By early evening the strong winds teasing the north of the country had moved south, gathering sufficient force along the way for weather forecasters to issue warnings about motorists limiting their journeys and children being kept indoors. Lying on the sofa, her tender, bulging ankles propped on a cushion, her head throbbing with an intensity that made it hard to watch telly, let alone think straight, Jessica felt each squeak and rattle of the flat's ill-fitting windows like a drill in her temples. Maureen, snapping unconvincing sympathies between putting in her rollers and packing for a week's holiday with her new boyfriend, had instructed her daughter to take some tablets and get some sleep. In her weak state Jessica had readily complied, only to discover that this new supersonic headache was beyond the reach of Panadol and that closing her eyes made her feel sort of seasick, like the room was swaying because the wind had got the entire tower block in its clutches and was trying to prise it out of its concrete roots . . .

'Jess . . . I've been calling, are you deaf or what?'

'Sorry, I . . .' Jessica switched off the television and stared bleary-eyed at her mother, who was standing in the doorway to her bedroom holding up two flimsy dresses, one sequined and black, the other a shiny red.

'Well?'

'They . . . Are they new?'

Maureen rolled her eyes. 'Why do you think I'm showing them to you, dummy? Stan bought them for me, didn't he, to wear in the evenings and that . . . It's his own villa but he says we'll be out to dinner every night and he wants me to look . . .' Maureen broke off and shook the dresses at the sofa. 'I'm not having this, okay?'

'Not having what?' rasped Jessica, struggling to concentrate on whatever might be coming next.

'Stan's said it often enough and he's right.'

'Said what?' asked Jessica weakly, rubbing her knuckles into her temples, desperate to clear her head.

'That making me feel bad is your number-one speciality. My first decent bleeding holiday in years and you have to take to the sofa like Madam Muck, pressing the guilt button with your headache and sore legs and whatnot. Well, it's not going to stop me, okay? I'm going to walk out that door when the taxi comes and I'm going to have me a good time. You got yourself into this mess and there's nothing I can do now to get you out of it. You ruined my life once, girl, and I'm not going to let you do it again.'

Jessica opened her mouth, then closed it without a word.

'That's it, go on, do the silent thing, make me feel as bad as you possibly can.' When still Jessica did not reply, Maureen squeezed her eyes shut and blew out a long, wheezy breath towards the ceiling, as if her patience had reached its limits. 'It's only a week. The rent's paid, there's food in the fridge, and all you're doing these days is lounging around, isn't it? So it's not like me going will make a difference, will it?'

'No, it bloody won't,' Jessica blurted, glaring at her. 'I want you to have your sodding holiday with sodding Sidney –'

'His name, as you know bloody well, is Stan – *Stanley*.'

'Whatever.'

'Fuck me.' Maureen turned back towards her open suitcase. 'I don't know why I bother.'

Half an hour later she was tottering towards the front door in a new pair of spindly high heels, her hair a riot of white-blonde curls, her suitcase banging against the paintwork. As she opened the front door it caught on a gust of wind and flung itself back against the wall with such a thunderous crack that Jessica, momentarily forgetting her bulk and her discomfort, sprang forwards and peered with some concern down the hallway. 'You okay?' She could just see her mother in the outer passageway, her hair already a crazy tangle from the wind as she tried to reach over her suitcase to get the door closed.

'I'll live.'

'I'll do it.' Jessica heaved herself off the sofa and lumbered down the hall. She felt dizzy but rather liked the blasts of cold air on her face and in her hair. Reaching the front door, she grabbed the handle just in time to stop it swinging back against the wall again. 'Have a nice time, then.'

'I've got to go or the taxi will piss off. I'll send a postcard, okay?'

Jessica nodded, although she knew it wouldn't happen. Her mum hated writing anything, mostly because she was no good at it.

She peered over the balcony and watched until Maureen had emerged from the lift shaft and got herself and her baggage into the car waiting below. Then, unable to bear the thought of shutting herself back into the suffocating stuffiness of the flat, she grabbed her handbag and keys and set off down the passageway. She would treat herself to something in Blockbuster, she decided, then maybe stop by Mr Patel's for a sweet drink and something stronger to sort out her head.

By the time she stepped out of the lift Jessica was wishing she had thought to bring her coat. The stuffy hemmed-in feeling had gone and she was shivering with cold. The wind made walking even harder than usual. It played games the whole way, pushing her from behind one minute, then leaning into her face the next, like it was trying to bully her into turning back. She had gone a few yards down the street when her headache, which had stalled at a bearable point, suddenly shifted to a higher gear, so violently that Jessica, reeling against a lamp-post, half wondered if one of the estate's more delightful members had crept up behind her and sunk a fist into the back of her skull. Across the street an old man yanking at a dog lead looked at her, then glanced away. She tried to gesture at him, to explain that she was having difficulty standing, but could make no sound above the roaring of the wind in her ears. Her fingers were on the cold, gritty metal of the lamp-post but for some reason she couldn't get a proper grip. Her arms, her legs, were jerking, buckling, bringing her down. Then there was nothing but the hard cold solidity of the pavement and the warm darkness spilling like water inside her head.

'What weather!' exclaimed Serena, cheerfully, swivelling in her seat to check on Pamela, whose eyes were closed, and to see that Elizabeth and Cassie were still following safely in the car behind. Both Roland and Ed had elected to stay on at Clem's where, with Theo in exuberant form and the arrival of Jonny,

Flora and Daisy, there had been a party in the making. Maisie had made an early, sheepish exit to see her boyfriend, while Peter, in spite of much pleading, had left them all at the gallery, assuring Roland that he would claim his painting the moment the exhibition ended and promising to see them all at Christmas.

By the time the remaining group arrived at the flat, both Clem's complexion and the general atmosphere among the family had returned to normal. A mood of celebration had descended, aided greatly by champagne and Theo slipping his completed film into Flora and Daisy's DVD player. Teenagers and adults alike had clustered spellbound round the television throughout the showing, then burst into applause as the final strains of Jonny's soundtrack swelled round the last shot of the bedraggled but reunited lovers and the ensuing list of credits. With Theo, Clem and Jonny taking their bows, Roland beaming and Ed so thrilled for his sister and his cousin, the older members of the party had gawped and murmured admiringly. 'I love happy endings,' cried Serena, 'and it's such a clever story . . . Oh, Charlie, aren't the children so *clever*?' She seized her husband's hand, relishing both that he shared her wonderment and the sheer joy of finding that they could feel the same things again, at the same time and so effortlessly. And then, as if all that wasn't cause for jubilation enough, Clem had chosen the moment of their departure to produce a letter from a publisher, full of encouraging remarks about some writing she had submitted, saying if there was ever a completed manuscript they would like to see it.

'Manuscript? What manuscript?' Charlie had boomed. 'How dare you do something else so amazing and not tell us? And what on earth are you doing becoming a press officer when you're already such an accomplished actress and a *novelist*?'

'Because, Daddy darling, I'm not accomplished at anything yet, and I need to pay my bills,' Clem had replied demurely, poking his ample stomach with one finger as she reached up to give him a farewell kiss.

Serena, savouring it as they drove home, pondered what a mercurial and wily thing happiness was, how it could descend so quietly and in such an avalanche when one had spent months scratching for the tiniest evidence of it. Shadows remained, of course – lowering over them all in the form of the accidental grandchild, and the demise of Peter and Helen's marriage – they had been as stiff and ashen-faced that afternoon as statues – but for those precious minutes, with the strange dry storm beating at the car windows and Charlie's firm hands on the steering-wheel, Serena felt an acute sense of contentment and safety such as she had not experienced in a long while.

Even when they rounded the bend in the lane and the car's headlights fell upon the splintered remains of the old oak, its thick, gnarled torso lying across the lawn like a felled giant, it was the sense of being protected rather than threatened that struck Serena first. 'Oh, Charlie, the poor old tree. How lucky that no one was nearby to get hurt.'

'What a shame, but it will make good firewood, I suppose.' Charlie turned carefully past the debris of branches into the drive. 'We'll need professional help to get it cleared. Poor old Sid wouldn't know where to start.'

There was a whimper of dismay from the back seat.

'It's all right, Mum, it hasn't done any damage,' Charlie told her, his voice full of good cheer and confidence. 'The roof is still on the house, that's the main thing.'

'Yes, dear, of course.' Exhausted after her long day, too moved to say more, Pamela pressed a hand to her mouth and stared at the wreckage through the back window as Charlie eased the car into the garage.

'I'll phone the council first thing,' offered Serena, briskly, once they were inside, greeting Poppy and peeling off their coats. 'I think she's really upset,' she added, after Pamela had taken herself upstairs and she and Charlie were sitting at the kitchen table with mugs of soup and some hastily made ham sandwiches. 'She's always loved that tree.' She sighed, blowing a few ripples across the top of her soup. 'She hides it well, but she's still pretty fragile without John and likely to remain so. It makes me think that maybe this move to Crayshott is what she needs, after all – it really is the most beautiful place, her rooms are lovely and, of course, there are all those nursing staff . . . just in case.' She took a bite of sandwich, adding absently, 'In fact, I respect your mother enormously for forging on with the whole plan when we told her not to. That takes real courage, if you think about it. And it might be good for us, too, don't you think?' she added carefully, peeling off a piece of crust and crumbling it between her fingers. 'Charlie?' She raised her eyes timidly to her husband's. 'Just being you and me . . . will be good, won't it?'

Charlie put down his sandwich. He had been watching the beam of one of the ceiling lights move across his wife's face and hair, lighting up the threads of silver among the chestnut and the flecks of grey in her eyes. It was quite something, he mused, to have known the physical terrain of another creature for so long, to know it so well. The lines of ageing were sharp and clear under the blaze of the electric bulb, but so, too, were the traces of the youthful beauty that underlay it. And when those last traces were gone the memory of them would remain in his perception of her, as vivid as reality, impossible to erase.

He picked up her hand and held the palm to his cheek. 'You are incredible,' he said quietly. 'Did you know that?'

'No, I'm not,' Serena replied, her voice surprised and shy.

'Yes, you are.' Charlie moved aside the plates and mugs of soup and picked up her other hand. It was a little cooler than the first. There was a faint white scar across one of the knuckles, an ancient memento of some domestic accident, a kitchen burn, or the slip of a knife. He couldn't remember and it didn't matter. They were full of scars, most of which were invisible. He kissed it. 'If the floor wasn't so hard I'd get down on my knees.'

'Silly.' She laughed softly. 'Whatever for?'

'To make a speech.'

'Silly,' she said again. 'You made a speech at Clem's, telling Roland he was a star. It was lovely.'

'But there are things I want to tell you. I want, for example, to say, from the bottom of my heart, how truly sorry I am for all that I've put you through, all the doubt – all the . . . Hey –' he broke off, frowning. 'Is that your phone?'

'It doesn't matter.' Serena tried to keep her hands on his face, caring for nothing now but his soothing voice and the closeness, which, after weeks of slow flowering, had blossomed that afternoon into something on which she felt that she might again be able to rely. But Charlie was already plucking the offending item out of her handbag, which lay on the table next to them, and joking that his speech would be all the better for the accompaniment of a little wine. 'I might nick something good off one of Peter's racks.' He chuckled, and added, as he headed for the cellar, 'If it's Ed tell him, no, I haven't forgotten his driving test is tomorrow afternoon and, yes, I will pick him up from the station.'

But it wasn't Ed, it was a doctor from St George's Hospital in Tooting, saying that one Jessica Blake had been admitted by ambulance suffering from severe eclampsia, that she had consented to a general anaesthetic for an emergency Caesarean section and presented this phone number as belonging to the only person whom she wished to be informed of the situation. It was only fair to emphasize, the doctor continued, that the condition of both mother and baby was of the gravest possible nature.

Serena could hear Charlie whistling as he came back up the cellar steps. It was clear to her that she had to get back into the car and drive to London, to St George's, Tooting. It was a hospital she knew well since it was where she had had checkups, then given birth to Tina – an almost comically easy process, two hours from start to finish with a pain that she had ridden like an expert surfer, too close to exultation to mind the suffering; the sort of labour one didn't mention much to other women for fear of appearing smug.

It was also clear to Serena that Charlie would not understand, that all his beautiful gentleness would turn to despair, soured by new justification for the very mistrust they had fought so hard to leave behind.

'I'll confess my crime to my dear brother at Christmas,' announced Charlie, grinning broadly as he entered the kitchen, a dusty bottle cradled in both hands. At the sight of Serena, already in her coat, her handbag over her shoulder, he stopped in astonishment. 'What the . . .'

'Charlie.' Serena gripped the strap of her handbag. 'It's my turn for a speech. I'm going to say something and I want you to promise to forgive me before I say it.'

Charlie laughed uncertainly. 'I'm not sure I can do that. You might be about to announce a long-held secret love for Sid or the milkman.' He stepped towards her. 'I say.' He laughed again, with even less conviction. 'Darling, you're not leaving me, are you?'

'Never.' Serena's lips sealed the word, making it hard for a moment to say anything else. 'It wasn't Ed on the phone, Charlie, it was Jessica – or, rather, a doctor.'

'*Jessica?* Since when did Jessica have your mobile number?'

Serena could hear the dismay curdling his voice. He had dropped the wine bottle on to the table with a thump, heedless of its delicate contents. 'Since I gave it to her,' she said quietly. 'I sent her some baby clothes and gave her my number. I told her to call if ever she needed help.'

Charlie scratched his head in a mockery of perplexity. 'Let me guess . . . she needs a little *money*, does she?'

'No, Charlie, she's dangerously ill.'

Charlie groaned and rolled his eyes. 'Of *course* she is.'

'No, Charlie, she really is. That was a doctor who called –'

'And where, pray, if Jessica is so *ill*, is her own mother – the lovely Maureen? Shouldn't she be the one on call in such an emergency?'

'I don't know,' Serena admitted. 'But this doctor said Jessica's got eclampsia – she has dangerously high blood pressure and has had some sort of fit – and they're about to operate to try to get the baby out before it's too late, and when they asked who she wanted them to call she said me.'

Unmoved, Charlie shook his head. 'Has it never occurred to you, Serena dearest, that this odious child planned the whole thing from the start? That is,' he continued, in response to Serena's evident bafflement, 'that after years of hovering in the shadows of Ashley House, like a kid with her nose pressed against a sweet-shop window, Jessica deliberately set out to *entrap* Ed, hoping, somehow, to worm her way into our family. I mean, at one point she was even implying Peter had tried something on with her, wasn't she? Or have you conveniently forgotten that particularly preposterous detail?'

'I haven't forgotten anything,' replied Serena, coldly, glancing at her watch, and adding, as her desperation mounted, 'although, given the way Peter has behaved, maybe it wasn't quite so preposterous.'

'*What?*' Charlie slapped his palm against his forehead. 'Jesus Christ, now I've heard it all, I really have.'

'I'm sorry,' Serena muttered. 'I shouldn't have said that and I didn't mean it. I wasn't thinking.'

'Hah,' interjected Charlie. 'Now, there I agree with you.'

'But I have *got* to go,' she wailed, edging towards the hall. 'You said it yourself, Jessica's a *child*. Of course she didn't plan the whole thing. She's got herself into a terrible mess and needs help to get out of it, and if my compulsion to offer that help is connected to my – our – loss, then so be it. *So be it.*'

'So be it indeed,' said Charlie, softly. They stood staring at each other from opposite sides of the kitchen, all the closeness of the day like a lost dream.

'I'll take the Volvo. I'll be back as soon as I can. I . . . What are you doing?' Charlie had seized the kitchen pad off the hook next to the kettle and was scrawling something across it with a felt-tip pen.

'I'm writing a note to my mother in case she wakes up before we get back and wonders where we are . . . *if* that's all right with you.'

'We? But, Charlie, I'll go alone – it's okay.'

'In this weather? Don't be ridiculous.' He tore off the message and propped it against the kettle, impatiently shoving the tea-jar against the paper when it slipped out of position. Then he pushed past her out of the kitchen, snatching the car keys from her hands and taking such long, aggressive strides down the hall that even Poppy – usually so delightfully oblivious to all nuances of human mood – shrank against the wall.

By the time the Volvo crept back along the pot-holed lane, many more branches had been torn from their moorings, converting the already uneven ground into an almost unnavigable sea of wood. Charlie began slowly, then speeded up, driving at logs and twigs alike as if ploughing an ice-breaker through a frozen waste. Serena, white-faced and rigid beside him, gripped the dashboard and fixed her thoughts on the scalpel slicing a window into Jessica's womb, willing it to be fast and successful. Charlie, she feared, had darker thoughts about what might constitute the best outcome. He hadn't expressed them, but she had *felt* him think them and it sickened her.

In Hull, Keith scowled as he tried to concentrate over the thunder of the rain now drumming on the flat roof of Irene's kitchen. There were only a few lines on the page; still such a long way to go. His hand ached from gripping the pen, forcing it to form words that he would never have the courage to say out loud.

The little party in Camberwell was enjoying a third, riotous viewing of Theo's digitally filmed masterpiece, yelling the lines before the characters and singing along with even the most poignant sections of Jonny's soundtrack. Lost to such noisy merriment, they paid no heed to the inconvenience of a howling wind until the entire street was pitched into darkness by a power-cut. Even then, carefree and young as they were, they responded to it as an adventure rather than a catastrophe. Amid much squealing and thumping, an assortment of candle stumps was eventually assembled and lit; Theo, with shy, wary glances at his relatives, then delved into his rucksack and produced two fat, battered joints that Julian had given him. Jonny let out a squawk of delight and groped his way into Clem's bedroom to fetch his guitar. Soon they were sprawled round the furniture, smoking and singing softly, Clem leading the way on harmonies while the boys beat out the rhythm on their thighs, all aware of a spreading, pleasurable cohesion that reached far beyond the usual barriers of being cousins or siblings, lovers or friends.

Ed, surveying the flickering light cast by the candles and the pale, serene faces humming tunes, misty in the layers of floating smoke, decided it was almost like being in church – a nice church, where there was no pressure to believe, just a mystical sense of unity that took you out of yourself to the sense of something better. He remembered in the same instant, and with rather less peace of mind, the desperate prayer he had made seven months before in the thick of his nightmare with Jessica. *Get me out of this and I'll believe in you until the day I die.* He wasn't out of anything and yet . . . he was *through* it somehow, he thought, with a future he couldn't wait to embrace and a restored belief in himself and his family. Had that been God's doing or his own? He sucked in a fresh lungful of the pungent smoke as he pondered the question, blowing it out in neat rings that held their shape for several seconds before wavering and thinning into small, smeary clouds. He had always imagined that divine intervention would prove its existence in some irrefutable clear-cut fashion, more like the proverbial bolt from the heavens – a striking, instant solution. But it occurred to him now that maybe everyday miracles weren't like that, but evolved slowly out of a combination of effort and circumstance and . . . love? Ed's cynical eighteen-year-old self resisted the word even as it formed in his mind. He loved himself, and his family, and his life, all right. But as for the bigger stuff – love with a capital L, belief with a capital B – even after the way things had turned out, with his prayer sort of answered, it felt like a too big, too impossible leap to make. And anyway, he reminded himself, reaching out to pat the back of Roland, who had inhaled too deeply and was choking, his aunt Helen was the only really churchy one of the family and it hadn't done her a lot of good.

On the other side of London, huddled on the furthest edge of Julian's bed after the first serious row of their four-month acquaintance, Maisie, too, was pondering weightier issues than the pummelling of wind and rain against the windowpanes. Transplanting a holiday romance to the chillier, more obstacled environs of everyday life was proving harder than she could have imagined. Jealous of her new friends at Bristol, of her partying with her family – of any air she breathed in his absence, in fact – her boyfriend appeared to have transmogrified from a desirable, interesting fellow creature into something whining, selfish and altogether repellent. Lying in the dark, listening to the unhappy sighs next to her, recognizing in them a plea for reassurance, which she had no inclination to give, Maisie wished with all her heart that she had stayed on at her sister's flat for the party with her cousins and friends. The more she tried to sleep, the harder the wish burned until, surrendering to the directness for which she had always been famed, she burst out, 'I'm sorry, Julian, I just don't love you any more,' and reached for her shoes.

Back in Sussex, Cassie had accepted the offer of Roland's bed for the night and was curled in one corner of her elder sister's cosy sofa, clutching a mug of tea. Elizabeth lay at full stretch on the floor next to her, laid low not by over-indulgence in the day's many causes for celebration but by the sound of Keith's voice on her answering-machine. '"Thank you for the cutting. I need to see you,"' she groaned, repeating the message for the umpteenth time. 'I mean, what *is* that? Has he gone mad? So he wants to see me, after all this time, after insisting that we *couldn't* see each other, and of course I should stop him but I don't want to so I can't and I don't know what to do.'

Cassie smiled a little wanly. She was pleased for her sister – pleased and afraid: Elizabeth's history in matters of the heart read like a bad novel – but also a little tired of hearing the phone message repeated and, beneath all that, if she was honest, just the tiniest bit jealous. Forty-odd years of being prettier, more confident and conventionally more successful than her hapless elder sibling had not prepared her for this new sensation of being the more misfortunate. In addition to which, witnessing the true extent of Elizabeth's fervour for Keith, the obsessive agonizing, the writhing on the carpet, the moans of desire and despair, it occurred to Cassie that she herself probably wasn't capable of loving anyone so much. The closest she had come was with Dan Lambert, the doctor; the *married* doctor, who had ultimately chosen his family over her. Before him boyfriends had been things to fit into a busy schedule. After him there had only been Stephen, wooing her with the obstinacy she had eventually found so endearing, until she, too, began to believe . . . in something that didn't exist, Cassie reminded herself bitterly, setting down her mug and asking her sister whether she minded awfully if they went to bed.

'And, anyway,' she couldn't resist adding, after Elizabeth had given her a clean towel and a glass of water, and was leading the way up the cottage's creaking little staircase, 'I don't see *why* it's all such a problem between you and Keith. It's perfectly clear that you're in love with him.'

'Is it?' Elizabeth spun round, spilling a few drops of water from her glass across her jumper.

'Can't stop talking about him, can't stop thinking about him, saying what you ought to do when it's perfectly clear it makes no difference . . . Sounds like a bad case of love to me.'

'Oh, it is, it is,' Elizabeth gushed. 'When we're together it's just so . . . *easy*, so natural, like no one else . . .'

'So what's the problem?' repeated Cassie.

All the openness in Elizabeth's face vanished. Like the slamming of a book, Cassie mused, watching the performance and the laboured way with which her sister turned to continue her journey up the stairs. 'So he has family ties up north. It doesn't sound like a big deal to me.'

'I can't explain,' said Elizabeth, in a muffled voice, then checked that the bathroom was more or less clean, muttered goodnight and closed her bedroom door. She couldn't explain, not to Cassie, not to anyone. She had played her last card during the ill-fated excursion to Hull, when she had repeated to Keith that what he had done made no difference to her and offered to tell her family herself about the little Pakistani girl. She missed him too much, she had explained, to let anything about his past stand in their way. With Roland a sixth-former, she would have more time for trips up north, she had continued, more time to get to know his sons. The memory of his explosive response still made her shudder. *His history not hers.* The words were etched on Elizabeth's heart, along with recognition of Keith's right to utter them. The killing of the little girl, the two years in jail, were indeed his story – to forgive himself for or torture himself with as he chose. She was an outsider, one who had reached the limits of her capacity to beg or offer help.

Lying in the dark, the duvet tucked round her neck and her arms crossed under her head, Elizabeth tried to shift her thoughts to all that had happened before the phone message – the fun of the family gathering, the thrill of seeing Roland's pictures, the extraordinary and, in retrospect, hilarious business of the portrait of Clem – but her mind kept returning to the terse, enigmatic sentence on her answering-machine. What *cutting* and why should it make Keith want to see her? It was like a cryptic crossword clue and she'd never been any good at those.

She turned on her side to try to sleep. Love indeed, she scoffed, remembering Cassie's words. A fifty-four-year-old divorcee with dried-out hair, a saggy body, veins round her nose and useless Italian had no business even contemplating such a thing. But it was no good. The sound of Keith's voice on the answering-machine had opened up all the old feelings and the bubble of hope, now swelling round Elizabeth's heart and making it hard to breathe, refused to deflate. She slept at last, but fitfully, her eyes flicking open each time one of the branches outside brushed against her window, half hoping to find Keith clambering into the bedroom, laughing and wet, clutching some fairytale resolution to her desires.

Charlie tried to drop her off at the main entrance, muttering about finding somewhere to park. Serena almost agreed. The sight of the familiar concrete bulk of the hospital was a shock, far worse than she had expected. She could remember, as if it were yesterday, walking out of the same large doors cradling

Tina, wrapped like a little human pupa in a new yellow baby blanket, her small pixie face turned into her mother's swollen breasts, nuzzling for warmth and milk. She could remember the singing of her heart, the lovely confidence of how they would enjoy this fourth, unplanned, child. She could remember Charlie skipping along next to them, one arm across her back, the other holding an umbrella over their heads, shielding his wife and newborn from the September drizzle as if it were a monsoon. There was no question of an umbrella now: the wind was too strong, whipping the rain in so many directions that there was no hope of protection on any side.

'I will not get out,' she said. 'There are loads of spaces. We'll park the car and walk together.'

'Suit yourself.' Charlie reversed with unnecessary speed, swinging the Volvo back and round so violently that Serena rocked between the door and the gear-stick.

Inside the hospital he hung back, forcing her to walk ahead, to be the one to check the signs for directions, to press the right lift button and the intercom guarding the maternity unit. Then, when they were through to the staff base, he left all the questions and explanations to her, wandering past the photographs of the medical personnel lining the walls, his arms pinned behind his back, peering at the images as if they were back at the exhibition and he was assessing the merits of one of Nathan Chalmer's paintings.

The sister-in-charge had an inky black bun, skin the colour of burnished toffee and a pink dot in the middle of her forehead. Serena watched the dot move as the woman explained calmly and kindly that Jessica was out of theatre, that before the operation she had been given magnesium to stop the fits she had been experiencing and something else to lower her blood pressure. Although she was still groggy, she appeared to be doing well.

'And the baby?' It was more an exhalation of breath than a

sentence. Next to her Serena was aware of Charlie, now nose-deep in one of the many cards of gratitude pinned to a corkboard next to the desk. As she released the words he stiffened and clenched his hands.

'A little girl.' The midwife smiled, with an effort. 'She's small, just over a kilo, but from what we can work out she's five or six weeks premature so that's not surprising. She has what we call respiratory-distress syndrome. We have her in NICU –'

'What's that?' Serena swallowed.

'Our neonatal intensive care unit – she really couldn't be in better hands.' The midwife smiled more broadly, revealing over-crowded white teeth. 'Now, I expect you would like to see Mum. She said you were the grandparents. Congratulations.' She directed the word towards Charlie, who had shuffled over to the desk at last, with his head bowed as if ready to receive a blow rather than good news. 'It's very early days but there's no reason why she shouldn't make it. Such a fighter – you should have heard her screams when she came out.'

'Jessica's mother, Mrs Blake, is she here too?' Charlie raised his head to deliver the question, then cast an anxious glance over his shoulder as if the last thing he wanted was Maureen to appear round the corner.

The midwife shook her head. 'She's on holiday in Spain, apparently. Talk about bad timing . . .'

'Indeed.' Charlie grimaced. 'I might leave you to it,' he murmured to Serena, 'find myself a cup of tea.'

'You will not,' she whispered fiercely. 'I can't do this alone. I just can't.'

'We shouldn't be doing it at all,' he hissed back, composing his features as the midwife, having led them down the corridor, opened a door to what she called the recovery room and stepped back for them to go inside.

Jessica was lying on her back with her eyes closed. Propped next to her on a bedside table was a photograph of a tiny frog-like baby, its scrawny face only just visible beneath a peculiar miniature sock of a white hat.

'Ugly rat, isn't it?'

'Oh, no, Jessica, no, she isn't ugly at all, just very, very small,' said Serena, stopping short of the bed. She felt badly that an embrace was called for but, with the tubes of two drips in the way and the expression of flat hostility on Jessica's face, had no idea how to manage it.

'Sorry to drag you up here.'

'No need – it's fine, isn't it, Charlie?' Serena shot a frantic look across the bed to where Charlie was standing, much like a soldier in a sentry-box, straight-backed, his face set and inscrutable.

'Thought I was dying.'

'It must have been awful for you – I remember being warned about pre-eclampsia during my pregnancies. It's desperately serious – you poor thing. How are you feeling now?'

'Like shite.'

'Such a shame your mother's away.'

Jessica made a snorting sound and shifted position, flinching visibly. 'All of you were right, for what it's worth,' she muttered next. 'I should have got rid of it.'

'Now, that's silly –'

'Not you,' Jessica shot back, 'I always knew you weren't keen on an *abortion*.' She scowled at Charlie, then returned her attention to Serena. 'You should have been, though. So should I. A fucking baby – almost killed me, didn't it?'

'I know you feel like this now,' began Serena, softly, shuffling nearer to the bed. 'It's hardly surprising when you've been through so much.' She touched Jessica's forearm above where one of the drips had been taped into the veins on her wrist. 'You'll feel differently soon, when you get to know her.'

Jessica made a clicking sound and turned her head to the wall. 'You sound like one of the bleeding nurses.'

'She's your child. You'll love her – you'll see. Millions of women would give anything to be in your shoes.'

Jessica snorted. 'Oh, yeah, and who are they?'

Serena struggled for a moment. 'Cassie – Ed's aunt – for a start. She's wanted a baby for years.'

'Well, this one might not live, anyway, so what's the point?' Jessica sneered. 'Be easier all round, if you think about it. Not like her dad wants anything to do with her, is it?'

Serena wrung her hands and stole another glance at Charlie, who had drawn in his cheeks as if attempting to prevent some involuntary act of self-combustion. The truth, put like that, was so stark, so incontrovertible. She could think of no comfort for it. It remained perfectly clear to her that Ed had had every right to choose as he had. The road Jessica had taken, which had brought her to this pitiful state, was entirely of her own making. 'Are we allowed to see the . . . Does she have a name yet?' she inquired gently.

Jessica made a face, almost as if she was embarrassed to concede that she had given the matter any thought. 'I was thinking Gemma . . . I've always kind of liked it.'

'Gemma. That's a sweet name, isn't it, Charlie?'

'And as for seeing her, you'll have to ask one of the nurses, I suppose,' Jessica continued sulkily. 'They, like, *rule* this place. When I'm a bit better they say they want me to get some milk out – with a bloody *pump*. I said no bloody way – I'm not a cow, am I?'

'No,' interjected Charlie, his voice tight and dark, 'you're a mother, whose baby needs –'

'Don't you start.' Jessica rolled on to her side, half hiding her face in the pillow. 'They *also* said,' she went on fiercely, 'that bottles are fine, that it's up to me, so you can just fuck off with all that breast is best crap. It's up to *me*, okay?' She punched her hand against her chest and buried her face more deeply in the pillow. Charlie, exasperated almost to breaking-point, moved towards the door, nodding at Serena to follow.

'Try not to worry, Jessica.' Serena touched the girl's shoulder, which was trembling. 'They said you need to stay in here for a few days yet,' she soothed, 'and then your mother will be back. Everything will work out fine, you'll see.' The shoulder continued to tremble but Jessica kept her face buried. 'I'll get one of the nurses,' Serena murmured, then turned to follow Charlie out of the room.

'We're leaving,' he said, the moment they were in the corridor. 'We're leaving now.'

'Not before we've seen the baby.'

'You're getting sucked in, I can feel it – I knew you would.'

'I'm not getting sucked in. I want to see the baby. She might die, Charlie. She's Ed's daughter and she might die.'

'Stop it,' he rasped. 'Stop it this instant.'

'We will ask to see the baby and then we will go. I promise. I just want to see her.'

Charlie dropped his face into his hands. 'How can you? This hospital – how can you?'

'How can I what?'

'Be so fucking calm.' He groaned.

Serena was so amazed that she almost laughed. She tried to reach for his arm but he stumbled away from her against the corridor wall, knocking into a large print of Monet's water-lilies. They both watched, too shocked at their own conversation to move, as the picture swung violently from side to side before steadying.

'I don't want to be here,' he gasped. 'This hospital – any hospital. Babies – I can't do it, I tell you, I fucking can't do it. I wasn't – I'm not – *prepared*. I need to get some air!' Catching sight of the pretty Indian midwife gliding down the corridor towards them, he made a monumental effort to compose himself, swiping his damp cheeks and clearing his throat.

'You can see the baby now,' she announced, 'just a peek, and you'll need to scrub up. If you'd like to come with me?' She set off at a brisk walk towards the lifts.

Dazed, not knowing what else to do, Charlie and Serena followed. 'Darling, I'm so sorry. I had no idea,' Serena murmured. 'I thought you were still just angry with me. Look, don't come . . . You don't have to come.'

Charlie had his head down and was placing his feet carefully between the swirls on the carpet. 'I was angry – I *am* angry. I still think we have no business being here, but then, arriving here, it all came back to me – Christ, just the smell of the place . . .' He choked on the words. 'It was like I was living it all again . . . like losing her again . . .'

Serena squeezed his hand. 'I felt it too. But then I reminded myself that this was the hospital where Tina was born, not where she died. And it was a lovely birth – do you remember? She came out like a little slippery fish, so sweet and easy, no fuss. Nothing will ever take the joy of that away. If anything, coming here tonight has made me see it more clearly. She was ours and we couldn't have loved her more. All this is so utterly different, so much harder and uglier. I feel for this child – for Jessica. I desperately want her and the baby to be okay, of course I do. The baby is our flesh and blood, whether we get to know her or not, so of course I want the best for her. I'm going to tell the nurses I'm worried about Jessica's state of mind – make sure she gets help. But that's all, the full extent of the *getting sucked in*. Okay?' Serena squeezed his hand more tightly. 'Can you manage that, Charlie?'

He nodded, and a few minutes later they had washed their hands in soap, then alcohol and were being led, in comical plastic aprons and gloves, into a room full of humming machines and screens, each connected to what looked at first glance like see-through plastic boxes.

'Here she is.' One of the neonatal nurses indicated the nearest box. Serena had to look twice to register that what lay in the middle, beneath the transparent lid, was a baby. She looked scrawnier even than she had in the little photograph, more like a premature puppy than a baby girl. Tubes protruded from every possible part of her body – nose, mouth, arms, legs. Even the too-big hat – twice the size of her head – was keeping a tube in place. Round each of her miniature ankles and wrists was an ID tag saying 'Blake', followed by a series of numbers and her date of birth. Serena had been coping well until she saw the tags.

'We should tell them she has a name,' she whispered, biting her lip, groping for Charlie's hand.

Charlie couldn't speak. The machines were thrumming in his ears, full of quiet beeps and buzzes, like mesmerizing music. Through the maze of wires and tubes he watched the fierce, fast rise and fall of the tiny chest. The beat of life. He couldn't stop watching, couldn't stop willing it to go on. Such a small being, such a mighty fight. There were no words for it, only the humbling recognition that all the issues which for months had seemed so huge – money, paternal responsibility, even the ache for their darling Tina – had to give way for the infinitely more important battle going on in the cot in front of them.

'I didn't know they made nappies that small,' he gasped. 'Her hands and feet, they're like . . .'

'Little flowers,' murmured Serena, 'little bunched-up flowers. I wish we could touch.'

'Christ, I don't – I'd be too scared I'd drop or squash her, poor little mite.'

'Mum will get to touch her soon,' remarked the nurse. 'She's not quite as fragile as she looks and a little cuddle does wonders.'

Twenty minutes later, when they were back in the car, Charlie said, 'I'm glad we came. Thank you for making me.' He turned on the ignition but made no move to start driving. 'They said they'd call, didn't they, if there was any . . . change?'

'Yes.'

He put the car into gear, then shifted it back to neutral and reached for Serena. They hugged awkwardly across the gearstick and handbrake, but with an intensity that required no words. It was an embrace as threaded with pain as it was with love. Stroking his cheek afterwards, as he drove, Serena wondered that she could ever have been naïve enough to imagine the two emotions as separate. Death and love could not be separated either, she thought; a sense of loss was what death left behind, what gave life its treasure trove of meaning.

That night she dreamt of Tina, not fleetingly, or with pain, but vividly with a sense of endless joy. It was precisely the sort of dream she had longed to have in the months after her daughter's death, when she had ransacked every memory for images of what she had lost, feeding off them like a beast sucking at a shrinking water-hole, not slaking her thirst so much as stoking it. And here, suddenly, when she had stopped waiting for it, stopped looking for it, was her darling child, in her green dungarees and corduroy slip-on booties, one half off as usual, tottering towards her, her dimpled arms outstretched, her baby teeth paraded proudly in her smile. Lost as she was in the depths of her subconscious, Serena had tensed, preparing for the disappointment, the non-arrival that was the hallmark of any dream of longing. But instead Tina arrived in her arms, warm, moving and loving, wanting to touch and be touched, the smell of her baby skin as fresh and satiating as oxygen. Heady with the pleasure of it, Serena groaned in her sleep, moving closer to Charlie, who nuzzled and kissed her head. And when Tina left her arms, she was ready for it, as relaxed as any mother releasing a child in the certain knowledge that he or she would return, that they were not lost but merely out of sight, ready always to be held again.

She woke early, suffused with elation and a sense of blessing so strong that when a call to St George's revealed that both

Jessica and Gemma were going from strength to strength she was somehow unsurprised. It seemed perfectly normal, too, to open the front door a few hours later and find Keith hovering on the doorstep, clutching an envelope addressed to her and Charlie and saying – as he thrust it into her hands – that if the post was still vacant and they still wanted him after they'd read it, he'd like his job back. 'Of course we want you,' she called, laughing as he bolted back up the steps, then taking the letter inside to enjoy over a cup of coffee.

January

The dawn light seeped out slowly that New Year's morning, as if reluctant to illuminate the jewelled beauty of the night frost, sparkling like fairy dust along the tops of fence posts and roofs. Zigzagging across the lawns of Ashley House, dainty trails of animal prints told a story that its sleeping occupants would never know. Only Genevieve, who had a bad cold and had been put to bed long before the chimes of Big Ben heralded the end of the year, woke early enough to see the patterns etched in the frosted grass from her bedroom window. At five years old, it was the crisp white ground that interested her more. Certain it was snow, she knelt on her bed and rubbed eagerly at the steam of her hot breath on the glass to get a better look. If more fell she would build a snowman, she decided. All by herself, not letting Chloë help even if she asked. It would be a beautiful lady snowman, like the one in the book Aunt Cassie had given her for Christmas, with long straw hair and blue stone eyes and a ruby mouth that came to life when it was kissed.

Except Chloë wasn't here, Genevieve remembered. She was at home with Mum. They were there and she was here, alone and with a horrible cold and a sore on her lip that she wasn't supposed to touch even when it itched. For a moment Genevieve thought she might cry. Her father had said she was to be good and quiet in the morning and wait for him or Theo to fetch her for breakfast. He had warned that it might be later than usual because they were all staying up for a grown-up party, the sort of party she could stay up for when she was a little bit older and wasn't taking medicine. As her lip trembled the bedroom door – propped open, at her insistence, with a heavy metal elephant that Granny had said Great-uncle Eric had brought all the way from India – swung a little wider and Samson appeared, mewing softly and curling his tail round the elephant, as if it was an old friend. Forgetting to be sad, Genevieve squatted on the floor to make some mewing noises of her own, which Samson liked so much that he butted his head against her nose and made her sneeze. A little startled, he trotted back to the door, then glanced at her as if he was expecting to be followed.

He wanted his breakfast too, of course, Genevieve thought, feeling important as she slid her feet into her slippers and put on her dressing-gown. To feed the cat would be fun. It would also be *useful*. The night before, helping pour a saucer of milk and chopping up the soggy lumps of catfood, her aunt Serena had said over and over again what a good and *useful* little girl she was and how Samson was very old and needed lots of food and love.

Downstairs the house felt a lot colder and emptier, and when she poured the milk too much came out and spilt all over the table. Finding a tin of catfood in the larder but unable to reach the opener – which was stuck high up on the wall next to the fridge – Genevieve put a handful of Frosties into a bowl for the cat instead. But Samson seemed to prefer the milk, lapping it off the table and the saucer, then even licking the top of the milk bottle to show he wanted more. Genevieve poured out another dollop for him, put some into the cereal for herself, then carefully carried the bowl into the television room, which, with the fat sofa cushions and the curtains still closed, felt as snug as the den at home.

When he found her some twenty minutes later, curled up next to the old ginger cat in front of the television, Peter chuckled with pleasure. 'I wondered where you were.'

'I gave Samson breakfast and I've had mine, too, and I've been nice and quiet like you said.'

'Good girl.' Peter, who had already shaved and dressed, perched on the arm of the sofa and stroked her bouncy red hair, always at its wildest and loveliest after a night's sleep.

'There was some snow but now it's melted,' she babbled, 'and I put the telly on.'

'What are you watching, then?' Peter murmured, narrowing his eyes to bring the screen into focus, then laughing because – almost certainly by accident rather than design – his daughter had activated the DVD-player, which still contained Theo's film.

'That's Clemmy,' said Genevieve, pointing. 'And she likes *him* a *lot*,' she added, with some distaste, shifting her finger to indicate the actor called Ben.

Peter smiled. 'That is your cousin, yes, but they're only acting – *pretending* to like each other. It's a story – made up and filmed by your brother, who is extremely talented and who, if this is anything to go by, should make a lot more films just like it.'

'*Theo!*' squealed Genevieve, spotting her brother hovering in the doorway and leaping off the sofa to hug his legs.

Theo patted his little sister's back, grateful for the diversion as he pondered the oddity of longing for compliments and not knowing what to do with them when they arrived. His father, smiling in the new sheepish way he had, as if being sorry had become an integral part of his features, looked equally perplexed. 'I was just saying –'

'I know. I heard. Thanks.'

'It was hard last night, with everybody else there . . . you know.'

'I know.' Theo tried an encouraging smile, at the same time experiencing a fresh wave of sadness at how all their roles had been changed, as if the entire family had been shuffled like a pack of cards ready for a new game that no one yet knew how to play. There wasn't really any anger now: there had been too much suffering for that. Nor was he sure yet how to respond to this new, humble, eager-to-please version of his father. Sometimes he even caught himself longing for the blinkered, authoritarian figure, who had prevailed over the first nineteen years of his life. At least he had known exactly where he stood then, how to be. Unable to express any of these confusions, Theo ventured instead that he was thinking of making pancakes.

'Pancakes? Splendid. So long as Gen and I are away by midmorning. I promised Mum I'd have her back in good time for lunch.' Peter pulled his daughter on to his lap so that she was facing him and began a gentle version of ride-a-cock-horse, wiggling his legs to make her lose her balance. 'Since when could you cook pancakes?' he called, as Theo headed off towards the kitchen. 'Theo?' When there was still no reply Peter stopped bouncing his knees and pulled a face at his daughter.

'He said a friend taught him,' explained Genevieve, breathless and happy from the game. 'He made them last time he came home. Chloë had jam on hers and I had Golden Syrup *and* sugar.'

'And what did Mum have?' asked Peter, gently, keeping his legs very still now, glad that his daughter could have no inkling of the ache in his heart.

Except that she seemed to know, because instead of answering the question she put one finger on each side of his mouth as if to tug it into a smile and said, 'I wish you still lived with us.'

'So do I, Genny.'

'Well, why don't you?' She punched his chest.

'Because . . . because . . .' Because, oh, God, he had fallen in love or lust, or something, and got caught, because he had forgotten to cherish all that he should have held dear, because he was weak and foolish. 'Because grown-ups sometimes can't love each other like they're supposed to . . .'

'Well, *I* love you,' she declared, 'and so does Chloë, and Theo.' She bunched her left hand into a fist and uncurled one chubby finger with each name. 'And Mummy –' She faltered, the third finger wagging uncertainly. 'Mummy *cries* now and she never used to.'

'Mummy cries?' echoed Peter, feebly. Helen never sounded remotely tearful to him, on their doorstep hand-overs, on the phone, she was like a businesswoman with her eye on a target – going through things, ticking them off, as if life was an agenda of points to be addressed. She was still working on the summary of her finances – outgoings and incomings – taking so long about it that his lawyer had warned Peter to expect the worst. 'Mummy cries?' he prompted again, sickened by his own shameless need, but too much at its mercy to care. But Genevieve, out of her depth or, perhaps, merely responding to the rich smell of frying butter wafting from the kitchen, had already slipped off his lap and skipped away.

Upstairs, Serena was pulling clothes out of the wardrobe and laying them across the bed while Charlie pretended to sleep.

'Cassie and Elizabeth are going to the sales. The question is, should I go with them? This blue dress is nice – and warm too, which will be important, I suppose, and somewhere –' She flung another couple of items, still wrapped in plastic from the dry-cleaner's, on to the duvet '– there's a jacket that would go really well with it. A sort of tweed, dark blue flecked with white – do you remember it? Or did I throw it out? I wouldn't have, would I? It was so pretty, with velvet collar and cuffs. Charlie, have you seen it?'

Charlie opened one eye, peered at the pile of clothes spread across the bed, then closed it again.

'Charlie? You're not remotely asleep – you haven't been for hours. You woke at six o'clock and drank about a gallon of water because you had a headache from last night and you've been tossing and turning ever since.' Serena returned to the wardrobe, riffling noisily through the remaining hangers. 'I know they said it will only be a register office but one still has to look the part, doesn't one? And anything half decent in the sales goes on the first day . . .'

In acknowledgement of defeat, Charlie had raised himself during this last outburst into a sitting position and discovered that his hangover wasn't as bad as he had feared. He waggled his feet, making the heap of clothes and polythene heave and rustle like something coming alive. 'You'd look lovely in a bin-liner.'

Serena cocked her head at him and tapped her foot. 'Which is a very sweet thing to say, but not entirely helpful.' Then smiling, sighing, giving in to her real mood, which was close to blissful, she cleared a space on the bed and sat down. 'It's overcast, look, but still beautiful.' She cast a dreamy glance out of the window. The downs were draped in mist, as fine spun as white gauze against the mottled grey of the sky. 'A January wedding, after all. Who would have thought it? Dear Keith, dear Lizzy, I'm so pleased for them.'

Charlie humphed. 'We'll lose him again, you know, when it all goes pear-shaped.'

'Oh, you gloom-merchant, have a little faith. They're fantastic together, like shy teenagers but with heaps of heartache and self-knowledge thrown in. And all those months of wanting to be together, but staying apart because of . . .' Serena caught her breath, awestruck still at the courage behind Keith's revelation, then his and Elizabeth's concern for the effect it would have on her and Charlie. Reading Keith's letter that December morning, the afterglow of her extraordinary dream still upon her, she had felt as if she were floating above the webbed complexity of the world, seeing the grand design clearly at last. Keith's confession – for that was what it amounted to – had made her weep, not so much for the death of the little girl, tragic and terrible though it was, but for how the accident had blighted his life. So punished, so burdened, so remorseful . . . It had induced something bordering on gratitude for the simplicity of her and Charlie's loss, unhampered as it had been by any equivalent burdensome certainty of wrongdoing. It had made Serena wonder, too, for the first time in ages, about the man on the motorbike that had hit their daughter, about whatever darkness he carried in his own heart. But even as she summoned the familiar phantom of the leather-clad figure to mind – the haunting screech of his fat wheels, the throaty roar of his engine – the images slipped away, floating free of her, releasing her, just as her darling Tina had done during the night.

Serena had had Charlie pulled out of a meeting to read Keith's letter to him over the phone. After an initial grumble, he had responded exactly as she had hoped, expostulating dismay and surprise that Keith should have felt the parallels of the two accidents so keenly and declaring that the poor man should be reassured and employed forthwith. Of the dream, not to mention her growing conviction that it bore a powerful connection to their visit to St George's, Serena made no mention, nor ever would. Charlie might have understood, but she didn't want to risk it. More importantly, she had no need of his understanding. The experience was too private, too perfect . . . close to indescribable.

Venturing outside after the call, the letter clasped in her hand, she had found Keith sitting on the fallen torso of the oak in the drive, staring into the tangle of broken branches still strewn across the grass.

'There was no need . . .' she began. And then, when he flinched, not looking at her, she had said thank you, and if he could start work that week – that day, even – it would suit them fine.

Keith had tugged his hair, patted his knees, stood up and said that first he needed to see Elizabeth, then tie things up at home. As he trudged back towards his car, a muddy grey Ford, which he had parked at the bend in the lane, Serena had shaken open the pages of his letter and shouted, 'Look. It's over.' While he watched she tore each page into two, four, then six, until the strips were flapping like trapped bunting in her hands.

Keith had grinned. 'Thank you,' he called back, his voice cracked and high, as he turned and jogged back towards his car.

Even with such a prelude to his re-employment, the announcement of a *wedding* – delivered suddenly during the ritual midnight hugs under mistletoe the night before – had come as a tremendous shock to the entire family. Amid the stunned silence that had greeted the news, Elizabeth had whispered, 'Please be pleased.' She had fixed her gaze on Keith, taking a step closer to him but keeping a firm grip on Roland, who stood at her side and, from the pleading expression in his brown eyes, had clearly been privy to the news beforehand.

'Of course we're pleased,' Charlie had boomed, his rich voice thawing the tableau. Moments later they were all firing questions, chinking glasses and hugging again, energized by goodwill that might have arisen out of duty but quickly grew into something more solid and heartfelt. Keith and Elizabeth, brought to life by its warmth, were soon fielding questions about dates and venues, and brimming with gratitude at Serena and Charlie's insistence that the only place to have even the modest reception they had described was Ashley House. 'If that's okay with you, Pamela, of course,' Serena had remembered to add, offering a shy smile at her mother-in-law whom Peter had settled on the sofa with a cup of camomile tea. 'Oh, I'll be long gone,' Pamela had replied, waving one heavily braceleted arm at the room. 'Don't worry about me.'

Serena exchanged a look of mild alarm with Elizabeth, then rushed over to the sofa to insist that they would always worry about her, no matter where she lived. 'And you will come to the wedding, Mum, won't you?' Elizabeth had urged. 'The thirty-first of January – it's all booked, so make sure you put it in your diary.'

'Charlie and I will take you,' said Serena brightly.

'Or I could,' ventured Peter.

'And we'd like to invite Helen,' continued Elizabeth, in a hushed voice that signified the delicacy of the suggestion, 'if that's okay with you, Peter?'

'Of course . . . Quite right to ask her,' Peter had stuttered, so obviously not okay that Serena had burned with compassion for him.

'Do you know what?' she said now, poking disconsolately at the pile of clothes on the bed. 'I feel truly sorry for your brother. I never thought I'd say it, but I do. He's so lost and he's trying so hard, it's pitiful. I suppose you never know how strong someone is until they run into trouble.'

'You certainly don't,' agreed Charlie, giving her a fond smile, which needed no verbal elaboration. 'But Peter will be all right. He's bloody good at his job, he earns a bomb, his children still love him. Someone else will snap him up – you'll see. But I'm glad you've softened towards him . . . All those years of you two not really getting on – I hated it.'

'I did too.' Serena was silent for a moment. 'But I expect you're right. He'll be okay, once the dust has settled. And now, talking of dust . . .' She leant across the bed, scooped up the outfits and dropped them on to the floor by the wardrobe. 'I've decided. I *am* going to buy something new. A wedding always deserves something new. And I don't care about the sales. There's too much going on in the next couple of weeks as it is, seeing off the girls, giving Ed a hand with his application forms, helping your mother and sister move into their new homes, not to mention plucking the pheasant that Sid will, no doubt, leave on the kitchen doorstep after the New Year's Day shoot . . .' She had begun hanging the clothes back in the wardrobe as she talked, patting off specks of dust and shaking out creases. 'No, I shall go shopping *after* the sales when it's nice and quiet and I've got time to try on ten things in a row without feeling guilty. And as for money, I shall use that lovely Christmas cheque you gave me.'

'Ah . . . the cheque.'

'Don't you want me to?'

'No . . . I mean, yes, by all means.' Charlie was smiling mysteriously. 'It's just that I should perhaps confess now that the *cheque* was written not because your useless husband couldn't think of a proper gift but because the gift wasn't quite ready – in fact, ten days ago I wasn't sure if it was even going to be possible.'

'And?' gasped Serena watching him get out of bed and calmly – infuriatingly – unhook his dressing-gown from the back of the bathroom door. 'Don't stop there – you can't!' she cried, hurling a pillow at him, which missed and landed at his feet.

'I can and I shall.' Charlie tied the cord of his dressing-gown loosely round his waist and tapped his nose. 'Prepare to be surprised – and soon. You have been warned.' He made a run for the bathroom, closing the door against another pillow, more accurately lobbed this time.

On the top floor of the house Maisie, Clem and Ed continued to sleep, stirred neither by the faint sweet smell of frying pancakes nor the orchestral creak of floorboards and gurgling waterpipes triggered by Keith and Elizabeth taking it in turns to visit the bathroom.

'We should get dressed.'

'Not yet. Come here.' Elizabeth had scrambled back into bed and lifted the duvet. 'Just for a bit.'

Keith, already in his shirt and boxers, tunnelled in next to her and pulled the covers over their heads like a tent. 'Just for a bit, then. They're all getting up downstairs. Someone's cooking breakfast. Wouldn't want them thinking we're up to anything.'

Elizabeth giggled. 'Why not? We're grown-ups and we're getting *married*. We're allowed to be up to something.' She nibbled his shoulder and snuggled closer. 'Cassie moves into her cottage this week so you can have the barn.'

'Trying to get rid of me already, eh?'

'Silly – just for three weeks, like we agreed . . . like a proper bride and groom. All that grime from you doing up the loft for Roland – you'll be well out of it. He's so thrilled by the way.'

'It was the least I could do. Sending me that advert – the cheeky sod.'

'He's very clever, very special, and he likes you.'

'I like him.'

'Keith?'

'Yes?'

Elizabeth hesitated. She had been going to say that she wished she had seen what he had written to Charlie and Serena. She did wish it, but not, she perceived suddenly, for any reason other than curiosity. All that mattered was that Keith had found the courage to overcome his shame, to forgive himself sufficiently to let her share his life.

'What is it, sweetheart?'

'I'm scared about meeting your boys.'

'Don't be. It'll be fine, you'll see. I'll make Roland's old room as nice as I can, but not push them into staying until they feel ready. One step at a time, eh? We'll feel our way along . . . together.'

Inspired by the warm darkness of the bedclothes over their heads they had been talking in whispers. They fell silent now and held each other instead, both in awe of the complicated path that had brought them together and the simple, obvious route that lay ahead.

* * *

Jessica pushed the pram quickly along the narrow stretch of pavement skirting St Margaret's, then ducked down the lane past the church. By the time she crossed the village green, she was walking so fast and the ground was so uneven that Gemma, rolling about under her blanket in her pink hat, mouth plugged with her pink plastic dummy, looked more like a doll than a baby. She was enjoying herself, though, Jessica could tell, from the way she kept her eyes closed and chomped on the dummy, like she was dreaming of a feed. She only ever seemed really peaceful when she was on the move, pressed to Jessica's chest in her sling, parked in her baby-carrier on the bus, or on the train journey down from London, the day before, when she had slept the whole way, rocked by the rhythm of the engine and the rattling of the carriage against the track. It was when the world went still that Gemma cried. Sometimes, jigging the pram in a trance of fatigue during the night, Jessica wondered if she had given birth to something only capable of contentment when she was, in some sense, in flight.

Having broached the subject with the midwife, who called round in the days after Gemma's three-week stay in hospital, she had been told to give it time and that after so many months of bobbing around in the womb all newborns were partial to a bit of jigging. When the health visitor took over and Jessica asked how come she was so good at stopping the bawling – dangling Gemma in that clever way over her forearm or perching her on one of her plump shoulders – the woman had laughed, looking pleased, and said that getting old wasn't any good unless you got wiser with it. They were keeping a beady eye on her as well as the baby, though, Jessica knew, which was why she made sure the flat was as neat as a pin and said nothing about her Mum staying on in Spain or how she had had no idea that you could love something and want to throttle it too.

There was no one on the green and nothing at the little playground but a glove, lying forgotten on the bench, and an empty plastic bag, flapping like a trapped bird under the skirt of the roundabout. With Gemma so small, so many months off being able to sit up and play, there was no reason to bring her there except as a place to come – a destination – away from her granddad's snores and the poky cottage. He had been pleased enough when Jessica phoned to say they were coming. He had even held Gemma a couple of times, puckering his bristly lips and cooing nonsense, but at the first whimper he'd handed her back, sucking his teeth and saying he had stuff to do, which seemed to mean nodding off in front of the telly or going down the road for a pint. He didn't have much to say about her mum staying on in Spain with Stan either, just shaken his head and made a growling sound, like he disapproved but didn't think it worth saying so.

As Jessica got out her cigarettes and lighter, a sharp wind gusted across the green, almost like it had been waiting to pounce when it would be least welcome. After working the lighter till her fingers were raw and tears of frustration pricking her eyes, she stomped off towards a nearby clump of trees, leaving the pram and her handbag by the bench. It was much nicer by the trees. With her face pressed close to the trunk of the fattest one, her hands cupped round the precious little yellow flame, she lit the cigarette. Then she leant against the tree as she inhaled, smelling the mulchy scent of the bark and tipping her chin up so that all she could see was the mesh of black branches overhead, criss-crossing the sky like cracks in concrete. Giddy after a while, from the smoke and looking up, she stared through the trees at the green's little pond instead, where she'd once swum for a dare as a kid and got a nosebleed from the shock of the cold. Its surface was choppy from the wind, and empty, apart from a lone brown duck, bobbing along like a cork and swivelling its head, like it was as wary as her of being seen.

She was so absorbed in the sense of being alone that it was

a shock to turn and see a woman by the bench, peering into the pram. She was wearing a long brown overcoat and a cream silk scarf with long ends that kept flapping across her face. Jessica, reluctant to approach but fearing for her handbag, walked slowly back across the grass, tucking her chin behind the zip on her anorak.

'Hello,' said Cassie, guiltily, as she straightened. 'I thought it was you. We didn't know you were down – Sid never said.'

'I told him not to, didn't I? I'm not staying long.'

'Just showing him his granddaughter, are you? It's Gemma, isn't it?' Cassie stooped over the pram again, her face softening. 'She's beautiful, Jessica, really beautiful.'

'Whatever.'

'Serena told me you'd quite a time of it . . . I'm so glad you're both –'

Jessica pushed past her and seized the handle of the pram, so roughly that Gemma, who had been stirring, popped her eyes open and then, after a glance at the two faces, whimpered. 'We've got to go.'

'I've moved into the village,' continued Cassie, 'the grey cottage next to the rectory – do you know the one?'

Jessica nodded. She tried to push the pram but had forgotten the brake was on. It lurched and Gemma began to cry properly.

'I just wanted to say – I mean, I know it's difficult, the whole situation, but if ever there's –'

'Look, I don't want anything from you lot, okay?' Jessica stamped on the brake pedal to release it. 'Neither does *she*. We're not animals in a fucking zoo, you know, for you Harrisons to gawp at when you're not too busy having your fancy get-togethers.'

'I'm not getting married any more,' said Cassie, quietly, driven by something like pity. 'My sister is, though, which is sort of unexpected, but I don't think it's going to be at all fancy.'

'Like I'm interested,' Jessica muttered, but not moving away.

'Could I pick her up?' said Cassie next. 'I'll keep the blanket round her so she won't get cold.'

'I don't think so – she needs her bottle.' But Cassie already had her hands in the pram and was scooping the bundle into her arms. The dummy fell out and landed on a clump of muddy grass. 'Great! Now she really *will* bawl her head off,' snapped Jessica, bending down to pick it up and dropping it into her handbag.

Cassie was cradling and murmuring to the baby, stroking her cheeks with her fingertips, telling her she was beautiful and precious.

'Give her back, okay? Just give her back.' Jessica had meant to sound cross and in control but the words came out as a screech. 'Fucking give her back!'

Dismayed and astonished in equal measure, Cassie handed the baby to her at once. 'I'm sorry, Jessica, I was only – I never meant –'

Jessica managed not to cry until she was almost at the pond. The pram bumped furiously all the way, its wheels sticking on grass and in the mud, which got thicker and stickier the closer they got to the water's edge. It was only then that she dared to look back, letting out a groan of relief when she saw that the green and its miserable little playground were as empty as when she had arrived. 'Stupid cow,' she yelled, though the words died on her lips, almost as if they knew there was no real force behind them. She glared at Gemma, who had somehow got her pink bonnet half over her face and who, with sickening predictability, had started to cry again the moment the pram had stopped. 'How come you don't squawk for anyone else?' she shouted, shaking the pram. 'How come they all think you're so fucking *precious?* How come you don't seem that way to me? How the fuck am I ever going to have a *life* again?' Jessica shook the pram harder, pushing it forwards so that the wheels were at the edge of the pond. Close to, the water was dark and more crinkled than ever from the chivvying of the wind. Jessica stared into it with unblinking eyes, seeing with sudden lucidity the awful repeating treadmill of her life: unplanned – unwanted – by her mum, and here she was with her own unplanned squawking kid, fucking it up just as Maureen had done, resentment stifling anything that might have been good.

The water was lapping at the wheels of the pram now, making funny smacking sounds, like wet kisses. Jessica thought of Ed's granny, who had been rescued, and the writer woman with stones in her pockets, who hadn't. Life was such a fight – every day, all the time; Gemma, with all her screaming, seemed to understand that. She looked again at her daughter. The pink hat was still half over her eyes, but she had gone still and quiet, like she knew they were on the edge of something and was doing her best to behave.

That afternoon Serena called at Rectory Cottage to pick Cassie up for a visit to Crayshott Manor. Pamela had phoned the night before to issue the invitation, which, though welcome, had been delivered in a manner that did not allow refusal or negotiation of days and times.

Serena found her sister-in-law clutching a hammer and a duster, staring rather wildly at half-empty cardboard boxes and piles of books and pictures.

'It's smaller than it looks, this place . . . and no obvious niches for anything. I'm resigned to being a spinster for the rest of my life, but I could really do with *someone* to hold up pictures in different spaces, then bang a nail in straight.'

'I can do all of that,' said Serena, peeling off her coat and pushing up the sleeves of her jumper. 'We could make a start now – we've got a little time.'

Cassie laughed, shaking her head – now a mass of exuberant

corkscrew curls – in exasperated affection. 'You're too kind, did you know that? It's unusual, endearing, but *really* unhealthy because people like me – and the rest of the world – will always want to take advantage of it.' She put down the hammer and folded the duster. 'I've got the rest of my life to sort this place out. My mother, on the other hand, has requested our company for a cup of tea at three forty-five and is bound not to be nearly so welcoming if we arrive any later.'

When they were in the car Cassie told Serena about her encounter with Jessica that morning. 'She's such a child herself, it's unspeakably sad.'

'Believe me, Cass, I know,' replied Serena, quietly. 'Accepting the situation has been harder than you can possibly imagine.'

'Ed could *visit* at least, couldn't he? Get to know her, have some sort of relationship . . .'

Serena was shaking her head. 'Of *course*, in an ideal world, I'd like Ed to know his daughter – for us to know our grand-daughter, for that matter. But the world isn't ideal and it's not up to us. Believe me, I've done what I can, but Jessica chose to have this baby and she must deal with it. Ed has been forced into a position he would have given anything to avoid and wants only to be allowed to get on with his life. And I don't blame him. He's eighteen, on a gap year, going to university. He's just passed his driving test and he's got a girlfriend called Melanie. He has set aside a thousand pounds of his trust fund to buy a car and is paying out a hundred pounds a month from the rest as maintenance. Maybe, one day, he will feel up to getting to know Gemma. Of course, part of me longs for that, but Ed is a grown-up now and it's up to him.' She glanced at Cassie, who was staring forlornly out of the window. 'Letting one's children live their own lives is the hardest thing,' she added softly, 'but all one can do in the end.' Wanting to lighten the atmosphere she asked next if her sister-in-law had any inkling of the surprise gift Charlie had mentioned at the weekend. 'If you know, just give me a clue,' she pleaded. 'The more I ask the less he says. It's so exasperating.'

Cassie, who did know, chuckled quietly. As it happened, the gift was arriving that very afternoon. 'You're extremely naughty to ask and you'll get nothing out of me. It's Charlie's surprise and he's very pleased with it.'

They found Pamela in an old coat and gardening gloves patting miniature white and crimson cyclamen into the window-boxes lining the sills outside her room. Poppy was lying next to her, one paw protectively over a large bone.

'She sneaks off to the kitchens, looking all sorry for herself, and they give her that,' announced Pamela, indignantly, shaking her trowel at the bone. 'If it carries on she's going to get very fat, aren't you, darling?'

'She looks happy, though,' said Serena, while Cassie crouched down to make a fuss of the dog.

'Oh, she is. We both are, aren't we, Poppy? The food is splendid – all the vegetables home-grown. One of my bathroom taps was leaking but a nice man came to sort it out – and so quickly too. We had a concert last night, a delightful girl played the cello – reminded me of Elizabeth. Do you remember, Cassie, how good she was before she decided it was too much hard work?' Pamela paused, smiling as she peeled off her gloves. 'All you children, all your talents . . . John and I always felt so blessed.'

'That's exactly how Charlie and I feel about our lot,' said Serena, while Cassie kept her head down, patting the dog.

Once Pamela had put away her gardening things and – needlessly, as it seemed to the two younger women – fussed at Poppy's perfectly clean paws with a cloth, they retreated inside for tea. The sitting room, with its oak-panelled walls, high ceiling and little fireplace, was both elegant and cosy. Pamela took evident delight in showing it off, pointing out how well her belongings looked and lauding the merits of a fire that burned like real coal but sprang to life at the flick of a switch. 'So warm and no mess – I wouldn't go back to all that black dust and kindling if you paid me.' Poppy's bed took pride of place on the hearth, along with a pair of dark blue velvet Queen Anne chairs, which had once lived in the music room at Ashley House, and the leather footstool from the drawing room, worn smooth by John Harrison's heels. Two mahogany and glass bookcases from Pamela's bedroom fitted snugly on either side of the fireplace, each sporting a vase of flowers and several silver-framed family photographs.

Continuing to talk from the cubby-hole of a kitchen in the far corner of the room, Pamela made a pot of tea, which she served on a tray with what remained of the hand-painted china set that she and John had received from his parents as a wedding present.

'It's perfect,' cried Cassie, getting up to relieve her mother of the tray, then parking herself on the footstool. 'Like a little piece of Ashley House – all the best of it rolled into one.'

Serena, watching her mother-in-law relaxing into her familiar routines – tutting at Poppy, pouring the careful dribble of milk into her tea, smoothing the non-existent creases from her lap, patting at the tight, silky sculpture of her bun – recalled in disbelief the disoriented unhappy creature who had stumbled into the lake less than a year before. The world had heaved and threatened and then – slowly – grown safe again, like a dangerous beast subsiding into a deep sleep, not just for Pamela but for her too, for Cassie, for all of them. It was, Serena mused dreamily, as if the giant kaleidoscope of family life had turned, shifting a period of senseless chaos into a new shape, which none of them could have envisaged: a baby, a bombing, the suffering of separations, new unions. It was only by looking back on it all that one could gain any perception of a journey made, a sense of cohesion and purpose. 'Now,' she said, while Cassie refilled their teacups, 'the wedding . . . My goodness,' she checked the date on her watch, 'only ten days to go. Charlie and I thought we'd pick you up around midday, bring you home for a spot of lunch . . .'

'No need, dear, thank you. I've arranged everything with Peter. He's coming down with Theo – Helen is bringing the girls separately, of course. He has promised to treat me to lunch somewhere nice beforehand, then take me back afterwards for the reception at Ashley House.'

'Oh, splendid. So long as you're happy. Good.' Serena took a sip of tea, fighting the absurd idea that she had been rebuffed and reminding herself that she would be busy enough with preparations for the wedding party.

'Not that I'm not grateful, dear,' added Pamela, smoothly, setting down her cup and looking at her watch in a way that made it clear to her visitors that it was time they took their leave.

'She's got sort of *bossy*, don't you think?' Serena laughed, when they were speeding back towards Barham. 'In that way old people do when they've decided that they're past the point of having to pussyfoot around.'

Cassie nodded and grinned. 'I've every intention of following suit – God, all those years of trying to *please* people. Such a waste when you look back on it.' She fell silent, thinking, inevitably, of Stephen. She knew from Keith, who had stammered out the information with a pink face, that he was in Cuba, devising a new case for his literary alter ego, Jack Connolly. 'I'll make sure I stay in touch, if you like,' he had added, 'so you know what he's up to.' There was no need, Cassie had assured him, but Keith's snippet had promoted a new peace of mind, because now she could picture Stephen *somewhere*, instead of floating in limbo like a spirit that refused to be laid to rest.

'You have to try to please other people a little bit,' ventured Serena, dimly aware that she was defending herself in some way.

'Not me,' said Cassie, stoutly. 'My clients, yes, but I'm going to keep them to a minimum too from now on. I want to make my own little house as perfect as I can. And to make myself the number-one priority in my life – *moi*. All singletons agree it's the one great privilege of being alone.'

'But you'll meet someone soon, I'm sure,' said Serena, fearing for what lay beneath Cassie's bravado. 'You're still so good-looking.'

Her sister-in-law made a gagging noise, then burst out laughing. 'You're such a mother hen, Serena. Stop *clucking*. I don't want – I don't *need* anyone. The truth is, I never really did. In fact, that's probably been half my trouble – Oh, look!' she exclaimed, as they rounded the bend in the lane to find a large green lorry parked across the drive and several men in hard hats standing next to it. 'The council have come to cut the tree up at last. I suppose it was too big for Keith to manage. The wood's all yours, presumably?'

'Absolutely. It'll keep us in log fires for years,' Serena murmured, as she eased her car through the narrow gap between the lorry and the gatepost. 'Charlie took the day off to oversee the project. He and Keith are going to stack it all in the shed next to my studio. Oh, they've brought a dog. Just as well Poppy isn't here – she'd go mad. She hates Alsatians.' As she was speaking Charlie appeared at the back gate, looking anxious. The Alsatian bounded towards him and veered away as he tried to stroke it. 'It looks rather wild,' said Serena, and clicked her fingers to catch the animal's attention. The dog pricked its ears and turned towards her and Cassie. 'You are handsome, aren't you?' said Serena, letting the animal sniff her hand before she stroked it. 'Don't you like him?' she added, glancing at Cassie who was hanging back uncertainly. 'He likes *me*,' she boasted, as Charlie sauntered across the front lawn to join them and the dog continued to lick her hand. 'And such a soft mouth – you lovely boy.'

'It's not a boy, it's a girl.'

'So it is.' Serena chuckled, peering at the dog's belly.

'She's called Petra.'

'Well, you've obviously had a busy afternoon,' she teased. 'I hope you've done a bit of wood-stacking as well as making friends with other people's pets.'

'She doesn't belong to anyone else. She's ours – well, yours, actually. She's your surprise. She's a failed police dog – wasn't any good at chasing burglars, too soppy.'

'So that's why you wanted to come back here,' Serena exclaimed, rounding on her sister-in-law. 'All that tosh about collecting a few more boxes – you wanted to see my reaction.'

'Serena, darling, you are pleased, aren't you?' urged Charlie.

'I . . . don't know what I am – astonished, I think.' Serena looked from her husband and his sister, both grinning sheepishly now, to Petra, who was rolling on the lawn paddling her huge paws like a stranded tortoise. 'She is lovely but an *Alsatian*. The Ashley House dogs have always been Labradors or spaniels . . . and poor Samson!' She gasped, pressing her hands to her mouth. 'He'll have a heart-attack or something, won't he?'

Charlie shook his head. 'They've already met. Samson swiped her twice across the nose and she backed off like a lamb. Like I said, she's a *failed* police dog. They're hard to come by, I can tell you – questionnaires and interviews – I've had more of a grilling than I did when I applied for the civil service. She's only two,' he added, 'still a baby. She'll need loads of exercise, but seems pretty obedient . . . You are pleased, aren't you?'

Serena answered by slipping an arm round his waist and reaching up to kiss his cheek. Charlie turned and their lips met instead, so lingeringly that Cassie had to look away. Approaching with forms to be signed, and no knowledge of the poignancy of this man bestowing a young animal on his wife, the three men from the council whooped and wolf-whistled until the pair pulled apart.

* * *

Maybe she should get a dog too, Cassie mused, walking home later that night, her overcoat buttoned up to her jaw to keep out the cold. Serena and Charlie had offered her a lift but she had insisted she wanted to walk. It was only a couple of miles, probably less, but she was glad of the torch Charlie had pressed into her hands, especially when she hit the part of the lane where the trees, although leafless and gaunt, blocked the paltry light of the clouded moon. She could have something small that would curl up on her lap, she decided, and thin-coated, so she wouldn't be forever vacuuming hair off carpets and cushions. She would spoil it with love and titbits and let it sit in her handbag – play the part of the happy spinster she had described to Serena, full of selfishness and self-knowledge.

The torchbeam was both a comfort in the dark and a practical assistant in the business of keeping her suede boots from the worst of the mud and puddles. Once she was on the narrow pavement that ran the length of the village, Cassie had less need of it and walked with more confidence, idly using the beam to draw patterns in her path or to illuminate interesting patches on hedges and garden walls. By the time she reached her cottage gate she was humming and almost too warm. She was through it and only a few feet from the latticed porch when, with a clatter that made her jump, an empty milk bottle fell and rolled down the path towards her. Cassie stood very still for a few seconds, heart pounding, then gingerly steered the torchbeam into the porch. A cat, of course, she told herself. A cat had knocked over one of her empties. Then the arrow of yellow light fell upon the dark hood of a pram and next to it, Jessica's huddled figure, crouched on the doorstep.

'God, you gave me a fright.'

'Sorry.' Jessica squinted, holding a hand up against the glare.

'Are you okay? Has something happened?'

'No, I – I just . . .'

'You'd better come inside.'

'No.'

Cassie laughed a little impatiently, her nerves still jangling. 'Has something happened?' she said again, glancing into the darkness of the pram as she fished out her keys and edged round it to get to the door.

'No . . . yes . . .' Jessica clenched her hands as she stood up, seeing again the choppy darkness of the pond as she had lowered the pram wheels into the water. 'I want you to have her,' she blurted. 'Gemma. I want you to have her. I was going to just leave her here and then I thought you might call the police or something. I've written a letter – it's in there with all her stuff.' She pointed under the pram and at some bulging bags suspended from its handles. 'So it will be *legal* and all that.'

'My dear child,' gasped Cassie, half inside the house now, groping for the hall light, 'you're *exhausted*. Now, bring Gemma inside and I'll put the kettle on. We'll have a good talk, okay? See what we can work out here . . . Jessica?' The girl hadn't moved. Her hair, mousy now and tousled, had fallen across her face so Cassie couldn't even make out her expression.

'Don't talk to me like I'm a nutter.'

'I'm not,' Cassie protested, unable to keep the exasperation from her voice.

'I want you to have her. If you don't want her that's another thing. If you don't get her social services will. I don't want her. I love her but I don't want her, and that means one day . . .' Jessica drew in her breath sharply, as the emotions she had felt by the pond stabbed again, cold and sharp, like a dagger of ice. 'My mum didn't want me either so I know, *see*?' She hissed the word. 'I know you want a kid – Ed's mum told me. I don't want a kid and I've got one. It's fucking simple, if you think about it. And you're family, you're her *aunt*, and if you take her she'll have a fucking great life instead of a crap one and maybe . . .' She paused to prevent the rest of the sentence coming out too tremulously. '. . . maybe Ed will get to know her a bit and her *grandparents* and all that.'

'Jessica, my dear,' whispered Cassie, 'you can't just *give* a baby away, like it – like she – was a –'

'Yes, you can,' she snapped. 'People do it all the time. You read about it in the papers and in books. That Silas Marner, he got given a kid. And there was a girl in my block who thought she had a sister who turned out to be her mum, and a boy at school who lived with his granny because his mum and dad did drugs, so don't tell me people don't do it. And you're her aunt,' she said again, her voice trembling.

'Sweetheart, you said yourself you *love* Gemma,' Cassie pleaded, trying a different tack. 'You might feel like this now but, believe me, you'd miss her terribly, want her back in no time. It would be the most dreadful mistake.'

'There you go,' Jessica cried, 'talking *down* to me, like you don't think I've thought it through, like you don't think I can see straight. I haven't been for months – I shouldn't have kept her but I did, and then today I nearly . . . Today I saw straight for the first time in my life.' Jessica closed her eyes and took another deep breath, pushing her hair off her face. 'It's in the letter, that I want you to have her. If you say no I'll get social services to have her adopted. I've made up my mind.'

Cassie, clinging now to the front door, felt suddenly very cold and giddy. 'But your grandfather,' she tried weakly, breaking off as Gemma, stirred from her nap by voices or perhaps the dank night air, began to snuffle and mew, like a kitten.

Jessica glanced sharply at the pram. The crying would start soon, she knew. She had to get away before that. She had limits after all, in spite of her certainty.

'Granddad will be dead soon, won't he?' she sneered. 'He can hardly look after himself, these days. Anyway, he's always liked you Harrisons more than anything in the world. I've left him a note. When he gets back from the pub and reads it he'll be jumping for joy.' She was still facing Cassie but had stepped off the porch. 'Like I said, her stuff's all there – bottles, nappies and that. There's a whole pack of new dummies. She likes her dummy – you'll get no peace without it.'

'Jessica – please!' Cassie reached across the pram, as if physical strength might succeed where persuasion had failed, but Jessica was already backing down the path.

'I'm going back to London now. Please don't call unless you decide you don't want her.' And with that she ran out of the gate and up the street, her footsteps echoing long after the outline of her anorak had merged into the dark.

Peter was glad of the excuse to phone Helen, glad, too, of the unguarded incredulity of her response, as if he was seeing a glimpse of something behind the new wall of civility that sat between them like bulletproof glass.

'And has Cassie kept her?'

'It would appear so, for the time being.'

'And what do Charlie and Serena have to say about it?'

'They're kind of shell-shocked, I think, torn between seeing the sense of it and wanting whatever is best for the . . . for Gemma.'

'Pretty name.'

'Yes, I thought so too.'

A silence followed, while Peter fiddled with his pen-stand and tried to think of something to say that might prolong not only the conversation but the small tremor of intimacy it had allowed.

'It's obvious what will happen, though,' Helen continued, her voice hardening. 'Jessica will change her mind and come charging back to reclaim the poor mite just as Cassie has got too embroiled to want to give her up. It will be heartache all round . . . again.'

'Maybe.'

'Oh, really? And what do you think will happen?'

The hardness was teetering on sarcasm now. In the background Peter could hear Genevieve saying something. He strained his ears – something about tea and television. 'I don't know what will happen,' he confessed. 'But apparently Jessica said that if Cassie doesn't want the child she'll give her up to social services. She said, too, that she doesn't want to be contacted. She put it all in a letter. She's even sent Ed's first maintenance cheque back.'

'Hang on . . .' Muffled noises followed while Helen put her hand over the receiver and said something to settle Genevieve. 'It's unbelievable,' she said, back on the line, 'how early some lives go off the rails.'

'Rather than going off them later, you mean?'

'Don't start, Peter,' she warned, in such a low whisper that he had to press the receiver to his ear to hear her. 'Now is not the time.'

Peter, who wanted badly to ask if that meant there *would* be a time – and for what exactly – inquired instead after his daughters.

'They're good,' Helen replied, speaking normally again. 'Genevieve's happy so long as she is allowed to wear those horrible pink shoes with *everything* and Chloë has agreed, at last, that her aunt's wedding warrants something more than a pair of jeans and a T-shirt. I'm taking her shopping tomorrow and have high hopes of returning with a dress.'

He laughed. 'Good luck.'

'Thank you,' she replied, her voice too dry for Peter to be sure whether the words had been accompanied by so much as a smile. He held his breath, hoping for a clue, or for further funny revelations about their children, or any sign that she knew he knew how she felt. Instead she said she had lots to be getting on with and would see him in Chichester at the North Street register office the following Saturday.

'Theo's coming with me – we're taking my mother out to lunch first.'

'I know. That's fine.'

'My lawyer says he still hasn't –'

'No, I've been so busy. Tell him it won't be long.'

Spying a distorted image of Peter's wide face and long nose through the peephole in the front door of her flat a couple of hours later, Jessica's instinctive response was to drop to her knees. When the bell rang a second time, longer and more shrilly, she put her hands to her ears, muttering expletives. A moment later the flap of the letterbox opened above her head.

'Jessica, please, if you're in there, I haven't come to cause trouble. I can understand why you don't want to let me in. It's not about Gemma. Gemma's fine. My sister's taking good care of her. I want to talk to you about something else. I want to help –'

'I don't want your bleeding help,' she shouted at last, tipping her face up towards the flap to be sure of being heard. 'Leave me alone. I'm all right. Fuck off.'

'I know you're all right – that is, I hope you are.' Peter, crouching awkwardly with his knees burning and his back at an uncomfortable angle, pressed his mouth closer to the flap. 'Please, could you let me in for a few minutes?' The door swung open so suddenly that he pitched forwards on to all fours, landing on the doormat.

Jessica looked down at him, her mouth curled into a sneer. 'Yeah? And what do you want to talk *about*? You've got one minute starting . . .' she folded her arms and tapped her foot '. . . *now*.'

'I want to help you,' muttered Peter, clambering to his feet, aware that he was going to have to work hard to retain the impulse that had driven him, on a dank January evening, to the ugly concrete block of flats where the disastrous dual family conference had taken place seven months before. He had forgotten what an adversary the girl was, how forcefully antagonistic. It dawned on him that he had been expecting her ordeal to have softened her in some way, made her more accessible. Instead she looked more sure of herself than before, aided considerably by the fact that she had lost not only the bulk of her pregnancy but the puppy fat she had been carrying. Noting the flattering tight blue jeans and crisp white T-shirt, the lank hair freshly dyed a charcoal black that set off the blazing ferocity of her green eyes, Peter had to remind himself that she was seventeen, adrift and badly in need of help. 'What you did – your child –'

'I thought you weren't going to talk about that.'

'No . . . sorry.' Peter cleared his throat. 'Your mother – I was so sorry to hear that she –'

'Good riddance.' Her foot was tapping faster. 'Is that it? Or . . .' Jessica smiled slyly, narrowing her eyes '. . . or was it something else you were after?'

'Something else? Heavens, no,' Peter muttered, his voice thick with dismay and disgust. 'How could you?' He stopped, recalling the vile insinuation she had made during the dreadful family meeting, but saw in the same instant that such a mind-set could only be the by-product of mistreatment and suffering. The thought steadied him. 'Jessica, I can assure you I want nothing. I have come here simply to acknowledge the ordeal you have been through by offering you the chance of a fresh start. That is to say, if you wanted to take A levels . . .' There were snorts of derision at this but Peter pressed on. '. . . or maybe a vocational course of some kind, I would pay the necessary fees.'

'I've got a job, thank you *very* much.'

'A job,' he echoed, struggling to keep the wind in his sails. 'Something you like, I hope?'

Jessica hesitated as her newly acquired working life, dodging Jerry's groping at the hair salon, shimmered like a bad dream. 'I'm training to be a hairdresser.'

'Ah, I see and you have the money for that, do you?'

Jessica clutched her head with her hands. 'Why are you so fucking keen to give me money?' Her tone was scoffing, but also incredulous. 'What's it *for*, eh? What do you want in return?'

'Nothing.' Peter shook his head wearily: he had not considered that the notion of giving something for nothing should be so unimaginably foreign to her. 'You haven't had the easiest start in life. With the unwitting assistance of my nephew you have somehow . . .' Remembering his conversation with Helen, he had been tempted to say 'gone off the rails' but feared that this damaged, touchy creature – now at least deigning to talk to him – might take offence. 'Believe it or not, and I know you might find this hard to understand, helping you would help me. What I would get in return is the knowledge that I'm doing some good for somebody who deserved a few more choices than have so far come her way. It would be between you and me,' he continued, perceiving from the flicker in her eyes that she was interested. 'We would tell no one.'

He still had his foot in the door, keeping it open out of a dim instinct that she needed space – the reassurance of not being trapped – for any understanding between them to have a chance of taking root.

'So I choose a course or something anywhere I like and you pay for it?'

Peter nodded. 'That's about it.'

'Cos it would make you feel better.'

'Yup.'

'Like I'm your private *charity* or something.'

Peter was on the point of denying this accusation when he saw that she was now rolling her eyes and grinning.

'You're potty, you are.'

'Er . . . yes, probably.' Peter smiled sheepishly. 'I'm also quite wealthy, and I've had a devil of a year doing nothing but making people I care for miserable, and to perform this one small favour for you would go a long way towards helping me atone for at least some of that.' He stopped, warned off by her expression of irritated puzzlement.

'I'm not sure I want to go back to studying.' She frowned. 'To be honest, I'm not that keen on hairdressing either . . . but I'd quite fancy doing a beautician's course or something. Would you pay for that?'

'Of course.' Peter, aware that the battle had been fought and won, felt sufficiently relaxed to give a little bow. 'I shall be at your service. Here . . .' He took a business card out of his pocket. 'Look into it and call me when you've made your mind up or if you just want to talk it through. Okay?'

Slowly, cautiously, she took the card but didn't look at it. 'And it's like . . . between you and me?'

'Absolutely.'

'Well, thanks, then. I might do it, I suppose.'

'Splendid. Excellent.' Peter held out his hand, keeping it there as she hesitated, studying it – like an animal sniffing out foe or friend – then slid her palm briefly across his, no more firmly than a feather brushing his skin.

'And Gemma's okay, is she?' she asked, folding her arms tightly across her chest.

'Oh, yes . . .' Peter began, prevented from saying more because a lump the size of a tennis ball swelled at the back of his throat. 'If you wish you hadn't, you must say . . .'

Jessica shook her head twice, so vehemently that the flat, blackened hair spun out from her ears. 'I wanted the best for her – a mum who'll love her right and a big family and that.'

'You're a remarkable girl.'

Jessica shrugged, whether out of modesty or because she could not comprehend the compliment Peter found it hard to be sure. 'So I might call you,' was all she said, waving the business card at him as he walked away.

'When you're ready.'

In the three easy strides it seemed to take to reach the lifts Peter felt as if he was walking on air. Going down in the dingy box he had a merry conversation with a toothless pensioner about the weather, animated by warmth that had nothing to do with the double lining of his cashmere overcoat.

Back in the contrastingly sumptuous surroundings of his own flat in Barons Court, he hung Roland's curious whisk of oils above the hall table, then cooked himself a pork chop, two rashers of bacon and a scoop of frozen vegetables, which he washed down with several glasses of good claret. Undressing for bed a little later, he took his wallet out of his breast pocket and carefully – tenderly – examined the worn, out-of-date photos of his family that he carried next to his heart. There was a picture of Delia there too, hidden at the back – a good one, showing off the soft slope of her fair hair and the striking feline set of her eyes. Peter waited for the usual reflex of physical longing. It came at last, but was so faint – so suffused with remorse – that it was easy to crumple the image in his fist, then drop it into the wastepaper basket next to his bed. 'Life goes on,' he murmured, fetching a final glass of wine to accompany his night-time reading and get him to a point where fatigue overrode the discomfort of sleeping alone.

Anyone inclined to align the notion of good weather with good fortune might have felt a dampening of spirits on glimpsing the canvas of steely grey pressing on the South Downs the following Saturday morning. Serena, however, striding across the fields with Petra, her head full of mental lists for the catering requirements of the wedding party, hardly noticed it. The finger food was already stacked on trays in the larder – well away from the prying paws of Samson and his new canine accomplice – and she had left Charlie setting out glasses and bottles along a crisp linen tablecloth she had laid over the dining-table. Still to do were the beds: Keith's sister Irene and his two boys were staying the night, as were Peter and Theo. Roland, too, wanting to keep out of the way of the honeymoon night, which his mother and prospective stepfather had elected to spend in Midhurst, had asked if he might stay over. They wouldn't be having a proper holiday until the spring, Elizabeth had explained, when they were going to take all three of their children to visit Maria in Umbria. Helen, perhaps not surprisingly, had refused Serena and Charlie's tactful offer of the barn for the night and insisted that she and the girls would leave for London straight after the reception. Cassie had also warned that she might not stay long, that it would depend on Gemma. The whirligig of Serena's thoughts paused there. Few events in her life had shaken her more deeply – or caused her more pleasure – than the thrusting of her son's unwanted child into the arms of her sister-in-law.

'But I'm also madly jealous,' she had confessed to Charlie, once all the obvious questions had been asked and Sid had assured them several times that his granddaughter was fine and that the arrangement had his wholehearted support. 'A baby girl – Ed's baby girl, for God's sake, *our* granddaughter – and Cassie gets to bring her up.'

Once, not long ago, such an admission would have been like gouging the scab off a deep wound. It was a measure of how far they had come – of how close and mended they were – that Charlie had merely smiled, nodded, stroked her arm and said of course she felt that way, and it was only natural, but that like any set of deserving grandparents they were going to get all the best of it and none of the worst. Cassie would do the hard stuff and they could hover in the background, ready to spoil Gemma whenever it was required.

In all the furore it was Ed who had somehow been forgotten. Poor, angry, bewildered Ed. Serena sat down on a tree stump with a sigh and clicked her fingers at Petra, who gave a reluctant last sniff to a rabbit-hole, then dropped obediently at her side. Squinting back towards the house, Serena could just make out the blue curtains bunched to each side of her son's bedroom window. His reaction to the news had been instant and unequivocal. 'Jessica's won,' he had shouted. 'Can't you see? She's won. She wanted a piece of our lives and she's got it.' He had slammed the door and pounded the stairs to his bedroom. Half an hour later Melanie's little red Fiat had appeared in the drive for the few minutes it took Ed to thunder back down the stairs and get into it. He had remained with his girlfriend's family ever since, phoning once to ask if he was expected to buy his aunt a wedding present and again to say he would make his own way to the register office.

It was understandable, Serena reasoned now, patting Petra's glossy head as she got up from her perch and headed back towards the house. He had thought his huge, terrible problem solved – or at least removed – only to find that it had been lobbed back at his feet. For, under the guardianship of his aunt, the daughter whose existence he had opposed from the moment of her conception would now be brought up on the doorstep of his own home, incorporated into family functions with all the rights of any other little Harrison. However much Ed was away, studying, working, forging his own life, he would have to *know* her, even if the task of disclosing her true parentage remained years away.

But, as with all problems, these days, Serena found herself soothed by the perspective of the past. Ed had not disappeared this time. He was sulking at his girlfriend's house; a very nice girlfriend, with a place to study English at Edinburgh, a sharp sense of humour and a fascinatingly tiny diamond stud in her nose. He would come round eventually, she was sure, rejoin the muddle of family life, shifting as it did from one day to the next. Cassie had been desperate to talk to him – had even mooted door-stepping him at Melanie's – but Serena and Charlie, advising her during the course of their own reintroduction to

Gemma, had suggested she let the initial shock of the news wear off first. 'But I want to take her to the wedding,' Cassie had cried, still a little hysterical from her new responsibilities and lack of sleep. 'That will be a bigger shock than anything, won't it, when he *sees* her? And she's got his eyes too, don't you think? Large, blue and deep-set – they're the spitting image.'

All three adults had peered into the pram, whose comfort, in its occupant's opinion at least, had been heightened by the addition of a little square of honey-coloured sheepskin. 'Did yours like dummies?' Cassie had asked, tugging at the little pink plastic loop sticking out of Gemma's mouth, which caused a fierce suction protest in response.

'No, just their thumbs and bits of blanket, and Tina loved that bunch of plastic keys – do you remember, Charlie? We didn't dare go anywhere without it for months.'

'Of course,' he had whispered, 'I remember every bit of her.'

Serena, still only half-way across the field, breath swirling in front of her in bursts of white mist, felt tears prick her eyes as she recalled the moment and the little person in the white sleepsuit who lay at the heart of it. Watching the busily pumping legs and fists, the strengthening focus of the blue button eyes, Serena had felt both incredulous and ashamed at the fear her conception had caused. So small, so brave, so perfect. It was impossible now not to delight in her; impossible too, for Serena at least, not to feel that, from the first fighting moments of the harrowing birth, all that fear had been turned on its head. Small and fragile Gemma might be, but she was rebalancing – redeeming – them all, much as the tiniest light can signal a way through the thickest dark.

Roland, standing among his cousins in the first row facing the registrar's desk, was aware of the tight leather of his new shoes pinching his toes. His feet had grown, just as he had feared they would when Cassie bought them. Only pulled out of their box – dusty from so many months' residence at the back of his wardrobe – that morning, there had been no question of purchasing another pair. Yet it seemed fitting, somehow, that he should wear them – his *wedding* shoes – in spite of the radical change to both the venue and the participants. His mother, tottering round the kitchen that morning, making tea and not drinking it, buttering toast and not eating it, stabbing at her hair with clips and combs, had muttered about her own footwear (cream stilettos to match her new skirt and jacket) and the unlikelihood of getting through the day without breaking an ankle.

Her ankles looked steady enough now, though, Roland observed, watching as she slipped a gold band on to Keith's finger and told him, in a strong, clear voice, that she would be his until her dying day. Forgetting the discomfort of his toes, he became aware instead of a swelling in his chest. He had made it happen, after all, cutting out the advert and posting it to Keith, much as a gambler might send a die spinning across a board. Aware of how much his mother liked the man – seeing how hard she had tried to hide her despondency after the trip to Hull with his aunt – baffled as to why a few miles' separation should be so terminal, the idea of sending the newspaper clipping had dropped into his mind like inspiration, a sudden *seeing* of what could, should, be done. And then when it had all worked so well, Roland had experienced a rush of satisfaction similar to the final brushstroke on a painting when the work was done and something beautiful had emerged. In addition to which, their gratitude to him had been thrilling, more than making up for the inevitable sense of displacement at having a third place set at the table and finding strange socks lying on top of the laundry basket. Converting the attic had helped too – an obvious ploy of Keith's to win his affections but done so swiftly and so well: with two dormer windows, the light up there was as good as it would be in the classiest studio and Roland had felt nothing but gratitude. Best of all, Keith loved his mother: it shone out of him, in every cup of tea he made for her, in the way he watched her talk, in the alertness of his responses to each colour in her messy rainbow of moods.

Roland's trance of contentment was broken by a cry from the back row, a cross between a shout and a squawk, not proper crying so much as a noisy assertion of a small presence based on the recent discovery that vocal cords could do many things. It took considerable self-discipline – a reminder of the correct decorum – for Roland to resist turning round. Next to him Ed stiffened. Maisie and Clem, positioned in the row behind, both sneaked a glance over their shoulders, while Chloë and Genevieve, ignoring their mother's glare, stood on tiptoe to get a good view of their aunt and the new baby.

Cassie, hot and anxious, wishing she had worn cotton instead of her thick wool suit, tried the tip of her finger instead of the dummy. Gemma sucked hard, making little smacking noises and blinking in surprise. Looking up, Cassie relaxed as Charlie caught her eye and winked. She wanted so badly not to make a hash of things, not that day, not any day. She had never been more exhausted in her life, more out of control, more happy. The cottage remained in a state of merry chaos, the half-unpacked boxes now jostling for space among the paraphernalia concomitant upon mothering a child. During the first few days, she had been prepared for Jessica to come charging down the front path saying that the letter offering guardianship of her daughter meant nothing, that she had changed her mind, and so Cassie had done her best to keep her heart and her bank balance in check, buying no toys, no clothes, doing only what was strictly necessary, dimly imagining that such resistance might protect her from the agony of disappointment. But it hadn't lasted. Half-love was not possible, Cassie had discovered, not for a charge so sweet, or for a carer whose heart was so primed and eager. It was all or nothing, like falling in love, the headlong kind she had despaired of finding, as impossible to resist as gravity. It might go wrong, but so might anything. Life was so miraculously unpredictable – the arrival of Gemma had taught her that – and she had resolved to go with the flow, wherever it might lead.

They had got to the signing stage now. Serena and Peter had stepped forward as witnesses. Gemma had settled against her shoulder, her cheek tucked snugly into the hollow above Cassie's collarbone, her breathing as quick and warm as little kisses against Cassie's neck. Relieved, truly relaxed now, Cassie let her gaze shift from the signing to the ramrod back of her nephew, who had arrived – deliberately, no doubt – too late for a proper introduction. She felt sorry for him but also a little impatient. It was tricky, of course, but keeping his back turned wouldn't solve anything. If he tried to scoot off after the ceremony she had every intention of running after him, not just to get the introduction over with but to reassure him that he had nothing to be afraid of, that families were often untidy but no less happy and functional for that. In addition, she had something to give him. Tucked alongside the envelope addressed to her – buried among the packets of nappies and baby clothes – there had been another, thinner, one, saying *'Ed,'* with *'PRIVATE'* printed carefully next to it. Cassie had been carrying it around in her handbag for days, wanting many times to defy Serena's advice about not ringing the doorbell of Melanie's family home but refraining out of respect for the word *'private'* and the certainty that Ed would not like to receive such a document within sight of any audience, least of all his new girlfriend.

As Peter kissed his sister, then bent forward to sign his name, Helen's eyes flicked to the vase of flowers on a small pedestal behind the desk. It was important to concentrate on real objects, she scolded herself, rather than the hazy swirl of feelings that the ceremony had evoked. It was a civil procedure, after all, nothing grand, nothing sacrosanct, and between two people who had made such vows before and who, one assumed, had broken them. All in all, it was nothing to get too emotional about, though she wished them well, of course. How could one not? Launching themselves back into the stormy sea of compromise and commitment, the impossible challenge of blending two contrary lives, two sets of hopes, two . . . Helen could feel herself swaying slightly as the flowers – white lilies, pink roses, feathery green foliage – blurred with her tears. She was not going to cry. She was not. Stupid, sentimental, crocodile tears – she wanted none of it. Checking that neither of her daughters was watching, she ran her sleeve quickly under her eyes and reassembled her expression in preparation for when Peter returned to his seat.

And then, suddenly, it was all over. Charlie led a round of applause while Elizabeth and Keith kissed as bashful newlyweds. As everyone left their seats Keith's boys, who had sat so still and wide-eyed on either side of Irene throughout the proceedings, set off round the room, like exploding fire-crackers, shrieking as they dodged chairs and their aunt. Keith, moving more quickly and with more confidence than his sister, soon had one child pinned under each arm, where they remained long enough for Elizabeth to give them each a small parcel.

'Bribery,' she whispered, kissing Charlie who, like all the adults, was jostling for the chance to offer congratulations. 'I've discovered it works wonders . . . but the moment we get back you'll have to dig out a pump.'

'A pump?' said Serena, butting in for her own kiss.

'I've given them a football each – really good ones – but they need blowing up.'

'Ed's bike's got one, I'm sure –' Charlie began, breaking off as Peter pushed through the throng to greet his sister and the registrar called out that, much as she hated to break up a party, it was time for them to vacate the room.

In the mayhem it was easy for Cassie to tap on Ed's shoulder and slip Jessica's note into his hand. He shot her a look of something like terror, then sidled away. She returned to Gemma, whom Pamela had seized the moment the ceremony was over and settled in the crook of her arm with the deft, gentle – unteachable – authority of a great-grandmother. As Cassie approached, signalling that they should follow the others out of the room, Pamela cradled her charge more tightly, scolding her that one visit a week simply wasn't enough and what was she going to do about it?

Helen, surveying the scene through still misty eyes, amazed as they all were at Pamela's easy accommodation of the latest twist in the mesh of family life, felt suddenly, horribly, on the outside of it all. The group was moving towards the door now. Genevieve and Chloë had been swept along with them. In the hallway outside she could make out the bobbing heads of the next wedding party. She could see the back of Peter's head too, the neat line of his recent haircut, the crisp fold of his suit collar. He was patting Keith's shoulder, saying something that made him laugh. Desolation swept through her, so violently that she put out a hand to steady herself. It was over. Peter was gone, and it was over. He had begged forgiveness and she had refused. They were both moving on, moving away. Helen looked again towards the family group, steeling herself for the effort of catching up and joining in with it. As she did so Peter dropped his arm from Keith's back and glanced over his shoulder – looking for her, clearly . . . or was he? Helen stood very still. She felt bleak and forgotten. She wanted to be remembered, to be looked at, to be cared about – all the things that Peter's sister and her new man still had the luxury of taking for granted. Peter's eyes found hers at last, but only briefly. There was a flicker of a smile – no more than a twitch, nothing warm or reassuring – before he was swept away by his family.

She caught up with him in the street outside. The light, muted by cloud all day, was already receding and it had turned much colder. The shoppers hurrying by had their heads hunched inside their coats. The bulk of the family party was already moving off down the street towards the Festival Theatre carpark. Peter was holding Genevieve's hand and saying something to Chloë. Next to them Theo, as tall as his father now, was stooping to respond to some pleasantry offered by his grandmother. The group pulled apart as Helen approached. Pamela, tugging on her gloves, said they had better be going, hadn't they?

'Where did you park?' Helen asked.

Peter nodded at the entrance to an alleyway across the street. 'St Cyriac's. What about you?'

'The same . . . but I think I've left my gloves in the register office.'

'We'll wait, if you like.'

'Don't worry. Perhaps you could take the girls and I'll follow.' She hurried back inside, returning, gloves found, a few minutes later, to find Peter waiting alone next to a lamp-post.

'I let Theo take charge. He's good at that.'

'Like you.'

'Hmm . . . probably, poor sod.'

'Peter?'

'Yes?'

'Could we . . . could we . . . er . . . drive in convoy?'

'Convoy?' he echoed stupidly.

'The one-way system . . . I always get lost.'

'Of course. No problem.'

As they turned to cross the road towards the alleyway a motorbike roared up from the roundabout by the theatre. Noisy, within the speed limit, it offered no threat, but Peter reached instinctively for Helen's elbow to ensure there was no danger of her stepping into its path. Helen shook it off and took his hand instead, his big, firm, familiar hand, with the Harrison signet ring slotted on to the little finger, where it had worn a groove for itself. 'Peter, I don't know how to say this . . . don't really know what I want to say except . . .' They had reached the other side of the street, which was busier. A woman in a Puffa jacket had parked her buggy across the entrance to the alleyway and was talking loudly into her mobile phone: 'You tell him from me I don't give a flying fuck *what* the fuck he thinks . . .'

'Except?' Peter prompted, trying to keep the hope from his voice, convinced he was to hear more about convoys and one-way systems.

They stepped awkwardly round the buggy, which contained shopping-bags rather than a child. 'I cannot forgive you,' Helen murmured, once they were in the alleyway, 'but I'm beginning to understand that the day may come when I shall wish that I had.'

'Right. I see,' Peter muttered, seeing nothing, in fact, but grey cobbled paving-stones and the shine of his black brogues, polished that morning with spit and a tea-towel.

'Those words you gave me . . .'

'Words?'

'On the envelope, at the gallery.'

Peter groaned. 'Oh, *those* words. I'm sorry about that.'

'They moved me deeply. *Love is what you arrive at.* I thought that was very good. I've had it sitting on the desk at home, next to all my stuff for the lawyer.'

'Ah, the lawyer.'

They were nearing the end of the alleyway now. Ahead they could see the start of the car-park and Genevieve swinging on her brother's arm.

'I think it's what has been stopping me.'

'Stopping you?'

'Sending the stuff to the lawyer – my income and outgoings. They've been ready for weeks, only I can't bring myself to post them.'

'Oh, Helen.' She stopped walking. 'Oh, Helen,' he repeated, while the girl with the buggy of shopping strode past, still yelping into her phone.

'I'm not promising anything. I don't know *anything*. I just . . . Since you wrote those words and then today, I just don't want – can't – bring myself to give you up. I've been praying too, which I know you won't like to hear but –'

'Praying?' Peter was almost weeping. 'Helen, my darling, you pray all you like. If this is what it does, I might try it myself. Oh, my darling, I'm so sorry, so very sorry for everything. I will make it up to you, I promise.'

They were hugging when Chloë came running into the alleyway, her new dress, which was shorter than her mother would have liked, riding high above her knees, exposing her skinny shins and the curious tasselled suede boots that she had insisted were necessary to complete the outfit. 'Oh, blimey,' she gasped, stopping several yards short and looking appalled rather than pleased. 'We were just wondering where you'd got to.'

'Well, now you know,' said Helen, sounding arch but grinning with a goofiness that made her look not far off fourteen herself.

There was something almost bridal about the way Peter and Helen held hands to complete the journey through the archway and out into the car-park. Warned by Chloë, the little group waiting among the cars tried not to stare too hard or look curious; all, that is, except Genevieve, who pointed an accusing finger, shouting, 'You kissed. Chloë saw you! You kissed!'

'Bloody hell,' said Maisie, sighing happily, 'what a day.' She reached across her sister and swiped Ed's cigarette from his fingers. 'I need a drag.'

'I thought you'd given up.'

'I have.' She inhaled deeply, then handed it back to her brother. 'You've never smoked, have you, Theo?'

Theo shook his head, then stuck an elbow into Roland's ribcage as his cousin emitted a hoot of scorn. 'Not tobacco, anyway.'

'Really?' Maisie was trying to bat the smoke away from a scowling Clem and raised her eyebrows. 'Well, next time make sure I'm there, okay?'

Theo, worried on account of Chloë, who had crept out to join her cousins in the cloisters, said, 'Enough, okay?'

'I know what you're talking about – I'm not *that* pathetic.' Chloë pressed a little nearer to Clem, who had won her heart during the afternoon with several sips of wine and at least two admiring remarks about her new boots.

'Why did you dump Julian, anyway, sis?' asked Ed, lazily, tossing the cigarette into a flowerpot and tucking his hands under his armpits. Like all of them he was cold. It was hardly appropriate weather to be sitting out on the cloister bench and in deckchairs admiring the view. In fact, there wasn't a view, except of the lawns and the winter skeleton of the pergola. Beyond that the countryside was smothered in a thick mist that looked as if it had rolled down like a stage curtain from the sky. He had come outside originally to have a kick-around with Craig and Neil. When Keith had called them in he had turned to find his sisters and cousins ranged in a small grandstand in the cloisters, chuckling at his eagerness to show off his rusty schoolboy skills.

'Because he was an arse,' retorted Maisie, after a pause, prompting a round of guffaws, especially from Theo, who said, 'Good girl,' and patted her leg.

'So you can play the field at Bristol, more like,' said Ed. He could feel Jessica's note under his crossed arms, pressed next to the packet of cigarettes in his breast pocket. He had opened it with trembling fingers in the privacy of his bedroom, his heart thick with the dread of threats and recriminations, the certainty of continued entanglement, only to find something quite different, something almost *noble,* he decided now, recalling each brief word. *You were right, I shouldn't have had her, but now she's here I just wanted her safe. I know you'll keep an eye on her. Whatever you might think, I did love you, Ed Harrison, once upon a time. Goodbye and good luck and all that.*

So, nothing to dread, after all. Just as the baby – his baby – hadn't turned out to be so dreadful either. He'd had a proper look at her at last, peering into the pram, which Cassie had parked in the hall outside the drawing room, after he had come down from the bedroom. She was like any other baby, small and peaky-faced, like a little gnome. His aunt Cassie had caught him but not said anything, which was decent and just the way he would have wanted her to play it. And then, a little later, after Gemma had woken up and his grandmother had brought her into the drawing room, she'd been passed round like a parcel, admired and gurgled at, and he had held her for a little bit and no one had said anything stupid or made him feel bad. Just like none of them was saying anything now. It had made Ed think that in giving the baby to his aunt, Jessica had probably done the right thing, that his life would be a lot easier, a lot less burdened – not just financially but because it was preferable to know where his daughter was instead of living with the terror of being presented with her at some inconvenient, unguarded moment. She was *present* already, and it felt sort of okay. God alone knew what and when they would tell her about how she got into the world, but with his faith restored in the supporting network of his family, Ed was sure that wouldn't be so bad either.

The conversation had shifted to marriage. Chloë, bored and self-conscious, had sloped back inside.

'It's great about your mum and dad, Theo,' ventured Clem.

Her cousin made a face. 'Early days. Dad's behaved like a total tosser. Frankly, I think Mum's barking mad.'

'But then it is barking mad, isn't it?' put in Maisie. 'Look at Aunt Elizabeth trying it for a *third* time. I mean, what *is* that?'

'Keith's nice,' said Clem, shooting an encouraging smile at Roland.

'I know Keith's nice but a *third* marriage – I don't get it.'

'Third time lucky?' suggested Ed, also glancing at Roland, recalling suddenly the likely deeper cause of his cousin's reticence and pitying him on account of it.

'They're soul-mates,' said Roland, quietly. 'I believe in soul-mates.'

Which was a bloody clever response, Ed decided, grinning at his cousin, the pity receding.

'How lovely, Roland, and how *true*,' exclaimed Clem, thinking, as she knew Maisie was, of their own parents, so close these days it was almost embarrassing.

'It's just luck if you find one,' Roland added, so confidently that, for a moment, Ed thought he might go further. But then Maisie and Clem announced, in that uncanny twin-unison they showed sometimes, that they were freezing, and the next moment they were all folding away the deckchairs and entering the steamy heat of the drawing room where canapés and wine glasses had been cleared to make way for fruit cake and cups of tea.

Pamela's eyes were closing when the bedroom door opened and her youngest granddaughter appeared, eyes wide with shyness and self-importance. Genevieve approached the bed slowly, aware as she had been all day of the lovely swish of her party dress against her tights and the prettiness of her beloved footwear. 'Mummy told me to ask you if you wanted some tea.'

Pamela held out her hand, rejoicing at the way the child took it so easily, so trustingly, giving not a moment's thought to the contrast between the soft whiteness of her skin and the papery veined glove that clasped it. 'That was very kind of her, but tell her I'm going to have a little sleep first. I shall come down and have tea soon.'

'And I brought you these,' Genevieve said, flinging out her other hand, which she had kept pinned tightly behind her back, to reveal a fistful of snowdrops, wilted already from having been guarded so well. 'They were by the big broken tree and Mummy said I could pick them.'

'How lovely, dear, thank you so much.' Pamela took the flowers and placed them gently in the half-glass of water on her bedside table. 'See how pretty they look.'

Genevieve beamed, then frowned. 'It's sad about the tree.'

'Yes, it is, but it was too old to stand up to those strong winds.'

Genevieve tugged at one of her gingery curls and popped her thumb into her mouth, which she wasn't supposed to do but which she knew her grandmother wouldn't mind. 'Will you die soon, do you think?' she asked, through her thumb.

'Everybody dies in the end,' Pamela began, then added quickly, 'but I certainly don't think it will happen to me today, or tomorrow, or for quite a while probably. I don't *feel* like dying in the least.'

The thumb had been removed to make way for a wide grin. 'Where's Poppy?'

'She's at our new house, which I want you to visit very soon. Mummy says you're all staying the night now, so perhaps you could come tomorrow?'

Her granddaughter nodded. 'Poppy wouldn't like Petra, would she?'

'No, I don't think she would.' Pamela could feel her eyes growing heavy again. 'Now, I think I'd better have my sleep. Thank you, dear, for the flowers. I'll be down soon for my tea.'

''Bye, Granny.'

'Don't I get a kiss?'

'Of course you do.' Genevieve deposited a noisy wet smack on her grandmother's cheek, then skipped off to the door.

'Leave it open, would you, darling?'

Pamela turned out the bedside light and closed her eyes. She had lied about dying to the dear child, of course. She was ready for it, but only in the sense that she was no longer afraid. John wanted her, too, she was aware of that more than ever now, not in their conversations – they didn't talk so much, these days – but in a constant gentle tugging at her heart.

With the door open she could hear strains of merriment coming up the stairs – or were they the voices of past parties, past generations? The before, the now, the after, it was all one in the end.

Outside fog continued to roll off the downs, floating and thickening round the contours of the countryside like ghostly lava. Ashley House, lights burning on all floors as the night drew in and the party spread, faced the silent onslaught like some glittering rock rising out of a foaming sea, as rooted and indomitable as the spirits of those it protected, as stubborn as the misty old hills.